F&SF MAM
The n   story

Alex Dally MacFarlane is a writ
not researching narrative maps in the legendary traditions of
Alexander III of Macedon, she writes stories, found in *Clarkes-
world Magazine, Strange Horizons, Beneath Ceaseless Skies, Solaris
Rising 3, Heiresses of Russ 2013: The Year's Best Lesbian Specula-
tive Fiction, The Year's Best Science Fiction & Fantasy: 2014* and
other anthologies. Her poetry can be found in *Stone Telling, The
Moment of Change* and *Here, We Cross.* She is the editor of *Aliens:
Recent Encounters* (2013) and *The Mammoth Book of SF Stories by
Women.*

THE MAMMOTH BOOK OF

SF Stories
by Women

Edited by Alex Dally MacFarlane

ROBINSON | RUNNING PRESS
PHILADELPHIA · LONDON

ROBINSON

First published in Great Britain in 2014 by Robinson

A CIP catalogue record for this book
is available from the British Library.

ISBN 978-1-47211-166-1 (paperback)
ISBN 978-1-47211-171-5 (ebook)

Typeset in Plantin light by Hewer Text UK Ltd, Edinburgh
Printed and bound in Great Britain by CPI Group (UK) Ltd, Croydon, CR0 4YY

Robinson
is an imprint of
Constable & Robinson Ltd
100 Victoria Embankment
London EC4Y 0DY

An Hachette UK Company
www.hachette.co.uk

www.constablerobinson.com

First published in the United States in 2014 by Running Press Book Publishers,
A Member of the Perseus Books Group

Books published by Running Press are available at special discounts for bulk
purchases in the United States by corporations, institutions and other organizations.
For more information, please contact the Special Markets Department at the
Perseus Books Group, 2300 Chestnut Street, Suite 200, Philadelphia, PA 19103,
or call (800) 810-4145, ext. 5000, or email special.markets@perseusbooks.com.

US ISBN: 978-0-7624-5470-9
US Library of Congress Control Number: 2014936347

9 8 7 6 5 4 3 2 1

Digit on the right indicates the number of this printing

Running Press Book Publishers
2300 Chestnut Street
Philadelphia, PA 19103-4371

Visit us on the web!
www.runningpress.com

CONTENTS

PERMISSIONS

INTRODUCTION

Such pleasure in selection!
The anthologist more than any other knows
the universe is multiple.
        —Sofia Samatar, "Snowbound in Hamadan"

I would like to say that women writing science fiction belong to an unarguably long history. Say: Margaret Cavendish, Mary Shelley, Alice Ilgenfritz Jones and Ella Merchant, Rokeya Sakhawat Hossain – and more. Women fascinated by science and the stars are attested throughout human civilization. Hypatia of Alexandria (350/370 to 415 CE), philosophist, astronomer, mathematician. Mariam Al-Ijliya (tenth-century CE), who designed and constructed innovative astrolabes. Mary Anning (1799 to 1847 CE), excavating dinosaur bones on the Dorset coast.

Women do belong to these histories. The difficult word is "unarguably". Perennial arguments question how long women have been writing science fiction compared to men, whether their science fiction is truly science fiction, what the definition of science fiction is – to the exclusion of sciences like biology, sociology or linguistics, to the exclusion of non-Western narrative approaches used by women who are not white or not Western. To the exclusion, too, of a wider understanding of gender around the world. Sometimes these arguments are men yelling at clouds. Sometimes they are publishers not buying science fiction books by women, or lists of classic science fiction that are almost entirely by men.

This is not a book of classic science fiction by women.

The universe of science fiction is multiple: I could have collected stories from an entire century – or more – or I could have condensed my scope. And then, in any breadth of time, which stories to collect? There are so many.

Science fiction is always changing: at its best, it is always exciting, always saying something new. To say that the best science fiction of recent years is pushing the genre into new places is not a new statement – but I am incredibly excited by what the science fiction of recent years is doing. More than before, writers from around the world and of many backgrounds – gender, sexuality, ethnicity – are being published in English, in original and in translation. Their voices are changing science fiction, taking it into more futures and looking at our present and past in more ways. If science fiction is defined as looking at as many worlds as possible, it is an excellent time to be a reader.

I wanted to take a snapshot of this.

The stories in *The Mammoth Book of SF Stories by Women* are all (bar one) from the last twenty years. Some of the writers have been working in the science fiction field for far longer than that – writers like Ursula K. Le Guin, Karen Joy Fowler, Élisabeth Vonarburg, Angélica Gorodischer, Nancy Kress. Many started publishing quite recently – Zen Cho, Karin Tidbeck, Benjanun Sriduangkaew, Sofia Samatar. Their approaches to science fiction are varied. Their stories are consistent in one quality: they all excite me.

This is not a solution.

It is a snapshot, a collection of stories by women working in science fiction today. I hope it brings these writers to new readers. It cannot deal a one-hit kill to sexism in the science fiction industry. It cannot solve another problem – the tendency to forget the contributions of women from earlier decades; although some of its contents deal very directly with the past: Karen Joy Fowler writing about Mary Anning's life and discoveries, Sofia Samatar writing about Henrietta Swan Leavitt and the other women employed as human computers by Harvard College Observatory in the 1870s, Tori Truslow's re-imagining of the Moon to examine the erasure of women's poetic scholarship. They look at history, they remember it, but they are no replacement for it.

They are an addition – as is this anthology.

It is also important to note that the conversation about gender is more complex than just men and women. Non-binary gender exists around the world and always has done, which tends to be forgotten. An anthology such as *The Mammoth Book of SF Stories by Women* is, by elevating the work of women, limiting itself to them (although the complexity of gender identity means that some writers in this anthology are not binary-gendered). It can only be one part of what needs to be a much wider conversation.

What is this book?

A contribution to the conversation about writing and gender that has gone on for centuries. A collection of thirty-three excellent science fiction stories by women. Look: Sedoretu on the planet O. A train journey to the Moon. Alternate universes. Post apocalypses. An exomoon that stops birds from singing. Living spaceships born in gas giants. Cartographic wasps. Callowhales on Venus. Constellations.

Look at what women have written. Enjoy.

GIRL HOURS

Sofia Samatar

For Henrietta Swan Leavitt

Notes

In the 1870s, the Harvard College Observatory began to employ young women as human computers to record and analyze data. One of them, Henrietta Swan Leavitt, discovered a way to measure stellar distances using the pulsing of variable stars.

Quotations are from George Johnson's *Miss Leavitt's Stars: The Untold Story of the Woman Who Discovered How to Measure the Universe* (W. W. Norton, 2005).

Harlow Shapley, director of the observatory, reckoned the difficulty of astronomical projects in "girl hours" – the number of hours a human computer would take to obtain the data. The most challenging projects were measured in "kilo-girl-hours."

Conclusion

You were not the only deaf woman there.
Annie Cannon, too, was hard of hearing.
On the day of your death she wrote: *Rainy day pouring at night.*

Oh bright rain, brave clouds, oh stars,
oh stars.

Two thousand four hundred fires
and uncharted, unstudied,
the hours, the hours, the hours.

Body

The body is a computer.

The body has two eyes. For the body, the process of triangulation is automatic. The body can see the red steeple of the church beyond the trees. Blackbirds unfold as they grow nearer, like messages.

The body never intended to be a secret.

The body was called a shining cloud, and then a galaxy. The body comforted mariners, spilt milk in the southern sky. The body was thought to be only 30,000 light years away.

The body is untrustworthy. It falls ill.

> *The thought of uncompleted work, particularly of the Standard Magnitudes, is one I have had to avoid as much as possible, as it has had a bad effect nervously.*

The body sits at a desk. A high collar, faint stripes in the white blouse. In this rare photograph, the body is framed in light. The gaze is turned down, the hand poised to make a mark. The body says: "Take photographs, write poems. I will go on with my work."

The body is not always the same, the body varies in brightness, its true brightness may be ascertained from the rhythm of its pulsing, the body is more remote than we imagined, it eats, it walks, it traverses with terrible slowness the distance between Wisconsin and Massachusetts, the body is stubborn, snowbound, the body has disappeared, the body has left the country, the body has traveled to Europe and will not say if it went there alone, the body is generous, dedicated, seated again, reserved, exacting,

brushed and buttoned, smelling of healthy soap,
and not allowed to touch the telescope.

The body gives time away with both hands.

The body, when working, does not know that time has passed.

The body died in 1921.

The body's edges are so far from one another that it is hardly a body at all. We gather the stars, and we call them a body. Cygnus. The Swan.

Introduction

Twelve o'clock.
My husband and children asleep.

To chart one more star, to go on working:
this is a way of keeping faith.

Draw me a map.
Show me how to read music.
Teach me to rise without standing,
to hold the galaxy's calipers
with the earth at one gleaming tip,
to live vastly and with precision,
to travel
where distance is no longer measured in miles but in lifetimes,
in epochs, in breaths, in light years, in girl hours.

EXCERPT FROM A LETTER BY A SOCIAL-REALIST ASWANG

Kristin Mandigma

I apologize for this late reply. Our mail service has been erratic recently due to a spate of troublesome security-related issues. I don't think I need to elaborate. You must have read the latest reports. These government spooks are hopelessly incompetent but they (very) occasionally evince flashes of human-like logic. I expect it will only take them a matter of time before they figure it out, with or without their torturous diagrams, at which point I may have to seriously consider the advisability of having one of our supporters open *another* German bank account. As a diversion, if nothing else, and I have had nothing entertaining to watch on cable television (which I believe has also been bugged because it persists in showing me nothing but Disney) for a while. Just between the two of us – I do believe that if fatuous, single-minded politicians were not an irrevocable fact of life, like having to use the toilet, we would have to invent them.

Now, to your letter. I confess to having read it with some consternation. I am well acquainted with your penchant for morbid humor, and yet the suggestion that I might write a short "piece" for a speculative fiction magazine struck me as more perverse than usual. What on earth is speculative fiction anyway? I believe you are referring to one of those ridiculous publications which traffic in sensationalizing the human imagination while actually claiming to enrich it by virtue of setting it loose from the moorings of elitist literary fiction? Or whatever? And for elitist substitute "realist," I suppose. You argue that speculative fiction is merely a convenient "ideologically neutral" term to describe a certain grouping of popular genre fiction, but then follow it up. with a defensive polemic on its revolutionary significance with regard to encapsulating the "popular" Filipino experience. To which I ask: As opposed to what?

I believe, Comrade, that you are conflating ideology with bourgeois hair-splitting. When it comes down to it, how is this novel you sent along with your letter, this novel about an interstellar war between monster cockroaches and alienated capitalist soldiers, supposed to be a valid form of social commentary? I do not care if the main character is a Filipino infantryman. I assume he is capitalist, too. Furthermore, since he is far too busy killing cockroaches on godforsaken planets in a spaceship (which is definitely not a respectable proletarian occupation), his insights into the future of Marxist revolution in the Philippines must be suspect at best. And this Robert Heinlein fellow you mention, I assume, is another imperialist Westerner? I thought so. Comrade, I must admit to being troubled by your choice of reading fare these days. And do not think you can fob me off with claims that your favorite novel at the moment is written by a socialist author. I do not trust socialists. The only socialists I know are white-collar fascist trolls who watch too many Sylvester Stallone movies. Sellouts, the lot of them. Do not get me started on the kapre, they are all closet theists. An inevitable by-product of all that repulsive tobacco, I should say.

With regard to your question about how I perceive myself as an "Other," let me make it clear that I am as fantastic to myself as rice. I do not waste time sitting around brooding about my mythic status and why the notion that I have lived for 500 years ought to send me into a paroxysm of metaphysical Angst for the benefit of self-indulgent, overprivileged, cultural hegemonists who fancy themselves writers. So there are times in the month when half of me flies off to – as you put it so charmingly – eat babies. Well, I ask you, so what? For your information, I only eat babies whose parents are far too entrenched in the oppressive capitalist superstructure to expect them to be redeemed as good dialectical materialists. It is a legitimate form of population control, I dare say.

I think the real issue here is not my dietary habits but whether or not my being an aswang makes me any less of a Filipino and a communist. I think that being an aswang is a category of social difference – imposed by an external utilitarian authority – like sexuality and income bracket. Nobody conceives of being gay just as a literary trope, do they? To put it in another way: I do not conceive of my biological constitution as a significant marker of my identity. Men, women, gays, aswang, talk-show hosts, politicians, even these speculative fiction non-idealists you speak of – we are all subject to the evils of capitalism, class struggle, the eschatological workings of history, and the inevitability of socialist relations. In this scheme of things, whether or not one eats dried fish or (imperialist) babies for sustenance should be somewhat irrelevant.

I would also like to address in more depth your rather confused contention that the intellectual enlightenment of the Filipino masses lies not in "contemporary" (I presume you meant to say "outdated" but were too busy contradicting yourself) realistic literature, but in a new artistic imaginative "paradigm" (again, this unseemly bourgeois terminology!). As I have said, I would emphatically beg to differ. Being an aswang – not just the commodified subject, but the fetishistic object of this new literature you speak of – has not enlightened me in any way about the true nature of society, about modes of production, about historical progress. I am a nationalist not because I am an aswang, but despite of it. You only have to consider the example of those notorious Transylvanian vampires. No one would ever call them patriots, except insofar as they speak like Bela Lugosi.

Before I end this letter, I must add another caveat: my first reaction upon meeting Jose Rizal in Paris during the International Exposition was not to eat him, as malicious rumors would have you believe. In fact, we spoke cordially and had an extended conversation about Hegel in a cafe. I do think that he is just another overrated ilustrado poseur – brilliant, of course, but with a dangerous touch of the Trotskyite utopian about him. I prefer Bonifacio, for obvious reasons.

In closing, let me say, as Marx does, that "one has to leave philosophy aside." You must inure yourself against these pernicious novels about cockroaches and spaceships (and did you mention dragons? All dragons are either Freudians or fascists), for they can only lead you to a totalizing anthropogenetic attitude toward the world. Concentrate on the real work that needs to be done, Comrade.

(For all that, let me thank you for the sweaters. I can only hope you did not buy them in that cursed cesspool of superexploitation, SM Shoemart. It is getting quite cold here in America, hivemind of evil, and it has been increasingly impractical for me to fly out without any sort of protective covering.)

Long live the Philippines! Long live the Revolution!

SOMADEVA: A SKY RIVER SUTRA

Vandana Singh

I am Somadeva.

I was once a man, a poet, a teller of tales, but I am long dead now. I lived in the eleventh century of the Common Era in northern India. Then we could only dream of that fabulous device, the udan-khatola, the ship that flies between worlds. Then, the sky-dwelling Vidyadharas were myth, occupying a reality different from our own. And the only wings I had with which to make my journeys were those of my imagination . . .

Who or what am I now, in this age when flying between worlds is commonplace? Who brought me into being, here in this small, cramped space, with its smooth metallic surfaces, and the round window revealing an endless field of stars?

It takes me a moment to recognize Isha. She is lying in her bunk, her hair spread over the pillow, looking at me.

And then I remember the first time I woke up in this room, bewildered. Isha told me she had re-created me. She fell in love with me fifteen centuries after my death, after she read a book I wrote, an eighteen-volume compendium of folktales and legends, called the *Kathāsaritsāgara*: The Ocean of Streams of Story.

"You do remember that?" she asked me anxiously upon my first awakening.

"Of course I remember," I said, as my memories returned to me in a great rush.

The *Kathāsaritsāgara* was my life's work. I wandered all over North India, following rumors of the Lost Manuscript, risking death to interview murderers and demons, cajoling stories out of old women and princes, merchants and nursing mothers. I took these stories and organized them into patterns of labyrinthine complexity. In my book there are stories within stories – the chief narrator tells a story and the characters in that story tell other stories and so on. Some of the narrators refer to the stories of previous narrators; thus each is not only a teller of tales but also a participant. The story-frames themselves form a complex, multi-referential tapestry. And the story of how the *Kathāsaritsāgara* came to be is the first story of them all.

I began this quest because of a mystery in my own life, but it became a labor of love, an attempt to save a life. That is why I wove the stories into a web, so I could hold safe the woman I loved. I could not have guessed that fifteen centuries after my death, another very different woman would read my words and fall in love with me.

The first time I met Isha, she told me she had created me to be her companion on her journeys between the stars. She wants to be the Somadeva of this age, collecting stories from planet to planet in the galaxy we call Sky River. What a moment of revelation it was for me, when I first knew that there were other worlds, peopled and habited, rich with stories! Isha told me that she had my spirit trapped in a crystal jewel-box. The jewel-box has long feelers like the antennae of insects, so that I can see and hear and smell, and thereby taste the worlds we visit.

"How did you pull my spirit from death? From history? Was I reborn in this magic box?"

She shook her head.

"It isn't magic, Somadeva. Oh, I can't explain! But tell me, I need to know. Why didn't you write yourself into the *Kathāsaritsāgara*? Who, really, is this narrator of yours, Gunādhya? I know there is a mystery there . . . "

She asks questions all the time. When she is alone with me, she is often animated like this. My heart reaches out to her, this lost child of a distant age.

Gunādhya is a goblin-like creature who is the narrator of the *Kathāsaritsāgara*. According to the story I told, Gunādhya was a minion of Shiva himself who was reborn on Earth due to a curse. His mission was to tell the greater story of which the *Kathāsaritsāgara* is only a page: the Brhat-kathā. But he was forbidden to speak or write in Sanskrit or any other language of humankind. Wandering through a forest one day, he came upon a company of the flesh-eating Pishāch. He hid himself and listened to them, and learned their strange tongue. In time he wrote the great Brhat-kathā in the Pishāchi language in a book made of the bark of trees, in his own blood.

They say that he was forced to burn the manuscript, and that only at the last moment did a student of his pull out one section from the fire. I tracked that surviving fragment for years, but found only a few scattered pages, and the incomplete memories of those who had seen the original, or been told the tales. From these few I reconstructed what I have called the *Kathāsaritsāgara*. In all this, I have drawn on ancient Indic tradition, in which the author is a compiler, an embellisher, an arranger of stories, some written, some told. He fragments his consciousness into the various fictional narrators in order to be a conduit for their tales.

In most ancient works, the author goes a step further: he walks himself whole into the story, like an actor onto the stage.

This is one way I have broken from tradition. I am not, myself, a participant in the stories of the *Kathāsaritsāgara*. And Isha wants to know why.

Sometimes I sense my narrator, Gunādhya, as one would a ghost, a presence standing by my side. He is related to me in some way that is not clear to me. All these years he has been coming into my dreams, filling in gaps in my stories, or contradicting what I've already written down. He is a whisper in my ear; sometimes my tongue moves at his command. All the time he is keeping secrets from me, tormenting me with the silence between his words. Perhaps he is waiting until the time is right.

'I don't know,' I tell Isha. 'I don't know why I didn't put myself in the story. I thought it would be enough, you know, to cast a story web, to trap my queen. To save her from death . . . "

"Tell me about her," Isha says. Isha knows all about Sūryavati but she wants to hear it from me. Over and over.

I remember . . .

A high balcony, open, not latticed. The mountain air, like wine. In the inner courtyard below us, apricots are drying in the sun in great orange piles. Beyond the courtyard walls I can hear men's voices, the clash of steel as soldiers practice their murderous art. The king is preparing to battle his own son, who lusts for the

throne and cannot wait for death to take his father. But it is for the
Queen that I am here. She is standing by the great stone vase on
the balcony, watering the holy tulsi plant. She wears a long skirt of
a deep, rich red, and a green shawl over the delicately embroidered tunic. Her slender fingers shake; her gaze, when it lifts to
me, is full of anguish. Her serving maids hover around her, unable
to relieve her of her pain. At last she sits, drawing the edge of her
fine silken veil about her face. A slight gesture of the hand. My
cue to begin the story that will, for a moment, smooth that troubled brow.

It is for her that I have woven the story web. Every day it gives
her a reason to forget despair, to live a day longer. Every day she
is trapped in it, enthralled by it a little more. There are days when
the weight of her anxiety is too much, when she breaks the spell
of story and requires me for another purpose. Then I must, for
love of her, take part in an ancient and dangerous rite. But today,
the day that I am remembering for Isha, Sūryavati simply wants
to hear a story.

I think I made a mistake with Sūryavati, fifteen centuries ago.
If I'd written myself into the *Kathāsaritsāgara*, perhaps she would
have realized how much I needed her to be alive. After all, Vyāsa,
who penned the immortal *Mahābhārata*, was as much a participant in the tale as its chronicler. And the same is true of Vālmīki,
who wrote the *Rāmāyana* and was himself a character in it, an
agent.

So, for the first time, I will write myself into *this* story. Perhaps
that is the secret to affecting events as they unfold. And, after all,
I, too, have need of meaning. Beside me, Gunādhya's ghost nods
silently in agreement.

Isha sits in the ship's chamber, her fingers running through her
hair, her gaze troubled. She has always been restless. For all her
confidence I can only guess what it is she is seeking through the
compilation of the legends and myths of the inhabited worlds. As
I wander through the story-labyrinths of my own making, I hope
to find, at the end, my Isha, my Sūryavati.

Isha is, I know, particularly interested in stories of origin, of
ancestry. I think it is because she has no knowledge of her natal
family. When she was a young woman, she was the victim of a

history raid. The raiders took from her all her memories. Her memories are scattered now in the performances of entertainers, the conversations of strangers, and the false memories of imitation men. The extinction of her identity was so clean that she would not recognize those memories as her own, were she to come across them. What a terrible and wondrous age this is, in which such things are possible!

In her wanderings, Isha hasn't yet been able to find out who her people were. All she has as a clue is an ancient, battered set of books: the eighteen volumes of the *Kathāsaritsāgara*. They are, to all appearances, her legacy, all that was left of her belongings after the raid. The pages are yellow and brittle, the text powdery, fading. She has spent much of her youth learning the lost art of reading, learning the lost scripts of now-dead languages. Inside the cover of the first volume is a faint inscription, a name: Vandana. There are notes in the same hand in the margins of the text. An ancestor, she thinks.

This is why Isha is particularly interested in stories of origin. She thinks she'll find out something about herself by listening to other people's tales of where they came from.

I discovered this on my very first journey with her. After she brought me into existence, we went to a world called Jesanli, where the few city-states were hostile toward us. None would receive us, until we met the Kiha, a nomadic desert tribe who had a tradition of hospitality. None of the inhabitants of this planet have much by way of arts or machinery, civilization or learning. But the Kiha have stories that are poetic and strange. Here is the first of them.

> Once upon a time our ancestors lived in a hot and crowded space, in near darkness. They were not like us. They were not men, nor women, but had a different form. The ancestors, having poor sight, lived in fear all the time, and when one intruded too close to another, they immediately sprang apart in terror. It was as though each moment of approach brought the possibility of a stranger, an enemy, entering their personal domain. Imagine a lot of people who cannot speak, forced to live in a small, cramped, dark cave, where

every blundering collision is a nightmare – for that is what it was like for them. Their fear became part of them, becoming a physical presence like a burden carried on the back.

But every once in a while two or more of them would be pushed close enough together to actually behold each other dimly through their nearly useless eyes. During these moments of recognition they were able to see themselves in the other person, and to reach out, and to draw together. In time they formed tight little family units. Then they had no more need to carry around their burdens of fear, which, when released, turned into light.

Yes, yes. You heard that right. Although they continued to live in their furnace-like world and be cramped together, what emanated from them – despite everything   was light.

Isha's eyes lit up when she heard this story. She told the Kiha that the story had hidden meanings, that it contained the secret of how the stars burn. They listened politely to her explanation and thanked her for her story. She wanted to know where they had first heard the tale, but the question made no sense to them. Later she told me that for all their non-technological way of life, the Kiha must have once been sky-dwellers.

They had told Isha the story to repay a debt, because she brought them gifts. So when she explained their story back to them, they had to tell her another story to even things out. They did this with reluctance, because a story is a gift not easily given to strangers.

Here is the second story.

In the beginning there was just one being, whose name was That Which Is Nameless. The Nameless One was vast, undifferentiated, and lay quiescent, waiting. In that place there was no darkness, for there was no light.

Slowly the Nameless One wearied of its existence. It said into the nothingness: "Who am I?" But there was no answer because there was no other. It said unto itself: "Being alone is a burden. I will carve myself up and make myself companions."

So the Nameless One gathered itself and spread itself

violently into all directions, thinning out as it did so. It was the greatest explosion ever known, and from its shards were born people and animals and stars.

And so when light falls on water, or a man shoots an arrow at another man, or a mother picks up a child, That Which Was Once Nameless answers a very small part of the question: Who am I?

And yet the Once Nameless still reaches out, beyond the horizon of what we know and don't know, breaking itself up into smaller and smaller bits like the froth from a wave that hits a rocky shore. What is it seeking? Where is it going? Nobody can tell.

I could tell that Isha was excited by this story also; she wanted to tell the Kiha that the second story was really about the birth of the universe – but I restrained her. To the Kiha, what is real and what is not real is not a point of importance. To them there are just stories and stories, and the universe has a place for all of them.

Later Isha asked me: "How is it possible that the Kiha have forgotten they once traversed the stars? Those two stories contain the essence of the sciences, the vigyan-shastras, in disguise. How can memory be so fragile?"

She bit her lip, and I know she was thinking of her own lost past. In my life, too, there are gaps I cannot fill.

The stories in the *Kathāsaritsāgara* are not like these tales of the Kiha. Queen Sūryavati was of a serious mien, spending much time in contemplation of Lord Shiva. To lighten her burdens I collected tales of ordinary, erring mortals and divines: cheating wives, sky-dwelling, shape-shifting Vidyadharas, and the denizens, dangerous and benign, of the great forests. These were first told, so the story goes, by Shiva himself. They are nothing like the stories of the Kiha.

Isha has so much to learn! Like Sūryavati, she is a woman of reserve. She conceals her pain as much as she can from the world. Her interaction with the Kiha is impersonal, almost aloof. Now if it were left to me, I would go into their dwelling places, live with them, listen to gossip. Find out who is in love with whom, what joys and sorrows the seasons bring, whether there is enmity between clans. I have never been much interested in the cosmic dramas of gods and heroes.

However, the third Kiha tale is quite unlike the first two. I don't know what to make of it.

Once, in the darkness, a man wandered onto a beach where he saw a fire. He came upon it and saw that the fire was another man, all made of light, who spun in a circle on the beach as though drunk. The first man, warmed by the glow of the fire-man, wanted to talk to him, but the fire-man didn't take any notice of him. The fire-man kept spinning, round and round, and the first man kept yelling out questions, spinning round and round with the fire-man so he could see his face. And there were three small biting insects who dared not bite the fire-man but wanted to bite the cheeks of the other man, and they kept hovering around the other man, and he kept waving them off, but they would go behind him until he forgot about them, and then they'd circle around and bite him again.

Then?

Then nothing. They are all, all five of them, still on that dark beach, dancing still.

Isha thinks this story is a more recent origin story. She speculates that the ancestral people of the Kiha come from a world which has three moons. A world that floated alone in space until it fell into the embrace of a star. There are worlds like that, I've heard, planets wandering without their shepherd stars. It is not unlikely that one of these was captured by a sun. This story was told to Isha by a child, who ran up to us in secret when we were leaving. She wanted to make us a gift of some sort, but that was all she had.

If Isha is right, then the Kiha told us the stories in the wrong order. Arrange them like this: Birth of the universe, birth of their sun, coming into being of their world.

But these old stories have as many meanings as there are stars in the sky. To assign one single interpretation to them is to miss the point. Take the second story. It could be as much a retelling of a certain philosophical idea from the ancient Indic texts called the

Upanishads as a disguised theory of cosmological origin. In my other life I was learned in Sanskrit.

But it is also important what *we* make of these stories. What meaning we find in them, as wanderers by the seashore find first one shell, then another, and form them into a chain of their own making.

Here is the start of a story I have made by braiding together the Kiha tales.

> In the beginning, Isha made the world. Wishing to know herself, she broke herself up into parts. One of them is me, Somadeva, poet and wanderer. We circle each other for ever, one maker, one made . . .

Sometimes I wonder if I have made her up as much as she has concocted me. If we are fictions of each other, given substance only through our mutual narratives.

Perhaps the Kiha are right: stories make the world.

I wake and find myself on that high stone balcony. The Queen is watching me. A small fire in an earthen pail burns between us, an angeethi. Over it, hanging from an iron support, is a black pot containing the brew.

"Did it take you too far, my poet?" she asks, worried. "You told me of far worlds and impossible things. You spoke some words I couldn't understand. An entertaining tale. But I only want a glimpse of what is to come in the next few days, not eons. I want to know . . ."

I am confused. When I first opened my eyes I thought I saw Isha. I thought I was on the ship, telling Isha a story about Sūryavati. She likes me to recite the old tales, as she lies back in her bunk, running her fingers slowly over her brow. I wish I could caress that brow myself.

So how is it that I find myself here, breathing in pine-scented Himalayan air? How is it my mouth has a complex aftertaste that I cannot quite identify, which has something to do with the herbal brew steaming in the pot? My tongue is slightly numb, an effect of the poison in the mix.

Or is it that in telling my story to Isha I have immersed myself so deeply in the tale that it has become reality to me?

The Queen's eyes are dark, and filled with tears.

"Dare I ask you to try again, my poet? Will you risk your life and sanity one more time, and tell me what you see? Just a step beyond this moment, a few days hence. Who will win this war . . . "

What I cannot tell her is that I've seen what she wants to know. I know what history has recorded of the battle. The Prince, her son, took his father's throne and drove him to his death. And the Queen . . .

It is past bearing.

What I am trying to do is to tell her a story in which I am a character. If I can have a say in the way things turn out, perhaps I can save her. The King and his son are beyond my reach. But Sūryavati? She is susceptible to story. If she recognizes, in the fictional Somadeva's love for Isha, the real Somadeva's unspoken, agonized love, perhaps she'll step back from the brink of history.

My fear is that if events unfurl as history records, I will lose my Sūryavati. Will I then be with Isha, wandering the stars in search of stories? Or will I die here on this earth, under the shadow of the palace walls, with the night sky nothing but a dream? Who will survive, the real Somadeva or the fictional one? And which is which?

All I can do is stall Sūryavati with my impossible tales – and hope.

"I don't know how far the brew will take me," I tell her. "But for you, my queen, I will drink again."

I take a sip.

I am back on the ship. Isha is asleep, her hair in tangles over her face. Her face in sleep is slack, except for that habitual little frown between her brows. The frown makes her look more like a child, not less. I wonder if her memories come to her in her dreams.

So I begin another story, although I remain a little confused. Who is listening: Isha or Sūryavati?

I will tell a story about Inish. It is a place on a far world and one of the most interesting we have visited.

I hesitate to call Inish a city, because it is not really one. It is a collection of buildings and people, animals and plants, and is referred to by the natives as though it has an independent consciousness. But also it has no clear boundary because the mini-settlements at what might have been its edge keep wandering off and returning, apparently randomly.

Identities are also peculiar among the inhabitants of Inish. A person has a name, let us say Mana, but when Mana is with her friend Ayo, they together form an entity named Tukrit. If you meet them together and ask them for their names, they will say "Tukrit," not "Ayo and Mana." Isha once asked them whether Ayo and Mana were parts of Tukrit, and they both laughed. "Tukrit is not bits of this or that," Mana said. "Then who just spoke, Mana or Tukrit?" Isha asked. "Tukrit, of course," they said, giggling in an indulgent manner.

"I am Isha," Isha told them. "But who am I when I'm with you?"

"We are *teso*," they said, looking at each other. Isha knew what that meant. "*Teso*" is, in their language, a word that stands for anything that is unformed, not quite there, a possibility, a potential.

It is hard for outsiders to understand whether the Inish folk have family units or not. Several people may live in one dwelling, but since their dwellings are connected by little corridors and tunnels, it is hard to say where one ends and another begins. The people in one dwelling may be four older females, one young woman, three young men and five children. Ask them their names and depending on which of them are present at that time, they will say a different collective name. If there are only Baijo, Akar, and Inha around, they'll say, "We are Garho." If Sami, Kinjo, and Vif are also there, then they are collectively an entity known as "Parak." And so on and so forth.

How they keep from getting confused is quite beyond Isha and me.

"Tell me, Isha," I said once. "You and I . . . what are we when we are together?"

She looked at me sadly.

"Isha and Somadeva," she said. But there was a faint query in her tone.

"What do you think, Somadeva?" she said.

"*Teso*," I said.

Here is a story from Inish.

There was Ikla. Then, no Ikla but Bako walking away from what was now Samish. While walking, Bako found herself being part of a becoming, but she could not see who or what she was becoming with. Ah, she thought, it is a *goro* being; one that does not show itself except through a sigh in the mind. She felt the *teso* build up slowly, felt herself turn into a liquid, sky, rain. Then there was no *teso*, no *goro*, no Bako, but a fullness, a ripening, and thus was Chihuli come into happening.

And this Chihuli went shouting down the summer lanes, flinging bits of mud and rock around, saying, "There is a storm coming! A storm!" And Chihuli went up the hill and sank down before the sacred stones and died there. So there was nothing left but Bako, who looked up with enormous eyes at the sky, and felt inside her the emptiness left by the departure of the *goro* being.

Bako, now, why had the *goro* being chosen her for a happening? Maybe because she had always felt *teso* with storms, and since storms were rare here and people had to be warned, there was a space inside her for the kind of *goro* being that lived for storms and their warning. So that is how the right kind of emptiness had brought Chihuli into being.

Pods kept forming around Bako but she resisted being pulled in. It was because of the coming storm, because she could sense the *teso* with it. Nobody else could. With others it was other beings, wild things and bright eyes in the darkness, sometimes even the slowtrees, but only with Bako was there the emptiness inside shaped like a storm. And so she felt the *teso*, the way she had with the *goro* being.

The air crackled with electricity; dark clouds filled the sky, like a ceiling about to come down. Everywhere you looked, it was gray: gray water, gray beings, looking up with wondering, frightened eyes. Only for Bako, as the *teso* built, was the excitement, the anticipation. Many had felt that before when they found their special pod, their mate-beings. The feeling of ripening, of coming into a fullness. The wild sweetness of it. Now Bako felt something like that many times over.

Samish came sweeping up the hill where she was

standing, trying to swoop her back with them, so they could be Ikla again, and the *teso* with the storm would become nothing more. But she resisted, and Samish had to go away. This was a thing stronger than the love-bonds they had known.

Came the storm. A magnificent storm it was, rain and thunder, and the legs of lightning dancing around Bako. Rivers swollen, running wild over land, into homes, sweeping everything away. Hills began to move, and the beings ran from their homes. Only Bako stood in the rain, on the highest hill, and the storm danced for her.

The *teso* became something. We call it T'fan. T'fan played with the world, spread over half the planet, wrapped her wet arms around trees and hills. The storm went on until the beings thought there would be no more sun, no more dry land. Then one day it ceased.

Samish gathered itself up, and went tiredly up the hill to find Bako, or to mourn the death of Ikla.

Bako was not there. What was there was standing just as they had left Bako, arms outstretched to the sky. She looked at them with faraway eyes, and they saw then that although the sky was clearing, the storm was still in her. Tiny sparks of lightning flashed from her fingertips. Her hair was singed.

They saw then that the storm had filled her empty spaces so completely that there would never be Ikla again. They did not even feel *teso*. They walked away from her and prepared for mourning.

T'fan stands there still, her eyes filled with storms, her fingers playing with lightning. Her hair has singed away almost completely. She needs no food or water, and seems, in the way of storms, to be quite content. When storms come to her people they cluster around her and she comes to life, dancing in their midst as though relatives have come again from far away. Then T'fan goes away and is replaced by something larger and more complex than we can name.

"What does that story mean, I wonder," Isha said.

"Sometimes stories are just stories," I told her.

"You've never told me what happened to Sūryavati, after you

took the next sip, told her the next tale," she told me, turning away from the consequences of my remark. The fact that you can't wrest meaning from everything like fruit from trees – that meaning is a matter not only of story but of what the listener brings to the tale – all that is not something she can face at the moment. She is so impatient, my Isha.

I steeled myself.

"The Queen was distraught with grief when her son took the kingdom and destroyed his father," I said. "She threw herself on his funeral pyre. I could not save her."

But in this moment I am also conscious of the Queen herself, her eyes dark with grief and yearning. Her hand, with its long fingers – a healed cut on the right index finger, the henna patterns fading reaches up to wipe a tear. And yet in her gaze leaps a certain vitality, an interest. Her mind ranges far across the universe, carried by my tales. In that small fire in her eyes is all my hope.

Perhaps all I've found is a moment of time that keeps repeating, in which, despite the predations of history, I am caught, with Isha and Sūryavati, in a loop of time distanced from the main current. Here my stories never end; I never reach the moment Sūryavati awaits, and Isha never finds out who she is. Gunādhya remains a whisper in my mind, his relation to me as yet a secret. Here we range across the skies, Isha and I, Vidyadharas of another age, and Sūryavati's gaze follows us. Who is the teller of the tale, and who the listener? We are caught in a web, a wheel of our own making. And if you, the listener from another time and space, upon whose cheek this story falls like spray thrown up by the ocean – you, the eavesdropper hearing a conversation borne by the wind, if you would walk into this story, take it away with you into your world, with its sorrows and small revelations, what would become of you? Would you also enter this circle? Would you tell me your story? Would we sit together, Sūryavati, Isha, and I, with you, and feel *teso* within us – and weave meaning from the strands of the tale?

I am Somadeva. I am a poet, a teller of tales.

THE QUEEN OF EREWHON

Lucy Sussex

"Hey you! Story-eater! Devourer of lives! Leave us alone! GET OUT!"

Those are the first sounds on the tape: Idris spitting at me, refusing to be interviewed. I wind on a little, until I hear a different voice – Sadry speaking.

Sadry: . . . ghosts. The house at Erewhon could have been full of them for all anyone knew, for there were only our family of three and the hired hands rattling around the building. Erewhon had followed the Rule for generations, not that I knew that. I was only a child; I think three. Things hadn't got explained to me yet. I had no idea how odd my upbringing was, for the High country, with only one father.

One night I thought I heard crying, so I got out of bed, curious. I wandered along the upstairs corridor which all the sleeping rooms led off. When I got a little older, I learnt why this space was called "Intrigue" in all the Rule houses. It kinks and curves, with crannies for people to hide and overhear – hence the name.

Me: A public space?

Sadry: Or a private one. I followed the sound to the outside wall, to a window with a recessed ledge. The shutters were closed and the winter curtains drawn, but between both was a space where someone might sit comfortably and that was from where the sound came. Now it sounded human, and female. I heard soft words, a male voice responding. Two people were hidden there! Curious, I stood and listened. But it was bitter frost weather, and rather than give myself away by teeth-chatter, I retreated until just round the corner I found a basket. It was filled with rags, either bought from Scavengers or our old clothes (Highlanders never throw anything away). So I climbed into it without making a sound, for it was an old Tech thing, of *perlastic*, rather than wicker. I curled up warmly in the contents and listened in comfort, not that I could understand much. Eventually I fell asleep, and woke in dawnlight to find my mother bending over me. And unthinkingly I blurted out the last words I had heard, which were: "I only want to be married to the one I love best, not all the others."

My mother said: "Where did you hear that?" and so I pointed at the ledge.

"The two lovers, there, last night."

She looked at me hard, then flung the curtain back. It wasn't me who screeched, it was her – at the sight of dust thick and undisturbed on the ledge. Then she scooped me up in her arms and went running down Intrigue, to the room she and my father shared, a small room, his younger son's room.

Idris: What did *he* do?

Sadry: Took us both into bed, calmed us down, for now I was hysterical too, and then very gently questioned me. What did the voices sound like? Could I imitate them? When I was as dry of information as a squeezed fruit, he said: "It could have been any unhappy Queen of Erewhon."

And then he told me about living under the Rule, of his first wife, his brother, and their husband-lover.

Polyandry. The first time I heard the word I thought it a girl's name: *Polly Andree*. The misapprehension, though instantly corrected, stuck in my mind, so that I persistently thought of the woman at the centre of these group marriages as a Polly. And here I was in Polyandry Central, as anthropologists called it, the Highlands of Suff, and I still couldn't shake my personal terminology. It was a bad slip to make when trying to convince Bel Innkeeper to find me space, in a town already filled to bursting for the Assizes.

"We call them *Queens*," she said.

I'd listened to tapes of Suff accents but the actuality was something else, my comprehension of it being delayed, with embarrassing pauses at the ends of sentences. When I finally understood, I replied, too hastily: "I know. Like bees."

All the while we had talked on the inn's back verandah a steady stream of fat brown bees had zoomed to and from some nearby hive, so this comment was both dead obvious and instantly regrettable.

Bel snorted. "You Northerners! Think you know everything, with your new-Tech ways! Ever seen a hive, ever seen a Rule House? No, that's why you're here, to find all about the funny Suffeners, isn't it?"

I said, carefully: "Okay, I'm what you call a story-eater, an anthropologist. But I can understand you've had a gutful of being studied and written up. I'm not here to sensationalize you, but to observe the court case."

Bel stopped folding the inn washing and gave me her undivided attention. "Why?"

"Because it's important."

"It's brought everyone down from the mountains and into this valley! How'm I supposed to house 'em all? And you, too."

She rocked on the balls of her feet, thinking. "Well, since you're here, I'd better be hospitable. And teach you about queen bees, too." She pointed at an outbuilding. "That's the honey-hut, and the one free space I've got. Take it or leave it!"

The hut was tiny: between pallet and beekeeping equipment there was barely any room for me. Above the bed was what I at first took to be a Tech photoimage, but it proved to be a window looking onto the mountains, made of the glass and wooden surround of a picture frame. In fact the whole building was constructed of scavenged oddments from the days of affluence: flattened tins, scraps of timber, and other usables slapped together in a crude but habitable mess. I was used to recycling, even in the neo-industrial North, but I had never seen such a higgledy-piggledy assortment before. It was to prove typical of much of the town itself.

I lay on the pallet and dozed for a while, lulled by the soporific hum from the nearby hives. When I woke, I tested my tape recorder – a precious thing, not because it was a genuine Tech artefact, but because it was a copy, its workings painstakingly rediscovered. Of course, it wasn't as good; nothing was, for we would never be as rich, nor as spendthrift, as our forebears. For over a century now, since the Crash, we had been adapting to an economy of scarcity. It was the adaptations, rather than the antiques, or the neo copies, that interested me – particularly the Rule Houses, and at their centre, the Queen Polly Andree. How would it feel, to have multiple husbands? And what would happen if you grew tired of them?

Sadry: My father said, "Nobody knows how the Rule began, just as nobody knows who bred the mountain Lori to be our herd animals. A Northerner, a story-eater, once told me the Rule was a pragmatic evolution, practiced by other mountain peoples. He said large populations cannot be sustained in marginal highland. One wife for several men – who are linked by blood, or ties of love – limits breeding, and means the family land can be passed undivided through the generations. It made sense; more than what the Lowlanders say, which is that we Highlanders deliberately chose complicated sex lives! Yet he spoke as if we were specimens, like a strain of Lori. That annoyed me, so I wouldn't give him what he had come for, which was my history.

"When I was the age you are now, my brother Bryn and I were contracted to marry Nissa of Bulle, who would grow to be our wife and Queen of Erewhon. When I was twelve and Bryn fifteen – the same age as Nissa – we travelled to Bulle to 'steal' our bride, as is custom. When we got back Erewhon celebrated with the biggest party I ever saw and afterwards Nissa spent the night with Bryn. I was too young to be a husband to her, though we would play knucklebones, or other children's games. That way Nissa and I grew friends, and then, after several years, husband and wife. But we lived without passion, all three of us. So when love did strike Nissa and Bryn, it did like a thunderbolt. And the lightning cracked through this house, destroying nearly everybody within it."

Market day in the Highlands is a spectacle, even without the added excitement of an Assizes and a sensational lawsuit. I woke early, to the sounds of shouts, goods being trundled down the main street, the shrill cries of Lori. When I came in the meal area of the Inn was full. Bel was cutting buckwheat bread; she handed me a slice, spread with Lori butter, at the same time jerking her head at the open door. I took the hint and went outside.

Immediately I found myself in the middle of a herd of Lori, who assessed the stranger intelligently from under their black topknots, then parted and pattered around me. The animal was a miracle of genetic engineering, combining the best of sheep, llama and goat, but with three-toed feet causing less damage to mountain soils than hooves. Like the other Highland animals it was dark, resistant to skin cancer; a boon in an area cursed with thin ozone, even so long after the Crash. Various studies had posited that the Lori designer might have been the social architect who engineered the lives of Highlanders with the Rule. If so, I wondered why human genes had not been manipulated as well, given that these people had insufficient protective melanin, varying as they did from pale to brown.

Sufferers met by sunlight would be shrouded in the robes of Lori homespun that served all purposes, from formal to cold-weather wear, wide flax hats and the kohl that male and female daubed around their eyes in lieu of the precious Tech sunglasses. But inside, or under protective awnings such as those strung over the market square, hats would be doffed, robes flipped back like cloaks, displaying bare skin, gaudy underobes and the embroidered or beaded or tattooed emblems of the Highland Houses. It was a paradox: outwardly, dour puritanism; inwardly, carnival.

I stood on the fringes, observing the display of goods and people. Nobody in sight was armed, well not visibly, but I had read too many accounts of bloodshed and the consequent blood-price not to sense the underlying menace in the marketplace. The most obvious source was the young men, who tended towards ostentatious ornament, an in-your-face statement of aggressive sexual confidence. The women were less showy, but had an air of defensibility, as if being hardbitten was a desirable female trait in the Highlands. Small wonder, I thought, recalling the mock kidnap in the marriage ceremony, and how common real raids had been until recently.

I felt a little too conspicuously a visitor, so bought a second-hand robe, the wool soft but smelly, and draped it over my shoulders. Thus partially disguised, I wandered among the stalls. A one-eyed man watched over Scavenged Tech rubbish, cans, wires, tires; a nursing mother examined the parchments of designs offered by the tattooist; a group of teenage boys, herders from their staffs, noisily tried on strings of beads; and two husky young men haggled over a tiny jar proffered for sale by an elderly woman. Hungry for overheard talk, information, I lingered by the tattoos, my interest not feigned, for I was particularly taken with one design, a serpent eating its own tail. Conversation ebbed around me, and I learnt the one-eyed Scavenger had found a new site, that the herders weren't impressed by the selection of beads, that the mother wished to mark that she now had children by all three of her husbands with a celebratory tattoo, and that the men were buying a philtre or aphrodisiac, for use on a third party. Now I was slipping into the flow of Suff speak, I quickly comprehended the old woman's spiel: "If Celat had tried *my* potion on Erewhon, none of this would have happened"

All within earshot involuntarily glanced up at the bulk of the biggest building in the town, the Courthouse/lock-up. I had, in my wanderings through the market, seen many emblems of greater or lesser Houses, a distinction the Highlanders made by the size of the landholdings. The signs were displayed on people and also the stalls, signalling the goods that were the specialties of each House. I had been making a mental checklist, and had noted two emblems unseen: the blue swirl of Erewhon, and the red swordblade of Celat. Those entitled to bear them currently resided within the lock-up, while the merits of their respective cases were decided. On the one hand, unlawful detention and threatened rape; on the other, abduction, arson and murder. No wonder the town was packed.

Sadry: The place of graves at Erewhon is a birch grove and as we walked through it, hand in hand, my parents named each tree: "This is Bryn's, this Moli the trader's, by chance at Erewhon that night and for ever after." It was a peaceful spot, even with the new thicket of saplings, Nissa's work. I could believe that any ghost here would sleep and not walk – which was precisely why I had been brought there.

Idris: Nissa and her lover were buried in the snow, weren't they? Or at Bulle?

Sadry: I don't know . . .

[A clattering interruption at this point, the turnkeys bringing in

that night's meal, the sound also coming from below, as the Celats, housed on the ground floor, were simultaneously fed.]

Sadry: On that day, or one soon after, I saw above the birches a line of pack Lori winding their way down the mountainside. Their flags had the device of a bee: Westron, our nearest neighbours. And that proved to be the first of many visits from the local and not so local Houses.

Me: Including the Celats?

Sadry: *[nods]* The message would be always be the same: Erewhon has been decimated, and you need an alliance. That meant, me + whoever was the highest bidder. But my father said to all and sundry that they had made such offers before, when he was the sole survivor of Erewhon House. And had he not responded by a second marriage with a lowland woman, outside the Rule? I, as his only child and heiress of Erewhon, also should have the opportunity of making a choice, when I was old enough.

Me: They agreed to that?

Sadry: With grumbling, yes.

Ever since contact was re-established between North and Suff, nearly a century after the Crash, anthropologists had been fascinated by the Rule. Much of their interest was prurient, with accounts of giant beds for the Queen and her consorts (a lurid fantasy, given the Intrigue configuration). I had in my pack a report positing the mechanisms by which Highland men could apparently switch from het monogamy, albeit with a brother or brothers involved in the marriage; to bisex, when an additional unrelated male entered the House, a partner for both husbands and wife; to homosex, with the Queen relationship purely platonic. It was not exactly light reading, but I persisted with it, lying on the pallet, the hum of bees filling my ears. In the end the graphs and diagrams were too much for me, and I simply stared at the wall and thought.

On, for instance, how easily the complex relationships in a Rule marriage could turn nasty, Nissa of Erewhon being merely an extreme example. Yet divorce, with people "walking out and down", i.e. to the Lowlands or to join the itinerant traders, was uncommon. Highlanders had a vested interest in conciliation, in preserving the group marriages: that was why many houses contained Mediators, skilled negotiators. The ideal was embodied in a toy I had bought at the market that little girls wore dangling from their belts: a lady-doll on a string, with a dependent number of men-dolls.

Why, I wondered, dandling the puppets, did sexual options not exist for women as well as men, with, say, linked girl-dolls? Were the Queens simply too busy with their men? Feeling frustrated I wandered outside and found Bel attending to the hives.

"Come see!" she said, and so I donned over my Highland robes the spare veil and gloves hanging behind the hut door. Bel had lifted the roof off a hive, and I stared over her black shoulder at the teeming mass of insects.

"I think I understand," I finally said, "why a hive is unlike a Rule House."

She nodded, invisible behind her veil. "Ever see a Hive where the drones bossed the show? Or without any other female bees? It would be impossible . . . "

"As a House with two Queens?" I finished.

She straightened, holding a comb-frame in her gloved hand, staring across the valley at the Courthouse roof.

"You're learning, story-eater."

Sadry: Highlanders say, when you die, you go downriver and that is what happened to me. My life at Erewhon with my parents, then my father only (after my mother went, as the Lowlanders say, underground) that is upriver to me. Everything since is the next life.

[She spoke with such intensity that I almost reached out and touched her, to belie the words.]

I went out alone after a stray Lori, the best yearling we had. Our herders had given up searching and my father was ill in bed, but I stubbornly kept looking. Most likely the animal had drowned, so I followed the Lori paths along a stream raging with snowmelt. Almost at its junction with the great river that runs from Erewhon to the lowlands, I saw a patch of colour in a large thornbush overhanging the torrent: a drowned bird, swept downstream until it had caught in the thorns. But though it was shaped like the black finches of the Highlands, the feathers were white-gold-red: a throwback to the days before the hole in the sky opened. I wanted the feathers for ornament, so leant on the thornbush, to better reach out – but the bank collapsed beneath me.

The water wasn't deep and the bush cartwheeled in its flow, taking me, my robes entangled in the branches, into the great river. Up and down I was ducked, alternately breathing and drowning, torn by thorns, or dashed against riverstones. All I could do was grab at air when I could . . .

[She paused and I again noted the fine white lines on her exposed skin, a tracery of thornmarks. Worst was the scar tissue in the palm of one hand, where she must have clutched at the bush despite the pain, in the process defacing and almost obscuring her birth marker, the Erewhon tattoo.]

I think miles went by, hours – for the next thing I recall was the evening moon. I gazed up at it, slowly comprehending that I lay still, out of the helter-skelter race of the river, and that something wet and sluggish held me fast. From the taste of silt in my mouth I knew that the bush had stuck in the mudflats where the river widens. In the moonlight I saw solid land, shoreline, but when I tried to struggle towards it I found I had no strength left. But I lived! And surely my father's herders would soon find me.

Idris: You'd forgotten . . .

Sadry: On whose land the mudflats were. So I shivered through that night, until the morning sun warmed me. I had no protection against it, so covered my face with all I had, which was mud. Then I waited for help.

Idris: The next bit is my story . . .

Sadry: *[laughing]* Tell it, then.

Idris: The river had lately brought we Celats a fine young Lori, fresh-drowned. So in hopes of further luck, I scavenged in the mudflats again. The bush sticking up like a cage, I noticed that first. Next I saw a faint movement like a crab, a human hand, then eyes looking at me out of the mud. I had to use the pack Lori to drag her out, she was stuck so fast, half-dead as she was. And the bird too, the one that had brought her to me; I found that when I washed the mud from her robes.

[She pulled from beneath her underobe a thong, pendant from it a love-charm fashioned from tiny feathers, white-gold-red. Sadry almost simultaneously revealed a duplicate charm. I wondered again at the mixture of toughness and sentimentality of the Highlanders,

then at the strength of this pair, one to survive near death from drown-ing and then exposure, the other to save her . . . In my cosy north, teenage girls are babies, but these two had a life's hard experience.]

In the courtroom, they looked tiny, my quarry, against the black-clad might of the Highland Rule. The tribunal hearing this case consisted of a Judge from Chuch, the Suff capitol, a Northern Government representative, and the only empowered woman in sight, Conye of Westron. This Queen had been the subject of a classic study, so I knew her story well – but still boggled at the fact that this dignified old lady with the multiple tattooes had seven husbands.

I bent towards Bel, sitting beside me in the public gallery. "Now *she* is like the Queen of a Hive!" I murmured.

"Only because she outlived all her drones!" Bel replied.

Around us, Suffeners commented too, court etiquette permit-ting this background buzz, along with eating and the nursing of babies or pets.

"—I ain't disrespecting new dead, but old Erewhon was mad to say no to Westron—"

"—had a bellyful of the Rule, hadn't he—"

"—but risking all that House lore being lost—"

"Excuse me," said a male voice, from behind me. "You're the anthropologist?"

I turned to see a fellow Northerner, nervously holding out an ID. It read: Fowlds, journalist.

"I'm normally posted in Chuch, so I can't make head or tail of this mountain law," he said.

"And you'd like an interpreter? Meet Bel!"

The Innkeeper grinned, speaking slowly and precisely:

"The two girls in that dock are one party; the two men another. They tell their stories, and the judges decide who are to be believed."

"Ah," he said. "And who is likely to be credible?"

Around us Suffeners sucked sweets and eavesdropped happily.

"Well," said Bel, "on the one hand we have a House wealthy and respected, but eccentric – maybe to the point of having gone just too far. That's Sadry of Erewhon, second generation Rule-breaker. On the other hand, Idye and Mors of Cclat, a lesser

House. Now they are Scavengers, but once Celat were mercenar-
ies, hired trouble, before your North outlawed feuding."

It had been a condition of autonomy, I recalled, which had
incidentally obviated the need to have a concentration of fighting
men in the fortified Houses. And thus the need to create bonds
between them, a prime function of the Rule?

"But the other girl is Idris of Celat? What is she doing with
Erewhon?"

"That's what the tribunal is trying to establish," said Bel, as
thunderous drumrolls sounded through the court, signalling the
formal start of proceedings.

Sadry: I knew that somebody found me, but merely thought I had
crossed into downriver, this life revisited, with a ghost Lori carrying me on its back to a ghost House. Somebody washed me and
bandaged my cuts – I asked her if she was an angel spirit, but she
only laughed. I slept, ate buckwheat mush when it was spooned
into my mouth, slept again. The next time I woke, the room
seemed full of men, all staring at me.

"Idris, do you know who she is?" said one, in a voice soft and
smooth as a stroked cat.

"How could I?" said the angel.

"She looks like rotting bait," said another, so big and hairy I
thought him an ogre.

"Idris, has she been instructing you how to treat her wounds?"
asked the first.

Mutinous silence. Of course I had, for sick as I was, I was still
an Erewhon healer.

"Only one way to find out!" said the third, twin of the second,
but clearly the leader. He unwrapped the bandage on my right
hand, to reveal the palm, which he inspected closely, picking at
the scab with his nails.

"Blue! The missing heir of Erewhon!"

Big hands lifted the pallet, carrying it and me out the door and
along the Intrigue space. Somewhere along the way my raw hand
struck rough stonewall, and a red haze of pain washed over me.
Even the jolt as the pallet met floor again, in a larger room, I
barely noticed.

"Where's that girl? Idris?"

"Here!" – but spoken as if through clenched teeth.

"Get her good and better, and soon, okay?"

And with that they left. The pain had cleared my head: now I could see that the angel crying as she re-bandaged my hand was only a girl my age, in a room too stuffed with Scavengers' rubbish to be ghostly.

"Which House is this?" I asked, after a while.

"Celat."

"Oh," I said. "Trouble."

"The thugs were Idye and Iain, my brothers; the smoothie Mors, Mediator of this House, and their lover."

"No Queen?" I asked, trying to recall what I knew of Celat.

"This is her room."

Idris stared into my face, as if expecting a reaction. Something was wrong, I could tell that.

She sighed, and added: "Our mother is years downriver." Her words and tone were like a trail, down which I chased a hunting beast.

"We've been too poor and disreputable for any marrying since."

The trail was warm now, and I guessed what I would find at the end of it would be unpleasant.

"Until you came along," Idris finished. "That's why they moved the bed. Don't you understand? They want you for Queen of Celat *and* Erewhon."

Indeed, an ogre with three male heads, ferocious game. I knew I had to fight it, or marry it, but how? More thinking aloud than anything else, I said:

"I'd sooner marry you!"

Idris: *[triumphantly]* And I said: Do you mean that? Do you really mean that?

The hearing began with a reading of the various charges and counter-charges, then a series of witnesses appeared. I began to get a sense of Suff law, as the bare bones of the case, what was not disputed by either side, was established. But the mix of ritual and informality in the proceedings disconcerted me, as when Bel waved wildly at some witnesses, a married trio from Greym House. They waved back, before resuming their evidence: that they, being river fishers, had found a hat with blue ties in their net.

"At least there's no argument she fell in the water," Fowlds commented.

Mors of Celat rose and bowed at the judges. I thought him a personable young buck, not as loutish as Idye beside him, with a feline, glossy look – if you liked that sort of thing. An answer to a virgin's prayers? Not from the look of black hatred that passed between him and the two girls.

"Can he address the court? I mean, he's an accused," Fowlds murmured.

Bel had gone rushing out of the gallery, leaving me to interpret as best I could.

"As a Mediator Mors is privileged to argue points of law."

"They're marriage counsellors, right?"

"Among other things," I said. "Things get fraught, you need someone like that. Otherwise you might end up like Nissa's Erewhon."

"Oh, the case people keep on mentioning," he said.

"They're similar, that's why."

"But wasn't that a mass poisoning . . . " he began, but I shushed him as Mors began to speak.

"I bring the attention of this court to the law of the Scavengers . . . "

"Cheeky beggar!" somebody muttered.

"Huh?" said Fowlds. I was feeling confused myself.

"Er, I believe it's basicallly finder's keepers."

"But it's not been applied to living humans since feuding days," Bel finished, from behind my shoulder.

"But there's a precedent?"

"Oh yes. Oh my!"

Idris had leapt up, shouting:

"I found Sadry, so she's mine! Not yours, not anybody else's."

Conye of Westron rose, and moving effortlessly despite her age, placed herself between the pair, her arms stretched out, invoking quiet.

"Another Mediator," said Bel. "She'll adjourn the court now, and let people cool off. It's getting late, so I guess they'll call it a day."

"See you in court tomorrow, then," said Fowlds. He bent

towards me. "You're an anthropologist, so is it true that these mountain guys are hot trots?"

"Why don't you find out?" I said.

"Oh I will!" – and he wandered away.

Bel said: "Come and meet a non-bee Queen."

Sadry: Idris's brothers left us alone, but Mors would bring some small comfort, like fresh milk, sit on the end of the pallet, and talk, playing mediator.

Idris: The thin part of the wedge.

Sadry: The thick part being your brothers. I put no trust in him, but he was too engaging for me to keep sulking. It became a game, to talk and parry his flirtation. That way courtship lay, I knew.

I asked: "What brought you to Celat?" and he looked rueful: "Love. Or a potion. Or perhaps both."

Idris: *[sarcastic]* "Men are such romantics."

Sadry: I said: "And you've stayed here?" – looking pointedly around the Scavengers' mess.

He said: "I mediate when Idye and Iain get into trouble."

"Like now?" I said.

He sighed. "This wasn't my idea. But as a challenge, I find it – seductive."

"As opposed to rape?"

He said, lightly: "You know that is the last resort."

I must have gone white, for he added: "But that would mean I'd failed. And I'd hate that."

When he had gone, I said to Idris: "I suppose he's not too bad."

On the wall hung the one precious thing I had seen in Celat, a Tech mirror. Idris abruptly lifted it down and set it on my chest, holding it with both hands, so all I could see was my scratched face.

"You think, you really think pretty Mors courts you for love, when you look, as Idye charmingly said, like rotten bait!"

"No," I said, sobered. She touched my cheekbones.

"I can see under the surface, but *they* can't. That protects you for the moment. But when you heal . . . "

I said: "Get word to my father!"

She hesitated, before replying: "Mors came from the market with the news your father's dead. Of sickness or worry, they say. And so Erewhon is vacant and everyone's looking for you."

I cried at that, and she kissed away my tears. After a while I said: "Then we must get out of here all by ourselves."

The Queen proved to be the fisher-girl from Greym, whom we found, together with her husbands, in Bel's private attic rooms. The trio were replete with honeycake and a keg of the weak Highland beer. Close to they seemed painfully young, in their mid-teens at most, the two obvious brothers and the girl touchingly in love with each other. Bel introduced them as Milas and Meren and Jossy, saying of the latter: "Pregnant, she tells me, but she won't say by whom . . . "

Jossy grinned with gap-toothed embarrassment. The boys were more forthcoming: "Aw, she's just kiddin' you, Cos."

Indeed, I thought, the Rule was strict regarding sexual access, precisely to prevent squabbles over paternity. Then I did a delayed doubletake at the last word spoken. Cos meant *cousin* . . .

I stared at Bel. "I thought you were a Lowlander."

"Not always," she said. "Once I could have been a Queen."

Milas coughed. "Aw, that's old history now."

I was starting to catch on. "You walked out and down from Greym? Why?"

Bel replied with a question. "You like men?" she said, looking at Jossy. "You like lots of sex with men?"

Jossy giggled; the boys exchanged glances, tolerant of their eccentric relative.

"I'll take that as a yes," Bel said. Then, more to me: "But if you don't, then there's no sense living in misery. I had a pretty young cousin, who would never question the Rule. So I gave my husbands to her."

"Our mam," said the boys proudly.

"These are her twins. I had no children, so I walked free."

She smiled at them, on her face the lines of a hard life, lived good-naturedly and without regret.

"What did you do?" I asked.

"Came down to the village and this Inn, where I asked for work as a kitchenhand, anything. And here I stayed, with Bel, who owned the Inn. When she went underground, I took her name and carried on the business."

She poured out more beer, and sliced the remaining cake. As she did, I noticed a tattoo extending from the palm of her hand to the wrist: an oval enclosing two stylized bees, under a gabled roof.

"Two Queens in a House?" I asked softly, as she passed me the cake.

"No," she replied, "Two worker bees in their Inn."

I took her hand, to better examine the device, and then noticed the pigment of one bee was faded, and that it was drawn differently from the other. It also looked vaguely familiar – and I whistled softly as I recognized a birth marker, the bee of Westron modified into an emblem that was all Bel's own.

"With your bee-skills, I should have guessed you were born at Westron."

I released her hand.

"As you're a relative, I wonder if you might get me an interview with Queen Conye. She's an interesting woman."

A guarded nod. Press on, I thought.

"I'd like that," I said. "Almost as much as I'd like to talk to Sadry and Idris."

"Easier said than done," she said.

"Well, yes."

"Conye's cranky on me, for letting the House down." She paused, and what she said next nearly floored me. "But I can get you into the lock-up." She turned to the Greym three: "And you didn't hear that, did you?"

"No, Cos," muttered one of the boys, and I began to realize the powers of this extraordinary woman.

Sadry: "Erewhon's symbol is a blue swirl, the river of life, for it is knowledge of illness that is the strength of our House, just as Dusse has botany, herbalism, and Westron the secret of mead.

[I nodded, thinking that it was as if when setting up the Rule someone had determined that the precious Tech knowledge and goods be apportioned equally between Houses.]

Sadry: In our cellars, cut deep into the mountainside, we hoard the artefacts of Tech medicine.

Me: I heard you had a pharmacopeia.

Sadry: Yes, a book of the coloured beads that the Tech people didn't wear but ate, to keep themselves well. That we salvaged ourselves, other books the Scavengers bring us. Our oldest book, though, isn't medical – it's called Erewhon, but it's not about my House, but a dream, a nowhere place. In this book things are reversed: the sick are criminals, and the criminals regarded as ill.

Idris: Are we criminal, or ill?

Bel: Both, probably, in the eyes of the men.

Sadry: The book-Erewhon seemed strange, but not much stranger than the Rule. Or the way I would live in my home, with Idris, if the court permits us.

[I thought, but did not say, that while Bel could live in the Lowlands, a happy impossibility in Highland terms, two Queens in the same mountain House was probably intolerable for the Rule-followers. Sadry was Queen of Erewhon by inheritance, but if this case went against her she could end up Queen of Nowhere.]

The Greym three had had a big, exciting day and they drooped like flowers with the dusk. Bel brought them blankets, letting them doze on her private floorspace. After she blew out the candles (Highland style, of rush and tallow), we two retired to the downstairs bar, where she ejected the last drinkers. Now we had the place to ourselves I wanted to interview this runaway Queen, but instead Bel went out. Alone, I stretched out on the hearthrug and watched the fire, thinking of the Houses and their troubles. As I lay there, unbidden came to mind the memory of an interview tape I had once heard, with an anonymous woman of Bulle.

Bulle woman: The Rule is, share and share body alike in marriage. That's why Queens seldom have a night to themselves once they wed. It's best if you're stolen by brothers, because they're like beans in the pod, so you treat them the same. But if you've got one you like less, or one you love most . . . that means trouble. Poor silly Nissa!

Interviewer: It was the lover that was the problem, wasn't it?

Bulle woman: His name was Yeny. I met him once, and wasn't surprised that Bryn Erewhon was head over heels, why he brought him into the marriage. The trouble was Nissa fell for Yeny too, and she wanted him all for herself, like a Lowlander. The sensible thing would have been to let those two walk out and down, but Bryn was stubborn, I guess, like Erewhoners are. He called in a Mediator, but that didn't work. So Nissa took the matters into her own hands.

Slowly, imperceptibly, I slipped into dream-sleep, images appearing and disappearing before my slitted eyes. First I saw the blue sign of Erewhon, the river twisting into a figure of eight, an infinity symbol, then the self-devouring serpent I had admired at the tattooist's. A log collapsed in the fireplace, and I opened and closed one eye, importing the flamescape into my dream, for now I flew above red mountains. Below my eagle-I were Houses, and I zoomed in and somehow through the thatch roof of Erewhon, to see Nissa (who looked amazingly like Sadry) zig-zagging through Intrigue. She went down a flight of stone steps to the courtyard where a Scavenger waited with goods for identification and sale: sheets of dirty foil, on one side covered with symmetrical white studs. The dream-watcher followed Nissa into the cellars, where she consulted a tattered book. When she came out again, she paid the Scavenger, and tucked the drugs into her underrobes.

I felt her cold hand – then realized it was Bel, shaking me awake.

"Come on! I've bribed you an hour's talk!"

"Wh . . . ?" I started to say, then received a spare robe full in the face, and with it the realization of where we were going.

"Hurry! Wrap yourself up!" she said.

Doubly shrouded we slipped into the darkness of the street, the mountain air chill even in summer. The village at first seemed asleep, with the mountains looming over it as if over a cradle, the gleam of snow at their peaks like watchful eyes. But as we moved swift and silent as Loris, I noticed cracks of light under shutters, heard babies' cries or soft talk, and saw distantly, in the gap between two buildings, a group of men carousing around a bonfire, among them Fowlds.

"He'll get slipped a philtre and good and proper fucked," Bel commented.

"That's what he wants," I said.

After what seemed an age Bel finally led me into a dark door-way I slowly realized was a back entrance to the Courthouse. Inside, someone waited for us, their robe thrown completely over their head, almost like Bel beekeeping. The apparition led us up stairs of scavenged Tech concrete to the second floor, where a door was unlocked for us, then locked behind us.

Sadry was awake, spinning Lori wool on a spindle, the Highland cure for fidgets, or using up time. I could see for the first time her scars, and her composed, indeed, queenly mien. Idris slept, her head on Sadry's knee; she stirred as we approached, knuckling her eyes. For a long moment there was silence, before Bel fumbled under her robe and produced delicacies: fresh Lori cheese, fruit, cured meat.

"Greetings Bel Innkeeper, greetings Northerner," Sadry said, her voice neutral as she accepted the gifts.

I had nothing to offer, but nonetheless pulled out my tape recorder from under my robes. Idris goggled at the device, then said to Sadry: "What, our words to be set down and used against us?"

"For an interview," I said, alarmed, "It's standard practice."

"I didn't agree to a Tech toy," Sadry said. She looked at Bel. "Your intermediary never mentioned it . . . "

Idris reached forward, as if to snatch away the device, and I clutched it, inadvertently activating Record. She spoke, her voice a snarl, rising . . . until Bel clapped a hand over her mouth.

"Hush," she said. "Would you wake the guards? When the Northerner is like me, and like you!"

Idris's eyes rolled.

I said, my voice trembling, now I was so near to my goal, and yet not there yet: "I . . . we . . . my friends . . . we monitor . . . looking for . . . breakers of the rules . . . even in such a male-dominated society . . . you see, it's so important that you exist, we need a record . . . of women loving women . . . that's why I want your story!"

The gaze of these two girl lovers met, considering my plea.

I started the interview story-eater style, using the polite Highland opener of recounting my latest dream. One dream demands another, and so Sadry responded with her ghost story, continuing the theme of Nissa, which recurred as if haunting the conversation:

Sadry: My father said he got sick of it, Bryn moping, Nissa

storming, and Yeny in the middle (who was not *his* lover) unable to make up his mind. So he went off herding . . .

Idris: It saved him from a dose of worm-cure!

[I thought of my dream again. If Bel had not shaken me awake, I possibly might have continued the dream, with Nissa–Sadry one snowy night serving her in-laws a Bulle herbal remedy, but combined with what from the pharmacopeic texts in the library she knew to be sleeping pills. Presumably she wanted everyone in the House to sleep long enough for her and her lover to elope. Murder meant feuding, and mass murder surely a civil war. Her bad luck then, or her curse, as the Highlanders said, that the pills were contaminated, or when combined with the herbs, toxic. Ten people died at Erewhon, two more when Nissa's flight ended in an avalanche – incidentally saving, as the Bulle woman had noted, that House from a ruinous bloodprice.]

Me: What saved Mors?

[They eyed me. This I knew was the nub of the case, whether the story of Nissa had repeated with Sadry.]

Idris: He was called away to Mediate, in a dispute over some Lori.

Me: And with only two men left in the house, you acted.

Idris: They got drunk as pigs.

Me: On pissweak Highland beer?

Idris *[defensively]*: Maybe they had mead.

Me: That's a luxury. You said Celat was poor.

Sadry: What is this? An interview or an interrogation?

Bel: It will help you! And you need help.

[Long pause]

Me: What happened?

Idris: I cooked for my brothers that night, and then went upstairs with sop for Sadry. We could hear roistering below, and I barred the door of the Queen's room with what I could find and move . . . without Mors to Mediate, Sadry wasn't safe.

Sadry: The House went quiet.

Idris: I went down to see what was going on, and found my brother Iain passed out at the table. Idye was the same, sprawled in the courtyard. Without losing a moment, I went out to the field where our two best and biggest Lori grazed. I brought them into the courtyard, found halters and saddlecloths, then tied them by the door, while I went into the house for my Queen.

Sadry: I could barely walk, so she near carried me downstairs, and got me onto the Lori.

Idris: I went upstairs to get extra robes against the night air, but having a sudden idea, grabbed rags and a haybale I had been using to re-stuff a pallet. With them I formed a mock Sadry under the blanket in the Queen's room.

Sadry: That done, just like that! we stole away into the darkness, heading for Erewhon.

Idris: *[hesitant]* We don't know what happened next.

Me: I hear Idye was too drunk to remember a thing.

Idris: I was right to take her! Iain went into the Queen's room!

Me: He was fuddled.

Sadry: He meant harm.

Idris: But in igniting the dummy Queen, he harmed nobody but himself.

Me: And the House.

[I thought again of the Inn fire, of the log imploding in a shower of sparks. Celat House and its flammable rubbish had burnt like Bel's kindling, leaving ashes – in which Mors and a party from a neighbouring House had found the charred form of Iain, a metal candleholder and long-bladed hunting knife by his side. Idye had survived, simply because he had slumped in the courtyard, out of the flame's reach.]

Sadry: We defended ourselves.

Me: I understand that, but to the extent of doing a Nissa?

Idris: That is for the court to decide.

Bel: We should stop now. The guard's shift ends soon, and I could only afford one bribe!

And she turned the recorder off. End of conversation, with the two defendants, but not with Bel, for when we got back to the Inn she stoked the fire and poured out beer for us.

I took a couple of mouthfuls, and said: "This stuff really is feeble. I reckon Idris nobbled her brothers' beer!"

Bel shrugged. "All the village thinks so, but with what?"

Now it was my turn to shrug. "I've seen a pharmacopoeia book in a museum. It described everything the Tech culture took for their ailments. So, if something drastically increased the effects of alcohol, Sadry would have known it and told Idris."

Bel pulled off her outer layer of robe. "Maybe."

"But how did they get hold of it?" I wondered.

"The House was full of Scavenged goods, remember?"

"Good point. Anything could have been stored there." I rolled out on the rug again, watching flames.

Bel hunkered down beside me. "Well, if we are play judges, and have solved the mystery, what do we do now, given the important difference between this case and Nissa's? Idris and Sadry survived, and that means they are answerable for bloodprice."

"Even for an accidental death," I replied, with a sinking feeling.

"And the fratricide makes it worse. Not to mention burning the House, and stealing Idris, the one thing Celat had to barter on the marriage market."

I supped more beer. "Extenuating circumstances. Sadry escaped enforced marriage."

"But she also broke the Rule."

"Into little pieces," I finished, putting down the mug. "They don't stand much of a chance, do they?"

Bel put her hand on my shoulder. "That was why I took you to the lock-up, to collect their story, and disseminate it over the North."

I turned, and her grip grew firmer, kneading me.

"And, because I wanted you to be grateful to me."

I laughed and quoted Idris: "'Do you mean that? Do you really mean that?'"

I had come to the mountains a detached, dispassionate observer, with a story to eat. But, almost despite myself, the case study of Sadry and Idris, and the other like-minded women of the Highlands had come to involve me. Taking Bel's hand in mine, I touched her bees and felt them slightly raised – a cicatrice. Tonight, we would play Queens of the Inn, and the two bees would crawl all over my skin. And tomorrow, to celebrate, I would go to the market tattooist and mark myself with the snake – for now this mountain herstory was part of me, and I was a serpent eating my own tale.

TOMORROW IS SAINT VALENTINE'S DAY

Tori Truslow

Elijah Willemot Wynn: A Life • **Chapter 7**

> *Your Strangenesses are numberless*
> *For each I love you all the more*
> *It is not* me *that turns from you*
> *But my unenchanting form.*
> —Catherin Northcliffe, *The Mortal Lover*, 1891

Merish song was attributed unique physical qualities even in folklore, and as with much folklore this has proved to have a factual root. We now know that their songs move through the air as particles rather than as waves, penetrating and becoming stuck under the shells of moon-floating molluscs. A layer of tissue forms over the song-grain, and a kind of pearl is formed. What remains unexplained is the remarkable fact that shells containing these pearls have recently been found on mortal shores, and when held to the ear have echoed mer-songs from over a hundred years ago.
> —Tony Peacock, "Defining Elemental Sound",
> Modern Faery Studies, June 2008

After the lecture tour and all the controversy that bubbled in its wake, it was suggested to Wynn by his colleagues that he leave England for a time. Not surprisingly, he embraced this advice and made preparations to visit the Tychonic Institute in Denmark. Before he could leave, however, came the announcement that was to open a new door for him, one that would lead to so many captivating insights and the promise of lasting good relations between humans and merfolk. Had he lived longer, history might have followed a very different course. But whatever did happen to Elijah Willemot Wynn? Previous biographers have latched onto wild conspiracies, but in the light of cutting-edge new research, the facts speak for themselves. We are now entering a darker chapter in his life: the academic alienation and the increasingly bizarre theories leading up to his disappearance – but alongside that, the unorthodox personal life, and at the start of it all: New Year's Day, 1880.

On that day, it was announced that at long last members of the public would be able to buy tickets for the Great Ice Train. Wynn was among the first to book his place. It was the moment he had dreamed of all his life: the journey to

the moist star,
Upon whose influence Neptune's empire stands.[1]

The train departed on Friday the thirteenth of February – a date now infamous in history. Horace Hunt, who was also on that fatal journey, recorded it in his memoirs:

We stood shivering in our thick coats on that desolate Northern platform . . . the train rose out of the water like a ghost. We stood, gaping idiotically at it – but not Elijah. He mounted the step and strode into the carriage. Emboldened, we followed – several slipped and fell on the frozen steps, but at last we were all aboard. I had followed Elijah into the first carriage. Directly before us was the captain's car, completely filled by the intricate engine, pipes connecting jars and tanks of strange half-substantial things. The sea glowed all around us . . . we gazed up through the ceiling to our destination and felt a queer tug as the Moon opened her

---

1 *Hamlet* 1.1.118-9. How Shakespeare knew of the mer-people's tidal migration to the moon remains a mystery, but these lines show that the Bard knew even more of Faery than we have given him credit for. *Hamlet* is not usually considered an elficological play, but in *Rosencrantz and Guildenstern are Faeries* C.C. Temple uncovers a wealth of hidden references and makes a compelling argument for *Hamlet* as a *radically* Faery-based text.

pores. A watery clicking came from the engine; the enchanted molecules of unfrozen water thrummed through the sides of the train as it was lifted with all its captive passengers into the heavens. We were utterly silent, awe-struck by the sight of the Arctic sea beneath, the vast starry expanse above, all seen through the pipes and gears of ice in the glass-green walls of this glacier shaped so much like a train.

We gathered speed and were soon moving faster than the fastest locomotive on Earth. The rattling was just as loud as any train at home, so loud that I thought the carriages would splinter and leave us in the void above our darkened planet. To be sitting on the thick silver fur that lined seats of ice with all that space and darkness in every direction was beyond belief. I suppose I sat gaping at the sublimity of it for some time, but I eventually roused myself and had started to form some great thought that might have changed the course of philosophy and religion, when I saw the lunar surface was growing closer and closer ahead – why was the captain not slowing us down? He paid no heed to the shapes so frantically dancing in the engine's bulbous jars – the smoke in one tank had materialised into a tangling of cuttle-fish which all turned jet-black – the captain had gone as pale as the Moon's face, staring as if he could not comprehend where he was . . . [1]

Hunt and Wynn were among a small handful of survivors. Many were killed by great shards of ic e as the train shattered; many more when the wet lunar air entered their lungs. Before Kristoffersen's successful refining of sailor's stone, the only way mortals could survive on the moon was to receive a kiss from a merwoman. An explorer of those early days recalled "a row of sirens, lovely naked bodies with hideous scaly legs and flat disk-like eyes, waiting on the platform to bestow their briny kisses of life".[2] The train crashed outside the city's dome, with no platform

---

1 Hunt, *Diary of a Man in the Moon*, 17

2 Ulysses Wright, quoted in *Early Accounts of Moon Exploration,* ed. S. Banerjee, 87

and no waiting merwomen. As the moon was soaking up seawater, however, merfolk would have been appearing in their moon-forms nearby. Some noticed the peril of those still living and rushed to plant kisses on the men who held their breath.

Wynn was reached by a young mermaid who had been gathering sea-flowers for her garden, who

> *Bedecked with microscopic nacre scales*
> *Outshined the galaxy's starry spray.*[1]

Dizzy and bruised, he let her take him into the dome.

The city, until six years before, had been mobile, washing between moon and sea with the tides. Since the construction of the dome, the merfolk could enjoy the same permanence there as in their enchanted sea-palaces – but the moon-form of their city was then a tight cluster of palatial seashells and nothing more. This would remain as the centre of the new town, but the settlement that Wynn crashed in front of was at that time still a network of industrious, rough-cut hamlets and villages around a gilded heart.

Wynn's rescuer and her family lived in an isolated crater by the dome's circumference. He limped across the short distance, his feet lacerated by the fragmented train. Thus it was that he arrived at the setting of his most vivid passages: badly crippled and leaving a trail of misty blood in the air.

> They are citizens of Melzun, a family of gardeners toiling to make this young city beautiful. They live in a hollow fringed by thick multihued polypi, surrounded by glimmering rock-pools and pearly boulders that serve as anchors to the long-tendrilled flowers that caress this strange, moist, salty air.
>
> At the bottom of the hollow, lined with living sponge, my pretty little saviour and her sisters laid out food in silver bowls. They eat lying down on their stomachs, which appears uncomfortable – but I think they are used to grazing on their bellies. We ate elongated mushrooms that

1 Northcliffe, 'The Moon-Jewel'

reminded me of oysters, and some of the polypi from their garden – gelatinous and red; I was apprehensive of them at first but they were delicious, although it is impossible to describe the flavour; they tasted *bright* – and fruits rather like oranges, but turquoise, with a taste something like spiced rum. It seems everything that grows here takes on a subtle salty taste, but it is not unpleasant.

I spoke very falteringly in the mertongue, trying to some-how explain that I needed to find the RAEI [Royal Anthro-Elficological Institute] building. They insisted that I rest till I am recovered from the accident – they will take me to the town when I am better. So here I sit on a bed of slowly beating sponge, gazing out of this hole at the sky where sleeping nautili float weirdly in the starlight, writing this – though I don't know when I'll be able to send it . . .

(Letter to Robert Creschen, 1880)

His wounds healed well, "with the aid of an unpleasant, squirm-ing unguent", though even then the long journey on foot to the gilt shell-buildings of central Melzun must have been painful. Wynn forgot his discomfort as they drew nearer, becoming wildly excited by the symptoms of mer–human cooperation he saw around him. Man-made streetlamps held blue mer-conjured fire and drew "silent fish on gossamer wings to kiss their own reflec-tions". He was equally impressed by the old shell-buildings and those newly built in more human styles – in particular, the water-house, stocked with "great tanks of clean water that we mortals may drink, but securely sealed so no merman will touch it and dissolve". He got as far as the first step leading to the RAEI and stopped, enraptured, at the sight of an omnibus rounding the corner, "exactly like a London bus, but with wheels encircled by delicate anemone fronds and pulled by a beast rather like an over-grown mackerel in the shape of a horse" (Letter to Nellie Bell, 1880).

The Institute, however, was a bitter disappointment, stuffed to the top with stuffy government scholars who squinted at fins through lenses and made futile attempts to render merish archi-tecture on paper. They did not warm to Wynn, regarding him as an amateur and his ideas dangerous. He endured their

old-fashioned methods and their comments on his lack of alchem-
ical knowledge for a month, before deciding that he would make
more progress living amongst the merfolk and observing the
routine of their lives. He returned to the family that had shown
him such kindness on his arrival.

Wynn reports that they were just as welcoming the second
time, even building him some sort of room out of fine yellow coral
in their now-thriving garden. Why they were so keen for him to
stay and study them remains a mystery. It was there that he wrote
his most celebrated works, uncovering a great deal of information
on mer-culture in conversation with his hosts. Not long after his
arrival, he witnessed the event that inspired a series of writings
eventually to be collected in *Festivals and Rites of Passage among
the Merfolk*:

The youngest daughter sat at the heart of the house, her
hair entangled by tentacled flowers that writhed from the
limpet-starred ceiling and her face scintillating with fins
plucked from countless scarab-like fish. She was given a
bowl, into which her sisters placed various lunar fruits. She
ate these sitting upright, an awkward position for her species
to eat in. Her family stood around, holding censers filled
with a bladderwrack-like plant that smelled, when burned,
like a summer's sea-breeze, singing songs that appeared to
ripple through the smoke in colours never seen on Earth.

When she had eaten, she joined in the song, at which the
woman of the house stepped forward with a silver tray holding fish-bones strange to the eye, as if they were of mercury,
flowing inwardly while keeping their outward shape. The
tentacles from the ceiling gripped the girl's arms as the
woman pierced her back, between the spikes of her vertebrae, with these unearthly bones. The child cried out, and
the air around the holes was coloured by red spray.

I observed the parents' own piercings, quicksilver spines
which seemed part of their flesh, significantly larger than
the girl's ornaments. After the ceremony, which ended with
more singing and the drinking of a heady liquor made from
pearls, the mother explained to me that they *are* a part of
her. After piercing, one tidal cycle between mortal

moon-form and elemental sea-form transforms the jewels first into a part of the merman's soul and then of his living body. From what phrases of their singing I could glean, I believe this is somehow connected to their longevity, an area which still demands meaningful research. A merman can live for an astonishing 300 years, yet no established elficologist has provided a convincing study of this. I submit that my discovery of the piercing ritual is a possible key to understanding it.

                                    (FRPM, first edition, 34)

The dig at the RAEI did not pass unnoticed, but by the time complaints were aired, Wynn had quite different matters on his mind. In his essays and books, he continued to call his favourite subject for observation "the youngest daughter of the house", but in letters to friends, as the years went by, the descriptions of her changed. From "my pretty little saviour", she was transformed into a variety of whimsical creatures, including "the bright pearlskinned flower-enchanting heart's light of this cold moon" (Letter to Catherin Northcliffe, 1882). By the time she was eighteen, he had a name for her: "Opal", which he claimed was wonderfully similar to the first syllables of her merish name (never recorded). It is hard to miss the significance of this, especially given her love of flowers and a curiosity about humanity that prompted him to travel to Earth and back just to bring her books – including the plays of Shakespeare. By all accounts she was a charming and innocent girl who loved to sing – Wynn would have lost no time in imagining her part in the favourite play of his youth and naming her after the "mermaid-like" Ophelia. Perhaps "Opal" herself embraced this association, uncommonly enamoured as she was of human poetry.

As her womanhood bloomed, so did their romance. This is largely documented in the poems of Catherin Northcliffe, who controversially gained the title of Lunar Laureate in 1885, and treated Wynn's adopted household as an idyllic writing retreat for some time. Two years previously, Wynn had written to her (then still in England) about Opal dancing:

in a splendid squid-silk tent all sewn with dusky pearls. Since she came in on the last tide her arms are encrusted with the tiny peaks of silver barnacles that flare in the deep blue lamplight, like sequins or perhaps armour. Her tiny peacock-scaled feet twist in ways that jolt my eye, suggesting, in the corners of my vision, that they are not tiny at all. I never used to think of my feet, and now I do so only to regret their condition. What must it be to have toes that are really the fleshy, scaly shell of a vast, unworldly tail-fin? There is a subject for you! A mortal, upon seeing a mermaid dance, yearning to have such legs, such power, such strangeness. I will await the poem, sealed in a mottled glass bottle, on the next tide.

(Letter to Catherin Northcliffe, 1883)

Northcliffe was captivated. Their correspondence from then on focused on little other than the merfolk and their culture. When she came to the moon she stayed with Wynn for long periods of time. The mermaid figures in her poems are doubtless almost all Opal. The mortal lovers are often a version of Wynn.

How far Wynn allowed the physical aspect of the relationship to progress is unknown. Some poems from Northcliffe's "Siren" cycle hint at bizarre debaucheries, but one of her unpublished poems, apparently narrated from Wynn's perspective, is far more frank:

A mortal maid and an undine
I spied amidst the coral ferns
And knew not if I greater yearned
To kiss the pink-lipp'd or the green.

"Twin cups of rarest love I see"
I cried – "I cannot choose my way"
Twin bosoms, scale and skin, laughed "Nay,
Love can full fill these vessels three!

Think you we two would willing part
That only one should take thy hand?
Come lay here on this lucent sand

And learn to share thy brimming heart. "[1]

Northcliffe, however, is known for her flights of fancy – and besides, better-substantiated accounts of mer–human sexual encounters[2] are harrowing enough to suggest that Wynn would have reacted far more strongly than he did if her poems were true. They are clearly Northcliffe's fantasy, fuelled at once by her jealous desire to compete with Opal in Wynn's estimation and her own, presumably repressed, lesbian attraction towards Opal.

It is far more likely that Wynn kept Opal at a physical distance, enjoying an idealised, non-sexual – yet always deeply passionate, in its way – romance.

But even that was no match for their ultimate incompatibility.

> My Opal has come back from the sea wearing living beads in her hair, bubbles of light clasped amongst her locks, winking red, yellow and mauve. I have seen this on other merwomen, a sign of yearning for children. I have been feeling not dissimilar pangs myself. But what can we do? I cannot carry her eggs in my belly and she could not nurture my seed in her womb. Oh, if I could only change that!
>
> (Letter to Robert Creschen, 1887)

Of course, he could not. But he grew obsessed with the idea, returning to the RAEI and bombarding its scholars with wild new theories. A doctor there, one of the first to notice the adverse effects of the lunar atmosphere on the human brain, kept notes on Wynn's behaviour, from his initial visit as "a pseudo-elficologist raving about how he would become a merman if we gave over our valuable resources to his lunatic scheme" to the letters the RAEI started to receive from Wynn after his return to Opal's family:

> He wrote again yesterday, saying he had, with the help of the poetess, undergone a version of the merfolk's ritual piercing. This, he supposes, would transform him over time

---

1   Northcliffe, 'The Three of Cups', c.1886
2   As collected in *True Nightmares: Sex on the Moon* vols I, II and III, ed. Jared Norman

into one of them, if we were to help him travel between this plane of being and another over and again. It seems the mercury in those bones has only been fuel to his insanity[1].

After several fruitless months of mimicking every aspect of merish life and repeatedly asking the RAEI for various forms of aid, Wynn went suddenly quiet. Very little is known about his activities over the following year; the next record of his movements that we have is a final letter to the RAEI in October, 1888, stating that he was leaving and knew he would find better help in England. What was he up to in the meantime? In all likelihood, he wrote: friends that he spoke to upon his return to Earth report that he mentioned a work-in-progress entitled "This Too Solid Flesh", the manuscripts of which are lost. Robert Creschen was one of those Wynn met, and though Creschen only gives a cursory mention of their meeting in his diary, it was not long after that he penned his first literary success, horror classic *The Mermaid Wife* (1894). If this work was influenced by Wynn's experiences, as it undoubtedly was, some disturbing conclusions about his final months on the Moon can be drawn from it. The passage wherein Creschen's fictional Wynn-figure, William Elverson, relates his misfortunes to the narrator is particularly chilling:

"You think you know things, that the concrete world and the aether are mapped in formulae by your alchemists." He leaned close, gin and nightmares rank on his breath. "If you had seen a shadow, a mere reflection, heard a whisper of what I have, you would not set foot on that train. Your eye would flinch from the sight of the Moon in the sky. The night and the sea would be devilish to you, and you would not walk another easy step in your life. She ruined my mind, Crescent, and even that was not enough. She wanted to spread her corruption into our race, wanted to debase my humanity and my bloodline; she would have – good God! – shared me with a merman so he could carry the demons we created."[2]

1 Notes collected from the RAEI by Lucien Farrell, British Library
2 Creschen, *The Mermaid Wife*, 149

Underneath Creschen's melodramatic association of merfolk with demons, there is conceivably some truth in the suggestion of a surrogate father, and it is not unreasonable to conclude that such a demand would be sufficient to drive Wynn away for good. Once on Earth again, he became much calmer, and deeply absorbed in study.

And that is where Opal's story has ended – until now. But in February 1889, something happened to change Wynn completely. From then on his friends noted "inexplicable strangeness, prolonged waking dreams, frighteningly alien movements and utterances"[1] which increased until the time of his disappearance. What was it that sent those first fine cracks across the surface of his sanity?

What else? He received word of Opal's suicide – a suicide we could not have known about until last year's discovery of merish song-shells. These shells, holding songs sung on the moon over a century ago, are currently stumping our scientists by washing up on Earth's beaches. One of these shells has just been dated to the thirteenth of February, 1889: the day before Wynn's mental well-being took a drastic turn for the worse; the ninth anniversary of their first meeting. The song within the shell is English, which no other mermaids are known to have sung in. Now, her voice flies hauntingly across the years to us, and the song is all too familiar:

Tomorrow is Saint Valentine's day
All in the morning betime,
And I a maid at your window,
To be your Valentine.

Then up he rose and donned his clothes
And dupped the chamber door,
Let in the maid, that out a maid
Never departed more.[2]

---

1   Creschen, *Memoirs*, 624
2   *Hamlet* 4.5.48-55, recorded in song-shell, Luna 13 February 1889, accessed by the author at the St. Ives Ocean Observatory

The responses so far to this discovery have been speculative, tenuous at best.

What seems to be an echo, perhaps a sort of feedback caused by the metaphysical transportation of the song-particles, has been seized on by some scholars who claim it is in fact a male voice singing faintly alongside her. Isobel Cutter even claims that it proves her (already widely discredited[1]) theory that Wynn succeeded at becoming a merman, writing that:

> The fluidity between mortal and merish form needed to be activated somehow, and with no outside help his only option was astral projection. To hear him singing a duet with Opal seems impossible – unless, of course, he was successfully projecting onto the moon. Northcliffe's later work mentions a ghostly lover slowly becoming more solid – perhaps this is Wynn, at last becoming the merman he longed to be. His Earthly disappearance, in that light, is unsurprising – his Earth-bound self would have eventually become purely elemental.[2]

As discussed, Northcliffe is hardly a reliable historic source – her refusal to join the human exodus from the moon at the turn of the century and the subsequent brain-damage and physical decay she must have suffered renders her late work (or at least, what has been recovered of it) particularly questionable. But besides this and Cutter's flimsy science, the theory conveniently ignores the source of the song.

Here was a mermaid who had loved a man – who had been named after Ophelia by that man, maybe even driven mad by him; who knows what lasting psychological damage may have been caused by this passion for a man of the wrong species, and one who could only ever fail to live up to her society's ideal of masculinity? The answer, then, to the question of *what possible reason she could have to sing one of Ophelia's mad songs* is woefully

1   See the author's review of Cutter's *Children of the Air: The Lost Lunar Settlers* in the *Times Literary Supplement*, 19 September 2006

2   Cutter, "Notes on a Late Nineteenth Century Song-Shell", Metaphysics Quarterly, October 2008

clear: unable to find him after his return to England, she chose to end her life in a way that she hoped would connect them. He had seen her as an Ophelia, so she would live out his ideal to the very end. We can imagine her wreathing herself in living flowers and walking, singing as she went, to the centre of Melzun, to the water-house with its tanks of clean water. We can picture her slipping quietly inside, opening a tank and climbing in and – singing still – closing the lid on herself even as she began to disintegrate, turning the fresh water to brine. Later, the tank would have been checked, found to be contaminated, and drained off outside the dome. And when the moon next released its absorbed water back into the sea, Opal's particles would have returned with it, nothing more than foam on the high tide.

Here, perhaps, Northcliffe is at last a dependable chronicler – for what else could she have been alluding to in the last section of her final, incomplete work, "The Mortal Lover?"

> *Night, its pearls strewn on the air*
> *Confines me to this reeling shore—*
> *These long grey tides ebb you from here*
> *Transformed beyond the dreams of form.*

SPIDER THE ARTIST

Nnedi Okorafor

Zombie no go go, unless you tell am to go
Zombie!
Zombie!
Zombie no go stop, unless you tell am to stop
Zombie no go turn, unless you tell am to turn
Zombie!
Zombie no go think, unless you tell am to think
         —from *Zombie* by Fela Kuti, Nigerian
musician and self-proclaimed voice of the voiceless.

My husband used to beat me. That was how I ended up out there that evening behind our house, just past the bushes, through the tall grass, in front of the pipelines. Our small house was the last in the village, practically in the forest itself. So nobody ever saw or heard him beating me.

Going out there was the best way to put space between me and him without sending him into further rage. When I went behind the house, he knew where I was and he knew I was alone. But he was too full of himself to realize I was thinking about killing myself.

My husband was a drunk, like too many of the members of the Niger Delta People's Movement. It was how they all controlled their anger and feelings of helplessness. The fish, shrimps and crayfish in the creeks were dying. Drinking the water shriveled women's wombs and eventually made men urinate blood.

There was a stream where I had been fetching water. A flow station was built nearby and now the stream was rank and filthy, with an oily film that reflected rainbows. Cassava and yam farms yielded less and less each year. The air left your skin dirty and smelled like something preparing to die. In some places, it was always daytime because of the noisy gas flares.

My village was shit.

On top of all this, People's Movement members were getting picked off like flies. The "kill-and-go" had grown bold. They shot People's Movement members in the streets, they ran them over, dragged them into the swamps. You never saw them again.

I tried to give my husband some happiness. But after three years, my body continued to refuse him children. It's easy to see the root of his frustration and sadness . . . but pain is pain. And he dealt it to me regularly.

My greatest, my only true possession was my father's guitar. It was made of fine polished Abura timber and it had a lovely tortoiseshell pick guard. Excellent handwork. My father said that the timber used to create the guitar came from one of the last timber trees in the delta. If you held it to your nose, you could believe this. The guitar was decades old and still smelled like fresh cut wood, like it wanted to tell you its story because only it could.

I wouldn't exist without my father's guitar. When he was a young man, he used to sit in front of the compound in the evening and play for everyone. People danced, clapped, shut their eyes and listened. Cell phones would ring and people would ignore them. One day, it was my mother who stopped to listen.

I used to stare at my father's fast long-fingered hands when he played. Oh, the harmonies. He could weave anything with his music – rainbows, sunrises, spider webs sparkling with morning dew. My older brothers weren't interested in learning how to play. But I was, so my father taught me everything he knew. And now it was my long fingers that graced the strings. I'd always been able to hear music and my fingers moved even faster than my father's. I was good. Really good.

But I married that stupid man. Andrew. So I only played behind the house. Away from him. My guitar was my escape.

That fateful evening, I was sitting on the ground in front of the fuel pipeline. It ran right through everyone's backyard. My village was an oil village, as was the village where I grew up. My mother lived in a similar village before she was married, as did her mother. We are Pipeline People.

My mother's grandmother was known for lying on the pipeline running through her village. She'd stay like that for hours, listening and wondering what magical fluids were running through the large never-ending steel tubes. This was before the Zombies, of course. I laughed. If she tried to lie on a pipeline now she'd be brutally killed.

Anyway, when I was feeling especially blue, I'd take my guitar and come out here and sit right in front of the pipeline. I knew I was flirting with death by being so close but when I was like this, I didn't really care. I actually welcomed the possibility of being done with life. It was a wonder that my husband didn't smash my guitar during one of his drunken rages. I'd surely have quickly thrown myself on the pipeline if he did. Maybe that was why he'd rather smash my nose than my guitar.

This day, he'd only slapped me hard across the face. I had no idea why. He'd simply come in, seen me in the kitchen and *smack!* Maybe he'd had a bad day at work – he worked very hard at a local restaurant. Maybe one of his women had scorned him. Maybe I did something wrong. I didn't know. I didn't care. My nose was just starting to stop bleeding and I was not seeing so many stars.

My feet were only inches from the pipeline. I was especially daring this night. It was warmer and more humid than normal. Or maybe it was my stinging, burning face. The mosquitoes didn't even bother me much. In the distance, I could see Nneka, a woman who rarely spoke to me, giving her small sons a bath in a large tub. Some men were playing cards at a table several houses down. It was dark, there were small, small trees and bushes here and even our closest neighbor was not very close, so I was hidden.

I sighed and placed my hands on the guitar strings. I plucked out a tune my father used to play. I sighed and closed my eyes. I would always miss my father. The feel of the strings vibrating under my fingers was exquisite.

I fell deep into the zone of my music, weaving it, then floating on a glorious sunset that lit the palm tree tops and . . .

Click!

I froze. My hands still on the strings, the vibration dying. I didn't dare move. I kept my eyes closed. The side of my face throbbed.

Click! This time the sound was closer. *Click!* Closer. *Click!* Closer.

My heart pounded and I felt nauseous with fear. Despite my risk taking, I knew this was *not* the way I wanted to die. Who would want to be torn limb from limb by Zombies? As everyone in my village did multiple times a day, I quietly cursed the Nigerian government.

Twing!

The vibration of the guitar string was stifled by my middle finger still pressing it down. My hands started to shake, but still I kept my eyes shut. Something sharp and cool lifted my finger. I wanted to scream. The string was plucked again.

Twang!

The sound was deeper and fuller, my finger no longer muffling the vibration. Very slowly, I opened my eyes. My heart skipped. The thing stood about three feet tall, which meant I was eye-to eye with it. I'd never seen one up close. Few people have. These things are always running up and down the pipeline like a herd of super-fast steer, always with things to do.

I chanced a better look. It really *did* have eight legs. Even in the darkness, those legs shined, catching even the dimmest light. A bit more light and I'd have been able to see my face perfectly reflected back at me. I'd heard that they polished and maintained themselves. This made even more sense now, for who would have time to keep them looking so immaculate?

The government came up with the idea to create the Zombies, and Shell, Chevron and a few other oil companies (who were just as desperate) supplied the money to pay for it all. The Zombies were made to combat pipeline bunkering and terrorism. It makes me laugh. The government and the oil people destroyed our land and dug up our oil, then they created robots to keep us from taking it back.

They were originally called Anansi Droids 419 but we call them "*oyibo* contraption" and, most often, Zombie, the same name we call those "kill-and-go" soldiers who come in here harassing us every time something bites their brains.

It's said that Zombies can think. Artificial Intelligence, this is called. I have had some schooling, a year or two of university, but my area was not in the sciences. No matter my education, as soon as I got married and brought to this damn place I became like every other woman here, a simple village woman living in the delta region where Zombies kill anyone who touches the pipelines and whose husband knocks her around every so often. What did I know about Zombie intellect?

It looked like a giant shiny metal spider. It moved like one too. All smooth-shifting joints and legs. It crept closer and leaned in to inspect my guitar strings some more. As it did so, two of its back legs tapped on the metal of the pipeline. *Click! Click! Click!*

It pushed my thumb back down on the strings and plucked the string twice, making a muted *pluck!* It looked at me with its many blue shining round eyes. Up close I could see that they weren't lights. They were balls of a glowing metallic blue undulating liquid, like charged mercury. I stared into them fascinated. No one else in my village could possibly know this fact. No one had gotten close enough. *Eyes of glowing bright blue liquid metal*, I thought. *Na wa.*

It pressed my hand harder and I gasped, blinking and looking away from its hypnotic eyes. Then I understood.

"You . . . you want me to play?"

It sat there waiting, placing a leg on the body of my guitar with a soft *tap.* It had been a long time since anyone had wanted me to play for him. I played my favorite highlife song, "Love Dey See Road" by Oliver De Coque. I played like my life depended on it.

The Zombie didn't move, its leg remaining pressed to my guitar. Was it listening? I was sure it was. Twenty minutes later, when I stopped finally playing, sweat running down my face, it touched the tips of my aching hands. Gently.

Some of these pipelines carry diesel fuel, others carry crude oil. Millions of liters of it a day. Nigeria supplies 25 percent of United States oil. And we get virtually nothing in return. Nothing but death by Zombie attack. We can all tell you stories.

When the Zombies were first released, no one knew about them. All people would hear were rumors about people getting torn apart near pipelines or sightings of giant white spiders in the night. Or you'd hear about huge pipeline explosions, charred bodies everywhere. But the pipeline where the bodies lay would be perfectly intact.

People still bunkered. My husband was one of them. I suspected that he sold the fuel and oil on the black market; he would bring some of the oil home, too. You let it sit in a bucket for two days and it would become something like kerosene. I used it for cooking. So I couldn't really complain. But bunkering was a very, very dangerous practice.

There *were* ways of breaking a pipeline open without immediately bringing the wrath of Zombies. My husband and his comrades used some sort of powerful laser cutter. They stole them from the hospitals. But they had to be very, very quiet when cutting through the metal. All it took was one bang, one vibration, and the Zombies would come running within a minute. Many of my husband's comrades had been killed because of the tap of someone's wedding ring or the tip of the laser cutter on steel.

Two years ago a group of boys had been playing too close to the pipeline. Two of them were wrestling and they fell on it. Within seconds the Zombies came. One boy managed to scramble away. But the other was grabbed by the arm and flung into some bushes. His arm and both of his legs were broken. Government officials *said* that Zombies were programmed to do as little harm as possible but . . . I didn't believe this, *na* lie.

They were terrible creatures. To get close to a pipeline was to risk a terrible death. Yet the goddamn things ran right through our backyards.

But I didn't care. My husband was beating the hell out of me during these months. I don't know why. He had not lost his job. I knew he was seeing other women. We were poor but we were not starving. Maybe it was because I couldn't bear him children. It is my fault I know, but what can I do?

I found myself out in the backyard more and more. And this particular Zombie visited me every time. I loved playing for it. It would listen. Its lovely eyes would glow with joy. Could a robot feel joy? I believed intelligent ones like this could. Many times a day, I would see a crowd of Zombies running up and down the pipeline, off to do repairs or policing, whatever they did. If my Zombie was amongst them, I couldn't tell.

It was about the tenth time it visited me that it did something very, very strange. My husband had come home smelling practically flammable, stinking of several kinds of alcohol – beer, palm wine, perfume. I had been thinking hard all day. About my life. I was stuck. I wanted a baby. I wanted to get out of the house. I wanted a job. I wanted friends. I needed courage. I knew I had courage. I had faced a Zombie, many times.

I was going to ask my husband about teaching at the elementary school. I'd heard that they were looking for teachers. When he walked in, he greeted me with a sloppy hug and kiss and then plopped himself on the couch. He turned on the television. It was late but I brought him his dinner, pepper soup heavy with goat meat, chicken and large shrimp. He was in a good drunken mood. But as I stood there watching him eat, all my courage fled. All my need for change skittered and cowered to the back of my brain.

"Do you want anything else?" I asked.

He looked up at me and actually smiled. "The soup is good today."

I smiled, but something inside me ducked its head lower. "I'm glad," I said. I picked up my guitar. "I'm going to the back. It's nice outside."

"Don't go too close to the pipeline," he said. But he was looking at the TV and gnawing on a large piece of goat meat.

I crept into the darkness, through the bushes and grasses, to the pipeline. I sat in my usual spot. A foot from it. I strummed softly, a series of chords. A forlorn tune that spoke my heart. Where else was there to go from here? Was this my life? I sighed. I hadn't been to church in a month.

When it came clicking down the pipe, my heart lifted. Its blue liquid eyes glowed strong tonight. There was a woman from whom I once bought a bolt of blue cloth. The cloth was a rich blue that reminded me of the open water on sunny days. The woman said the cloth was "azure." My Zombie's eyes were a deep azure this night.

It stopped, standing before me. Waiting. I knew it was my Zombie because a month ago, it had allowed me to put a blue butterfly sticker on one of its front legs.

"Good evening," I said.

It did not move.

"I'm sad today," I said.

It stepped off the pipeline, its metal legs clicking on the metal and then whispering on the dirt and grass. It sat its body on the ground as it always did. Then it waited.

I strummed a few chords and then played its favorite song, Bob Marley's "No Woman No Cry." As I played, its body slowly began to rotate, something I'd come to understand was its way of expressing pleasure. I smiled. When I stopped playing, it turned its eyes back to me. I sighed, strummed an A minor chord, and sat back. "My life is shit," I said.

Suddenly, it rose up on its eight legs with a soft whir. It stretched and straightened its legs until it was standing a foot taller than normal. From under its body in the center, something whitish and metallic began to descend. I gasped, grabbing my guitar. My mind told me to move away. Move away fast. I'd befriended this artificial creature. I knew it. Or I thought I knew it. But what did I *really* know about why it did what it did? Or why it came to me?

The metallic substance descended faster, pooling in the grass beneath it. I squinted. The stuff was wire. Right before my eyes, I watched the Zombie take this wire and do something with five of its legs while it supported itself on the other three. The legs scrambled around, working and weaving the shiny wire this way and that. They moved too fast for me to see exactly what they were creating. Grass flew and the soft whirring sound grew slightly louder.

Then the legs stopped. For a moment all I could hear was the sounds of crickets and frogs singing, the breeze blowing in the palm and mangrove tree tops. I could smell the sizzling oil of someone frying plantain or yam nearby.

My eyes focused on what the Zombie had done. I grinned. I grinned and grinned. "What is that?" I whispered.

It held it up with two of its front legs and tapped its back leg twice on the ground as it always seemed to when it was trying to make a point. A point that I usually didn't understand.

It brought three legs forward and commenced to pluck out what first was a medley of my favorite songs, from Bob Marley to Sunny Ade to Carlos Santana. Then its music deepened to something so complex and beautiful that I was reduced to tears of joy, awe, ecstasy. People must have heard the music, maybe they looked out their windows or opened their doors. But we were hidden by the darkness, the grass, the trees. I cried and cried. I don't know why, but I cried. I wonder if it was pleased by my reaction. I think it was.

I spent the next hour learning to play its tune.

Ten days later, a group of Zombies attacked some oil workers and soldiers deep in the delta. Ten of the men were torn limb from limb, their bloody remains scattered all over the swampy land. Those who escaped told reporters that nothing would stop the Zombies. A soldier had even thrown a grenade at one, but the thing protected itself with the very force field it had been built to use during pipeline explosions. The soldier said the force field looked like a crackling bubble made of lightning.

"*Wahala!* Trouble!" the soldier frantically told television reporters. His face was greasy with sweat and the sides of his eyes were twitching. "Evil, evil things! I've believed this from start! Look at me with grenade! *Ye ye!* I could do nothing!"

The pipeline the men had barely even started was found fully assembled. Zombies are made to make repairs, not fully assemble things. It was bizarre. Newspaper write-ups said that the Zombies were getting too smart for their own good. That they were rebelling. Something had certainly changed.

"Maybe it's only a matter of time before the damn things kill us all," my husband said, a beer in hand, as he read about the incident in the newspaper.

I considered never going near my Zombie again. They were unpredictable and possibly out of control.

It was midnight and I was out there again.

My husband hadn't laid a heavy hand on me in weeks. I think he sensed the change in me. I had changed. He now heard me play more. Even in the house. In the mornings. After cooking his dinners. In the bedroom when his friends were over. And he was hearing songs that I knew gave him a most glorious feeling. As if each chord, each sound were examined by scientists and hand-picked to provoke the strongest feeling of happiness.

My Zombie had solved my marital problems. At least the worst of them. My husband could not beat me when there was beautiful music sending his senses to lush, sweet places. I began to hope. To hope for a baby. Hope that I would one day leave my house and wifely duties for a job as music teacher at the elementary school. Hope that my village would one day reap from the oil being reaped from it. And I dreamt about being embraced by deep blue liquid metal, webs of wire and music.

I'd woken up that night from one of these strange dreams. I opened my eyes, a smile on my face. Good things were certainly coming. My husband was sleeping soundly beside me. In the dim moonlight, he looked so peaceful. His skin no longer smelled of alcohol. I leaned forward and kissed his lips. He didn't wake. I slipped out of bed and put on some pants and a long-sleeve shirt. The mosquitoes would be out tonight. I grabbed my guitar.

I'd named my Zombie Udide Okwanka. In my language, it means "spider the artist." According to legend, Udide Okwanka is the Supreme Artist. And she lives underground where she takes fragments of things and changes them into something else. She can even weave spirits from straw. It was a good name for my Zombie. I wondered what Udide named me. I was sure it named me something, though I doubted that it told the others about me. I don't think it would have been allowed to keep seeing me.

Udide was waiting for me there, as if it sensed I would come out this night. I grinned, my heart feeling so warm. I sat down as it left the pipeline and crept up to me. It carried its instrument on top of its head. A sort of complex star made of wire. Over the weeks, it had added more wire lines, some thin and some thick. I often wondered where it put this thing when it was running about with the others, for the instrument was too big to hide on its body.

Udide held it before its eyes. With a front leg, it plucked out a sweet simple tune that almost made me weep with joy. It conjured up images of my mother and father, when they were so young and full of hope, when my brothers and I were too young to marry and move away. Before the "kill-and-go" had driven my oldest brother away to America and my middle brother to the north . . . when there was so much potential.

I laughed and wiped away a tear and started strumming some chords to support the tune. From there we took off into something so intricate, enveloping, intertwining . . . *Chei!* I felt as if I were communing with God. *Ah-ah*, this machine and me. You can't imagine.

"Eme!"

Our music instantly fell apart.

"Eme!" my husband called again.

I froze, staring at Udide who was also motionless. "Please," I whispered to it. "Don't hurt him."

"Samuel messaged me!" my husband said, his eyes still on his cell phone, as he stepped up to me through the tall grass. "There's a break in the pipeline near the school! Not a goddamn Zombie in sight yet! Throw down that guitar, woman! Let's go and get . . ." He looked up. A terrified look took hold of his face.

For a very long time it seemed we all were frozen in time. My husband standing just at the last of the tall grass. Udide standing in front of the pipeline, instrument held up like a ceremonial shield. And me between the two of them, too afraid to move. I turned to my husband. "Andrew," I said with the greatest of care. "Let me explain . . ."

He slowly dragged his gaze to me and gave me a look, as if he were seeing me for the first time. "My own wife?!" he whispered. "I . . ."

Udide raised its two front legs. For a moment it looked almost like it was pleading with me. Or maybe offering me a hug. Then it clicked its legs together so hard that it produced a large red spark and an ear splitting *ting!*

My husband and I clapped our hands over our ears. The air instantly smelled like freshly lit matches. Even through the palms of my hands, I could hear the responses from down the pipeline. The clicking was so numerous that it sounded like a rain of tiny pebbles falling on the pipeline. Udide shuddered, scrambled back and stood on it, waiting. They came in a great mob. About twenty of them. The first thing that I noticed was their eyes. They were all a deep angry red.

The others scrambled around Udide, tapping their feet in complex rhythms on the pipe. I couldn't see Udide's eyes. Then they all ran off with amazing speed, to the east.

I turned to my husband. He was gone.

Word spread like a disease because almost everyone had a cell phone. Soon everyone was clicking away on them, messaging things like, "Pipeline burst, near school! No Zombies in sight!"

and "Hurry to school, bring bucket!" My husband never let me have my own cell phone. We couldn't afford one and he didn't think I needed one. But I knew where the elementary school was.

People now believed that the Zombies had all gone rogue, shrugging off their man-given jobs to live in the delta swamps and do whatever it was they did there. Normally, if bunkerers broke open a pipeline, even for the quietest jobs, the Zombies would become aware of it within an hour and repair the thing within another hour. But two hours later this broken pipe continued to splash fuel. That was when someone had decided to put the word out.

I knew better. The Zombies weren't "zombies" at all. They were thinking creatures. Smart beasts. They had a method to their madness. And most of them did *not* like human beings.

The chaos was lit by the headlights of several cars and trucks. The pipeline here was raised as it traveled south. Someone had taken advantage of this and removed a whole section of piping. Pink diesel fuel poured out of both ends like a giant fountain. People crowded beneath the flow like parched elephants, filling jerry cans, bottles, bowls, buckets. One man even held a garbage bag, until the fuel ate through the bag, splashing fuel all over the man's chest and legs.

The spillage collected into a large dark pink pool that swiftly flowed toward the elementary school, gathering on the playground. The fumes hit me even before I got within sight of the school. My eyes watered and my nose started running. I held my shirt over my nose and mouth. This barely helped.

People came in cars, motorcycles, buses, on foot. Everyone was messaging on their cell phones, further spreading the word. It had been a while since people who did not make a career out of fuel theft had gotten a sip of free fuel.

There were children everywhere. They ran up and down, sent on errands by their parents or just hanging around to be a part of the excitement. They'd probably never seen people able to go near a pipeline without getting killed. Hip-hop and highlife blasted from cars and SUVs with enhanced sound systems. The baseline vibrations were almost as stifling as the fumes. I had not a doubt that the Zombies knew this was going on.

I spotted my husband. He was heading toward the fountain of

fuel with a large red bucket. Five men started arguing amongst each other. Two of them started pushing and shoving, almost falling into the fountain.

"Andrew!" I called over all the noise.

He turned. When he saw me, he narrowed his eyes.

"Please!" I said. "I'm . . . I'm sorry."

He spat and started walking away.

"You have to get out of here!" I said. "They will come!"

He whirled around and strode up to me. "How the hell are you so sure? Did you bring them yourself?"

As if in response, people suddenly started screaming and running. I cursed. The Zombies were coming from the street, forcing people to run toward the pool of fuel. I cursed, again. My husband was glaring at me. He pointed into my face with a look of disgust. I couldn't hear what he said over all the noise. He turned and ran off.

I tried to spot Udide amongst the Zombies. All of their eyes were still red. Was Udide even amongst them? I stared at their legs, searching for the butterfly sticker. There it was. Closest to me, to the left. "Udide!" I called.

As the name came out of my mouth, I saw two of the Zombies in the center each raise two front legs. My smile went to an "O" of shock. I dropped to the ground and threw my hands over my head. People were still splashing across the pool of fuel, trying to get into the school. Their cars continued blasting hip-hop and highlife, the headlights still on, lighting the madness.

The two Zombies clicked their legs together, producing two large sparks. *Ting!*

WHOOOOOOOOSH!

I remember light, heat, the smell of burning hair and flesh and screams that melted to guttural gurgles. The noise was muffled. The stench was awful. My head to my lap, I remained in this hellish limbo for a long, long time.

I'll never teach music at the elementary school. It was incinerated along with many of the children who went to it. My husband was killed, too. He died thinking I was some sort of spy fraternizing with the enemy . . . or something like that. Everyone died. Except me. Just before the explosion happened, Udide ran to me. It protected me with its force field.

So I lived.

And so did the baby inside me. The baby that my body allowed to happen because of Udide's lovely soothing music. Udide tells me it is a girl. How can a robot know this? Udide and I play for her every day. I can only imagine how content she is. But what kind of world will I be bringing her into? Where only her mother and Udide stand between a flat-out war between the Zombies and the human beings who created them?

Pray that Udide and I can convince man and droid to call a truce; otherwise the delta will keep rolling in blood, metal and flames. You know what else? You should also pray that these Zombies don't build themselves some fins and travel across the ocean.

THE SCIENCE OF HERSELF

Karen Joy Fowler

None but a woman can teach the science of herself.
Jane Austen

In 1814, Anne Elliot came to Lyme Regis and watched Louisa Musgrove fall from the steps of the breakwater onto the rocks below. It was late November so even though the weather was good, the beach was empty of bathers and bathing machines. To their left, they could see the steep road spilling through the village, landing on the expanse of level beach. It was, Austen tells us, a vista both lovely and wonderful. The water was a dark Byronic blue. Seagulls wheeled in the air above them, shrieking. The air smelled of salt.

There might have been a scavenger or two, combing the tide-line for flotsam. Perhaps a fisherman had hauled his boat out, flipped it belly-up for repairs and was hammering in the distance. Anne Elliot noticed none of these. Nor did she see a young girl, well known to the locals, selling snakestones, vertiberries, and devil's toenails from a stand. This girl might have identified the Elliot party as tourists, might have even been approaching them with a basket of curious rocks just in time to see Louisa fall.

Or not. Strangely dressed, lower class, odd in affect, and desperately poor, she was not really the kind of girl who wanders into an Austen novel.

In 1803, Austen had come herself to Lyme Regis and met this same girl's father. His name was Richard Anning. He was a cabinetmaker. Austen needed some repair work done on the lid to a box; he was recommended to her. We know these things because she found the price he asked so offensively high that she noted it in her diary.

Not noted: Richard Anning was a Dissenter from the Church of England, a Congregationalist, and an outlier even there, an activist who'd organized a protest over the food shortages occasioned by the Napoleonic Wars and worked with the dominant church on issues of Poor Law.

Also not noted: his second career. Richard Anning was a fossil hunter. There is no mention of fossils in Austen's descriptions of the charms of Lyme Regis yet it was said that smugglers could identify the beach in the dark simply by raking with their fingers through the sand. Two hundred million years ago, Lyme Regis lay at the bottom of a tropical sea, but no one knew this yet or would have believed it if they had.

Austen came again the following year. She and her sister Cassandra were uncommonly hardy, continuing their ocean bathing long into October. In 1804, they witnessed together the great fire that destroyed some fifty houses in Lyme.

Five years after Austen's second visit and five years before Anne's, Richard Anning died. He left behind a wife, two living children – a son, Joseph, thirteen at the time, and a daughter, Mary, ten – and eight dead and in the graveyard. Also a debt of £120. Within a year, the family was on parish relief.

Lyme's most notable manmade feature is the Cobb, the large wall of stone that curves around the harbor and has done so since at least 1328. The day they arrived, the Elliot party walked on top of the Cobb until they tired of the wind, and then descended to its shelter by a particularly steep set of stairs known as Granny's Teeth. They talked of poetry and ships, war and a young curate's prospects.

Anne stayed in Lyme only one night. Many of the inns and boarding houses, the indoor baths and the Assembly Rooms were closed. In the summer, they might have gone into the sea, a bell ringing to warn men to stay away as the ladies bathed. In November, Lyme had dwindled to its actual residents. Winter was the wrong season for tourists.

Winter was the season for fossil hunting. Ninety-five miles of crumbling cliffs stretch like wings on either side of Lyme Regis. These cliffs contain shale, lime and sandstone in an unstable proportion particular to Lyme and called the Blue Lias. In the winter, storms strip and shift the terrain, exposing new bits of cliff face, tumbling old bits back into the sea. A fossil can appear after one storm, scrubbed free by the wind and rain, only to disappear again after the next. Diligence and persistence are required, but also courage. There can be no waiting for the weather to clear, no waiting for the tides to recede. The fossil hunter must wade and climb. Landslips are common, the waves treacherous.

The chief peril is the hanging cliffs. At any moment they may give, crushing anyone underneath. Later in her life, Mary Anning's beloved dog Tray was killed in just this way only a few feet from where she stood. Richard Anning was often criticized for taking his children into this dangerous terrain; he did so even on the Lord's Day. He himself had at least one serious fall and the resulting injuries usually share the blame with tuberculosis for his early death.

That young Joseph and Mary continued this work without him, that their mother, who had already lost so many of her children, allowed it, shows how desperate their finances were. Mary made her first sale in the period just after her father died. A Londoner gave her half a crown for a very fine ammonite, enough to feed them for a week. She was eleven years old.

Sometime later that same year, her older brother Joseph found a massive ichthyosaurus skull in a fallen rock. The skull measured almost four feet from snout to neck. He called Mary to come and see and they knelt together in the whipping wind and rain. The sockets of its eyes were twelve inches across.

The children were used to not knowing what it was that they had found. Ammonites were called snakestones because people thought they might be petrified snakes. Belemnites were caused by lightning and known therefore as thunderbolts. The world was vast and mysterious and no one knew how it was about to tip over.

But Mary had never seen a fossil so big as this one. What did she think as she looked into the eye-sockets of that enormous skull? Did she suddenly wonder if the bay was still hiding other such beasts, beasts alive and hunting? That when she waded in the tidewaters, searching for her stones, those enormous, predatory eyes were watching her legs? Or did she already know more than enough about monsters – her life so hard, her heart so full of grief? She had been very close to her father.

Did she see only the money such an object would bring?

We do know what Joseph thought. He thought that fossil hunting was not for him and from then on he mostly left it to his little sister. He apprenticed as an upholsterer, trading any present income for future earnings. By the time those occurred, he would be married with a child of his own.

A mudslide buried the skull before it could be moved, the creature having raised its enormous head only briefly and then returned to the deep. Tides and storms prevented further searching for almost a year, and it was Mary, aged twelve now, who finally found it again, and also the rest of the skeleton in the cliffs high above.

The event was reported in a local newspaper:

A few days ago, immediately after the late high tide, was discovered, under the cliffs between Lyme Regis and Charmouth, the complete petrifaction of a crocodile, 17 feet in length, in a very perfect state.

This was the first ichthyosaurus ever to be found so complete. The Annings sold it to Henry Hoste Henley, the lord of the manor of Colway. Henley was also their landlord; no competitive bids were entertained. They got £23 for the specimen minus the wages of the workmen who dug it out.

Henley sold it in turn to a collector named William Bullock and Bullock exhibited it in his Museum of Natural Curiosities in Piccadilly. In 1814, Everard Home, a surgeon and recent Baronet, wrote the first of six papers, all riddled with errors, arguing that the creature's anatomy suggested a closer relationship to fish than to crocodiles. It had a fish's delicate spine, four fin-shaped limbs, and a fish's tail. But the plates in its eyes were more like a bird's. In short, no one had ever seen a creature like it. It remained a mystery that opened into more mysteries, an infinite, unsettling puzzle box. What world did we live in? Whose world did we live in?

In 1819, it was sold again, in auction to Charles Konig of the British Museum, as a "crocodile in a fossil state." Konig was the first to suggest the name ichthyosaurus, or fish lizard.

More papers were written and delivered and debated. Over in France, Georges Cuvier was gaining support for his extinction theory. His research, he said, seemed to prove the existence of a world previous to ours, destroyed by some catastrophe. But many scientists still hoped for an explanation in keeping with Biblical dogma. The catastrophe could well have been the Biblical flood, except that the animals had all been saved, two by two by two. God would never be so profligate, so wasteful as to make a creature only to lose its kind entirely. The theory of extinction suggested mistakes, or at the very least divine inattention. The church responded to each new theory with increasing alarm.

In any case, these perplexing matters were now comfortably in the hands of rich, and often titled, men. The price of Mary's specimen had risen to £45, and her role in recovering and cleaning it had already been forgotten by everyone outside Lyme Regis.

She was the second Anning girl to be named Mary. The first had died at the age of four, when, her mother having left the room for only a minute, she'd tried to add wood chips to the fire and her clothes had caught. It was Christmastime.

Five months later, her mother gave birth to the second Mary and this Mary also had a perilous childhood. The Annings lived so close to the water that the house often flooded. On one occasion the family had to climb out through an upstairs window to avoid being drowned in their own kitchen.

On another, a family friend, a woman named Elizabeth Haskings, took the baby Mary to nearby Rack Field for a show of horsemanship. The riders wheeled and danced their horses. They wore red vests, and red ribbons were threaded through the horses' manes. Half the town had turned out to see them.

Mary lay against Elizabeth, her breath on Elizabeth's neck, one hand clutching her collar. Mary was small for her age, limp in Elizabeth's arms, and damp with her own heat. A wind came up and Elizabeth moved to the shelter of a nearby elm. The hooves of the horses pounded on the dirt like thunder. The sky opened white and struck, lightning without rain. Elizabeth Haskings was killed instantly along with two fifteen-year-old girls, friends from the village. John Haskings, Elizabeth's widower, wrote later: "The Child was taken from my wifes arms and carried to its parents in appearance dead but they was advised to put it in warm water and by so doing it soon recovered."

The crowd at Rack Field had followed to the Anning's house and waited outside. When the physician came to tell them that the baby had survived – *a miracle*, he said – the cheering could be heard even over the sound of the surf, all the way down to the Cobb.

Decades later, her nephew wrote that Mary had been born a sickly, listless child, but the lightning bolt turned her bright and lively. Perhaps there was simply no other way to explain a woman of her class and time, intelligent but little educated, no money, and an outcast Dissenter, who taught herself French so as to read Cuvier, followed the shifting theories of pre-Darwinian science with acuity, and had her own ideas about the objects she had found, touched, pried from the rocks, cleaned and polished for presentation. Like the fossils, she defied explanation.

Mary had begun fossil hunting at the age of five. She'd followed her father so tenaciously among the cliffs that he'd made a pick and hammer especially for her, something to fit her little hands. Back in his workroom, he taught her to chip away the rock, and then to clean and polish the fossil that emerged. Sometimes the work was so delicate it had to be done with a sewing needle. Her father teased her that she was, like any other girl, learning her needlework.

After his death, she roamed the beaches in her odd get-up – filthy clogs, multiple tattered skirts, one on top of the next for warmth, and then a patched cloak flung over the whole. She wore a man's top hat, stuffed with paper and shellacked for protection from falling rocks. Quite thin, but seen from a distance, kitted out for fossil hunting, she resembled a small round hut with a hat for a chimney.

She was not always alone on the beach. In 1812, someone new came to Lyme, a boy with prospects, sixteen years old to Mary's thirteen, and, like Tom Bertram in *Mansfield Park*, heir to a sugar plantation in Jamaica. Austen would have seen the possibilities. The only sure way out of poverty for Mary was to marry up.

She might have been more marriageable if she hadn't made a habit of picking up creatures that washed ashore and dissecting them on the Anning kitchen table. She was not a pretty girl and she had no pretty ways.

The boy's name was Henry De la Beche. Recently booted from military school for insubordination, he'd come to join his mother and her third husband at their home on Broad Street. There is no record of how he and Mary met, but we can imagine it as Austen might have written it – the older boy, in disgrace, but with the confidence of wealth, education, and good looks. Then Mary, who should have been quiet and deferential in his company, but was not.

At thirteen, she was already the expert on the Blue Lias. People talked later of how sharp her eye was, how she would set her chisel into the cliff at some spot no different from any other spot and after a few blows, reveal the small skeleton of an ancient fish. If it was fossils Henry wanted, he did best to listen to her, keep in her good graces.

He did want fossils. He was as keen on fossils as a boy could be, given that he didn't need to find them in order to eat. Soon after meeting Mary, he had decided on a career in geology. They were often seen scouring the cliffs after a storm, their heads bent together over some find, their hands touching accidentally as they worked a specimen free. Mary's fingers would be rough and scraped, her nose red from the wind and salt. Mr. Elliot, Anne's father, would have been the first to note that she was seldom out in such weather as would improve her looks.

Sometimes an older woman, Miss Elizabeth Philpot, a noted collector who also lived in Lyme, joined them. But often it was just the two of them, alone in the wind and the water, scrambling about the cliffs.

He did not marry her. At twenty-one, he came into his fortune and used it to travel to sites of geological interest, to meet prominent scholars in the field. He was able, as she was not, to join the prestigious Geological Society of London. He was writing papers by then; one entitled "Memoir on the genus Ichthyosaurus," consisted mostly of descriptions of Mary's finds.

Mary had continued to uncover skeletons. These, varying greatly in size and with subtle differences, particularly in regard to their teeth, suggested four distinct sub-species of ichthyosaurus. She learned of his marriage to the beautiful Letitia Whyte only after it had occurred. They continued as good friends, the carpenter's daughter and the plantation owner's son, although he was much less often in Lyme now.

By then she had other partners. Her terrier, Tray. Elizabeth Philpot on many occasions. And, when she was only sixteen, an Oxford professor named William Buckland. He had written to her first, asking for the privilege of accompanying her on her hunts. Buckland was a noted eccentric, a jokester, whose rooms at Oxford were filled with birds and mice, guinea pigs, snakes, and frogs. As a young man, he'd vowed to eat his way through the animal kingdom and was infamous for serving mice on toast to unsuspecting guests. The bluebottle fly, he said, was the worst tasting animal he'd found.

Other geologists – the Anglican clergyman, William Conybeare, and Jean Andre De Luc – came often to Lyme Regis during these same years and these men sought Mary out, young and poor as she was. She listened to them and they to her. She grew accustomed to the company of her betters. The residents of Lyme noticed.

These guests sometimes brought her papers from the various scientific societies. Mary copied these out, including the drawings, which she did very deftly. She read well and had a good hand. She deeply regretted not being able to go to the museums in London to see what could be seen.

She noticed that the men who'd bought the fossils from her were being credited with finding them. In addition to thinking well of herself, she began to feel hard done by. For all the flattering attention, her family's finances had not improved.

At thirteen, a neighbor had given her a book on geology, the first book she'd ever owned, and over the subsequent years she had read it to tatters, carried on with her dissections, and learned to make her careful drawings, her beautiful, detailed descriptions of the fossils she found. She was becoming impressively learned. She was every inch a scientist.

She was a complete romantic. Fond of poetry, her fourth commonplace book (the first through third are lost) began with Lord Byron's "January 22nd, Missolonghi" copied onto the page.

Tis time this heart should be unmoved,
    Since others it has ceased to move:
Yet though I cannot be beloved,
    Still let me love.

Though perhaps she chose this poem not for the rejected melancholy of its opening verses, but for its later impulse toward glorious self-sacrifice. Anna Maria Pinney, a wealthy sixteen-year-old who met Mary when Mary was in her thirties and was clearly dazzled, wrote in her diary: "Had she lived in an age of chivalry she might have been a heroine with fearless courage, ardour, and peerless truth and honour."

Awake (not Greece – she is awake!)
    Awake, my Spirit! Think through *whom*
Thy life-blood tracks its parent lake
    And then strike home!

One morning, Mary was out early, the remnants of the storm still gusting about her, stinging her cheeks with salt. The year was 1815. The Napoleonic Wars would soon see their final battle. Anne Elliot was off somewhere, enjoying her happy ending.

Something large had washed up on the Lyme beach. Smugglers' brandy often came ashore. Mary usually hid any contraband she found until it could be quietly retrieved. Lyme looked after Lyme and not the excise men. But this was not a box. She approached it cautiously. Perhaps she was finally to see one of her crocodiles in the flesh. Perhaps it was only a seal.

What she found was the body of woman, lying with her face to the sky, her long hair tangled with seaweed, her eyes open and milky. Her sodden clothes were beautifully and expensively made.

Mary knelt and cleaned the sand from her face, untangled the seaweed from her hair, pulled her skirts so that her legs were covered. The woman was still beautiful and Mary immediately associated her with Ophelia or some other storied creature. There was something so intimate in her ministrations as to make her feel that she had known this woman. The finding and the loss of her seemed like the exact same thing since they had happened at the exact same moment.

She saw the body taken into the church and then went there daily, to pray over her and to bring fresh flowers. As long as the woman went unidentified there was no one she belonged to more than Mary. Mary invented many pasts for her, many ways she might have ended on the beach. Tragic love stories, desperate gestures.

Eventually she was identified as a Lady Jackson, lost in the wreck of The *Alexander* with her husband and children. The *Alexander,* inbound from Bombay, had gone down in a gale on Easter Monday in a part of Chesil Beach known as Deadman's Cove. There were only five survivors, none of whom spoke English, and no account of the ship's final hours, so close to home after a journey of 155 days, has survived. Friends came from London to take charge and Mary felt the loss not just of the body, but of the stories she had told herself about the body. No Lady Jackson had been listed on the ship's manifest. There remained just that bit of mystery.

Fifteen years later, Mary recounted this to Anna Maria Pinney. Mary had been just sixteen when she found Lady Jackson. Pinney was just sixteen when Mary told her about it. The romance may well have doubled in the double adolescent telling of it. Anne Elliot would have recommended less poetry in the diet and more prose to the both of them.

When she was nineteen, Mary met Lieutenant Colonel Thomas James Birch, a retired officer of fifty-two, comfortably well off and a great collector of fossils. He began visiting Lyme, calling on Mary and her mother and usually making several purchases.

On one such occasion, he found both Mary and her mother in tears. He made them sit, brought cups of tea. He feared something dreadful had happened to Joseph, but the problems turned out to be financial. After years of support, there was to be no more money from the parish. Mary had not found a valuable fossil for many months. "We are selling the furniture," Mary's mother told him. There was little enough of it, but all made by her dead husband. "And once that's gone, we've no rent, we've no roof over our heads."

Birch's sympathies were aroused, but also his anger. As valuable as Mary's contributions to science had been, it wasn't right that the Annings should be facing eviction. He would not have it.

He put the whole of his own collection up for auction, 102 items in all, an extraordinary grouping that he had gathered over years and continents. Many of these were things that Mary had found. The sale created enormous excitement. It lasted three days and drew bidders from Germany, France, Austria, and, of course, England. Cuvier himself bought several pieces. When it was over, Birch had earned more than £400, all of which he gave to the Anning family. For the first time in their lives, the Annings were financially secure.

The auction had also drawn a great deal of attention to Mary. Most of it was scientific. That such a young girl was capable of the arduous, dangerous work of fossil collecting! That she had found so many exemplary specimens!

Some of it was romantic. What had possessed Birch to make such an astonishing gesture? Rumors arose about the young girl and the old man; it was whispered that she *attended* to him on his visits to Lyme. Fortunately, according to Pinney's diaries, Mary "glories in being afraid of no one." She went out and bought herself a bonnet, though as a Dissenter it cannot have been a gaudy one.

Three years later, Mary made her greatest find. She was out on a particularly treacherous section of cliff known as the Black Ven when she saw something, some bit of shine, still mostly covered with shale. It was December, the day after a great storm, and she was working in a blustery wind with an intermittent icy spray of rain. She spent all morning chipping away the slate, her fingers numb and stiff with cold. When she was done, she had a skull unlike any she had ever seen.

She left her dog Tray to guard the spot and called on men from the village to help her before the tide returned. They worked into the evening until the whole skeleton had been revealed, nine feet long and six feet wide, but with a strangely elongated neck and a strangely tiny head. The creature had paddles instead of feet and would have resembled a turtle if not for the neck.

Conybeare had speculated on the possibility of this creature from fragments he'd found and now here was the whole of it. He responded with jubilation, writing to Henry De la Beche who was off in Jamaica attending his plantation. "The Annings have discovered an entire Plesiosaurus," Conybeare wrote. Mary had made meticulous drawings of the skeleton and one of these went to Henry, her childhood friend.

Another found its way to Georges Cuvier. Cuvier said that the neck was far too long – thirty-five vertebrate – when no creature that walked on four legs had more than seven. Birds might have as many as twenty-five, reptiles no more than eight and this was clearly a reptile. Mary, he suggested, had taken the head of a snake and put it on the body of an ichthyosaur. He felt he could even identify the place in the neck where she had made the joining.

Skeletons in the Blue Lias were often found scattered; there was always the danger of mistakenly welding two creatures together. But Cuvier was not alleging a mistake. He was accusing Mary of deliberate fraud.

A special meeting of the Geological Society of London was called, which, as a woman, Mary could not have attended even if she'd had the money to go to London. She paced the beach at dawn, prayed in the church at noon, picked at her dinner as she waited to hear. Sleep was impossible. She was still so young. The wrong finding would destroy her reputation and end her career.

The skeleton had been shipped by sea to London, but didn't arrive in time and Mary's drawings had to suffice. The meeting went late, hot with debate, a duel of science against science. Around this same time, Mary wrote a letter, which contained the following: "The world has used me so unkindly, I fear it has made me suspicious of all mankind."

By the end of the meeting, Cuvier had completely recanted. On closer inspection, he accepted Mary's specimen as the genuine article.

The village of Lyme Regis did not fare as well; the year ended in an epic storm. The first floor of the Anning's house flooded and all their fossils had to be moved to the upstairs where Tray whimpered and the family huddled as the wind howled outside. Dozens of ships along the coast went down, scores of people drowned. Trees were pulled from the ground and hurled down the hills. The great Cobb itself cracked and let the ocean through.

Mary had at least two close friendships with younger women. Both were diarists; both are remembered only because they left a record of Mary. Both appear to have been thoroughly infatuated, at least initially. Frances Augustus Bell was the first of these. Sickly herself, she was greatly impressed with Mary's strength and courage. On one occasion, out on the cliffs with a dangerous tide already at their ankles, she says that Mary simply seized her and carried her up the cliffs to safety. She describes Mary as a person impossible to dislike.

But Anna Maria Pinney, who knew Mary later and wrote more of her, said that she "gossiped and abused almost everyone in Lyme" and that the company of her own class had become distasteful to her. Her likes and her dislikes, Pinney said, were equally violent and unshakeable.

Visitors to Lyme vary greatly in their descriptions of her over the years:

"A clever funny Creature."

"A prim, pedantic, vinegar-looking, thin female, shrewd and rather satirical in her conversation."

"A strong, energetic spinster of about 28 years" (she would have been thirty-eight at this time) *"tanned and masculine in expression . . ."*

"She would serve us with the sweetest temper, bearing with all our little fancies and never finding us too troublesome as we turned over her trays of curiosities."

"It is certainly a wonderful instance of divine favour – that this poor, ignorant girl . . . understands more of the science than anyone else in this kingdom."

By the time she was twenty-seven, Mary had saved enough money to buy a shop with a glass display window in the front. She named it Anning's Fossil Depot and she and her mother lived in the rooms above. In 1844, King Frederick Augustus II of Saxony visited her there and for £15 purchased an entire ichthyosaurus skeleton. His physician who accompanied him wrote the following:

We had alighted from the carriage and were proceeding on foot, when we fell in with a shop in which the most remarkable petrifications and fossil remains – the head of an

Ichthyosaurus, beautiful ammonites, etc. – were exhibited in the window. We entered and found the small shop and adjoining chamber completely filled with fossil productions of the coast . . .

He asked Mary Anning for her name and address, which she wrote in his notebook. "I am well-known throughout the whole of Europe," she told him since he seemed not to know this already.

In 1833, an entry in Anna Maria Pinney's diary alludes to a deep sorrow, given in strictest confidence and too delicate to set down in its details. Whatever it was, Pinney kept the secret, noting only that, eight years earlier, Mary had hoped to see herself raised from her low situation and had seen those hopes cruelly dashed.

The world dislikes a story in which a woman is merely accomplished, brave, and consequential. Eight years before, Letitia De la Beche had sought a legal separation from Henry alleging ill treatment, which may have simply been his long years without her in Jamaica. A year later, she'd taken up residence with her lover, Major General Wyndham. We've no reason beyond the faint hint of Pinney's diary to believe that Mary wanted Henry. If she did, like Anne Elliot, she'd had this second chance. But Henry took off for the continent to escape the scandal and Mary found a pterosaur, the first in England, instead.

In 1830, Henry had come to Mary with an offering. He'd painted a watercolor for her entitled *Duria Antiquior, A More Ancient Dorset.* This crowded Jurassic landscape, largely underwater, included every creature Mary had found, and most of them trying to eat each other. It was an astonishing act of imagination, beautifully rendered.

But it was not the painting that was Henry's chief gift. Mary had lost her money in a bad investment; the market for fossils had slowed, and once again her finances were precarious. Lithographic prints had been made from Henry's painting and were being briskly sold. All the proceeds were to be Mary's. Henry hoped her fossil sales would be boosted as well by the advertising.

Meanwhile her old friend William Buckland persuaded the

British Association for the Advancement of Science to grant her an annuity of £25 a year. No other woman had ever been half so acknowledged. When secured, it was enough to keep her and her mother, too, even if she never made another great find.

A decade passed and a few years more. Mary Anning continued to uncover fossils – ichthyosaurs, plesiosaurs, and pterosaurs, but also the *Squaloraja polyspondyla*, the fish *Dapedius,* the shark *Hybodus*. In 1839, she wrote a letter to the *Magazine of Natural History*, part of which was published. She was correcting a claim made in one of their articles, that a recent *Hybodus* fossil was the first of its kind, a new genus, since she had already discovered several others. She was among the earliest to recognize coprolites for what they were – petrified feces – and sold sketches made from the ink she discovered still in the ink sacs of belemnite fossils.

She narrowly escaped a drowning. She was nearly crushed by a runaway carriage. She was only a few feet away from the cliff collapse that killed Tray, her constant companion.

Prominent scientists such as Louis Agassiz and Richard Owen continued to seek her out, to, in Owen's words, "take a run down to make love to Mary Anning at Lyme." Owen routinely omitted her role when discussing her finds, but in the early 1840s, Agassiz named two fish fossils for her – *Acrodus anningiae* and *Belenostomus anningiae*. He was the only person to so acknowledge her while she was still alive to enjoy it. He even threw in *Eugnathus philpotae*, for her good friend, the collector Elizabeth Philpot. Both women had impressed him enormously.

Mary was part now of the great debates, even if only from the counter of her fossil shop. The theory of catastrophism waned in favor of uniformitarianism, geological change coming slowly and uniformly rather than in a series of catastrophes. Biblical stories fell beneath Agassiz's glaciers and Lyell's recurring cycles of climate change. Darwin was about to speak.

Henry De la Beche was named director of the British Geological Survey. As such he was more interested in finding the materials to fuel the British Empire – tin, iron, and coal – than in fossils. William Buckland was named Dean of Westminster, and occupied with problems of cholera and sewage. Lyme was hit, first with disastrous landslips that caused whole houses to fall from the cliffs, and then with fire. Mary lost her dog and then her mother. She found a lump in one of her breasts.

These things Mary Anning and Jane Austen shared: that they made their own way in the world, and that they are remembered. Tourists come to Lyme to see the inn where Austen stayed or the place where Mary Anning's shop once stood, and some, like Lord Tennyson, come to see the exact spot where Louisa Musgrove fell. They shared this, too, that they both died young: Austen at forty-one and Mary at forty-seven.

Austen's death came in 1817, the same year Mary's first ichthyosaurus was named, the same year *Persuasion* was published. Austen had worked on Anne's story until illness prevented her and would have worked on it more had she been able. Its publication was posthumous.

Mary Anning made it into Jules Verne's books in the guise of her monsters, but never into Austen's. She wouldn't have made sense there with her bits of gothic history, her lightning, her science, her creatures. She wouldn't make sense in any story until the story changed.

Austen's story does not.

Anne Elliot is standing in the shelter of the Cobb, her cloak pulled tightly around her. The seagulls float above on currents, glide with their wings outstretched through the air. The day is cloudless, but the sun is thin. Anne is certain that Captain Wentworth no longer loves her and yet, Austen tells us, she is coming into a second bloom. She has recently been admired by a young man in passing who will propose to her before the story's end. All Anne has to do to see young Mary approaching in her curious clothes with her curious rocks is turn.

But the moment is already past. Austen is tired; she is dying. Her pen moves and Anne's mouth opens in fear and horror. Into the charming setting of Lyme Regis, just as Austen remembers it from her visits long ago, Louisa Musgrove falls.

THE OTHER GRACES

Alice Sola Kim

See: I don't even need to wake you up anymore. Maybe you're exhausted, your eyeballs feeling tender and painful and peeled of their membranes, but when the alarm goes off at 6:00 a.m., you jump out of bed and skitter across the chilly floor to the bathroom.

Every morning is thrilling; every morning you make an effort because this might be the day. It is April and you are a high school senior. Very soon you will be getting the letter that tells you that you've gotten into an Ivy League college. Any Ivy! Who gives a shit which one?

It wasn't easy to get in. You're all wrong for them. Your parents didn't put on identical polo shirts and take you on winding car tours through the Northeast to check out Princeton and Yale. No, you're part of the special category, species, family, genus, *thing* known as yellow trash. Yellow trash aren't supposed to go Ivy League – you've fooled them all, you cheater, you fake! Get ready for your new life.

It's all so thrilling. Too bad you thought you couldn't write about that in your college application essays. All of the things that make you what you had decided should be called yellow trash – the shouting matches in motel courtyards, the dirty hair, the histories of mental illness, the language barriers, the shoes, the silver fillings.

Grace, didn't you know? They eat that shit up. But you wanted a real do-over. You didn't want to be admitted only because they knew what you were. You like to think there's some honor in that.

Even though you may or may not have cheated on the SAT.

Breakfast is last night's dinner of chilly white rice and kimchi, which keeps your stomach full and your breath nasty, good things for a city girl on the go without a car. You like to think that this blast of prickly, fermented stink-breath might someday protect you from the next weirdo at the bus stop who sidles up to you to ask, "China or Japan?" So far, the most you've been able to do is flick up a middle finger in conjunction with a spat-out "*America*, asswipe!" And even that you've only been able to pull off once, but hey – good for you. If you were born unable to be pretty and quiet, then be loud and smelly. Own it.

When you leave the house for the day, your mother is gone and your brother is still at work. When you return, your brother will already be perched on the couch, watching TV. You pause at the door and rest your head on the jamb. The house is so quiet, all yours for now, and you will miss it.

Catch the bus, Grace! The bus!

It takes two city buses to get to your high school. You had started there right before your parents got divorced. You could walk seven blocks to go to a nearby, similarly shitty high school, but faced with the choice of shitty-familiar and shitty-new, you chose shitty-familiar.

Running across the street, you jam the hood of your sweatshirt over your damp head, creating tropical conditions under which your hair will steam and saran-wrap itself to your skull before giving up and drying itself. Why do people even use hair-dryers? They make you go deaf. You're just happy to have shampoo. It was not that long ago when your family could not afford shampoo and so used soap. People – as in, other ten-year-old girls – noticed. Perhaps being poor either turns one into an animal or a classy ascetic with eye-popping cheekbones; it made you into an animal, the fur on your head as oily and felted as a grizzly's.

The bus comes; you lunge inside, stepping tall; the doors slide shut like folding arms. On the sweating brown seat, you pull out a book to read – a little volume titled *Science Fiction Terror Tales* – but instead you wedge it under your thigh and close your eyes.

Last night you dreamed a familiar dream, so familiar that all you have to do is drift off in order to call it back. It's a Grace convention up in there, populated with girls and women who look exactly like you. GraceCon always meets in a different location

– in hammocks that don't connect to anything you can see, a rainforest, the bottom of a swimming pool. Last night was the swimming pool. Graces were turning somersaults, sitting cross-legged on the bottom of the pool, knifing through the water. You just hung there, inhaling as if the heavy blue water was both fresh air and a nice cold drink.

Always, in the dreams, the Graces look at you and go, "대황. 대황 대황 대황." You ask them, "대황?" Your accent is perfect. You sound like an ingénue on one of those K-dramas that your mother is addicted to. "대황," they answer. In the dreams, you understand every word.

On the bus, when you jerk awake, your face feels tired. It's the same way your face always felt after elementary school slumber parties – your eyebrows were unused to being hoisted so high, and your mouth-corners felt as though they had been pushed wide and pinned. Back then, your face didn't move much; when anyone in your family smiled, your pops got paranoid. He thought the joke was on him; now it is; it is.

Origin story. You first figured out that you were yellow trash when you were thirteen and attended a summer music day camp two hours away, in a nice neighborhood with a good school district. We both know that you're not that good at the violin. But already you were thinking about college applications, and searching for cheap and easy ways to make yourself appealing to admissions officials.

Anyway, you were getting off the bus in that nice neighborhood when the handle of the violin case slipped out of your hand. You stopped to wipe your sweaty hand on your t-shirt. Someone pushed up behind you and said, "Out of my way, chink."

Who does that? Surely the dickhead utterer of such words must have been green-skinned, a thousand feet tall, dragging a spiked club behind it as it picked and ate its own boogers. But, no, it was just some pretty white girl, a little older than you, high-ponytailed and tall. She didn't even look at you as she walked past. It was all so very racist that you felt as though you were watching a movie of yourself. A movie about racism! Oh, but for you it was playing in Extreme Feel-O-Vision, in that you felt everything, all the hurt and shock, and that despite your best efforts to blend in, to embody a Whiter Shade of Asian, this thing just happened to you, it had happened before, and it would happen again.

It was unfair how everyone could look at her and not see a – let's be blunt, Grace, a *racist asshole* – but just about anyone could look at you and see a chink.

You walked to the middle school where the music camp met, and spent a few minutes in quiet shock as everyone around you chattered and warmed up. Ann Li, who played the cello, asked you what was wrong.

"Someone called me a chink on the way over here," you said.

Ann opened her mouth, so you felt encouraged to spill. You said, "I didn't even do anything to her. I hate people."

"Wow," she said. She gave you a look of pity. "No one's ever called me a chink before."

At this, you crumpled like a soda can. *Never?* Bitch please! You thought: if you believe *that* then I have a very lovely, like, pagoda or whatever to sell you. Admit it, you wondered how it could be that you got chinked about once a month but Ann never had in her entire life. Wasn't there enough racism to go around?

It was then you realized that there are many different kinds of Asian girls. One kind is yellow trash; that is what you are. No matter how you brush your hair and wear Neutrogena lip shimmer and speak perfect English with nary a trace of fobbiness and play a string instrument like, say, Ann Li, you are not like her and you will never be like her, because you are yellow trash and *people can tell*. Even if it takes them a while.

Because at first they only see an Asian girl carrying a violin case, and if they think about you at all, it's to wonder at what a dweeby little princess you must be. But then they realize that the violin is borrowed from the scanty school music equipment room, deep scratches next to the f-holes as if Wolverine himself had given classical music a brief try before roaring in frustration, that you can only ever understand about half of what your parents are saying (if that), that your father is a nutcase, that your mother – who, let it be known, is amazing at her job – periodically has clients who want to speak to her manager because does her manager know that *this woman totally cannot speak English?*, that your brother likes to spit on the floor inside the house, that you are trashy and weird and something is deeply wrong with you and it will never be right unless you do something drastic, like go away to an Ivy League college and return transmuted, if at all.

You like to think that the Ivy League is mystical, miraculous – that, in a biography, it erases everything that comes before it, or else imbues an ignoble childhood with a magical sense of purpose. And it goes without saying that it charms the life that comes after it.

Grace, you moron!

But I understand. Things were rough; you got single-minded.

Your high school is named after a Native American chief and is said to be one of the most ethnically diverse high schools in the state, which unfortunately gives ethnic diversity a terrible name because the high school is truly rubbish. They don't offer AP classes, which is a big part of what drove you to cheat on the SAT, because the SAT is then the only objective measure by which admissions officials will be able to determine if your waving and withered cold hand is the one they want to catch and yank out of the sea.

(You've thought this through. You chew your nails, a lot, and spit out keratin explosively like so many bitten-off ends of cigars. You like to think you fret in style.)

The school day is a long gray expanse. At lunch, you sit in the hallway with some friends. Tama is your best friend here. Tama's half-black, half-white, her skin paler than yours. She's stupid-pretty. Not as in ridiculously pretty, but as in pretty in a way that initially makes people think she's not smart, with her jutting upper lip and her lashes so thick they pass for eyeliner. You and Tama have an unequal friendship of the type where she is your best friend and you are probably not hers.

You break Fritos in your mouth and listen to Tama talk about her mother's new painting. It is something sexually explicit involving satyrs and plums. Tama's parents are both artists.

You pull out *Science Fiction Terror Tales*, an act that might be rude if you were there, but you are not there. They, your friends, like you when you're there, but they don't miss you when you're not there. I don't read science fiction anymore, but I like to watch you do it. You get so lost, Grace. You're split in two: you're immersed in a story about a man who is confused about if he's really a man or a robot (truth: he's a bomb), but you're also dreamy for the better days to come.

Right now, you're a weirdo in a hooded sweatshirt, a skinny girl shapeless but for a gigantic ass. Think of a boa constrictor that's just eaten a goat. Stand the boa constrictor on its pointy end. The goat, sliding deeper into its body in one thick lump, is your ass. The rest of you, in this example, is the boa constrictor, which was chosen because obviously boa constrictors do not have tits.

But someday, far into the future, you will look fine. You will have money to spend on your clothes instead of going to the thrift store and pretending that the stuff there is cool but really every-thing's been picked over by tattooed twenty-somethings and all that's left are racks of sad tank tops with droopy armpits and flared stretch denim. Your hair will be washed with shampoo like the snot of unicorns and cruel hairstylists who are rude to every-one else but kind and complimentary to you will shear you into acceptability. Someday you'll learn on your own the things that no one bothered to teach you. You'll be a lovely young woman.

Yes you will.

Riding the bus home after school, you think about those letters that might be in the mailbox right now. Why not? You've got a perfect 4.0 (albeit the easiest 4.0 ever), crazy extracurriculars, a brilliant essay all about, like, making realizations about things and stuff at important moments, and an SAT score of 2,400. A perfect score.

Around this time last year, you received a strange invitation to join a group on a social networking website. The group was called The Other Graces, and when you saw its members, you looked around the library in a panic and scooted your chair closer to the computer. Because the other members of The Other Graces looked just like you, but older, all different ages and hairstyles and clothing.

Well, you joined. The next day, you received a message from Grace Prime, as she called herself. Grace Prime got right to it:

> you have been chosen for a mentorship by the other graces
> the other graces are grace chos from alternate timelines of a
> high fidelity to yours

we have decided to help you with your dream of acing the sat
in order to do so i will have to open a subspace corridor into
your brain
please respond with your answer within two business days
all best
grace prime

You wrote back and asked her what a subspace corridor was and what it would do inside your brain. You told her that you needed more information before proceeding, duh. Grace Prime called you at home later that night. How she got your number you still don't know.

"It's a way of traveling between universes," said Grace Prime. "You won't feel anything. Well, you may experience a side effect of odd dreams, just here and there, but that's the nature of the beast. It's an invasion, dear. A kindly invasion. You don't need to be afraid."

The cordless handset rested on your face. You tapped your feet on the wall. "You'll all be inside my brain? For how long?"

Grace Prime's voice was old. Quavering-old, creaky-screen door old, gargling-with-Listerine-for-a-thousand-years old. But strong and scary. "Once created, the subspace corridor remains open for a time before fading away. It has to close on its own. It'll take time, but eventually your mind will be all yours again."

"I don't want a bunch of strangers running through my brain," you said. You laid back on your bed, stuck your big toe into a dent on the wall from that time you threw a desk drawer at it. (See, you've caused trouble too.)

Grace Prime sighed. "Grace, privacy is overrated. Especially among those who've already thought your thoughts, or near enough. You think about that. We're no strangers. Think about what that means. Do you want a perfect score on the SAT or not? And those subject tests are killer. You've not exactly had a classical education. You need the help. But it's your decision to make."

You listened to the TV for a while. The way it sounded from the other room, the walls muffling its noise, made you think of someone being kidnapped. Oh, Grace: you composed an ecstatic letter in your head, like a *Penthouse* Forum letter except not to *Penthouse*: *Dear Amazing Stories – you'll never believe what happened to me . . .*

Then, slowly, you agreed to everything.

"Good," Grace Prime said. "You won't regret it. We get results. We change lives."

"Now what?"

"Now I tell you the truth," she said. "The subspace connection was already opened. It was the only way we could talk." She coughed, but not in an embarrassed way. "I'm sorry. I do hate to trick a Grace."

Your head jerked up, just a little. The phone stayed stuck to your cheek. "We're talking on the phone. You called me on the phone."

"Unfortunately not," she said. "Sorry."

The dial tone became louder, turned up and up, until it was all you could hear. And then you realized that it was all you had ever been hearing.

You never spoke to Grace Prime again. Grace Prime, ancient, weird, brilliant – you wonder how she's been. Moved on to another young Grace, you imagine. She may have lied to you, but the subspace corridor worked.

On the morning of the SAT, you got to the testing site and tied your hair back as solemnly as a kamikaze pilot, sitting monolith-straight in a room full of slouchers. The answers came to you unbidden, if not of you then from you. The room was silent but your mind was stuffed migraine-full. You wondered, as you do now, if the feeling of the panoply of Graces in your head, their voices as familiar as your own thoughts, is what it is like to be your father, who gets transmissions from a place he calls the Information Center. Sometimes you imagine how nice a place called the Information Center would be, so straightforward and honest, but then you remember that the Information Center only whispers lies to your father, lies that keep him awake all hours of the night, listening and scheming.

With the assistance of the other Graces over the subspace corridor, you aced test after test after test – Biology Molecular, English Literature, World History, Chemistry. That is how it happened. That is how you know you will get into any college you want. You know.

I am still with you, after all these months – *I can't pull myself away* – and I know this too.

The price you pay is that you'll never know how smart you really are.

When you finally get home, you yank open the mailbox door, prepared to gut it of its contents. There's nothing in there. Your face is tingly and your clothes are sticking to you, sweaty and wet as a pupal skin.

As expected, your brother Luke is sitting on the couch, watching the History Channel. Your mother and father are short, good-looking people, and it's unclear who, if anyone, inherited their looks. Both of you are patchy and unfinished. Luke is twenty-four. He finished college in a prudent and cheap way, by attending community college for two years and moving on afterward to the state university. Yet here he is. It just goes to show that escape must be a drastic endeavor. You must seek out the best of everything. Otherwise you will loop ever closely back to the source, an orbit decaying into sodden trash.

"Where's the mail?" you say.

He rolls his eyes your way. "Kitchen table."

There's nothing there but catalogs and bills. "Nothing for me?"

"Nope."

"Are you sure?"

He sighs deeply. You know Luke is tired from his nocturnal job, making X-ray copies for hospitals. He also works at a discount department store. But you think this is no excuse for being such a butthead, a terrible brother, a faker, a conspiracy theorist.

"Uh," he finally says. "Dad came by earlier. I saw him through the window. He took something out of the mailbox."

"ARE YOU KIDDING ME? WHY DIDN'T YOU STOP HIM? DID YOU SEE WHAT IT WAS?"

"He would have made me let him into the house," your brother says simply. "It was a big envelope. Stop fucking yelling."

The last time your father got into the house, he went around cleaning everything up, which meant collecting a bunch of papers and magazines from your and your mother's rooms and ripping them up. Then he walked around the living room and took all the Christmas and birthday and congratulations cards that your mother had received over the years and put on the walls and he ripped those up too. You came home to three big grocery bags full of ripped-up paper clustered neatly by the front door, and your brother in his room with the door closed.

Your mother's not much of a yeller, but that night she really went off on your brother, which at first appeared ineffectual because Luke already has the mien of one who has just been yelled at, regardless. But after that, he never let your father into the house again.

Standing there in the living room, shoes still on (and your mother would kill you if she knew!), you consider your options. You're not going to call your mother. It will only stress her out, and then she will stress you out, and then you will feel sorry that you ever said anything. After their divorce, you discovered that your father had given your mother some kind of head injury, years and years ago. It's hard to picture now. He is like King Mr. Head Injury himself now, a man who got knocked straight out of a world in which he was a millionaire and people were conspiring against him in buzzing clusters, into this world, where he's a bum and no one believes a thing he says. He's not capable of hurting anyone now, but you must remember: once he was.

You worry so much that this head injury might bite your mother in the ass in thirty or so years. For now, her memory just sucks, kind of. She forgets when she's promised to take you shopping, because shopping makes her tired and always, always you demand far too much. Once upon a time she had three jobs (a main job at the shipping company, an occasional job at the nearby fried fish fast-food place, and the jewelry counter at JC Penney's on the weekends). Now she only needs one job, but the tiredness persists, deepened into something chronic.

It's also a language barrier thing – this occasionally drifty quality to her; after all, if your life began happening in the Korean language, you wouldn't be able to remember or express anything for shit.

You'll only call your mother when you tell her the good news about college. She'll be thrilled. She is the saddest and least trashy out of any of you. This is why life is hardest for her – you allow yourself to behave badly while she abstains.

"I need a ride downtown," you say to your brother.

"I'm busy," he says.

"It's the History Channel! They show everything five billion times!"

"Ancient astronauts," says Luke. "In the Chariots of the Gods. Chariots of the Gods." He grins stiffly and holds his head back in a way that makes him look seedy and double-chinned, unpleasantly taxidermied.

"Come on, Luke."

He's gotten into a state. He does this all the time and it is so awful. He'll repeat phrases from his conspiracy theory books over and over again, perform weird tics and squeaks (this is where the spitting on the floor thing comes in). You know he doesn't have Tourette's, you *know*, but he likes to act like he does. Later you'll understand that damage manifests itself in so many different ways. Later, you might have sympathy for Luke, with his fake Tourette's. Today, however, all you can think is that he is disgusting

"Ancient astronauts."

"Man, fuck you," you say, "Just shut up." You grab your backpack and move out the door.

"Don't tell me to shut up," Luke says, suddenly angry.

You hate your brother! Yes you do, right now! You become even more furious when, turning back to Luke, you spy a glob of spit on the floor by the couch. He could stop himself from spitting in the house, but he just doesn't. The sight of it grosses you out but even more so it makes you feel existentially depressed and low and lonesome, all for your brother.

For there are times when you are near-friends, when you sit and watch *The Simpsons* reruns together and he forgets to spit on the floor and act crazy, or times when you ask him polite questions about his conspiracy theories and try to listen quietly, or times when he delivers unto you tiny kindnesses such as a new pair of ugly black socks from the department store where he works, but that's just not enough, it's not. The one time it's vital for you to get downtown very quickly and it takes about an hour to get there on the bus and the bus smells like poisonous buttmushrooms when it rains (which it did last night), Luke completely shuts you down?

FUCK this STUPID family. You sail out the door; your brother gets up to lock it behind you; you kick the door; he opens it and yells at you again; you run away as the screen door squeaks shut and the door-door slams; and then, you assume, your brother lapses back into his History Channel stupor, because there's really nothing else to do.

You, as well as I, have had those times where you don't feel like trying anymore. You've thrown your SAT study books across the room. Big, flimsy blocks – they don't make much noise when they hit. You've laughed at your own words in the application essay: wah wah, please take me. I'm ethnic enough for you. But not ethnic in all the wrong ways. I'm poor enough for you. But not so poor I can't pay (let them find the truth out later).

You've made your blood go hot and speedy at the thought of what these colleges have done to you without their knowing it, making you bow and scrape, making you rewrite and redo your life, until you want to cursive your anger across the skies, or better yet, hack those .edus to scrawl in crude MS Paint on the home page banners I WOULDN'T GO TO YOUR FUCKING SCHOOL IF YOU PAID ME A MILLION DOLLARS TIMES A BILLION DOLLARS SO YOU CAN EAT MY ASS KTHXBYE. ALL BEST, GRACE CHO.

And yet, and yet. Every time, you picked the books up and brushed them off. You read each sentence in your essay aloud, searching for the perfect words, tamping down the parts of your brain that cringed at your asshattery, your mendaciousness.

Because:

Remember your brother. Remember your father, remember your mother.

Remember the Asian imposters at Stanford. Two recent news stories made you laugh, they scared you so much: an eighteen-year-old girl named Azia Kim (Azia? Seriously?) posed as a Stanford University freshman for almost a whole year. She lived in the dorms! She joined the ROTC! Just a week after, a woman named Elizabeth Okazaki was discovered to be posing as a visiting scholar in the physics department at – yes! – Stanford again, hanging out at Varian Physics Laboratory and accomplishing the heroic feat of being even weirder and creepier than a pack of physics grad students. Azia and Elizabeth were both kicked off campus.

To a certain extent, you had to admire them. They were too dumb or unlucky or crazy or poor to realize this one stupid dream of theirs, but that didn't stop them.

To a much greater extent, you had to separate yourself from any identification with them, because you were getting into college in a legit way (or, rather, your cheating would be so technologically advanced and devious that no one would ever find out), and they had ruined Stanford for you – you imagined campus police looking out for girls *just like you*, chasing you across the moist green lawns and under the Spanish tiles and demanding ID, except you were already late to class, and everyone was staring, and, and . . .

You didn't apply to Stanford.

Your father's shelter is on the outskirts of downtown, in an emptied neighborhood scattered with unsuccessful coffee shops, corner stores, dead brick businesses, and bus stops. The shelter is unobtrusive and looks like a tax office from the outside, except for a faded sign that reads FRANCIS-HOLT HOUSE. The buzzer is broken, so you wait outside the door, peering in through the glass until a resident spots you and lets you in. You've never seen him before – a middle-aged black man wearing a maroon t-shirt with a stretched-out neck.

After opening the door, he smiles kindly and says, "Would you like some money?" He opens his hands and three or four mashed together dollar bills fall to the ground. You help him pick them up, and then go down the hallway to the elevator. When you pass the main office, you wave at the girl inside and tell her you're there to see your father. Of course you don't tell her why you're here and what you might do, so she smiles and says that he's up in his room.

Everyone in this house has got something weird with their heads. Which should go without saying, but every time you come here it's as if you've stepped onto a stage, into a company of committed improv actors who incorporate you into skits with Oulipo-type parameters of which no one has informed you; you're just playing but they are utterly serious.

You take the elevator up to the fourth floor. The hallway is stuffy. It smells of madness, which is something like the smell of people who don't have the right soap and products to get fully clean in the shower, and who wear clothes that come in huge batches from churches. You knock on your father's door. He answers right away.

You say hello, leaning to give him a careful hug.

He smiles. You haven't seen him in a few months, so every time you visit you fear that he'll look like just another bum, just another crazy on the street. Always, he looks okay. His hair is neatly parted, and he is clad in clean-as-is-possible slacks and button-down shirts. The thing about yellow trash that you remember is that yellow trash can be visually deceptive.

"Grace," he says. "대황 [*you*] 대황 [*messy*] 대황 [*very tired-looking*]."

Every time you see him you are relieved that he looks so good but he gets upset at how awful you look.

"How are you doing?" you say.

"Ah," he says, like ten light bulbs have exploded above his head. "대황. 대황 [*Come in*]."

Your father has mellowed out extremely. There's a night you remember, a long time ago, when he left home. You and your mother and your brother went to retrieve him and had a huge shouting fight in a motel courtyard. People were smiling as they watched. The same people that liked watching your family fight probably liked watching that show *COPS*. Why would they smile?

His place now looks like a motel room, everything petite and self-contained, an answer to the question, *How little do you need in order to feel like a respectable human being in today's America?* You stand by the round table next to his bed. Your father is on medication that makes his feet dance forward and back in a shuffling samba. You looked it up; it's called tardive dyskinesia, and it is the result of an evil White Elephant party in which one gives up psychosis in order to win a case of pseudo-Parkinson's. All the way home from the library you chanted "tardive dyskinesia, tardive dyskinesia" until it turned into "retarded synesthesia," which could have been yet another mental ailment lying in wait for your father.

"Come on, Dad, let's sit down." You put your hand on his elbow and help him down into the chair. He doesn't need the help, but it makes you feel better and maybe him too. He used to harsh you out every time you saw him, especially back when he still had money and his illness still seemed more like an overabundance of cruelty and suspicion than anything else.

These days, during the good visits, you two can walk arm-in-arm down the street to get tacos; this never, ever would have been manageable before. So you have hope, now. Which is a terrible thing, Grace. I feel sorry for you.

"Dad," you say, "Luke saw you get some of the mail from our box."

He nods, and grins so widely you can see the spaces where teeth are missing.

"Was there anything for me?"

He opens his black satchel, which he keeps clean and polished, and pulls out a big flat envelope. On that envelope are the colors of a school you've dreamed about. Inside that envelope must be a Yes, or at the very least a strong Maybe. Around that envelope are your father's fingers.

He says, "I am very proud of you," a sentence that you can understand in English or in Korean. You bask in it, you do, his pride and the fact that you finally understood something completely. Everything's so tenuous. Everything's about to be undone.

"Thanks, Dad," you say. You and your father smile at each other, and he reaches over to pat you on the shoulder. "Can I see it?" you say.

"No," he says loudly, "대황 대황 [*keep safe*] 대황 Information Center. 대황 대황."

He slides the envelope back into the satchel and rests his arm over it. "대황 [*this is*] 대황 [*very good school*]. 대황 대황 but you careful. 대황 대황 Information Center 대황 대황 대황 [*your mother*] 대황 대황 대황 대황 Catholic Church 대황 대황 대황 대황 대황 대황 lawyer 대황 대황 대황 대황 대황 [*money*] 대황 대황 대황 대황 대황 대황 Luke 대황 대황 대황 [*millions*] 대황 대황 [*television news anchors*] 대황 대황 대황 대황 sometimes you are not smart 대황 대황 대황 대황 [*I need to make you study*] 대황 대황 대황 대황 I will call school 대황 대황. I'm coming with you. We go together."

You know that's not true and he can't, he just can't. It's all crazy talk. How's this guy going to get on a plane and follow you anywhere? He couldn't even ride the bus if he didn't get a pass from the shelter.

But at the same time everything he is saying is so true that your heart and your head want to explode. You feel like crying, but your body is set up to not-cry; it's set up to shunt that impulse into thinking about crying, all the crying you will have to do later, in your room at home. But by then it will be all gone. That's the problem with saving it up.

"OK? OK?" he is saying.

Heliumed with despair – because despair can make one oddly light, isn't that right? Everything lost, and what remains is so stupid and pointless it's lighter than popcorn – you rise up and stand over your father. He is small and thin in his paper-bag-cinched slacks and you feel huge. You're taller than both of your parents because you were bred on meat and white bread and hateful, indigestible milk. This can happen to guys who are afflicted with Bad Dads. They take it until they're fifteen, sixteen, until they discover that they're big enough to start hitting back. You're a girl, but over the years you've been getting angry and big too. Slowly. So slowly that you had no idea it was happening.

He looks up at you. The reds of his eyes are showing, the skin underneath them lymphy and bagged. "Why you are so bad to me," he says.

"I'm not bad," you say.

"You know what happen 대황 대황," he says, "You don't help stop. You blame me. 대황."

"I don't know what I did. I don't know what that is." You're sinking again. You sink lower, catching your head in your arms, entirely exhausted.

There are things you've got to do now. You're too tired to do them. You've got to call the school and ask them for another packet, have them send it to your high school or your mom's workplace. They'll say, "Why?" maybe, and you will tell them a lie. Or maybe you'll say, "None of your fucking business!" and slam the phone down and then they'll un-admit you. Maybe it's all your father's fault that you are yellow trash and you will stay that way forever, but there must have been some way things could have been better. A way that is lost now. Plenty of people deal with plenty of things and they don't turn out trash.

He reaches into the briefcase and takes out the envelope again. This time he opens it and pulls out the letter to show you. He hands you the letter. It's nice. A seal's been punched into the paper, and someone is congratulating you. You barely read it.

"That's fine," you say, and slide it back to him.

The letter's not the thing. I told you, Grace. This story ends well, so never you worry; you don't need the fucking letter anyway. You're in, you're in, and no one can tell you that you're not. Don't cry please.

He says, "You study law, or medicine. If you study law you can do English too in undergrad 대황 대황."

"Uh huh." A wailing rises up in your head.

Your father talks about getting an apartment – or, hey, even a house, because he'll have money to burn – near the campus, where he can visit you every day. And there comes a moment when you almost wish it could be true, all these delusions of his – houses and money and college degrees for anyone who wants those things so badly that they've dreamed themselves onto the streets and into homeless shelters.

"We can get cat or dog," he says. "대황 [*which do you want?*] 대황 대황 cat is cleaner."

"I hate cats," you say. This is the worst. A pet. Something he could very nearly have. But he will never, ever have a pet.

"대황 [*What?*]" he says.

"Okay, I'll have a cat. We can have one."

"Ca-li-co," he says, "대황 [*those are the prettiest*]." How does he know that word?

Forget a wife, and kids, and a life to keep warm and solvent – I can't even imagine this man taking care of a pet. Suddenly I laugh. It surprises even me, but you get pissed off. You shake your head. *That's enough*, you think, *no more looking*. No more judging. Suddenly you lift a fist and punch the side of your head with a loud, inorganic-sounding thock. Inside your skull clangs and aches. It surprises even me. *Get out, get out, get out*, you think. Go away.

Doing something crazy in front of someone crazy is interesting; you wonder, how will they explain this? Your father is staring at you with wide eyes, and you know he's not getting up to help you. He's figuring out how this all fits into the connected flow charts and diagrams and blueprints and toppling spires in his constructed world. Someone's gotten to his daughter. Someone's put poison into her drinking water and made her go crazy. His daughter is not his daughter.

"Dad," you say, "When you hear the Information Center, do you—"

But you interrupt by hitting yourself again. *Go away, go away, GO AWAY.* This time it takes. With a shock, I realize that it's my turn to feel, and what I feel is this: me and everything else receding into a rapidly shrinking circle, a tiny angry pupil.

The corridor's closing; I'm an ant up a vacuum cleaner.

Then I come to, and it's just me, all me – alone in my fancy house, chair tipped back onto the floor. There's a broken glass beside me. I want to see how it ends. But I think I know how it ends. I think it's you who doesn't, Grace. My back is killing me. I get up from the floor; I stumble to the kitchen and palm some pills down my throat and drink cold water from the dispenser.

I look at the clock on the wall.

Only minutes have passed for me, just a few of them, but for you, oh you, Grace, for you it's been years and years and years.

BOOJUM

Elizabeth Bear & Sarah Monette

The ship had no name of her own, so her human crew called her the *Lavinia Whateley*. As far as anyone could tell, she didn't mind. At least, her long grasping vanes curled – affectionately? – when the chief engineers patted her bulkheads and called her "Vinnie," and she ceremoniously tracked the footsteps of each crew member with her internal bioluminescence, giving them light to walk and work and live by.

The *Lavinia Whateley* was a Boojum, a deep-space swimmer, but her kind had evolved in the high tempestuous envelopes of gas giants, and their offspring still spent their infancies there, in cloud-nurseries over eternal storms. And so she was streamlined, something like a vast spiny lionfish to the earth-adapted eye. Her sides were lined with gasbags filled with hydrogen; her vanes and wings furled tight. Her color was a blue-green so dark it seemed a glossy black unless the light struck it; her hide was impregnated with symbiotic algae.

Where there was light, she could make oxygen. Where there was oxygen, she could make water.

She was an ecosystem unto herself, as the captain was a law unto herself. And down in the bowels of the engineering section, Black Alice Bradley, who was only human and no kind of law at all, loved her.

Black Alice had taken the oath back in '32, after the Venusian Riots. She hadn't hidden her reasons, and the captain had looked at her with cold, dark, amused eyes and said, "So long as you carry your weight, cherie, I don't care. Betray me, though, and you will be going back to Venus the cold way." But it was probably that – and the fact that Black Alice couldn't hit the broad side of a space freighter with a ray gun – that had gotten her assigned to Engineering, where ethics were less of a problem. It wasn't, after all, as if she was going anywhere.

Black Alice was on duty when the *Lavinia Whateley* spotted prey; she felt the shiver of anticipation that ran through the decks of the ship. It was an odd sensation, a tic Vinnie only exhibited in pursuit. And then they were underway, zooming down the slope of the gravity well toward Sol, and the screens all around Engineering – which Captain Song kept dark, most of the time, on the theory that swabs and deckhands and coal-shovelers didn't need to know where they were, or what they were doing – flickered bright and live.

Everybody looked up, and Demijack shouted, "There! There!" He was right: The blot that might only have been a smudge of oil on the screen moved as Vinnie banked, revealing itself to be a freighter, big and ungainly and hopelessly outclassed. Easy prey. Easy pickings.

We could use some of them, thought Black Alice. Contrary to the e-ballads and comm stories, a pirate's life was not all imported delicacies and fawning slaves. Especially not when three-quarters of any and all profits went directly back to the *Lavinia Whateley*, to keep her healthy and happy. Nobody ever argued. There were stories about the *Marie Curie*, too.

The captain's voice over fiber optic cable – strung beside the *Lavinia Whateley*'s nerve bundles – was as clear and free of static as if she stood at Black Alice's elbow. "Battle stations," Captain Song said, and the crew leapt to obey. It had been two Solar since Captain Song keelhauled James Brady, but nobody who'd been with the ship then was ever likely to forget his ruptured eyes and frozen scream.

Black Alice manned her station, and stared at the screen. She saw the freighter's name – the *Josephine Baker* – gold on black across the stern, the Venusian flag for its port of registry wired stiff from a mast on its hull. It was a steelship, not a Boojum, and they had every advantage. For a moment she thought the freighter would run.

And then it turned, and brought its guns to bear.

No sense of movement, of acceleration, of disorientation. No pop, no whump of displaced air. The view on the screens just flickered to a different one, as Vinnie skipped – apported – to a new position just aft and above the *Josephine Baker*, crushing the flag mast with her hull.

Black Alice felt that, a grinding shiver. And had just time to grab her console before the *Lavinia Whateley* grappled the freighter, long vanes not curling in affection now.

Out of the corner of her eye, she saw Dogcollar, the closest thing the *Lavinia Whateley* had to a chaplain, cross himself, and she heard him mutter, like he always did, *Ave, Grandaevissimi, morituri vos salutant.* It was the best he'd be able to do until it was all over, and even then he wouldn't have the chance to do much. Captain Song didn't mind other people worrying about souls, so long as they didn't do it on her time.

The captain's voice was calling orders, assigning people to boarding parties port and starboard. Down in Engineering, all they had to do was monitor the *Lavinia Whateley*'s hull and prepare to repel boarders, assuming the freighter's crew had the gumption to send any. Vinnie would take care of the rest – until the time came to persuade her not to eat her prey before they'd gotten all the valuables off it. That was a ticklish job, only entrusted to the chief engineers, but Black Alice watched and listened, and although she didn't expect she'd ever get the chance, she thought she could do it herself.

It was a small ambition, and one she never talked about. But it would be a hell of a thing, wouldn't it? To be somebody a Boojum would listen to?

She gave her attention to the dull screens in her sectors, and tried not to crane her neck to catch a glimpse of the ones with the actual fighting on them. Dogcollar was making the rounds with sidearms from the weapons locker, just in case. Once the *Josephine Baker* was subdued, it was the junior engineers and others who would board her to take inventory.

Sometimes there were crew members left in hiding on captured ships. Sometimes, unwary pirates got shot.

There was no way to judge the progress of the battle from Engineering. Wasabi put a stopwatch up on one of the secondary screens, as usual, and everybody glanced at it periodically. Fifteen minutes ongoing meant the boarding parties hadn't hit any nasty surprises. Black Alice had met a man once who'd been on the *Margaret Mead* when she grappled a freighter that turned out to be carrying a division's-worth of Marines out to the Jovian moons. Thirty minutes ongoing was normal. Forty-five minutes. Upward of an hour ongoing, and people started double-checking their weapons. The longest battle Black Alice had ever personally been part of was six hours, forty-three minutes, and fifty-two seconds. That had been the last time the *Lavinia Whateley* worked with a partner, and the double-cross by the *Henry Ford* was the only reason any of Vinnie's crew needed. Captain Song still had Captain Edwards's head in a jar on the bridge, and Vinnie had an ugly ring of scars where the *Henry Ford* had bitten her.

This time, the clock stopped at fifty minutes, thirteen seconds. The *Josephine Baker* surrendered.

Dogcollar slapped Black Alice's arm. "With me," he said, and she didn't argue. He had only six weeks seniority over her, but he was as tough as he was devout, and not stupid either. She checked the Velcro on her holster and followed him up the ladder, reaching through the rungs once to scratch Vinnie's bulkhead as she passed. The ship paid her no notice. She wasn't the captain, and she wasn't one of the four chief engineers.

Quartermaster mostly respected crew's own partner choices, and as Black Alice and Dogcollar suited up – it wouldn't be the first time, if the *Josephine Baker*'s crew decided to blow her open to space rather than be taken captive – he came by and issued them both tag guns and x-ray pads, taking a retina scan in return. All sorts of valuable things got hidden inside of bulkheads, and once Vinnie was done with the steelship there wouldn't be much chance of coming back to look for what they'd missed.

Wet pirates used to scuttle their captures. The Boojums were more efficient.

Black Alice clipped everything to her belt and checked Dogcollar's seals.

And then they were swinging down lines from the *Lavinia Whateley*'s belly to the chewed-open airlock. A lot of crew didn't like to look at the ship's face, but Black Alice loved it. All those teeth, the diamond edges worn to a glitter, and a few of the ship's dozens of bright sapphire eyes blinking back at her.

She waved, unselfconsciously, and flattered herself that the ripple of closing eyes was Vinnie winking in return.

She followed Dogcollar inside the prize.

They unsealed when they had checked atmosphere – no sense in wasting your own air when you might need it later – and the first thing she noticed was the smell.

The *Lavinia Whateley* had her own smell, ozone and nutmeg, and other ships never smelled as good, but this was . . . this was . . .

"What did they kill and why didn't they space it?" Dogcollar wheezed, and Black Alice swallowed hard against her gag reflex and said, "One will get you twenty we're the lucky bastards that find it."

"No takers," Dogcollar said.

They worked together to crank open the hatches they came to. Twice they found crew members, messily dead. Once they found crew members alive.

"Gillies," said Black Alice.

"Still don't explain the smell," said Dogcollar and, to the gillies: "Look, you can join our crew, or our ship can eat you. Makes no never mind to us."

The gillies blinked their big wet eyes and made fingersigns at each other, and then nodded. Hard.

Dogcollar slapped a tag on the bulkhead. "Someone will come get you. You go wandering, we'll assume you changed your mind."

The gillies shook their heads, hard, and folded down onto the deck to wait.

Dogcollar tagged searched holds – green for clean, purple for goods, red for anything Vinnie might like to eat that couldn't be fenced for a profit – and Black Alice mapped. The corridors in the steelship were winding, twisty, hard to track. She was glad she chalked the walls, because she didn't think her map was quite right, somehow, but she couldn't figure out where she'd gone wrong. Still, they had a beacon, and Vinnie could always chew them out if she had to.

Black Alice loved her ship.

She was thinking about that, how, okay, it wasn't so bad, the pirate game, and it sure beat working in the sunstone mines on Venus, when she found a locked cargo hold. "Hey, Dogcollar," she said to her comm, and while he was turning to cover her, she pulled her sidearm and blasted the lock.

The door peeled back, and Black Alice found herself staring at rank upon rank of silver cylinders, each less than a meter tall and perhaps half a meter wide, smooth and featureless except for what looked like an assortment of sockets and plugs on the surface of each. The smell was strongest here.

"Shit," she said.

Dogcollar, more practical, slapped the first safety orange tag of the expedition beside the door and said only, "Captain'll want to see this."

"Yeah," said Black Alice, cold chills chasing themselves up and down her spine. "C'mon, let's move."

But of course it turned out that she and Dogcollar were on the retrieval detail, too, and the captain wasn't leaving the canisters for Vinnie.

Which, okay, fair. Black Alice didn't want the *Lavinia Whateley* eating those things, either, but why did they have to bring them *back?*

She said as much to Dogcollar, under her breath, and had a horrifying thought: "She knows what they are, right?"

"She's the captain," said Dogcollar.

"Yeah, but – I ain't arguing, man, but if she doesn't know . . . " She lowered her voice even farther, so she could barely hear herself: "What if somebody *opens* one?"

Dogcollar gave her a pained look. "Nobody's going to go opening anything. But if you're really worried, go talk to the captain about it."

He was calling her bluff. Black Alice called his right back. "Come with me?"

He was stuck. He stared at her, and then he grunted and pulled his gloves off, the left and then the right. "Fuck," he said. "I guess we oughta."

For the crew members who had been in the boarding action, the party had already started. Dogcollar and Black Alice finally tracked the captain down in the rec room, where her marines were slurping stolen wine from broken-necked bottles. As much of it splashed on the gravity plates epoxied to the *Lavinia*

Whateley's flattest interior surface as went into the marines, but Black Alice imagined there was plenty more where that came from. And the faster the crew went through it, the less long they'd be drunk.

The captain herself was naked in a great extruded tub, up to her collarbones in steaming water dyed pink and heavily scented by the bath bombs sizzling here and there. Black Alice stared; she hadn't seen a tub bath in seven years. She still dreamed of them sometimes.

"Captain," she said, because Dogcollar wasn't going to say anything. "We think you should know we found some dangerous cargo on the prize."

Captain Song raised one eyebrow. "And you imagine I don't know already, cherie?"

Oh shit. But Black Alice stood her ground. "We thought we should be *sure*."

The captain raised one long leg out of the water to shove a pair of necking pirates off the rim of her tub. They rolled onto the floor, grappling and clawing, both fighting to be on top. But they didn't break the kiss. "You wish to be sure," said the captain. Her dark eyes had never left Black Alice's sweating face. "Very well. Tell me. And then you will know that I know, and you can be *sure*."

Dogcollar made a grumbling noise deep in his throat, easily interpreted: *I told you so*.

Just as she had when she took Captain Song's oath and slit her thumb with a razorblade and dripped her blood on the *Lavinia Whateley*'s decking so the ship might know her, Black Alice – metaphorically speaking – took a breath and jumped. "They're brains," she said. "Human brains. Stolen. Black-market. The Fungi—"

"Mi-Go," Dogcollar hissed, and the captain grinned at him, showing extraordinarily white strong teeth. He ducked, submissively, but didn't step back, for which Black Alice felt a completely ridiculous gratitude.

"Mi-Go," Black Alice said. Mi-Go, Fungi, what did it matter? They came from the outer rim of the Solar System, the black cold hurtling rocks of the Öpik-Oort Cloud. Like the Boojums, they could swim between the stars. "They collect them. There's a black market. Nobody knows what they use them for. It's illegal, of course. But they're . . . alive in there. They go mad, supposedly."

And that was it. That was all Black Alice could manage. She stopped, and had to remind herself to shut her mouth.

"So I've heard," the captain said, dabbling at the steaming water. She stretched luxuriously in her tub. Someone thrust a glass of white wine at her, condensation dewing the outside. The captain did not drink from shattered plastic bottles. "The Mi-Go will pay for this cargo, won't they? They mine rare minerals all over the system. They're said to be very wealthy."

"Yes, Captain," Dogcollar said, when it became obvious that Black Alice couldn't.

"Good," the captain said. Under Black Alice's feet, the decking shuddered, a grinding sound as Vinnie began to dine. Her rows of teeth would make short work of the *Josephine Baker*'s steel hide. Black Alice could see two of the gillies – the same two? She never could tell them apart unless they had scars – flinch and tug at their chains. "Then they might as well pay us as someone else, wouldn't you say?"

Black Alice knew she should stop thinking about the canisters. Captain's word was law. But she couldn't help it, like scratching at a scab. They were down there, in the third subhold, the one even sniffers couldn't find, cold and sweating and with that stench that was like a living thing.

And she kept wondering. Were they empty? Or were there brains in there, people's brains, going mad?

The idea was driving her crazy, and finally, her fourth off-shift after the capture of the *Josephine Baker*, she had to go look.

"This is stupid, Black Alice," she muttered to herself as she climbed down the companionway, the beads in her hair clicking against her earrings. "Stupid, stupid, stupid." Vinnie biolumi-nesced, a traveling spotlight, placidly unconcerned whether Black Alice was being an idiot or not.

Half-Hand Sally had pulled duty in the main hold. She nodded at Black Alice and Black Alice nodded back. Black Alice ran errands a lot, for Engineering and sometimes for other depart-ments, because she didn't smoke hash and she didn't cheat at cards. She was reliable.

Down through the subholds, and she really didn't want to be doing this, but she was here and the smell of the third subhold was already making her sick, and maybe if she just knew one way or the other, she'd be able to quit thinking about it.

She opened the third subhold, and the stench rushed out.

The canisters were just metal, sealed, seemingly airtight. There shouldn't be any way for the aroma of the contents to escape. But it permeated the air nonetheless, bad enough that Black Alice wished she had brought a rebreather.

No, that would have been suspicious. So it was really best for everyone concerned that she hadn't, but oh, gods and little fishes, the stench. Even breathing through her mouth was no help; she could taste it, like oil from a fryer, saturating the air, oozing up her sinuses, coating the interior spaces of her body.

As silently as possible, she stepped across the threshold and into the space beyond. The *Lavinia Whateley* obligingly lit the space as she entered, dazzling her at first as the overhead lights – not just bioluminescent, here, but LEDs chosen to approximate natural daylight, for when they shipped plants and animals – reflected off rank upon rank of canisters. When Black Alice went among them, they did not reach her waist.

She was just going to walk through, she told herself. Hesitantly, she touched the closest cylinder. The air in this hold was so dry there was no condensation – the whole ship ran to lip-cracking, nosebleed dryness in the long weeks between prizes – but the cylinder was cold. It felt somehow grimy to the touch, gritty and oily like machine grease. She pulled her hand back.

It wouldn't do to open the closest one to the door – and she realized with that thought that she was planning on opening one. There must be a way to do it, a concealed catch or a code pad. She was an engineer, after all.

She stopped three ranks in, lightheaded with the smell, to examine the problem.

It was remarkably simple, once you looked for it. There were three depressions on either side of the rim, a little smaller than human fingertips but spaced appropriately. She laid the pads of her fingers over them and pressed hard, making the flesh deform into the catches.

The lid sprang up with a pressurized hiss. Black Alice was

grateful that even open, it couldn't smell much worse. She leaned forward to peer within. There was a clear membrane over the surface, and gelatin or thick fluid underneath. Vinnie's lights illuminated it well.

It was not empty. And as the light struck the grayish surface of the lump of tissue floating within, Black Alice would have sworn she saw the pathetic unbodied thing flinch.

She scrambled to close the canister again, nearly pinching her fingertips when it clanked shut. "Sorry," she whispered, although dear sweet Jesus, surely the thing couldn't hear her. "Sorry, sorry." And then she turned and ran, catching her hip a bruising blow against the doorway, slapping the controls to make it fucking *close* already. And then she staggered sideways, lurching to her knees, and vomited until blackness was spinning in front of her eyes and she couldn't smell or taste anything but bile.

Vinnie would absorb the former contents of Black Alice's stomach, just as she absorbed, filtered, recycled, and excreted all her crew's wastes. Shaking, Black Alice braced herself back upright and began the long climb out of the holds.

In the first subhold, she had to stop, her shoulder against the smooth, velvet slickness of Vinnie's skin, her mouth hanging open while her lungs worked. And she knew Vinnie wasn't going to hear her, because she wasn't the captain or a chief engineer or anyone important, but she had to try anyway, croaking, "Vinnie, water, please."

And no one could have been more surprised than Black Alice Bradley when Vinnie extruded a basin and a thin cool trickle of water began to flow into it.

Well, now she knew. And there was still nothing she could do about it. She wasn't the captain, and if she said anything more than she already had, people were going to start looking at her funny. Mutiny kind of funny. And what Black Alice did *not* need was any more of Captain Song's attention and especially not for rumors like that. She kept her head down and did her job and didn't discuss her nightmares with anyone.

And she had nightmares, all right. Hot and cold running; enough, she fancied, that she could have filled up the captain's huge tub with them.

She could live with that. But over the next double dozen of shifts, she became aware of something else wrong, and this was worse, because it was something wrong with the *Lavinia Whateley*.

The first sign was the chief engineers frowning and going into huddles at odd moments. And then Black Alice began to feel it herself, the way Vinnie was . . . she didn't have a word for it because she'd never felt anything like it before. She would have said *balky*, but that couldn't be right. It couldn't. But she was more and more sure that Vinnie was less responsive somehow, that when she obeyed the captain's orders, it was with a delay. If she were human, Vinnie would have been dragging her feet.

You couldn't keelhaul a ship for not obeying fast enough.

And then, because she was paying attention so hard she was making her own head hurt, Black Alice noticed something else. Captain Song had them cruising the gas giants' orbits – Jupiter, Saturn, Neptune – not going in as far as the asteroid belt, not going out as far as Uranus. Nobody Black Alice talked to knew why, exactly, but she and Dogcollar figured it was because the captain wanted to talk to the Mi-Go without actually getting near the nasty cold rock of their planet. And what Black Alice noticed was that Vinnie was less balky, less *unhappy*, when she was headed out, and more and more resistant the closer they got to the asteroid belt.

Vinnie, she remembered, had been born over Uranus.

"Do you want to go home, Vinnie?" Black Alice asked her one late-night shift when there was nobody around to care that she was talking to the ship. "Is that what's wrong?"

She put her hand flat on the wall, and although she was probably imagining it, she thought she felt a shiver ripple across Vinnie's vast side.

Black Alice knew how little she knew, and didn't even contemplate sharing her theory with the chief engineers. They probably knew exactly what was wrong and exactly what to do to keep the *Lavinia Whateley* from going core meltdown like the *Marie Curie* had. That was a whispered story, not the sort of thing anybody talked about except in their hammocks after lights out.

The *Marie Curie* had eaten her own crew.

So when Wasabi said, four shifts later, "Black Alice, I've got a job for you," Black Alice said, "Yessir," and hoped it would be something that would help the *Lavinia Whateley* be happy again.

It was a suit job, he said, replace and repair. Black Alice was going because she was reliable and smart and stayed quiet, and it was time she took on more responsibilities. The way he said it made her first fret because that meant the captain might be reminded of her existence, and then fret because she realized the captain already had been.

But she took the equipment he issued, and she listened to the instructions and read schematics and committed them both to memory and her implants. It was a ticklish job, a neural override repair. She'd done some fiber-optic bundle splicing, but this was going to be a doozy. And she was going to have to do it in stiff, pressurized gloves.

Her heart hammered as she sealed her helmet, and not because she was worried about the EVA. This was a chance. An opportunity. A step closer to chief engineer.

Maybe she had impressed the captain with her discretion, after all.

She cycled the airlock, snapped her safety harness, and stepped out onto the *Lavinia Whateley*'s hide.

That deep blue-green, like azurite, like the teeming seas of Venus under their swampy eternal clouds, was invisible. They were too far from Sol – it was a yellow stylus-dot, and you had to know where to look for it. Vinnie's hide was just black under Black Alice's suit floods. As the airlock cycled shut, though, the Boojum's own bioluminescence shimmered up her vanes and along the ridges of her sides – crimson and electric green and acid blue. Vinnie must have noticed Black Alice picking her way carefully up her spine with barbed boots. They wouldn't *hurt* Vinnie – nothing short of a space rock could manage that – but they certainly stuck in there good.

The thing Black Alice was supposed to repair was at the principal nexus of Vinnie's central nervous system. The ship didn't have anything like what a human or a gilly would consider a brain; there were nodules spread all through her vast body. Too slow, otherwise. And Black Alice had heard Boojums weren't supposed to be all that smart – trainable, sure, maybe like an Earth monkey. Which is what made it creepy as hell that, as she picked her way up Vinnie's flank – though *up* was a courtesy, under these circumstances – talking to her all the way, she would have sworn Vinnie was talking back. Not just tracking her with the lights, as she would always do, but bending some of her barbels and vanes around as if craning her neck to get a look at Black Alice.

Black Alice carefully circumnavigated an eye – she didn't think her boots would hurt it, but it seemed discourteous to stomp across somebody's field of vision – and wondered, only half-idly, if she had been sent out on this task not because she was being considered for promotion, but because she was expendable.

She was just rolling her eyes and dismissing that as borrowing trouble when she came over a bump on Vinnie's back, spotted her goal – and all the ship's lights went out.

She tongued on the comm. "Wasabi?"

"I got you, Blackie. You just keep doing what you're doing."

"Yessir."

But it seemed like her feet stayed stuck in Vinnie's hide a little longer than was good. At least fifteen seconds before she managed a couple of deep breaths – too deep for her limited oxygen supply, so she went briefly dizzy – and continued up Vinnie's side.

Black Alice had no idea what inflammation looked like in a Boojum, but she would guess this was it. All around the interface she was meant to repair, Vinnie's flesh looked scraped and puffy. Black Alice walked tenderly, wincing, muttering apologies under her breath. And with every step, the tendrils coiled a little closer.

Black Alice crouched beside the box, and began examining connections. The console was about three meters by four, half a meter tall, and fixed firmly to Vinnie's hide. It looked like the thing was still functional, but something – a bit of space debris, maybe – had dented it pretty good.

Cautiously, Black Alice dropped a hand on it. She found the access panel, and flipped it open: more red lights than green. A tongue-click, and she began withdrawing her tethered tools from their holding pouches and arranging them so that they would float conveniently around.

She didn't hear a thing, of course, but the hide under her boots vibrated suddenly, sharply. She jerked her head around, just in time to see one of Vinnie's feelers slap her own side, five or ten meters away. And then the whole Boojum shuddered, contracting, curved into a hard crescent of pain the same way she had when the *Henry Ford* had taken that chunk out of her hide. And the lights in the access panel lit up all at once – red, red, yellow, red.

Black Alice tongued off the *send* function on her headset microphone, so Wasabi wouldn't hear her. She touched the bruised hull, and she touched the dented edge of the console. "Vinnie," she said, "does this *hurt?*"

Not that Vinnie could answer her. But it was obvious. She was in pain. And maybe that dent didn't have anything to do with space debris. Maybe – Black Alice straightened, looked around, and couldn't convince herself that it was an accident that this box was planted right where Vinnie couldn't . . . quite . . . reach it.

"So what does it *do?*" she muttered. "Why am I out here repairing something that fucking hurts?" She crouched down again and took another long look at the interface.

As an engineer, Black Alice was mostly self-taught; her implants were second-hand, black market, scavenged, the wet work done by a gilly on Providence Station. She'd learned the technical vocabulary from Gogglehead Kim before he bought it in a stupid little fight with a ship named the *V. I. Ulyanov*, but what she relied on were her instincts, the things she knew without being able to say. So she *looked* at that box wired into Vinnie's spine and all its red and yellow lights, and then she tongued the comm back on and said, "Wasabi, this thing don't look so good."

"Whaddya mean, don't look so good?" Wasabi sounded distracted, and that was just fine.

Black Alice made a noise, the auditory equivalent of a shrug. "I think the node's inflamed. Can we pull it and lock it in somewhere else?"

"No!" said Wasabi.

"It's looking pretty ugly out here."

"Look, Blackie, unless you want us to all go sailing out into the Big Empty, we are *not* pulling that governor. Just fix the fucking thing, would you?"

"Yessir," said Black Alice, thinking hard. The first thing was that Wasabi knew what was going on – knew what the box did and knew that the *Lavinia Whateley* didn't like it. That wasn't comforting. The second thing was that whatever was going on, it involved the Big Empty, the cold vastness between the stars. So it wasn't that Vinnie wanted to go home. She wanted to go *out*.

It made sense, from what Black Alice knew about Boojums. Their infants lived in the tumult of the gas giants' atmosphere, but as they aged, they pushed higher and higher, until they reached the edge of the envelope. And then – following instinct or maybe the calls of their fellows, nobody knew for sure – they learned to skip, throwing themselves out into the vacuum like Earth birds leaving the nest. And what if, for a Boojum, the solar system was just another nest?

Black Alice knew the *Lavinia Whateley* was old, for a Boojum. Captain Song was not her first captain, although you never mentioned Captain Smith if you knew what was good for you. So if there *was* another stage to her life cycle, she might be ready for it. And her crew wasn't letting her go.

Jesus and the cold fishy gods, Black Alice thought. Is this why the *Marie Curie* ate her crew? Because they wouldn't let her go?

She fumbled for her tools, tugging the cords to float them closer, and wound up walloping herself in the bicep with a splicer. And as she was wrestling with it, her headset spoke again. "Blackie, can you hurry it up out there? Captain says we're going to have company."

Company? She never got to say it. Because when she looked up, she saw the shapes, faintly limned in starlight, and a chill as cold as a suit leak crept up her neck.

There were dozens of them. Hundreds. They made her skin crawl and her nerves judder the way gillies and Boojums never had. They were man-sized, roughly, but they looked like the pseudoroaches of Venus, the ones Black Alice still had nightmares about, with too many legs, and horrible stiff wings. They had ovate, corrugated heads, but no faces, and where their mouths ought to be sprouted writhing tentacles.

And some of them carried silver shining cylinders, like the canisters in Vinnie's subhold.

Black Alice wasn't certain if they saw her, crouched on the Boojum's hide with only a thin laminate between her and the breathsucker, but she was certain of something else. If they did, they did not care.

They disappeared below the curve of the ship, toward the

airlock Black Alice had exited before clawing her way along the ship's side. They could be a trade delegation, come to bargain for the salvaged cargo.

Black Alice didn't think even the Mi-Go came in the battalions to talk trade.

She meant to wait until the last of them had passed, but they just kept coming. Wasabi wasn't answering her hails; she was on her own and unarmed. She fumbled with her tools, stowing things in any handy pocket whether it was where the tool went or not. She couldn't see much; everything was misty. It took her several seconds to realize that her visor was fogged because she was crying.

Patch cables. Where were the fucking patch cables? She found a two-meter length of fiber optic with the right plugs on the end. One end went into the monitor panel. The other snapped into her suit comm.

"Vinnie?" she whispered, when she thought she had a connection. "Vinnie, can you hear me?"

The bioluminescence under Black Alice's boots pulsed once.

Gods and little fishes, she thought. And then she drew out her laser cutting torch, and started slicing open the case on the console that Wasabi had called the *governor*. Wasabi was probably dead by now, or dying. Wasabi, and Dogcollar, and . . . well, not dead. If they were lucky, they were dead.

Because the opposite of lucky was those canisters the Mi-Go were carrying.

She hoped Dogcollar was lucky.

"You wanna go *out*, right?" she whispered to the *Lavinia Whateley*. "Out into the Big Empty."

She'd never been sure how much Vinnie understood of what people said, but the light pulsed again.

"And this thing won't let you." It wasn't a question. She had it open now, and she could see that was what it did. Ugly fucking thing. Vinnie shivered underneath her, and there was a sudden pulse of noise in her helmet speakers: screaming. People screaming.

"I know," Black Alice said. "They'll come get me in a minute, I guess." She swallowed hard against the sudden lurch of her stomach. "I'm gonna get this thing off you, though. And when they go, you can go, okay? And I'm sorry. I didn't know we were keeping you from . . . " She had to quit talking, or she really was going to puke. Grimly, she fumbled for the tools she needed to disentangle the abomination from Vinnie's nervous system.

Another pulse of sound, a voice, not a person: flat and buzzing and horrible. "We do not bargain with thieves." And the scream that time – she'd never heard Captain Song scream before. Black Alice flinched and started counting to slow her breathing. Puking in a suit was the number one badness, but hyperventilating in a suit was a really close second.

Her heads-up display was low-res, and slightly miscalibrated, so that everything had a faint shadow-double. But the thing that flashed up against her own view of her hands was unmistakable: a question mark.

<?>

"Vinnie?"

Another pulse of screaming, and the question mark again.

<?>

"Holy shit, Vinnie! . . . Never mind, never mind. They, um, they collect people's brains. In canisters. Like the canisters in the third subhold."

The bioluminescence pulsed once. Black Alice kept working.

Her heads-up pinged again: <ALICE> A pause. <?>

"Um, yeah. I figure that's what they'll do with me, too. It looked like they had plenty of canisters to go around."

Vinnie pulsed, and there was a longer pause while Black Alice doggedly severed connections and loosened bolts.

<WANT> said the *Lavinia Whateley*. <?>

"Want? Do I *want* . . . ?" Her laughter sounded bad. "Um, no. No, I don't want to be a brain in a jar. But I'm not seeing a lot of choices here. Even if I went cometary, they could catch me. And it kind of sounds like they're mad enough to do it, too."

She'd cleared out all the moorings around the edge of the governor; the case lifted off with a shove and went sailing into the dark. Black Alice winced. But then the processor under the cover drifted away from Vinnie's hide, and there was just the monofilament tethers and the fat cluster of fiber optic and superconductors to go.

<HELP>

"I'm doing my best here, Vinnie," Black Alice said through her teeth.

That got her a fast double-pulse, and the *Lavinia Whateley* said, <HELP>

And then, <ALICE>

"You want to help *me?*" Black Alice squeaked.

A strong pulse, and the heads-up said, <HELP ALICE>

"That's really sweet of you, but I'm honestly not sure there's anything you can do. I mean, it doesn't look like the Mi-Go are mad at *you*, and I really want to keep it that way."

<EAT ALICE> said the *Lavinia Whateley*.

Black Alice came within a millimeter of taking her own fingers off with the cutting laser. "Um, Vinnie, that's um . . . well, I guess it's better than being a brain in a jar." Or suffocating to death in her suit if she went cometary and the Mi-Go *didn't* come after her.

The double-pulse again, but Black Alice didn't see what she could have missed. As communications went, *EAT ALICE* was pretty fucking unambiguous.

<HELP ALICE> the *Lavinia Whateley* insisted. Black Alice leaned in close, unsplicing the last of the governor's circuits from the Boojum's nervous system. <SAVE ALICE>

"By eating me? Look, I know what happens to things you eat, and it's not . . . " She bit her tongue. Because she *did* know what happened to things the *Lavinia Whateley* ate. Absorbed. Filtered. Recycled. "Vinnie . . . are you saying you can save me from the Mi-Go?"

A pulse of agreement.

"By eating me?" Black Alice pursued, needing to be sure she understood.

Another pulse of agreement.

Black Alice thought about the *Lavinia Whateley*'s teeth. "How much *me* are we talking about here?"

<ALICE> said the *Lavinia Whateley*, and then the last fiber optic cable parted, and Black Alice, her hands shaking, detached her patch cable and flung the whole mess of it as hard as she could straight up. Maybe it would find a planet with atmosphere and be some little alien kid's shooting star.

And now she had to decide what to do.

She figured she had two choices, really. One, walk back down the *Lavinia Whateley* and find out if the Mi-Go believed in surrender. Two, walk around the *Lavinia Whateley* and into her toothy mouth.

Black Alice didn't think the Mi-Go believed in surrender.

She tilted her head back for one last clear look at the shining black infinity of space. Really, there wasn't any choice at all. Because even if she'd misunderstood what Vinnie seemed to be trying to tell her, the worst she'd end up was dead, and that was light-years better than what the Mi-Go had on offer.

Black Alice Bradley loved her ship.

She turned to her left and started walking, and the *Lavinia Whateley*'s bioluminescence followed her courteously all the way, vanes swaying out of her path. Black Alice skirted each of Vinnie's eyes as she came to them, and each of them blinked at her. And then she reached Vinnie's mouth and that magnificent panoply of teeth.

"Make it quick, Vinnie, okay?" said Black Alice, and walked into her leviathan's maw.

Picking her way delicately between razor-sharp teeth, Black Alice had plenty of time to consider the ridiculousness of worrying about a hole in her suit. Vinnie's mouth was more like a crystal cave, once you were inside it; there was no tongue, no palate. Just polished, macerating stones. Which did not close on Black Alice, to her surprise. If anything, she got the feeling Vinnie was holding her . . . breath. Or what passed for it.

The Boojum was lit inside, as well – or was making herself lit, for Black Alice's benefit. And as Black Alice clambered inward, the teeth got smaller, and fewer, and the tunnel narrowed. Her throat, Alice thought. I'm inside her.

And the walls closed down, and she was swallowed.

Like a pill, enclosed in the tight sarcophagus of her space suit, she felt rippling pressure as peristalsis pushed her along. And then greater pressure, suffocating, savage. One sharp pain. The pop of her ribs as her lungs crushed.

Screaming inside a space suit was contraindicated, too. And with collapsed lungs, she couldn't even do it properly.

alice.

She floated. In warm darkness. A womb, a bath. She was comfortable. An itchy soreness between her shoulder blades felt like a very mild radiation burn.

alice.

A voice she thought she should know. She tried to speak; her mouth gnashed, her teeth ground.

alice. talk here.

She tried again. Not with her mouth, this time.

Talk . . . here?

The buoyant warmth flickered past her. She was . . . drifting. No, swimming. She could feel currents on her skin. Her vision was confused. She blinked and blinked, and things were shattered.

There was nothing to see anyway, but stars.

alice talk here.

Where am I?

eat alice.

Vinnie. Vinnie's voice, but not in the flatness of the heads-up display anymore. Vinnie's voice alive with emotion and nuance and the vastness of her self.

You ate me, she said, and understood abruptly that the numbness she felt was not shock. It was the boundaries of her body erased and redrawn.

!

Agreement. Relief.

I'm . . . in you, Vinnie?

=/=

Not a "no." More like, this thing is not the same, does not compare, to this other thing. Black Alice felt the warmth of space so near a generous star slipping by her. She felt the swift currents of its gravity, and the gravity of its satellites, and bent them, and tasted them, and surfed them faster and faster away.

I am you.

!

Ecstatic comprehension, which Black Alice echoed with passionate relief. Not dead. Not dead after all. Just, transformed. Accepted. Embraced by her ship, whom she embraced in return.

Vinnie. Where are we going?

out, Vinnie answered. And in her, Black Alice read the whole great naked wonder of space, approaching faster and faster as Vinnie accelerated, reaching for the first great skip that would hurl them into the interstellar darkness of the Big Empty. They were going somewhere.

Out, Black Alice agreed and told herself not to grieve. Not to go mad. This sure beat swampy Hell out of being a brain in a jar.

And it occurred to her, as Vinnie jumped, the brainless bodies of her crew already digesting inside her, that it wouldn't be long before the loss of the *Lavinia Whateley* was a tale told to frighten spacers, too.

THE ELEVEN HOLY NUMBERS OF THE MECHANICAL SOUL

Natalia Theodoridou

a=38. This is the first holy number.

Stand still. Still. In the water. Barely breathing, spear in hand. One with the hand.

A light brush against my right calf. The cold and glistening touch of human skin that is not human. Yet, it's something. Now strike. Strike.

Theo had been standing in the sea for hours – his bright green jacket tied high around his waist, the water up to his crotch. Daylight was running out. The fish was just under the point of his spear when he caught a glimpse of a beast walking towards him. Animalis Primus. The water was already lapping at its first knees.

He struck, skewering the middle of the fish through and through. It was large and cumbersome – enough for a couple of days. It fought as he pulled it out of the water. He looked at it, its smooth skin, its pink, human-like flesh. These fish were the closest thing to a human being he'd seen since he crashed on Oceanus.

Theo's vision blurred for a moment, and he almost lost his balance. The fish kept fighting, flapping against the spear.

It gasped for air.

He drove his knife through its head and started wading ashore.

Animalis Primus was taking slow, persistent steps into the water. Its stomach bottles were already starting to fill up, its feet were tangled in seaweed. Soon, it would drown.

Theo put the fish in the net on his back and sheathed his spear to free both his hands. He would need all of his strength to get the beast back on the beach. Its hollow skeleton was light when dry, but wet, and with the sea swelling at dusk – it could take them both down.

When he got close enough, Theo placed his hands against the hips of the advancing beast to stop its motion, then grabbed it firmly by its horizontal spine to start pushing it in the other direction. The beast moved, reluctantly at first, then faster as its second knees emerged from the water and met less resistance. Finally its feet gained traction against the sand, and soon Theo was lying on his back, panting, the fish on one side, the beast on the other, dripping on the beach and motionless. But he was losing the light. In a few moments, it would be night and he would have to find his way back in the dark.

He struggled to his feet and stood next to the beast.

"What were you doing, mate?" he asked it. "You would have drowned if I hadn't caught you, you know that?"

He knelt by the beast's stomach and examined the bottles. They were meant to store pressurized air – now they were full of water. Theo shook his head. "We need to empty all these, dry them. It will take some time." He looked for the tubing that was supposed to steer the animal in the opposite direction when it came in contact with water. It was nowhere to be found.

"All right," he said. "We'll get you fixed soon. Now let's go home for the night, ja?"

He threw the net and fish over his shoulder and started pushing Animalis Primus towards the fuselage.

b=41,5. This is the second holy number.

Every night, remember to count all the things that do not belong here. So you don't forget. Come on, I'll help you.

Humans don't belong here. Remember how you couldn't even eat the fish at first, because they reminded you too much of people, with their sleek skin, their soft, scaleless flesh? Not any more, though, ja? I told you, you would get over it. In time.

Animals don't belong here, except the ones we make.

Insects.

Birds.

Trees. Never knew I could miss trees so much.

Remember how the fish gasped for air? Like I would. Like I am.
It will be light again in a few hours. Get some sleep, friend. Get some sleep.

The wind was strong in the morning. Theo emerged from the fuselage and tied his long grey hair with an elastic band. It was a good thing he'd tethered Animalis Primus to the craft the night before.

He rubbed his palms together over the dying fire. There was a new sore on the back of his right hand. He would have to clean it with some saltwater later. But there were more important things to do first.

He walked over to the compartment of the craft that he used as a storage room and pulled free some white tubing to replace the damaged beast's water detector. He had to work fast. The days on Oceanus waited for no man.

About six hours later, the bottles in Animalis Primus were empty and dry, a new binary step counter and water detector installed. All he had to do now was test it.

Theo pushed the beast towards the water, its crab-like feet drawing helixes in the wet sand. He let the beast walk to the sea on its own. As soon as the detector touched the surf, Animalis Primus changed direction and walked away from the water.

Theo clapped. "There you go, mate!" he shouted. "There you go!"

The beast continued to walk, all clank and mechanical grace. As it passed by Theo, it stopped, as if hesitating.

Then, the wind blew, and the beast walked away.

Dusk again, and the winds grew stronger. Nine hours of day, nine hours of night. Life passed quickly on Oceanus.

Theo was sitting by the fire just outside the fuselage. He dined on the rest of the fish, wrapped in seaweed. Seaweed was good for him, a good source of vitamin C, invaluable after what was left of the craft's supplies ran out, a long time ago. He hated the taste, though.

He looked at the beasts, silhouetted against the night sky and the endless shore:

Animalis Acutus, walking sideways with its long nose pointed at the wind,

Animalis Agrestis, the wild, moving faster than all of them combined,

Animalis Caecus, the blind, named irrationally one night, in a bout of despair,

Animalis Echinatus, the spiny one, the tallest,

Animalis Elegans, the most beautiful yet, its long white wings undulating in the wind with a slight, silky whoosh,

and Animalis Primus, now about eight years old, by a clumsy calculation. The oldest one still alive.

Eight years was not bad. Eight years of living here were long enough to live.

$c=39,3$. *This is the third holy number.*

Now listen, these beasts, they are simple Jansen mechanisms with a five-bar linkage at their core. Mechanical linkages are what brought about the Industrial Revolution, ja? I remember reading about them in my Archaic Mechanics studies.

See, these animals are all legs, made of those electrical tubes we use to hide wires in. Each leg consists of a pair of kite-like constructions that are linked via a hip and a simple crank. Each kite is made up of a pentagon and a triangle, the apex of which is the beast's foot. The movement is created by the relative lengths of the struts. That's why the holy numbers are so important. They are what allows the beasts to walk. To live.

Each beast needs at least three pairs of legs to stand by itself, each leg with its very own rotary motion. All the hips and cranks are connected via a central rod. That's the beast's spine.

And then, of course, there are the wings. The wind moves the wings, and the beasts walk on their own.

They have wings, but don't fool yourself into thinking they can fly, ja?

Wings are not all it takes to fly.

In the morning, Theo was so weak he could barely use the desalination pump to get a drink of water and wash his face. He munched on seaweed, filling up on nutrients, trying to ignore the taste. After all these years, he had still not got used to that taste. Like eating rot right off of the ocean bed.

The beasts were herding by the nearest sand dune today, mostly immobilized by the low wind. The sun shone overhead, grinding down Theo's bones, the vast stretches of sand and kelp around him. The beach. His beach.

He had walked as far from the sea as he could, the first months on Oceanus. All he had found was another shore on the other side of this swath of land. All there was here was this beach. All there was, this ocean.

He poured some saltwater on the new wounds on his knees. The pain radiated upwards, like a wave taking over his body.

The winds suddenly grew stronger. There was the distant roar of thunder.

Theo let himself be filled by the sound of the sand shifting under the force of the wind, by the sound of the rising waves, by this ocean that was everything. The ocean filled him up, and the whole world fell away, and then Theo fell away and dissolved, and life was dismantled, and only the numbers were left.

a=38 b=41,5 c=39,3 d=40,1 e=55,8 f=39,4 g=36,7 h=65,7 i=49 j=50 k=61,9 a=38 b=41,5 c=39,3 d=40,1 e=55,8 f=39,4 g=36,7 h=65,7 i=49 j=50 k=61,9 a=38 b=41,5 c=39,3 d=40,1 e=55,8 f=39,4 g=36,7 h=65,7 i=49 j=50 k=61,9 a=38 b=41,5 c=39,3 d=40,1 e=55,8 f=39,4 g=36,7 h=65,7 i=49 j=50 k=61,9 a=38 b=41,5 c=39,3 d=40,1 e=55,8 f=39,4 g=36,7 h=65,7 i=49 j=50 k=61,9 a=38 b=41,5 c=39,3 d=40,1 e=55,8 f=39,4 g=36,7 h=65,7 i=49 j=50 k=61,9 a=38 b=41,5 c=39,3 d=40,1 e=55,8 . . .

At night, like every night, Theo sent messages to the stars. Sometimes he used the broken transmitter from the craft; others, he talked to them directly, face to face.

"Stars," he said, "are you lonely? Are you there, stars?"

d=40,1. This is the fourth holy number.

You know, at first I thought this was a young planet. I thought that there was so little here because life was only just beginning. I could still study it, make all this worthwhile. But then, after a while, it became clear. The scarcity of lifeforms. The powdery sand, the absence of seashells, the traces of radiation, the shortage of fish. The fish, the improbable fish. It's obvious, isn't it? We are closer to an end than we are to a beginning. This ecosystem has died. We, here; well. We are just the aftermath.

Stars, are you there?

Day again, and a walk behind the craft to where his companions were buried. Theo untangled the kelp that had been caught on the three steel rods marking their graves, rearranged his red scarf around Tessa's rod. Not red any more – bleached and worn thin from the wind and the sun and the rain.

"It was all for nothing, you know," he said. "There is nothing to learn here. This place could never be a home for us."

He heard a beast approaching steadily, its cranks turning, its feet landing rhythmically on the sand. It was Animalis Primus. A few more steps and it would tread all over the graves. Theo felt blood rush to his head. He started waving his hands, trying to shoo the beast, even though he knew better. The beast did not know grave. All it knew was water and not-water.

"Go away!" he screamed. "What do you want, you stupid piece of trash?" He ran towards the beast and pushed it away, trying to make it move in the opposite direction. He kicked loose one of its knees. Immediately, the beast stopped moving.

Theo knelt by the beast and hid his face in his palms. "I'm sorry," he whispered. "I'm so sorry."

A slight breeze later, the beast started to limp away from the graves, towards the rest of its herd.

Theo climbed to his feet and took a last look at his companions' graves.

"We died for nothing," he said, and walked away.

At night, Theo made his fire away from the craft. He lay down, with his back resting on a bed of dry kelp, and took in the night, the darkness, the clear sky.

He imagined birds flying overhead.

Remember birds?

e=55,8. This is the fifth holy number.

A few years ago the sea spit out the carcass of a bird. I think it was a bird. I pulled it out of the water, all bones and feathers and loose skin. I looked at it and looked at it, but I couldn't understand it. Where had it come from? Was it a sign of some sort? Perhaps I was supposed to read it in some way? I pulled it apart using my hands, looked for the fleshy crank that used to animate it. I found nothing. I left it there on the sand. The next morning it was gone.

Did you imagine it?

Perhaps I imagined it. Or maybe this planet is full of carcasses; they just haven't found me yet.

How do you know it was a bird?

Have you ever seen birds?

Are you sure?

Theo's emaciated body ached as he pulled himself up from the cold sand. He shouldn't sleep outside, he knew that much.

How much of this sand is made of bone?

Had the winds come during the night, he could have been buried under a dune in a matter of minutes. Animalis Elegans was swinging its wings in the soft breeze, walking past him, when a brilliant flash of light bloomed in the sky. A comet. It happened, sometimes.

Are you there? he thought.

Are you lonely?

f=39,4. This is the sixth holy number.

Animalis (Latin): that which has breath. From *anima* (Latin): breath. Also spirit, soul.

Breath is the wind that moves you; what does it matter if it fills your lungs of flesh or bottles? I have lungs of flesh, I have a stomach. What is a soul made of?

Do you have a soul? Do I?

The breath gives me voice. The fish is mute, the comet breathless; I haven't heard any voice but my own in so long.

Are you there? Are you lonely?

When I was a little boy I saw a comet in the sky and thought:

Wings are not enough to fly, but if you catch a comet with a bug net, well . . . Well, that might just do the trick.

Breath gives life. To live: the way I keep my face on, my voice in, my soul from spilling out.

Night already. Look, there is a light in the black above. It is a comet; see its long tail? Like a rose blooming in the sky.

If we catch it, maybe we can fly.

Tomorrow, I think I'll walk into the sea, swim as far as I can. *And then what?*

Then, nothing. I let go.

Instead of walking into the sea, in the morning Theo started building a new animal. He put up a tent just outside the fuselage, using some leftover tarpaulin and steel rods from the craft. He gathered all his materials inside: tubes, wire, bottles, cable ties, remains of beasts that had drowned in the past, or ones which had been created with some fundamental flaw that never allowed them to live in the first place. Theo worked quickly but carefully, pausing every now and then to steady his trembling hands, to blink the blurriness away. New sores appeared on his chest, but he ignored them.

This one would live. Perhaps it would even fly.

The rest of the beasts gathered outside the makeshift tent, as if to witness the birth of their kin.

g=36,7. This is the seventh holy number.

Come here, friend. Sit. Get some rest. I can see your knees trembling, your hip ready to give, your feet digging into the mud. Soon you will die, if you stay this way.

I see you have a spine, friend.

I, too, have a spine.

Theo was out fishing when the clouds started to gather and the sea turned black. Storms were not rare on Oceanus, but this one looked angrier than usual. He shouldered his fishing gear and started treading water towards the shore. He passed Animalis Elegans, its wings undulating faster and faster, and Animalis Caecus, which seemed to pause to look at him through its mechanical blindness, its nose pointed at the sky.

Theo made sure the half-finished beast was resting as securely as possible under the tarpaulin, and withdrew into the fuselage for what was to come.

$h=65,7$. This is the eighth holy number.

Once, a long long time ago, there was a prophet in old Earth who asked: when we have cut down all the trees and scraped the galaxy clean of stars, what will be left to shelter us from the terrible, empty skies?

Theo watched from his safe spot behind the fuselage's porthole as the beasts hammered their tails to the ground to defend their skeletons against the rising winds. Soon, everything outside was a blur of sand and rain. The craft was being battered from all sides; by the time the storm subsided, it would be half-buried in sand and kelp. And there was nothing to do but watch as the wind dislodged the rod that marked Tessa's grave and the red scarf was blown away, soon nowhere to be seen. It disappeared into the sea as if it had never existed at all, as if it had only been a memory of a childish story from long-ago and far-away. There was nothing to do as the wind uprooted the tarpaulin tent and blew the new animal to pieces; nothing to do as Animalis Elegans was torn from the ground and dragged to the water, its silken wings crushed under the waves.

Theo walked over to the trapdoor, cracked it open to let in some air. The night, heavy and humid, stuck to his skin.

$i=49$. This is the ninth holy number.

The night is heavy and humid like the dreams I used to have as a boy. In my dream, I see I'm walking into the sea, only it's not the sea any more, it's tall grass, taller than any grass I've ever seen in any ecosystem, taller than me, taller than the beasts. I swim in the grass, and it grows even taller; it reaches my head and keeps growing towards the sky, or maybe it's me getting smaller and smaller until all I can see is grass above and around me. I fall back, and the grass catches me, and it's the sky catching me like I always knew it would.

The storm lasted two Oceanus days and two Oceanus nights. When the clouds parted and the winds moved deeper into the ocean, Theo finally emerged from the fuselage. Half the beach had turned into a mire. Animalis Elegans was nowhere in sight. Animalis Primus limped in the distance. The beach was strewn with parts; only three of the beasts had survived the storm.

"No point in mourning, ja?" Theo muttered, and got to work.

He gathered as many of the materials as had landed in the area around the craft and dismantled the remains of the new animal that would never be named.

He had laid everything on the tarpaulin to dry, when a glimpse of white caught his eye. He turned towards the expanse of sea that blended into mire, and squinted. At first he thought it was foam, but no; it was one of Elegans's wings, a precious piece of white silk poking out of a murky-looking patch in the ground.

He knew better than to go retrieve it, but he went anyway.

j=50. This is the tenth holy number.

Listen, listen. It's okay. Don't fret. Take it in. The desolation, take it all in. Decomposition is a vital part of any ecosystem. It releases nutrients that can be reused, returns to the atmosphere what was only borrowed before. Without it, dead matter would accumulate and the world would be fragmented and dead, a wasteland of drowned parts and things with no knees, no spine, no wings.

Theo had his hands on the precious fabric, knee-deep in the muck, when he realized he was sinking, inch by inch, every time he moved. He tried to pull himself back out, but the next moment the sand was up to his thighs. He tried to kick his way out, to drag himself up, but his knees buckled, his muscles burned and he sank deeper and deeper with every breath he took.

This is it, then, he thought. *Here we are, friend. Here we are.*

He let out a breath, and it was almost like letting go.

k=61,9. This is the last holy number.

So here we are, friend: I, *Homo Necans*, the Man who Dies; you, ever a corpse. Beautiful, exquisite corpse. I lay my hands on you, caress your inanimate flawlessness. I dip my palms into you, what you once were. And then, there it is, so close and tangible I can almost reach it.

Here I am.

In your soul up to my knees.

The sand around Theo was drying in the sun. It was up to his navel now. Wouldn't be long. The wind hissed against the kelp and sand, lulling him. His eyes closed and he dozed off, still holding on to the wing.

He was woken by the rattling sound of Animalis Primus limping towards him.

The beast approached, its feet distributing its weight so as to barely touch the unsteady sand.

"I made you fine, didn't I?" Theo mused. "Just fine."

Primus came to a halt next to Theo, and waited.

He looked up at the beast, squinting at the sun behind it. "What are you doing, old friend?" he asked.

The beast stood, as if waiting for him to reach out, to hold on.

Theo pulled a hand out of the sand and reached for the beast's first knees. He was afraid he might trip the animal over, take them both down, but as soon as he got a firm grasp on its skeleton, Primus started walking against the wind, pulling Theo out of the sand.

He let go once he was safely away from the marsh. He collapsed on the powdery sand, trying to catch his breath, reel it back in, keep it from running out. Animalis Primus did not stop.

"Wait," Theo whispered as he pulled himself half-way up from the ground, thousands of miniscule grains sticking to his damp cheek. The beast marched onwards, unresponsive. "Wait!" Theo shouted, with all the breath he had left. He almost passed out.

The wind changed direction. Theo rested his head back on the sand, spent, and watched as Animalis Primus walked away – all clank and mechanics and the vestige of something like breath.

MOUNTAIN WAYS

Ursula K. Le Guin

Note for readers unfamiliar with the planet O:

Ki'O society is divided into two halves or moieties, called (for ancient religious reasons) the Morning and the Evening. You belong to your mother's moiety, and you can't have sex with anybody of your moiety.

Marriage on O is a foursome, the sedoretu – a man and a woman from the Morning moiety and a man and a woman from the Evening moiety. You're expected to have sex with both your spouses of the other moiety, and not to have sex with your spouse of your own moiety. So each sedoretu has two expected heterosexual relationships, two expected homosexual relationships, and two forbidden heterosexual relationships.

The expected relationships within each sedoretu are:

The Morning woman and the Evening man (the "Morning marriage")

The Evening woman and the Morning man (the "Evening marriage")

The Morning woman and the Evening woman (the "Day marriage")

The Morning man and the Evening man (the "Night marriage")

The forbidden relationships are between the Morning woman and the Morning man, and between the Evening woman and the Evening man, and they aren't called anything, except sacrilege.

It's just as complicated as it sounds, but aren't most marriages?

In the stony uplands of the Deka Mountains the farmholds are few and far between. Farmers scrape a living out of that cold earth, planting on sheltered slopes facing south, combing the yama for fleece, carding and spinning and weaving the prime wool, selling pelts to the carpet-factories. The mountain yama, called ariu, are a small wiry breed; they run wild, without shelter, and are not fenced in, since they never cross the invisible, immemorial boundaries of the herd territory. Each farmhold is in fact a herd territory. The animals are the true farmholders. Tolerant and aloof, they allow the farmers to comb out their thick fleeces, to assist them in difficult births, and to skin them when they die. The farmers are dependent on the ariu; the ariu are not dependent on the farmers. The question of ownership is moot. At Danro Farmhold they don't say, "We have 900 ariu," they say, "The herd has 900."

Danro is the farthest farm of Oro Village in the High Watershed of the Mane River on Oniasu on O. The people up there in the mountains are civilized but not very civilized. Like most ki'O they pride themselves on doing things the way they've always been done, but in fact they are a wilful, stubborn lot who change the rules to suit themselves and then say the people "down there" don't know the rules, don't honor the old ways, the true ki'O ways, the mountain ways.

Some years ago, the First Sedoretu of Danro was broken by a landslide up on the Farren that killed the Morning woman and her husband. The widowed Evening couple, who had both married in from other farmholds, fell into a habit of mourning and grew old early, letting the daughter of the Morning manage the farm and all its business.

Her name was Shahes. At thirty, she was a straight-backed, strong, short woman with rough red cheeks, a mountaineer's long stride, and a mountaineer's deep lungs. She could walk down the road to the village center in deep snow with a sixty-pound pack of pelts on her back, sell the pelts, pay her taxes and visit a bit at the village hearth, and stride back up the steep zigzags to be home before nightfall, a forty-kilometer round trip and 600 meters of altitude each way. If she or anyone else at Danro wanted to see a new face they had to go down the mountain to other farms or to the village center. There was nothing to bring anybody up the hard road to Danro. Shahes seldom hired help, and the family wasn't sociable. Their hospitality, like their road, had grown stony through lack of use.

But a traveling scholar from the lowlands who came up the Mane all the way to Oro was not daunted by another near-vertical stretch of ruts and rubble. Having visited the other farms, the scholar climbed on around the Farren from Ked'din and up to Danro, and there made the honorable and traditional offer: to share worship at the house shrine, to lead conversation about the Discussions, to instruct the children of the farmhold in spiritual matters, for as long as the farmers wished to lodge and keep her.

This scholar was an Evening woman, over forty, tall and long-limbed, with cropped dark-brown hair as fine and curly as a yama's. She was quite fearless, expected nothing in the way of luxury or even comfort, and had no small talk at all. She was not one of the subtle and eloquent expounders of the great Centers. She was a farm woman who had gone to school. She read and talked about the Discussions in a plain way that suited her hearers, sang the offerings and the praise-songs to the oldest tunes, and gave brief, undemanding lessons to Danro's one child, a ten-year-old Morning half-nephew. Otherwise she was as silent as her hosts, and as hardworking. They were up at dawn; she was up before dawn to sit in meditation. She studied her few books and wrote for an hour or two after that. The rest of the day she worked alongside the farm people at whatever job they gave her.

It was fleecing season, midsummer, and the people were all out every day, all over the vast mountain territory of the herd, following the scattered groups, combing the animals when they lay down to chew the cud.

The old ariu knew and liked the combing. They lay with their legs folded under them or stood still for it, leaning into the comb-strokes a little, sometimes making a small, shivering whisper-cough of enjoyment. The yearlings, whose fleece was the finest and brought the best price raw or woven, were ticklish and frisky; they sidled, bit, and bolted. Fleecing yearlings called for a profound and resolute patience. To this the young ariu would at last respond, growing quiet and even drowsing as the long, fine teeth of the comb bit in and stroked through, over and over again, in the rhythm of the comber's soft monotonous tune, "Hunna, hunna, na, na . . . "

The traveling scholar, whose religious name was Enno, showed such a knack for handling new-born ariu that Shahes took her out to try her hand at fleecing yearlings. Enno proved to be as good with them as with the infants, and soon she and Shahes, the best fine-fleecer of Oro, were working daily side by side. After her meditation and reading, Enno would come out and find Shahes on the great slopes where the yearlings still ran with their dams and the new-borns. Together the two women could fill a forty-pound sack a day with the airy, silky, milk-colored clouds of combings. Often they would pick out a pair of twins, of which there had been an unusual number this mild year. If Shahes led out one twin the other would follow it, as yama twins will do all their lives; and so the women could work side by side in a silent, absorbed companionship. They talked only to the animals. "Move your fool leg," Shahes would say to the yearling she was combing, as it gazed at her with its great, dark, dreaming eyes. Enno would murmur "Hunna, hunna, hunna, na," or hum a fragment of an Offering, to soothe her beast when it shook its disdainful, elegant head and showed its teeth at her for tickling its belly. Then for half an hour nothing but the crisp whisper of the combs, the flutter of the unceasing wind over stones, the soft bleat of a calf, the faint rhythmical sound of the nearby beasts biting the thin, dry grass. Always one old female stood watch, the alert head poised on the long neck, the large eyes watching up and down the vast, tilted planes of the mountain from the river miles below to the hanging glaciers miles above. Far peaks of stone and snow stood distinct against the dark-blue, sun-filled sky, blurred off into cloud and blowing mists, then shone out again across the gulfs of air.

Enno took up the big clot of milky fleece she had combed, and Shahes held open the long, loose-woven, double-ended sack.

Enno stuffed the fleece down into the sack. Shahes took her hands.

Leaning across the half-filled sack they held each other's hands, and Shahes said, "I want—" and Enno said, "Yes, yes!"

Neither of them had had much love, neither had had much pleasure in sex. Enno, when she was a rough farm girl named Akal, had the misfortune to attract and be attracted by a man whose pleasure was in cruelty. When she finally understood that she did not have to endure what he did to her, she ran away, not knowing how else to escape him. She took refuge at the School in Asta, and there found the work and learning much to her liking, as she did the spiritual discipline, and later the wandering life. She had been an itinerant scholar with no family, no close attachments, for twenty years. Now Shahes's passion opened to her a spirituality of the body, a revelation that transformed the world and made her feel she had never lived in it before.

As for Shahes, she'd given very little thought to love and not much more to sex, except as it entered into the question of marriage. Marriage was an urgent matter of business. She was thirty years old. Danro had no whole sedoretu, no child-bearing women, and only one child. Her duty was plain. She had gone courting in a grim, reluctant fashion to a couple of neighboring farms where there were Evening men. She was too late for the man at Beha Farm, who ran off with a lowlander. The widower at Upper Ked'd was receptive, but he also was nearly sixty and smelled like piss. She tried to force herself to accept the advances of Uncle Mika's half-cousin from Okro Farm down the river, but his desire to own a share of Danro was clearly the sole substance of his desire for Shahes, and he was even lazier and more shiftless than Uncle Mika.

Ever since they were girls, Shahes had met now and then with Temly, the Evening daughter of the nearest farmhold, Ked'din, round on the other side of the Farren. Temly and Shahes had a sexual friendship that was a true and reliable pleasure to them both. They both wished it could be permanent. Every now and then they talked, lying in Shahes's bed at Danro or Temly's bed at Ked'din, of getting married, making a sedoretu. There was no use going to the village matchmakers; they knew everybody the matchmakers knew. One by one they would name the men of Oro and the very few men they knew from outside the Oro Valley, and one by one they would dismiss them as either impossible or inaccessible. The only name that always stayed on the list was Otorra, a Morning man who worked at the carding sheds down in the village center. Shahes liked his reputation as a steady worker; Temly liked his looks and conversation. He evidently liked Temly's looks and conversation too, and would certainly have come courting her if there were any chance of a marriage at Ked'din, but it was a poor farmhold, and there was the same problem there as at Danro: there wasn't an eligible Evening man. To make a sedoretu,

Shahes and Temly and Otorra would have to marry the shiftless, shameless fellow at Okba or the sour old widower at Ked'd. To Shahes the idea of sharing her farm and her bed with either of them was intolerable.

"If I could only meet a man who was a match for me!" she said with bitter energy.

"I wonder if you'd like him if you did," said Temly.

"I don't know that I would."

"Maybe next autumn at Manebo . . . "

Shahes sighed. Every autumn she trekked down sixty kilometers to Manebo Fair with a train of pack-yama laden with pelts and wool, and looked for a man; but those she looked at twice never looked at her once. Even though Danro offered a steady living, nobody wanted to live way up there, on the roof, as they called it. And Shahes had no prettiness or nice ways to interest a man. Hard work, hard weather, and the habit of command had made her tough; solitude had made her shy. She was like a wild animal among the jovial, easy-talking dealers and buyers. Last autumn once more she had gone to the fair and once more strode back up into her mountains, sore and dour, and said to Temly, "I wouldn't touch a one of 'em."

Enno woke in the ringing silence of the mountain night. She saw the small square of the window ablaze with stars and felt Shahes's warm body beside her shake with sobs.

"What is it? What is it, my dear love?"

"You'll go away. You're going to go away!"

"But not now – not soon—"

"You can't stay here. You have a calling. A resp—" the word broken by a gasp and sob, "responsibility to your school, to your work, and I can't keep you. I can't give you the farm. I haven't anything to give you, anything at all!"

Enno – or Akal, as she had asked Shahes to call her when they were alone, going back to the girl-name she had given up – knew only too well what Shahes meant. It was the farmholder's duty to provide continuity. As Shahes owed life to her ancestors she owed life to her descendants. Akal did not question this; she had grown up on a farmhold. Since then, at school, she had learned about the joys and duties of the soul, and with Shahes she had learned the joys and duties of love. Neither of them in any way invalidated the duty of a farmholder. Shahes need not bear children herself, but she must see to it that Danro had children. If Temly and Otorra made the Evening marriage, Temly would bear the children of Danro. But a sedoretu must have a Morning marriage; Shahes must find an Evening man. Shahes was not free to keep Akal at Danro, nor was Akal justified in staying there, for she was in the way, an irrelevance, ultimately an obstacle, a spoiler. As long as she stayed on as a lover, she was neglecting her religious obligations while compromising Shahes's obligation to her farmhold. Shahes had said the truth: she had to go.

She got out of bed and went over to the window. Cold as it was she stood there naked in the starlight, gazing at the stars that flared and dazzled from the far grey slopes up to the zenith. She had to go and she could not go. Life was here, life was Shahes's body, her breasts, her mouth, her breath. She had found life and she could not go down to death. She could not go and she had to go.

Shahes said across the dark room, "Marry me."

Akal came back to the bed, her bare feet silent on the bare floor. She slipped under the bedfleece, shivering, feeling Shahes's warmth against her, and turned to her to hold her; but Shahes took her hand in a strong grip and said again, "Marry me."

"Oh if I could!"

"You can."

After a moment Akal sighed and stretched out, her hands behind her head on the pillow. "There's no Evening men here; you've said so yourself. So how can we marry? What can I do? Go fishing for a husband down in the lowlands, I suppose. With the farmhold as bait. What kind of man would that turn up? Nobody I'd let share you with me for a moment. I won't do it."

Shahes was following her own train of thought. "I can't leave Temly in the lurch," she said.

"And that's the other obstacle," Akal said. "It's not fair to Temly. If we do find an Evening man, then she'll get left out."

"No, she won't."

"Two Day marriages and no Morning marriage? Two Evening women in one sedoretu? There's a fine notion!"

"Listen," Shahes said, still not listening. She sat up with the bedfleece round her shoulders and spoke low and quick. "You go away. Back down there. The winter goes by. Late in the spring, people come up the Mane looking for summer work. A man comes to Oro and says, is anybody asking for a good finefleecer? At the sheds they tell him, yes, Shahes from Danro was down here looking for a hand. So he comes on up here, he knocks at the door here. My name is Akal, he says, I hear you need a fleecer. Yes, I say, yes, we do. Come in. Oh come in, come in and stay forever!"

Her hand was like iron on Akal's wrist, and her voice shook with exultation. Akal listened as if to a fairytale.

"Who's to know, Akal? Who'd ever know you? You're taller than most men up here – you can grow your hair, and dress like a man – you said you liked men's clothes once. Nobody will know. Who ever comes here anyway?"

"Oh, come on, Shahes! The people here, Magel and Madu – Shest— "

"The old people won't see anything. Mika's a halfwit. The child won't know. Temly can bring old Barres from Ked'din to marry us. He never knew a tit from a toe anyhow. But he can say the marriage ceremony."

"And Temly?" Akal said, laughing but disturbed; the idea was so wild and Shahes was so serious about it.

"Don't worry about Temly. She'd do anything to get out of Ked'din. She wants to come here; she and I have wanted to marry for years. Now we can. All we need is a Morning man for her. She likes Otorra well enough. And he'd like a share of Danro."

"No doubt, but he gets a share of me with it, you know! A woman in a Night marriage?"

"He doesn't have to know."

"You're crazy. Of course he'll know!"

"Only after we're married."

Akal stared through the dark at Shahes, speechless. Finally she said, "What you're proposing is that I go away now and come back after half a year dressed as a man. And marry you and Temly and a man I've never met. And live here the rest of my life pretending to be a man. And nobody is going to guess who I am or see through it or object to it. Least of all my husband."

"He doesn't matter."

"Yes, he does," said Akal. "It's wicked and unfair. It would desecrate the marriage sacrament. And anyway, it wouldn't work. I couldn't fool everybody! Certainly not for the rest of my life!"

"What other way have we to marry?"

"Find an Evening husband – somewhere—"

"But I want you! I want you for my husband and my wife. I don't want any man, ever. I want you, only you till the end of life, and nobody between us, and nobody to part us. Akal, think, think about it, maybe it's against religion, but who does it hurt? Why is it unfair? Temly likes men, and she'll have Otorra. He'll have her, and Danro. And Danro will have their children. And I will have you, I'll have you for ever and ever, my soul, my life and soul."

"Oh don't, oh don't," Akal said with a great sob.

Shahes held her.

"I never was much good at being a woman," Akal said. "Till I met you. You can't make me into a man now! I'd be even worse at that, no good at all!"

"You won't be a man, you'll be my Akal, my love, and nothing and nobody will ever come between us."

They rocked back and forth together, laughing and crying, with the fleece around them and the stars blazing at them. "We'll do it, we'll do it!" Shahes said, and Akal said, "We're crazy, we're crazy!"

Gossips in Oro had begun to ask if that scholar woman was going to spend the winter up in the high farmholds, where was she now, Danro was it or Ked'din? – when she came walking down the zigzag road. She spent the night and sang the offerings for the mayor's family, and caught the daily freighter to the suntrain station down at Dermane. The first of the autumn blizzards followed her down from the peaks.

Shahes and Akal sent no message to each other all through the winter. In the early spring Akal telephoned the farm. "When are you coming?" Shahes asked, and the distant voice replied, "In time for the fleecing."

For Shahes the winter passed in a long dream of Akal. Her voice sounded in the empty next room. Her tall body moved beside Shahes through the wind and snow. Shahes's sleep was peaceful, rocked in a certainty of love known and love to come.

For Akal, or Enno as she became again in the lowlands, the

winter passed in a long misery of guilt and indecision. Marriage was a sacrament, and surely what they planned was a mockery of that sacrament. Yet as surely it was a marriage of love. And as Shahes had said, it harmed no one – unless to deceive them was to harm them. It could not be right to fool the man, Otorra, into a marriage where his Night partner would turn out to be a woman. But surely no man knowing the scheme beforehand would agree to it; deception was the only means at hand. They must cheat him.

The religion of the ki'O lacks priests and pundits who tell the common folk what to do. The common folk have to make their own moral and spiritual choices, which is why they spend a good deal of time discussing the Discussions. As a scholar of the Discussions, Enno knew more questions than most people, but fewer answers.

She sat all the dark winter mornings wrestling with her soul. When she called Shahes, it was to tell her that she could not come. When she heard Shahes's voice her misery and guilt ceased to exist, were gone, as a dream is gone on waking. She said, "I'll be there in time for the fleecing."

In the spring, while she worked with a crew rebuilding and repainting a wing of her old school at Asta, she let her hair grow. When it was long enough, she clubbed it back, as men often did. In the summer, having saved a little money working for the school, she bought men's clothes. She put them on and looked at herself in the mirror in the shop. She saw Akal. Akal was a tall, thin man with a thin face, a bony nose, and a slow, brilliant smile. She liked him.

Akal got off the High Deka freighter at its last stop, Oro, went to the village center, and asked if anybody was looking for a fleecer.

"Danro."—"The farmer was down from Danro, twice already."—"Wants a finefleecer."—"Coarsefleecer, wasn't it?"— It took a while, but the elders and gossips agreed at last: a finefleecer was wanted at Danro.

"Where's Danro?" asked the tall man.

"Up," said an elder succinctly. "You ever handled ariu yearlings?"

"Yes," said the tall man. "Up west or up east?"

They told him the road to Danro, and he went off up the zigzags, whistling a familiar praise-song.

As Akal went on he stopped whistling, and stopped being a man, and wondered how she could pretend not to know anybody in the household, and how she could imagine they wouldn't know her. How could she deceive Shest, the child whom she had taught the water rite and the praise-songs? A pang of fear and dismay and shame shook her when she saw Shest come running to the gate to let the stranger in.

Akal spoke little, keeping her voice down in her chest, not meeting the child's eyes. She was sure he recognized her. But his stare was simply that of a child who saw strangers so seldom that for all he knew they all looked alike. He ran in to fetch the old people, Magel and Madu. They came out to offer Akal the customary hospitality, a religious duty, and Akal accepted, feeling mean and low at deceiving these people, who had always been kind to her in their rusty, stingy way, and at the same time feeling a wild impulse of laughter, of triumph. They did not see Enno in her, they did not know her. That meant that she was Akal, and Akal was free.

She was sitting in the kitchen drinking a thin and sour soup of summer greens when Shahes came in – grim, stocky, weather-beaten, wet. A summer thunderstorm had broken over the Farren soon after Akal reached the farm. "Who's that?" said Shahes, doffing her wet coat.

"Come up from the village." Old Magel lowered his voice to address Shahes confidentially: "He said they said you said you wanted a hand with the yearlings."

"Where've you worked?" Shahes demanded, her back turned as she ladled herself a bowl of soup.

Akal had no life history, at least not a recent one. She groped a long time. No one took any notice, prompt answers and quick talk being unusual and suspect practices in the mountains. At last she said the name of the farm she had run away from twenty years ago. "Bredde Hold, of Abba Village, on the Oriso."

"And you've finefleeced? Handled yearlings? Ariu yearlings?"

Akal nodded, dumb. Was it possible that Shahes did not recognize her? Her voice was flat and unfriendly, and the one glance she had given Akal was dismissive. She had sat down with her soupbowl and was eating hungrily.

"You can come out with me this afternoon and I'll see how you work," Shahes said. "What's your name, then?"

"Akal."

Shahes grunted and went on eating. She glanced up across the table at Akal again, one flick of the eyes, like a stab of light.

Out on the high hills, in the mud of rain and snowmelt, in the stinging wind and the flashing sunlight, they held each other so tight neither could breathe; they laughed and wept and talked and kissed and coupled in a rock shelter, and came back so dirty and with such a sorry little sack of combings that old Magel told Madu that he couldn't understand why Shahes was going to hire the tall fellow from down there at all, if that's all the work was in him, and Madu said what's more he eats for six.

But after a month or so, when Shahes and Akal weren't hiding the fact that they slept together, and Shahes began to talk about making a sedoretu, the old couple grudgingly approved. They had no other kind of approval to give. Maybe Akal was ignorant, didn't know a hassel-bit from a cold-chisel; but they were all like that down there. Remember that travelling scholar, Enno, stayed here last year; she was just the same, too tall for her own good and ignorant, but willing to learn, same as Akal. Akal was a prime hand with the beasts, or had the makings of it anyhow. Shahes could look farther and do worse. And it meant she and Temly could be the Day marriage of a sedoretu, as they would have been long since if there'd been any kind of men around worth taking into the farmhold; what's wrong with this generation, plenty of good men around in my day.

Shahes had spoken to the village matchmakers down in Oro. They spoke to Otorra, now a foreman at the carding sheds; he accepted a formal invitation to Danro. Such invitations included meals and an overnight stay, necessarily, in such a remote place, but the invitation was to share worship with the farm family at the house shrine, and its significance was known to all.

So they all gathered at the house shrine, which at Danro was a low, cold, inner room walled with stone, with a floor of earth and stones that was the unlevelled ground of the mountainside. A tiny spring, rising at the higher end of the room, trickled in a channel of cut granite. It was the reason why the house stood where it did, and had stood there for 600 years. They offered water and accepted water, one to another, one from another, the old Evening couple, Uncle Mika, his son Shest, Asbi who had worked as a pack-trainer and handyman at Danro for thirty years, Akal the new hand, Shahes the farmholder, and the guests: Otorra from Oro and Temly from Ked'din.

Temly smiled across the spring at Otorra, but he did not meet her eyes, or anyone else's.

Temly was a short, stocky woman, the same type as Shahes, but fairer-skinned and a bit lighter all round, not as solid, not as hard. She had a surprising, clear singing voice that soared up in the praise-songs. Otorra was also rather short and broad-shouldered, with good features, a competent-looking man, but just now extremely ill at ease; he looked as if he had robbed the shrine or murdered the mayor, Akal thought, studying him with interest, as well she might. He looked furtive; he looked guilty.

Akal observed him with curiosity and dispassion. She would share water with Otorra, but not guilt. As soon as she had seen Shahes, touched Shahes, all her scruples and moral anxieties had dropped away, as if they could not breathe up here in the mountains. Akal had been born for Shahes and Shahes for Akal; that was all there was to it. Whatever made it possible for them to be together was right.

Once or twice she did ask herself, what if I'd been born into the Morning instead of the Evening moiety? – a perverse and terrible thought. But perversity and sacrilege were not asked of her. All she had to do was change sex. And that only in appearance, in public. With Shahes she was a woman, and more truly a woman and herself than she had ever been in her life. With everybody else she was Akal, whom they took to be a man. That was no trouble at all. She was Akal; she liked being Akal. It was not like acting a part. She never had been herself with other people, had always felt a falsity in her relationships with them; she had never known who she was at all, except sometimes for a moment in meditation, when her *I am* became *It is,* and she breathed the stars. But with Shahes she was herself utterly, in time and in the body, Akal, a soul consumed in love and blessed by intimacy.

So it was that she had agreed with Shahes that they should say nothing to Otorra, nothing even to Temly. "Let's see what Temly makes of you," Shahes said, and Akal agreed.

Last year Temly had entertained the scholar Enno overnight at her farmhold for instruction and worship, and had met her two or three times at Danro. When she came to share worship today she met Akal for the first time. Did she see Enno? She gave no sign of it. She greeted Akal with a kind of brusque goodwill, and they talked about breeding ariu. She quite evidently studied the newcomer, judging, sizing up; but that was natural enough in a woman meeting a stranger she might be going to marry. "You don't know much about mountain farming, do you?" she said kindly after they had talked a while. "Different from down there. What did you raise? Those big flatland yama?" And Akal told her about the farm where she grew up, and the three crops a year they got, which made Temly nod in amazement.

As for Otorra, Shahes and Akal colluded to deceive him without ever saying a word more about it to each other. Akal's mind shied away from the subject. They would get to know each other during the engagement period, she thought vaguely. She would have to tell him, eventually, that she did not want to have sex with him, of course, and the only way to do that without insulting and humiliating him was to say that she, that Akal, was averse to having sex with other men, and hoped he would forgive her. But Shahes had made it clear that she mustn't tell him that till they were married. If he knew it beforehand he would refuse to enter the sedoretu. And even worse, he might talk about it, expose Akal as a woman, in revenge. Then they would never be able to marry. When Shahes had spoken about this Akal had felt distressed and trapped, anxious, guilty again; but Shahes was serenely confident and untroubled, and somehow Akal's guilty feelings would not stick. They dropped off. She simply hadn't thought much about it. She watched Otorra now with sympathy and curiosity, wondering what made him look so hangdog. He was scared of something, she thought.

After the water was poured and the blessing said, Shahes read from the Fourth Discussion; she closed the old boxbook very carefully, put it on its shelf and its cloth over it, and then, speaking to Magel and Madu as was proper, they being what was left of the First Sedoretu of Danro, she said, "My Othermother and my Otherfather, I propose that a new sedoretu be made in this house."

Madu nudged Magel. He fidgeted and grimaced and muttered

inaudibly. Finally Madu said in her weak, resigned voice, "Daughter of the Morning, tell us the marriages."

"If all be well and willing, the marriage of the Morning will be Shahes and Akal, and the marriage of the Evening will be Temly and Otorra, and the marriage of the Day will be Shahes and Temly, and the marriage of the Night will be Akal and Otorra."

There was a long pause. Magel hunched his shoulders. Madu said at last, rather fretfully, "Well, is that all right with everybody?" – which gave the gist, if not the glory, of the formal request for consent, usually couched in antique and ornate language.

"Yes," said Shahes, clearly.

"Yes," said Akal, manfully.

"Yes," said Temly, cheerfully.

A pause.

Everybody looked at Otorra, of course. He had blushed purple and, as they watched, turned greyish.

"I am willing," he said at last in a forced mumble, and cleared his throat. "Only—" He stuck there.

Nobody said anything.

The silence was horribly painful.

Akal finally said, "We don't have to decide now. We can talk. And, and come back to the shrine later, if . . . "

"Yes," Otorra said, glancing at Akal with a look in which so much emotion was compressed that she could not read it at all – terror, hate, gratitude, despair? – "I want to – I need to talk – to Akal."

"I'd like to get to know my brother of the Evening too," said Temly in her clear voice.

"Yes, that's it, yes, that is—" Otorra stuck again, and blushed again. He was in such an agony of discomfort that Akal said, "Let's go on outside for a bit, then," and led Otorra out into the yard, while the others went to the kitchen.

Akal knew Otorra had seen through her pretense. She was dismayed, and dreaded what he might say; but he had not made a scene, he had not humiliated her before the others, and she was grateful to him for that.

"This is what it is," Otorra said in a stiff, forced voice, coming to a stop at the gate. "It's the Night marriage." He came to a stop there, too.

Akal nodded. Reluctantly, she spoke, to help Otorra do what he had to do. "You don't have to—" she began, but he was speaking again:

"The Night marriage. Us. You and me. See, I don't— There's some— See, with men, I—"

The whine of delusion and the buzz of incredulity kept Akal from hearing what the man was trying to tell her. He had to stammer on even more painfully before she began to listen. When his words came clear to her she could not trust them, but she had to. He had stopped trying to talk.

Very hesitantly, she said, "Well, I . . . I was going to tell you . . . The only man I ever had sex with, it was . . . It wasn't good. He made me— He did things— I don't know what was wrong. But I never have— I have never had any sex with men. Since that. I can't. I can't make myself want to."

"Neither can I," Otorra said.

They stood side by side leaning on the gate, contemplating the miracle, the simple truth.

"I just only ever want women," Otorra said in a shaking voice.

"A lot of people are like that," Akal said.

"They are?"

She was touched and grieved by his humility. Was it men's boastfulness with other men, or the hardness of the mountain people, that had burdened him with this ignorance, this shame?

"Yes," she said. "Everywhere I've been. There's quite a lot of men who only want sex with women. And women who only want sex with men. And the other way round, too. Most people want both, but there's always some who don't. It's like the two ends of," she was about to say "a spectrum," but it wasn't the language of Akal the fleecer or Otorra the carder, and with the adroitness of the old teacher she substituted "a sack. If you pack it right, most of the fleece is in the middle. But there's some at both ends where you tie off, too. That's us. There's not as many of us. But there's nothing wrong with us." As she said this last bit it did not sound like what a man would say to a man. But it was said; and Otorra did not seem to think it peculiar, though he did not look entirely convinced. He pondered. He had a pleasant face, blunt, unguarded, now that his unhappy secret was out. He was only about thirty, younger than she had expected.

"But in a marriage," he said. "It's different from just . . . A marriage is—Well, if I don't – and you don't—"

"Marriage isn't just sex," Akal said, but said it in Enno's voice, Enno the scholar discussing questions of ethics, and Akal cringed.

"A lot of it is," said Otorra, reasonably.

"All right," Akal said in a consciously deeper, slower voice. "But if I don't want it with you and you don't want it with me why can't we have a good marriage?" It came out so improbable and so banal at the same time that she nearly broke into a fit of laughter. Controlling herself, she thought, rather shocked, that Otorra was laughing at her, until she realized that he was crying.

"I never could tell anybody," he said.

"We don't ever have to," she said. She put her arm around his shoulders without thinking about it at all. He wiped his eyes with his fists like a child, cleared his throat, and stood thinking. Obviously he was thinking about what she had just said.

"Think," she said, also thinking about it, "how lucky we are!"

"Yes. Yes, we are." He hesitated. "But . . . but is it religious . . . to marry each other knowing . . . Without really meaning to . . . " He stuck again.

After a long time, Akal said, in a voice as soft and nearly as deep as his, "I don't know."

She had withdrawn her comforting, patronizing arm from his shoulders. She leaned her hands on the top bar of the gate. She looked at her hands, long and strong, hardened and dirt-engrained from farm work, though the oil of the fleeces kept them supple. A farmer's hands. She had given up the religious life for love's sake and never looked back. But now she was ashamed.

She wanted to tell this honest man the truth, to be worthy of his honesty.

But it would do no good, unless not to make the sedoretu was the only good.

"I don't know," she said again. "I think what matters is if we try to give each other love and honor. However we do that, that's how we do it. That's how we're married. The marriage – the religion is in the love, in the honoring."

"I wish there was somebody to ask," Otorra said, unsatisfied. "Like that travelling scholar that was here last summer. Somebody who knows about religion."

Akal was silent.

"I guess the thing is to do your best," Otorra said after a while. It sounded sententious, but he added, plainly, "I would do that."

"So would I," Akal said.

A mountain farmhouse like Danro is a dark, damp, bare, grim place to live in, sparsely furnished, with no luxuries except the warmth of the big kitchen and the splendid bedfleeces. But it offers privacy, which may be the greatest luxury of all, though the ki'O consider it a necessity. "A three-room sedoretu" is a common expression in Okets, meaning an enterprise doomed to fail.

At Danro, everyone had their own room and bathroom. The two old members of the First Sedoretu, and Uncle Mika and his child, had rooms in the center and west wing; Asbi, when he wasn't sleeping out on the mountain, had a cozy, dirty nest behind the kitchen. The new Second Sedoretu had the whole east side of the house. Temly chose a little attic room, up a half-flight of stairs from the others, with a fine view. Shahes kept her room, and Akal hers, adjoining; and Otorra chose the southeast corner, the sunniest room in the house.

The conduct of a new sedoretu is to some extent, and wisely, prescribed by custom and sanctioned by religion. The first night after the ceremony of marriage belongs to the Morning and Evening couples; the second night to the Day and Night couples. Thereafter the four spouses may join as and when they please, but always and only by invitation given and accepted, and the arrangements are to be known to all four. Four souls and bodies and all the years of their four lives to come are in the balance in each of those decisions and invitations; passion, negative and positive, must find its channels, and trust must be established, lest the whole structure fail to found itself solidly, or destroy itself in selfishness and jealousy and grief.

Akal knew all the customs and sanctions, and she insisted that they be followed to the letter. Her wedding night with Shahes was tender and a little tense. Her wedding night with Otorra was also tender; they sat in his room and talked softly, shy with each other but each very grateful; then Otorra slept in the deep windowseat, insisting that Akal have the bed.

Within a few weeks Akal knew that Shahes was more intent on

having her way, on having Akal as her partner, than on maintaining any kind of sexual balance or even a pretense of it. As far as Shahes was concerned, Otorra and Temly could look after each other and that was that. Akal had of course known many sedoretu where one or two of the partnerships dominated the others completely, through passion or the power of an ego. To balance all four relationships perfectly was an ideal seldom realized. But this sedoretu, already built on a deception, a disguise, was more fragile than most. Shahes wanted what she wanted and consequences be damned. Akal had followed her far up the mountain, but would not follow her over a precipice.

It was a clear autumn night, the window full of stars, like that night last year when Shahes had said, "Marry me."

"You have to give Temly tomorrow night," Akal repeated.

"She's got Otorra," Shahes repeated.

"She wants you. Why do you think she married you?"

"She's got what she wants. I hope she gets pregnant soon," Shahes said, stretching luxuriously, and running her hand over Akal's breasts and belly. Akal stopped her hand and held it.

"It isn't fair, Shahes. It isn't right."

"A fine one you are to talk!"

"But Otorra doesn't want me, you know that. And Temly does want you. And we owe it to her."

"Owe her what?"

"Love and honor."

"She's got what she wanted," Shahes said, and freed her hand from Akal's grasp with a harsh twist. "Don't preach at me."

"I'm going back to my room," Akal said, slipping lithely from the bed and stalking naked through the starry dark. "Good night."

She was with Temly in the old dye room, unused for years until Temly, an expert dyer, came to the farm. Weavers down in the Centers would pay well for fleece dyed the true Deka red. Her skill had been Temly's dowry. Akal was her assistant and apprentice now.

"Eighteen minutes. Timer set?"

"Set."

Temly nodded, checked the vents on the great dye-boiler, checked the read-out again, and went outside to catch the morning sun. Akal joined her on the stone bench by the stone doorway. The smell of the vegetable dye, pungent and acid-sweet, clung to them, and their clothes and hands and arms were raddled pink and crimson.

Akal had become attached to Temly very soon, finding her reliably good-tempered and unexpectedly thoughtful – both qualities that had been in rather short supply at Danro. Without knowing it, Akal had formed her expectation of the mountain people on Shahes – powerful, wilful, undeviating, rough. Temly was strong and quite self-contained, but open to impressions as Shahes was not. Relationships within her moiety meant little to Shahes; she called Otorra brother because it was customary, but did not see a brother in him. Temly called Akal brother and meant it, and Akal, who had had no family for so long, welcomed the relationship, returning Temly's warmth. They talked easily together, though Akal constantly had to guard herself from becoming too easy and letting her woman-self speak out. Mostly it was no trouble at all being Akal and she gave little thought to it, but sometimes with Temly it was very hard to keep up the pretense, to prevent herself from saying what a woman would say to her sister. In general she had found that the main drawback in being a man was that conversations were less interesting.

They talked about the next step in the dyeing process, and then Temly said, looking off over the low stone wall of the yard to the huge purple slant of the Farren, "You know Enno, don't you?"

The question seemed innocent and Akal almost answered automatically with some kind of deceit – "The scholar that was here . . . ?"

But there was no reason why Akal the fleecer should know Enno the scholar. And Temly had not asked, Do you remember Enno, or did you know Enno, but, "You know Enno, don't you?" She knew the answer.

"Yes."

Temly nodded, smiling a little. She said nothing more.

Akal was amazed by her subtlety, her restraint. There was no difficulty in honoring so honorable a woman.

"I lived alone for a long time," Akal said. "Even on the farm where I grew up I was mostly alone. I never had a sister. I'm glad to have one at last."

"So am I," said Temly.

Their eyes met briefly, a flicker of recognition, a glance planting trust deep and silent as a tree-root.

"She knows who I am, Shahes."

Shahes said nothing, trudging up the steep slope.

"Now I wonder if she knew from the start. From the first water-sharing . . . "

"Ask her if you like," Shahes said, indifferent.

"I can't. The deceiver has no right to ask for the truth."

"Humbug!" Shahes said, turning on her, halting her in midstride. They were up on the Farren looking for an old beast that Asbi had reported missing from the herd. The keen autumn wind had blown Shahes's cheeks red, and as she stood staring up at Akal she squinted her watering eyes so that they glinted like knife blades. "Quit preaching! Is that who you are? 'The deceiver?' I thought you were my wife!"

"I am, and Otorra's too, and you're Temly's – you can't leave them out, Shahes!"

"Are they complaining?"

"Do you want them to complain?" Akal shouted, losing her temper. "Is that the kind of marriage you want? Look, there she is," she added in a suddenly quiet voice, pointing up the great rocky mountainside. Farsighted, led by a bird's circling, she had caught the movement of the yama's head near an outcrop of boulders. The quarrel was postponed. They both set off at a cautious trot towards the boulders.

The old yama had broken a leg in a slip from the rocks. She lay neatly collected, though the broken foreleg would not double under her white breast but stuck out forward, and her whole body had a lurch to that side. Her disdainful head was erect on the long neck, and she gazed at the women, watching her death approach, with clear, unfathomable, uninterested eyes.

"Is she in pain?" Akal asked, daunted by that great serenity.

"Of course," Shahes said, sitting down several paces away from the yama to sharpen her knife on its emery-stone. "Wouldn't you be?"

She took a long time getting the knife as sharp as she could get it, patiently retesting and rewhetting the blade. At last she tested it again and then sat completely still. She stood up quietly, walked over to the yama, pressed its head up against her breast and cut its throat in one long fast slash. Blood leaped out in a brilliant arc. Shahes slowly lowered the head with its gazing eyes down to the ground.

Akal found that she was speaking the words of the ceremony for the dead, *Now all that was owed is repaid and all that was owned, returned. Now all that was lost is found and all that was bound, free.* Shahes stood silent, listening till the end.

Then came the work of skinning. They would leave the carcass to be cleaned by the scavengers of the mountain; it was a carrion-bird circling over the yama that had first caught Akal's eye, and there were now three of them riding the wind. Skinning was fussy, dirty work, in the stink of meat and blood. Akal was inexpert, clumsy, cutting the hide more than once. In penance she insisted on carrying the pelt, rolled as best they could and strapped with their belts. She felt like a grave robber, carrying away the white-and-dun fleece, leaving the thin, broken corpse sprawled among the rocks in the indignity of its nakedness. Yet in her mind as she lugged the heavy fleece along was Shahes standing up and taking the yama's beautiful head against her breast and slashing its throat, all one long movement, in which the woman and the animal were utterly one.

It is need that answers need, Akal thought, as it is question that answers question. The pelt reeked of death and dung. Her hands were caked with blood, and ached, gripping the stiff belt, as she followed Shahes down the steep rocky path homeward.

"I'm going down to the village," Otorra said, getting up from the breakfast table.

"When are you going to card those four sacks?" Shahes said.

He ignored her, carrying his dishes to the washer-rack. "Any errands?" he asked of them all.

"Everybody done?" Madu asked, and took the cheese out to the pantry.

"No use going into town till you can take the carded fleece," said Shahes.

Otorra turned to her, stared at her, and said, "I'll card it when I choose and take it when I choose and I don't take orders at my own work, will you understand that?"

Stop, stop now! Akal cried silently, for Shahes, stunned by the uprising of the meek, was listening to him. But he went on, firing grievance with grievance, blazing out in recriminations. "You can't give all the orders, we're your sedoretu, we're your household, not a lot of hired hands. Yes, it's your farm but it's ours too; you married us, you can't make all the decisions, and you can't have it all your way either," and at this point Shahes unhurriedly walked out of the room.

"Shahes!" Akal called after her, loud and imperative. Though Otorra's outburst was undignified it was completely justified, and his anger was both real and dangerous. He was a man who had been used, and he knew it. As he had let himself be used and had colluded in that misuse, so now his anger threatened destruction. Shahes could not run away from it.

She did not come back. Madu had wisely disappeared. Akal told Shest to run out and see to the pack-beasts' feed and water.

The three remaining in the kitchen sat or stood silent. Temly looked at Otorra. He looked at Akal.

"You're right," Akal said to him.

He gave a kind of satisfied snarl. He looked handsome in his anger, flushed and reckless. "Damn right I'm right. I've let this go on for too long. Just because she owned the farmhold—"

"And managed it since she was fourteen," Akal cut in. "You think she can quit managing just like that? She's always run things here. She had to. She never had anybody to share power with. Everybody has to learn how to be married."

"That's right," Otorra flashed back, "and a marriage isn't two pairs. It's four pairs!"

That brought Akal up short. Instinctively she looked to Temly for help. Temly was sitting, quiet as usual, her elbows on the table, gathering up crumbs with one hand and pushing them into a little pyramid.

"Temly and me, you and Shahes, Evening and Morning, fine," Otorra said. "What about Temly and her? What about you and me?"

Akal was now completely at a loss. "I thought . . . When we talked . . . "

"I said I didn't like sex with men," said Otorra.

She looked up and saw a gleam in his eye. Spite? Triumph? Laughter?

"Yes. You did," Akal said after a long pause. "And I said the same thing."

Another pause.

"It's a religious duty," Otorra said.

Enno suddenly said very loudly in Akal's voice, "Don't come onto me with your religious duty! I studied religious duty for twenty years and where did it get me? Here! With you! In this mess!"

At this, Temly made a strange noise and put her face in her hands. Akal thought she had burst into tears, and then saw she was laughing, the painful, helpless, jolting laugh of a person who hasn't had much practice at it.

"There's nothing to laugh about," Otorra said fiercely, but then had no more to say; his anger had blown up leaving nothing but smoke. He groped for words for a while longer. He looked at Temly, who was indeed in tears now, tears of laughter. He made a despairing gesture. He sat down beside Temly and said, "I suppose it is funny if you look at it. It's just that I feel like a chump." He laughed, ruefully, and then, looking up at Akal, he laughed genuinely. "Who's the biggest chump?" he asked her.

"Not you," she said. "How long . . . "

"How long do you think?"

It was what Shahes, standing in the passageway, heard: their laughter. The three of them laughing. She listened to it with dismay, fear, shame, and terrible envy. She hated them for laughing. She wanted to be with them, she wanted to laugh with them, she wanted to silence them. Akal, Akal was laughing at her.

She went out to the workshed and stood in the dark behind the door and tried to cry and did not know how. She had not cried when her parents were killed; there had been too much to do. She thought the others were laughing at her for loving Akal, for wanting her, for needing her. She thought Akal was laughing at her for being such a fool, for loving her. She thought Akal would sleep with the man and they would laugh together at her. She drew her knife and tested its edge. She had made it very sharp yesterday on the Farren to kill the yama. She came back to the house, to the kitchen.

They were all still there. Shest had come back and was pestering Otorra to take him into town and Otorra was saying, "Maybe, maybe," in his soft lazy voice.

Temly looked up, and Akal looked round at Shahes – the small head on the graceful neck, the clear eyes gazing.

Nobody spoke.

"I'll walk down with you, then," Shahes said to Otorra, and sheathed her knife. She looked at the women and the child. "We might as well all go," she said sourly. "If you like."

TAN-TAN AND DRY BONE

Nalo Hopkinson

If you only see Dry Bone: one meager man, with arms and legs
thin so like matches stick, and what a way the man face just a-hang
down till it favour jackass when him sick!

Duppy Dead Town is where people go when life boof them,
when hope left them and happiness cut she eye 'pon them and
strut away. Duppy Dead people drag them foot when them walk.
The food them cook taste like burial ground ashes. Duppy Dead
people have one foot in the world and the next one already cross-
ing the threshold to where the real duppy-them living. In Duppy
Dead Town them will tell you how it ain't have no way to get away
from Dry Bone the skin-and-bone man, for even if you lock you
door on him, him body thin so like the hope of salvation, so fine
him could slide through the crack and all to pass inside your
house.

Dry Bone sit down there on one little wooden crate in the open
market in Duppy Dead Town. Him a-think about food. Him
hungry so till him belly a-burn him, till it just a-prowl round
inside him rib cage like angry bush cat, till it clamp on to him
backbone, and a-crouch there so and a-growl.

And all the time Dry Bone sitting down there in the market,
him just a-watch the open sky above him, for Dry Bone nah like
that endless blue. Him 'fraid him will just fall up into it and keep
falling.

Dry Bone feel say him could eat two-three of that market
woman skinny little fowl-them, feathers and all, then wash them
down with a dry-up breadfruit from the farmer cart across the
way, raw and hard just so, and five-six of them wrinkle-up string
mango from the fruit stand over there. Dry Bone coulda never get

enough food, and right now, all like how him ain't eat for days, even Duppy Dead people food looking good. But him nah have no money. The market people wouldn't even prekkay 'pon him, only a-watch him like stray dog so him wouldn't fast himself and thief away any of them goods. In Duppy Dead Town them had a way to say if you only start to feed Dry Bone, you can't stop, and you pickney-them go starve, for him will eat up all your provisions. And then them would shrug and purse-up them mouth, for them know say hunger is only one of the crosses Duppy Dead pickney go have to bear.

Duppy Dead ain't know it waiting; waiting for the one name Tan-Tan.

So – it had Dry Bone sitting there, listening to he belly bawl. And is so Tan-Tan find he, cotch-up on the wooden crate like one big black anansi-spider.

Dry Bone watch the young woman dragging she sad self into the market like monkey riding she back. She nah have no right to look downpressed so; she body tall and straight like young cane, and she legs strong. But the look on she pretty face favour puppy what lose it mother, and she carrying she hand on she machète handle the way you does put your hand on your friend shoulder. Dry Bone sit up straight. He lick he lips. A stranger in Duppy Dead Town, one who ain't know to avoid he. One who can't see she joy for she sorrow; the favourite meat of the one name Dry Bone. He know she good. Dry Bone know all the souls that feed he. He recognize she so well, he discern she name in the curve of she spine. So Dry Bone laugh, a sound like the dust blowin' down in the dry gully. "Girl pickney Tan-Tan," he whisper, "I go make you take me on this day. And when you pick me up, you pick up trouble."

He call out to Tan-Tan, "My beautiful one; you enjoying the day?"

Tan-Tan look at the little fine-foot man, so meager you could nearly see through he. "What you want, Grandpa?" she ask.

Dry Bone smile when she say "Grandpa." True, Duppy Dead townspeople have a way to say that Dry Bone older than Death it own self. "Well doux-doux darlin', me wasn't going to say nothing; but since you ask, beg you a copper to buy something to eat, nuh? I ain't eat from mornin'."

Now, Tan-Tan heart soft. Too besides, she figure maybe if she help out this old man who look to be on he last legs, she go ease up the curse on she a little. For you must know the story 'bout she, how she kill Antonio she father, she only family on New Half-Way Tree. Guilt nearly breaking she heart in two, but to make it worse, the douen people nah put a curse on she when she do the deed? Yes, man: she couldn't rest until she save two people life to make up for the one she did kill. Everywhere she go, she could hear the douen chant following she:

> It ain't have no magic in do-feh-do,
> If you take one, you mus' give back two.

Tan-Tan reach into she pocket to fling the old man couple-three coppers. But she find it strange that he own people wasn't feeding he. So she raise she voice to everyone in the marketplace: "How oonuh could let this old man sit here hungry so? Oonuh not shame?"

"Lawd, missus," say the woman selling the fowl, "you ain't want to mix up with he. That is Dry Bone, and when you pick he up, you pick up trouble!"

"What stupidness you talking, woman? Hot sun make you bassourdie, or what? How much trouble so one little old man could give you?"

A man frying some hard johnnycake on a rusty piece of galvanized iron look up from he wares. "You should listen when people talk to you, girl pickney. Make I tell you: you even self touch Dry Bone, is like you touch Death. Don't say nobody ain't tell you!"

Tan-Tan look down at the little old man, just holding he belly and waiting for somebody to take pity on he. Tan-Tan kiss she teeth *steuups*. "Oonuh too craven, you hear? Come, Daddy. I go buy you a meal, and I go take you where I staying and cook it up nice for you. All right?"

Dry Bone get excited one time; he almost have she now! "Thank you, my darlin'. Granny Nanny bless you, doux-doux. I ain't go be plenty trouble. Beg you though, sweetheart: pick me up. Me old bones so weak with hunger, I ain't think I could make the walk back to your place. I is only a little man, half-way a duppy meself. You could lift me easy."

"You mean to say these people make you stay here and get hungry so till you can't walk?" Tan-Tan know say she could pick he up; after he the smallest man she ever see.

The market go quiet all of a sudden. Everybody only waiting to see what she go do. Tan-Tan bend down to take the old man in she arms. Dry Bone reach out and hold on to she. As he touch she, she feel a coldness wrap round she heart. She pick up the old man, and is like she pick up all the cares of the world. She make a joke of it, though: "Eh-eh, Pappy, you heavier than you look, you know!"

That is when she hear Dry Bone voice good, whispering inside she head, *sht-sht-sht* like dead leaf on a dead tree And she realize that all this time she been talking to he, she never see he lips move. "I name Dry Bone," the old man say, "I old like Death, and when you pick me up, you pick up trouble. You ain't go shake me loose until I suck out all your substance. Feed me, Tan-Tan."

And Tan-Tan feel Dry Bone getting heavier and heavier, but she couldn't let he go. She feel the weight of all the buriens she carrying: alone, stranded on New Half-Way Tree with a curse on she head, a spiteful woman so ungrateful she kill she own daddy.

"Feed me, Tan-Tan, or I go choke you." He wrap he arms tight round she neck and cut off she wind. She stumble ever to the closest market stall. The lady selling the fowl back away, she eyes rolling with fright. Gasping for air, Tan-Tan stretch out she hind and feel two dead fowl. She pick them up off the woman stand. Dry Bone chuckle. He loosen up he arms just enough to let she get sone air. He grab one fowl and stuff it into he mouth, feathers and all. He chew, then he swallow. "More, Tan-Tan. Feed me." He choke she again.

She body crying for breath, Tan-Tan stagger from one market stall to the next. All the higglers fill up a market basket for she. Them had warn she, but she never listen. None of them would take she money. Dry Bone let she breathe again. "Now take me home, Tan-Tan."

Tan-Tan grab the little man round he waist and try to dash he off, but she hand stick to he like he was tar baby. He laugh in she mind, the way ground puppy does giggle when it see carrion.

Nalo Hopkinson

"You pick me up by your own free will. You can't put me down. Take me home, Tan-Tan."

Tan-Tan turn she feet towards she little hut in the bush, and with every step she take along the narrow gravel path into the bush, Dry Bone only getting heavier. Tan-Tan mother did never want she; Lone make Antonio kidnap she away to New Half-Way Tree. Even she daddy who did say he love she used to beat she, and worse things too besides. Tan-Tan never see the singing tree she always pass by on she way home, with the wind playing like harp in the leaves, or the bright blue furry butterflies that always used to sweet she, flitting through the bush carrying the flowers they gather in their little hands. With Dry Bone on her back and the full market basket in her arms, Tan-Tan had was to use she shoulders to shove aside the branches to make she way to she hut. Branches reach out bony fingers to pull at she dreads, but she ain't feel that pain. She only feel the pain of knowing what she is, a worthless, wicked woman that only good to feed a duppy like Dry Bone. How anybody could love she? She don't deserve no better.

"Make haste, woman," Dry Bone snarl. "And keep under the trees, you hear? I want to get out from under the open sky."

By the time them reach the thatch hut standing all by itself in the bush, Tan-Tan back did bend with the weight of all she was carrying. It feel like Dry Bone get bigger, oui? Tan-Tan stand up outside she home, panting under the weight of she burdens.

"Take me inside, Tan-Tan. I prefer to be out of the air."

"Yes, Dry Bone." Wheezing, she climb up the verandah steps and carry he inside the dark, mean one-room hut, exactly the kind of place where a worthless woman should live. One break-seat chair for sit in; a old ticking mattress for when sleep catch she; two rusty hurricane lamp with rancid oil inside them, one for light the inside of the hut, and one for light outside when night come, to keep away the ground puppy and mako jumbie-them; a dirty coal-pot, and a bucket full of stale water with dead spider and thing floating on top. Just good for she. With all the nice things she steal from people, she ain't keep none for sheself, but only giving them away all the time.

Dry Bone voice fill up the inside of she head again: "Put me on the mattress. It look softer than the chair. Is there I go stay from now on."

"Yes, Dry Bone." She find she could put he down, but the weight ain't lift from off she. Is like she still carrying he, a heaviness next to she heart, and getting heavier.

"I hungry, Tan-Tan. Cook up that food for me. All of it, you hear?"

"Yes, Dry Bone." And Tan-Tan pluck the fowl, and chop off the head, and gut out the insides. She make a fire outside the hut. She roast the fowl and she boil water for topi-tambo root, and she bake a breadfruit.

"I want johnnycake too."

So Tan-Tan find she one bowl and she fry pan, and she little store of flour and oil, and she carry water and make dumpling and put it to fry on the fire. And all she working, she could hear Dry Bone whispering in she head like knowledge: "Me know say what you is, Tan-Tan. Me know how you worthless and your heart hard. Me know you could kill just for so, and you don't look out for nobody but yourself. You make a mistake when you pick me up. You pick up trouble."

When she done cook the meal, she ain't self have enough plate to serve it all one time. She had was to bring a plate of food in to Dry Bone, make he eat it, and take it outside and fill it up again. Dry Bone swallow every last johnnycake whole. He chew up the topi-tambo, skin and all, and nyam it down. He ain't even wait for she to peel the roast breadfruit, he pop it into he maw just so. He tear the meat from the chicken bone, then he crunch up the bone-them and all. And all he eat, he belly getting round and hard, but he arms and legs only getting thinner and thinner. Still, Tan-Tan could feel the weight of he resting on she chest till she could scarcely breathe.

"That not enough," Dry Bone say. "Is where the fowl guts-them there?"

"I wrap them up in leaf and bury them in the back," Tan-Tan mumble.

"Dig them up and bring them for me."

"You want me to cook them in the fire?"

"No, stupid one, hard-ears one," Dry Bone say in he sandpaper voice. "I ain't tell you to cook them. I go eat them raw just so."

She own-way, yes, and stupid too. Is must be so. Tan-Tan hang she head. She dig up the fowl entrails and bring them back. Dry

Bone suck down the rank meat, toothless gums smacking in the dark hut. He pop the bitter gall bladder in he mouth like a sea grape and swallow that too. "Well," he say, "that go do me for now, but a next hour or two, and you going to feed me again. It ain't look like you have plenty here to eat, eh, Tan-Tan? You best go and find more before evening come."

That is all she good for. Tan-Tan know she must be grateful Dry Bone even let she live. She turn she weary feet back on the path to Duppy Dead Town. She feel the weight on she dragging she down to the ground. Branch scratch up she face, and mosquito bite she, and when she reach where she always did used to find Duppy Dead Town, it ain't have nothing there. The people pick up lock, stock and barrel and left she in she shame with Dry Bone. Tears start to track down Tan-Tan face. She weary, she weary can't done, but she had was to feed the little duppy man. *Lazy*, the voice in she head say. *What a way this woman could run from a little hard work!* Tan-Tan drag down some net vine from out a tree and weave sheself a basket. She search the bush. She find two-three mushroom under some rockstone, and a halwa tree with a half-ripe fruit on it. She throw she knife and stick a fat guinea lizard. Dry Bone go eat the bones and all. Maybe that would full he belly.

And is so the days go for she. So Dry Bone eat, so he hungry again one time. Tan-Tan had was to catch and kill and gut and cook, and she only get time to sneak a little bite for sheself was when Dry Bone sleeping, but it seem like he barely sleep at all. He stretch out the whole day and night on Tan-Tan one bed, giving orders. Tan-Tan had to try and doze the long nights through in the break-seat chair or on the cold floor, and come 'fore-day morning, she had was to find sheself awake one time, to stoke up the fire and start cooking all over again. And what a way Dry Bone belly get big! Big like a watermelon. But the rest of he like he wasting away, just a skin-and-bone man. Sometimes, Tan-Tan couldn't even self see he in the dark hut; only a belly sticking up on the bed.

One time, after he did guzzle down three lizard, two breadfruit, a gully hen and four gully hen eggs, Dry Bone sigh and settle back down on the bed. He close he eyes.

Tan-Tan walk over to the bed. Dry Bone ain't move. She wave she hand in front of he face. He ain't open he eyes. Maybe he did fall to sleep? Maybe she could run away now? Tan-Tan turn to creep out the door, and four bony fingers grab she round she arm and start to squeeze. "You can't run away, Tan-Tan. I go follow you. You have to deal with me."

Is must be true. Dry Bone was she sins come to haunt she, to ride she into she grave. Tan-Tan ain't try to get away no more, but late at night, she weep bitter, bitter tears.

One day, she had was to go down to the river to dip some fresh water to make soup for Dry Bone. As she lean out over the river with she dipping bowl, she see a reflection in the water: Master Johncrow the corbeau-bird, the turkey buzzard, perch on a tree branch, looking for carrion for he supper. He bald head gleaming in the sun like a hard-boil egg. He must be feeling hot in he black frock coat, for he eyes look sad, and he beak drooping like candle wax. Tan-Tan remember she manners. "Good day to you, Sir Buzzard," she say. "How do?"

"Not so good, eh?" Master Johncrow reply. "I think I going hungry today. All I look, I can't spy nothing dead or even ready to dead. You feeling all right, Tan-Tan?" he ask hopefully.

"Yes, Master Buzzard, thanks Nanny."

"But you don't look too good, you know. Your eyes sink back in your head, and your skin all grey, and you walking with a stoop. I could smell death round here yes, and it making me hungry."

"Is only tired I tired, sir. Dry Bone latch on to me, and I can't get any rest, only feeding he day and night."

"Dry Bone?" The turkey buzzard sit up straight on he perch. Tan-Tan could see a black tongue snaking in and out of he mouth with excitement.

"Seen, Master Buzzard. I is a evil woman, and I must pay for my corruption by looking after Dry Bone. It go drive me to me grave, I know, then you go have your meal."

"I ain't know about you and any corruption, doux-doux." Johncrow leap off the tree branch and flap down to the ground beside Tan-Tan. "You smell fresh like the living to me." Him nearly big as she, he frock-coat feathers rank and raggedy, and she could smell the carrion on he. Tan-Tan step back a little.

"You don't know the wicked things I do," she say.

"If a man attack you, child, don't you must defend yourself? I know this, though: I ain't smell no rottenness on you, and that is my favourite smell. If you dead soon, I go thank you for your thoughtfulness with each taste of your entrails, but I go thank you even more if you stay alive long enough to deliver Dry Bone to me."

"How you mean, Master Crow?"

"Dry Bone did dead and rotten long before Nanny was a girl, but him living still. Him is the sweetest meat for a man like me. I could feed off Dry Bone for the rest of my natural days, and him still wouldn't done. Is years now I trying to catch he for me larder. Why you think he so 'fraid the open sky? Open sky is home to *me*. Do me this one favour, nuh?"

Tan-Tan feel hope start to bud in she heart.

"What you want me to do, Master Crow?"

"Just get he to come outside in your yard, and I go do the rest."

So the two of them make a plan. And before he fly off Master Johncrow say to she, "Like Dry Bone not the only monkey that a-ride your back, child. You carrying round a bigger burden than he. And me nah want that one there. It ain't smell dead, but like it did never live. Best you go find Papa Bois."

"And who is Papa Bois, sir?"

"The old man of the bush, the one who does look after all the beast-them. He could look into your eyes, and see your soul, and tell you how to cleanse it."

Tan-Tan ain't like the sound of someone examining she soul, so she only say politely, "Thank you, Master Johncrow. Maybe I go do that."

"All right then, child. Till later." And Master Buzzard fly off to wait until he part of the plan commence.

Tan-Tan scoop up the water for the soup to carry back to she hut, feeling almost happy for the first time in weeks. On the way home, she fill up she carry sack with a big, nice halwa fruit, three handful of mushroom, some coco yam that she dig up, big so like she head, and all the ripe hog plum she could find on the ground. She go make Dry Bone eat till he foolish, oui?

When she reach back at the hut, she set about she cooking with a will. She boil up the soup thick and nice with mushroom and coco yam and cornmeal dumpling. She roast the halwa fruit in the coal pot, and she sprinkle nutmeg and brown sugar on top of it too besides, till the whole hut smell sweet with it scent. She wash the hog plum clean and put them in she best bowl. And all the time she work, she humming to sheself:

> *Corbeau say so, it must be so,*
> *Corbeau say so, it must be so.*

Dry Bone sprawl off on she bed and just a-watch she with him tiny jumbie-bead eye, red with a black centre. "How you happy so?"

Tan-Tan catch sheself. She mustn't make Dry Bone hear Master Johncrow name. She make she mouth droop and she eyes sad, and she say, "Me not really happy, Dry Bone. Me only find when me sing, the work go a little faster."

Dry Bone still suspicious, though. "Then is what that you singing? Sing it louder so I could hear."

"Is a song about making soup." Tan-Tan sing for he:

> *Coco boil so, is so it go,*
> *Coco boil so, is so it go.*

"Cho! Stupid woman. Just cook the food fast, you hear?"

"Yes, Dry Bone." She leave off singing. Fear form a lump of ice in she chest. Suppose Dry Bone find she out?

Tan-Tan finish preparing the meal as fast as she could. She take it to Dry Bone right there on the bed.

By now, Dry Bone skin did draw thin like paper on he face. He eyes did disappear so far back into he head that Tan-Tan could scarce see them. She ain't know what holding he arms and legs-them together, for it look as though all the flesh on them waste away. Only he belly still bulging big with all the food she been cooking for he. If Tan-Tan had buck up a thing like Dry Bone in the bush, she would have take it for a corpse, dead and rotting in the sun. Dry Bone, the skin-and-bone man. To pick he up was to pick up trouble, for true.

Dry Bone bare he teeth at Tan-Tan in a skull grin. "Like you cook plenty this time, almost enough for a snack. Give me the soup first." He take the whole pot in he two hand, put it to he head, and drink it down hot-hot just so. He never even self stop to chew the coco yam and dumpling; he just swallow. When he put down the pot and belch, Tan-Tan see steam coming out of he mouth, the soup did so hot. He scoop out all the insides of the halwa fruit with he bare hand, and he chew up the hard seed-them like them was fig. Then he eat the thick rind. And so he belly getting bigger. He suck down the hog plum one by one, then he just let go Tan-Tan best bowl. She had was to catch it before it hit the ground and shatter.

Dry Bone lie back and sigh. "That was good. It cut me hunger little bit. In two-three hour, I go want more again."

Time was, them words would have hit Tan-Tan like blow, but this time, she know what she have to do. "Dry Bone," she say in a sweet voice, "you ain't want to go out onto the verandah for a little sun while I cook your next meal?"

Dry Bone open he eyes up big-big. Tan-Tan could see she death in them cold eyes. "Woman, you crazy? Go outside? Like you want breeze blow me away, or what? I comfortable right here." He close he eyes and settle back down in the bed.

She try a next thing. "I want to clean the house, Master. I need to make up the bed, put on clean sheets for you. Make me just cotch you on the verandah for two little minutes while I do that, nuh?"

"Don't get me vex." Tan-Tan feel he choking weight on she spirit squeeze harder. Only two-three sips of air making it past she throat.

The plan ain't go work. Tan-Tan start to despair. Then she remember how she used to love to play masque Robber Queen when she was a girl-pickney, how she could roll pretty words around in she mouth like marble, and make up any kind of story. She had a talent for the Robber Queen patter. Nursie used to say she could make yellow think it was red. "But Dry Bone," she wheeze, "look at how nice and strong I build my verandah, fit to sit a king. Look at how it shade off from the sun." She gasp for a breath, just a little breath of air. "No glare to beware, no open sky to trouble you, only sweet breeze to dance over your face, to soothe you as you lie and daydream. Ain't you would like me to carry you out there to lounge off in the wicker chair, and warm your bones little bit, just sit and contemplate your estate? It nice and warm outside today. You could hear the gully hens-them singing *co-corico*, and the guinea lizards-them just a-relax in the sun hot and drowse. It nice out there for true, like a day in heaven. Nothing to cause you danger. Nothing to cause you harm. I could carry you out there in my own two arm, and put you nice and comfortable in the wicker chair, with two pillow at your back for you to rest back on, a king on he own throne. Ain't you would like that?"

Dry Bone smile. The tightness in she chest ease up little bit. "All right, Tan-Tan. You getting to know how to treat me good. Take me outside. But you have to watch out after me. No make no open sky catch me. Remember, when you pick me up, you pick up trouble! If you ain't protect me, you go be sorry."

"Yes, Dry Bone." She pick he up. He heavy like a heart attack from all the food he done eat already. She carry he out onto the verandah and put he in the wicker chair with two pillow at he back.

Dry Bone lean he dead-looking self back in the chair with a peaceful smile on he face. "Yes, I like this. Maybe I go get you to bring me my food out here from now on."

Tan-Tan give he some cool sorrel drink in a cup to tide he over till she finish cook, then she go back inside the hut to make the next meal. And as she cooking, she singing soft-soft,

> *Corbeau say so, it must be so,*
> *Corbeau say so, it must be so.*

And she only watching at the sky through the one little window in the hut. Suppose Master Johncrow ain't come?

"Woman, the food ready yet?" Dry Bone call out.

"Nearly ready, Dry Bone." Is a black shadow that she see in the sky? It moving? It flying their way? No. Just a leaf blowing in the wind. "The chicken done stew!" she called out to the verandah. "I making the dumpling now!" And she hum she tune, willing Master Johncrow to hear.

A-what that? Him come? No, only one baby raincloud scudding by. "Dumpling done! I frying the banana!"

"What a way you taking long today," grumbled Dry Bone.

Yes! Coasting in quiet-quiet on wings the span of a big man,

Master Johncrow the corbeau-bird float through the sky. From her window Tan-Tan see him land on the banister rail right beside Dry Bone, so soft that the duppy man ain't even self hear he. She heart start dancing in she chest, light and airy like a masque band flag. Tan-Tan tiptoe out to the front door to watch the drama.

Dry Bone still have he eyes closed. Master Johncrow stretch he long, picky-picky wattle neck and look right into Dry Bone face, tender as a lover. He black tongue snake out to lick one side of he pointy beak, to clean out the corner of one eye. "Ah, Dry Bone," he say, and he voice was the wind in dry season, "so long I been waiting for this day."

Dry Bone open up he eye. Him two eyes make four with Master Johncrow own. He scream and try to scramble out the chair, but he belly get too heavy for he skin-and-bone limbs. "Don't touch me!" he shout. "When you pick me up, you pick up trouble! Tan-Tan, come and chase this buzzard away!" But Tan-Tan ain't move.

Striking like a serpent, Master Johncrow trap one of Dry Bone arm in he beak. Tan-Tan hear the arm snap like twig, and Dry Bone scream again. "You can't pick me up! You picking up trouble!" But Master Johncrow haul Dry Bone out into the yard by he break arm, then he fasten onto the nape of Dry Bone neck with he claws. He leap into the air, dragging Dry Bone up with him. The skin-and-bone man fall into the sky in truth.

As Master Johncrow flap away over the trees with he prize, Tan-Tan hear he chuckle. "Ah, Dry Bone, you dead thing, you! Trouble sweet to me like the yolk that did sustain me. Is trouble you swallow to make that belly so fat? Ripe like a watermelon. I want you to try to give me plenty, plenty trouble. I want you to make it last a long time."

Tan-Tan sit down in the wicker chair on the verandah and watch them flying away till she couldn't hear Dry Bone screaming no more and Master Johncrow was only a black speck in the sky. She whisper to sheself:

> *Corbeau say so, it must be so,*
> *Please, Johncrow, take Dry Bone and go,*
> *Tan-Tan say so,*
> *Tan-Tan beg so.*

Tan-Tan went inside and look at she little home. It wouldn't be plenty trouble to make another window to let in more light. Nothing would be trouble after living with the trouble of Dry Bone. She go make the window tomorrow, and the day after that, she go re-cane the break-seat chair.

Tan-Tan pick up she kerosene lamp and went outside to look in the bush for some scraper grass to polish the rust off it. That would give she something to do while she think about what Master John-crow had tell she. Maybe she would even go find this Papa Bois, oui?

Wire bend,
Story end.

THE FOUR GENERATIONS OF CHANG E

Zen Cho

The First Generation

In the final days of Earth as we knew it, Chang E won the moon lottery.

For Earthlings who were neither rich nor well-connected, the lottery was the only way to get on the Lunar Habitation Programme. (This was the Earthlings' name for it. The moon people said: "those fucking immigrants".)

Chang E sold everything she had: the car, the family heirloom enamel hairpin collection, her external brain. Humans were so much less intelligent than Moonites anyway. The extra brain would have made little difference.

She was entitled to the hairpins. Her grandmother had pressed them into Chang E's hands herself, her soft old hands folding over Chang E's.

"In the future it will be dangerous to be a woman," her grandmother had said. "Maybe even more dangerous than when my grandmother was a girl. You look after yourself, OK?"

It was not as if anyone else would. There was a row over the hairpins. Her parents had been saving them to pay for Elder Brother's education.

Hah! Education! Who had time for education in days like these? In these times you mated young before you died young; you plucked your roses before you came down with some hideous mutation or discovered one in your child, or else you did something crazy – like go to the moon. Like survive.

Chang E could see the signs. Her parents' eyes had started following her around hungrily, for all the world as if they were

Bugs Bunny and she was a giant carrot. One night Chang E would wake up to find herself trussed up on the altar they had erected to Elder Brother.

Since the change Elder Brother had spent most of his time in his room, slumbering Kraken-like in the gloomful depths of his bed. But by the pricking of their thumbs, by the lengthening of his teeth, Mother and Father trusted that he was their way out of the last war, their guard against assault and cannibalism.

Offerings of oranges, watermelons and pink steamed rice cakes piled up around his bed. One day Chang E would join them. Everyone knew the new gods liked best the taste of the flesh of women.

So Chang E sold her last keepsake of her grandmother and pulled on her moon boots without regret.

On the moon Chang E floated free, untrammelled by the Earth's ponderous gravity, untroubled by that sticky thing called family. In the curious glances of the moon people, in their condescension ("your Lunarish is very good!") she was reinvented.

Away from home, you could be anything. Nobody knew who you'd been. Nobody cared.

She lived in one of the human ghettos, learnt to walk without needing the boots to tether her to the ground, married a human who chopped wood unceasingly to displace his intolerable homesickness.

One night she woke up and saw the light lying at the foot of her bed like snow on the grass. Lifting her head, she saw the weeping blue eye of home. The thought, exultant, thrilled through her: *I'm free! I'm free!*

The Second Generation

Her mother had had a pet moon rabbit. This was before we found out they were sentient. She'd always treated it well, said Chang E. That was the irony: how well we had treated the rabbits! How little some of them deserved it!

Though if any rabbit had ever deserved good treatment, it was her mother's pet rabbit. When Chang E was little, it had made herbal tea for her when she was ill, and sung her nursery rhymes in its native moon rabbit tongue – little songs, simple and savage, but rather sweet. Of course Chang E wouldn't have been able to sing them to you now. She'd forgotten.

But she was grateful to that rabbit. It had been like a second mother to her, said Chang E.

What Chang E didn't like was the rabbits claiming to be intelligent. It's one thing to cradle babies to your breast and sing them songs, stroking your silken paw across their foreheads. It's another to want the vote, demand entrance to schools, move in to the best part of town and start building warrens.

When Chang E went to university there was a rabbit living in her student hall. Imagine that. A rabbit sharing their kitchen, using their plates, filling the pantry with its food.

Chang E kept her chopsticks and bowls in her bedroom, bringing them back from the kitchen every time she finished a meal. She was polite, in memory of her nanny, but it wasn't pleasant. The entire hall smelled of rabbit food. You worried other people would smell it on you.

Chang E was tired of smelling funny. She was tired of being ugly. She was tired of not fitting in. She'd learnt Lunarish from her immigrant mother, who'd made it sound like a song in a foreign language.

Her first day at school Chang E had sat on the floor, one of three humans among twenty children learning to add and subtract. When her teacher had asked what one and two made, her hand shot up.

"Tree!" she said.

Her teacher had smiled. She'd called up a tree on the holographic display.

"This is a tree." She called up the image of the number three. "Now, this is three."

She made the high-pitched clicking sound in the throat which is so difficult for humans to reproduce.

"Which is it, Changey?"

"Tree," Chang E had said stupidly. "Tree. Tree." Like a broken down robot.

In a month her Lunarish was perfect, accentless, and she rolled her eyes at her mother's singsong, "Chang E, you got listen or not?"

Chang E would have liked to be motherless, pastless, selfless.

Why was her skin so yellow, her eyes so small, when she felt so green inside?

After she turned sixteen, Chang E begged the money off her dad, who was conveniently indulgent since the divorce, and went in secret for the surgery.

When she saw herself in the mirror for the first time after the operation she gasped.

Long ovoid eyes, the last word in Lunar beauty, all iris, no ugly inconvenient whites or dark browns to spoil that perfect reflective surface. The eyes took up half her face. They were like black eggs, like jewels.

Her mother screamed when she saw Chang E. Then she cried.

It was strange. Chang E had wanted this surgery with every fibre of her being – her nose hairs swooning with longing, her liver contracting with want.

Yet she would have cried too, seeing her mother so upset, if her new eyes had let her. But Moonite eyes didn't have tear ducts. No eyelids to cradle tears, no eyelashes to sweep them away. She stared unblinking and felt sorry for her mother, who was still alive, but locked in an inaccessible past.

The Third Generation

Chang E met H'yi in the lab, on her first day at work. He was the only rabbit there and he had the wary, closed-off look so many rabbits had.

At Chang E's school the rabbit students had kept themselves to themselves. They had their own associations – the Rabbit Moonball Club, the Lapin Lacemaking Society – and sat in quiet groups at their own tables in the cafeteria.

Chang E had sat with her Moonite friends.

"There's only so much you can do," they'd said. "If they're not making any effort to integrate . . . "

But Chang E had wondered secretly if the rabbits had the right idea. When she met other Earthlings, each one alone in a group of Moonites, they'd exchange brief embarrassed glances before subsiding back into invisibility. The basic wrongness of being an Earthling was intensified in the presence of other Earthlings. When you were with normal people you could almost forget.

Around humans Chang E could feel her face become used to smiling and frowning, every emotion transmitted to her face with that flexibility of expression that was so distasteful to Moonites. As a child this had pained her, and she'd avoided it as much as possible – better the smoothness of surface that came to her when she was hidden among Moonites.

At twenty-four, Chang E was coming to understand that this was no way to live. But it was a difficult business, this easing into being. She and H'yi did not speak to each other at first, though they were the only non-Moonites in the lab.

The first time she brought human food to work, filling the place with strange warm smells, she kept her head down over her lunch, shrinking from the Moonites' glances. H'yi looked over at her.

"Smells good," he said. "I love noodles."

"Have you had this before?" said Chang E. H'yi's ears twitched. His face didn't change, but somehow Chang E knew he was laughing.

"I haven't spent my entire life in a warren," he said. "We do get out once in a while."

The first time Chang E slept over at his, she felt like she was coming home. The close dark warren was just big enough for her. It smelt of moon dust.

In H'yi's arms, her face buried in his fur, she felt as if the planet itself had caught her up in its embrace. She felt the wall vibrate: next door H'yi's mother was humming to her new litter. It was the moon's own lullaby.

Chang E's mother stopped speaking to her when she got married. It was rebellion, Ma said, but did she have to take it so far?

"I should have known when you changed your name," Ma wept. "After all the effort I went to, giving you a Moonite name. Having the throat operation so I could pronounce it. Sending you to all the best schools and making sure we lived in the right neighbourhoods. When will you grow up?"

Growing up meant wanting to be Moonite. Ma had always been disappointed by how bad Chang E was at this.

They only reconciled after Chang E had the baby. Her mother came to visit, sitting stiffly on the sofa. H'yi made himself invisible in the kitchen.

The carpet on the floor between Chang E and her mother may as well have been a mare. But the baby stirred and yawned in Chang E's arms – and stolen glance by jealous, stolen glance, her mother fell in love.

One day Chang E came home from the lab and heard her mother singing to the baby. She stopped outside the nursery and listened, her heart still.

Her mother was singing a rabbit song.

Creaky and true, the voice of an old peasant rabbit unwound from her mouth. The accent was flawless. Her face was innocent, wiped clean of murky passions, as if she'd gone back in time to a self that had not yet discovered its capacity for cruelty.

The Fourth Generation

When Chang E was sixteen, her mother died. The next year Chang E left school and went to Earth, taking her mother's ashes with her in a brown ceramic urn.

The place her mother had chosen was on an island just above the equator, where, Ma had said, their Earthling ancestors had been buried. When Chang E came out of the environment-controlled port building, the air wrapped around her, sticky and close. It was like stepping into a god's mouth and being enclosed by his warm humid breath.

Even on Earth most people travelled by hovercraft, but on this remote outpost wheeled vehicles were still in use. The journey was bumpy – the wheels rendered them victim to every stray imperfection in the road. Chang E hugged the urn to her and stared out the window, trying to ignore her nausea.

It was strange to see so many humans around, and only humans. In the capital city you'd see plenty of Moonites, expats and tourists, but not in a small town like this.

Here, thought Chang E, was what her mother had dreamt of. Earthlings would not be like moon humans, always looking anxiously over their shoulder for the next way in which they would be found wanting.

And yet her mother had not chosen to come here in life. Only in death. Where would Chang E find the answer to that riddle?

Not in the graveyard. This was on an orange hill, studded with white and grey tombstones, the vermillion earth furred in places with scrubby grass.

The sun bore close to the Earth here. The sunshine was almost a tangible thing, the heat a repeated hammer's blow against the temple. The only shade was from the trees, starred with yellow-hearted white flowers. They smelled sweet when Chang E picked them up. She put one in her pocket.

The illness had been sudden, but they'd expected the death. Chang E's mother had arranged everything in advance, so that once Chang E arrived she did not have to do or understand anything. The nuns took over.

Following them, listening with only half her attention on their droning chant in a language she did not know to a god she did not recognize, she looked down on the town below. The air was thick with light over the stubby low buildings, crowded close together the way human habitations tended to be.

How godlike the Moonites must have felt when they entered these skies and saw such towns from above. To love a new world, you had to get close to the ground and listen.

You were not allowed to watch them lower the urn into the ground and cover it with soil. Chang E looked up obediently.

In the blue sky there was a dragon.

She blinked. It was a flock of birds, forming a long line against the sky. A cluster of birds at one end made it look like the dragon had turned its head. The sunlight glinting off their white bodies made it seem that the dragon looked straight at her with luminous eyes.

She stood and watched the sky, her hand shading her eyes, long after the dragon had left, until the urn was buried and her mother was back in the earth.

What was the point of this funeral so far from home, a sky's worth of stars lying between Chang E's mother and everyone she had ever known? Had her mother wanted Chang E to stay? Had she hoped Chang E would fall in love with the home of her ancestors, find a human to marry, and by so doing somehow return them all to a place where they were known?

Chang E put her hand in her pocket and found the flower. The petals were waxen, the texture oddly plastic between her finger-tips. They had none of the fragility she'd been taught to associate with flowers.

Here is a secret Chang E knew, though her mother didn't.

Past a certain point, you stop being able to go home. At this point, when you have got this far from where you were from, the thread snaps. The narrative breaks. And you are forced, pastless, motherless, selfless, to invent yourself anew.

At a certain point, this stops being sad – but who knows if any human has ever reached that point?

Chang E wiped her eyes and her streaming forehead, followed the nuns back to the temple and knelt to pray to her nameless forebears.

She was at the exit when remembered the flower. The Lunar Border Agency got funny if you tried to bring Earth vegetation in. She left the flower on the steps to the temple.

Then Chang E flew back to the moon.

STAY THY FLIGHT

Élisabeth Vonarburg

By day, I go fast, nowhere but fast, not moving, impossible, too focused, unfurled wings, tilted head, eyes on the sun, when there is some. Now for instance, no clouds, nothing but light, rain of light, torrents, maelstroms, hurricanes of light. And me inside it, through my every pore, my skin you'd say, yes, beneath the hair. Naked skin: only on the face, the torso. Get some light too, but less efficient. The hair mostly, soaking up light, and my wings' feathers, a million antennas, if you will, conduits, minuscule, avid mouths, tongues, hands, a million fingers, stretching toward the sun, all that energy, everywhere: I'm charging. Inside, metamorphosed light: food, strength, lightning strikes, from cell to cell, vortexes, in my whole body, a continuous vibration, electric sponge, I absorb life. Fast inside, my body is fast. Accelerated metabolism inside, chemical exchanges, neurons, everything, faster. I am charging, I burn, my own matter, my life, at lightning speed, behind each thought, a condensed frenzy, white hot, ablaze, crackling. Outside unmoving, almost: you don't, see me move, doesn't feel like, I'm moving either, but I'm revolving, with the magnet-sun, like the flowers, but no flower, I: lioness, winged woman. Statue, you say, not quite, but what else, convenient word: on a pedestal, after all, immobile, almost, by day.

You are immobile, for me, by day, almost, less than I for you, but slow. Everything around me, becomes slow, after dawn: the sun rises, heaves itself up, slows down, crawls, an imperceptible movement, in the sky, the birds' songs too, in the Park, draw out, lowering down, deeper and deeper, to a basso continuo, some modulations, but spaced out, wind, when there is some, leaves, music, solemn, meditating, I like. Behind me, lower still, the sound of the city. Sometimes a blending, images, sounds, leaves moving, shadows, like a music almost, clouds, when there are some, flowers, opening with the day. Sometimes I try, to seize the moment, when it changes, flowers, shadows, clouds: hard, impossible almost. Then I look elsewhere, or close my eyes, and come back later: more open, the petals, closer to the pistils, the bee, but everything caught, in invisible amber, time, all slowed down. With telescopic vision, perhaps, I could, with a millionfold, magnification, see the sap moving up, the flesh of the flower, stiffening, or in the clouds, patient, the accretion of molecules. But it's human vision I have, that's all, not superhuman. "Look": not quite, either, hard to will it, by day. Simply: eyes open, I see, my eyes see, like everything else, the other senses, smell, taste, hearing, touch, everything, at a normal speed, but my brain, no, too focused on energy, on charging: registers, transmits, a drop every decade. If I want to look, to change the direction, in which I look, great effort, lasts for centuries.

A little mist, on the sun; the color of the sky changes; and my speed changes; less light: I slow down, a little; leaves, shadows, clouds, insects: a little bit faster; I could almost see the bee's wings moving. A slow day, perhaps? Slow days, for me, the days of soft sun, of mist or clouds, passing: I charge up more slowly, I live, and die, more slowly.

The first passers-by, at the back of the alley, in a few centuries, will walk in front of me, will stop. Tourists, it's summer, always nice, in here anyhow: the South, warm, just enough wind, in summer, to break up the mist. Sometimes very humid, all that hovering water, invisible, ghost of the melted ice, far away at the poles. Sometimes it rains, I drink, head tilted up, don't need to, but it's nice. Glinting gravel, after the rain, puddles in alleys, kids splashing about, the birds, bathing, in slow motion, droplets, wavelets, glimmerings, soon dry, those waters, tides of the sky. Elsewhere, more rains, I know, but here, sometimes, you can forget, the other tides, everywhere, eating at the earth. Not me: I stand in the main alley, at the highest point of the Park, facing the Seaside Promenade, I see them, from up here, the tides.

I see them, I look at them, from time to time. My inward clock always knows. This decade: one minute outside, in the slow world, this year one second, I know, exactly. When I am facing in the right direction, I look at the sea, every five minutes, I must parcel out time in order to see: the ocean, swelling up, an unending breath, rising, past the ancient marks, on the pier, the blue, the red lines. The black line, would never get past it, they thought: on a rebuilt cliff, fifty meters high, the city. And there it is: vanished, the black line. Heaving, overflowing the sculpted stone parapets, through their interlacing design, the sea, draped on the Promenade, a shimmering of heat, around the trees, mercury under the sun. It rolls, trembling, under the feet of the passers-by, behind the wheels of the horse-drawn buggies, suspended droplets clinging to the raised hooves, the sea inside the city, slow, irresistible.

More passers-by, not only tourists: the regulars, at this hour. You like to go to the Park, on the heights, far from the sea, turning your back on it, walking up to me. You spread slowly between the statues, you fold up, sitting down in the grass, on the benches, endlessly, almost statues yourselves, if I don't perceive you for too long: *The Bird Lover, The Dog Lady*; several dogs, not necessarily hers, *The Dog Walker? The Lovers*: just *The Girl Student, The Philosopher*, alone, then the encounter, the month-long first sentence, the week-long first smile, then seeing them leave, together, throughout a century, and come back, another century, their hands, seeking each other, sea anemones, in a magnetic current. A few hours, another title: *The Kiss*. Are going to change again: their bodies move differently, the space they inhabit together, not the same anymore, their eyes, elsewhere. *The Break-Up*, perhaps?

The mist is gone, the sun revolves, unmoving, in the sky. Tropism, I move too, don't see the Promenade any longer, but The Sleeper's bench, real statue, that is, blue dress, crossed legs, her cheek against her hand. Today, next to her, a youngster, a true human, skin the color of light tobacco, eyes closed, no shirt. Soaking up some sun, but what difference? Doesn't move either for me, or so little, a breath every hour.

I see elsewhere, clouds, shadows, leaves, other passers-by ambling on, imperceptibly, for several eternities. Or I close my eyes, to see the crackling energy, behind my lids, flashing through, life in my cells, death.

Eyes open again, bench vanished: the Hummingbirds' Dome now, the great central lawn; less ardent light; longer shadows; the color of the sky changes faster; the hummingbirds' wings vibrate; behind the transparent dome, I am beginning to see them move, from flower to flower; in the trees, the free birds' symphony wells up again to higher notes; where soon the song of this or that bird stands out, that I recognize; you go on walking, gracefully swimming along the alleys, buoyant; the sun's orb sinks behind the leaves fluttering in the breeze as in a river. This endless day is coming to an end. Inside me the energy pulse slows down, gets lighter, fades away. There is a very brief moment when everything stops, when I feel as if suspended, time for the symbols to reverse, for the fluxes to reorganize, for other instructions to move me.

Sunset is coming, a time for questions. Your questions.

But first let me enjoy my newfound body. Let me yawn hugely and turn my head, this way, that way, to uncrick my neck. Fold my wings, unfold them again, stand up and stretch – front claws gripping the edge of the pedestal, back arched, hindquarters up in the air, braced on my back legs, tail lashing. And then adopt the posture in which I will answer you. Sitting back, wings folded, tail coiled around the haunches, the human head very straight between the animal shoulders, the chest very obvious with its two little round breasts just above the place where the pelt begins. This posture is disturbing to some of you, it took me a long time to understand one of the reasons why: too much woman. They prefer me in a recumbent posture, head on the front legs, either lying at length on my belly or curled upon myself. And eyes shut. But this is not appropriate, I can feel it, and in the end I always answer you sitting straight. Thus my face is at the same height as yours when you stand. Perhaps this is what disturbs you, who walk by averting your eyes or feigning not to see me.

You don't ask many questions, nowadays. You never did ask many questions. Mainly at first, when I was a novelty. Or at least something to be outraged about, since talking statues had been made before, in the very beginning, fifty years earlier. But to make one just when bio-sculpture was on the verge of being outlawed, only Angkaar could pull that off and stay unpunished. He was famous, a subject for controversy for so long that it was now a routine. And he was old, dying, everybody knew. He had friends in high places: they let him make his last statue, and then they passed the law.

His face is in my first memory, and in the one after that, and in all the others until he put me to sleep and I woke up on that pedestal in the Park, in front of a wondering, shocked crowd. He let no one interfere with his ultimate creation: advances in the technology allowed it. But when I opened my eyes for the very first time, there was only his face, an ivory parchment, finely engraved with lines, stretched taut on a delicate bony architecture, the wide rounded forehead, the mouth, sinuous and weary, and eyes like carbuncles, their fire too dark in a face too white. His voice, throaty, always a little breathless.

I remember all the learning – you say «programming», you say «conditioning». He wanted to me to remember it, to remember him. He wanted me to know what I was, and how I had come to be. An artefact. A living sculpture. An artificial creature, a harmonious meeting of the organic and the electronic. My body, my brain, their development, their assembling: artificial, but organic. My movements, my reflexes, my memory, the algorithms of my thought: programmed. My thoughts themselves? Yes, some of them. There begins the uncertainty which is Angkaar's gift to me.

There are very narrow physical limits to what I can do on my pedestal, besides the independent movement of each of my limbs: sit up, lie down in two different postures, stand up on all fours, beat my wings, move my head and torso. I cannot «jump down». Those terms have no physical referent for me, neither my joints nor my muscles hold them in memory. Of course, I feel no need to do those things. The few movements available to me are satisfying enough, and even more, they give me an intense pleasure, as do all my sensations.

In the beginning, I thought there were also limits to my thoughts. Then I slowly understood that those were more limits to my emotions. Your questions made me aware of it. And my answers. At first, I never knew what I was going to say. After all, you have to enter my perceptual field for me to answer you; you must be inside the magic circle, about four meters in diameter, materialized on the ground around my pedestal by small black triangular tiles. Beyond that limit, I don't perceive you well enough; your expressions, your body language, yes, but not your electrical and chemical language, the emotions that surround you like an aura only I can perceive: I need that to answer you. Thus, in the beginning, I was waiting for my own words, my oracles, just as you were, believing just as you did that all my brief responses were programmed. But with time I was able to see that they never repeat. That since they evolve they take into account everything I have learned during these nearly ten years of my existence. And I concluded that somehow they must fit themselves to your questions. That in a more obscure fashion they must even answer them. I cannot say whether I am the only one speaking, however. No doubt there is also my creator, a residual echo slowly fading inside me. I have learned to know him better that way, through the gaps: in what I cannot feel although I can think it, in the distance between your curiosity and my enigmas. Between my questions and the answers you are not giving me, too.

But sunset is the time for your questions, not mine. Our respective speeds mesh for such short periods, no wonder Angkaar programmed me to be laconic. It was also in accord with his project, my nature, the title inscribed on my pedestal and that I have never read. I had never seen myself, either. I don't know if that was my creator's intention. He told me what I was, and I have in memory everything there is to know about sphinxes, but he never held out a mirror to me during my learning period, and I find in myself no desire to see my countenance.

When I did see myself, however . . .

The painter arrived in the morning and he revolved as I did, for I saw him each time I opened my eyes or looked back from the limits of the Park, the far stretches of the city or the heights of the sky. I knew him: I had seen him several times with Angkaar. First at my unveiling. (Memories: Angkaar had hidden me under an opaque thermosensitive glaze, the fading light of the sunset dissolved its chemical bounds as I was awakened.)

Then I saw the painter on strolls through the Park with a rapidly weakening Angkaar, the last few times in an electric wheelchair. Angkaar loved to go to the Park during his last weeks, no doubt because it showed several works of his. "There will be others", he had cryptically told the media on the eve of my unveiling. No one had understood then. Neither had I.

He used to come at sunset, of course. He stopped in front of me. He listened to the questions people asked. He never asked any. For a long time I believed it was because he already knew all the answers. I now know it was because he didn't. The painter (was he already a painter then? Perhaps) never asked anything either. He just held Angkaar's hand, or his arm, later the back of the wheelchair. He was the younger man, hardly past his thirties, very dark, very slender, with the anxious expression of one who always expects to be rejected. Angkaar was very pleasant with him, though, or was it merely indifference? They never entered my perceptual circle. Alex. His name was Alex. And one day Alex came back alone. At sunset. He stayed before me, just outside the circle, for a long time, looking hard at me with an expression I didn't understand (later, I learned that it was hatred). Then he said: "He's dead." Since it was not a question, there was no answer. He stayed there until the Park lights came up, then he turned away abruptly and was gone.

I saw him again two years later; he had an easel and a canvas – there was a revival of archaic techniques at that time; the Park was full of would-be landscape painters. He always arrived when the sun was rising in the east, always went when the sun slid down through the trees in the west: he wanted no words between us. He was doing sketches. After four days, he vanished. A week later he came back. He waited for the last painters to pack up and leave, then he took his canvas – a big thing almost a square meter wide – and he came up to me. With faltering steps, almost. Stopped just inside the circle. Placed the canvas so that I could see it. He was afraid. He was hurt.

It was a hyperrealist kind of painting, with every color shifted to shades of red. The winged silhouette was chained to the pedestal, supine, but with the torso rearing up. The left wing was dangling, broken. The right wing was half-unfolded. Blood had dripped from the shoulder to the left breast, was dripping from the parted lips. The head was slightly tilted to one side, as though the embroidered headdress was too heavy, or as though the rage that had caused the creature to tear at her own flesh had exhausted itself. The face was that of an ageless woman, with great, slanted amber eyes, a short, slightly hooked nose, wide, high cheekbones.

After a while, Alex asked: "Who is it?"

I heard myself answer: "Yourself."

He stiffened, then seemed to crumple. Without a word, he

turned away and left with his canvas. I availed myself of the absence of other questioners to ponder the complex feeling that had filled me at the sight of the picture. Despite my answer to Alex's question, I had immediately assumed, through logical processing, that it was my image. Or at least an approximate likeness, since I have no broken wing. It was not really me . . . and it was me nevertheless. Why was I so *sure* of it, beyond all logic? Angkaar had never shown me any pictures corresponding to the purely verbal description present in my memory. A creature with the body of a lion, the wings of an eagle, but a human face and torso, and female. Lion, eagle, woman, I had already seen them, separately. But not their fusion. *Sphinx.* Do words correspond to some vast pool of intangible but eternal images, which I would have accessed? That was a curiously pleasant idea. The other component of my feeling, then, was it also pleasure? Alex's painting was appalling, full of both cruelty and despair. But at the same time . . . beautiful. Did that mean I was beautiful? Or merely that Alex saw me thus, in spite of his pain, or perhaps because of it? Then what I felt was not pleasure, it was curiosity. And yet, indeed, pleasure of a sort: to discover questions I had never asked myself yet. Not who I was, but how you saw me: who I was, what I was, for you.

And this strange idea, also new to me, that perhaps you never saw me at all, really. That I was your mirror.

I believed I knew what you thought of me, though, what you felt in front of me. I heard you; I still do when you talk while passing by me, or stopping, when our times are in synch. That's how I completed the education provided by Angkaar. At first you were admiring, the more secretly pleased for being officially shocked. Then, just after artefacts were outlawed, you took to censoring me in a more or less sincere tone; there were a few protests, even; far less fierce than at the beginning of bio-sculpture about sixty years ago: no one tried to blow me up; not even one graffiti. There were doubts as to the exact nature of my programmation, I gather: Angkaar was known for not being very tolerant of vandals; perhaps he had seen to my defensive capacities. On the other hand, you seem not to have much energy left to waste in symbolic gestures anymore; you apparently exhausted it in building dams and new cities that would protect you against the rising oceans

– but the tides go on nibbling at them as if the sea did not care. No one even tried to shoot me from a distance. Perhaps they thought I was bullet-proof. There were only some protesters with placards: STOP THE SACRILEGE.

You kept on coming to see me, actually, because I was the one and only talking artefact that was semi-mobile, but also because I was the oldest artefact known to be still «functioning» (you never say «living»): five years, an amazing longevity. Then, later, the Sleeper in Blue walked into the Park and turned to stone on her bench, and Angkaar's statement became clear: there *were* others. Among you, artefacts, perfectly humanoid ones that you never even suspected were not human: inorganic matter could go on existing much longer than official scientists had let on. You came to see me in bigger crowds, then – perhaps reassured by my honestly non-human appearance, and my so limited mobility. And you asked me questions, the questions you didn't ask in the beginning because I was too new.

But since the functioning of artefacts had briefly came back into fashion, I expected you to ask them. I had studied enough inner traces of Angkaar in myself, made enough correlations with what I had learned from you without your knowledge. I know that you fear death, that time is still for you an unresolved enigma. "What walks on four legs in the morning, on two at noon and on three in the evening?" someone asked me once, thinking he was clever. I heard myself answer: "An animal victimized by civilization." I chalked that one up to Angkaar's opinion about humanity; he'd chosen to turn the legend on itself, which was telling enough in itself. He'd taught me Oedipus's answer to the Greek Sphinx, of course; perhaps, at that time, humans had more answers.

Someone enters my field of vision. I know her: she walked by a moment ago, in full sunlight. She is not one of the regulars. Neither is she a tourist. I can see her much better now – paradoxically, when I go fast and you are slow, I see you for too long and in too much detail; I can't get a good impression of you. Self-confidence, strength, a supple gait, an athletic build despite the aristocratic, cheetah-like slenderness. Beautiful, you'd say. Perhaps too self-composed? She doesn't enter the circle. She doesn't really stop in front of me, she merely slows down for a few seconds, she looks at me, turning her head toward me as she walks by, thoughtful, then she is gone, without asking me anything. Green eyes, golden skin, short light hair: one more human, one more image, one more mystery. The Park is emptying. My time is over. The shadows are almost touching me. No one asked me a question today.

You asked me once; after much dithering; talking circles around the word «death»; which would have been acknowledging my being alive; asked me whether I knew when I was to end, and why. And in my equally convoluted way; because of my programming then; not of any discomfort; I made you understand; yes, I know I am limited in time; yes, the artorganic matter of my body ages at an accelerated rate; a little faster by day; a little slower by night. "Do you know how you will end?" you asked then; I waited with interest for my answer: did I know? Had Angkaar given me that knowledge? I'd heard you before; talking about his previous biosculptures; he had never been at pain; to give them a spectacular ending. Protracted fireworks? Lightning-fast sublimation? The Sleeper in Blue had not yet come; to stop forever on her bench; at that time; I didn't know; I could have added that: metamorphosis; into a real statue. I heard myself say: "All comes in time to those who are prepared"; you seemed disappointed; I could understand: a mere variant; on a tired old proverb; really, Angkaar! Only later did I understand; its appropriateness; come to think of it; you die so badly; most of you; surprised, furious, or reluctant; no insistence on esthetics.

Angkaar killed himself, too; he didn't wait; for mechanical progress; to rob him of his death.

But my death; he devised it; and I know nothing of it.

At last I understood; the tone of your comments among yourselves; when you talked about it; near me; you wondered; if I hated him; if I was scared. You never dared; ask me; you were too afraid; of my answer. I would say no, however; I don't hate Angkaar; and I am not afraid; to end – to die? – because he programmed me so? – certainly – but I understand – that limitation – as a kindness on his part – are you so happy – to know how you are mortal?

But it is not yet – time – for my questions – no time for yours – either – the sky darkens – our times go out of synch – you walk faster – in the alleys – and I without light – without the sun – I almost – stop – slowed down – metabolism – I am digesting – my feast of the day past – really immobile – now – evening birds – sing higher notes – in the sky – the stars explode – sudden dust – close to the trees – a diffuse light – time for me – to blink – and the moon bursts out – from the clouds – tonight – she sails through – their jagged outlines – blue and silver – lightning – shadows – running on the ground – and you run too – the night-time regulars – different from – those of the day – searching – one another – always a surprise – the pattern – of your nocturnal – paths – suddenly revealed – to me – through speed – I see you – searching – without knowing – one another – the precise – frantic dance – of your signals – coming up – to one another – you talk – very little – what do you say? – I can't hear – but the ritual – always the same – a few words – a gesture – very important – body-language – arms – folded or dangling – hands – in the pockets – or raked through hair – contacts – furtive – eyes averted – then you go – together – in the bushes – or outside the Park – for the night – a night – you burn – your whole life – in one night – you are – so afraid – I know –

No one – now – hour of the cats – in the grasses – quick – slithering – careful – between the trees – birds of prey – lethal flight – silent – and soon – nothing at all – the solitary hour – the solitary minute – the moon – is gone – I think – I still perceive – glacial – thoughts – stretched – over a million – years –

And now – muted pulse – of light – in the sky – other birds – singing together – in the fading – darkness – slower and lower – they sing – for the sun is growing; like a luminous mushroom; the tide of shadows is turning; little by little, the molten glass of my thoughts, becomes fluid again, dawn has come.

Dawn is here, the time for questions: my own. There is no one, usually, to listen to them: the night-time regulars have left the Park, the daytime regulars have not arrived yet. Only the birds, an errant cat or dog, the leaves, whispering. I am alone, usually, to taste this instant when I live at the world's speed – on my pedestal still, but it doesn't matter. I look at the sun rising above the trees. I feel the energy coursing through my veins, my cells and synapses, speeding up; I stretch and I yawn, I stand up and sit down, rituals of my own. And I think of all the questions I would try to ask, if there were anyone to share my dawn.

And today there is someone. A woman. The young woman of yesterday's sunset. Here she is, back in my dawn. She takes one of the chairs lining the lawns, hoists it in one movement upon her shoulder – those are metal chairs, and very heavy – and she comes to me. She is young, I'd say in her twenties. She puts the chair down near my pedestal, she sits, facing east. Legs a-stretch, arms folded. She looks at the sun glimmering through the top of the trees. Very calm. Inhumanly, I'd say. My occasional visitors never are so calm. She knows I am going to talk to her, though. No, she's *waiting* for me to talk to her.

I am not so sure I want to, suddenly – to ask her questions, since at dawn I can, for lack of questions to *answer*, which is for sunset. Only during the slow days can I talk normally, without being a prisoner of my matrices of questions and answers. Angkaar told no one; he wanted me to have a measure of freedom. But usually it makes you too uneasy, and finally I desisted. I am a statue, after all: why would you want to talk to a statue as you would a normal person? There are not enough slow days, anyhow.

Should I really ask her something? She seems so sad, suddenly. But the tropism is too strong, I can't resist it for very long. And at dawn, I can ask anything I want, those are really *my* questions.

"Long night?"

She doesn't even flinch, turns her head a little to look up at me: "Not just for you."

"Why?"

She says nothing. I'd really appreciate it if humans were forced to answer questions as I am: I have so little time to ask mine. She stands up and faces me, leaning on my pedestal. I am lying down, and her face is above mine. She holds out her hand, touches my cheek.

You don't touch me very often. Despite all your boasting, most of you humans are afraid of me, and those who wouldn't be, the children, are too small to be able to touch me, except when standing on a chair – and there is always an adult to see them and keep them away from me. But Angkaar did touch me. And a few other humans, even so. I know what I perceive when I am physically touched: the electro-chemical signature of your emotions, a little clearer than when you are at a distance in the circle.

Not so with her. Emotions, yes, but distant, shifted somehow.

Muted? Was what I thought to be calmness merely this gap, this ... slowness, between stimulus and response?

An artefact, about to end.

And I have no questions for her any more.

After looking at me for a while, eye to eye, she sits down again, offering her face to the rising sun.

With her I look at the jagged leaves, the jagged light. Never did I feel more acutely that my time is limited. So much curiosity, so little time to satisfy it ... All of a sudden, I understand you better for not asking questions. At last I ask: "What about me?"

She looks at me again, with, yes, a slightly distant tenderness, not answering. Or is that her answer, when she says: "I'll be there"?

And the sun rises some more, my heart beats faster, I can feel the vibration, inside, rising, signaling the full light of day. Does she feel it too? She puts a hand on my outstretched paws, a slow movement, getting even slower, which alerts me: dawn is over, too late now for my questions, I will have to wait for tomorrow, if she comes back tomorrow, I don't even know her name, but then I don't have a name either. And while the shadows begin to crawl, on the ground, like the sun, crawls in the sky, while the birds' songs slide, into the sound of the city, lower and deeper, while this unknown, my sister, as if weightless, stands up and walks away, swimming more and more, languidly in the alley, leading down to the sea, and the rising tide, I dream, of all that she and I will not see, the submerged city, the tide that will not ebb, the streets almost deserted, only a few wistful vagrants left, while my inner time pulses and contracts, while the outer time stretches endlessly, I imagine the future, after me, without me, but she will be there, she said, a promise, she knows when, the end for me, for her, I trust.

A real cloud-bank is drifting, from the sea; rising up; stretching on. It will be a slow day, at least a slow morning, and for me the innocent pleasure of sharing time with you.

Perhaps today someone will ask me if I am afraid of ending. Sifted through the programs that prompt my convoluted sentences, my answer will mean "no". Or perhaps I will tell you: "Even less now," and that will satisfy my creator's sarcastic ghost. You might also ask me how I am going to end. I will try to tell you that I don't know, that deep down it is not important after all. Soon. I'll end soon. But she will come. Perhaps in full daylight: amidst my ultimate conflagration I'll see her floating toward me with a long smile, or perhaps at night, and suddenly she'll be there, the lightning warmth and sadness of her smile, her hand on my petrifying flesh. At sunset, and I will answer her? At dawn, and she will answer me?

But perhaps it will be a slow day, as now, when we can talk without constraints. Even that will not be necessary. Simply, without too much haste or slowness, together in time, we will have all of it to know, unspeaking, one moment, an eternity.

ASTROPHILIA

Carrie Vaughn

After five years of drought, the tiny, wool-producing household of Greentree was finished. First the pastures died off, then the sheep, and Stella and the others didn't have any wool to process and couldn't meet the household's quota, small though it was with only five of them working at the end. The holding just couldn't support a household and the regional committee couldn't keep putting credits into it, hoping that rains would come. They might never come, or the next year might be a flood. No one could tell, and that was the problem, wasn't it?

None of them argued when Az and Jude put in to dissolve Greentree. They could starve themselves to death with pride, but that would be a waste of resources. Stella was a good weaver, and ought to have a chance somewhere else. That was the first reason they gave for the decision.

Because they dissolved voluntarily, the committee found places for them in other households, ones not on the verge of collapse. However, Az put in a special request and found Stella's new home herself. "I know the head of the place, Toma. He'll take good care of you, but more than that his place is prosperous. Rich enough for children, even. You could earn a baby there, Stella." Az's wrinkled hands gripped Stella's young ones in her own, and her eyes shone. Twenty-three years ago, Greentree had been prosperous enough to earn a baby: Stella. But those days were gone.

Stella began to have doubts. "Mama, I don't want to leave you and everyone—"

"We'll be fine. We'd have had to leave sooner or later, and this way we've got credits to take with us. Start new on a good footing, yes?"

"Yes, but—" She hesitated, because her fears were childish. "What if they don't like *me*?"

Az shook her head. "Winter market I gave Toma the shawl you made. You should have seen him, Stella, his mouth dropped. He said Barnard Croft would take you on the spot, credits or no."

But what if they don't like *me*, Stella wanted to whine. She wasn't worried about her weaving.

Az must have seen that she was about to cry. "Oh, dear, it'll be all right. We'll see each other at the markets, maybe more if there's trading to be done. You'll be happy, I know you will. Better things will come."

Because Az seemed so pleased for her, Stella stayed quiet, and hoped.

In the spring, Stella traveled to Barnard Croft, 300 miles on the Long Road from Greentree, in the hills near the coast.

Rain poured on the last day of the journey, so the waystation driver used a pair of horses to draw the wagon, instead of the truck. Stella offered to wait until the storm passed and the solar batteries charged up, but he had a schedule to keep, and insisted that the horses needed the exercise.

Stella sat under the awning on the front seat of the wagon, wrapped in a blanket against the chill, feeling sorry for the hulking draft animals in front of her. They were soaked, brown coats dripping as they clomped step by step on the muddy road. It might have been faster, waiting for the clouds to break, for the sun to emerge and let them use the truck. But the driver said they'd be waiting for days in these spring rains.

She traveled through an alien world, wet and green. Stella had never seen so much water in her whole life, all of it pouring from the sky. A quarter of this amount of rain a couple of hundred miles east would have saved Greentree.

The road curved into the next green valley, to Barnard Croft. The wide meadow and its surrounding rolling hills were green, lush with grass. A handful of alpaca grazed along a stream that ran frothing from the hills opposite. The animals didn't seem to mind the water, however matted and heavy their coats looked. There'd be some work, cleaning that mess for spinning. Actually, she looked forward to it. She wanted to make herself useful as soon as she could. To prove herself. If this didn't work, if she didn't fit in here and had to throw herself at the mercy of the regional committee to find some place prosperous enough to take her, that could use a decent weaver . . . no, this would work.

A half-a-dozen whitewashed cottages clustered together, along with sheds and shelters for animals, a couple of rabbit hutches, and squares of turned black soil with a barest sheen of green – garden plots and new growth. The largest cottage stood apart from the others. It had wide doors and many windows, shuttered now against the rain – the work house, she guessed. Under the shelter of the wide eaves sat wooden barrels for washing wool, and a pair of precious copper pots for dyeing. All comfortable, familiar sights.

The next-largest cottage, near the garden plots, had a smoking chimney. Kitchen and common room, most likely. Which meant the others were sleeping quarters. She wondered which was hers, and who'd she'd be sharing with. A pair of windmills stood on the side of one hill; their trefoil blades were still.

At the top of the highest hill, across the meadow, was a small, unpainted shack. It couldn't have held more than a person or two standing upright. This, she did not recognize. Maybe it was a curing shed, though it seemed an unlikely spot, exposed as it was to every passing storm.

A turn-off took them from the road to the cottages, and by the time the driver pulled up the horses, eased the wagon to a stop, and set the brakes, a pair of men wrapped in cloaks emerged from the work house to greet them. Stella thanked the driver and jumped to the ground. Her boots splashed, her long woolen skirt tangled around her legs, and the rain pressed the blanket close around her. She felt sodden and bedraggled, but she wouldn't complain.

The elder of those who came to greet her was middle-aged and worn, but he moved briskly and spread his arms wide. "Here she is! Didn't know if you would make it in this weather." This was Toma. Az's friend, Stella reminded herself. Nothing to worry about.

"Horses'll get through anything," the driver said, moving to the back of the wagon to unload her luggage.

"Well then," Toma said. "Let's get you inside and dried off."

"Thank you," Stella managed. "I just have a couple of bags. And a loom. Az let me take Greentree's loom."

"Well then, that is a treasure. Good."

The men clustered around the back of the wagon to help. The bags held her clothes, a few books and letters and trinkets. Her equipment: spindles and needles, carders, skeins of yarn, coils of roving. The loom took up most of the space – dismantled, legs and frames strapped together, mechanisms folded away in protective oilskin. It would take her most of a day to set up. She'd feel better when it was.

A third figure came running from the work house, shrouded by her wrap and hood like the others. The shape of her was female, young – maybe even Stella's age. She wore dark trousers and a pale tunic, like the others.

She came straight to the driver. "Anything for me?"

"Package from Griffith?" the driver answered.

"Oh, yes!"

The driver dug under an oil cloth and brought out a leather document case, stuffed full. The woman came forward to take it, revealing her face, sandstone-burnished skin and bright brown eyes.

Toma scowled at her, but the woman didn't seem to notice. She tucked the package under her arm and beamed like sunshine.

"At least be useful and take a bag," Toma said to her.

Taking up a bag with a free hand, the woman flashed a smile at Stella, and turned to carry her load to the cottage.

Toma and other other man, Jorge, carried the loom to the work house. Hefting the rest of her luggage, Stella went to the main cottage, following the young woman at a distance. Behind her, the driver returned to his seat and got the horses moving again; their hooves splashed on the road.

Around dinner time, the clouds broke, belying the driver's prediction. Some sky and a last bit of sunlight peeked through.

They ate what seemed to her eyes a magnificent feast – meat, eggs, preserved fruits and vegetables, fresh bread. At Greentree, they'd barely got through the winter on stores, and until this meal Stella hadn't realized she'd been dimly hungry all the time, for weeks. Months. Greentree really had been dying.

The folk of the croft gathered around the hearth at night, just as they did back home at Greentree, just as folk did at dozens of households up and down the Long Road. She met everyone: Toma and Jorge, who'd helped with the loom. Elsta, Toma's partner, who ran the kitchen and garden. Nik and Wendy, Jon and Faren. Peri had a baby, which showed just how well off Barnard was, to be able to support a baby as well as a refugee like Stella. The first thing Peri did was put the baby – Bette – in Stella's arms, and Stella was stricken because she'd never held a wriggly baby before and was afraid of dropping her. But Peri arranged her arms just so and took the baby back after a few moments of cooing over them both. Stella had never thought of earning the right to have her implant removed, to have a baby – another mouth to feed at Greentree would have been a disaster.

Elsta was wearing the shawl Stella had made, the one Az had given Toma – her audition, really, to prove her worth. The shawl was an intricate weave made of finely spun merino. Stella had done everything – carded and spun the wool, dyed it the difficult smoky blue, and designed the pattern herself. Elsta didn't have to wear it, the croft could have traded it for credits. Stella felt a small spark of pride. Wasn't just charity that brought her here.

Stella had brought her work basket, but Elsta tsked at her. "You've had a long trip, so rest now. Plenty of time to work later." So she sat on a blanket spread out on the floor and played with Bette.

Elsta picked apart a tangle of roving, preparing to draft into the spindle of her spinning wheel. Toma and Jorge had a folding table in front of them, and the tools to repair a set of hand carders. The others knit, crocheted, or mended. They no doubt made all their own clothing, from weaving the fabric to sewing, dark trousers, bright skirts, aprons, and tunics. Stella's hands itched to work – she was in the middle of knitting a pair of very bright yellow socks from the remnants of yarn from a weaving. They'd be ugly but warm – and the right kind of ugly had a charm of its own. But Elsta was probably right, and the baby was fascinating. Bette had a set of wooden blocks that she banged into each other; occasionally, very seriously, she handed them to Stella. Then demanded them back. The process must have had a logic to it.

The young woman wasn't with them. She'd skipped dinner as

well. Stella was thinking of how to ask about her, when Elsta did it for her.

"Is Andi gone out to her study, then?"

Toma grumbled, "Of course she is." The words bit.

Her study – the shack on the hill? Stella listened close, wishing the baby would stop banging her blocks so loudly.

"Toma—"

"She should be here."

"She's done her work, let her be. The night's turned clear, you know how she gets."

"She should listen to me."

"The more you push, the angrier she'll get. Leave her be, dearest."

Elsta's wheel turned and purred, Peri hummed as she knit, and Bette's toys clacked. Toma frowned, never looking up from his work.

Her bags sat by one of the two beds in the smallest cottage, only half unpacked. The other bed, Andi's, remained empty. Stella washed, brushed out her short blonde hair, changed into her nightdress, and curled up under the covers. Andi still hadn't returned.

The air smelled wrong, here. Wet, earthy, as if she could smell the grass growing outside the window. The shutters cracked open to let in a breeze. Stella was chilled; her nose wouldn't stop running. The desert always smelled dusty, dry – even at night, the heat of the sun rose up from the ground. There, her nose itched with dust.

She couldn't sleep. She kept waiting for Andi to come back.

Finally, she did. Stella started awake when the door opened with the smallest squeak – so she must have slept, at least a little. Cocooned under the covers, she clutched her pillow, blinking, uncertain for a moment where she was and what was happening. Everything felt wrong, but that was to be expected, so she lay still.

Andi didn't seem to notice that she was awake. She hung up her cloak on a peg by the door, sat on her bed while she peeled off shoes and clothes, which she left lying on the chest at the foot of her bed, and crawled under the covers without seeming to notice – or care – that Stella was there. The woman moved quickly

– nervously, even? But when she pulled the covers over her, she lay still, asleep in moments. Stella had a suspicion that she'd had practice, falling asleep quickly in the last hours before dawn, before she'd be expected to rise and work.

Stella supposed she would get a chance to finally talk to her new roommate soon enough, but she had no idea what she was going to say to her.

The next day, the clouds had more than broken. No sign of them remained, and the sun blazed clear as it ever had in the desert, but on a world that was wet, green, and growing. The faint sprouts in the garden plots seemed to have exploded into full growth, leaves uncurling. The angora in the hutches pressed twitching noses to the wire mesh of their cages, as if they could squeeze out to play in the meadow. Every shutter and window in the croft was opened to let in the sun.

The work house was wide and clean, whitewashed inside and out. It smelled of lanolin, fiber and work. Lint floated in beams of sunlight. Two – now three – looms and a pair of spinning wheels sat facing each other, so the weavers and spinners could talk. Days would pass quickly here. The first passed quickly enough, and Stella finished it feeling tired and satisfied.

Andi had spent the day at the wash tubs outside, cleaning a batch of wool, preparing it to card and spin in the next week or so. She'd still been asleep when Stella got up that morning, but must have woken up soon after. They still hadn't talked. Not even hello. They kept missing each other, being in different places. Continually out of rhythm, like a pattern that wove crooked because you hadn't counted the threads right. The more time passed without them speaking, the harder Stella found it to think of anything to say. She wanted to ask, *Are you avoiding me?*

Stella had finished putting away her work and was headed for the common room, when she noticed Andi following the footpath away from the cottages, around the meadow and up the hill to the lonely shack. Her study, Elsta had called it. She walked at a steady pace, not quite running, but not lingering.

After waiting until she was far enough ahead that she was not likely to look over her shoulder, Stella followed.

The trail up the hill was a hike, and even walking slowly Stella was soon gasping for breath. But slowly and steadily she made progress. The path made a couple of switchbacks, and finally reached the crest of the hill and the tiny weathered shack planted there.

As she suspected, the view was worth the climb. The whole of Barnard Croft's valley was visible, as well as the next one over. The neighboring croft's cottages were pale specks, and a thread of smoke climbed from one. The hills were soft and rounded, cut through with clefts like the folds in a length of fabric. Trees along the creek gave texture to the picture. The Long Road was a gray track painted around the green rise. The sky above stretched on, and on, blue touched by a faint haze. If she squinted, she thought she could see a line of gray on the far western horizon – the ocean – and the breeze in that direction had a touch of salt and wild. From this perspective, the croft rested in a shallow bowl that sat on the top of the world. She wondered how long it would take to walk around the entire valley, and decided she would like to try some sunny day.

The shed seemed even smaller when she was standing next to it. Strangely, part of the roof was missing, folded back on hinges, letting in light. The walls were too high to see over, and the door was closed. Stella hesitated; she shouldn't be here, she was invading. She had to share a room with this woman, she shouldn't intrude. Then again – she had to share a room with this woman. She only wanted to talk. And if Andi didn't like it, well . . .

Stella knocked on the door before she could change her mind. Three quick, woodpecker-like raps.

When the door swung out, she hopped back, managed not to fall over, and looked with wide eyes to see Andi glaring at her.

Then the expression softened, falling away to blank confusion. "Oh. Hi."

They stared at each other for a long moment. Andi leaned on the door, blocking the way; Stella still couldn't see what was inside.

"May I come in?" she finally asked, because Andi hadn't closed the door on her.

"Oh – sure." The woman seemed to shake herself out of a daydream, and stepped back to open the door wide.

The bulk of the tiny room was taken up by a device mounted

on a tripod as tall as she was. A metallic cylinder, wide as a bucket, pointed to the ceiling. A giant tin can almost, except the outer case was painted gray, and it had latches, dials, levers, all manner of protrusions connected to it. Stella moved around it, studying it, reminding herself not to touch, however much the object beckoned.

"It's a telescope, isn't it?" she asked, looking over to Andi. "An old one."

A smile dawned on Andi's face, lighting her mahogany eyes. "It is – twelve-inch reflector. Century or so old, probably. Pride and joy." Her finger traced up the tripod, stroking it like it was a favorite pet.

Stella's chest clenched at that smile, and she was glad now that she'd followed Andi here. She kept her voice calm. "Where'd you get it? You couldn't have traded for it—"

"Oh no, you can't trade for something like this. What would you trade for it?" Meaning how many bales of wool, or bolts of cloth, or live alpacas, or cans full of fish from the coast was something like this worth? You couldn't put a price on it. Some people would just give it away, because it had no real use, no matter how rare it was. Andi continued, "It was Pan's, who ran the household before Toma. He was one of the ones who helped build up the network with the observatories, after the big fall. Then he left it all to me. He'd have left it to Toma, but he wasn't interested." She shrugged, as if unable to explain.

"Then it actually works?"

"Oh yes." That smile shone again, and Stella would stay and talk all night, to keep that smile lit up. "I mean, not now, we'll have to wait until dark, assuming the weather stays clear. With the roof open it's almost a real observatory. See how we've fixed the seams?" She pointed to the edges, where the roof met the walls. Besides the hinges and latches that closed the roof in place, the seams had oilskin weatherproofing, to keep rain from seeping through the cracks. The design was clever. The building, then, was shelter for the equipment. The telescope never moved – the bottom points of the tripod were anchored with bricks.

Beside the telescope there wasn't much here: a tiny desk, a shelf filled with books, a bin holding a stack of papers, and a wooden box holding pencils. The leather pouch Andi had received yesterday was open, and packets of paper spread over the desk.

"Is that what you got in the mail?"

She bustled to the desk and shuffled through the pages. "Assignment from Griffith. It's a whole new list of coordinates, now that summer's almost here. The whole sky changes – what we see changes, at least – so I make observations and send the whole thing back." The flush in her brown face deepened as she ducked away. "I know it doesn't sound very interesting; we mostly just write down numbers and trade them back and forth—"

"Oh no," Stella said, shaking her head to emphasize. "It's interesting. Unusual—"

"And useless, Toma says." The smile turned sad, and last night's discussion became clear to Stella.

"Nothing's useless," Stella said. "It's like you said – you can't just throw something like this away." This wasn't like a household that couldn't feed itself and had no choice but to break up.

Three sharp rings of a distant brass bell sounded across the valley. Stella looked out the door, confused.

"Elsta's supper bell," Andi explained. "She only uses it when we've all scattered." She quickly straightened her papers, returned them to their pouch, and latched the roof back in place. Too late, Stella thought to help, reaching up to hold the panel of wood after Andi had already secured the last latch. Oh well. Maybe next time.

Stella got a better look at Andi as they walked back to the croft. She was rough in the way of wind and rain, her dark hair curly, pulled back by a scrap of gray yarn that was unraveling. The collar of her shirt was untied, and her woven jacket had slipped off a shoulder. Stella resisted an urge to pull it back up, and to brush the lock of hair that had fallen out of the tie behind her ear.

"So you're really more of an astronomer than a weaver," Stella said. She'd tried to sound encouraging, but Andi frowned.

"Drives Toma crazy," Andi said. "If there was a household of astronomers, I'd join. But astronomy doesn't feed anyone, does it? Well, some of it does – meteorology, climatology, solar astronomy, maybe. But not what we're doing. We don't earn anyone a baby."

"What are you doing?"

"Astronomical observation. As much as we can, though it feels like reinventing the wheel sometimes. We're not learning anything that people didn't already know back in the day. We're just – well, it feels like filling in the gaps until we get back to where we were. Tracking asteroids, marking supernovae, that sort of thing. Maybe we can't do much with the data. But it might be useful someday."

"There, you see – it's planning ahead. There's use in that."

She sighed. "The committees mostly think it's a waste of time. They can't really complain, though, because we – those of us in the network – do our share and work extra to support the observatories. A bunch of us designate ration credits toward Griffith and Kitt Peak and Wilson – they've got the region's big scopes – to keep staff there maintaining the equipment, to keep the solar power and windmills running. Toma always complains, says if I put my extra credits toward the household we could have a second baby. He says it could even be mine. But they're my credits, and this is important. I earn the time I spend with the scope, and he can't argue." She said that as a declaration, then looked straight at Stella, who blushed. "They may have brought you here to make up for me."

Stella didn't know what to say to that. She was too grateful to have a place at all, to consider that she may have been wanted.

Awkwardly, Andi covered up the silence. "Well. I hope you like it here. That you don't get too homesick, I mean."

The words felt like a warm blanket, soft and wooly. "Thanks."

"We can be kind of rowdy sometimes. Bette gets colicky, and you haven't heard Wendy sing yet. Then there's Jorge and Jon – they share a bed as well as a cottage, see, and can get pretty loud, though if you tease them about it they'll deny it."

"I don't mind rowdy. But I did almost expect to find a clandestine still in that shed."

Andi laughed. "I think Toma'd like a still better, because at least you can drink from it. Elsta does make a really good cider, though. If she ever put enough together to trade it would make up for all the credits I waste on the observatories."

As they came off the hill and approached the cluster of cottages, Andi asked, "Did you know that Stella means star in Latin?"

"Yes, I did," she answered.

Work was work no matter where you were, and Stella settled into her work quickly. The folk of Barnard were nice, and Andi was easy to talk to. And cute. Stella found excuses to be in the same room with her, just to see that smile. She hadn't expected this, coming to a new household. But she didn't mind, not at all.

Many households along the Long Road kept sheep, but the folk at Barnard did most of the spinning and weaving for trade. All the wool came to them. Barnard also produced a small quantity of specialty fibers from the alpaca and angora rabbits they kept. They were known for the quality of all their work, the smoothness of their yarns, the evenness of their weaving. Their work was sought after not just along the Long Road, but up and down the coast.

Everyone spun, wove, and dyed. Everyone knew every step of working with wool. They either came here because they knew, or because they'd grown up here learning the trade, like Toma and Nik, like Bette would in her turn. As Andi had, as Stella found out. Andi was the baby that Toma and Elsta had earned together.

Stella and Andi were at the looms, talking as they worked. The spring rains seem to have broken for good, and everyone else had taken their work outside. Wendy sat in the fresh air with her spinning wheel. A new batch of wool had arrived, and Toma and Jorge worked cleaning it. So Stella had a chance to ask questions in private.

"Could you get a place at one of the observatories? How does that work?"

Andi shook her head. "It wouldn't work out. There's three people at Kitt and two each at Griffith and Wilson, and they pick their successors. I'm better use to them here, working to send them credits."

"And you have your telescope, I suppose."

"The astronomers love my telescope," she said. "They call my setup Barnard Observatory, as if it's actually important. Isn't it silly?"

"Of course it isn't."

Andi's hands flashed, passing the shuttle across. She glanced up every now and then. Stella, for her part, let her hands move by habit, and watched Andi more than her own work. Outside, Wendy sang as she spun, in rhythm with the clipping hum of her wheel. Her voice was light, dream-like.

The next time Andi glanced up, she exclaimed, "How do you *do* that? You're not even watching and it's coming out beautiful."

Stella blinked at her work – not much to judge by, she thought. A foot or two of fabric curling over the breast beam, only just starting to wind onto the cloth beam. "I don't know. It's what I'm good at. Like you and the telescope."

"Nice of you to say so. But here, look at this – I've missed a row." She sat back and started unpicking the last five minutes of her work. "I go too fast. My mind wanders."

"It happens to everyone," Stella said.

"Not you. I saw that shawl you did for Elsta."

"I've just gotten good at covering up the mistakes," Stella said, winking.

A week after her arrival, an agent from the regional committee came to visit. A stout, gray-haired, cheerful woman, she was the doctor who made regular rounds up and down the Long Road. She was scheduled to give Bette a round of vaccinations, but Stella suspected the woman was going to be checking on her as well, to make sure she was settling in and hadn't disrupted the household too much.

The doctor, Nance, sat with Bette on the floor, and the baby immediately started crying. Peri hovered, but Nance just smiled and cooed while lifting the baby's arms and checking her ears, not seeming at all bothered.

"How is the world treating you then, Toma?" Nance turned to Toma, who was sitting in his usual chair by the fire.

His brow was creased with worry, though there didn't seem to be anything wrong. "Fine, fine," he said brusquely.

Nance turned. "And Stella, are you doing well?"

"Yes, thank you," Stella said. She was winding yarn around Andi's outstretched hands, to make a skein. This didn't feel much like an inspection, but that only made her more nervous.

"Very good. My, you're a wiggler, aren't you?" Bette's crying had finally subsided to red-faced sniffling, but she continued to fling herself from Nance's arms in an attempt to escape. After a round with a stethoscope, Nance let her go, and the baby crawled away, back to Peri.

The doctor turned her full attention to Toma. "The committee wants to order more banners, they expect to award quite a few this summer. Will you have some ready?"

Toma seemed startled. "Really? Are they sure?"

Barnard supplied the red-and-green patterned cloth used to make the banners awarded to households who'd been approved to have a baby. One of the things Nance had asked about when she first arrived was if anyone had tried bribing him for a length of the cloth over the last year. One of the reasons Barnard had the task of producing the banners – they were prosperous enough not to be vulnerable to bribes. Such attempts happened rarely, but did happen. Households had been broken up over such crimes.

The banner the household had earned for Bette was pinned proudly to the wall above the mantel.

Nance shrugged. "The region's been stable for a couple of years. No quota arguments, most households supporting them-selves, just enough surplus to get by without draining resources. We're a healthy region, Toma. If we can support more children, we ought to. And you – with all these healthy young women you have, you might think of putting in for another baby." The doctor beamed.

Stella and Andi looked at each other and blushed. Another baby so soon after the first? Scandalous.

Nance gathered up her kit. "Before I go, let me check all your birth control implants so we don't have any mishaps, eh?"

She started with Elsta and Toma and worked her way around the room.

"Not that I could have a mishap," Andi muttered to Stella. "They ought to make exceptions for someone like me who isn't likely to get in that kind of trouble. Because of her *preferences,* you know?"

"I know," Stella said, blushing very hard now. "I've had that thought myself."

They stared at each other for a very long moment. Stella's mouth had suddenly gone dry. She wanted to flee the room and stick her head in a bucket of cool water. Then again, she didn't.

When Nance came to her side to prod her arm, checking that the implant was in place, Stella hardly felt it.

"Looks like you're good and covered," Nance said. "For now, 'eh? Until you get that extra banner." She winked.

The doctor stayed for supper and still had enough daylight left to walk to the next waystation along the road. Elsta wrapped up a snack of fruit and cheese for her to take with her, and Nance thanked her very much. As soon as she was gone, Toma muttered.

"Too many mouths to feed – and what happens when the next flood hits? The next typhoon? We lose everything and then there isn't enough? We have enough as it is, more than enough. Wanting more, it's asking for trouble. Getting greedy is what brought the disasters in the first place. It's too much."

Everyone stayed quiet, letting him rant. This felt to Stella like an old argument, words repeated like the chorus of a song. Toma's philosophy, expounded by habit. He didn't need a response.

Stella finished winding the skein of yarn and quietly excused herself, putting her things away and saying goodnight to everyone.

Andi followed her out of the cottage soon after, and they walked together to their room.

"So, do you want one?" Stella asked her.

"A baby? I suppose I do. Someday. I mean, I assumed as well off as Barnard is I could have one if I wanted one. It's a little odd, thinking about who I'd pick for the father. That's the part I'm not sure about. What about you?"

Besides being secretly, massively pleased that Andi hadn't thought much about fathers . . . "I assumed I'd never get the chance. I don't think I'd miss it if I didn't."

"Enough other people who want 'em, right?"

"Something like that."

They reached their room, changed into their nightclothes, washed up for bed. Ended up sitting on their beds, facing each other and talking. That first uncomfortable night seemed far away now.

"Toma doesn't seem to like the idea of another baby," Stella prompted.

"Terrified, I think," she said. "Wanting too much gets people in trouble."

"But it only seems natural, to want as much as you can have."

Andi shook her head. "His grandparents remembered the old days. He heard stories from them about the disasters. All the people who died in the floods and plagues. He's that close to it

– might as well have lived through it himself. He thinks we'll lose it all, that another great disaster will fall on us and destroy everything. It's part of why he hates my telescope so much. It's a sign of the old days when everything went rotten. But it won't happen, doesn't he see that?"

Stella shrugged. "Those days aren't so far gone, really. Look at what happened to Greentree."

"Oh – Stella, I'm sorry. I didn't mean that there's not anything to it, just that . . . " She shrugged, unable to finish the thought.

"It can't happen here. I know."

Andi's black hair fell around her face, framing her pensive expression. She stared into space. "I just wish he could see how good things are. We've earned a little extra, haven't we?"

Unexpected even to herself, Stella burst, "Can I kiss you?"

In half a heartbeat Andi fell at her, holding Stella's arms, and Stella clung back, and either her arms were hot or Andi's hands were, and they met, lips to lips.

One evening, Andi escaped the gathering in the common room and brought Stella with her. They left as the sun had almost set, leaving just enough light to follow the path to the observatory. They took candles inside shaded lanterns for the trip back to their cottage. At dusk, the windmills were ghostly skeletons lurking on the hillside.

They waited for full dark, talking while Andi looked over her paperwork and prepared her notes. Andi asked about Greentree, and Stella explained that the aquifers had dried up in the drought. Households remained in the region because they'd always been there. Some survived, but they weren't particularly successful. She told Andi how the green of the valleys near the coast had almost blinded her when she first arrived, and how all the rain had seemed like a miracle.

Then it was time to unlatch the roof panels and look at the sky.

"Don't squint, just relax. Let the image come into focus," Andi said, bending close to give directions to Stella, who was peering through the scope's eyepiece. Truth be told, Stella was more aware of Andi's hand resting lightly on her shoulder. She shifted closer.

"You should be able to see it," Andi said, straightening to look at the sky.

"Okay . . . I think . . . oh! Is that it?" A disk had come into view, a pale, glowing light striped with orange, yellow, cream. Like someone had covered a very distant moon with melted butter.

"Jupiter," Andi said proudly.

"But it's just a star."

"Not up close it isn't."

Not a disk, then, but a sphere. Another planet. "Amazing."

"Isn't it? You ought to be able to see some of the moons as well – a couple of bright stars on either side?"

"I think . . . yes, there they are."

After an hour, Stella began shivering in the night-time cold, and Andi put her arms around her, rubbing warmth into her back. In moments, they were kissing, and stumbled together to the desk by the shack's wall, where Andi pushed her back across the surface and made love to her. Jupiter had swung out of view by the time they closed up the roof and stumbled off the hill.

Another round of storms came, shrouding the night-time sky, and they spent the evenings around the hearth with the others. Some of the light went out of Andi on those nights. She sat on a chair with a basket of mending at her feet, darning socks and shirts, head bent over her work. Lamplight turned her skin amber and made her hair shine like obsidian. But she didn't talk. That may have been because Elsta and Toma talked over everyone, or Peri exclaimed over something the baby did, then everyone had to admire Bette.

The day the latest round of rain broke and the heat of summer finally settled over the valley, Andi got another package from Griffith, and that light of discovery came back to her. Tonight, they'd rush off to the observatory after supper.

Stella almost missed the cue to escape, helping Elsta with the dishes. When she was finished and drying her hands, Andi was at the door. Stella rushed in behind her. Then Toma brought out a basket, one of the ones as big as an embrace that they used to store just-washed wool in, and set it by Andi's chair before the hearth. "Andi, get back here."

Her hand was on the door, one foot over the threshold, and Stella thought she might keep going, pretending that she hadn't heard. But her hand clenched on the door frame, and she turned around.

"We've got to get all this new wool processed, so you'll stay in tonight to help."

"I can do that tomorrow. I'll work double tomorrow—"

"Now, Andi."

Stella stepped forward, hands reaching for the basket. "Toma, I can do that."

"No, you're doing plenty already. Andi needs to do it."

"I'll be done with the mending in a minute and can finish that in no time at all. Really, it's all right."

He looked past her, to Andi. "You know the rules – household business first."

"The household business is *done*. This is makework!" she said. Toma held the basket out in reproof.

Stella tried again. "But I *like* carding." It sounded lame – no one liked carding.

But Andi had surrendered, coming away from the door, shuffling toward her chair. "Stella, it's all right. Not your argument."

"But—" The pleading in her gaze felt naked. She wanted to help; how could she help?

Andi slumped in the chair without looking up. All Stella could do was sit in her own chair, with her knitting. She jabbed herself with the needle three times, from glancing up at Andi every other stitch.

Toma sat before his workbench, looking pleased for nearly the first time since Stella had met him.

Well after dark, Stella lay in her bed, stomach in knots. Andi was in the other bed and hadn't said a word all evening.

"Andi? Are you all right?" she whispered. She stared across the room, to the slope of the other woman, mounded her under blanket. The lump didn't move, but didn't look relaxed in sleep. But if she didn't want to talk, Stella wouldn't force her.

"I'm okay," Andi sighed, finally.

"Anything I can do?"

Another long pause, and Stella was sure she'd said too much. Then, "You're a good person, Stella. Anyone ever told you that?"

Stella crawled out from under her covers, crossed to Andi's bed, climbed in with her. Andi pulled the covers up over them both, and the women held each other.

Toma sent Andi on an errand, delivering a set of blankets to the next waystation and picking up messages to bring back. More makework. The task could just as easily have been done by the next wagon messenger to pass by. Andi told him as much, standing outside the work house the next morning.

"Why wait when we can get the job done now?" Toma answered, hefting the backpack, stuffed to bursting with newly woven woolens, toward her.

Stella was at her loom, and her hand on the shuttle paused as she listened. But Andi didn't say anything else. Only glared at Toma a good long minute before taking up the pack. She'd be gone most of the day, hiking there and back.

Which was the point, wasn't it?

Stella contrived to find jobs that kept Toma in sight, sorting and carding wool outside where he was working repairing a fence, when she should have been weaving. So she saw when Toma studied the hammer in his hand, looked up the hill, and started walking the path to Andi's observatory.

Stella dropped the basket of wool she was holding and ran.

He was merely walking. Stella overtook him easily, at first. But after fifty yards of running, she slowed, clutching at a stitch in her side. Gasping for breath with burning lungs, she kept on, step after step, hauling herself up the hill, desperate to get there first.

"Stella, go back. Don't get in the middle of this."

Even if she could catch enough of her breath to speak, she didn't know what she would say. He lengthened his stride, gaining on her. She got to the shed a bare few steps before him.

The door didn't have a lock; it had never needed one. Stella pressed herself across it and faced out, to Toma, marching closer. At least she had something to lean on for the moment.

"Move aside, Stella. She's got to grow up and get on with what's important," Toma said.

"This *is* important."

He stopped, studied her. He gripped the handle of the hammer like it was a weapon. Her heart thudded. How angry was he?

Toma considered, then said, "Stella. You're here because I wanted to do Az a favor. I can change my mind. I can send a message to Nance and the committee that it just isn't working out. I can do that."

Panic brought sudden tears to her eyes. He wouldn't dare, he couldn't, she'd proven herself already in just a few weeks, hadn't she? The committee wouldn't believe him, couldn't listen to him. But she couldn't be sure of that, could she?

Best thing to do would be to step aside. He was head of the household; it was his call. She ought to do as he said, because her place here *wasn't* secure. A month ago that might not have mattered, but now – she *wanted* to stay, she *had* to stay.

And if she stepped aside, leaving Toma free to enter the shed, what would she tell Andi afterward?

She swallowed the lump in her throat and found words. "I know disaster can still happen. I know the droughts and storms and plagues do still come and can take away everything. Better than anyone, I know. But we have to start building again some-time, yes? People like Andi have to start building, and we have to let them, even if it seems useless to the rest of us. Because it isn't useless, it – it's beautiful."

He stared at her for a long time. She thought maybe he was considering how to wrestle her away from the door. He was bigger than she was, and she wasn't strong. It wouldn't take much. But she'd fight.

"You're infatuated, that's all," he said.

Maybe, not that it mattered.

Then he said, "You're not going to move away, are you?"

Shaking her head, Stella flattened herself more firmly against the door.

Toma's grip on the hammer loosened, just a bit. "My grand-parents – has Andi told you about my grandparents? They were children when the big fall came. They remembered what it was like. Mostly they talked about what they'd lost, all the things they had and didn't now. And I thought, all those things they missed, that they wanted back – that was what caused the fall in the first place, wasn't it? We don't need it, any of it."

"Andi needs it. And it's not hurting anything." What else could she say? She had to say something that would make it all right. "Better things will come, or what's the point?"

A weird crooked smile turned Toma's lips, and he shifted his grip on the hammer. Holding it by the head now, he let it dangle by his leg. "God, what a world," he muttered. Stella still couldn't tell if he was going to force her away from the door. She held her breath.

Toma said, "Don't tell Andi about this. All right?"

She nodded. "All right."

Toma turned and started down the trail, a calm and steady pace. Like a man who'd just gone out for a walk.

Stella slid to the ground and sat on the grass by the wall until the old man was out of sight. Finally, after scrubbing the tears from her face, she followed him down, returning to the cottages and her work.

Andi was home in time for supper, and the household ate together as usual. The woman was quiet and kept making quick glances at Toma, who avoided looking back at all. It was like she knew Toma had had a plan. Stella couldn't say anything until they were alone.

The night was clear, the moon was dark. Stella'd learned enough from Andi to know it was a good night for stargazing. As they were cleaning up after the meal, she touched Andi's hand. "Let's go to the observatory."

Andi glanced at Toma, and her lips pressed together, grim. "I don't think that's a good idea."

"I think it'll be okay."

Andi clearly didn't believe her, so Stella took her hand, and together they walked out of the cottage, then across the yard, past the work house, and to the trail that led up the hill to the observatory.

And it was all right.

INVISIBLE PLANETS

Hao Jingfang

Translated by Ken Liu

"Tell me about the fascinating planets you've seen. But I don't want to hear anything cruel or disgusting," you say.

Good. I nod and smile. *Of course. No problem.*

CHICHI RAHA

Chichi Raha is a fascinating place, its flowers and lakes unforgettable to all visitors. There, you cannot see a single inch of exposed soil because the land is covered by vegetation: the *anua* grass, as fine as silk thread; the *kuqin* tree, tall enough to scrape the clouds; and many varieties of unnameable, unimaginably strange fruits, exuding seductive aromas.

The Chichi Rahans have never needed to worry about making a living. Their life expectancy is high, their metabolism is slow, and they have no natural enemies. They fill their bellies on a diet of various fruits and make their homes inside a type of tree with large, hollow trunks. The average diameter of these tubes is just wide enough to allow an adult Chichi Rahan to lie down comfortably. When the weather is good, the branches hang loosely, but when it rains, the branches rise so that the leaves form a canopy like an umbrella.

Those who visit Chichi Raha for the first time are always confused by how civilization could have developed on such a world. From the perspective of the visitors, in a place lacking crisis and competition, life should be able to survive very well without intelligence. But there is indeed civilization here, and indeed it is beautiful, vigorous, full of creativity.

Many visitors think that they would like to retire here. Most of them think that their greatest difficulty would be a matter of diet. So, anxiously and carefully, they taste every type of local fruit. But after they've lived here for a while, after they've attended enough local banquets, they discover – somewhat to their surprise – that while they enjoy the food, they cannot tolerate life here, especially those who are old.

It turns out that all Chichi Rahans learn to lie from birth. Indeed, lying is their most important occupation. They spend the entire span of their existence fabricating stories concerning both events that have occurred and events that have not. They write them down, paint them, sing them, but never remember them. They do not care if there's a correspondence between their words and the facts, their only standard being whether the tale is interesting. If you ask them about the history of Chichi Raha, they will tell you a hundred versions. No one will contradict the version told by another, because each moment, they are already engaged in self-contradiction.

On this world, everyone is always saying, "Yes, I will," but nothing is ever done. No one takes such promises seriously, though promises do make life more interesting. Only in extremely rare circumstances do the inhabitants do as they promise. And such occasions are celebrated. For example, if two of them make an appointment and both happen to keep it then they will most likely become a couple and live together. Of course, such occurrences are rare. Most live alone all their lives. The inhabitants do not feel any lack because of this. Indeed, they hear about the over-population problems of other planets and feel that their own world is the only one that understands the secret of good living.

So, Chichi Raha developed a brilliant literature, art, and history, and became a famous center of civilization. Many visitors come with the hope that they might hear a local tell family stories in the grass beneath the crown of one of the house-trees.

At one time, some questioned whether a stable society could develop on a planet like this. They imagined Chichi Raha as a chaotic place with no government or commerce. But they were wrong. The planet has an advanced political culture, and the business of exporting fruits has gone on for several centuries without interruption. The habit of lying has never caused problems for these developments, and may have even helped them. The only thing that Chichi Raha lacks is science. Here, every intelligent mind knows a bit of the universe's secret, but the bits never get the chance to be pieced together.

PIMACEH

This is another planet where you can't be sure about history. As you wander through its museums, restaurants, and hotels, you will hear many versions of its past. Eventually, you will be trapped in a miasma of confusion because every speaker's expression will be so sincere that you can't help but believe, and yet there is no way to reconcile all the different stories.

The scenery of this world is legendary. Strictly speaking, the planet is not even spherical. The southern hemisphere is far lower in elevation than the northern, and an almost perpendicular cliff, going all the way around the equator, divides the planet into two completely different halves. Above the cliff: ice and snow; below: an endless ocean. The city of Pimaceh is built on this world-encircling cliff. From the sky to the sea, the lightly recessed houses and the perfect straight up-and-down avenues are like parts of a giant painting.

No one knows how this place was built. All that you will hear are the various romances told by the current inhabitants. Every story is exciting: some are heroic legends; some are tragic and austere; some are full of doomed loves. The particular effect depends on the teller, but no one can give a version that convinces everyone. And so, as it passes from teller to teller, Pimaceh becomes more and more mysterious and charming.

Many visitors, entranced by the wondrous sights and stories, linger and do not wish to leave. This is an open and accommodating planet, and every visitor is welcomed with open arms. The visitors – now settlers – then build their own houses on the cliff and pass on the stories they hear to new visitors. Content, they gradually become locals.

This state of happiness will last until one day, when they will realize the truth about themselves. They'll suddenly understand that countless hints have already revealed Pimaceh's true history to them: everyone on this world is a visitor. There are no natives at all.

Yes, Pimaceh did once have a glorious history, but for some reason it had been abandoned. The original inhabitants had left for unknown reasons, leaving behind only a lovely ghost town that astounded interstellar travelers who later stumbled upon it. They also left behind fragments of a language that no one could decipher, like metaphors that filled in the blank spaces between the buildings. These took root in the minds of those who came after, and blossomed into the most lush and beautiful imaginary pasts for the planet.

No one knew who was the first to discover this uninhabited world. The history of the visitors has also faded, consciously or not, as it passed from generation to generation. All the visitors who have settled wish to think of themselves as the people of Pimaceh. They protect this planet and steadfastly play the role of hosts – until one day they themselves begin to believe that this is their native land and the country where they will die.

Almost no one can discover Pimaceh's secret except a few true wanderers who have been to all corners of the universe. They can sense that the inhabitants here emphasize slightly too often the fact that they are the *People of Pimaceh*. On planets where real natives have remained in charge, this is one of those things easily forgotten.

BINGWAUGH

Setting Pimaceh aside, in the sea of stars, you'll probably have to go all the way to Bingwaugh to see such a variety of different species from all over, each with its own culture and civilization, colliding, striking against each other, creating sparks.

Bingwaugh is not too big and not too small. Its seasons are indistinct and its climate mild. The surface of the planet is composed mostly of plains, with few mountains and little variation in elevation. The horizon is a gentle, smooth curve. Here is everything that an average planet should have, but nothing more: good soil, decent mineral deposits, various fauna and flora, and even the sort of circular fields surrounded by low bushes where tourists like to sing and dance. There's nothing remarkable at all.

The inhabitants of Bingwaugh are similarly average. They are mammals: not too big; a solid, good people, easily satisfied. Their social organization is loose, and everyone lives in harmony.

If one *had* to pick something unique about them, it would be their pleasant disposition. Rarely are they seen arguing, whether amongst themselves or with the multiplicity of interstellar visitors. They're great listeners. Adults and children alike would open their eyes wide and listen to you lecture, nodding frequently, their faces often breaking into expressions of intoxications at the wisdom you're imparting.

Having discovered this characteristic of Bingwaugh, all the ambitious adventurers in the universe rushed to take advantage of it. Who doesn't want to rule over such a people and place? Plenty of resources, comfortable living environment, and a great location at the intersection of so many trade routes.

So, educators came, missionaries came, politicians came, revolutionaries and reporters all came. They described to the locals their visions of heaven, lectured them on their ideals, and again and again, the inhabitants of Bingwaugh nodded and sighed with heartfelt admiration and accepted the new philosophies. Some remote planets even sent over "Supervisors" to rule over these new converts. The inhabitants never objected, not even a peep.

But, after these triumphant developments, the interstellar guests would always be disappointed. Indeed, the longer they stayed on Bingwaugh, the more their disappointment grew.

As it turns out, the locals have never truly accepted any alien propaganda. Even when they agree with a new faith, they never actually do as they're told. As enthusiastically as they admire the new systems of laws being presented to them, just as enthusiastically they don't follow any of the alien laws at all.

Faced with this attitude from the locals, the ambitious colonizers can do nothing. This is because they realize that this contrast between what the locals say and what they do is not at all the result of some deep conspiracy, but simply a matter of habit. If you ask them directly, they'll reply, very puzzled, "Yes, what you say sounds like Truth. But the world is full of Truths. So what if you have a Truth?"

Some planets, unable to tolerate this state of affairs, attempted to conquer Bingwaugh by force. But immediately, some other planets would intervene. The balance of power is such that every possible conflict is always resolved outside the boundaries of the atmosphere of Bingwaugh.

So, though it is a place where foreigners love to congregate, Bingwaugh is also one of the planets that has best preserved its native culture.

Do you like these stories?

"Yes . . . and no. Why is every planet filled with visitors from across the stars? I don't like this. It makes them sound like zoos."

You're right. I don't like it, either. The uniqueness of each planet disappears over time in this manner, like a fingerprint being rubbed away. All right, let's hear some stories about real natives.

AMIYACHI AND AIHUOWU

Let me tell you about two planets still ruled by their original inhabitants. On each, there are two different intelligent species. Yet each species believes itself to be the only master of its respective world.

Amiyachi orbits a double star: one a bright blue giant, the other a dim white dwarf. The two are similar in mass, but differ widely in volume and the type of emitted radiation. So, Amiyachi's orbit is shaped like an irregular gourd. It dances a waltz along the hyperbolic paraboloid of the gravitational fields of the two stars.

Whenever Amiyachi is near the blue giant, it enters a long summer. But when it's near the white dwarf, it enters an equally long winter. The summer is when the planet's flora multiply and grow and stretch their vines like madness. In winter, most are dormant, and only a few hardy weeds quietly bloom over the empty earth.

Summer and winter, in each season Amiyachi is ruled by a different species: one dances through the lush forests of summer, the other marches alone over the barren plains of winter. The summer Amiyachians live in houses made of woven vines, and when the weather turns cold, the houses disappear as the vines wither and die. The winter Amiyachians live in caves dug into thick mountains, and when the weather turns hot, the mouths of the caves are hidden behind dense clumps of grass and fern, leaving no visible trace.

Whenever the summer Amiyachians are about to hibernate, they secrete a liquid covering to protect themselves and sink underground. The liquid stimulates a kind of insect, known as the *wususu,* to begin mating. The multiplying *wususu* then bring to life the cold-resistant shrub *aludon*. The flowering of this plant, unremarkable in appearance, begins the long and slow process of awakening the winter Amiyachians.

When the winter Amiyachians are near the end of their season's journey, they give birth. The new babies, protected by a hard membrane, develop and grow in the soil. The ionic reactions of their growth change the pH level of the soil and cause other plants to germinate and grow, announcing the beginning of the planet's summer, as well as the reign of the summer Amiyachians.

Thus, the two intelligent species of Amiyachi remain unaware of each other. Neither knows that its civilization's existence depends on the existence of the other, two sides of the same coin. Both races have composed works praising the divine wisdom of the gods, allowing them to be reborn as they awake from their slumber. But they have never realized that they're both children called forth by the gods, as well as the gods themselves.

As for Aihuowu, the situation is entirely different. On the surface of this world, the two intelligent species and their civilizations are very aware of each other's existence, yet neither is aware that the other is just like itself, possessing feelings, logic, and morality.

The reason is simple: The two species exist in different frames of time.

Aihuowu is a planet with a strange orbit. The angle between its axis of rotation and the plane of its orbit is very small, and the axis of rotation itself processes slowly. Thus, the surface of the planet can be divided into four regions: The narrow strip near the equator has night and day in accordance with the rotation of the planet, while the polar regions have their own periods of brightness and darkness based on the procession of the axis of rotation. A day near the pole is hundreds of times longer than a day near the equator, and so the lives born in each of these regions experience time at rates hundreds of times apart.

For the Aihuowuans near the equator, the mysterious poles seem to have very long nights and very long days. But for the polar Aihuowuans, the equator passes through darkness and light rapidly, in flashes. The equatorial Aihuowuans are dainty and agile, with hundreds of thousands of individuals living in dense colonies. The polar Aihuowuans, on the other hand, have slow metabolic rates matched to their long days and long nights, and their bodies are scaled large to fit their sense of time.

Sometimes, the equatorial Aihuowuans come to the poles for adventure and exploration. They always get lost in the maze-like forests full of gigantic trees, and mistake the occasional houses they encounter as unscalable cliffs. But when the polar Aihuowuans wander near the equator, they often miss the details and carelessly destroy the houses and fields of the equatorial Aihuowuans. They live on the same planet, but belong to entirely separate worlds.

Sometimes, the equatorial Aihuowuans venture to speculate that the giant creatures of the poles might also possess intelligence. But in their hearts, they believe that even if such slow-moving creatures, who in a hundred years might not shift more than a few feet, were intelligent, it would be a simple and rudimentary kind of intelligence. The polar Aihuowuans have similar suspicions of intelligence concerning the equatorial species. But then they sigh and shake their heads, realizing that such tiny creatures that are born and die in a single day would be incapable of experiencing real civilization.

And so the two intelligent species of Aihuowu experience the same process of learning, working, love, and war. Their histories play out at two time scales, each echoing the other. But they remain opaque to each other, unaware that when it comes to time, everyone is only measuring the universe using the ruler of their own lifespan.

"Wait a minute," you interrupt. "How can you know about all these civilizations? When did you go to Amiyachi? And what scale of time did you use to experience Aihuowu?"

I know. Of course I know. If you had been there, you would know as well. This is the difference between visitors and natives. This is the point of traveling.

"It is? This is why you travel?"
Yes, and no.
If you really want to know why I travel, then let me tell you about a planet devoted to travel.

LUNAJI

The people of Lunaji build the galaxy's most beautiful cars, boats, airships, and passenger catapults. The complexity and refinement of these vehicles far exceed the imaginations of visitors from other worlds, and also far exceed the technological levels of all other industries on this planet.

Those who are intuitive immediately jump to the conclusion that travel is especially meaningful for the Lunajians. But there's a deeper explanation that most cannot figure out. They can't imagine why so many intelligent beings would devote their entire lives to traveling and preparing for travel, rather than the accomplishment of some other, more rewarding task. Only those who know the life cycle of the Lunajians have some understanding of this seemingly irrational restlessness.

Lunaji has a large basin, where the concentration of oxygen is higher than anywhere else. The soil is rich and moist; small waterfalls pour into a clear, pristine lake; flowers are in bloom every season of the year; and heavily laden, spherical fruit trees surround soft lawns, strewn with mushrooms in all the colors of the rainbow. Every Lunajian spends their childhood here, none knowing how they arrived in this world. From the moment they open their eyes, this basin is all they know.

From time to time, some wish to discover the secret origin of their lives, or seek the home of the gods. Then they start to grow up, tall enough to climb over the rocks blocking the gentle slope at the edge of the basin. They walk into the maze-like, dense forest, climbing up the slope toward the world outside the basin. They can't tell you their ages, because the age at which each one begins to mature is different.

After exiting the basin, they keep on walking, wandering, seeking – finding nothing. They meet others who left the basin before them, but they also are still searching, still traveling, still baffled by the mystery of their own lives. So, a Lunajian's life is one long migration. They go from one place to another, never settling. They build boats, cars, and airplanes with the purpose of accelerating their own pace so that they can cover every square inch of the planet, until they reach the edge of the sky.

Sometimes, by coincidence, some follow an obscure path and arrive at a meadow in the wilderness. There, a lovely silver flower blooms, giving off an intoxicating aroma. The fragrance makes every Lunajian nearby dizzy, and causes unprecedented tender feelings to spring up between them. For the first time, they feel attraction for one another, embrace, clasp, give and receive. Then, they give birth by the edge of a brook, from where the babies are borne by the water to the basin beneath the falls.

The parents? They die and sink into the muddy earth.

And so, such a simple cycle turns out to be the entirety of the meaning of the ceaseless travels of the Lunajians.

YANYANNI

Since we're on the topic of growing up, I want to tell you a few more stories. The first is about Yanyanni.

You can always tell a Yanyannian's age at a glance. Like trees, they never cease to grow. Every year, they become taller than they were the year before. An adult is several times the height of a child, and a young person is several feet shorter than an elder. The oldest person is always head and shoulders above the surrounding crowd, a lonely tower.

So, in the world of the Yanyannians, there is no such thing as a friendship that crosses age gaps. Even talking to someone who is very different in age can be a chore. A long conversation would leave both interlocutors with sore necks and shoulders, as the younger looks up while the older looks down. Indeed, there's not much to talk about between people of very different ages. Their houses are of different heights and the shelves from which they do their shopping are different. One can only see the belt of the other, and neither can see the other's expressions.

It's not true, however, that the Yanyannians can grow without limit. One day, they wake up and discover that their height hasn't increased. Then they know that they are about to die. The knowledge does not make them sad, however. Growing taller is actually a very tiring process. Many have been exhausted by it and simply find an excuse to stop. Death for the Yanyannians takes a long time, but no one knows exactly how long. It's never been precisely measured. To simplify things, they list the age of death as the day when growth ceases. In their eyes, the passage of time is a measure of change. When growth ceases, time stops.

The tallest house on Yanyanni was built more than a century ago. At the time, there was an old man who, year after year, grew and grew until his head touched the ceiling of the tallest building then in existence. So the people erected a tower for him designed to hold a single man. The base of the tower took up the space for a park. After his death, no one else ever managed to reach his record of longevity, and so the tower was divided into two stories and turned into a museum.

Legend has it that the old man left a diary next to each window of the tower, recording his life during the years when his height corresponded to that window. Afterward, others climbed ladders to retrieve these diaries for reading, but after a while, the diaries became lost.

Now, visitors wander past the empty windows and imagine how a man who could cross a river with a single step might brush his teeth and eat his food.

TISU ATI AND LUTIKAWULU

Tisu Ati and Lutikawulu are a pair of opposites. These two planets, 100,000 light years apart, are like the two ends of a dipole: they negate each other and also define each other.

Tisu Atians are much smaller than the inhabitants of most planets. Their skin is especially soft, and their bodies can rapidly shift shapes. On this Lamarckian world, the development of gene expression reached its pinnacle – no, surpassed the pinnacle. All of evolution has been compressed into an individual's brief life.

The Tisu Atians can alter their bodies in accordance with their desires. Those who practice climbing mountains develop longer and longer arms, until their arms are longer than their bodies. Those who operate machinery develop five or six arms, until an individual can simultaneously control the opening and closing of numerous valves. On the street, no two Tisu Atians look alike.

Everywhere, one can see a mouth so large as to take up half a face, a waist thinner than a strand of noodle, or a round sphere covered by a layer of armor-like scales. These changes are unique to each individual, and it's impossible to detect anyone's parentage based on appearance. Even the parents themselves, if sufficient time has passed, have a hard time picking their children out of a crowd.

But "in accordance with their desires" is not quite accurate. It's not true that every Tisu Atian can attain the appearance they have in their minds. Most of the time, they're vague in their self-images. It's only when someone takes an extra large step or bumps into something that that person realizes their legs have grown another 30 percent or their back has grown a row of little spikes. Of course, in a few years, one has turned into a long-legged strider able to go up an entire flight of stairs in a single step, or a warrior whose body is covered by hard and sharp spikes.

So, many Tisu Atians are even more cautious than the inhabitants of other planets. They speak carefully; they work carefully. They're terrified of the possibility that in a moment of carelessness, the silly face they made before going to bed will become permanent, will turn into a tumor impossible to remove.

On the busy streets of Lutikawulu, you can tell at a glance each person's career and daily life. This may be the only point on which Tisu Ati and Lutikawulu agree.

The Lutikawuluans also look very different from each other: runners, singers, sculptors, thinkers, etc. The difference between them can be clearly gleaned from differences in musculature, body shape, size, and facial features, just like on Tisu Ati.

But on Lutikawulu, the journey of life is the exact opposite of life on Tisu Ati. This is a Darwinian planet, where everyone is in agreement that any effort expended in directing the path of evolution is useless. The Lutikawuluans have stable genomes that evolve slowly in accordance with the principles of random variation and natural selection. But because the Lutikawuluans reproduce asexually, genetic changes in their somatic cells do continue to be expressed through inheritance. The cells, as they divide and change, pass on their adaptations without reservation to the next generation. And so children inherit the alterations in their parents.

As a result, a blacksmith's son is born stronger than other

children, and a clocksmith's daughter is born with better vision and more nimble fingers. These differences, accumulated over thousands of years, slowly add up to the level of speciation. Every occupation has evolved into its own independent species. And even when some occupations have disappeared, the features associated with them continue to be expressed and continue to evolve.

All of these different species are united by their language. It's only through the common tongue and identical numbers of chromosomes that they can recognize themselves as possessing a common origin. Other than these, they have nothing in common. No one is jealous of another's work, just as a monkey would not be jealous of a dinosaur. As the proverb says, *the birds have the sky while the fish have the sea.* They pass by each other in the same town, but it's as if they see each other without seeing each other.

While the Tisu Atians have replayed evolution a hundred million times, they have always refused real evolution. No matter how they alter their own appearance, their children always begin in the same place, keeping the same original, primitive shape. The Lutikawuluans are just the opposite. No individual ever experiences any change, but when seen through the lens of eons, they are each points along numerous diverging curves.

"You lie," you say, pouting. "How can the same universe follow two opposite sets of rules?"

Why not? My dear, there's nothing that's impossible. Numerous steps, each meaningless by itself, when added together become a rule, a principle. Perhaps in this moment you laugh, or frown, and the future is divided into two paths, two sets of rules. But how can you, the you of this moment, know?

"Is that true?" you ask, leaning your head. And for a while you are quiet.

I look at you and laugh lightly. The swing you sit on sways back and forth, and the breeze causes the locks of hair next to your ears to flutter. The key to your question is the method of reproduction, of course, but this kind of answer is too dry. I have no wish to give it.

You know something? The real key isn't about whether what I say is true, but whether you believe it. From start to end, the direction of narrative is not guided by the tongue, but by the ear.

CHINCATO

The tongue and the ear have the most meaning on Chincato. For the people of this planet, speech is not a mere way to pass the time, but a necessity for existence.

There's nothing special about Chincato, save its thick atmosphere. It's so dense that no light can penetrate it, and the surface of the planet is covered by darkness. Chincato's life is born from warm, thick, deep-sea currents, full of organic material and warmed by bubbling lava, and it gains its energy from the heat at the heart of the planet. For the Chincatoans, the boiling crater of the underwater volcano is their sun, the home of the gods, the source of wisdom and strength. Outside the crater, they can find organic sugars, which are their food, the foundation of their life.

The Chincatoans do not have organs that sense light, or eyes. They rely on sound to locate each other. Their ears are both for listening and observing. Actually, to be precise, they don't have ears. They listen with their entire body. The upper halves of their bodies are covered by trapezoidal diaphragms, each of which is strung with thousands of hairs of different lengths, and each of which can resonate with the sound of a particular frequency. Using timing differences between when each trapezoidal diaphragm hears a sound and their positions, the brain of a Chincatoan can deduce the location of the source of the sound, its distance, and even its precise shape.

So, all day long, the Chincatoan talk and listen without pause. They emit sounds to feel the presence of others, and also to let others know of their own existence. They cannot be silent. Silence is dangerous and makes them panic. Only by continuously talking can they ascertain their own position, be sure that they're still alive. They compete with each other to speak louder, because only by doing so can they make themselves appear brighter, more noticeable by others.

Some children are born with defects in their voice organs. These children almost cannot survive. They're always in danger of being run over by others, much bigger and faster. And then no one would even know that such a child once existed.

"That is so sad.Your stories have become shorter and shorter, but why have they also become so much sadder?"

Sad? Is it that the story I'm telling is sad, or is that that the story you're hearing is sad?

"What's the difference?"

Very different. I've been to a planet where the people can make sounds at ten thousand different frequencies, but can only hear a small portion of the frequency range. The sensitivity of their ears is not matched to the versatility of their vocal cords, and so they never hear as much as they can speak. But the most interesting part is that the range of frequencies that each of them can hear is different. While they all think they're hearing the same song, a thousand individuals would actually hear a thousand different songs, but none of them knows that.

"You're making things up again. How can such a place exist?" You bite your lips and widen your eyes. "I'm now suspicious that you haven't been to these planets you've been telling me about. Have you made them all up to amuse me?"

My darling, starting with the Odyssey, *every knight errant has told romances of faraway places to court the ladies they love. Can you tell which stories are real and which are not? I travel through these planets like Marco Polo wandering through the cities of the Orient, like Kubla Khan riding through his endless realm: Everything happens in the blink of an eye. You can say that I really have been to those places, or that I have never left. The planets I speak of are scattered at every corner of the universe, but sometimes collect themselves into the same place, as though they have always been together.*

Hearing this, you giggle. "I understand now. They are gathered together by your stories, and now you tell these stories to me, so they are gathered in my mind. Isn't that right?"

Looking at your happy face, I sigh. The sound is so quiet that you cannot see anything strange in my smile. How can I explain this to you? How do I make you understand? Stories cannot gather anything together, if they're fated to separate.

Yes, I say quietly. *We have been sitting here for an afternoon telling stories, and together, we possess a universe. But these stories are not something I tell you. This afternoon, you and I are both tellers, and both listeners.*

JINJIALIN

Jinjialin is the last story I will tell you today. It's a short tale. I'll be finished soon.

The people of Jinjialin possess bodies unlike the bodies of the people of any other planet. They are like soft balloons, or maybe like jellyfish floating through the air, transparent and loose. The surface of the Jinjialinians is membranous, like a cell's outermost layer. When two membranes touch, they can merge into one.

When two Jinjialinians encounter each other, parts of their bodies briefly merge and mix the materials inside. When they separate, the materials are redistributed. Thus, the people do not care much about their physical bodies. Even they cannot tell how much of their current bodies come from strangers they met along the road. They believe that they are still themselves, and it's no big deal to exchange some materials.

But they don't realize that this sense of "self" is an illusion. At the moment when two of them merge, the two original selves cease to exist. They become a combined person, and, when separated, two new persons. The new persons do not know all that transpired before their encounter and each believes that the self is the self, never having changed at all.

Do you understand? When I am done telling you these stories, when you're done listening to these stories, I am no longer I, and you are no longer you. In this afternoon we briefly merged into one. After this, you will always carry a bit of me and I will always carry a bit of you, even if we both forget this conversation.

"You're saying that Jinjialin is our own world?"

Our own world? Which one? Can any planet have belonged to us? Or can we have belonged to any planet?

Do not ask me about the coordinates of these planets. Those numbers are the oldest mystical proverbs of the universe. They are the air between your fingers. You reach out to grab them, but when you open your hands, there's nothing. You and I and they meet for a moment, and we are fated to again separate. We're only travelers, singing songs whose meanings are obscure, wandering through the dark sky. That is all. You know they are singing in the wind, singing in the wind of a distant homeland.

ON THE LEITMOTIF OF THE TRICKSTER CONSTELLATION IN NORTHERN HEMISPHERIC STAR CHARTS, POST-APOCALYPSE

Nicole Kornher-Stace

The One Who Got Away
Area: 513.842 sq. deg. (appx. 1.29%)
from the Palisade Chart: pine pitch, birch bark
Winter

Seven stars: three major, four minor. Six represent the head, heart, hands and feet of an androgynous child; the seventh, an object gripped in the child's left fist. Regrettably, this object's identity remains a puzzle that has thwarted both the restoration efforts of our team and the scrutiny of every expert in the field: this sector of the chart, including roughly 1/3 of the lower-left quadrant of the One (to say nothing of its neighbor, the Flensed Bride, foxed down to her caption – see fig. 1), is obliterated. A further unhappy consequence of this damage: it is impossible to tell whether the child in question is hugging itself (as children will, against cold or loneliness or fear) or if its wrists are tied.

Any scholar of the charts will forgive me – posthumously, at least – for saying that the trickster constellations prove, time and time again, the *trickiest* to study: whereas the constellations out of history (e.g. the Payload, the Comet, the Exodus, the Pest), those shaped by daily circumstance (the Huntsman, the Pitfall, the Bear), and those obviously conjured by minds seeking to realize them with wish (the Wellspring, the Garden) tend to leave us careful breadcrumb trails to follow, in the form of Songkeepers, journals, and old books, the trickster constellations set us a puzzle on the best of days, an ambush on the worst, and it is utterly in keeping with the trickster's own motif that, at times, even the most meticulous of combings comes up emptyhanded, yielding little but a tag-end or a fragment of a tale – or, in the case of this odd little constellation, nothing.

In default of contextual evidence, the imagination picks at clues, thumb-and-forefinger, as if at a spider in the stewpot, or undetonated ordnance in the path. From this figure's caption we can glean it "got away," but from what? When? And how? Is it a refugee? An escaped prisoner? A ghost?

Of a certainty this was the constellation mothers made offerings to, when their infants' fevers spiked, and the one whose name lost wanderers invoked on lonely roads – but why? Those who threw themselves upon this trickster's questionable mercies did not lead easy lives. Their very bones assure us of this: soft with radiation, pitted with disease. Their toothless skulls give tongue to songs of loss. Was the object of these prayers then to be returned unto oneself, one's place, one's family – or to be spirited away from all of these, propelled headlong into some gentler tale?

If so, this may explain occasional depictions of the One alongside a waterspout or cyclone, natural phenomena which folk belief endows with an almost mystic sense of *quid pro quo*; they were widely thought to serve as conduits or tunnels drawing souls from this plane into another, and those from others into this, thus counterpoising each potential world against the rest.

Similar formations in other charts: the Changeling (Trench Chart, NQ3), Death (Sail Chart, NQ3).

When Archivist Wasp found the bottle on her doorstep, she knew at once the ghosts had left it there, because it smelled of salt. Most of what she found there in the dawn still wore a stink of dirt and ash, from where someone had exhumed it; or of dirt and sweat and cooking, the close smells of a little house, from where someone had sewn or pieced or woven it in the few hours of ashy light each day allotted. A heel of acorn-flour bread, a clutch of stunted onions and a seashell; a scarf knitted of nettle yarn and a pair of horseleather gloves, clumsily stitched and too short in the fingers, but warming as she tugged them on. A bright orange plastic pitcher, clouded with its ancientness and warped with some past heat, which sloshed with rainwater as she dethroned it from its place of honor in the cairn of offerings. The movement dislodged a sharpening-stone and a sort of torque someone had fashioned out of scavengings: empty cartridges and tarnished rings and bits of colored glass flanking a single tiny locket with a blue-and-white enamel windmill on the front. And someone had shored up her sagging doorframe with the same bits of salvage that the rest of the Archivist-hut had been pieced of for as long as Wasp had known. Underneath it all, at the time of the first Archivist, it could have been made of anything.

Fear-gifts, blood-gifts, bribes. Most days she left the lot of it to the snuffling shrine-dogs who prowled her hut to ensure her obedience – first subtracting maybe a few dried apples, maybe a bullet for a gun she may yet find, maybe some corpse's stolen shoes – only to have new cairns rebuilt by eager hands during the night. After all, there was no other sword between the living and the ghosts than her; no other intercessor, no other keeper of the door. She could purge a poltergeist, send the shades of cradle-deaths to quicken fallow wombs, tether a ghost in place with salt to ward a scraggled field against the tithing of the crows. And it was she who gleaned the shards of histories and pieced them, tipped voice like sips of water down the throat of a dead world.

And she'd gladly let the gifts rot down to mulch, and their givers along with them.

But the bottle smelled cold and clean and salt as seas she knew were salt because the ghosts had told her so. The smell on it, and the whitegreen of the glass, put her in mind of licking icicles. Though the icicles she knew were riddled with flaws and streaks of grit, she believed the ghost who'd said the icicles of the Well-Before had frozen clear as windowpanes.

("As what?" Wasp had asked. "Windowpanes," the ghost had repeated. Then, "Crystal," it had offered to her blank look. "Plastic sheeting?" At last she'd understood. In her head – for she possessed neither paper nor the letters to put on it – she'd written *windowpanes*. Written *crystal*. And tipped the ghost out of its jar to go its way.)

She turned the bottle back and forth in the light, watching how the glass warped the roll of paper within. Of course the ghosts had not brought it there, any more than the sea could bring her shells; only that their migrations had disinterred it from wherever it had been concealed and someone had found it, plucked it from the ground as though it might well bite, and brought it to the only person any of them knew who'd bite back harder.

Also odd: the sheet of paper inside the bottle was nothing like the ones she'd seen from time to time on traders' wagons or bound into books in the Songkeeper's hut, burned or drowned or gnawed or sweet with rot. She sat on the rock that was her front step – gingerly, still sore from her last escape attempt, a week ago now by the moon – and studied it, flattened against the tamped-earth path to her hut. The paper unrolled to the length of one of Wasp's long strides and was peppered with as many dots as there were windfalls in an orchard, skulls in a slagpit, or beans in a bowl.

A map, thought Wasp, who had seen such things before. *A map of stars.*

And then she grew very thoughtful, did Wasp with the ache still in her calves from the fleeing, with the rawness still in her lungs and a lattice of welts from the thornfield she had pushed through with the clamor of the hunt right on her heels, with the smell of the shrine-dogs still in her hair from the last time they'd run her down. With the scars on her ankles from the first time the Catchkeep-priest had had to drag her back, spitting and slashing, and smashed her feet between two stones. Sheer dumb luck, perhaps, or force of rage, she'd healed.

The next day, hunting, she packed the saltlick and the fruit and blade and bells as usual, but left her jars behind. She brought the map instead.

Catchkeep
Area: 300.492 sq. deg. (appx. 0.73%)
from the Dogwagon Chart: leather tooling, horsehide
Autumn

Sixteen stars: six major, ten minor, most of the latter representing teeth. This dog's jaw is like a beartrap, too huge for her head, dwarfing even the massive barrel of her chest and the bulging muscles of her thighs. Even today it proves no challenge to see her as the crafters of this chart must have done, the ones who venerated her deeply enough to hold her fellow dogs in such high regard – the pistons of her legs, the forges of her eyes, the fey flux of that awful guileful grin – and in truth it remains almost instinctive in the modern heart to cheer her on each night as she runs the moon to earth behind the hills. But she is Catchkeep, ghostherder and sentinel, constant as the stars that shape her nightly steeplechase; and when the lot of us is done to dust, she will not miss our rallying.

Of all this trickster's stories – "Catchkeep Chases the Comet's Tail," "Catchkeep's Biting Contest with Grandmother Shark," etc. – the one that comes to us the most well-preserved by far is "Catchkeep's Bequest," wherein a few short paragraphs (or, more pertinent to the experience of its original audience, a few minutes' telling) find that inimitable bitch whelping the First Litter, passing the Earth itself as afterbirth, then fashioning the world's first people out of dogs' skeletons rearranged to stand upright, inadvertently killing many when she tries to scruff those who dare disobey. It ends with Catchkeep commandeering the first makeshift vehicle of these people, who grew foolhardy or daft enough to try to tame her, and in so doing forming her sister constellation, the Empty Wagon (NQ3, fig. 2) – possibly a glorification of that people's own wagons, constructed of rusted-out automobile chassis welded to whatever scaffolding and stretched with whatever rotten fabric or brittle leather was to hand?

"The lot of you," said Catchkeep, "can go screw." And she took their wagon and drove it hard across the hills until all the dogs fell down dead in their traces, glowing bright as arclights through the ash. Then she lifted each of them in her great jaws and tossed them up into the sky, gently as a bitch tumbling pups, and they dug in their footholds on the dark and paced their circles and curled up to sleep the sleep of stars.

What she is perhaps best known as, however, is a herder of spirits: both those of the dead and the unborn. In this aspect she earns the fear of the diseased, the chased, and the condemned, whose souls it is her charge to bear away; also the veneration of the fallow-wombed, whose custom it was to set out the choicest bits of meat after their evening meal, in hopes of luring Catchkeep to the door.

Her former, baneful aspect is illustrated in a scrap of doggerel, perhaps a fraction of a larger piece of verse, found scrawled on a

bit of scorch-edged paper rolled into a tube and tied off with a
string, worn in a horsehide pouch as a crude little talisman against
her inexorable teeth:

> *Catchkeep* [illegible], *running free,*
> *Herding the souls out over the trees:*
> *Cold ghosts you are. Till ghost I be,*
> *You have no power over me.*

Similar formations in other charts: the Lurcher (Hothouse
Chart, NQ4), the Hunt (Pennon Chart, NQ4).

She turned the first four away with her blessing, for they were
faceless, the height of her knees, and moved vaguely, as if underwater – but the fifth ghost Wasp saw up on the lightning-blasted
ledge of Execution Hill was a tall one, easily a head higher than
herself, and there was something about it that caught her eye. Not
exactly awareness, never that; but a sort of daunted yearning that
it broadcast, which she understood too well.

Before she put out the saltlick, she sat her heels a moment to
watch it. It fascinated her, the way the ghosts moved, pacing their
confines like tethered dogs, sounding their boundaries, back and
forth. She saw much of herself in them, so she never watched for
long.

This particular ghost was walking down a corridor she could
not see, turning invisible doorknobs. Its mouth moved, shaping
the same word again and again, but no sound came out. A name,
Wasp thought. It could have been anyone's. A lover's, a child's, a
friend's. Wasp's mouth twisted: scorn or envy.

She wondered what had done it in, this restive ghost. If she
waited long enough she would probably get her answer, but she'd
lost her stomach for that long ago.

Hurriedly she laid the saltlick out and the ghost nosed forward,
browsing at the air.

She never knew quite why the saltlick worked. Never quite
cared. Another fragment of the ritual, she figured, another step in
the dance of call-and-response that kept her here – not exactly
like the ghosts, for no Archivist trapped *her* in jars for questioning, and not exactly unlike them, for her path was prescribed in

lines as clearly-drawn as any one of theirs. The saltlick worked, the Songkeepers said, because it put the ghosts in mind of the flesh they used to wear. The salt of sweat, of tears, of blood. It drew them. It made them remember. But there was no Archivist to lay a trail of salt for Wasp. Her rescue, or else her entrapment, was her own.

The ghost reached the saltlick and began to feed.

She gave it a moment.

"I am the Archivist," Wasp said, when the ghost had slowed. She gagged against the cloy of rote, but spat it anyway. "Catchkeep's emissary, ambassador, and avatar on earth. Her bones and stars my flesh; my flesh and bones her stars. I greet you."

The ghost looked up at her. This part used to frighten her a little: the sea change in the ghosts' eyes as the salt waylaid them, clogged their feet with the memory of clay. The look they'd wear, as though waking from a dream and seeing something wholly frightening which Wasp could not. It had not taken her long to learn that they were only seeing her.

She set the rolled map on the ground and toed it toward the ghost, who for its part was not cowering as most did but instead had drawn itself up to its full height and was peering down its nose at her as at a turd in the path it would have to step around.

Wasp hid her smile. She'd been lucky. She'd gone out to Execution Hill expecting to keep coming back a week, a month, before she'd found one quite like this. This was the sort of ghost that had retained or salvaged enough of itself to be searching for something, or someone, or somewhere, and the draw of it was stronger even than the salt. This one sought a *someone*, she was sure, and from the look of it, the days it'd lived out were long past. Then it was looking for a ghost. And it wouldn't find it on its own.

She hoped it was smart enough, or dumb enough, to bargain with.

"You're seeking," she said. The other ghosts walked or flew or fell through their last moments to all sides of her, oblivious, but this one, *this one* heard. It eyed that map the way a half-starved dog eyes carrion, and she held it up at arm's-length, keeping the salt between them; the ghost lunged and came up short, collared by the empty air. "Well. So am I."

The Cinder Girl
Area: 1119.303 sq. deg. (appx. 2.71%)
from the Sinkhole Chart: razor scarring, human skin
Autumn

Twenty-three stars: eight major, fifteen minor, including neither the visual binary blue supergiant representing her heart nor the nebula colloquially known as the Spool; while this latter's representation remains the subject of some debate, it is generally agreed to be *either* the Girl's navel or her womb. (If one can use *agreed* in fairness, conjuring as it does more a smiling accord over a glass of fine vintage than the panting stalemate reached by brawlers, each having succumbed less to his rival's blows than to his own growing lassitude.)

On some charts this constellation shares two major and one minor star with the Carrion Boy, whereas on others the Girl and Boy only border upon points (e.g. the Blood Quilt Chart, which depicts them handfast, or the Floodplain Chart, which shows them going at each other's throats with shivs).

The Lintel Chart (fig. 3) marks one striking departure: the two constellations are drawn together into one, torso to torso, while the stars designated elsewhere as the base of the Cinder Girl's childbed-pyre, her right knee, and the Carrion Boy's attendant crow are here shown to represent offerings – water, bullets, seed-fruit – heaped by persons unknown at their feet. The overall effect is that of a two-headed, four-armed monster god: arguably an attempt, in the spirit of the origin stories of the Well-Before, to explain away cases of severe mutation.

Apparently a light- or fire-bringer, the Cinder Girl was – and in some few rough backwaters of the Waste-that-was, still is – called upon, with that wayworn trinity of incantation, song, and sacrifice, to conjure out the sun from where it floundered in its yearlong skirts of ash. In fact, whatever demarcating line is sketched in between sun and Girl is vague; most indications hint there's no line there at all: she either *is* the sun, or else is swollen with it, as any mother is with any child.

Consider then this chart: carved into the flesh, from soles to brow, of a girl of childbearing age – more: one who has recently *borne* a child – but with interruptions in the chart over the girl's heart and abdomen, wherein are illustrated the binary blue supergiant called the Beartrap (see above) and the Spool Nebula, respectively. These breaks in the chart demonstrate a level of artistry ratcheted up several notches from that shown in the execution of its remainder, and the entirety of the scarring was performed very shortly before the death of its recipient via living interment in the ash.

The suggestion of apotheosis is not a subtle one. Pared down to its particulars, what we have in the Sinkhole Chart is a pair of extraordinarily well-preserved corpses – those of the abovementioned girl and her infant – the former being illustrated with both the hallmarks of the constellation whose avatar she likely is and the chart in which that constellation may be found, the latter (we are given to conjecture) as a stand-in for the sun the Cinder Girl gives birth to, and which is her death by immolation. (It remains also a matter of supposition that the ash burial edged out the conflagration in the affections of this girl's acolyte-executioners simply because they wished the chart to be preserved.)

The observant eye will glean hints toward this circuit of ritual human sacrifice – for crops, for rain, for the fertility of barren wombs – from the story cycles "Bones and Coins," "A Greener Grave," and "Cinder Girl Tricks the Honey Thief."

Similar formations in other charts: the Bonewitch (Palimpsest Chart, NQ2), the Chooser (Fallows Chart, NQ2), the Queen (White Chart, NQ2).

By that evening, Wasp had learned her letters. The next day she could spell her name.

"Wasp," the ghost sneered, chafing at its leash of salt. "What sort of name is that supposed to be?"

"The one I was given," she answered placidly. Wasp could understand the ghost's frustration: it wasn't like it had come all this way up from the world Below just to teach a teenage girl to read. Still, a bargain was a bargain. And she was turning out to be a fast learner. "Because I was a fool and I let them make me fight for the privilege of being Archivist." She told it about the night that she was chosen out of all the novices and made to challenge the current Archivist for her place. All that training, all that bloodshed, just to be deemed strong enough, cutthroat and holy enough, to wring ghosts free of stories and with them piece the story of the world before.

As she spoke she rubbed the ridged scar on her neck, shades paler, pinker than her skin, where the then-Archivist had drawn first blood. Wasp hadn't been expected to get up from it. She smiled, remembering.

"After that they called me Wasp. Because I'd poisoned my blade and I stabbed her full of holes with it."

"How fierce," the ghost said, mocking. "How proud. All the thwarted dignity of a whipped dog. Have you ever seen a wasp? A live one?"

She had not.

"Nuisances," the ghost said. "You'd like them. They can do nothing else but sting."

(*You daft bitch*, the Catchkeep-priest said in Wasp's memory. *You malapert. Why do we keep you? You're no solace to anyone. You couldn't unpuzzle a snarl in your hair.*)

(*You keep me*, Wasp had replied, *because none of you can kill me.*)

Wasp gritted her teeth. Bent her head back to the map. Read *spool*. Read *blue*. Read *trap*. And dreamed of the constellation the Catchkeep-priest's blood would make upon his clammy robes.

The Carrion Boy
Area: 487.012 sq. deg. (appx. 1.19%)
from the Brainpan Chart: scrimshaw, whalebone
Summer

Ten stars: four major, six minor, and a further two to designate the eye and tail of the attendant crow toward which he is discovered making full-body placatory gestures. A random selection of charts lists the crow as either the Boy's sidekick (the Holly Chart), his anima (the Chalk Hills Chart), his nemesis (the Gatekeeper Chart), or virtually anything between (both the Riot Shield and Blast Charts – fig. 4 – provide striking deviations). Even the Boy's posture of deference, which renders this constellation unmistakable in any sky – balanced on one foot, head down, arms up and out, hands open, palms heavy with offerings or bribes – is variously interpreted, beyond its face value, as either a game, a gambit, or a trap.

More curiously still, six of this constellation's stars belong to binary systems (two visual, one eclipsing), and as the stars shift back and forth by virtue of their mutual orbits, they completely change the shape this constellation describes upon the earth-bound viewer's sky: slowly the crow's wings shift to become the boy's, and the crow vanishes altogether.

Setting aside the sheer technical achievement that this chart represents – albeit carved, one suspects, with a blade not much at ease in service to the arts, still it covers, in nearly microscopic detail, the entire frontal bone plate of the skull of a juvenile male *Orcinus orca*, incidentally providing an embarrassingly large component of the bone record of a splendid creature long-extinct – it appears to have served as, or been associated with, an object of some ritual significance. The skull itself was found interred in ash, alongside the corpse of a young man staked down, apparently alive, to a stretch of barren, heavily irradiated slag.

However, unlike what the host-canvas of the Sinkhole Chart (see above) experienced, this was no ash burial: what covered this chart and its – what? Ancillary? Chaperone? – was that which the winds had drifted in. One particularly intriguing aspect of this find was the presence of nine pairs of crows' wings, affixed between the stakes and their victim's flesh at wrists, elbows, knees, ankles, and neck, presumably to buoy up his manumitted soul to whatever fairer skies awaited it. Another was the assorted heap of limbs that lay atop the corpse: some crudely hacked, some removed with surgical precision, but all well-muscled and apparently quite healthy up until the very moment of subtraction.

No more colorful, perhaps, than the traditions upheld in the veneration of any of these tricksters, although quite probably more grotesque, and considerably more infamous, is the custom in the cult of the Carrion Boy toward ritual self-mutilation.

As always it is difficult to ascertain whether it was the custom that shaped the way of life of its practitioners, or the way of life that shaped the custom; puzzlingly, some few seem to spring up like daisies on a slag-spit, self-engendered and unreasoning. This is one of those.

Owing most probably to the striking lack of sheltering features in the landscape where these people chose to settle, a large fraction of their cultural experience was warfare: preparation, avoidance, aftermath, glorification. Upon reaching physical maturity, all young men and women (with the exception of those

pregnant, nursing, or convalescent) entered into a combat training regimen that only the most charitable would term rigorous. At
the culmination of the training, those whose lives it had not
claimed were made to choose a part of their own bodies for dedication to the Carrion Boy in a ritual taking place under that
constellation's ascendancy. The most common form this dedication took was amputation, but simple mangling of the flesh was
also widely used. All these gentle ministrations were performed
with the aid of song ("Carrion Boy Feeds the Crows" was a
particular favorite) and vast quantities of scorchweed wine.

One would soon have little doubt whether one's offering was
deemed acceptable to the Boy: accounts still survive of bodies
found turned literally inside out, bodies found tied literally into
knots, bodies hanged from points quite inaccessible to human
agency (see fig. 5 for artist's interpretation).

Similar formations in other charts: the Scapegoat (Stairwell
Chart, NQ2), the Juggler (Flotsam Chart, NQ2).

The slow burn of autumn congealed into winter, the edges of the
map grew sticky with apple-juice and the dirt from underneath
Wasp's bitten nails, and the ghost was getting restless. "This is not
a map to walk by, idiot," it told her, standing by in silence as she
lay out the saltlick and the apples and the little dish of blood. As
she crammed ghosts into jars and took them back to the hut where
she paced the tiny room of it nightlong, four paces by four, and
questioned them. Each with its story of a long drop on a short
rope, or a fall down the stairs, or a half-dozen bullets sinking
themselves, wet as kisses, in its erstwhile flesh. Or of a strange
deep sick-smelling sleep, stalked by the dreams of dreams. Or
nothing. "Or can you fly now? It will lead you nowhere."

Wasp said nothing. Not when the ghost berated her, not when
the snow caved her roof in, not when she neglected her duties at
the shrine and the dogs caught her at it and went to fetch the
Catchkeep-priest, and the Catchkeep-priest came to lash her raw
and lick the blood away. Blasphemy, for she was Catchkeep's
puppet, her blood the blood of stars. Even as the priest hissed his
wet breath down her neck the dogs were tonguing up that holy
blood from the floor where it had spattered. Half-dazed with pain
and rage, she thought she saw one lift its head and smirk.

She could feel Catchkeep rising up in her, all teeth. Wasp steeled her mind and shoved her down. She'd free *herself*.

"I had to lie," she told the ghost. "I thought I needed you to teach me how to read the map. So I could. So I." Something tightened in her throat and she ground down on it hard. "But it's just junk. A relic for the idiot Songkeepers. A few seconds of heat." And she tossed it on the fire. "There's nothing past here," she said, eyes averted. "Only more."

One evening she caught the ghost scratching at her door like a cat. She recalled how she had first seen it, walking down a hall she could not see, turning doorknobs. Even as she watched, it began to pace that hall again, two steps from her own door to the wall of the hut, then straight out through the wall. Sticking her head outside, she could count out twelve more paces in the snow before the ghost slammed into empty air at the end of its tether like a bird into a window. When its circuit snapped it back, the snow where it had walked was left unmarked by any prints. Until she fell asleep she watched it pace out through the wall into the snow and be returned, one arm outstretched, one hand rattling at locks that were not there.

Where the last light hit the ghost, it shone straight through.

The Bonesetter
Area: 442.122 sq. deg. (appx. 1.07%)
from the Railway Station Chart: spray paint, red brick
Spring

Thirteen stars: four major, nine minor, and barely visible through its pall of ash (best seen, in fact, in a wind too foul to allow for comfortable viewing: it scuds the cover sideways off the stars, like prying up a scab).

This constellation is a strange one. Crouched low on the horizon, hulking and spidery at once, it tiptoes hunchbacked through the fallen cities, downbent as though searching, by which it earns itself the alternate appellation Ragpicker (the best extant example being found in the Lighthouse Chart, fig. 6); sinister yet oddly delicate, its stars are among the last to prick the darkling sky, among the first to be annihilated by the coming of the sun.

As is also the case with the One Who Got Away (see above), few clues survive regarding the figure behind this constellation.

Unique to it, however, is that whatever evidence might have remained seems to have undergone systematic eradication, for reasons only guessed at, by people of whom nothing is known save their creation of the chart via which this constellation reaches our notice.

As always, uncertainty is hypothesis's breeding-ground: here the theorists swarm like flies to carrion, all too eager to spawn fresh execrations upon the heretofore unsullied lap of scholarly intent. They hold that this evidence was destroyed out of pure fear of the Bonesetter's return to earth out of the sky, where up until that point he had been chained, like many a chastised fellow-trickster from the stories of the Well-Before, by the very stars that outline him to mortal eyes.

They also hold that it is from this trickster that we get the songs "Marryings and Buryings" and "Scavengers' Circus," as well as the expression "a bonesetter's gambit," still in use today to describe apparently anything from anodyne to idiocy. But as the vast majority of these theories share an irritating tendency to go out on a limb and then saw it off behind them, all we can rely upon with any certainty is the chart itself; and, tricksterish in its own way, its lips are sealed.

Similar formations in other charts: the Ragpicker (Mural Chart, NQ1).

When the salt had worn it to translucence and a faint smell of copper, the ghost finally began to talk, though it told her nothing she did not already know. She'd netted enough ghosts by that point, left enough of them huddled in their terror on her shelf and telling each other tales of elsewhere to keep their longing for escape alive, to know just what it was about the map that drew it. Listening to it now she could almost see the pale ghost-roads that linked the stars; could almost see it walking them, both feet freed, heart light, and not alone.

She wondered after the other ghost, the one it sought. Had Wasp salted that ghost, caught it, crammed it in a jar, reeled its memories out hand over hand, and dumped it out amid the scorchweed and windfalls to wend its way back to its wandering? Or had it gone on, the way the tales said that they could go on, and left Wasp's captive ghost behind? Even if she freed this ghost now, would it go on chasing the other as a dog chases its tail, or the sun the moon: reaching always, all unreached?

At least it has something important to search for, she thought. *All I can think of to look for is a way out.*

Wasp blinked. For a fraction of a second she had seen something like a dream. In it, a daisy-chain of Archivists went back and back and back, an ancient hut their jar, their holiness shackling them as sure as salt. She had forgotten what it was she sought before she only sought escape. If she'd sought anything at all.

The daisy-chain could knot her up into it and continue on. Or she could end it here.

Before she knew what she was doing, the knife was in her fist. She crossed the tiny room to where the ghost sat slumped. Kicked the salt clear from its feet. Held out her hand.

It trusted neither her grin nor the glint in her eyes, but got up all the same.

The Archivist
Area: 65.002 sq. deg. (appx. 0.16%)
from the Ragtree Chart: plant-based pigment, human skin
Winter

Four stars, all minor: hardly enough to reasonably discern the image of what this tiny grouping is meant to represent; namely, a woman with a knife in one hand and a sort of scroll in the other, frozen in the act of stepping forward.

This trickster's status as culture-hero is provisional – her motives are dubious, her intentions suspect, the queues to her shrines no longer than the trails of corpses that rattle along in her wake through a half-dozen tales – but persistently widespread.

What makes it particularly strange is that she seems to have played culture-hero *to the very spirits of the deceased.*

If this woman truly was, as a fairly large body of conjecture suggests, one of the Archivists, the historian-priestesses of the bitch-god Catchkeep (see above), she would have been an extremely capable fighter, trained since early childhood to single combat and little else; and it is true her skybound avatar does hold her knife point-out, in brawling stance, against the vacuum of space.

But why the scroll? These priestesses are well known to us for their striking methodology, half clever, half quaint: while the quantities of information they gleaned from their informant ghosts was massive, nothing was committed to paper, for paper had they none. It is a reasonable supposition that to a one they were in fact illiterate. So this constellation, gazing blankly out at us from a face it does not have, begs the question – why should the ghosts have borne this woman any loyalty at all? Had she gone turncoat? Shirked her bound and holy duty to enslave them? Flouted Catchkeep's law?

The only clue we have can be found in a strange fragmented text discovered with the Ragtree Chart, interred beneath that tree itself. (The tree in question is a crab apple, and a curious one. Thrice the size it ought to be, at one point it appears to have grown up through a sort of hut, its footprint approximately four paces by four, constructed of automobile parts and leather and stones: most of the leather is long gone, but the framework that once supported it, in minor part, remains.)

The text itself is in grievous disrepair, scrawled on a few palm-sized fragments of scorched paper crushed into a glass bottle of palest green. Interestingly, it appears to have been penned by two different hands: first in a dire penmanship, blocky and childish, which peters out as though in great exhaustion midway through; the writing that continues after, while legible and even flowing, gives the observer the unmistakable impression that its scribe was able to maintain only through great concentration only the most tenuous grasp on his writing implement (which appears to have been a pin or needle dipped in blood) – as though he, or it, were made mostly of air.

If we are reading the text in its proper order, it tells us how an Archivist of Catchkeep, name of Wasp, in a total upheaval of all of the ritual structures of Catchkeep's worship, challenged her keeper/overseer in single combat and bested him. Gravely wounded, she used the last of her strength to free all of the dead man's captive ghosts and destroy every last one of the Archivist tools (see fig. 7 for a replica of a typical field kit) by which those ghosts and others had been hunted and enslaved.

It is not known what became of her – whether she died in her blood on the dirt floor of the priest of Catchkeep's house or else somehow healed her wounds and went on to become the sort of patron saint for ghosts the evidence suggests.

In the end, every wildly disparate theory sinks its roots in the same pot: the proto-tale rather uninspiredly entitled "Archivist Wasp Frees the Ghosts." Wherein, after destroying Catchkeep's priest and all his tools, our mortally wounded heroine conjures Catchkeep herself down out of the sky and tricks the dog-god into suffering the newly-released ghosts to climb up upon Her back. From there they are borne, clinging on like barnacles, aloft into the night. Meantime, our retired Archivist and a single anonymous ghost (though some sources insist that there were two) remain to see that none are left behind, vowing to rejoin the others when their work on earth is done.

And if they're not there yet, as every version of the story always ends, *they are here still.*

VALENTINES

Shira Lipkin

1.

The waiter's name is Valentine. He has long, slim fingers, and he writes down my order instead of pretending to commit it to memory. I like that, his pen on the paper bringing forth one simple thing about me. My lunch. Just a tiny fragment of information. I honor him by doing the same. "The waiter's name is Valentine," I write in my battered notebook, "and he has long, slim fingers."

Information is sacred. I don't remember why, or who told me. But I know that information is sacred, so I write it down, scraps of knowledge and observations. I used to write in leatherbound journals with elegant heavy pens, but the fetish for elegance has fallen by the wayside in my rush to commit everything to paper. Now I use cheap marbled composition books, purchased by the dozen. The pen is still important, though. It must write in smooth lines of black, not catch on the page. There is too much to capture.

I order chai tea and butternut squash soup. I write that down as well, just after Valentine does. I watch him walk to the kitchen, slender and graceful, and I wonder what Valentine does when he is not refilling coffee mugs. I wonder if he dances. I write that down: "Perhaps Valentine dances." I watch him flirt with the barista, their movements around each other a careful ballet of hot espresso and soup and witty banter, and I curl up in my armchair and wrap my hands around the mug of tea when Valentine brings it to me with his usual smile and nod. I observe. I record.

I write on the bus, on my way home. I write about the bus driver, and about the woman sitting across from me, wearing a too-heavy jacket ("perhaps she is sick"). I write about the barista and the patterns of her movement around the large copper espresso machine, the way she admires her reflection. When I get home, I carefully tear the pages from my notebook, and I tear fact from fact, isolating each bit of information, and I file them accordingly in the rows of small boxes nailed to my walls. Miniature pigeon coops filled with paper instead of birds. Facts. Ways to build the world. I copy things over when necessary, when I must file "perhaps Valentine dances" under both Valentine and Speculation. I must separate speculation, after all. My shreds and fragments of information comprise my image of Valentine (for example). I cannot allow speculation to color that. I can allow his grace, but not the possibility of his dancing.

With enough data, maybe I can figure out the world.

2.

The waiter's name is Val. His hands are stained a burnished yellow from nicotine, and are guitar-callused. He is bored and impatient, waiting for his shift to end. He does not write down my order – which is fair because it's just coffee and blackberry pie, and the pie is right at hand. He slices it and slaps it on the plate; it falls over just a bit, slides, and blackberry oozes out onto the plain white plate, the color almost shocking. I write that down, and the way the steam dances over the coffee mug. The mug is smooth and unadorned, the same bone-white, and the coffee is rich and dark and bitter. The diner is a diner, no more and no less, retro-50s tube with aproned waitresses and meat loaf and pie and Val, leaning forward by the register, staring at the door. Waiting for something else.

He talks to me. I think out of sheer boredom – I'm the only customer at the bar, the only person here alone. His dark hair is frosted blond at the ends, and his eyes are seaglass-blue. He is in a band, but he worries that now that the guys have day jobs, they'll stop playing music. He doesn't think he's good enough to go solo. He shrugs a lot – he has developed his own fake-casual rolling shrug, a silent "whatever". He asks why I care, and I tell him that these are the things that make him *him*. That we are collections of information. We are what we are because our dog died or our dad left or we won the lottery or whatever. And I like to figure out what people are by examining what they're made of.

When I close my eyes, I imagine Val made of paper, all the little strips of paper I'll file later under "music" and "loss" and "resentment," cross-reference him with others, see if I can figure out "loss."

See if I can figure out data loss.

When I open my eyes, Val has gone on to the next customer. I eat my pie and write.

3.

The waiter's name is V. It's a new restaurant, sci-fi themed; all of the waiters have names like Klaatu or Ripley. I point out that *V* is a series, not a character, and he laughs. "No one remembers character names from *V*. But everyone remembers the show. Everyone remembers the lizards."

He writes down my order, and I write down that everyone remembers *V*. I will file it under "television" and "things everyone remembers". "Things everyone remembers" is one of my bigger boxes; it is not nearly full. Not nearly as full as it needs to be.

Data loss. I do not remember the things everyone remembers. And I need to. In order to build a self, I need a foundation. So I write everything down, and I am always hoping that someone will let slip one of the things "everyone knows" or "everyone remembers." *V* and the Challenger explosion and 9/11 and the Smurfs. Sometimes when I get home, after I file the day's newly gathered information, I take the slips out of that box and spread them out on the floor to subcategorize them. Everybody knows this about politics. Everyone remembers that song.

My food arrives, a faux-Klingon dish I've already forgotten the name of. I must look it up later and record it. The drink V brings is not what I ordered – it's a neon-blue thing in a Klein bottle with dry ice fuming out of it. V grins and drapes himself over the chair beside me. "You looked like you could use it."

"What is it?"

"Dunno. Try some."

"I have . . . trouble. With things I don't know."

V looks around; seeing no manager, he takes a quick sip from my glass. "Perfectly safe."

I sip. It's sweet. V grins as I lower the glass. His hair is frosted silver, and I wonder if he's dyed it, or if he sprays it on every night. His hands seem to have a mind of their own; he gestures incessantly when he talks. Italian, he says, with a shrug very unlike Val's. I write that down: "Italians talk with their hands," and also, "V is Italian."

He has to get up eventually, as the restaurant gets busy. He brings me a spoon for dessert, with a wink like Valentine's.

1.

Valentine writes my order down with a flourish and gives me a wink like V's. I study him – none of his other mannerisms remind me of V. He does not talk with his hands. He is not flashy or flamboyant. His hands, unlike Val's, do not have guitar calluses; if Valentine plays anything it's a wind instrument, or maybe a violin.

This is speculation. I cannot allow speculation.

I study my own hands. They shake slightly, and I wonder if I ever played anything; if so, that data is lost. I should search my apartment. It has been too long since I've done anything there but file and sleep.

Valentine presents my chai with a smile. "Valentine," I ask, halting him in his graceful spin kitchenwards, "do I always order the same thing?"

"In the fall, yeah." He sits down beside me in a way not entirely unlike V's draping or Val's slouch. "Other soups, the rest of the year. But always chai and soup."

"Then why do you write it down?"

"Because you like it." I must look as puzzled as I feel, because he shrugs (unlike Val, like V) and continues. "You told me once that you don't see how anyone can hold that in their heads, not really. Things fade. I might forget what kind of tea, what kind of soup."

I stretch my hand, aching from holding the pen. "I think I forget."

2.

Val pours the coffee, thick plume of steam from the stream of dark liquid, the battered pot. "Do I always get the same thing?"

Val gives his rolling shrug. "Coffee, keep it comin'. Pie. Yeah, you do."

I write that down: "I always order the same thing."

I don't know how to file that. "My brain." That box is overflowing. I need to find a way to subcategorize it. I can't figure it out.

I ask Val if he's Italian. He's not. Mostly Norwegian, he says. I study him all shift for things that correlate with Valentine and with V. He notices, but ignores it.

I write. Everything. The clumping of the salt in its shaker. The reflection of sunlight on the silver edge of the clock. Val and the waitress, Thalia – she looks like the barista.

Everyone looks like everyone else these days. It feels like my world is compressing. I have to write more, write faster. I have to make sense of things.

3.

I don't remember entering the restaurant, but V is already sprawled across from me. He asks if I'm okay, and I tell him honestly that I don't know. I ask if he's in love with a waitress, and he laughs, says no, gestures at a waiter in Jedi robes. I tell him what I'm slowly, falteringly, worrying about: that all of them are the same person. He tells me all the ways he's different, but I find some things the same.

(A)

They all have a younger brother. They all had a dog, growing up. They are all waiters.

1.

I am so tired. Valentine brings me a chai without my asking, and he asks if I'm okay, and I tell him honestly that I don't know. He asks me when I last saw my doctor.

I say, "Doctor?"

He takes my hand and notices its tremor. He asks if he can walk me home.

4.

I am shy. I have never let anyone in.

Valentine enters, and his eyes widen at the sight of all of the little boxes lining the walls, perched on shelves, the bits of things everybody knows spread over the floor. "What is this?"

"Information," I whisper. "I – have chunks missing. Parts of the world I can't figure out. And I think – I think that bits of other worlds are melting in to cover the gaps. I think that maybe all Valentines are the same Valentine. I think the universe or the multiverse or whatever has this stopgap for data loss, and I think the human brain does pattern-patching on a subconscious level – finding the things that match you and filling holes with them. Do you think that's what happens?" And I pray for an "everybody knows," but he gives me something else.

He had been on duty when I had the seizure. He watched my body arc back; he called 911. Probably saved my life. The doctor told him I might lose some memory.

I lost more than that.

I lost swathes of long-term memory, the things everybody knew, the things I knew. I stopped being able to get all of my short-term memory into long-term. I started having trouble conceptualizing things.

I started writing. Data retrieval. Trying to make sense of the world.

I don't remember. I don't remember any of it. But Valentine so clearly does. And he is right there, holding my gaze and holding my hand, and the earth begins to tremble—

He tries to pull me to the doorway, but I refuse – I stand in the middle of the room and the whole building starts to shake, and I watch a year of carefully gathered and filed slips of information explode from the walls and shower around me like a snow globe, all of the fact and the speculation, all of the ways to learn people and make things make sense, all falling around me like ash, and I have a sort of hitching sob in my chest as I drop to my knees as the room settles, and he is there. V. Val. Valentine. His hair flashes silver, flashes blond, settles to dark, and his hands resolve from callused to slim, and he is folded back into himself; all Valentines are one Valentine. And I look up at him helplessly, all of my data scattered, and I ask: "Do you dance?"

DANCING IN THE SHADOW OF THE ONCE

Rochita Loenen-Ruiz

They came with their big ships, riding through the rifts in the Veil that protected the Once-country. We could not say if it was capture or salvation that came to us. They, who we called Compassionate, came for us and took us from the devastation left behind. Of the great number that was the Once-tribe, there were only a handful of us left. We watched as the world we knew and loved vanished in the chaos created by the rifts. And as we departed the Once-country, we wondered if we would ever see it again.

—*From Artifact Hala's account,*
Chaos and the Once-Country—

Hala's joints creaked as she unfolded herself from the regeneration egg. She paused and waited for her augmentations to adjust before moving again. Consciousness thrummed through her, a constant susurrus of memories through which she could sift and select when it was time for her to stand before her audience.

A visit to Ay-wan was in order, she thought. Hala's inner self was always comfortably chaotic, always thrumming with the reminder of what she was, but there was something about the chaos that disturbed her now.

Ay-wan would know what to do. If there was anyone who would pinpoint an error in her augmentations, it would be him.

She pondered Ay-wan briefly. When she'd arrived on Silhouette, he had been among the first to greet her. He had been old already, the lines of his face telling a story of grief and joy and inevitable sorrow.

"They've assigned you to my care," he'd said. And he'd taken

good care of her all throughout the augmentations, the installation of her arrays, and the surgical procedures that the
Compassionate deemed necessary.

They'd sent him to the shapers for a complete rejuvenation
five years ago, and now the skin of his face was stretched tighter
than the skin of a drum. It was eerie to see him looking that way
– not young, not old, more like a construct.

Her body signaled its readiness for movement. With a sigh, she
swung free of the egg and walked towards the mirror. They'd
added more transmitters to her array in this most recent surgery,
and she was thankful that they'd chosen to set the connectors
close to where her hairline ended. It was less unsightly this way
and it allowed her the temporary illusion of ordinariness.

"Old," she thought as she stared at her reflection. Her hair,
once compared to midnight by the young men of her tribe, still
shone; but there were silver tendrils among the black and it was
impossible to hide the crinkles at the side of her eyes.

"So what," she said to the mirror. "Age is a badge we wear with
honor."

In the old days, the Munhawe came into the fullness of their
power in their elder years. The patient growing into wisdom, the
waiting and the watching as the years passed, smoothing down
the sharp-edged impatience that was youth – all these necessary
things took time.

But with the Once-country fallen into chaos, and with the
Compassionate dominating the worlds where the remnant of the
Once-tribe were allowed succor, there wasn't really any need to
consider anything more than the roles that had been assigned to
the remnant.

She hadn't had the luxury of time to grow into the fullness of
her power. Instead, the Compassionate representative had her
fitted with tiny little machines that crawled around inside her
body, and an array of receivers and transmitters so she could tap
into that source from which the Munhawe drew their wisdoms,
their dreams, their prophecies, their healings and the skill to carry
the weight of history and legend.

Artifact.

That was the title they gave her along with the rest of those
who had been rescued. They had all been tested and fitted with

whatever augmentations the Compassionate saw fit to grant them, and then sent out to various worlds under the protection of Compassionate attachés.

In the beginning, she'd wanted to know where the others had been sent. But the attaché had looked at her with his cold blue eyes and told her that she should be honored to be selected as Artifact representative on Silhouette.

She'd accepted the reprimand, but she still missed her friends and wondered what had happened to the others.

She pressed her lips together and walked towards the console that projected her daily schedules. She was to appear at a benefit tonight. Funds were being raised for refugees located in various Once-worlds. She brushed away her nostalgia and her longing and tried to flow into the role that had been impressed on her.

No matter how hard she tried, no matter how much she reasoned with herself, she couldn't help but feel that she was nothing more than a museum exhibit trotted out for display every now and then. A trophy belonging to the Empire, a being that should have long ago been declared obsolete, but by some miracle still walked and talked, told stories and conjured visions of a place that might just as well be nothing more than a fairytale.

She folded her hands together in the proper form and moved from her bedroom. Her implants whispered loudly of memory, but she ignored them for now. They would quiet down as the day progressed and hopefully she would reach the state of calm that she needed each time she had to stand before a crowd.

Her stomach grumbled. Augmented or not, she was human and her body still desired food.

"So good of you to be here," the organizer of the 19:00 hour event gushed at her. "So many entry chips sold. There's bound to be a good audience. You'll want the dressing room first, I suppose?"

She had difficulty concentrating on the organizer's faces. Four on one, she thought. And she had a silly vision of bears piled up on top of each other as they strove to maintain balance on a one-wheeler, or wait, was it a two-wheeler? The memory did not belong to the history vaults of the Once-tribe, and it slipped through her fingers quicker than she could say fish.

It's not the Once-tribe's story all the time, she thought. *Artifact, I may be, but it doesn't mean I can't have memories of my own.*

She nodded and smiled as the organizers rushed her off in a flurry of nervous gasps, fluttering fingers and repeated bowing.

The dressing room was bigger than her living room. A long line of mirrors fitted with muted lights greeted her. Enhancers were plugged into the sockets – all on standby. Perhaps there was another performance after hers?

She sat down at one of the tables and unpacked the satchel she'd brought. The long length of woven cloth shone at her. Red and white threaded through with yellow, green, purple and black – the traditional wear of the Once-tribe's *Munhawe*.

"This will be yours when your time comes."

Her memory of her mother wearing the same colors came back to her so vividly she didn't see the mirror she gazed at. A year later, her mother had been dead, one of the countless victims of the bombings that took place after the Charter changes. They'd brought her back in a sealed casket, the skirt too tattered to be passed on.

Hala pushed back the memory. She smoothed her fingers over the woven cloth. They'd had this made for her and she could tell that the cloth had been enhanced.

She frowned and stared at her reflection. A deep breath and the connectors beneath her skin slid into view. There was no help for it. She'd never learned meditation the right way and without her augmentations, she couldn't enter the veils. She'd tried and failed to do so before.

"Are you all settled here?"

The four-headed organizer peered around the edge of the half-open door.

"Settled," Hala said. "Just getting myself psyched up."

"Good, good," the organizer said. Her faces smiled, and one of them whispered something to the other. "Do you want something to eat perhaps or to drink?"

"Ginger tea?" Hala asked.

"It will be arranged," the organizer said. "How much time will you need? The crowd isn't here yet, but the primary sponsors will be in before the rest."

"Half an hour," Hala said

It was disconcerting to watch the heads consult each other. After one of them whispered directives into a headpiece, all four nodded.

"Fifteen minutes then to mingle with the primaries. Your tea is coming. I'll check up on the other arrangements."

She watched as the organizer left. Her heads bobbed from side to side and her hands gesticulated at each other. At least the organizer would never lack for company, Hala thought. And she would never want for someone to talk to when the nights grew long and dark and lonely.

The door to the dressing room slid open again and this time one of the stewards came in. It was her tea, piping hot and filling the room with the sweet scent of ginger.

"Thank you," Hala said.

The steward nodded and departed as smoothly as he had entered and Hala was alone again. She sighed, lifted the cup to her nose and inhaled.

"Ah," she said.

The aroma brought back memories of her childhood and the mother who brewed ginger tea each time she had to do a long reading.

She blew on her tea, and sipped at it. It was good. Better than any she'd ever had before. She wondered briefly if the kitchen had a source and if they used real ginger instead of the amalgam that was available in machines for the masses.

Twelve hours spent in meditation.

Twenty-four hours spent replenishing her energy supply.

She was spruced up as well as she could ever be for an Artifact who was almost a septuagenarian.

She had prepared. Yes she had. But this question . . .

"I beg your pardon?" she said and she tapped the connector under her right ear discreetly.

Surely there must be a malfunction.

"I said, are you poor?" The woman who asked the question had a psychedelic array of hair plumes rigid with techno-spray, glittering under the bright lights of the dome.

"There's no need to be shy," the woman went on. "We see it on the news and we read it in the pages. The Once-country is sunk in poverty and Chaos holds sway over what remains of the populace. Without the Compassionate, there wouldn't be anything left of it by now. Want to see my display?"

Fragrance filled Hala's nostrils as the woman invaded her space.

"Look," the woman said.

Her screen flashed and the images appeared.

She knew what the vid was, of course. She'd seen them repeated countless times – and no matter that there was truth in the desolation shown on-screen, the Once-country was not all about mud and rain and blank-faced hopeless people living on Central City's streets.

"I came from a good family," Hala said as the vid came to an end.

"Oh," the woman seemed disappointed. "So you're not poor?"

Hala shook her head.

"But . . . "

"How do you measure poverty anyway?" Hala said. "What about yourself – do you consider yourself rich or poor?"

The woman took a deep breath and leaned away from Hala. Censure was in every line of her body.

"Well, I never," the woman said. "And we're doing all these things for you and your people. I should think you'd at least be a little grateful."

Hala sighed as the woman left her in a puff of sweet-smelling perfume.

"Well," said a voice behind her. "That's that then, and I suppose we can wave goodbye to a sizeable contribution from her. You do know how to deflate the pretentious, Hala."

She turned around and let out a squeal of joy.

"Bayninan! How . . . Why . . . when did you arrive?"

She fumbled for words not knowing what to ask first. The last time she'd seen Bayninan was when the Compassionate decreed that Hala would be sent to Silhouette. Bayninan's protests at the selection and segregation of the blooded had been rejected.

Hala was "blooded" – of the blood – and as a true descendant of the *Munhawe* she was expected to be an ambassador of goodwill, an Artifact. What flowed in the veins of the blooded was priceless and could not be entrusted to a planet still embroiled in the Chaos. For all that Bayninan was of the warrior class, she was deemed unfit to stand as companion to an Artifact. So she had been assigned to a different planet.

"I arrived two hours ago," Bayninan said. "A short sleep, and here I am. Fresh and fine and happy to be here in your time of need."

Hala threw her arms around the taller woman.

"I thought I'd never see you again," Hala said.

She pushed back the tears and the joy that threatened to overwhelm her.

"It took a long time to get myself into the representative's good books, and equally long to get myself enough credits to come here. I did promise I'd find you," Bayninan said. "You do remember that, don't you Hala?"

Hala smiled up at her. There was silver in Bayninan's hair, but the arms that embraced her felt strong and sure.

"How many years has it been?" Hala said. "I'm old and in need of a tune-up. You, on the other hand, look distinguished and very fine."

"You're not old," Bayninan replied. "You're at the right age."

Hala grimaced. Trust Bayninan to pick out what Hala was most insecure about. Even when they were growing up, Hala never needed to put her feelings into words. Bayninan simply knew.

"I've been the right age forever," she said. "And look."

She tucked her hair behind her ears so Bayninan could see where the shapers had given her more connectors.

"There's a slot at the back as well," Hala continued. "That's for maintenance when my receptors get foggy or some such technical thing that I don't really understand."

"My poor Hala," Bayninan said. "You've suffered by yourself."

"It hasn't been all bad," Hala said.

Bayninan smiled and leaned down to touch her forehead to Hala's.

"Well, I'm here now and I'll be here for as long as you need me."

Colorful clothing is worn by the upperclass, including the Munhawe, the Mama-oh, the Mumbaki, and the Chief of the Once-tribe. Belts carved from the teeth of the wild boar or from the crocodile are also an indication of class status. The white woven blouse with colorful embroidery is a later addition to traditional wear. Before the coming of the Compassionate, the women of the Once-tribe adorned their upper bodies with intricate beadworks. Breasts were displayed with pride.

The elder poet Sunyang wrote of the breast that sustains the life of the young.

"A woman's breasts are her adornment
Honorable and pure
They are the expression of the woman's modesty
For they are also the fountain of life."

                     —Artifact Hala on Life in the Once-tribe—

It was the same spiel and yet it was different somehow. Bayninan was here. Her heart leapt and sang, and her joy in their reunion manifested in a projection of goodwill.

"A beautiful poem," the organizer said.

Her words pulled Hala from the haze of joy. She was on the podium and the first sequence of her presentation was over. Beside her, the organizer beamed while the audience nodded and murmured to each other.

"Yes," Hala said. "The poem is lovely."

"And you agreed to show us a dance," the organizer prompted.

"Indeed," Hala said.

How could she have forgotten? She had intended to show them the communal dance, but her heart cried out for something more.

"It will be a celebratory dance," Bayninan said from beside her.

"Oooo . . . " the organizer said. She clapped her hands and her heads bobbed with excitement.

Hala stood there, her eyes riveted on Bayninan.

"Where will you find the garb of a warrior?" she choked out the words.

"I brought my brother's gear," Bayninan said. "It will do just as well as my own."

Was there a tinge of sorrow in Bayninan's voice? Hala wanted to ask her why she had Lakay's clothes with her, but before she could speak, the organizer swept Bayninan away.

"You must prepare," the organizer twittered. "How exciting and how fortuitous that you arrived on this day."

Hala listened to the organizer's excited announcements. She'd thought she had taken all the shock she could take in a day. But here was Bayninan looking every bit the warrior. The loincloth revealed the muscled length of her legs, her breasts were barely covered by the warrior's vest. A blanket was slung around her shoulders and the ivory of her belt bore the yellow sheen of age.

"I never thought I'd see you wearing this again," Hala said.

"Two women in skirts cannot dance the dance of blanket-sharing," Bayninan replied. "For tonight, let me be your warrior."

Was this Bayninan? Hala wondered. She watched as her friend walked with an easy gait to the other side of the podium. She bent down and picked up a shield and a spear. There was a smile in her eyes when she turned to look at Hala who stood there staring at her.

"Well?" There was the lift of the eyebrow and the sardonic twist of the mouth.

She'd never seen Bayninan like this before, never thought of what it meant for Bayninan to be one of the fighting women of the Once-tribe.

> First, the warrior dances to show off his prowess for his chosen one. He leaps and jumps around the fire and with his gestures, he lets the chosen one know that he has hunted for her, he has fought for her, and he has triumphed for her.
> —Acts of Courtship compiled by
> Munhawe Sunyang Chulipa—

It was the courtship dance. Even as her lips spilled out the words, she could not stop staring at Bayninan.

In Bayninan's hands, the prop became a weapon. She thrust at the ground in rhythm with the gongs. It was like watching the rite performed as it was in the days when the Once-tribe still was its own. The Warrior leapt and spun and landed in a crouch, her eyes were fierce beneath the hooked beak of the bird's head she wore as a headdress. Bayninan was the warrior now, and when Hala met her eyes, she couldn't explain why she suddenly felt as if she were prey.

Thrust and retreat. Bayninan's muscles gleamed like polished mahogany beneath the domed lights. There was the flex and the give and she drew the blanket from around her shoulders to shake it out.

It was the invitation.

Hala's hands twitched. She fed music into the air through her array: the song of the lover's flute twined with the rhythm of the gongs. Her feet shifted. Bayninan's eyes gleamed at her over the edge of the blanket.

A lover's dance, Hala thought.

She looked at her old friend in wonder, and allowed herself to succumb to the call of the gong. As she circled the imagined fire with the coyness of a maiden, she couldn't help but think of how very right Bayninan was. What better dance was there to celebrate this moment? Here, in the shadow of the gods, she was reunited with the one she loved the most. Bayninan's blanket closed around her shoulders, and she turned to accept its embrace in the way a maiden accepts the invitation of her first lover.

> *If I opened my palms to you*
> *Would you touch your palms to mine?*
> *If I reached out my hands*
> *Would you take them*
> *Would you give me the meaning to this life?*
> *—Song of the Maiden, Oral Records of the Once-Tribe—*

Rain seldom came to Silhouette, but it was here now. It poured down on the glass dome and spilled over into the ground beyond the domes where Silhouette's forest thrived in an atmosphere that was alien to and yet somehow similar to the Once-country they'd left behind.

Their celebration dance reached its end. Bayninan's hand was warm around her own. They clasped hands briefly before they parted and Hala stood alone again. She turned to face the wall. The crowd was at her back, and she could hear the wave of whispers. From soft wonderings the whispers grew into a crescendo of awe.

This, she thought, is for the Once-tribe.

She allowed her sight to blur as she accessed her array and passed through into the memory of the veils.

Here, in the space where the dance was born, she was alone. Here was the wind and the sky and the earth beneath her.

She paid obeisance to the sun as the song of the distant gongs coursed through her and filled the hall with their resonance. Her limbs trembled as the rhythm moved through her.

Tong-a-lit.

Her naked feet warmed the grey stone floor.

Even here, so many light years away from the Once-country, her spirit was connected to the earth and the sky. To the remembered horizon filled with the majesty of mountains and the green, green gold of ripening rice. She raised her arms in a gesture of remembered welcome.

"Come wind," she whispered.

Energy moved in her. It traveled through her bones, it moved through her flesh. She was aquiver with fire and lightning, bursting to the brim with the stories of beginnings.

Her ears resonated with the voices of the tribe sisters, and the et-et-du of the Once-tribe.

The gate to the veil's inner sanctum opened up and she walked into its familiar embrace.

Her people had wandered the Once-country long before the Compassionate came. It wasn't that they owned the land so much as the land owned them.

They tended her with care, they plowed her fields, and channeled her waters, they built their homes from what the land gave them and ate what the land brought forth. Season in and season out, the cycle went on in that way. Small wars were fought, alliances were made, and the Once-tribe grew as the gods meant it to. Their borders extended, their influence increased, their warriors were able hunters, and their women were strong in spirit and resilient in their minds.

The land was fecund and green and all manner of life grew there; even the spirits thrived and made their homes in the caves hidden by falls of water, and in rocky shelters where ferns and wild orchids grew.

There was the yell of children as they sprang from cliff into deep pools of green. Green, green, and around them, the bright smell of tiger grass and wild lilies – here the pitcher plants grew in profusion and the maiden's slippers swung in the wind as if waiting for the day when they would be released from the stem.

Beyond the pool of deep green, tall trees towered into the sky, and further in—

A voice called to her from the familiar green. A voice filled with melancholy and remembrance, summoning her and telling her to shed her fears and embrace what waited beyond the portals of this place.

"Sacrifice," the voice whispered.

At the sound of that voice, she blinked and she was back again. The hall was quiet. Sometime during the performance, she had turned to face the crowd. Now everyone was staring at her, and the look in their eyes sent a frisson of fear through her.

She had never experienced anything like this before. What had she said? What words had she chanted?

Below her the organizer's four heads had their eyes closed. Their mouths hung open and the multitude of hands stretched upward, open as if waiting for some gift.

"I . . . " her voice failed her and the crowd stirred as if waking from a deep, collective dream.

"It's all right." Bayninan was there again.

Hala felt suddenly tired. As if all the energy she'd stored up had been spent and she was nothing more than an empty husk.

"You did well," Bayninan whispered. "Just lean on me."

She was grateful for the words and grateful for her friend. She stared down at the crowd. They were wearing smiles now, but all she could think of was the look in their eyes when she'd come out of the trance. Like predators waiting for the first twitch.

She shivered and Bayninan wrapped the blanket around her.

"Here," Bayninan said. "A pod is waiting for us. We can go home now."

Hala woke to the sound of Bayninan's chanting. She burrowed deep in the cocoon of blankets and sheets, feeling as if she were young again and on the verge of a discovery.

"Et-et-doh-oh-oh, hi Bugan najawitaa-aha-aan . . . "

When they were younger, they followed the words of the chant, longing for the day when they would join the other chanters.

"Learn the words," her auntie said.

But by then the old language was so overlaid with the new that the words to the chants might just as well have been in an entirely different tongue.

"It doesn't matter what they mean," her auntie replied when Hala asked what the words meant. "Just memorize the words."

Hala had grown tired of it, but Bayninan had loved it. She remembered the serious look on Bayninan's face, her dedication to the exact holding of a tone and the measured beat of the chant.

Bayninan would have been a far better *Munhawe*. She would have fulfilled the duty with skill; no matter that she was not of the blood, Bayninan would have remembered the things that Hala would have forgotten without her augmentations. But the blood did not run in Bayninan.

"I love the chants," Bayninan had said. *"But I love the hunt and the chase more than I love the movements of the dance."*

Even when she'd been chosen, Hala had been conscious of her shortcomings. She was not a full-fledged *Munhawe*, and yet with the implants in her body, she could fulfill that role perfectly.

Lulled by the warmth and by the sound of Bayninan's voice, she fell back asleep, sinking into a dream of a bygone time. Her mother stood by the fire, stirring a pot filled with warm porridge. Her mother had no grey in her hair and she was chanting as she always did when a great event was about to take place.

"Coming of age," her mother said.

She looked up from the pot. Her smile was gentle and she beckoned with her hand to Hala.

"Come, inhale the spices," her mother said. "The smoke will cleanse your spirit."

"It's just porridge," Hala said.

"Is it?" her mother asked. "Is that all you think it is? Or is that all you will allow yourself to see?"

"I don't understand," Hala said.

"Come," her mother said. "You must look deeper and understand if you don't wish to die."

"Death," Hala said.

She closed her eyes and thought of death. She wondered if a dirge would be sung for her and she wondered if Bayninan would sing the *hudhud* for her burial. Would the Compassionate even allow it? A three-day dirge for an Artifact from the Once-tribe, for an exile from the Once-country – pain pierced her kneecap as she fell to the ground, and her eyes flew open.

"This is what I was telling you about," her mother's voice whispered through the trees.

She was in a forest now. It was the same one in which she'd played as a little girl. Clusters of ferns rose up above her, and beyond that the fat trunks of trees and the sheltering fronds of pine and banyan.

"Mother," she whispered.

"Understand," Her mother said. "You must open your eyes, Hala."

"Hala."

Bayninan's voice was loud in her ears, waking her once more. She blinked and rolled out of bed in a tangle of blankets and pillows.

"What?" she said.

"There's a man here for you," Bayninan said. "He says his name is Ay-wan."

She stared up at Bayninan. Her eyes saw her mother still and her ears rang with her mother's last admonition.

"Who?" She said.

"A man," Bayninan said. "He said his name is Ay-wan. He says you called for him."

Was it her imagination or did Bayninan put more emphasis on the word "man"?

"I know him," Hala said quickly. "Send him in."

> *Of course, there is the business of death and the dying*
> *But before that comes the litany of grief*
> *—Rituals of the Once-tribe, compiled records—*

"It's the augmentations," Ay-wan said.

He had spent the good part of an hour testing her reflexes. He sat opposite her now, his connector plugged into the slot at the back of her neck.

She tried to gauge his thoughts, but ever since his change it was as if there was a curtain pulled over his emotions.

"What's wrong with them?" Hala asked.

Ay-wan sighed and disconnected himself.

"You're breaking down," he said. "It's not unexpected but still . . . "

Hala pushed her hair back into place and breathed out in a huff.

"So impatient," Ay-wan murmured. "Your augmentations are deteriorating faster than they should. They're meant to last longer than human years, but the way yours are going they'll be corrupted in less than a year."

"What does that mean?" Hala demanded. "Speak in words that I can understand."

"You're dying," Ay-wan said. "And you'll be dead before year's end unless we take out your augmentations."

"Dying . . . " Hala's voice trailed off. She stared at Ay-wan willing him to change his diagnosis.

"We can always remove them," Ay-wan said. "They're not connected to your life support systems."

"But—" she couldn't finish.

Without the augmentations she wouldn't be the Artifact anymore. She wouldn't be able to access the knowledge that she needed to access. She would lose her ability to chant and to sing and to speak the old language. Would she even remember the steps of the dance once they were taken from her? A chilling thought came to her. Who would she be if she lost the ability to function as the Artifact?

"It's not an easy choice," Ay-wan said.

His fingers rubbed at the edges of his face. The skin there was pulled tight like skin over the surface of a drum.

"When you had your change," Hala asked. "Was it easy or difficult?"

Ay-wan turned towards her.

"What do you think?" he asked.

She met his gaze, and she flinched at the pain and the loneliness in his eyes.

"I am the last of my people," Ay-wan said. "This is the suffering I undertake in memory of what once was."

*There have been some side-effects noted. Hallucinations and
hysteria are common to those given augmentations. The stronger
the blood that runs in the Artifact, the stronger the reaction.*
                                —Augmentations and their Side-Effects,
                                  Medical Journal Suguran Foundation—

"One more appearance this week," Hala said.

Twice this week, she'd hibernated inside the regeneration egg.
Twice, she'd given Bayninan a lie.

"It's what I always do before and after an appearance," she'd
said.

She didn't know if Bayninan believed her, but she saw the
sadness in her friend's eyes.

"Where are we going?" Bayninan asked.

"You don't have to go," Hala said.

Bayninan's lips formed a grim line.

"Didn't I make myself clear already?" Bayninan said.

Hala avoided Bayninan's eyes.

"I'm not a child," she said. "Not an invalid. I don't need a
babysitter."

"Foolish," Bayninan said. "Who told you that I look at you as
a child or an invalid?"

Hala turned away from Bayninan.

"Do what you want," she said.

Her vision blurred and she caught herself before she stumbled.
Behind her, she heard Bayninan mutter a curse. Then Bayninan's
arms were around her, steadying her and helping her over the
threshold.

"Why won't you share with me?" Bayninan said. "Whatever it
is, you're not alone anymore."

For a moment, she was tempted to tell Bayninan. How easy it
would be to let this warrior be her strength. She flinched and
pulled away from Bayninan's hands.

"I'm fine," she said. "It's just a temporary glitch. Nothing that
can't be resolved."

She faced herself in the mirror, willing herself to be calm. For
tonight, she'd chosen to put on the clothing she'd received on the
day of her birth. The skirt had been woven by one of the

foremothers – the patterns more intricate than the patterns on the skirt she normally wore to such gatherings. There were no enhancements in the cloth, but it wasn't as if she needed enhancements in her clothing when her entire body hummed and bristled with the arrays installed by the Once-rule.

She brushed her hand over the horsehair that encircled her waist. She could feel the patterns woven into it – subtle figures embossed with skill in the same dark color as the band. Ivory buttons yellowed by age ran along the length of the belt and dangled down to where the edges of her skirt met and folded over each other.

It was the mark of her class. Out of deference to the Compassionate, she'd donned a vest, but over that, she wore a heavy necklace of bamboo beads and precious bloodstone. She had never worn it before and perhaps it was a sign of her augmentation's breakdown because when she'd picked up the necklace, it had burned. An image came into her mind, very sharp and very clear, of her mother wearing the same necklace, her eyes closed and her lips moving as if in prayer. Then it faded away. The feeling was like touching the edge of a memory that belonged with the piece. There was a message waiting there, she thought.

"The pod is here." Bayninan's voice broke into her thoughts.

She unclenched her hands and pulled herself away from the haze that beckoned.

"I'm ready," she said.

She met Bayninan's gaze. Was it only a few days ago that she'd been filled with such joy at their reunion? Why couldn't she dredge up even the slightest bit of that emotion now?

"I suppose you don't want me to be your warrior tonight," Bayninan said.

There was regret in Bayninan's smile.

Hala shook her head, her fingers reaching up to touch the deep red of the blood stones.

"Not tonight," she said.

Ay-wan's words haunted her while she shook hands and greeted political dignitaries from Silhouette's neighbor worlds. There were the ambassadors, clustered together in a circle, their wives dressed in sparkly costumes made up of tiny particles drenched in silver shine or platinum flair.

"This suffering I undertake," Ay-wan's words ghosted around her, overlaid with sorrow. As if the man who had spoken them wanted to say that given a choice, given descendants, he would have chosen something else.

She smiled and shook hands with the Consul from the Once-place named Siargao. An independent island, Siargao had been given the ultimatum to ally themselves with the Empire or risk destruction. There were tales of a hidden power in Siargao, but they had put up no struggle and signed the treaty.

"Ah," the Consul said. "So, you are the much spoken of Artifact. One of those rescued from the Chaos that plagued the Once-country, so the Compassionate attaché says. You will honor us with a dance perhaps. Maybe a telling or a showing of what it was like in your country before the Chaos took it?"

Hala smiled and murmured something noncommittal. It would not be good to offend one of the Empire's political allies. How she acted here would influence whatever privileges the Once-tribe had wrestled from the Compassionate.

"Never let it be said that we are not kind." Hala turned at the sound of the Compassionate attaché's voice.

The smile on his face was hard as glass. All his teeth showed, chills shot down her spine.

"Artifact Hala," the attaché said. "You've laid a good basis for our work here."

She couldn't bring herself to make a civil reply. She tried to speak polite words.

"You will give us a good performance tonight, won't you?" the attaché continued.

She opened her mouth, her mind flailing about for words.

"I—" she said.

"Yes?" There was a curious look on the attaché's face.

"I do this for the Once-tribe," she said. "In memory of the *Munhawe* and the Mama-oh who are lost to us."

In memory . . .

The words wrapped themselves around her like an embrace. The air around her seemed to coagulate into a hazy curtain through which she could see colors and hear snatches of words, music, and laughter.

And then, the gongs were pounding in her ears . . .

"Artifact," a voice pierced through the haze and she blinked and looked up into the face of the blue-haired representative from a place whose name she couldn't remember.

What he thought when she simply looked at him, she didn't know. Perhaps he thought she had gone into a trance induced by her boosters. She felt his hand at her elbow, knew he was moving her to where she was more visible.

On display again.

She shook her head at the whisper and tried to focus. Who had said those words? Vicious anger rose up inside her. If this was the Once-country, if this were the Once-tribe, she would demand satisfaction.

Artifact. Relic of a dead tribe.

Her head was pounding again and images superimposed themselves on the present. She could hear the gongs, she could smell the wood smoke. Was this what happened when one passed through the veils and communed with the spirits?

She lifted her eyes and looked at the expectant faces. Of course, she thought. To see the Artifact, to hear her speak, it was a thing to be spoken of among friends, wasn't it?

Those patterns are so unique. And her voice, and the chants – of course they all have their own charm. What a unique experience.

She closed her eyes and thought of the warm dear faces of her clansisters and her clanbrothers. The gongs were beating and the warriors were dancing down the path of the mountainside. They had come in from the kill, and they bore the heads of the invaders.

Look, sister, they said. *We have hunted well, this eve. See this head? How fragrant the locks of his hair are, and how shining and long. But he will look glorious standing guard at the doorposts of my home. Don't you think so, sister?*

The warrior grinned and passed before her, and the others passed as well, like waves washing over her, dancing down the mountainside bearing sheaves of rice from the harvest. Their feet sure on the steep slopes, the gongs beat a wild rhythm that made her want to dance and chant out loud of victory and challenge and the hunger to be free.

"Enough!" The roar tore apart her vision.

Around her, the veils shimmered and fell apart. The

Compassionate attaché stood before her, his blue eyes blazing with fury, his body quivering.

"You show us an outrage," he said.

As if from a very great distance, she heard her reply.

"I show what the spirits say I must show. I speak in remembrance of what has gone before."

Her vision blurred. The room whirled around her and before the darkness took her, she heard Bayninan's voice calling her name, and thought she saw a valiant warrior leaping over the heads of the gathered entourage to gather her into his arms.

"Hala."

When she was a child, her mother took her to the caves at Sagada. Time had wreaked its havoc on the caves and the Compassionate had taken what was left of the mummies and the coffins and the bones and sealed them in huge airless capsules that were put on display in various realms where the Empire held sway.

There was very little left to see of what had once been except for holos and vids that played across the cave walls at intermittent intervals. Her mother had taken her deeper into the caves and shining her light on the wall, she'd shown to Hala where generations of the Once-tribe had placed their mark in protest of the taking of what was theirs by right. There alongside her mother, she'd placed her own mark too. She'd dipped her hands in the pale white matter, a gift of the spirits her mother told her, and laid the imprint of her palms on the walls right under her mother's own.

"By this the spirits will know you," her mother said.

She came awake with a gasp.

She was in a room with walls the shade of lemons.

"You're awake," a voice said.

She turned.

Bayninan sat beside her bed, worry etched on her face.

She blinked and memory came back to her.

"Oh no," she groaned. "I messed up. The attaché must be furious."

"It was rather chaotic for a while," Bayninan said. "And he was very angry, but I said you hadn't been feeling well and the implants were not doing their job – I told him it might be a virus."

"And he accepted that?" Hala said.

Bayninan tilted her head to one side and smiled.

"I can be very good at persuading people when I want to," she said. "In the end, they were all very solicitous. The Consul from Siargao insisted that you be accommodated here."

Hala stared at Bayninan, wondering if her friend had always been this smooth-talking person with a twinkle in her eye.

"We're in the newest wing of the Sinuguran Foundation Center," Bayninan said with a smile.

"Oh no," Hala cried. "What have you done? We have to get out of here."

She sat up and swung her legs over the side of the bed.

"No," Bayninan said. "You need to rest. Lie down. All will be well, Hala. You'll see."

She stared up at this strange Bayninan who exuded more authority than she'd ever had before.

"What do you mean, all will be well?" she asked. "Do you know what the Suguran Foundation does, Bayninan? Do you understand what they are?"

Of course, Bayninan couldn't know or understand, Hala realized. How could Bayninan know that it was the Foundation that was at the heart of the implants and the boosters? If the Foundation realized that her augmentations were failing, they would take them away without asking. She would lose everything – the archive of memory, the names of the clans, the faces, the songs, the dances, even the memory of warm earth, the taste of steamed rice, and the scent of betelnut.

"Your augmentations are failing, Hala," Bayninan said. "I know the signs. They're like poison to you now, and if you don't get rid of them, you'll be dead before year's end."

"I can't," Hala said.

"It's no longer impossible," Bayninan replied. "There have been advancements and the other augmented have been restored to their own selves without harm."

"I can't," Hala insisted. "Without these, I'm nothing, Bayninan. I won't be able to access the veils, I won't be able to perform. I'll be nothing."

"You'll never be nothing," Bayninan said. "You'll always be Hala to me – always as you were meant to be."

"You don't understand," Hala cried out.

"I do," Bayninan replied. "But you don't need to be afraid. There's no risk to your life."

"But there is," Hala shouted. "You're not an Artifact. You don't get to say what it is that I will lose or that I will gain. You're not the one people turn to when they need to remember the long line of history. You're not the one people come to when they want access to the wealth of our culture, our chants and our songs and our dances. You don't understand at all."

"And for whom do you keep those histories, Hala?" Bayninan asked. "For whom do you recite the poems and chants? For whom do you dance and for whom do you speak? You say you do these things in memory of the Munhawe and the Mama-oh. But the Munhawe and the Mama-oh served the Once-tribe, Hala. I do not see any of the Once-tribe among your audience. For what purpose do you risk your life, Hala? Is it for the Once-tribe or is it for yourself?"

Bayninan's words fell like a scourge on Hala's shoulders. She stiffened in indignation – was this how her friend saw her? Was it how people looked at her? Was she nothing more than an old woman who put her heritage on display?

"Get out," she said. "Get out of my sight, Bayinan. Get out before I forget that I love you and that you are my friend."

Let us be clear on this. There was no invasion. With the sign-ing of the treaty, the Once-country was brought into the folds of the Empire. It was an acknowledgment of the Compassionate's sovereignty and the god-given right to lead those who were left behind into the light of the Compassionate's greater wisdom.

—from History of the Empire and the Once-Country—

Bayninan's departure left Hala with the luxury of solitude and time to think. It was very late in the evening – that much she knew. Silhouette's moon hovered in the night sky and the chimes sang out the eleventh hour. Not so long ago, she had been standing before delegates from the allies of the Compassionate Empire. They had admired her, of that she was certain, they had listened to her. Perhaps her words had confused some of them, perhaps some of them had been titillated, perhaps some of them had been amused, and the Compassionate attaché had most certainly been moved to anger.

She recalled fragments of what she had spoken and she wondered how she could have found the voice to sing the warrior's chant and the temerity to speak of the first invasion and the defeat of the Compassionate at the hands of the Once-tribe.

There was silence in her head now. None of the humming that accompanied her even when she was alone, none of the buzzing awareness that prickled at her skin even when in solitude. It was a strange feeling because no matter what, she'd always had the awareness of data streaming through her from the implants in her head.

Bayninan had spoken of some drug being applied to her system and she supposed it was that which quieted the data and made her feel suddenly so alone.

As she contemplated the darkness, she wondered if this was what it would be like if she consented to have her augmentations removed. She would no longer be the Artifact, as Bayninan had said. But was it really that important to be the Artifact? To recite auguries and poetry, to dance the dances and to explain symbols that held no significance to those who viewed her only as a novel thing, to be whispered of by people who had no understanding of the rhythm of harvest and planting or the variations of the gong?

She closed her eyes in weariness. Tears seeped from beneath her eyelids and spilled down her cheeks as she acknowledged Bayninan's words.

Alone with her thoughts, Hala acknowledged their truth. She'd clung to her role as Artifact, refusing to question it, but if she allowed herself to continue on as the Artifact, she would be betraying the blood that flowed in her veins.

"It's not deadly," Ay-wan said. "But it is still a procedure that carries risk."

Ay-wan had come to her on the second day of her confinement and she had given him permission to relay her corrupted state to the representative.

Now, he was talking her through the procedure that would change her life for ever.

"You mentioned no risk when we spoke of this in my home,"

Hala said. "And Bayninan said that removals had been successfully carried out on others who had been augmented."

A sliver of pain went through her. Bayninan had not been to see her since she'd sent her friend away. Instead, an emissary had come with the message that Bayninan was preparing for a return to the Once-country.

I will wait for word from you, Bayninan had written. *My promise still stands. If you send for me, I will come.*

What was Bayninan thinking? The Once-country was still in the grip of Chaos. Who would be there to greet them if they chose to return to the place of the Once-tribe? And why send a message when she could easily have come herself?

"You have lived with the augmentations for so long, lady," Ay-wan said. "Did you stop to consider that you were born of the blood? With the augmentations, you did not have to think of the consequences of your heritage. The machines suppressed what came naturally and the visions you brought forth for the public were what the Compassionate desired of the program."

Hala frowned.

"What do you mean by that?"

Ay-wan shrugged. Something flickered in his eyes. It was lonely and sad, and for a moment Hala wished she had made the effort to know more about him instead of sealing herself away from any intimate connections.

"There is this possibility that you could come into the role you were meant to fill," Ay-wan said after a pause. "It is also possible that you will never be anything more now than what you were before the augmentations."

Hala bowed her head and stared at her hands. She thought of the exhilaration brought on by the dance. The moments of joy and the way she had lived towards those moments. Outside of the performances, she had simply been going through the motions – moving from one performance to the next like a doll or a machine waiting for its master to utter the word of command.

She raised her eyes and stared out the window. There were fliers drifting above the dome outside; she'd seen them before and yet never really seen them. What else had she not seen while she was caught in the haze of her half-life as an Artifact, a person and yet not?

She thought of Bayninan looking at her with so much emotion and so much passion and wondered if her friend had also gone through the same process. She felt a pang at her own thoughtlessness. She'd never even bothered to wonder or to ask about Bayninan's life after their parting. What pain had Bayninan gone through, what suffering had she endured?

She bit her lip as she thought of their conversations. How spoiled she must have seemed. Now, as she contemplated the possibilities before her, she felt very small and unsure. Could she be brave enough to make her own way in the world as Bayninan had? Could she be strong enough to stand up and simply be Hala?

Beside her, Ay-wan cleared his throat.

She took a deep breath and turned to meet his gaze.

"I am ready," she said. "Whatever happens, I will embrace it."

The Once-Artifact named Hala has been released from her duties. The Empire in its benevolence has bestowed on her the gift of life and the choice to remain on Silhouette as a citizen or to go wherever it is that she wishes.

In her farewell speech, the former Artifact graciously acknowledged the good work of the Compassionate and regretted that she could no longer continue in her capacity. In the attached visual clip it is clear that she has not yet fully recovered from the extraction of her augmentations. Silhouette will miss her spectacular performances. Most memorable are her final presentations before she opted for the operation that saved her life.

At the farewell ceremony, the Compassionate attaché announced the arrival of a new Artifact from the Once-place called Siargao. The new Artifact will be arriving on the jump ship named Carollus. Siargao representative Pero Nimata says that the Once-place has prepared a spectacle to greet the new Artifact's arrival. It will be something to look forward to.

—Newsclip, Silhoutte Daily—

Author Note: This story has been two years in the making. JT Stewart planted the seed for this story on the afternoon she came to visit while I was at Clarion West. I cried, she talked. Her words continue to inspire me.

EJ-ES

Nancy Kress

> Jesse, come home
> There's a hole in the bed
> where we slept
> Now it's growing cold
> Hey Jesse, your face
> in the place where we lay
> by the hearth, all apart
> it hangs on my heart . . .
> Jesse, I'm lonely
> Come home.
> —"Jesse," Janis Ian, 1972

"Why did you first enter the Corps?" Lolimel asked her as they sat at the back of the shuttle, just before landing. Mia looked at the young man helplessly, because how could you answer a question like that? Especially when it was asked by the idealistic and worshipful new recruits, too ignorant to know what a waste of time worship was, let alone simplistic questions.

"Many reasons," Mia said gravely, vaguely. He looked like so many medicians she had worked with, for so many decades on so many planets . . . intense, thick-haired, genemod beautiful, a little insane. You had to be a little insane to leave Earth for the Corps, knowing that when (if) you ever returned, all you had known would have been dust for centuries.

He was more persistent than most. "What reasons?"

"The same as yours, Lolimel," she said, trying to keep her voice gentle. "Now be quiet, please, we're entering the atmosphere."

"Yes, but—"

"*Be quiet.*" Entry was so much easier on him than on her; he had not got bones weakened from decades in space. They *did* weaken, no matter what exercise one took or what supplements or what gene therapy. Mia leaned back in her shuttle chair and closed her eyes. Ten minutes, maybe, of aerobraking and descent; surely she could stand ten minutes. Or not.

The heaviness began, abruptly increased. Worse on her eyeballs, as always; she didn't have good eye-socket muscles, had never had them. Such an odd weakness. Well, not for long; this was her last flight. At the next station, she'd retire. She was already well over age, and her body felt it. Only her body? No, her mind, too. At the moment, for instance, she couldn't remember the name of the planet they were hurtling toward. She recalled its catalogue number, but not whatever its colonists, who were not answering hails from ship, had called it.

"*Why did you join the Corps?*"

"*Many reasons.*"

And so few of them fulfilled. But that was not a thing you told the young.

The colony sat at the edge of a river, under an evening sky of breathable air set with three brilliant, fast-moving moons. Beds of glorious flowers dotted the settlement, somewhere in size between a large town and a small city. The buildings of foamcast embedded with glittering native stone were graceful, well-proportioned rooms set around open atria. Minimal furniture, as graceful as the buildings; even the machines blended unobtrusively into the lovely landscape. The colonists had taste and restraint and a sense of beauty. They were all dead.

"A long time ago," said Kenin. Officially she was Expedition Head, although titles and chains-of-command tended to erode near the galactic edge, and Kenin led more by consensus and natural calm than by rank. More than once the team had been grateful for Kenin's calm. Lolimel looked shaken, although he was trying to hide it.

Kenin studied the skeleton before them. "Look at those bones – completely clean."

Lolimel managed, "It might have been picked clean quickly by predators, or carnivorous insects, or . . . " His voice trailed off.

"I already scanned it, Lolimel. No microscopic bone nicks. She decayed right there in bed, along with clothing and bedding."

The three of them looked at the bones lying on the indestructible mattress coils of some alloy Mia had once known the name of. Long clean bones, as neatly arranged as if for a first-year anatomy lesson. The bedroom door had been closed; the dehumidifying system had, astonishingly, not failed; the windows were intact. Nothing had disturbed the woman's long rot in the dry air until nothing remained, not even the bacteria that had fed on her, not even the smell of decay.

Kenin finished speaking to the other team. She turned to Mia and Lolimel, her beautiful brown eyes serene. "There are skeletons throughout the city, some in homes and some collapsed in what seem to be public spaces. Whatever the disease was, it struck fast Jamal says their computer network is gone, but individual rec cubes might still work. Those things last for ever."

Nothing lasts for ever, Mia thought, but she started searching the cabinets for a cube. She said to Lolimel, to give him something to focus on, "How long ago was this colony founded, again?"

"Three-hundred-sixty E-years," Lolimel said. He joined the search.

Three-hundred-sixty years since a colony ship left an established world with its hopeful burden, arrived at this deadly Eden, established a city, flourished, and died. How much of Mia's lifetime, much of it spent traveling at just under c, did that represent? Once she had delighted in figuring out such equations, in wondering if she'd been born when a given worldful of colonists made planetfall. But by now there were too many expeditions, too many colonies, too many accelerations and decelerations, and she'd lost track.

Lolimel said abruptly, "Here's a rec cube."

"Play it," Kenin said, and when he just went on staring at it in the palm of his smooth hand, she took the cube from him and played it herself.

It was what she expected. A native plague of some kind, jumping DNA-based species (which included all species in the galaxy, thanks to panspermia). The plague had struck after the colonists thought they had vaccinated against all dangerous micros. Of course, they couldn't really have thought that; even 360 years ago doctors had been familiar with alien species-crossers. Some were mildly irritating, some dangerous, some epidemically fatal. Colonies had been lost before, and would be again.

"Complete medical data resides on green rec cubes," the recorder had said in the curiously accented International of three centuries ago. Clearly dying, he gazed out from the cube with calm, sad eyes. A brave man. "Any future visitors to Good Fortune should be warned."

Good Fortune. That was the planet's name.

"All right," Kenin said, "tell the guard to search for green cubes. Mia, get the emergency analysis lab set up and direct Jamal to look for burial sites. If they had time to inter some victims – if they interred at all, of course – we might be able to recover some micros to create vacs or cures. Lolimel, you assist me in—"

One of the guards, carrying weapons that Mia could not have named, blurted, "Ma'am, how do we know we won't get the same thing that killed the colonists?"

Mia looked at her. Like Lolimel, she was very young. Like all of them, she would have her story about why she volunteered for the Corps.

Now the young guard was blushing. "I mean, ma'am, before you can make a vaccination? How do we know we won't get the disease, too?"

Mia said gently, "We don't."

No one, however, got sick. The colonists had had interment practices, they had had time to bury some of their dead in strong, water-tight coffins before everyone else died, and their customs didn't include embalming. Much more than Mia had dared hope for. Good Fortune, indeed.

In five days of tireless work they had the micro isolated, sequenced, and analyzed. It was a virus, or a virus analogue, that had somehow gained access to the brain and lodged near the limbic system, creating destruction and death. Like rabies, Mia thought, and hoped this virus hadn't caused the terror and madness of that stubborn disease. Not even Earth had been able to eradicate rabies.

Two more days yielded the vaccine. Kenin dispensed it outside the large building on the edge of the city, function unknown, which had become Corps headquarters. Mia applied her patch, noticing with the usual distaste the leathery, wrinkled skin of her forearm. Once she had had such beautiful skin, what was it that a long-ago lover had said to her, what had been his name ... Ah, growing old was not for the gutless.

Something moved at the edge of her vision.

"Lolimel ... did you see that?"

"See what?"

"Nothing." Sometimes her aging eyes played tricks on her; she didn't want Lolimel's pity.

The thing moved again.

Casually Mia rose, brushing imaginary dirt from the seat of her uniform, strolling toward the bushes where she'd seen motion. From her pocket she pulled her gun. There were animals on this planet, of course, although the Corps had only glimpsed them from a distance, and rabies was transmitted by animal bite ...

It wasn't an animal. It was a human child.

No, not a child, Mia realized as she rounded the clump of bushes and, amazingly, the girl didn't run. An adolescent, or perhaps older, but so short and thin that Mia's mind had filled in "child." A scrawny young woman with light brown skin and long, matted black hair, dressed carelessly in some sort of sarong-like wrap. Staring at Mia with a total lack of fear.

"Hello," Mia said gently.

"Ej-es?" the girl said.

Mia said into her wrister, "Kenin ... we've got natives. Survivors."

The girl smiled. Her hair was patchy on one side, marked with small white rings. *Fungus*, Mia thought professionally, absurdly. The girl walked right toward Mia, not slowing, as if intending to walk through her. Instinctively Mia put out an arm. The girl walked into it, bonked herself on the forehead, and crumpled to the ground.

"You're not supposed to beat up the natives, Mia," Kenin said. "God, she's not afraid of us at all. How can that be? You nearly gave her a concussion."

Mia was as bewildered as Kenin, as all of them. She'd picked up the girl, who'd looked bewildered but not angry, and then Mia had backed off, expecting the girl to run. Instead she'd stood there rubbing her forehead and jabbering, and Mia had seen that her sarong was made of an uncut sheet of plastic, its colors faded to a mottled gray.

Kenin, Lolimel, and two guards had come running. And *still* the girl wasn't afraid. She chattered at them, occasionally pausing as if expecting them to answer. When no one did, she eventually turned and moved leisurely off.

Mia said, "I'm going with her."

Instantly a guard said, "It's not safe, ma'am," and Kenin said, "Mia, you can't just—"

"You don't need me here," she said, too brusquely; suddenly there seemed nothing more important in the world than going with this girl. Where did that irrational impulse come from? "And I'll be perfectly safe with a gun."

This was such a stunningly stupid remark that no one answered her. But Kenin didn't order her to stay. Mia accepted the guard's tanflefoam and Kenin's vidcam and followed the girl.

It was hard to keep up with her. "Wait!" Mia called, which produced no response. So she tried what the girl had said to her: "Ej-es!"

Immediately the girl stopped and turned to her with glowing eyes and a smile that could have melted glaciers, had Good Fortune had such a thing. Gentle planet, gentle person, who was almost certainly a descendent of the original dead settlers. Or was she? InterGalactic had no record of any other registered ship leaving for this star system, but that didn't mean anything. Inter-Galactic didn't know everything. Sometimes, given the time dilation of space travel, Mia thought they knew nothing.

"Ej-es," the girl agreed, sprinted back to Mia, and took her hand. Slowing her youthful pace to match the older woman's, she led Mia home.

The houses were scattered, as though they couldn't make up their mind to be a village or not. A hundred yards away, another native walked toward a distant house. The two ignored each other.

Mia couldn't stand the silence. She said, "I am Mia."

The girl stopped outside her hut and looked at her.

Mia pointed to her chest. "Mia."

"Es-ef-eb," the girl said, pointing to herself and giving that glorious smile.

Not "ej-es," which must mean something else. Mia pointed to the hut, a primitive affair of untrimmed logs, pieces of foamcast carried from the city, and sheets of faded plastic, all tacked crazily together.

"Ef-ef," said Esefeb, which evidently meant "home." This language was going to be a bitch: degraded *and* confusing.

Esefeb suddenly hopped to one side of the dirt path, laughed, and pointed at blank air. Then she took Mia's hand and led her inside.

More confusion, more degradation. The single room had an open fire with the simple venting system of a hole in the roof. The bed was high on stilts (why?) with a set of rickety steps made of rotting, untrimmed logs. One corner held a collection of huge pots in which grew greenery; Mia saw three unfired clay pots, one of them sagging sideways so far the soil had spilled onto the packed-dirt floor. Also a beautiful titanium vase and a cracked hydroponic vat. On one plant, almost the size of a small tree, hung a second sheet of plastic sarong, this one an unfaded blue-green. Dishes and tools littered the floor, the same mix as the pots of scavenged items and crude homemade ones. The hut smelled of decaying food and unwashed bedding. There was no light source and no machinery.

Kenin's voice sounded softly from her wrister. "Your vid is coming through fine. Even the most primitive human societies have some type of art work."

Mia didn't reply. Her attention was riveted to Esefeb. The girl flung herself up the "stairs" and sat up in bed, facing the wall. What Mia had seen before could hardly be called a smile compared to the light, the sheer joy, that illuminated Esefeb's face now. Esefeb shuddered in ecstasy, crooning to the empty wall.

"Ej-es. Ej-es. Aaahhhh, *Ej-es!*"

Mia turned away. She was a medician, but Esefeb's emotion seemed too private to witness. It was the ecstasy of orgasm, or religious transfiguration, or madness.

"Mia," her wrister said, "I need an image of that girl's brain."

It was easy – too easy, Lolimel said later, and he was right. Creatures, sentient or not, did not behave this way.

"We could haul all the neuro equipment out to the village," Kenin said doubtfully, from base.

"It's not a village, and I don't think that's a good idea," Mia said softly. The softness was unnecessary. Esefeb slept like stone in her high bunk, and the hut was so dark, illuminated only by faint starlight through the hole in the roof, that Mia could barely see her wrister to talk into it. "I think Esefeb might come voluntarily. I'll try in the morning, when it's light."

Kenin, not old but old enough to feel stiff sleeping on the ground, said, "Will you be comfortable there until morning?"

"No, but I'll manage. What does the computer say about the recs?"

Lolimel answered – evidently they were having a regular all-hands conference. "The language is badly degraded International; you probably guessed that. The translator's preparing a lexicon and grammar. The artifacts, food supply, dwelling, everything visual, doesn't add up. They shouldn't have lost so much in 250 years, unless mental deficiency was a side-effect of having survived the virus. But Kenin thinks—" He stopped abruptly.

"You may speak for me," Kenin's voice said, amused. "I think you'll find that military protocol degrades, too, over time. At least, way out here."

"Well, I . . . Kenin thinks it's possible that what the girl has is a mutated version of the virus. Maybe infectious, maybe inheritable, maybe transmitted through fetal infection."

His statement dropped into Mia's darkness, as heavy as Esefeb's sleep.

Mia said, "So the mutated virus could still be extant and active."

"Yes," Kenin said. "We need not only neuro-images but a sample of cerebrospinal fluid. Her behavior suggests—"

"I know what her behavior suggests," Mia said curtly. That sheer joy, shuddering in ecstasy . . . It was seizures in the limbic system, the brain's deep center for primitive emotion, which produced such transcendent, rapturous trances. Religious mystics, Saul on the road to Damascus, visions of Our Lady or of nirvana. And the virus might still be extant, and not a part of the vaccine they had all received. Although if transmission was fetal, the medicians were safe. If not . . .

Mia said, "The rest of Esefeb's behavior doesn't fit with limbic seizures. She seems to see things that aren't there, even talks to her hallucinations, when she's not having an actual seizure."

"I don't know," Kenin said. "There might be multiple infection sites in the brain. I need her, Mia."

"We'll be there," Mia said, and wondered if that were going to be true.

But it was, mostly. Mia, after a brief uncomfortable sleep wrapped in the sheet of blue-green plastic, sat waiting for Esefeb to descend her rickety stairs. The girl bounced down, chattering at something to Mia's right. She smelled worse than yesterday. Mia breathed through her mouth and went firmly up to her.

"Esefeb!" Mia pointed dramatically, feeling like a fool. The girl pointed back.

"Mia."

"Yes, good." Now Mia made a sweep of the sorry hut. "Efef."

"Efef," Esefeb agreed, smiling radiantly.

"Esefeb efef."

The girl agreed that this was her home.

Mia pointed theatrically toward the city. "Mia efef! Mia eb Esefeb etej Mia efef!" *Mia and Esefeb come to Mia's home.* Mia had already raided the computer's tentative lexicon of Good Fortunese.

Esefeb cocked her head and looked quizzical. A worm crawled out of her hair.

Mia repeated, "Mia eb Esefeb etej Mia efef."

Esefeb responded with a torrent of repetitious syllables, none of which meant anything to Mia except "Ej-es." The girl spoke the word with such delight that it had to be a name. A lover? Maybe these people didn't live as solitary as she'd assumed.

Mia took Esefeb's hand and gently tugged her toward the door. Esefeb broke free and sat in the middle of the room, facing a blank wall of crumbling logs, and jabbered away to nothing at all, occasionally laughing and even reaching out to touch empty air. "Ej-es, Ej-es!" Mia watched, bemused, recording everything, making medical assessments. Esefeb wasn't malnourished, for which the natural abundance of the planet was undoubtedly responsible. But she was crawling with parasites, filthy (with water easily available), and isolated. Maybe isolated.

"Lolimel," Mia said softly into the wrister, "what's the best dictionary guess for 'alone'?"

Lolimel said, "The closest we've got is 'one.' There doesn't seem to be a concept for 'unaccompanied,' or at least we haven't found it yet. The word for 'one' is 'eket.'"

When Esefeb finally sprang up happily, Mia said, "Esefeb eket?"

The girl look startled. "Ek, ek," she said: *no, no.* Esefeb ek eket! Esefeb eb Ej-es!"

Esefeb and Ej-es. She was not alone. She had the hallucinatory Ej-es.

Again Mia took Esefeb's hand and pulled her toward the door. This time Esefeb went with her. As they set off toward the city, the girl's legs wobbled. Some parasite that had become active overnight in the leg muscles? Whatever the trouble was, Esefeb blithely ignored it as they traveled, much more slowly than yesterday, to Kenin's makeshift lab in the ruined city. Along the way, Esefeb stopped to watch, laugh at, or talk to three different things that weren't there.

"She's beautiful, under all that neglect," Lolimel said, staring down at the anesthetized girl on Kenin's neuroimaging slab.

Kenin said mildly, "If the mutated virus is transmitted to a fetus, it could also be transmitted sexually."

The young man said hotly, "I wasn't implying—"

Mia said, "Oh, calm down. Lolimel. We've all done it, on numerous worlds."

"Regs say—"

"Regs don't always matter 300 light years from anywhere else," Kenin said, exchanging an amused glance with Mia. "Mia, let's start."

The girl's limp body slid into the neuro-imager. Esefeb hadn't objected to meeting the other medicians, to a minimal washing, to the sedative patch Mia had put on her arm. Thirty seconds later she slumped to the floor. By the time she came to, an incision ten cells thick would have been made into her brain and a sample removed. She would have been harvested, imaged, electroscanned, and mapped. She would never know it; there wouldn't even be a headache.

Three hours later Esefeb sat on the ground with two of the guards, eating soysynth as if it were ambrosia. Mia, Kenin, Lolimel, and the three other medicians sat in a circle twenty yards away, staring at handhelds and analyzing results. It was late afternoon. Long shadows slanted across the gold-green grass, and a small breeze brought the sweet, heavy scent of some native flower.

Paradise, Mia thought. And then: *Bonnet Syndrome*.

She said it aloud, "Charles Bonnet Syndrome," and five people raised their heads to stare at her, returned to their handhelds, and called up medical deebees.

"I think you're right," Kenin said slowly. "I never even heard of it before. Or if I did, I don't remember."

"That's because nobody gets it anymore," Mia said. "It was usually old people whose eye problems weren't corrected. Now we routinely correct eye problems."

Kenin frowned. "But that's not all that's going on with Esefeb."

No, but it was one thing, and why couldn't Kenin give her credit for thinking of it? The next moment she was ashamed of her petty pique. It was just fatigue, sleeping on that hard cold floor in Esefeb's home. *Esefeb efef.* Mia concentrated on Charles Bonnet syndrome.

Patients with the syndrome, which was discovered in the eighteenth century, had damage somewhere in their optic pathway or brain. It could be lesions, macular degeneration, glaucoma, diabetic retinopathy, or even cataracts. Partially blind, people saw and sometimes heard instead things that weren't there, often with startling clarity and realism. Feedback pathways in the brain were two-way information avenues. Visual data, memory, and imagination constantly flowed to and from each other, interacting so vividly that, for example, even a small child could visualize a cat in the absence of any actual cats. But in Bonnet syndrome, there was interruption of the baseline visual data about what was and was not real. So all imaginings and hallucinations were just as real as the ground beneath one's feet.

"Look at the amygdala," medician Berutha said. "Oh merciful gods!"

Both of Esefeb's amygdalae were enlarged and deformed. The

amygdalae, two almond-shaped structures behind the ears, specialized in recognizing the emotional significance of events in the external world. They weren't involved in Charles Bonnet syndrome. Clearly, they were here.

Kenin said, "I think what's happening here is a strengthening or alteration of some neural pathways at the extreme expense of others. Esefeb 'sees' her hallucinations, and she experiences them as just as 'real' – maybe more real – than anything else in her world. And the pathways go down to the limbic, where seizures give some of them an intense emotional significance. Like . . . like orgasm, maybe."

Ej-es.

"Phantoms in the brain," Berutha said.

"A viral god," Lolimel said, surprising Mia. His tone, almost reverential, suddenly irritated her.

"A god responsible for this people's degradation, Lolimel. They're so absorbed in their 'phantoms' that they don't concentrate on the most basic care of themselves. Nor on building, farming, art, innovation . . . *nothing*. They're prisoners of their pretty fantasies."

Lolimel nodded reluctantly. "Yes, I see that."

Berutha said to Kenin, "We need to find the secondary virus. Because if it is infectious through any other vector besides fetal or sexual . . . " He didn't finish the thought.

"I know," Kenin said, "but it isn't going to be easy. We don't have cadavers for the secondary. The analyzer is still working on the cerebral-spinal fluid. Meanwhile—" She began organizing assignments, efficient and clear. Mia stopped listening.

Esefeb had finished her meal and walked up to the circle of scientists. She tugged at Mia's tunic.

"Mia . . . Esefeb etej efef." *Esefeb come home.*

"Mia eb Esefeb etej Esefeb efef," Mia said, and the girl gave her joyous smile.

"Mia—" Kenin said.

"I'm going with her, Kenin. We need more behavioral data. And maybe I can persuade another native or two to submit to examination," Mia argued, feebly. She knew that scientific information was not really her motive. She wasn't sure, however, what was. She just wanted to go with Esefeb.

"Why did you first enter the Corps?" Lolimel's question stuck in Mia's mind, a rhetorical fishbone in the throat, over the next few days. Mia had brought her medkit, and she administered broad-spectrum microbials to Esefeb, hoping something would hit. The parasites were trickier, needing life-cycle analysis or at least some structural knowledge, but she made a start on that, too. *I entered the Corps to relieve suffering, Lolimel.* Odd how naive the truest statements could sound. But that didn't make them any less true.

Esefeb went along with all Mia's pokings, patches, and procedures. She also carried out minimal food-gathering activities, with a haphazard disregard for safety or sanitation that appalled Mia. Mia had carried her own food from the ship. Esefeb ate it just as happily as her own.

But mostly Esefeb talked to Ej-es.

It made Mia feel like a voyeur. Esefeb was so unselfconscious – did she even know she had a "self" apart from Ej-es? She spoke to, laughed at (with?), played beside, and slept with her phantom in the brain, and around her the hut disintegrated even more. Esefeb got diarrhea from something in her water and then the place smelled even more foul. Grimly, Mia cleaned it up. Esefeb didn't seem to notice. Mia was *eket*. Alone in her futile endeavors at sanitation, at health, at civilization.

"Esefeb eb Mia etej efef—" How did you say "neighbors"? Mia consulted the computer's lexicon, steadily growing as the translator program deciphered words from context. It had discovered no word for "neighbor." Nor for "friend" nor "mate" nor any kinship relationships at all except "baby."

Mia was reduced to pointing at the nearest hut. "Esefeb eb Mia etej efef" *over there.*

The neighboring hut had a baby. Both hut and child, a toddler who lay listlessly in one corner, were just as filthy and diseased as Esefeb's house. At first the older woman didn't seem to recognize Esefeb, but when Esefeb said her name, the two women spoke animatedly. The neighbor smiled at Mia. Mia reached for the child, was not prevented from picking him up, and settled the baby on her lap. Discreetly, she examined him.

Sudden rage boiled through her, as unexpected as it was frightening. This child was dying. Of parasites, of infection, of something. A preventable something? Maybe yes, maybe no. The child didn't look neglected, but neither did the mother look concerned.

All at once, the child in her arms stiffened, shuddered, and began to babble. His listlessness vanished. His little dirty face lit up like sunrise and he laughed and reached out his arms toward something not there. His mother and Esefeb turned to watch, also smiling, as the toddler had an unknowable limbic seizure in his dying, ecstatic brain.

Mia set him down on the floor. She called up the dictionary, but before she could say anything, the mother, too, had a seizure and sat on the dirt floor, shuddering with joy. Esefeb watched her a moment before chattering to something Mia couldn't see.

Mia couldn't stand it any more. She left, walking as fast as she could back to Esefeb's house, disgusted and frightened and . . . what?

Envious?

"Why did you first enter the Corps?" To serve humanity, to live purposefully, to find, as all men and women hope, happiness. And she had, sometimes, been happy.

But she had never known such joy as that.

Nonetheless, she argued with herself, the price was too high. These people were dying off because of their absorption in their rapturous phantoms. They lived isolated, degraded, sickly lives, which were undoubtedly shorter than necessary. It was obscene.

In her clenched hand was a greasy hair sample she'd unobtrusively cut from the toddler's head as he sat on her lap. Hair, that dead tissue, was a person's fossilized past. Mia intended a DNA scan.

Esefeb strolled in an hour later. She didn't seem upset at Mia's abrupt departure. With her was Lolimel.

"I met her on the path," Lolimel said, although nothing as well-used as a path connected the huts. "She doesn't seem to mind my coming here."

"Or anything else," Mia said. "What did you bring?" He had to have brought something tangible; Kenin would have used the wrister to convey information.

"Tentative prophylactic. We haven't got a vaccine yet, and

Kenin says it may be too difficult; better to go directly to a cure to hold in reserve in case any of us comes down with this."

Mia caught the omission. "Any of *us*? What about them?"

Lolimel looked down at his feet. "It's, um, a borderline case, Mia. The decision hasn't been made yet."

"'Borderline' how, Lolimel? It's a virus infecting the brains of humans and degrading their functioning."

He was embarrassed. "Section Six says that, um, some biological conditions, especially persistent ones, create cultural differences for which Corps policy is non-interference. Section Six mentions the religious dietary laws that grew out of inherited food intolerances on—"

"I know what Section Six says, Lolimel! But you don't measure a culture's degree of success by its degree of happiness!"

"I don't think . . . that is, I don't know . . . maybe 'degree of success' isn't what Section Six means." He looked away from her. The tips of his ears grew red.

Poor Lolimel. She and Kenin had as much as told him that out here regs didn't matter. Except when they did. Mia stood. "You say the decision hasn't been made yet?"

He looked surprised. "How could it be? You're on the senior Corps board to make the decision."

Of course she was. How could she forget . . . she forgot more things these days, momentary lapses symbolic of the greater lapses to come. No brain functioned for ever.

"Mia, are you all—"

"I'm fine. And I'm glad you're here. I want to go back to the city for a few days. You can stay with Esefeb and continue the surveillance. You can also extend to her neighbors the antibiotic, antiviral, and anti-parasite protocols I've worked through with Esefeb. Here, I'll show you."

"But I—"

"That's an order."

She felt bad about it later, of course. But Lolimel would get over it.

At base everything had the controlled frenzy of steady, unremitting work. Meek now, not a part of the working team, Mia ran a DNA scan on the baby's hair. It showed what she expected. The child shared 50 percent DNA with Esefeb. He was her brother; the neighbor whom Esefeb clearly never saw, who had at first not recognized Esefeb, was her mother. For which there was still no word in the translator deebee.

"I think we've got it," Kenin said, coming into Mia's room. She collapsed on a stone bench, still beautiful after two and a half centuries. Kenin had the beatific serenity of a hard job well done.

"A cure?"

"Tentative. Radical. I wouldn't want to use it on one of us unless we absolutely have to, but we can refine it more. At least it's in reserve, so a part of the team can begin creating and disseminating medical help these people can actually use. Targeted microbials, an anti-parasite protocol."

"I've already started on that," Mia said, her stomach tightening. "Kenin, the board needs to meet."

"Not tonight. I'm soooo sleepy." Theatrically she stretched both arms; words and gesture were unlike her.

"Tonight," Mia said. While Kenin was feeling so accomplished. Let Kenin feel the full contrast to what she could do with what Esefeb could.

Kenin dropped her arms and looked at Mia. Her whole demeanor changed, relaxation into fortress. "Mia . . . I've already polled everyone privately. And run the computer sims. We'll meet, but the decision is going to be to extend no cure. The phantoms are a biologically based cultural difference."

"The hell they are! These people are dying out!"

"No, they're not. If they were heading for extinction, it'd be a different situation. But the satellite imagery and population equations, based on data left by the generation that had the plague, show they're increasing. Slowly, but a definite population gain significant to the point-oh-one level of confidence."

"Kenin—"

"I'm exhausted, Mia. Can we talk about it tomorrow?"

Plan on it, Mia thought grimly. She stored the data on the dying toddler's matrilineage in her handheld.

A week in base, and Mia could convince no one, not separately nor in a group. Medicians typically had tolerant psychological profiles, with higher-than-average acceptance of the unusual, divergent, and eccentric. Otherwise, they wouldn't have joined the Corps.

On the third day, to keep herself busy, Mia joined the junior medicians working on refining the cure for what was now verified as "limbic seizures with impaired sensory input causing Charles Bonnet syndrome." Over the next few weeks it became clear to Mia what Kenin had meant; this treatment, if they had to use it, would be brutally hard on the brain. What was that old ditty? *"Cured last night of my disease, I died today of my physician."* Well, it still happened enough in the Corps. Another reason behind the board's decision.

She felt a curious reluctance to go back to Esefeb. Or, as the words kept running through her mind, *Mia ek etej Esefeb efef.* God, it was a tongue twister. These people didn't just need help with parasites, they needed an infusion of new consonants. It was a relief to be back at base, to be working with her mind, solving technical problems alongside rational scientists. Still, she couldn't shake a feeling of being alone, being lonely: *Mia eket.*

Or maybe the feeling was more like futility.

"Lolimel's back," Jamal said. He'd come up behind her as she sat at dusk on her favorite stone bench, facing the city. At this time of day the ruins looked romantic, infused with history. The sweet scents of that night-blooming flower, which Mia still hadn't identified, wafted around her.

"I think you should come now," Jamal said, and this time Mia heard his tone. She spun around. In the alien shadows Jamal's face was set as ice.

"He's contracted it," Mia said, knowing beyond doubt that it was true. The virus wasn't just fetally transmitted, it wasn't a slow-acting retrovirus, and if Lolimel had slept with Esefeb . . . But he wouldn't be that stupid. He was a medician, he'd been warned . . .

"We don't really know anything solid about the goddamn thing!" Jamal burst out.

"We never do," Mia said, and the words cracked her dry lips like salt.

Lolimel stood in the center of the ruined atrium, giggling at something only he could see. Kenin, who could have proceeded without Mia, nodded at her. Mia understood; Kenin acknowledged the special bond Mia had with the young medician. The cure was untested, probably brutal, no more really than dumping a selection of poisons in the right areas of the brain, in itself problematical with the blood-brain barrier.

Mia made herself walk calmly up to Lolimel. "What's so funny, Lolimel?"

"All those sandwigs crawling in straight lines over the floor. I never saw blue ones before."

Sandwigs. Lolimel, she remembered, had been born on New Carthage. Sandwigs were always red.

Lolimel said, "But why is there a tree growing out of your head, Mia?"

"Strong fertilizer," she said. "Lolimel, did you have sex with Esefeb?"

He looked genuinely shocked. "No!"

"All right." He might or might not be lying.

Jamal whispered, "A chance to study the hallucinations in someone who can fully articulate—"

"No," Kenin said. "Time matters with this . . . " Mia saw that she couldn't bring herself to say "cure."

Realization dawned on Lolimel's face. "Me? You're going to . . . *me*? There's nothing wrong with me!"

"Lolimel, dear heart . . . " Mia said.

"I don't have it!"

"And the floor doesn't have sandwigs. Lolimel—"

"No!"

The guards had been alerted. Lolimel didn't make it out of the atrium. They held him, flailing and yelling, while Kenin deftly slapped on a tranq patch. In ten seconds he was out.

"Tie him down securely," Kenin said, breathing hard. "Daniel, get the brain bore started as soon as he's prepped. Everyone else, start packing up, and impose quarantine. We can't risk this for anyone else here. I'm calling a Section Eleven."

Section Eleven: *If the MedCorps officer in charge deems the risk to Corps members to exceed the gain to colonists by a factor of three or more, the officer may pull the Corps off-planet.*

It was the first time Mia had ever seen Kenin make a unilateral decision.

Twenty-four hours later, Mia sat beside Lolimel as dusk crept
over the city. The shuttle had already carried up most personnel
and equipment. Lolimel was in the last shift because, as Kenin did
not need to say aloud, if he died, his body would be left behind.
But Lolimel had not died. He had thrashed in unconscious
seizures, had distorted his features in silent grimaces of pain until
Mia would not have recognized him, had suffered malfunctions
in alimentary, lymphatic, endocrine, and parasympathetic nervous systems, all recorded on the monitors. But he would live. The
others didn't know it, but Mia did.

"We're ready for him, Mia," the young tech said. "Are you on
this shuttle, too?"

"No, the last one. Move him carefully. We don't know how
much pain he's actually feeling through the meds."

She watched the gurney slide out of the room, its monitors
looming over Lolimel like cliffs over a raging river. When he'd
gone, Mia slipped into the next building, and then the next. Such
beautiful buildings: spacious atria, beautifully proportioned
rooms, one structure flowing into another.

Eight buildings away, she picked up the pack she'd left there. It
was heavy, even though it didn't contain everything she had
cached around the city. It was so easy to take things when a base
was being hastily withdrawn. Everyone was preoccupied, everyone assumed anything not readily visible was already packed,
inventories were neglected and the deebees not cross-checked.
No time. Historically, war had always provided great opportuni-
ties for profiteers.

Was that what she was? Yes, but not a profit measured in
money. Measure it, rather, in lives saved, or restored to dignity, or
enhanced. *"Why did you first enter the Corps?"* Because I'm a
medician, Lolimel. Not an anthropologist.

They would notice, of course, that Mia herself wasn't aboard
the last shuttle. But Kenin, at least, would realize that searching
for her would be a waste of valuable resources when Mia didn't
want to be found. And Mia was so old. Surely the old should be
allowed to make their own decisions.

Although she would miss them, these Corps members who
had been her family since the last assignment shuffle, eighteen
months ago and decades ago, depending on whose time you

counted by. Especially she would miss Lolimel. But this was the right way to end her life, in service to these colonists' health. She was a medician.

It went better than Mia could have hoped. When the ship had gone – she'd seen it leave orbit, a fleeting stream of light – Mia went to Esefeb.

"Mia etej efef," Esefeb said with her rosy smile. *Mia come home.* Mia walked toward her, hugged the girl, and slapped the tranq patch on her neck.

For the next week, Mia barely slept. After the makeshift surgery, she tended Esefeb through the seizures, vomiting, diarrhea, pain. On the morning the girl woke up, herself again, Mia was there to bathe the feeble body, feed it, nurse Esefeb. She recovered very fast; the cure was violent on the body but not as debilitating as everyone had feared. And afterwards Esefeb was quieter, meeker, and surprisingly intelligent as Mia taught her the rudiments of water purification, sanitation, safe food storage, health care. By the time Mia moved on to Esefeb's mother's house, Esefeb was free of most parasites, and Mia was working on the rest. Esefeb never mentioned her former hallucinations. It was possible she didn't remember them.

"Esefeb ekebet," Mia said as she hefted her pack to leave. *Esefeb be well.*

Esefeb nodded. She stood quietly as Mia trudged away, and when Mia turned to wave at her, Esefeb waved back.

Mia shifted the pack on her shoulders. It seemed heavier than before. Or maybe Mia was just older. Two weeks older, merely, but two weeks could make a big difference. An enormous difference.

Two weeks could start to save a civilization.

Night fell. Esefeb sat on the stairs to her bed, clutching the blue-green sheet of plastic in both hands. She sobbed and shivered, her clean face contorted. Around her, the unpopulated shadows grew thicker and darker. Eventually, she wailed aloud to the empty night.

"Ej-es! O, Ej-es! Ej-es, Esefeb eket! Ej-es . . . etej efef! O, etej efef!"

THE CARTOGRAPHER WASPS
AND THE ANARCHIST BEES

E. Lily Yu

For longer than anyone could remember, the village of Yiwei had worn, in its orchards and under its eaves, clay-colored globes of paper that hissed and fizzed with wasps. The villagers maintained an uneasy peace with their neighbors for many years, exercising inimitable tact and circumspection. But it all ended the day a boy, digging in the riverbed, found a stone whose balance and weight pleased him. With this, he thought, he could hit a sparrow in flight. There were no sparrows to be seen, but a paper ball hung low and inviting nearby. He considered it for a moment, head cocked, then aimed and threw.

Much later, after he had been plastered and soothed, his mother scalded the fallen nest until the wasps seething in the paper were dead. In this way it was discovered that the wasp nests of Yiwei, dipped in hot water, unfurled into beautifully accurate maps of provinces near and far, inked in vegetable pigments and labeled in careful Mandarin that could be distinguished beneath a microscope.

The villagers' subsequent incursions with bee veils and kettles of boiling water soon diminished the prosperous population to a handful. Commanded by a single stubborn foundress, the survivors folded a new nest in the shape of a paper boat, provisioned it with fallen apricots and squash blossoms, and launched themselves onto the river. Browsing cows and children fled the riverbanks as they drifted downstream, piping sea chanteys.

At last, forty miles south from where they had begun, their craft snagged on an upthrust stick and sank. Only one drowned in the evacuation, weighed down with the remains of an apricot.

They reconvened upon a stump and looked about themselves.

"It's a good place to land," the foundress said in her sweet soprano, examining the first rough maps that the scouts brought back. There were plenty of caterpillars, oaks for ink galls, fruiting brambles, and no signs of other wasps. A colony of bees had hived in a split oak two miles away. "Once we are established we will, of course, send a delegation to collect tribute.

"We will not make the same mistakes as before. Ours is a race of explorers and scientists, cartographers and philosophers, and to rest and grow slothful is to die. Once we are established here, we will expand."

It took two weeks to complete the nurseries with their paper mobiles, and then another month to reconstruct the Great Library and fill the pigeonholes with what the oldest cartographers could remember of their lost maps. Their comings and goings did not go unnoticed. An ambassador from the beehive arrived with an ultimatum and was promptly executed; her wings were made into stained-glass windows for the council chamber, and her stinger was returned to the hive in a paper envelope. The second ambassador came with altered attitude and a proposal to divide the bees' kingdom evenly between the two governments, retaining pollen and water rights for the bees – "as an acknowledgment of the preexisting claims of a free people to the natural resources of a common territory," she hummed.

The wasps of the council were gracious and only divested the envoy of her sting. She survived just long enough to deliver her account to the hive.

The third ambassador arrived with a ball of wax on the tip of her stinger and was better received.

"You understand, we are not refugees applying for recognition of a token territorial sovereignty," the foundress said, as attendants served them nectars in paper horns, "nor are we negotiating with you as equal states. Those were the assumptions of your late predecessors. They were mistaken."

"I trust I will do better," the diplomat said stiffly. She was older than the others, and the hairs of her thorax were sparse and faded.

"I do hope so."

"Unlike them, I have complete authority to speak for the hive.

You have propositions for us; that is clear enough. We are prepared to listen."

"Oh, good." The foundress drained her horn and took another. "Yours is an old and highly cultured society, despite the indolence of your ruler, which we understand to be a racial rather than personal proclivity. You have laws, and traditional dances, and mathematicians, and principles, which of course we do respect."

"Your terms, please."

She smiled. "Since there is a local population of tussah moths, which we prefer for incubation, there is no need for anything so unrepublican as slavery. If you refrain from insurrection, you may keep your self-rule. But we will take a fifth of your stores in an ordinary year, and a tenth in drought years, and one of every hundred larvae."

"To eat?" Her antennae trembled with revulsion.

"Only if food is scarce. No, they will be raised among us and learn our ways and our arts, and then they will serve as officials and bureaucrats among you. It will be to your advantage, you see."

The diplomat paused for a moment, looking at nothing at all. Finally she said, "A tenth, in a good year—"

"Our terms," the foundress said, "are not negotiable."

The guards shifted among themselves, clinking the plates of their armor and shifting the gleaming points of their stings.

"I don't have a choice, do I?"

"The choice is enslavement or cooperation," the foundress said. "For your hive, I mean. You might choose something else, certainly, but they have tens of thousands to replace you with."

The diplomat bent her head. "I am old," she said. "I have served the hive all my life, in every fashion. My loyalty is to my hive and I will do what is best for it."

"I am so very glad."

"I ask you – I beg you – to wait three or four days to impose your terms. I will be dead by then, and will not see my sisters become a servile people."

The foundress clicked her claws together. "Is the delaying of business a custom of yours? We have no such practice. You will have the honor of watching us elevate your sisters to moral and technological heights you could never imagine."

The diplomat shivered.

"Go back to your queen, my dear. Tell them the good news."

It was a crisis for the constitutional monarchy. A riot broke out in District 6, destroying the royal waxworks and toppling the mouse-bone monuments before it was brutally suppressed. The queen had to be calmed with large doses of jelly after she burst into tears on her ministers' shoulders.

"Your Majesty," said one, "it's not a matter for your concern. Be at peace."

"These are my children," she said, sniffling. "You would feel for them too, were you a mother."

"Thankfully, I am not," the minister said briskly, "so to business."

"War is out of the question," another said.

"Their forces are vastly superior."

"We outnumber them 300 to one!"

"They are experienced fighters. Sixty of us would die for each of theirs. We might drive them away, but it would cost us most of the hive and possibly our queen—"

The queen began weeping noisily again and had to be cleaned and comforted.

"Have we any alternatives?"

There was a small silence.

"Very well, then."

The terms of the relationship were copied out, at the wasps' direction, on small paper plaques embedded in propolis and wax around the hive. As paper and ink were new substances to the bees, they jostled and touched and tasted the bills until the paper fell to pieces. The wasps sent to oversee the installation did not take this kindly. Several civilians died before it was established that the bees could not read the Yiwei dialect.

Thereafter the hive's chemists were charged with compounding pheromones complex enough to encode the terms of the treaty. These were applied to the papers, so that both species could inspect them and comprehend the relationship between the two states.

Whereas the hive before the wasp infestation had been busy but content, the bees now lived in desperation. The natural terms of their lives were cut short by the need to gather enough honey for both the hive and the wasp nest. As they traveled farther and farther afield in search of nectar, they stopped singing. They danced their findings grimly, without joy. The queen herself grew gaunt and thin from breeding replacements, and certain ministers who understood such matters began feeding royal jelly to the strongest larvae.

Meanwhile, the wasps grew sleek and strong. Cadres of scholars, cartographers, botanists, and soldiers were dispatched on the river in small floating nests caulked with beeswax and loaded with rations of honeycomb to chart the unknown lands to the south. Those who returned bore beautiful maps with towns and farms and alien populations of wasps carefully noted in blue and purple ink, and these, once studied by the foundress and her generals, were carefully filed away in the depths of the Great Library for their southern advance in the new year.

The bees adopted by the wasps were first trained to clerical tasks, but once it was determined that they could be taught to read and write, they were assigned to some of the reconnaissance missions. The brightest students, gifted at trigonometry and angles, were educated beside the cartographers themselves and proved valuable assistants. They learned not to see the thick green caterpillars led on silver chains, or the dead bees fed to the wasp brood. It was easier that way.

When the old queen died, they did not mourn.

By the sheerest of accidents, one of the bees trained as a cartographer's assistant was an anarchist. It might have been the stresses on the hive, or it might have been luck; wherever it came from, the mutation was viable. She tucked a number of her own eggs in beeswax and wasp paper among the pigeonholes of the library and fed the larvae their milk and bread in secret. To her sons in their capped silk cradles – and they were all sons – she whispered the precepts she had developed while calculating flight paths and azimuths, that there should be no queen and no state, and that, as in the wasp nest, the males should labor and profit equally with the females. In their sleep and slow transformation they heard her teachings and instructions, and when they chewed their way out of their cells and out of the wasp nest, they made their way to the hive.

The damage to the nest was discovered, of course, but by then the anarchist was dead of old age. She had done impeccable work, her tutor sighed, looking over the filigree of her inscriptions, but the brilliant were subject to mental aberrations, were they not? He buried beneath grumblings and labors his fondness for her, which had become a grief to him and a political liability, and he never again took on any student from the hive who showed a glint of talent.

Though they had the bitter smell of the wasp nest in their hair, the anarchist's twenty sons were permitted to wander freely through the hive, as it was assumed that they were either spies or on official business. When the new queen emerged from her chamber, they joined unnoticed the other drones in the nuptial flight. Two succeeded in mating with her. Those who failed and survived spoke afterward in hushed tones of what had been done for the sake of the ideal. Before they died they took propolis and oak-apple ink and inscribed upon the lintels of the hive, in a shorthand they had developed, the story of the first anarchist and her twenty sons.

Anarchism being a heritable trait in bees, a number of the daughters of the new queen found themselves questioning the purpose of the monarchy. Two were taken by the wasps and taught to read and write. On one of their visits to the hive they spotted the history of their forefathers, and, being excellent scholars, soon figured out the translation.

They found their sisters in the hive who were unquiet in soul and whispered to them the strange knowledge they had learned among the wasps: astronomy, military strategy, the state of the world beyond the farthest flights of the bees. Hitherto educated as dancers and architects, nurses and foragers, the bees were full of a new wonder, stranger even than the first day they flew from the hive and felt the sun on their backs.

"Govern us," they said to the two wasp-taught anarchists, but they refused.

"A perfect society needs no rulers," they said. "Knowledge and authority ought to be held in common. In order to imagine a new existence, we must free ourselves from the structures of both our failed government and the unjustifiable hegemony of the wasp nests. Hear what you can hear and learn what you can learn while we remain among them. But be ready."

It was the first summer in Yiwei without the immemorial hum of the cartographer wasps. In the orchards, though their skins split with sweetness, fallen fruit lay unmolested, and children played barefoot with impunity. One of the villagers' daughters, in her third year at an agricultural college, came home in the back of a pickup truck at the end of July. She thumped her single suitcase against the gate before opening it, to scatter the chickens, then raised the latch and swung the iron aside, and was immediately wrapped in a flying hug.

Once she disentangled herself from brother and parents and liberally distributed kisses, she listened to the news she'd missed: how the cows were dying from drinking stonecutters' dust in the streams; how grain prices were falling everywhere, despite the drought; and how her brother, little fool that he was, had torn down a wasp nest and received a faceful of red and white lumps for it. One of the most detailed wasp's maps had reached the capital, she was told, and a bureaucrat had arrived in a sleek black car. But because the wasps were all dead, he could report little more than a prank, a freak, or a miracle. There were no further inquiries.

Her brother produced for her inspection the brittle, boiled bodies of several wasps in a glass jar, along with one of the smaller maps. She tickled him until he surrendered his trophies, promised him a basket of peaches in return, and let herself be fed to tautness. Then, to her family's dismay, she wrote an urgent letter to the Academy of Sciences and packed a satchel with clothes and cash. If she could find one more nest of wasps, she said, it would make their fortune and her name. But it had to be done quickly.

In the morning, before the cockerels woke and while the sky was still purple, she hopped onto her old bicycle and rode down the dusty path.

Bees do not fly at night or lie to each other, but the anarchists had learned both from the wasps. On a warm, clear evening they left the hive at last, flying west in a small tight cloud. Around them swelled the voices of summer insects, strange and disquieting.

Several miles west of the old hive and the wasp nest, in a light-ning-scarred elm, the anarchists had built up a small stock of stolen honey sealed in wax and paper. They rested there for the night, in cells of clean white wax, and in the morning they arose to the building of their city.

The first business of the new colony was the laying of eggs, which a number of workers set to, and provisions for winter. One egg from the old queen, brought from the hive in an anarchist's jaws, was hatched and raised as a new mother. Uncrowned and unconcerned, she too laid mortar and wax, chewed wood to make paper, and fanned the storerooms with her wings.

The anarchists labored secretly but rapidly, drones alongside workers, because the copper taste of autumn was in the air. None had seen a winter before, but the memory of the species is subtle and long, and in their hearts, despite the summer sun, they felt an imminent darkness.

The flowers were fading in the fields. Every day the anarchists added to their coffers of warm gold and built their white walls higher. Every day the air grew a little crisper, the grass a little drier. They sang as they worked, sometimes ballads from the old hive, sometimes anthems of their own devising, and for a time they were happy. Too soon, the leaves turned flame colors and blew from the trees, and then there were no more flowers. The anarchists pressed down the lid on the last vat of honey and wondered what was coming.

Four miles away, at the first touch of cold, the wasps licked shut their paper doors and slept in a tight knot around the foun-dress. In both beehives, the bees huddled together, awake and watchful, warming themselves with the thrumming of their wings. The anarchists murmured comfort to each other.

"There will be more, after us. It will breed out again."

"We are only the beginning."

"There will be more."

Snow fell silently outside.

The snow was ankle-deep and the river iced over when the girl from Yiwei reached up into the empty branches of an oak tree and plucked down the paper castle of a nest. The wasps within, drowsy with cold, murmured but did not stir. In their barracks the soldiers dreamed of the unexplored south and battles in strange cities, among strange peoples, and scouts dreamed of the corpses of starved and frozen deer. The cartographers dreamed of the changes that winter would work on the landscape, the diverted creeks and dead trees they would have to note down. They did not feel the burlap bag that settled around them, nor the crunch of tires on the frozen road.

She had spent weeks tramping through the countryside, questioning beekeepers and villagers' children, peering up into trees and into hives, before she found the last wasps from Yiwei. Then she had had to wait for winter and the anesthetizing cold. But now, back in the warmth of her own room, she broke open the soft pages of the nest and pushed aside the heaps of glistening wasps until she found the foundress herself, stumbling on uncertain legs.

When it thawed, she would breed new foundresses among the village's apricot trees. The letters she received indicated a great demand for them in the capital, particularly from army generals and the captains of scientific explorations. In years to come, the village of Yiwei would be known for its delicately inscribed maps, the legends almost too small to see, and not for its barley and oats, its velvet apricots and glassy pears.

In the spring, the old beehive awoke to find the wasps gone, like a nightmare that evaporates by day. It was difficult to believe, but when not the slightest scrap of wasp paper could be found, the whole hive sang with delight. Even the queen, who had been coached from the pupa on the details of her client state and the conditions by which she ruled, and who had felt, perhaps, more sympathy for the wasps than she should have, cleared her throat and trilled once or twice. If she did not sing so loudly or so joyously as the rest, only a few noticed, and the winter had been a hard one, anyhow.

The maps had vanished with the wasps. No more would be made. Those who had studied among the wasps began to draft memoranda and the first independent decrees of queen and council. To defend against future invasions, it was decided that a detachment of bees would fly the borders of their land and carry home reports of what they found.

It was on one of these patrols that a small hive was discovered in the fork of an elm tree. Bees lay dead and brittle around it, no identifiable queen among them. Not a trace of honey remained in the storehouse; the dark wax of its walls had been gnawed to rags. Even the brood cells had been scraped clean. But in the last intact hexagons they found, curled and capped in wax, scrawled on page after page, words of revolution. They read in silence.

Then—

"Write," one said to the other, and she did.

THE DEATH OF SUGAR DADDY

Toiya Kristen Finley

Laffy Taffy – July 7

"Quit digging, girl!"

This was before all of the cryin, before that black hole started suckin me in, and my wrist wasn't so bad back then, neither.

I didn't mean to scratch that hard. Momma had her back to me, but she heard anyway. I pulled my sleeve over the bad spot on my wrist and went at it again. My nail wasn't sharp enough through the dress, though.

"Keisha." This time Momma turned all the way around. Folded her arms. Ms. Bentley's boyfriend watched Momma shuffle her hips and scratched under his chin.

"You know how impetigo spreads?" Momma said. "Now stop picking at your wrist before it gets raw."

This wasn't no mosquito bite, though. I couldn't leave it alone, neither. But there was nuthin wrong with my wrist, far as I could see. I rubbed it down with lotion and put Vaseline on top of that. All that did was give me greasy skin. My wrist still itched. I wanted to get home so I could try alcohol like Momma used when I got chiggers on my legs, but Momma liked to hang around after weddings, even for people she didn't know. This girl was the niece or granddaughter of somebody Grandmommy used to go to church with. That didn't mean Grandmommy thought she had to come and drag me along. At least Momma wasn't makin me wear them real lacy dresses no more. All the other eleven year olds – and some of the ten year olds, too – had relaxers, and they could run a comb through their hair without worryin about breakin any of it off. But I was stuck with twist ties and barrettes. Momma got the hint I wouldn't bother with em no more at the last weddin when I kept shakin my head and clankin those dumb barrettes together. Today she finally pressed my hair.

"It's not here," Ms. Bentley said. Her and Momma and Ms. Waters went through the Guestbook. The bride and groom had left the church about twenty minutes ago, and the front doors were wide open lettin the sticky and humidity in. Me and Ms. Bentley's boyfriend, I mean *companion,* as Momma called him in her voice to make stuff sound more important than it was, me and Ms. Bentley's companion stood in the doorway of the north ex, or whatever it's called, so Momma and Ms. Bentley'd get a clue. He fiddled with his keys in his pocket, tryin real hard not to frown. But he mumbled stuff to himself and smiled at me when he caught me watchin. Momma taught me how to act, though. I could stand there ladylike all day without buttin into grown people's business.

"Well," Ms. Waters said, "I guess not." She raised her eyebrow cuz she didn't believe it herself. Momma, Ms. Bentley, and Ms. Waters stood there and looked at each other for a second before Momma decided we could *finally* go.

Martin Hughes (r) scored 25 points in Fisk's 65–63 victory over the Tennessee State Tigers.

I pushed the liver around on my plate so it wouldn't touch the mashed potatoes. Then I wiped my fork on a napkin so the liver juice wouldn't dirty my peas. I stuffed peas in my mouth, and Momma glared at me.

"You better eat some of that meat, Keisha."

She didn't expect me to eat all of it. She never expected me to eat all my liver, only a mouthful so I never got why she bothered to give it to me. Liver was all spongy, what brains might taste like, cept the liver holds all the stuff that makes puke, and that just makes it worse. Momma cut off a piece the size of my pinky. She shook the plate so hard my peas rolled into the brown streaks.

"There. You can handle that . . . You know, we didn't see Sugar Daddy today."

Grandmommy sucked her teeth and snorted. "You probably missed that trifling, dirty old man. He must have slipped out."

"No, Mom, his name wasn't even in the Guestbook."

"Maybe he's out of town."

"When did that fool ever miss a summer wedding?"

"Can I git some more mashed potatoes?"

Grandmommy looked at me sideways. "I don't know. *Can* you *git* them? Who taught you to speak that way?"

I opened my mouth real wide and spoke slow. "*May. I. Get.* Some. More. Mashed. Po. Ta. Toes?"

"I still see that liver," Momma said.

I picked up the piece she cut off for me with my fingers and swallowed it whole.

"Keisha . . . " Momma said.

"I ate it!"

"Everything else was very sweet. They took communion together, and I really do prefer string quartets to the organ, but it was weird not seeing that chocolate or olive-green polyester suit in the back."

"Womanizing antics," Grandmommy mumbled. "They'll survive Sugar Daddy not attending. I'm surprised he never hit on her."

"Mom, you know she's too classy for him."

"Sugar Daddy?" I said.

"I remember when he came to my wedding. I remember the gift."

"Went to mine, too," Grandmommy said.

Grandmommy always brought up something else whenever Momma mentioned anything to do with Daddy. Daddy had moved down to Alabama, so Grandmommy couldn't keep an eye on him. But it was my fault I said I didn't know I could walk five miles without gettin tired. That happened last summer, when Daddy still didn't have enough for a car. I didn't hear everything Grandmommy said over the phone, but she did tell Daddy she'd come down there after him with a shotgun if he dragged me across Mobile again.

So, this summer I didn't get to see him at all, and I was stuck here with Grandmommy making me speak proper.

"May I be excused? I'll be back before the light's gone."

"You watch yourself with Tey and Marcus," Momma said.

Momma and Grandmommy don't like Tey and Marcus much

cuz of their father. Grandmommy swears their daddy sold coke or smack or one of them really bad drugs. He been in and out of jail so many times – he gotta be doin *sumthin*, Grandmommy said. Tey and Marcus's grandmother lived next door to Grandmommy for years, and she couldn't believe that woman would let her son turn into such a mess. (But at least she trusted their grandmother, which was the only reason I could play with Marcus and Tey.) I didn't see their father all that much. When he did come around, he'd drive his blue Pinto up and down Jefferson Street at 70 MPH. Late at night, if I heard gears shift three or four times, then a loud screech, I knew he was back in town, back from wherever he was hangin out, at least. Bein in jail was bad, but Marcus and Tey weren't too bad, so their own father couldna been, neither. I wonder if he was like Daddy. Daddy was fine til he got laid off. He spent all last summer lookin for a new job, but nobody bothered to hire him. He couldn't pay for the water for a while, so I had to pee in a bucket (I still ain't told Momma and Grandmommy bout that, and I ain't gonna), but he got a job now. He probably had enough to get a new car. I coulda spent the summer with him, like I'm supposed to. If I just kept my dumb mouth shut.

So, maybe Tey and Marcus's father wasn't so different. Maybe he lost his job and turned to dealin to take care of his two kids. Grandmommy figured he left em next door when he didn't have enough to support em. They showed up at the weirdest times durin the school year and summer and left again sometimes before I could say bye. But they're not bad kids. Not at all. The worst thing they did was sell bootlegs out the back of some dude's car. They thought it was cool cuz they got connections to the music business. I could care less. Those CDs weren't from no real rappers.

"Oooooo, Keisha back in her girlie braids!"

"Shut up, Tey!" Wasn't my fault Momma did my hair right after the weddin. "It looked good. You wish your nappy head could!"

"Your head nappier than mine," Tey said. "Probably why you gotta hide them naps under braids."

I rolled my eyes and watched Marcus light a pagoda. He'd been waitin a while for some to arrive. We were all bored of firecrackers and rockets after the 4th. The pagoda didn't get here in time. Tey smiled at me. I cut my eyes at him and folded my arms. The five stories spun in blues and reds and greens and yellows and whites. Like a water fountain should be, but all on fire and burnin bright. We could shoot fireworks all night if we wanted. Not too many cars came down our street.

"Granny went to a funeral today," Tey said. "How come there're so many weddings and funerals in the summer? Weddings are good, right? Why you wanna celebrate a good thing when everybody dies?"

"Marriage is only good at first. It don't end up that way," Marcus said.

"That still don't tell me nuthin. Why so many people die in the summer anyway? Do heat just fry old people?"

Marcus sucked his teeth. "That cat Granny went to see wasn't old."

"Old," Tey said, "but not *old* old. Forty something-or-other's still up there."

"Can we *do* something else?" I said. Momma was somewhere round forty, and I had no idea how old Grandmommy was. It wasn't never a good thing when a woman hid her age like that.

Sometimes I forgot my wrist bothered me, like a quiet, annoyin sound I could get used to in a room. But it got to itchin before we passed Discount 4 Less. Momma and Grandmommy didn't want me anywhere near the place. They'd be real pissed if they knew I was gettin candy right next door. Discount 4 Less on the corner used to be a Lee's Chicken way back in the day. I loved Lee's. Daddy used to get me a fish sandwich every Saturday at the one not far from where me and Daddy and Momma used to live. When Lee's shut down, somebody tried to turn it into a fashion boutique. Then it was a Meat 'N' Three. Didn't nobody have success until these foreign cats started sellin beer and tobacco cheap.

I stopped in the middle of the sidewalk and clenched my teeth real tight. I held my hand hard against my leg and scratched and scratched and dug and dug. I breathed air through my teeth til I started makin hissy sounds. The skin burned, and I scraped some of it away. But underneath the hurt, it was still itchin. I put my wrist in my mouth and nibbled a bit.

"Girl?" Marcus said.

"What's your problem?" Tey said.

"It keep on botherin me." I showed them where I clawed and the little red spots that popped up around it.

"That's what Vaseline's for. If it help your crusty knees, I'm sure it'll fix that."

I kicked at Tey. "Dumbass. I already done tried that."

Durin the summers, most of the teenagers didn't have the students from Tennessee State to hang out with – the freshmen and sophomores who'd put up with them, at least. So all the teenagers could do was bum around like me and Marcus and Tey, cept they didn't like lightin fireworks. All the teenagers round here sat around in cars at Hadley Parks blastin music or crowded outside of Alger's Market at the mini shopping center, right across from Discount 4 Less. The lady who owned Alger's let them mill around as long as they bought sumthin from her first. Plenty of cops cruised by to make sure those knuckleheads didn't cross over to the wrong side of the parkin lot for beer or smoke anythin worse than cigarettes.

Marcus spotted her first. He was always spottin her, watchin her whenever she visited Grandmommy. Ryan could always be found with those girls who got their hair done at the beauty shop every week and got their nails done up with designs, and hand massages, and knew how to look like ladies instead of hos. Grandmommy woulda beat Ryan *and* my aunt if she ever caught Ryan flashin her cleavage crack or a thong. Marcus liked to stare at her long enough just to let her know. She was only a year older, but Marcus was too ghetto for her. He still hadn't figured that out.

"Hey, Ryan!" I yelled. Me and Tey and Marcus were standin in front of the Alger's Market entrance, and Ryan was to our right, almost on top of us. Those girls weren't talkin too loud. Ryan just liked to ignore me. I didn't let her ignore me.

"Ryan, you see me here, girl."

Ryan pretended to laugh with her girlfriends. They made a couple of "Naw, for real?!" faces and slapped each other on the shoulder. Ryan turned her back toward us, flashed her big ol' booty in low-cut tight jeans. That's one thing I never understood about black girls. They could be real skinny like Ryan, but they had them round jello butts that stuck way out in the back.

Grandmommy said the Lord had to make sumthin for a man to hold on to, but I couldn't understand how anybody found that cute. I prayed God didn't make my booty big like that.

"*Ryan.*"

She hesitated a second and then darted her eyes towards me. "Oh, hey, KeKe." KeKe. KeKe! Didn't nobody but Ryan call me KeKe no more. I guess she thought that was better than Keisha. She was so proud she didn't have a name like LaShonda or DeVonaé or – Jesus, no! – *Keisha*. She had a nice white girl name. *Ryan*. And didn't let me forget it. Sometimes I wished Aunt Lil'd named her *La*Ryan so she woulda had to gotten over herself.

"I thought Auntie straightened your hair," she said, plinkin one of my barrettes with her fake fingernail.

"She did. It looked good, too!"

"C'mon, Keisha," Tey said.

"You can see I am having a con. ver. sa. tion," and I rolled my eyes. Tey sucked his teeth and went into the store. Marcus smiled at my cousin and followed his brother. Ryan didn't look at him.

"What are you doing with those two hood rats, KeKe?"

"We just gettin some candy. We goin straight back home. I promise."

"You know what Auntie and Grandma will do if they find out you were here with them."

"You know what Grandmommy'll do if she find out you wearin lipstick." If God gave a fourteen-year-old girl a jelly butt that attracted men, that was His business. But if she wore makeup to get attention, then she was askin for it.

Ryan grinned and tugged one of my braids. "So, how was the wedding?"

"Borin. Too many songs. Chants and stuff where we all had to follow . . . It was like real church. Momma made a big deal about some guy named Sugar Daddy not bein there. How come they call him after a candy bar?"

Ryan's girlfriends laughed. Ryan said to herself, "Ohhhh my God."

"What?"

"You're a 'tard, KeKe."

"Why?"

"Look, I gotta get home soon. Mom and Dad need me to housesit. I'll catch up with you later, okay?" She turned her back on me and started talkin to her girlfriends again.

Tey and Marcus got a bag full of Rain Blo gum, Junior Mints, candy necklaces, Lemon Heads, Gobstoppers, gummy worms, and Atomic Fireballs. All I could get were Nerds and a couple pieces of banana Laffy Taffy (my favorite). I could stick em down in my pocket and sneak into my room before Grandmommy or Momma realized I'd been to the store.

"You behavin now, baby?" Cashier Lady said when I put my candy up on the counter. That's what she always said to us kids and the teenagers, too. She was real fat, but not jiggly fat. She didn't have a lot of rolls. I remembered when she used to have bulges everywhere, hangin over her pants and shakin right over her elbows. Maybe I was six or seven then. She got smaller every year, sittin there behind the counter sweatin all over her stomach and arm pits and listenin to the oldies AM station.

"Yes, ma'am. I been good."

She turned to open the cash register, and I jumped. Splotches covered her cheek. One wider than my hand, but the others were tiny like somebody beat her with a handful of pebbles. It was like she had that disease where people were brown on the outside, but then they had bright pink dots all over their skin. Like somebody rubbed their black off, and they were really white underneath. Cept Cashier Lady's spots weren't quite like that. Her spots were white-white paper white, or gray like the papier-mâché we some-times used in art, kinda rough and dirty. If I touched her face, I bet it would feel like that, all soggy newspaper.

"You want a bag, baby?"

I shook my head and shoved my candy in my shorts pockets.

"Then you have a good one."

I nodded and looked away.

When we left the store, Ryan and her girlfriends were walkin up the other side of the street, past the interstate on-ramp. Ryan said sumthin I couldn't understand (Grandmommy'd get after her for talkin so loud), and then all the girls laughed. They were still laughin by the time they got under the overpass, and some boys honked at em as they cruised by. That made Ryan and her friends laugh even harder.

"Damn, that lady's face was wrecked." Marcus was the first to say anythin. We'd already passed Discount 4 Less and headed round the corner. Tey didn't say nuthin cuz he was suckin on a Gobstopper. He gave me a piece of Rain Blo, and I popped it in my mouth so I wouldn't have to say nuthin either.

SweeTarts – July 12

When Grandmommy, Ryan, and Aunt Lil got back from the funeral, Momma had lunch waitin. I didn't want to eat with em since Marcus finally got his BB gun. (I didn't tell Momma bout that cuz she probably never woulda let me see the boys again.) We'd been huntin round the alley when Momma called me in and made me wipe a washcloth across my face. I had to be sociable, she said. Especially with family. We ate nuthin but salad – three-bean salad and another salad with Italian dressing, mixed greens, baby tomatoes, black olives, and endamame. Momma and Aunt Lil were really into healthy stuff like endamame.

"Well, he didn't show up today, either," Grandmommy said. "Church's too small for him to hide. Horny old buzzard. He always shows up in that brown suit and tired old hat. To a *funeral.*"

"Maybe he doesn't have a black suit," Ryan said. "It's the sentiment that counts anyway, right? He doesn't have to go to everyone's funeral." She was so much better at pretendin to be interested in adult conversations than me.

"Honey, if he wanted to get himself a decent black suit, he certainly could. It's not about sentiment or paying respects with him. He wants to be seen," Grandmommy said.

I scratched the itch on my wrist. Sometimes it crawled up my arm, and I had learned to just live with it. Momma poked me in the side. I forgot to take my elbows off the table.

"You know, Momma, I remember he showed up in that brown polyester suit at my wedding," Aunt Lil said. "I can't believe he's recycled those same two suits all these years."

"He had the olive one at mine," Momma said.

"He seems to put a lot of money and effort into simply being seen. He doesn't *have to* go to all those funerals. He doesn't *have to* bring a present to every wedding," Ryan said.

"Sugar Daddy? What's his real name?"

Momma, Grandmommy, and Aunt Lil looked at me. Then they looked at each other and laughed.

"That's a shame," Momma said. "I can't remember. I probably could have recalled it if you hadn't asked."

"The man always wanted status he couldn't get. He's not an educator or a doctor – I can tell you *that* for certain – but he always finds his way to our weddings, or our children's weddings, or our grandchildren's. How many hours does he have to spend perusing the newspaper only so he can make sure we all know he's there? And if he could bring a present to every wedding, he certainly could have bought *one* decent black suit. Ryan, he's never bothered to show up anywhere else—"

"Aren't weddings and funerals open to everybody if they're in the paper?"

"—He can't find another way to fit in with all that running around he does," Grandmommy said.

"May not only be the weddings and funerals of doctors and teachers and lawyers he goes to. He could go to the janitors' weddings too, Grandma. Have you ever seen him at a janitor's wedding?" Ryan took a long drink of iced tea and hid her mouth down in the glass. Grandmommy looked at her funny and smirked, but didn't say nuthin.

"Did you have enough for the choir today?" Momma asked.

"It was a good turnout, actually," Aunt Lil said. "Not enough men, but you know how that is. Mr. Hughes didn't show up, though."

"He's the most reliable bass you've got," Momma said. Old Mr. Hughes was always there when the choir sang. Sometimes he was the only man standin in the middle of all them sopranos and altos.

Aunt Lil shrugged. "He's never stood me up. He promised he'd be there."

Once it was safe and Grandmommy started talkin bout song selection, Ryan put her glass down and went back to her three-bean salad. I'd put in my time bein sociable. Momma gave me a couple SweeTarts to kill the Italian dressing aftertaste in my mouth. I went back outside cuz I didn't know the next time I'd get to see Marcus use his BB gun before his father stole him and Tey away again.

Marcus said we'd try huntin in the vacant lot next to the Discount 4 Less. The trees across the alley and in front of the Elk's Lodge hung over the open space. Easy to pick off sparrows and starlings. The grass came up a little higher than my elbows, and I kept crunchin on broken bottles.

"We got any snakes, I'll shoot em," Marcus said. He added he was only kiddin bout the snakes, but I didn't need snake bites to go along with the white spot on my wrist. Maybe I scratched it too much and got impetigo after all.

Marcus told us to shut up and stand still. We couldn't see the garbage under our feet, and if we stepped on the wrong things, we'd mess up his shot. He didn't have great aim, I found out real quick, but he swore he was new at this. Each time he missed – truth be told – I was kinda relieved, but sad. I never saw nobody kill nuthin before, and I wanted to see as much in life as I could. (A person wasn't worth much if they wasn't well-rounded.) Watch sumthin flappin around one minute and then see it fall to the ground and never move again the next. One time while I waited for Daddy to pick me up for the weekend, the pit bull belongin to the boy up the street was just strollin through the neighborhood. I forgot sumthin and went to get it, and when I came back out on the porch, the pit bull was laid up on the side-walk. Hardly any blood at all. It would kinda be like that, cept I'd finally know what it looked like when sumthin died. Bugs didn't count. I wondered what happened when that boy found his dog I wondered if the person who hit him cared at all. I wondered how Marcus would act if he ever shot anythin.

He aimed at a sparrow perched on a limb across the alley. Its head poked out from a clump of leaves. Me and Tey leaned forward. Marcus waited. He looked at the sparrow. Then looked behind us back at Jefferson Street. Then he looked at the sparrow. Then back at Jefferson Street.

"What you waitin for?"

He shushed me.

"C'mon, man," Tey said.

The sparrow flew away. Marcus threw his gun-free hand in the air, rolled his head up towards the sky, and closed his eyes. "What did I tell you bout shuttin the hell up?"

"You took too damn long," Tey said.

"Y'all didn't see that car? Silver Buick sedan? It's only passed by here four or five times."

"No," we said.

"Why are those niggas spyin on us?" Marcus said.

"Why you think they want anythin to do with us? Paranoid," Tey said.

"Maybe cuz every time they come by, they stare right at us."

Marcus was right. The sedan passed, and maybe it was gone for two or three minutes. Then we'd see it on the other side of the street, and it'd turn back around. They eventually parked at Discount 4 Less. A woman with a long weave curled in spirals all over her head got outta the car. A strand of hair fell in her face, and she pushed it back with a six-inch-long acrylic nail. She didn't buy nuthin and came right back out. They turned down the alley and come straight at us.

Spiral Head rolled down her window. Another girl sat in the passenger's seat. Her head was covered in very neat micro braids. Momma wouldn't even let me get braids like that.

"Y'all know where we can find Mona's Beauty Salon?" Spiral Head sounded real country.

Marcus snorted. He and Tey looked at me. I shrugged and shook my head. "Sorry, never heard of it."

The girls raised their eyebrows. "My cousin told me Mona's was in the shopping center across from the Discount 4 Less and behind the Elk's Lodge," Spiral Head said. "We been up and down Jefferson, but we haven't seen a shopping center."

"Your cousin from around here?" Marcus asked.

"Naw. She goes to State. We'll be attendin in the fall. Just checkin out the area. Y'all sure Mona's not around here? She said it was next to a convenience store in the shopping center."

"Sorry, lady," Tey said.

"Got any idea where it is?"

We shook our heads. They looked at each other a little confused and upset, but they thanked us and went on down the alley.

"What we know bout a beauty salon?" Tey said under his breath.

Actually, I could sympathize. Sorta. Not that Momma'd ever let me get my hair done in a beauty salon at my age, but one of my grandfathers used to own a barber shop. I couldn't remember which grandfather, though. Grandmommy never talked about her ex-husband, and I'd only met him once when me and Daddy ran into him at Farmer's Market. Nobody really discussed Daddy's family either. All I knew about his father was he had water-wave hair, and he didn't have no grays when he died. One of my grandfathers was a postman, and one owned the barber shop. I get them mixed up. Actually, I'm not sure about the postman thing, neither. I think I remembered hearin it one time.

My grandfather had the barber shop back durin the 40s or 50s. It was so long ago, it didn't matter which decade. It used to be where the interstate is now. His barber shop and a bunch of other businesses. I had no idea what all those buildings used to look like. So, I could get why those girls were upset. Maybe Mona did hair real good, like my grandfather probably did. Maybe back then, after they tore down everythin, some country cat was comin to see the big city, and said he needed a good cut while he was here. It was startin to get a little scruffy up top. His cousin, or his best friend, or his brother who used to live here, told him to go see my grandfather. So, he's lookin forward to his hair cut, and all he found when he got here was lots of construction – or maybe the completed interstate by then. That would have pissed me off too.

"You heard a Mona's?" I asked Grandmommy when I got home. We got out the collard greens for dinner and started trimmin them since Momma wasn't off work yet.

"*Have* I heard of Mona's? No. Should I have?"

"I don't know . . . Where was my grandfather's barber shop?" I figured I should ask her instead of Daddy. If she picked up the line while I was talkin to him, she might think he called me. I didn't want her threatenin him with a shotgun again. "Did Daddy's father have the barber shop?"

Grandmommy blinked and put down the leaf she worked on. "Barber shop? Oh, yes! That was your other grandfather's. Why'd you drag that up?"

"I wanna know where it was. I never known, I never *have* known where it was."

"It was somewhere along the path of the interstate. Somewhere near a dime store . . . I think."

"But *where*?" I said.

"Keisha, I can't remember . . .You're leaving too much of the leaf on the stem. Watch what you're doing."

"He didn't start a new one?"

"Where was he going to put it? The white part of town?"

"So he didn't get a new one? Did they pay him for it?"

"Who? The government? You know the government never paid us for anything."

"So everybody lost their business and didn't get nuthin back? That ain't fair!"

"It *ain't*?" Grandmommy said. "There was no sense in reasoning out fair and unfair. It was always unfair—"

"Well, it *ain't* fair," I said rippin at the leaves. My fingers throbbed. My arm itched from my wrist all the way past my elbow. It wasn't fair, and I'd never know where his business was, and nobody seemed to care, neither.

The cryin started a few days after that. Don't know where it come from. I just know it wouldn't stop. I thought maybe I cried so much cuz the government took my grandfather's barber shop and never paid him back. But I couldna been that mad to cry so long and hard about it, and Tey started cryin too. Marcus wouldn't have nuthin to do with us no more, puttin up with us dumbass sissies.

At first Momma believed I got all weepy cuz I wasn't gettin enough sleep. The Department of Transportation did emergency work all day and all night to repair the overpass crossin Jefferson. Nobody knew what really happened. Not an earthquake or a freak electrical storm or a meteor or chunk of sumthin else fallen from the sky. Part of the overpass just wasn't *there* no more. When you looked at it from the street, part of the green siding and railing was gone. One lane looked like somebody took an eraser and scrubbed it a little bit thinner, and then the hand got shaky and scratched out most of the other lane. But it didn't look like nuthin was broken, only made that way to begin with.

Me and Tey weren't the only two cryin though. Sometimes we'd catch other kids in the neighborhood snifflin or wipin their eyes with the backs of their hands. Adults tried to make us explain it, but why? Sometimes sadness is all it is, and it comes from a deep hole nobody sees, and sometimes that hole can close up as soon as it opened. That's what it felt like. There was some huge hole somewhere – huger than a black hole – and it was so big and wide all we could do was cry because that's how deep and empty it felt. Like I could fall in that black hole and keep sinkin on forever. Try tellin a grownup any of that.

Tey and I sat on the curb in front of his grandmother's house and got all our cryin out for the day. We didn't look at each other or try to make one another feel better. We just wailed away with our eyes shut tight and our faces up to the sky. We didn't stop to blow our noses or keep our heads from achin. I had to wear long sleeves now, and that made it worse. I was sweaty, my hair got all poofy, and I ended up with snot and tears on my clothes. We always felt numb when we were done, like we could just pass out.

Tey wiped his face in his shirt and whined a little. I thought he might start up again, but he coughed, and that was the end of it. I was lightheaded. I rested against my knees and closed my eyes.

"Granny's got that itchin," Tey said. "She put everythin on it she can think of, but it don't go away. She said it don't bother her, but she always scratchin her chest."

He was gonna make me cry again. "Tey . . . " I pulled back my sleeve. He poked at my arm. A large splotch of white, paper-white white, trailed up from my wrist to my elbow. All along my arm, there were these spots, like somebody beat it with a handful of pebbles.

"Will that happen to Granny?"

I put my finger to my mouth, and now the tears were comin. "I don't know."

He whispered in my ear, "What the hell is that, Keisha?"

I shook my head. He looked back at his grandmother's house, then back at me.

"I'm sure it'll go away," he said.

But he knew we both couldn't know that. We'd never seen anythin like this before.

COMMUNITY NEWS

Alger MacAdams will be turning over the everyday responsibilities of his store to his only daughter, Ms. Marla MacAdams. Mr. MacAdams has been a regular, friendly face at Alger's Market since he opened the store in 1974. He had been considering handing over the reins to his daughter since his wife Diana died early last February. "Marla's been observing and helping me the last twenty-three years. She knows what to do, and I know she can do it on her own." MacAdams intends to remain active. He will still coordinate Second Avenue Baptist's food drives and tutor math at Hadley Park's Community Center. Alger's Market is located at 1507 B on Jefferson Street, next door to Mona's Beauty Salon behind Elk's Lodge 41.

Caption: Alger MacAdams and his daughter greet customers outside of Alger's Market.

Sugar Daddy – July 20

Everybody cried at Mrs. Probst's funeral. *Everybody.* And hardly anybody liked Mrs. Probst, far as I could tell. She cheated on all three of her husbands, she controlled the United Methodist Women, and the pastor did whatever she said. When Mama didn't think I was listenin, she called Mrs. Probst a bitch. I had my own beef with her. She changed the services and made church even longer. But Uncle David held me while I wept, and his tears drained through my hair. Momma had pressed my hair for the funeral and gotten it nice and straight, but the curls tightened and frizzed under Uncle David's chin. Aunt Lil cried so hard she could barely conduct the choir. Over in the soprano section, Ryan leaned on Grandmommy, and Grandmommy did everythin she could to stay upright. Momma lay in the aisle. She didn't even bother with appearin ladylike.

We coulda blamed this on the Holy Spirit – He did people that way sometimes, but not everybody all at once. He might fall on one or two people, they'd shake and wail, and then they'd fall out. We wished we could do that now. All we could hear was our own shriekin and screamin. Water puddled at our feet. Our noses clogged up, and our stomachs hurt.

Mr. Hughes didn't come. He wasn't at church last Sunday, neither. We didn't look for Sugar Daddy. He hadn't shown up to the last two weddings. We gave up on him comin here.

We planned to go straight to Swett's after the funeral, but we had to change our clothes first. None of us really talked while we ate. Momma said, "The old biddy didn't deserve all that hollering," and that was about it. We were too tired to talk, me and Momma, Grandmommy, Ryan, and Aunt Lil and Uncle David. We had a hard enough time gettin our forks to our mouths.

I can't lie. I wanted summer to be over with. I wanted to get back to school. I wouldn't have to answer so many questions from people who weren't from around here, questions about their friends or family we swore never lived here, even though strangers insisted the opposite. I wouldn't have to explain to em about some of the buildings in the area, why there was only half a building, or nuthin but a window or door hangin in space with no walls to hold it up. Maybe by the end of the summer, all this nonsense would go away, and I could go to sleep knowin Momma and Grandmommy hadn't disappeared on me by the time I woke up in the mornin. The white marks on my arm would heal up, and so would Tey's grandmother's, and I'd never have to worry that Daddy might come lookin for me one day, and nobody'd know who he was talkin bout.

I was lyin flat on my stomach with my arms at my sides. I hated sleepin in that position, but it was the only one that worked now. My stomach felt so hollow, like I hadn't eaten in years, and that black hole might rise up within me and snatch me from the inside out. I started lyin like this to stretch my stomach out, quiet it down so it quit all the grumblin.

Usually, Momma wouldn't let me catnap durin the day, especially not durin the summer when I could be runnin around gettin exercise. Not much use for that now. Sometimes Momma didn't feel like wakin me up after all of her cryin. I was happy when she did, though. Sometimes when I slept, I slipped down into that black hole. Didn't know if I'd ever wake outta it. When I opened my eyes, I felt like it had puked me up.

Momma knocked on my door and stuck her head in. "Tey wants to know if you can play."

I sighed and got up. He was worse off than me, so I couldn't leave him alone. He knew if his daddy came and got him and Marcus, their grandmother might disappear on em before the next time they came to see her.

We stood on my porch and stared at the street. We struggled for stuff to do. Sometimes we squished ants out on the sidewalk and watched other bugs carry them away, kinda like providin a bug Farmer's Market. But we got tired of that. Without Marcus supervisin us, Tey's grandmother wouldn't let us set off fireworks. Marcus still wouldn't put up with us, even though he tried to sneak his own tears by pullin his shirt collar up over his eyes. We couldn't play with the BB gun. We *wouldn't* play kick ball with the other kids in the neighborhood. We only made each other cry.

"We can catch crayfish," Tey said after a while.

I yawned. Nobody wanted us playin in the creek water, but the last couple days of July had been beat our ass. I didn't care if I got polluted water on me or not. "Okay. Let's go."

Tey got us some Mason jars, and we climbed over the short bridge on the other side of our street. The creek was more like a wide, really long gutter, and most of the time, I took for granted it was there, since there were a few houses down here we never visited. I didn't know if it ran into a lake, or a river, or whatever. I guess it was clean water once-upon-a-time. I never bothered askin when that was.

Tey moved some rocks around and swished his hand in the water. I sat on the concrete bank and put my head in my hands. He scooped the Mason jar down, cussed to himself when he didn't catch nuthin, and dumped the water out. He scooped the Mason jar down several times. I couldn't figure out what he was tryin to fish since I didn't see no life in that water.

He screwed up his face and held the jar to the sunlight. "*Unhhhh.*"

I stood up but didn't get in the water with him so Momma wouldn't know where I'd been. He jiggled the jar for me. Somthin feathery swirled.

"What, you got some toilet paper?"

"Ew, girl!"

We looked at it again with our noses almost to the glass. It *was* paper, with a few larger chunks and thousands and thousands of smaller pieces spinnin round like dust.

"Where'd it come from?" I said.

Tey kicked at the water. He pulled a large rock away from the bank. A sliver of newspaper tore apart and washed down the creek. We went down the bank and found more newspaper. Some of it dried up on rocks and broken concrete in a shriveled mess. By the time we knew where we were, the creek had taken us past some apartment buildings and down a dirt alley behind a street cut short by a fence in front of some railroad tracks. I never been down that way before, and neither had Tey. The houses were small, and some had been abandoned. Most of the backyards were junky, cept for one that had no grass at all. It was hard clay converted to a basketball court, with the baskets nailed to trees. The people watchin and playin were too busy to notice us passin through.

Tall weeds almost hid the back of the house at the end of the street. The air conditioner had been ripped out, and we could see it lyin in the high grass. There was a carport, but no car. The grass was high under there too. The backdoor was open just a little, and there was a bunch of paper thrown across the porch. Some of it had blown into the yard, down into the creek. Tey pulled the weeds out of his way and started towards the house. I yanked at his arm, and he smacked my hand.

"We gotta go back," I said. "We can't be trespassin."

"I bet nobody live here."

"*Soooo*? It's still trespassin."

He grabbed me and pulled me into the yard. This time we wouldn't have Marcus's BB gun to protect us from snakes. Tey stuck his head in the hole where the air conditioner used to be. "I bet this is how they robbed the house."

"We can use the door," I said, but Tey had already crawled in. He pulled me through, and we were in a kitchen. It reeked of old meat, the kind that gets forgotten at the back of the refrigerator. We pinched our noses with our shirts. Tey coughed, and I rubbed my eyes. Canisters and spices had been thrown on the floor. Our feet ground rice and pasta and salt into newspaper clippings.

"Damn, it stinks," I said.

Tey picked a piece of paper off the floor. Some of the type was smudged, but we made out an article on the closin of some gas station.

The table in the kitchen'd been flipped over, and it blocked our way into the dinin room. I brushed broken glass off the counter with my long sleeves, we hopped onto the counter, and jumped over the table. The china cabinet had been smashed open, and maybe a few plates were taken. We didn't find any busted up on the floor. The smell got worse in the hallway. There were so many books and binders everywhere we couldn't help but step on em. The basement door at the end of the hall was open. We peeked into the bedroom with more cutouts from newspapers and stacks of photo albums toppled over. Even without somebody sackin the place, there was hardly any room in there to move around or sleep.

"I don't think whoever robbed the place got anythin valuable," Tey said through his shirt. "Do you wanna go in there?" It's where the stink come from. I'd never seen a dead body before a mortician fixed it up nice, let alone reported I'd found one. I nodded.

Tey took one step into that den, started coughin, and ran into the basement. I stood in the doorway and didn't go no farther. He sat on the couch, head laid back, and his blood dirtied up the cushions. He didn't have nuthin on on top, but his pants were old, like sumthin they wore in the 70s. He was big, but not fat, how old men can get a little wide with a round belly. The bookcase had been thrown over him, or it landed across his legs when the robber pushed it outta the way. I figured he was already dead when that happened. He didn't look like he tried to avoid it. From where I stood, I couldn't tell if he'd been shot in the head or been hit, but he was readin the paper when he died, which I guess was the way it shoulda been. It was pinned against his legs and the bookcase. I couldn't tell if his eyes were wide open or closed. He was a dark man, and his face was just pudgy enough to keep the wrinkles from bein deep in his cheeks. He had big hands. His knuckles were thick, and the skin over them was rough.

"*Keishaaa . . .*"

Tey had turned the light on down in the basement. Scrapbooks and photo albums piled high to the ceilin. They were numbered by year. Tey sat on the dirty orange carpet flippin through a binder in his lap. I took the closest to me – "Students 2005." The man had pasted articles and pictures from *The Sentinel* and *Black Nashvillian*. There were pictures he'd taken from high schools. Track meets. Basketball games. Scores from all of TSU's and Fisk's wins. I recognized my middle-school auditorium. He had several shots of one of our choral nights. There was a National Merit Scholar list from *The Tennessean*. Four of the names were highlighted in blue. I knew one of them, Tony Diggs. Ryan went to school with him. She talked to him every once in a while cuz he wasn't too ghetto. Uncle David thought they'd make a good couple, if he let Ryan date.

"What you got?"

"Weddings. They *real* old," Tey said. He held the book up for me. Lots of black and white photos with the bride and groom headin down the aisle. Next to each one was the announcement for the weddin from the newspaper.

A couple of tears slipped down my cheeks. Sugar Daddy was upstairs. Tey stared at me all wide-eyed. If I started cryin again, he wouldn't be able to control himself, neither. I crawled in between the stacks lookin for the 50s and 40s. I pulled books out, and cobwebs flew in my face. We both sneezed. Sugar Daddy had articles for promotions and store openings and new partnerships and offices. Laundromats, and dress shops, and dime stores. Soda shops and diners. The clippings mentioned streets I never heard of before. There were photos of buildings I never seen.

"Keisha, I'm gettin sick."

"Wait."

Maybe he had a photo of my grandfather in front of his barber shop, maybe of my grandfather in his barber shop cuttin hair. Or my grandfather, whichever one, as a postman. Or Grandmommy's weddin. I turned up more dust and cobwebs. They burned my eyes. Me and Tey coughed and sneezed.

"*Keisha* . . . "

Sugar Daddy had to have them here somewhere. Seemed like he had everybody else. I saw a group photo of a fraternity with a head in the back that coulda been a young Mr. Hughes. There were pictures of protestors watchin the interstate construction. I looked for my family there among those people with picket signs and banners. I couldn't find them.

"Girl, I'm gonna puke all over you!"

"Okay! Okay! Okay!" I threw the book down and wiped the tears from my face with my sleeves. But my sleeves were covered in dirt, and my eyes only stung more.

In the backyard, I gathered all of the photos and newspaper cutouts I could find. I didn't care if I got bit. I didn't care if chiggers dug into my arms. The sun had gotten to some of the photos.

Peoples' faces disappeared behind fading colors the shape of cigarette burns. I could make out an eye, the side of a mouth, or hand, but the rest of em was gone. Houses missed roofs, or store windows had faded out. Tey was across the alley before he noticed I wasn't followin.

"What you doin?"

"We have to save them!" I showed him my handful of photos and articles.

"We have to tell somebody there's a old dead cat in that house."

I went back to the porch and put the photos and newspaper cutouts in a neat stack. I put a rock on top of them to make sure they didn't blow away. I gasped and ran farther down the creek, under the bridge where the train tracks went overhead. Way in the distance was the farm land on the TSU campus. I had no idea how far from home I was. There weren't no buildings out here.

"Pick up everythin you can find."

"Keisha, we gotta go."

"Pick em up!" I yelled.

Paper clogged a drain. It was soggy and looked like it never had words or faces on it at all. We took up a few of Sugar Daddy's photos out from the rocks and on the banks where the sun had baked some of em blank.

Tey sighed and rolled his eyes. "Keisha, come *on*! It's all ruined." He dropped the washed out photos back into the water.

I dug into the wet newspaper to see if I could make out any names, any faces. Put pages back together so I could bring the people back. There was nuthin that made sense. Just mush and clumps of black and grey. I crawled through the rocks. My knees turned up more drowned clippings and pictures the light bleached out.

"No! No! No!" I pounded on the rocks and cut my hands. I gathered all the photos I could and shuffled through them. "We have to save em all. We have to save em *all*! We can't lose no more. We have to put em back where Sugar Daddy had em!"

"Keisha? You okay? Keisha?" I heard him comin up behind me. He put his hand on my arm and drew it back real fast when I screamed.

I didn't mean to. I didn't mean to scream at all, but it came roarin outta me til I thought my throat might bleed. I found a man

I recognized in one of the photos. Sugar Daddy must have been on the opposite sidewalk when he took the picture on Jefferson Street. Maybe it was the day of TSU's Homecoming Parade. Girls were twirlin their batons in the street. The man watched them go by with a little girl sittin on his shoulders. The man had water-wave hair, and he wore thick, black frames. Sometimes I couldn't exactly remember Daddy's face, even though I should have, even though it hadn't been that long since I last saw him. But I didn't forget his chin. This man had a chin like Daddy's, and I sat on his shoulders with a big grin on my face, arms raised. The sun had gotten to this picture too. Some of the crowd had disappeared behind white spots. On my little arm, from the wrist and up to my elbow, I had been erased.

I couldn't breathe. I sucked in air and screamed like I lost my mind, and maybe I had. I gasped and sobbed so hard my head fell in and I sucked up water. Tey pulled me out and wrung the water out my braid. He looked over my shoulder at the photo tremblin in my hand. Then he fell on his knees beside me. All we could do was listen to me wail.

We just sat there in the middle of the creek with dirt and news-paper clingin to our skin. The sun dried our backs. I wiped the photo dry against my chest and tucked it in my undershirt before any of the rest of me faded away.

ENYO-ENYO

Kameron Hurley

Enyo meditated at mealtimes within the internod, huffing liquor vapors from a dead comrade's shattered skull. This deep within the satellite, ostensibly safe beneath the puckered skein of the peridium, she went over the lists of the dead.

She recited her own name first.

Enyo's memory was a severed ocular scelera; leaking aqueous humor, slowing losing shape as the satellite she commanded spun back to the beginning. The cargo she carried was unknown to her, a vital piece of knowledge that had escaped the punctured flesh of her memory.

She had named the ship after herself – *Enyo-Enyo* – without any hint of irony. The idea that Enyo had any irony left was a riotous laugh even without knowing the satellite's moniker, and her Second, Reeb, amused himself often at her shattering attempt at humor.

After the purging of every crew, Reeb came into Enyo's pulpy green quarters, his long face set in a black, graven expression she had come to call winter, for it came as often as she remembered that season in her childhood.

"Why don't we finish out this turn alone?" he would say. "We can manage the internod ourselves. Besides, they don't make engineers the way they did eight turns ago."

"There's the matter of the prisoner," she would say.

And he would throw up his dark, scarred hands and sigh and say, "Yes, there's the prisoner."

It was Enyo's duty, her vocation, her obsession, to tread down the tongue of the spiraling umbilicus from the internod to the holding pod rotation of the satellite, to tend to the prisoner.

Each time, she greeted the semblance of a body suspended in

viscous green fluid with the same incurious moue she had seen Justice wear in propaganda posters during the war. Some part of her wondered if the body would recognize it. If they could talk of those times. But who knew how many turns old it was? Who knew how many other wars it had seen? On a large enough scale, her war was nothing. A few million dead. A system destroyed.

The body's eyes were always closed, its sex indeterminate, its face a morass of dark, thread-like tentacles and fleshy growths. Most sessions, she merely came down and unlocked the feed cabinet, filled a clean syringe with dark fluid, and inserted it into the black fungal sucker fused to the transparent cell. Sometimes, when the body absorbed the fluid, it would writhe and twist, lost in the ecstasy of fulfillment.

Enyo usually went straight back to the internod to recite her lists of dead, after. But she had been known to linger, to sit at the flat, gurgling drive that kept her charge in permanent stasis.

She had stopped wondering where the body had come from, or who it had been. Her interest was in pondering what it would become when they reached its destination. She lost track of time in these intimate reveries, often. After half a rotation of contemplation, Reeb would do a sweep of the satellite. He would find her alive and intact, and perhaps he would go back to playing screes or fucking one of the engineers or concocting a vile hallucinogen the gelatinous consistency of aloe. They were a pair of two, a crew of three, picking up rim trash and mutilated memories in the seams between the stars during the long night of their orbit around the galactic core.

When they neared the scrap belt called Stile, Enyo was mildly surprised to see the collection of spinning habited asteroids virtually unchanged from the turn before.

"It's time," she told Reeb. "Without more fuel, we won't make it the full turn." And she would not be able to drop off the prisoner.

He gave her his winter look. She had left the last of his engineers on a paltry rock the color of foam some time before. He did not know why they needed the crew now; he did not have her sense of things, of the way time moved here. But he would be lonely. It's why he always agreed to take on another crew, even knowing their fate.

"How many more?" he said.

"This is the last turn," she said. "Then we are finished."

She let Reeb pick the new crew. He launched a self-propelled spore from the outernod well ahead of their arrival on the outskirts of Stile. The dusty ring of settlements within the asteroid belt circled a bloated, dying star. Had it been dying the last time they passed? Enyo could not remember.

Reeb's sister worked among the debris, digging through old spores and satellites, piecing together their innards, selling them as pirated vessels imbued with the spirit of cheap colonial grit.

Enyo had not seen Reeb's sister in many turns, when speaking of the war, of genocide – in terms outside the propagandic – was still new and unsettling and got them thrown out of establishments. Broodbreeders and creep cleaners called them void people, diseased, marked for a dry asphyxiation aboard a viral satellite, drifting ever aimless across limitless space. They were not far wrong. Sometimes Enyo wondered if they really knew who she was.

She heard Reeb's sister slide up the umbilicus into the internod. Heard her hesitate on the threshold, the lubrication of the umbilicus slick on her skin.

"This your satellite?" Reeb's sister asked.

Enyo had expected to feel nothing at her voice, but like the body in the tank, she was sometimes surprised at what was fed to her. Something in her flared, and darkened, and died. It was this snapshot of Reeb's sister that she always hoped was the true one. The real one. But she knew better.

She swiveled. Reeb's sister did not take up the tubal port as Reeb did, but inhabited it in the loose way the woman inhabited all spaces, wrapping it around herself like a shroud, blurring the edges of her surrounds – or perhaps Enyo's eyes were simply going bad again. The satellite changed them out every quarter turn. The woman had once had the body of a dancer, but like all of them, she had atrophied, and though she was naturally thin, it was a thinness borne of hunger and muscle loss. Her eyes were black as Reeb's, but their color was the only feature they shared. She was violet black to Reeb's tawny brown, slight in the hips and shoulders, delicate in the wrists and ankles, light enough, perhaps, to fly.

"Reeb says you need a sentient spore specialist," the woman said.

"Yes, we have one last pickup. I need you to aid in monitoring our spore for the drop. I'm afraid if you do not, the prisoner may escape."

"The prisoner?"

Enyo had forgotten. This woman had not met them yet. She did not know. Something inside of Enyo stirred, something dark and willfully forgotten, like a bad sexual encounter.

"Where are the others?" Enyo asked.

"Aren't you going to ask my name?"

"I already know it," Enyo said.

The day Reeb's sister was born, Enyo had named her "Dysnomia." She had cursed all three of them that day, and perhaps the universe, too. One could never be quite certain.

Nothing had ever been the same after that.

Because she could not go back. Only around.

The sound of the machines was deafening. Enyo stood ankle-deep in peridium salve and organic sludge. Ahead of her, Reeb was screaming. High pitched, squealing, like some broodmeat. But she could not see him.

Then the siren started. A deep-seated, body-thumping wail that cut deep into her belly. Now we turn, she thought. This is a very old snapshot.

Ahead of her, a few paces down the dripping corridor, Dax battered her small body against the ancient orbital entryway. Her tears mixed with sweat and grease and something far more dangerous, deceptive. Grew florets spiraled up the bare skin of her arms from wrist to elbow.

Enyo raised the fist of her weapon and called the girl back, "Don't go down there! Not there! The colonists are this way."

"I'm not leaving them!" Dax sobbed. Her white teeth looked brilliant in the darkness. What animal had she harvested them from? "I know what you did! I know you started this. You set this all in motion."

Enyo admitted that she had not expected it would be Dax who went back. Her memories were not always trustworthy.

The satellite took a snapshot.

Reeb's tastes were predictable in their disparity. He brought up his new crew to meet with Enyo in the internod. The first: a pale, freckled girl of a pilot whose yellow hair was startling in the ambient green glow of the dermal tissue of the room. Enyo could not remember the last time she'd seen yellow hair. The war, maybe. The girl carried no weapons, but her hands were lean and supple, and reminded Enyo of Reeb's hands when he was in his sixties: strong, deft, capable. Not what he was now, no, but what he would *become*.

The other crewmember was a mercenary: a tall, long-limbed woman as dark as the girl was light. Her head was shaved bald. She wore a silver circlet above her ears, and half of her left ear was missing. She carried a charged weapon at either hip, and a converted organic slaying stick across her back. She smelled of blood and metal.

"Do they have names?" Enyo asked Reeb.

"Dax Alhamin," the little pilot said, holding out her hand. It was a rude affectation picked up by many of the young, to touch when first meeting. They did not remember how the war had started, with a nit-infected warmonger who murdered superpod after superpod of colonists with a single kiss. Or perhaps they had simply forgotten. Enyo was never sure what side of the curtain she was on. The satellite distorted the universe at its leisure, often at her expense.

The other one, the mercenary, laughed at the open hand the girl proffered and said, "I'm Arso Tohl. I heard you have cargo that needs . . . liberating."

Dax pulled her hand back in. She was smiling broadly. Her teeth were too white to be real. Even if she was the twenty years she looked, no real person had teeth like that – not even a rim world god. Not even a warmonger.

"It's necessary," Enyo said. "We need to get back to the beginning."

"The beginning?" Dax said. "Where did you come from?"

"It doesn't matter where we came from," Reeb said. "Nor where we're going. That's not how a satellite like this works."

"I think I've heard of this satellite," Arso said. "Some prototype from the Sol system, isn't it? You're a long way from home. You were already old news when I was growing up."

Enyo closed her eyes. She ran through her litany of dead. At the end, she added two new names:

Arso Tohl and *Dax Alhamin.*

She opened her eyes. "Let's tell them how it works, Reeb," she said.

"Enyo-Enyo makes her own fate," Reeb said. "Her fate is ours, too. We can alter that fate, but only if we act quickly. Enyo guides that fate. Now you're part of it."

Arso snorted. "If that's so, you better hope this woman makes good decisions, then, huh?"

Reeb shrugged. "I gave up on hoping that many cycles ago."

"All that we are is sacrifice," Enyo's first squad captain told her. "Sacrifice to our countries. To our children. To ourselves. Our futures. We cannot hope to aspire to be more than that."

"But what if I am more than that?" Enyo said. Even then, she was arrogant. Too arrogant to let a slight go uncommented upon.

Her squad captain smiled; a bitter rictus, shiny metal teeth embedded in a slick green jaw grown just for her. The skin grafting hadn't taken. Enyo suspected it was because the captain forgot the daily applications of salve. People would take her more seriously, with a jaw like that.

"I know what you did, Enyo," her squad captain said. "I know who you are. This is how we mete out justice on the Venta Vera arm, to war criminals."

The captain shot her. It was the first time Enyo died.

As Enyo gazed up from the cold, slimy floor of the carrier, her blood steaming in the alien air, her captain leaned over her. The metal teeth clicked. Close enough to kiss.

The squad commander said, "That is how much a body is worth. One makes no more difference than any other. Even the body of the woman who started the war."

As her life bled out, Enyo's heart stopped. But not before Enyo reached up and ate half her captain's spongy artificial jaw.

Enyo secured her comrade's skull in the jellied dampener beside her. All around her, the spore trembled and surged against its restraints. Reeb had created it just an hour before and clocked in the elliptical path it must take to get them to the rocky little exoplanet where the cargo waited. The spore was ravenous and anxious. Dysmonia already lay immersed at the far end of the spore. She looked terribly peaceful.

Dax eased herself back into her own jellied dampener. Torso submerged, she remained sitting up a moment longer, cool eyes wide and finally, for the first time, fearful.

"Whose skull is that?" Dax asked.

Enyo patted the dampener. "Yours," she said.

Dax snorted. "You're so mad."

"Yes," Enyo said.

Arso pushed through the still-slimy exterior of the spore and into the core where they sat. She spit a glob of the exterior mush onto the floor, which absorbed it hungrily.

"You sure there's no one on that rock?" Arso said.

"Just the abandoned colonists," Reeb murmured from the internod. The vibrations tickled Enyo's ears. The tiny, threadlike strands tucked in their ear canals were linked for as long as the living tissue could survive on their blood.

"It was simply bad timing on their part," Reeb said. "The forming project that would have made Tuatara habitable was suspended when they were just a few rotations away. They were abandoned. No one to welcome them."

"No one but us," Enyo said, and patted the skull beside her. For a long moment, she thought to eat it. But there would be time for that later.

"Filthy business," Arso said.

Enyo unloaded the green fist of her weapon from the gilled compartment above her. It molded itself neatly to her arm, a glittering green sheath of death.

"You have no idea," Enyo said.

Enyo screamed and screamed, but the baby would not come. The rimwarder "midwife" she'd hired was young, prone to madness. The girl burst from the closet Enyo called home three hours into the birthing. Now Enyo lay in a bed soaked with her own perspiration and filth. The air was hot, humid. Above her screams, she heard the distant sound of people working in the ventilation tube.

So it was Enyo who took her own hand. Who calmed her own nerves, who coached her own belabored breath. Enyo. Just Enyo.

Why was it always the same, every turn? Why was she always alone, in this moment, but never the others?

She pushed. She screamed herself hoarse. Her body seemed to tear in two. Somewhere far away, in some other life, in some other snapshot, she was dimly aware of this moment, as if it were happening to some character in an opera.

The death dealers banged on the door and then melted it open. They saw she was simply birthing a child alone . . . so they left her. Sealed the room behind her. Like most rim filth, they hoped she would die there in childbed and spare them the trouble. They could come back and collect her dead flesh for resale later.

Enyo grit her teeth and pushed.

The baby came. One moment, just Enyo. The next . . . a squalling, writhing mass no more sentient in that moment than a programmable replicator, but hers nonetheless. A tawny brown child with her own black eyes.

"Reeb," she said.

She reached toward him. Her whole body trembled.

The second child was smaller, too thin. This was the one she would give away. The one who would pay her way to the stars.

This one she called Dysmonia.

Enyo voided the body for delivery. Capped all the tubes. A full turn about the galaxy in transit for a single delivery. A single body. Back to the beginning. How many times she had done this, she wasn't certain. The satellite, *Enyo-Enyo*, revealed nothing. Only told her when it was hungry. And when it was time to station itself, once again, on its place of origin.

She pushed the body's pod over and it floated beside her, light as a moth's wing. She placed her fingers on top of the pod and guided it down into the cargo bay. The body stirred gently.

The interior of *Enyo-Enyo* was mostly dark. Motionless. Not a sound. They were the last of the living on *Enyo-Enyo*, this turn. They usually were. The satellite was hungry. Always so hungry. Like the war.

At the airlock, she stopped to bundle up. Stiff boots, gloves, parka, respirator. The air here was breathable, *Enyo-Enyo* told her, but thin and toxic if exposed for long periods. She queued up the first phase of the release and waited for pressurization.

The vibrating door became transparent; blistering white light pushed away the darkness of the interior.

Ahead of her: a snow-swept platform. In the distance, a cavernous ruin of a mountain pockmarked with old munitions scars. A sea of frozen fog stretched from the platform to the mountain. As she watched, a thin, webbed bridge materialized between the mountain and the platform.

She waited. She had waited a full turn around the galaxy to come back here, to Eris. She could wait a couple terrestrial turns more.

The moisture of her breath began to freeze on the outer edges of her respirator. It reminded her of the first time she had come here to Eris.

Bodies littered the field, and Enyo moved among them, cloaked in clouds of blood-rain. The nits she had infected herself with collected the blood spilled around her and created a shimmering vortex of effluvia that, in turn, devoured all it touched.

"You must not fight her," the field commander shrieked, and Enyo knew some of the fear came from the waves of methane melting all around them as the frozen surface of Eris convulsed. "You must not stop her. She is small now. You must leave her alone, and she will stay small. If you fight her she will swell in size and grow large. She will be unstoppable."

But they fought her. They always fought her.

When she took the field, she flayed them of their fleshy spray-on suits and left them to freeze solid before they could asphyxiate, flailing in sublime methane.

There had to be sacrifices.

As she stood over the field commander, making long rents in her suit, the commander said, "If it's a war your people want, it's a war they'll get."

When it was over, Enyo gazed up at the thorny silhouette of the colonial superpod that the squad had tried to protect. Most of the Sol colonists started from here, on Eris. She would need the superpod, later, or she could never be here, now. Sometimes one had to start a war just to survive to the next turn.

Enyo crawled up into the sickening tissue of the superpod. She found the cortex without much trouble. The complicated bits of genetic code that went into programming the superpod should have been beyond her, but she had ingested coordinates from her squad commander's jaw, during some long-distant snapshot of her life that the satellite had created. Now the coordinates were a part of her, like her fingernails or eyelashes.

She kissed the cortex, and programmed the ship's destination. Tuatara.

Reeb worked on one of the harvester ships that circled the Rim every four cycles. Enyo was twenty, and he was eighty-two, he said. He said he had met her before. She said she didn't remember, but that was a lie. What she wanted to say was, "I remember giving birth to you," but that, too, was a lie. The difference between memory and premonition depended largely on where one was standing. At twenty, on the Mushta Mura arm, her "memories" were merely ghosts, visions, brain effluvia.

When she fucked Reeb in her twenty-year-old skin, it was with the urgency of a woman who understood time. Understood that there was never enough of it. Understood that this moment, now, was all of it. The end and the beginning. Distorted.

She said his name when she came. Said his name and wept for some nameless reason; some premonition, some memory. Wept for what it all had been and would become.

"The satellite is a prototype," the recruiter said. The emblem on her uniform looked familiar. A double red circle shot through with a blue dart.

They walked along a broad, transparent corridor that gave them a sweeping view of the marbled surface of Eris. Centuries of sculpting had done little to improve its features, though the burning brand in the sky that had once been its moon, Dysmonia, made the surface a bearable minus-twenty degrees Celsius during what passed for summer, and unaided breathing was often possible, if not always recommended. The methane seas had long since been tapped, leaving behind a stark, mottled surface of rocky protuberances shot through with the heads of methane wells. Beyond the domed spokes of the research hub's many arms, the only living thing out there was the hulking mop of the satellite. Enyo thought it looked like a spiky, pulsing crustacean.

"A prototype of what, exactly?" she asked. Her debriefing on Io had been remarkably . . . brief.

"There's much to know about it," the recruiter said. "We won't send you out until you've bonded with it, of course. That's our worry. That it won't take. But . . . there is an indication that you and the satellite are genetically and temperamentally matched. It's quite fortunate."

Enyo wasn't sure she believed in fortune or coincidence, but the job paid well, and it was only a matter of time before people found out who she was. The satellite offered escape. Redemption. "Sure, but what *is* it?"

"A self-repairing – and self-replicating, if need be – vehicle for exploring the galactic rim. It will take snapshots – exact replicas – of specified quadrants as you pass, and store them aboard for future generations to act out. Most of that is automated, but it will need a . . . companion. We have had some unfortunate incidents of madness, when constructs like these are cast off alone. It's been grown from . . . well, from some of the most interesting organic specimens we've found in our exploration of the near-systems."

"It's alien, then?"

"Partially. Some of it's terrestrial. Just enough of it."

"It's illegal to go mixing alien stuff with ours, isn't it?"

The recruiter smiled. "Not on Eris."

"Why Eris? Why not Sedna, or a neighboring system?"

"The concentrated methane that will give you much of your initial inertia comes from Eris. The edge of the Sol system is close enough for us to gain access to local system resources at a low cost, but far enough away to . . . well, it's far enough away to keep the rest of the system safe."

"Safe from what?"

"There's a danger, Enyo. A danger of what you could . . . bring back. Or perhaps . . . what you could become."

Enyo regarded the spiky satellite. "You should have hired some techhead, then." She was not afraid of the alien thing, not then, but the recruiter made her anxious. There was something very familiar about her teeth.

"You came highly recommended," the recruiter said.

"You mean I'm highly expendable."

They came to the end of the long spoke, and stepped into the transparent bubble of the airlock that sat outside the pulsing satellite.

"The war is over," the recruiter said, "but there were many casualties. We make do with what we have."

"It's breathing, isn't it?" Enyo said.

"Methane, mostly," the recruiter said.

"And out there?"

"It goes into hibernation. It will need less. But our initial probes along the galactic rim have indicated that methane is as abundant there as here. We'll go into more detail on the mechanics of its care and feeding."

"Feeding?" Enyo said.

"Oh yes," the recruiter said. She pressed her dark hand to the transparent screen. Her eyes were big, the pupils too large, like all the techs who had grown up on Eris. "You'll need to feed it. At least a few hundred kilos of organic matter a turn."

Enyo gazed up at the hulk of the thing. "And where exactly am I going to get organic matter as we orbit the far arms of the galaxy?"

"I'm sure you'll think of something," the recruiter said. She withdrew her hand, and flashed her teeth again. "We chose you because we knew you could make those kinds of decisions without regret. The way you did during the war. And long before it."

Enyo sliced open the slick surface of the superpod with her weapon. There was no rush of Tuataran atmosphere, no crumpling or wrinkling about the wound. No, the peridium had already been breached somewhere else. Arso and Dax hung back, bickering over some slight. Enyo wondered if they had known one another before Reeb picked them up. They had, hadn't they? The way she had known Arso. The snapshot of Arso. Some other life. Some other decision.

Inside, the superpod's bioluminescent tubal corridors still glowed a faint blue-green, just enough light for Enyo to avoid stepping on the wizened body of some unfortunate maintenance officer.

"Don't you need direction?" Reeb tickled her ear. But she already knew where the colonists were. She knew because she had placed them there herself, turns and turns ago.

Enyo crawled up through the sticky corridors, cutting through pressurized areas of the superpod, going around others. Finally, she reached the coded spiral of the safe room that held the colonists. She gestured to Arso.

"Open it," she said.

Arso snorted. "It's a coded door."

"Yes. It's coded for you. Open it."

"I don't understand."

"It's why you're here. Open it."

"I—"

Enyo lifted her weapon. "Should Enyo make you?"

Arso held up her hands. "Fine. No harm. Fucking dizzy core you've got, woman."

Arso placed her hand against the slimy doorway. The coating on the door fused with her spray-on suit. Pressurized. Enyo heard the soft intake of Arso's breath as the outer seal of the safe room tasted her blood.

The door went transparent.

Arso yanked away her hand.

Enyo walked through the transparent film and into the pressurized safe room. Ring after ring of personal pods lined the room, suffused in a blue glow. Hundreds? Thousands.

She glanced back at Dax. Both she and Arso were surveying the cargo. Dax's little mouth was open. Enyo realized who she reminded her of, then. The recruiter. The one with the teeth.

Enyo shot them both. They died quickly, without comment.

Then she walked to the first pod she saw. She tore away the head of her own suit and tossed it to the floor. She peered into the colonist's puckered face, and she thought of the prisoner.

Enyo bit the umbilicus that linked the pod to the main life system, the same core system responsible for renewing and replenishing the fluids that sustained these hibernating bodies.

The virus in her saliva infected the umbilicus. In a few hours, everything in here would be liquid jelly. Easily digestible for a satellite seeking to make its last turn.

As Reeb cursed in her ear, she walked the long line of pods, back and back and back, until she found two familiar names. Arso Tohl. Dax Alhamin. Their pods were side by side. Their faces perfectly pinched. Dax looked younger, and perhaps she was, in this snapshot. Arso was still formidable. Enyo pressed her fingers to the transparent face of the pod. She wanted to kiss them. But they would be dead of her kiss soon enough.

Dead for a second time. Or perhaps a fifth, a fiftieth, a five hundredth. She didn't know. She didn't want to know.

It's why she piloted *Enyo-Enyo*.

The woman waiting on the other side of the icy bridge was not one Enyo recognized, which did not happen often. As she guided the prisoner's pod to the woman's feet, she wondered how long it had been, this turn. How long since the last?

"What do you have for us?" the woman asked.

"Eris is very different," Enyo said.

The woman turned her soft brown face to the sky and frowned. "I suppose it must seem that way to you. It's been like this for centuries."

"No more methane?"

"Those wells went dry 500 years ago." The woman knit her brows. "You were around this way long before that happened. You must remember Eris like this."

"Was I? I must have forgotten."

"So what is it this time?" the woman said. "We're siphoning off the satellite's snapshots now."

"I brought you the prisoner," Enyo said.

"What prisoner?"

"*The* prisoner," Enyo said, because as she patted the prisoner's pod something in her memory ruptured. There was something important she knew. "The prisoner who started the war."

"What war?" the woman said.

"*The* war," Enyo said.

The woman wiped away the snow on the face of the pod, and frowned. "Is this some kind of joke?" she said.

"I brought her back," Enyo said.

The woman jabbed Enyo in the chest. "Get back in the fucking satellite," she said. "And do your fucking job."

Back to the beginning. Around and around.

Enyo wasn't sure how it happened, the first time. She was standing outside the escape pod, a bulbous, nasty little thing that made up the core of the internode. It seemed an odd place for it. Why put the escape pod at the center of the satellite? But that's where the thing decided to grow it. And so that's where it was.

She stood there as the satellite took its first snapshot of the quadrant they moved through. And something . . . shifted. Some core part of her. That's when the memories started. The memories of the other pieces. The snapshots.

That's when she realized what *Enyo-Enyo* really was.

Enyo stepped up into the escape pod. She sealed it shut. Her breathing was heavy. She closed her eyes. She had to go home, now, before it broke her into more pieces. Before it reminded her of what she was. War criminal. Flesh dealer. Monster.

As she sealed the escape pod and began drowning in life-sustaining fluid, she realized it was not meant for her escape. *Enyo-Enyo* had placed it there for another purpose.

The satellite took a snapshot.

And there, on the other side of the fluid-filled pod, she saw her own face.

The squalling children were imperfect, like Enyo. She had already sold Reeb to some infertile young diplomatic aid's broker in the flesh pits for a paltry sum. It was not enough to get her off the shit asteroid at the ass end of the Mushta Mura arm. She would die out here of some green plague, some white dust contagion. The death dealers would string her up and sell her parts. She'd be nothing. All this pain and anguish, for nothing.

Later, she could not recall how she found the place. Whispered rumors. A mangled transmission. She found herself walking into a chemically scrubbed medical office, like some place you'd go to have an industrial part grafted on for growing. The logo on the spiral of the door, and the coats of the staff, was a double circle shot through with a blue dart.

"I heard you're not looking for eggs or embryos," she said, and set Dysmonia's swaddled little body on the counter.

The receptionist smiled. White, white teeth. He blinked, and a woman came up from the back. She was a tall brown-skinned woman with large hands and a grim face.

"I'm Arso Tohl," the woman said. "Let's have a look."

They paid Enyo enough to leave not just the asteroid, but the Mushta Mura arm entirely. She fled with a hot bundle of currency instead of a squalling, temperamental child. When she entered the armed forces outside the Sol system, she did so because it was the furthest arm of the galaxy from her own. When a neighboring system paid her to start a war, she did so gladly.

She did not expect to see or hear from the butchers again.

Not until she saw the logo on the satellite recruiter's uniform.

Enyo ate her fill of the jellified colonists and slogged back to the satellite to feed it, to feed *Enyo-Enyo*. Reeb's annoying voice had grown silent. He always stopped protesting after the first dozen.

She found him sitting in the internode with the prisoner, his hands pressed against the base of the pod. His head was lowered.

"It was enough to make the next turn," Enyo said.

"It always is," he said.

"There will be other crews," she said.

"I know."

"Then why are you melancholy?" If she could see his face, it would be winter.

He raised his head. Stared at the semblance of a body floating in the viscous fluid. "I'm not really here, am I?"

"This turn? I don't know. Sometimes you are. Sometimes you aren't. It depends on how many snapshots *Enyo-Enyo* has taken this turn. And how she wants it all to turn out this time."

"When did you put yourself in here?" He patted the prisoner's pod.

"When things got too complicated to bear," she said. "When I realized who *Enyo-Enyo* was." She went to the slick feeding console. She vomited the condensed protein stew of the colonists into the receptacle. When it was over, she fell back, exhausted.

"Let's play screes," she said. "Before the next snapshot. We might be different people, then."

"We can only hope," Reeb said, and pulled his hands away from the prisoner.

SEMIRAMIS

Genevieve Valentine

The worst thing about being a sleeper embedded somewhere long-term was that inevitably, eventually, you started to care.

The worst thing about being embedded long-term as an administrator at the Svalbard Seed Vault was that when you inevitably started to care, you started to care about things like proper political geo-temperate arrangement of seeds, and there was just no one else in their right mind who was going to care about that with you.

That was half the reason I recruited Lise.

Ever since Svalbard had been put under review, it had been hell and a half trying to figure out how to recruit a domestic cover who could carry seeds off the island. And for something this long-term in a place as small as Longyearbyen, you needed domestic cover, or people started to suspect you for keeping apart.

The locals were out of the question, and once we were under review it was more than my life was worth to try to smuggle someone over if they didn't already have some international clearance.

("Under review": the Global Coalition was interested enough in Svalbard to station spies at the ports.)

Lise had been a loose affiliate of my organization, years back. She'd dropped off the map, but it only took two tries to contact her, and one meeting to convince her.

"Good choice," said the guy who'd met her, when he called weeks later to seal the deal. "She's got contacts at the mine at Sveagruva. She's already on a plane to Oslo; she'll catch a boat out to you next week."

The rest of the timeline was already set, for the short-term: quick public courtship, cohabitation. When our orders came in, she'd make the initial runs off the island, and then once there was a routine in place she could quietly vanish whenever things soured.

Until then she would live with me on Svalbard and keep an eye on Coalition business in town and whatever the mining company turned up.

I would keep making visits to the Seed Vault, taking inventory, ticking off names on my list, waiting for the day when I'd get the order to move out two or three seeds at a time and pass them off to whomever the highest bidders sent to collect.

(The day I was really waiting for was the day I could tell someone, "This one's drying up. We'll be looking for some decent soil, to grow it for re-harvest," and have their eyes light up, too.)

"Coalition Peacekeepers just showed up – they blocked the port," Lise says, knocking mud off her boots. "They've already dispatched a zoo team to look for polar bears."

I whistle. "How many of them?"

"Enough to make sure you don't get one fucking seed out of here," she says. "Good luck."

(She was a decent recruit – she'd done admin at the Millennium Seed Bank before it got militarized, had some clearance, had some brains – but she wasn't a believer, and it showed.)

I frown at the printout in front of me – scientific names and common names and country of origin marching in four-point font for 200 pages.

"We'll find a way around it," I say. "This could just be like the review. It could be years before we have to worry."

We plan in years.

She shoulders her rifle. "I'm going out."

Rifles are standard issue in Longyearbyen, one of the few places you can still get one. It's required outside the city, for protection against polar bears.

(She mostly goes out to the bird cliffs and takes shots at poachers.)

"Don't kill anyone," I say. We need to keep cover.

A gust of cold wind, and she's gone.

Absently, I check off *Acer palmatum* on the list, but my concentration is already gone, and I end up staring out the window at the shadows that gather inside shadows all over this place at night.

I don't notice the Peacekeeper boats have moved into place until someone inside one turns on a light.

We measure time two ways.

One is the paper calendar I get at Christmas from the woman who poses, twice a year, as my sister.

Longyearbyen went nearly paperless after the Global Coalition's Environmental Imperative was released. (We had to preserve any trees that would grow, it said; now that the waters were rising, arable land was sacrosanct.)

Tax on physical mail was obscene, but the calendar was how I received most of my instructions, so I paid.

One random day a year was "Semiramis (observed)" – the day I sent my ID over a landline, by voice.

I chose the name; she was the queen for whom they'd built the hanging gardens in Babylon.

By then I had started to care.

"Happy Semiramis," Lise always said when she checked off that calendar day, in a tone that made me feel like I was giving away too much.

It was the only paper in the house, save the printout of the Seed Vault inventory. That had been granted exemption – pulp for the good of the nation.

Lise was the one who started ticking off days on the calendar, the very first year she arrived.

I hadn't asked why. We didn't like each other enough back then to get into a round of questions, and by the time we'd reached a truce it wasn't worth asking. In this line of work, you learn just to live with people.

The other way we keep time is by tracking how much coal is worth.

Most of the coal mined on Svalbard went directly into the air conditioners at the Seed Vault, to keep the temperature at a constant zero Fahrenheit. The price of coal went up the warmer it got outside, and the more of it we needed, the less of it there was.

This was the calendar we kept for the rest of the world, to measure how bad things were getting.

Two years back, Lise had come home and said, "We passed gold on the index. Things must be rough down South."

"Did the Coalition do anything?"

"We got an embargo – no export under threat of treason," she said, shrugging. The coal was meant for the Vault, not for sale, and Svalbard was already under review; it wasn't as though anything got off the island anyway, unless the Norwegian government found some country down South with the money to buy.

(Down South: anywhere beneath the Arctic line, where water levels were rising and cities were being swallowed up. Shanghai and New York had gone early, London and Copenhagen a few years later. The Maldives had vanished right off the map. Their government operated out of Mumbai until that went under, too.

The whole South is just governments sprinting for high ground, these days.)

After the Peacekeepers come, I don't see her for two days.

The Sveagruva mine is battening down in the wake of the Peacekeepers, and she works long hours up there. Sometimes it's easier just to sleep over.

I go out to the Seed Vault every day, in the bright-green parka that makes me look like a tourist. I leave the Snow Cat and walk the last mile (less threatening), and try not to stare at the ships.

It's surprising how high the water has risen. My first year, passing ships had been so low I could look down onto their decks; now they're nearly eye level.

The Peacekeepers are already stationed outside, asking my business.

That's a mistake. If you ask someone about their business, they might tell you.

(Years back, when I was still so new that I worried how I'd ever overcome my apathy about seed packets in a fucking basement, some botanists came to drop off seeds. One of them talked at me for twenty minutes about the runaway metabolism of *Castanea sativa*.

"Can you imagine a future without chestnuts?" she said, and handed me the envelope, and sighed. "It's so precarious, now, with so few species allowed to grow at all. This is the last surviving breed – the very last."

I looked at the woman in mild terror. I already knew that I was doomed to be interested one day; that didn't mean it wasn't an awful thing to anticipate.

Norway sealed Svalbard to donations a year after that. By the time I'd developed interest, I was alone.)

I give the Peacekeepers a more detailed description of my business than anyone has ever wanted.

"It's the recalcitrant seeds that we really have to watch out for," I explain about five minutes in, and then I start on runaway metabolism and desiccation effects and where we'll be when we can't grow chestnuts any more, and the Peacekeepers look at me pretty much the way I'd expected them to.

Still, they move aside.

I ask them, "Where's home for you?"

"Scotland."

"How are things there?"

They don't answer.

(No answer: Under occupation, or under water.)

Inside, I'm relieved beyond reason the *Tuberaria guttata* seeds are doing well.

It had been drowned out of the Mediterranean and Wales and the States years back. This sample had been harvested from Scotland, and it doesn't sound like there are going to be many more chances at it.

When I come home, Lise is sitting in front of the little coal stove, still in her yellow coat.

It's a comfort. We've lived together for nearly eight years, and after a while you just get used to seeing someone.

(The first time I was embedded somewhere I fell in love with my domestic-cover operative. It went badly. I've learned not to overthink these things.)

I hang my coat. "How has it gone? Peacekeepers giving you trouble yet?"

"Their ships are upsetting the fish," she says. "The birds are just circling. Bad enough that the cliffs are disappearing underwater. Now they'll starve, too."

The bird-cliffs are covered this time of year, auks and terns and kittiwakes. I went out there once, with Lise, to check out escape routes. It was a chaos of feathers and noise and the green and yellow lights of the Aurora, and I left as soon as I realized it would be impossible to scale the cliffs.

Lise goes back all the time.

(One year, early on, she brought back a tern that had been on the bad end of a fight, and she fed and warmed it all night until it died. Then she took the body outside. What she did with it she never said, and I didn't ask. You learn to just live with people.)

I make coffee on the stove, keep one eye on her face as her expression gets darker.

By the time I sit next to her, I've made up my mind.

"I brought this," I say, and pull an envelope out of my pocket.

It's an archival envelope, unlabeled; inside is a single seed.

"*Tuberaria guttata*. Spotted rock rose. The flowers last less than a day. This one's from Scotland, but it sounds like they've drowned by now. These are going to be worth a lot of money."

She hasn't taken the seed out. She's just looking at it still tucked inside the envelope. I didn't think her expression could get darker, but I was wrong.

"Have the orders come in?" she asks.

I should have expected concern. She thinks she's been cut out of the loop.

"No, no," I say. "Still waiting to hear. I just – I wanted to bring this one out. Call it a dry run."

"Are you going to sell it?"

Suspicion I hadn't expected.

"No," I snap. "I just wanted you to see it."

She looks up at that. I freeze and wait; if she calls it a present, I'll deny it to the death.

But she only says, "Isn't it enough you'll be taking out the others?"

She's not a believer, and it shows.

I pluck the envelope out of her hand.

"Two million seeds," I say. "Will they really miss one?"

"There used to be two million birds," she says. Her voice is strained, like she's trying not to care.

We sit in silence until the fire goes down and the cabin's warm enough to sleep in.

(We sleep in the same bed. This is too long-term an arrangement to be a gentleman and sleep on the couch. You plan in years.)

It takes six weeks before Peacekeepers and Svalbard locals have finished jostling for territory.

It means the worst, of course – no one's under illusions. It means that "under review" has turned into "Coalition Protectorate" in some back room in some inland country, and the highest-bidding corporation will be moving in to take over the coal mines, and soon the Svalbard Seed Vault will be powered by Mainland Oil or MediaVox.

It means my orders are going to come through any day, so we can have a little of our own back before the MediaVox Seed Vault opens for business.

I go every day, now, just to keep the Peacekeepers used to my face.

Lise comes home from the mine, shoulders her rifle, goes out again. I don't know where. The Peacekeepers are crowding us out wherever they can.

By now I'm staying up nights, too, researching what nations have gone under one way or another.

It's really something how hard the Coalition works to keep its member nations separated. Once they get their import taxes and their offshore data charges and their streaming-feed embargoes on you, there's no communicating with anyone – you might as well be submerged in the sea.

You have to strike early, before the locals have submitted to all the red tape.

You have to act before they know to stop you.

Semiramis comes.

I make the call from the loudest pub in town.

"It's soon," my fake sister says. "Be ready to move out past the Peacekeepers."

I snap, "Then Lise will have to swim, because these boats aren't budging. We need time."

"We need at least one good run," she says, "to make this worth it. It has to be soon."

We argue about Peacekeepers for a minute or two in low voices, and then I talk nonsense about the weather for another five minutes, just in case.

(It's not all nonsense – I tell her about the sea level, and she says, "We moved," and I imagine the overpacked cities picking themselves up, buildings and all, and climbing the mountain as the water rises.)

When I come home, Lise doesn't tell me, "Happy Semiramis."

I can hardly be offended, but this is the first time I notice that she stopped marking days a long time ago. That worries me.

I don't mention yet that our time to act is coming. I have a feeling I'd better have a plan before I try to get her in on it.

I'm beginning to understand the frustration of not knowing everything. My fake sister hasn't told me what they think the Coalition will do to me, when they find out what's happened.

It's a when, not an if. Lise has been positioned to survive, as a condition of her participation. There's no such provision for me. Never has been. Sometimes when you take a job, it's your last one.

Still, I make a few more dry runs, just to keep in practice for when my orders come.

I pick some seeds that will grow in any soil (as dumb as it is, I still want to plant something, once, and watch it grow). I pick some seeds because they're rare enough to make a decent bribe if things go south.

I pick a bird of paradise, a seed with a sharp red tuft, for no reason except that it's been ten years since I've seen anything red; the Aurora is yellow and green, and the rest of the world is the tight dark of seeds, and envelopes paler than skin.

I should have planned a little more, for when this started to creep over me, but there's no knowing how it will creep up on you until you look at a tufted seed and blink at how bright it is.

I didn't even look up what happened to the Hanging Gardens until after I had picked the name. Turns out the ground swallowed them, but what can you do?

Every time I bring something home I hand her the envelope, so she can't say I held out on her.

She should know what she's doing when the time comes, and

she should know the worth of what she's carrying. I don't plead anybody's case – I'm not like that botanist with the chestnuts. This is business.

Usually she only glances inside. I tell her what they are and what long-gone country they came from, and she gets that drawn, sad look I'm starting to see in the mirror.

Once, she opens the envelope and says instantly, "Bird of paradise."

I'm so surprised I smile.

She hands it back "That's a slow grow. Good luck getting it to the blooming stage."

"You never know," I say.

(We plan in years.)

As part of the negotiations to keep everyone in Svalbard from turning on them, the Coalition ships finally move back out of fishing range.

They open a big enough gap on the north side of the water for seals and bears to pass; in return, the rifle-bearing locals promise to stop mistaking Peacekeepers for polar bears at night.

Thousands of birds have died from starvation in the meantime, Lise tells me that night.

"The shore under the cliff is a graveyard," she says.

"At least the seals will be fed," I say.

Her eyes are red. She doesn't answer.

I imagine her skidding through the slush all the way to the cliff, seeing what she saw, and the Peacekeeper boats just out of rifle range.

I make us coffee.

A week later, Sveagruva lets its employees go.

"It's just an interim measure," Lise parrots, "to preserve the facility until new management can be chosen."

I nod. "Very reassuring. Doesn't sound at all like a MediaVox move-in."

"Yeah," she says. "This coal brought to you by."

She already looks antsy about being cut off from information.

"Lise," I say, serious. "We'll figure a way off Svalbard for you. I'm not going to strand you here. That wasn't the deal."

She slings her rifle over her shoulder, disappears.

Our orders come in.

There are a hundred seeds on the list – one good run. They could be carried in someone's coat pocket, in the fingertips of a pair of gloves, if people were still allowed in or out.

The new coal boats have clearance, but Lise isn't employed there any more. Coalition companies start with clean slates.

"Somehow we have to get you on a ship," I say.

She says, like we were having a totally different conversation all along, "Are they going to sell the Vault, do you think?"

I have no answer. I don't like where this is going.

She sits back against the couch, stares at the tiny fire in our tiny stove.

"At first I thought they'd sell it off all in one piece, to one of the inland countries that can still grow something. That would be better than nothing. Any growth is better than letting things die – expensive wheat is better than no wheat. That, I would have been all right with. I would have let that happen."

She means, *I would have turned you in.*

She's using past tense, so I'm probably fine, but still I look around to make sure she's not within reach of her gun.

She sighs. "But seeing how they've managed things," and when she pauses I know she thinks of the birds, "I wonder if they're worse than we are, and we're better off just because we can call a theft a theft."

"Speak for yourself," I say, though it's true.

She pulls something from the inside of her jacket – a seed envelope.

The little rock rose seed tumbles into her open palm, and for a second I hold my breath like it will sprout.

(I need a drink.)

Lise doesn't look at me. "What color does it bloom?"

"Yellow."

She nods and curls her fingers around it. I think about telling her to give me my bribe back, but I don't. It was probably a gift. Happy Semiramis.

"I'll join up with the people from the Gene Ark, when they show," she says. "They never wait long to barge in and take tissue samples from native species, and they'll need the help. I can get out that way, and come back as soon as I can."

She says it like she'll actually make it back here, like we haven't done all this work for a shot at 100 seeds before the other, smarter thieves close in.

Still, 100 plants isn't bad. A hundred and one – she'll take hers with her.

"All right," I say.

After a while she says, "You know, I've never been inside the Vault."

I sit down beside her. Our shoulders are touching.

"It's a long hallway," I say, "and then some seeds."

We sit awake long after the fire goes out, watching shadows gathering inside shadows, waiting for morning.

(Inevitably, eventually, you start to care.)

IMMERSION

Aliette de Bodard

In the morning, you're no longer quite sure who you are.

You stand in front of the mirror – it shifts and trembles, reflecting only what you want to see – eyes that feel too wide, skin that feels too pale, an odd, distant smell wafting from the compartment's ambient system that is neither incense nor garlic, but something else, something elusive that you once knew.

You're dressed, already – not on your skin, but outside, where it matters, your avatar sporting blue and black and gold, the stylish clothes of a well-traveled, well-connected woman. For a moment, as you turn away from the mirror, the glass shimmers out of focus; and another woman in a dull silk gown stares back at you: smaller, squatter and in every way diminished – a stranger, a distant memory that has ceased to have any meaning.

Quy was on the docks, watching the spaceships arrive. She could, of course, have been anywhere on Longevity Station, and requested the feed from the network to be patched to her router – and watched, superimposed on her field of vision, the slow dance of ships slipping into their pod cradles like births watched in reverse. But there was something about standing on the spaceport's concourse – a feeling of closeness that she just couldn't replicate by standing in Golden Carp Gardens or Azure Dragon Temple. Because here – here, separated by only a few measures of sheet metal from the cradle pods, she could feel herself teetering on the edge of the vacuum, submerged in cold and breathing in neither air nor oxygen. She could almost imagine herself rootless, finally returned to the source of everything.

Most ships those days were Galactic – you'd have thought

Longevity's ex-masters would have been unhappy about the station's independence, but now that the war was over Longevity was a tidy source of profit. The ships came, and disgorged a steady stream of tourists – their eyes too round and straight, their jaws too square; their faces an unhealthy shade of pink, like under-cooked meat left too long in the sun. They walked with the easy confidence of people with immersers: pausing to admire the suggested highlights for a second or so before moving on to the transport station, where they haggled in schoolbook Rong for a ride to their recommended hotels – a sickeningly familiar ballet Quy had been seeing most of her life, a unison of foreigners descending on the station like a plague of centipedes or leeches.

Still, Quy watched them. They reminded her of her own time on Prime, her heady schooldays filled with raucous bars and wild weekends, and last-minute revisions for exams, a carefree time she'd never have again in her life. She both longed for those days back, and hated herself for her weakness. Her education on Prime, which should have been her path into the higher strata of the station's society, had brought her nothing but a sense of discon-nection from her family; a growing solitude, and a dissatisfaction, an aimlessness she couldn't put in words.

She might not have moved all day – had a sign not blinked, superimposed by her router on the edge of her field of vision. A message from Second Uncle.

"Child." His face was pale and worn, his eyes underlined by dark circles, as if he hadn't slept. He probably hadn't – the last Quy had seen of him, he had been closeted with Quy's sister Tam, trying to organize a delivery for a wedding – 500 winter melons, and six barrels of Prosper's Station best fish sauce. "Come back to the restaurant."

"I'm on my day of rest," Quy said; it came out as more peevish and childish than she'd intended.

Second Uncle's face twisted, in what might have been a smile, though he had very little sense of humor. The scar he'd got in the Independence War shone white against the grainy background – twisting back and forth, as if it still pained him. "I know, but I need you. We have an important customer."

"Galactic," Quy said. That was the only reason he'd be calling her, and not one of her brothers or cousins. Because the family somehow thought that her studies on Prime gave her insight into the Galactics' way of thought – something useful, if not the success they'd hoped for.

"Yes. An important man, head of a local trading company." Second Uncle did not move on her field of vision. Quy could *see* the ships moving through his face, slowly aligning themselves in front of their pods, the hole in front of them opening like an orchid flower. And she knew everything there was to know about Grandmother's restaurant; she was Tam's sister, after all; and she'd seen the accounts, the slow decline of their clientele as their more genteel clients moved to better areas of the station; the influx of tourists on a budget, with little time for expensive dishes prepared with the best ingredients.

"Fine," she said. "I'll come."

At breakfast, you stare at the food spread out on the table: bread and jam and some colored liquid – you come up blank for a moment, before your immerser kicks in, reminding you that it's coffee, served strong and black, just as you always take it.

Yes. Coffee.

You raise the cup to your lips – your immerser gently prompts you, reminding you of where to grasp, how to lift, how to be in every possible way graceful and elegant, always an effortless model.

"It's a bit strong," your husband says, apologetically. He watches you from the other end of the table, an expression you can't interpret on his face – and isn't this odd, because shouldn't you know all there is to know about expressions – shouldn't the immerser have everything about Galactic culture recorded into its database; shouldn't it prompt you? But it's strangely silent, and this scares you, more than anything. Immersers never fail.

"Shall we go?" your husband says – and, for a moment, you come up blank on his name, before you remember – Galen, it's Galen, named after some physician on Old Earth. He's tall, with dark hair and pale skin – his immerser avatar isn't much different from his real self; Galactic avatars seldom are. It's people like you who have to work the hardest to adjust, because so much about you draws attention to itself – the stretched eyes that crinkle in the shape of moths, the darker skin, the smaller, squatter shape more reminiscent of jackfruits than swaying fronds. But no matter: you can be made perfect; you can put on the immerser and become someone else, someone pale-skinned and tall and beautiful.

Though, really, it's been such a long time since you took off the immerser, isn't it? It's just a thought – a suspended moment that is soon erased by the immerser's flow of information, the little arrows drawing your attention to the bread and the kitchen, and the polished metal of the table – giving you context about everything, opening up the universe like a lotus flower.

"Yes," you say. "Let's go." Your tongue trips over the word – there's a structure you should have used, a pronoun you should have said instead of the lapidary Galactic sentence. But nothing will come, and you feel like a field of sugar canes after the harvest – burnt out, all cutting edges with no sweetness left inside.

Of course, Second Uncle insisted on Quy getting her immerser for the interview – just in case, he said, soothingly and diplomatically as always. Trouble was, it wasn't where Quy had last left it. After putting out a message to the rest of the family, the best information Quy got was from Cousin Khanh, who thought he'd seen Tam sweep through the living quarters, gathering every piece of Galactic tech she could get her hands on. Third Aunt, who caught Khanh's message on the family's communication channel, tutted disapprovingly. "Tam. Always with her mind lost in the mountains, that girl. Dreams have never husked rice."

Quy said nothing. Her own dreams had shriveled and died after she came back from Prime and failed Longevity's mandarin exams; but it was good to have Tam around – to have someone who saw beyond the restaurant, beyond the narrow circle of family interests. Besides, if she didn't stick with her sister, who would?

Tam wasn't in the communal areas on the upper floors; Quy threw a glance towards the lift to Grandmother's closeted rooms, but she was doubtful Tam would have gathered Galactic tech just so she could pay her respects to Grandmother. Instead, she went straight to the lower floor, the one she and Tam shared with the children of their generation.

It was right next to the kitchen, and the smells of garlic and fish sauce seemed to be everywhere – of course, the youngest generation always got the lower floor, the one with all the smells and the noises of a legion of waitresses bringing food over to the dining room.

Tam was there, sitting in the little compartment that served as the floor's communal area. She'd spread out the tech on the floor – two immersers (Tam and Quy were possibly the only family members who cared so little about immersers they left them lying around), a remote entertainment set that was busy broadcasting some stories of children running on terraformed planets, and something Quy couldn't quite identify, because Tam had taken it apart into small components: it lay on the table like a gutted fish, all metals and optical parts.

But, at some point, Tam had obviously got bored with the entire process, because she was currently finishing her breakfast, slurping noodles from her soup bowl. She must have got it from the kitchen's leftovers, because Quy knew the smell, could taste the spiciness of the broth on her tongue – Mother's cooking, enough to make her stomach growl although she'd had rolled rice cakes for breakfast.

"You're at it again," Quy said with a sigh. "Could you not take my immerser for your experiments, please?"

Tam didn't even look surprised. "You don't seem very keen on using it, big sis."

"That I don't use it doesn't mean it's yours," Quy said, though that wasn't a real reason. She didn't mind Tam borrowing her stuff, and actually would have been glad never to put on an immerser again – she hated the feeling they gave her, the vague sensation of the system rooting around in her brain to find the best body cues to give her. But there were times when she was expected to wear an immerser: whenever dealing with customers, whether she was waiting at tables or in preparation meetings for large occasions.

Tam, of course, didn't wait at tables – she'd made herself so good at logistics and anything to do with the station's system that she spent most of her time in front of a screen, or connected to the station's network.

"Lil' sis?" Quy said.

Tam set her chopsticks by the side of the bowl, and made an expansive gesture with her hands. "Fine. Have it back. I can always use mine."

Quy stared at the things spread on the table, and asked the inevitable question. "How's progress?"

Tam's work was network connections and network maintenance within the restaurant; her hobby was tech. Galactic tech. She took things apart to see what made them tick; and rebuilt them. Her foray into entertainment units had helped the restaurant set up ambient sounds – old-fashioned Rong music for Galactic customers, recitation of the newest poems for locals.

But immersers had her stumped: the things had nasty safeguards to them. You could open them in half, to replace the battery; but you went no further. Tam's previous attempt had almost lost her the use of her hands.

By Tam's face, she didn't feel ready to try again. "It's got to be the same logic."

"As what?" Quy couldn't help asking. She picked up her own immerser from the table, briefly checking that it did indeed bear her serial number.

Tam gestured to the splayed components on the table. "Artificial Literature Writer. Little gadget that composes light-entertainment novels."

"That's not the same—" Quy checked herself, and waited for Tam to explain.

"Takes existing cultural norms, and puts them into a cohesive, satisfying narrative. Like people forging their own path and fighting aliens for possession of a planet, that sort of stuff that barely speaks to us on Longevity. I mean, we've never even seen a planet." Tam exhaled, sharply – her eyes half on the dismembered Artificial Literature Writer, half on some overlay of her vision. "Just like immersers take a given culture and parcel it out to you in a form you can relate to: language, gestures, customs, the whole package. They've got to have the same architecture."

"I'm still not sure what you want to do with it." Quy put on her immerser, adjusting the thin metal mesh around her head until it fitted. She winced as the interface synced with her brain. She moved her hands, adjusting some settings lower than the factory ones – darn thing always reset itself to factory, which she suspected was no accident. A shimmering lattice surrounded her: her avatar, slowly taking shape around her. She could still see the room – the lattice was only faintly opaque – but ancestors, how she hated the feeling of not quite being there. "How do I look?"

"Horrible. Your avatar looks like it's died or something."

"Ha ha ha," Quy said. Her avatar was paler than her, and taller: it made her look beautiful, most customers agreed. In those moments, Quy was glad she had an avatar, so they wouldn't see the anger on her face. "You haven't answered my question."

Tam's eyes glinted. "Just think of the things we couldn't do. This is the best piece of tech Galactics have ever brought us."

Which wasn't much, but Quy didn't need to say it aloud. Tam knew exactly how Quy felt about Galactics and their hollow promises.

"It's their weapon, too." Tam pushed at the entertainment unit. "Just like their books and their holos and their live games. It's fine for them – they put the immersers on tourist settings, they get just what they need to navigate a foreign environment from whatever idiot's written the Rong script for that thing. But we – we worship them. We wear the immersers on Galactic all the time. We make ourselves like them, because they push, and because we're naive enough to give in."

"And you think you can make this better?" Quy couldn't help it. It wasn't that she needed to be convinced: on Prime, she'd never seen immersers. They were tourist stuff, and even while travelling from one city to another, the citizens just assumed they'd know enough to get by. But the stations, their ex-colonies were flooded with immersers.

Tam's eyes glinted, as savage as those of the rebels in the history holos. "If I can take them apart, I can rebuild them and disconnect the logical circuits. I can give us the language and the tools to deal with them without being swallowed by them."

Mind lost in the mountains, Third Aunt said. No one had ever accused Tam of thinking small. Or of not achieving what she set her mind on, come to think of it. And every revolution had to start somewhere – hadn't Longevity's War of Independence started over a single poem, and the unfair imprisonment of the poet who'd written it?

Quy nodded. She believed Tam, though she didn't know how far. "Fair point. Have to go now, or Second Uncle will skin me. See you later, lil' sis."

As you walk under the wide arch of the restaurant with your husband, you glance upwards, at the calligraphy that forms its sign. The immerser translates it for you into "Sister Hai's Kitchen," and starts giving you a detailed background of the place: the menu and the most recommended dishes – as you walk past the various tables, it highlights items it thinks you would like, from rolled-up rice dumplings to fried shrimps. It warns you about the more exotic dishes, like the pickled pig's ears, the fermented meat (you have to be careful about that one, because its name changes depending on which station dialect you order in), or the reeking durian fruit that the natives so love.

It feels . . . not quite right, you think, as you struggle to follow Galen, who is already far away, striding ahead with the same confidence he always exudes in life. People part before him; a waitress with a young, pretty avatar bows before him, though Galen himself takes no notice. You know that such obsequiousness unnerves him; he always rants about the outdated customs aboard Longevity, the inequalities and the lack of democratic government – he thinks it's only a matter of time before they change, adapt themselves to fit into Galactic society. You – you have a faint memory of arguing with him, a long time ago, but now you can't find the words, anymore, or even the reason why – it makes sense, it all makes sense. The Galactics rose against the tyranny of Old Earth and overthrew their shackles, and won the right to determine their own destiny; and every other station and planet will do the same, eventually, rise against the dictatorships that hold them away from progress. It's right; it's always been right.

Unbidden, you stop at a table, and watch two young women pick at a dish of chicken with chopsticks – the smell of fish sauce and lemongrass rises in the air, as pungent and as unbearable as rotten meat – no, no, that's not it, you have an image of a dark-skinned woman, bringing a dish of steamed rice to the table, her hands filled with that same smell, and your mouth watering in anticipation . . .

The young women are looking at you: they both wear standard-issue avatars, the bottom-of-the-line kind – their clothes are a garish mix of red and yellow, with the odd, uneasy cut of cheap designers; and their faces waver, letting you glimpse a hint of darker skin beneath the red flush of their cheeks. Cheap and tawdry, and altogether inappropriate; and you're glad you're not one of them.

"Can I help you, older sister?" one of them asks.

Older sister. A pronoun you were looking for, earlier; one of the things that seem to have vanished from your mind. You struggle for words; but all the immerser seems to suggest to you is a neutral and impersonal pronoun, one that you instinctively know is wrong – it's one only foreigners and outsiders would use in those circumstances. "Older sister," you repeat, finally, because you can't think of anything else.

"Agnes!"

Galen's voice, calling from far away – for a brief moment the immerser seems to fail you again, because you *know* that you have many names, that Agnes is the one they gave you in Galactic school, the one neither Galen nor his friends can mangle when they pronounce it. You remember the Rong names your mother gave you on Longevity, the childhood endearments and your adult style name.

Be-Nho, Be-Yeu. Thu – Autumn, like a memory of red maple leaves on a planet you never knew.

You pull away from the table, disguising the tremor in your hands.

Second Uncle was already waiting when Quy arrived; and so were the customers.

"You're late," Second Uncle sent on the private channel, though he made the comment half-heartedly, as if he'd expected it all along. As if he'd never really believed he could rely on her – that stung.

"Let me introduce my niece Quy to you," Second Uncle said, in Galactic, to the man beside him.

"Quy," the man said, his immerser perfectly taking up the nuances of her name in Rong. He was everything she'd expected; tall, with only a thin layer of avatar, a little something that narrowed his chin and eyes, and made his chest slightly larger. Cosmetic enhancements: he was good-looking for a Galactic, all things considered. He went on, in Galactic, "My name is Galen

Santos. Pleased to meet you. This is my wife, Agnes."

Agnes. Quy turned, and looked at the woman for the first time – and flinched. There was no one here: just a thick layer of avatar, so dense and so complex that she couldn't even guess at the body hidden within.

"Pleased to meet you." On a hunch, Quy bowed, from younger to elder, with both hands brought together – Rong-style, not Galactic – and saw a shudder run through Agnes's body, barely perceptible; but Quy was observant, she'd always been. Her immerser was screaming at her, telling her to hold out both hands, palms up, in the Galactic fashion. She tuned it out: she was still at the stage where she could tell the difference between her thoughts and the immerser's thoughts.

Second Uncle was talking again – his own avatar was light, a paler version of him. "I understand you're looking for a venue for a banquet."

"We are, yes." Galen pulled a chair to him, sank into it. They all followed suit, though not with the same fluid, arrogant ease. When Agnes sat, Quy saw her flinch, as though she'd just remembered something unpleasant. "We'll be celebrating our fifth marriage anniversary, and we both felt we wanted to mark the occasion with something suitable."

Second Uncle nodded. "I see," he said, scratching his chin. "My congratulations to you."

Galen nodded. "We thought—" he paused, threw a glance at his wife that Quy couldn't quite interpret – her immerser came up blank, but there was something oddly familiar about it, something she ought to have been able to name. "Something Rong," he said at last. "A large banquet for 100 people, with the traditional dishes."

Quy could almost feel Second Uncle's satisfaction. A banquet of that size would be awful logistics, but it would keep the restaurant afloat for a year or more, if they could get the price right. But something was wrong – something—

"What did you have in mind?" Quy asked, not to Galen, but to his wife. The wife – Agnes, which probably wasn't the name she'd been born with – who wore a thick avatar, and didn't seem to be answering or ever speaking up. An awful picture was coming together in Quy's mind.

Agnes didn't answer. Predictable.

Second Uncle took over, smoothing over the moment of awkwardness with expansive hand gestures. "The whole hog, yes?" Second Uncle said. He rubbed his hands, an odd gesture that Quy had never seen from him – a Galactic expression of satisfaction. "Bitter melon soup, Dragon-Phoenix plates, Roast Pig, Jade Under the Mountain . . . " He was citing all the traditional dishes for a wedding banquet – unsure of how far the foreigner wanted to take it. He left out the odder stuff, like Shark Fin or Sweet Red Bean Soup.

"Yes, that's what we would like. Wouldn't we, darling?" Galen's wife neither moved nor spoke. Galen's head turned towards her, and Quy caught his expression at last. She'd thought it would be contempt, or hatred; but no, it was anguish. He genuinely loved her, and he couldn't understand what was going on.

Galactics. Couldn't he recognize an immerser junkie when he saw one? But then Galactics, as Tam said, seldom had the problem – they didn't put on the immersers for more than a few days, on low settings, if they ever went that far. Most were flat-out convinced Galactic would get them anywhere.

Second Uncle and Galen were haggling, arguing prices and features; Second Uncle sounding more and more like a Galactic tourist as the conversation went on, more and more aggressive for lower and lower gains. Quy didn't care anymore: she watched Agnes. Watched the impenetrable avatar – a red-headed woman in the latest style from Prime, with freckles on her skin and a hint of a star-tan on her face. But that wasn't what she was, inside; what the immerser had dug deep into. That wasn't who she was at all.

Tam was right; all immersers should be taken apart, and did it matter if they exploded? They'd done enough harm as it was.

Quy wanted to get up, to tear away her own immerser, but she couldn't, not in the middle of the negotiation. Instead, she rose, and walked closer to Agnes; the two men barely glanced at her, too busy agreeing on a price. "You're not alone," she said, in Rong, low enough that it didn't carry.

Again, that odd, disjointed flash. "You have to take it off," Quy said, but got no further response. As an impulse, she grabbed the

Aliette de Bodard

other woman's arm; felt her hands go right through the immerser's avatar, connect with warm, solid flesh.

You hear them negotiating, in the background – it's tough going, because the Rong man sticks to his guns stubbornly, refusing to give ground to Galen's onslaught. It's all very distant, a subject of intellectual study; the immerser reminds you from time to time, interpreting this and that body cue, nudging you this way and that – you must sit straight and silent, and support your husband – and so you smile through a mouth that feels gummed together.

You feel, all the while, the Rong girl's gaze on you, burning like ice water, like the gaze of a dragon. She won't move away from you; and her hand rests on you, gripping your arm with a strength you didn't think she had in her body. Her avatar is but a thin layer, and you can see her beneath it: a round, moon-shaped face with skin the color of cinnamon – no, not spices, not chocolate, but simply a color you've seen all your life.

"You have to take it off," she says. You don't move; but you wonder what she's talking about.

Take it off. Take it off. Take what off?

The immerser.

Abruptly, you remember – a dinner with Galen's friends, when they laughed at jokes that had gone by too fast for you to understand. You came home battling tears; and found yourself reaching for the immerser on your bedside table, feeling its cool weight in your hands. You thought it would please Galen if you spoke his language; that he would be less ashamed of how uncultured you sounded to his friends. And then you found out that everything was fine, as long as you kept the settings on maximum and didn't remove it. And then . . . and then you walked with it and slept with it, and showed the world nothing but the avatar it had designed – saw nothing it hadn't tagged and labelled for you. Then . . .

Then it all slid down, didn't it? You couldn't program the network anymore, couldn't look at the guts of machines; you lost your job with the tech company, and came to Galen's compartment, wandering in the room like a hollow shell, a ghost of yourself – as if you'd already died, far away from home and all that it means to you. Then – then the immerser wouldn't come off, anymore.

"What do you think you're doing, young woman?"

Second Uncle had risen, turning towards Quy – his avatar flushed with anger, the pale skin mottled with an unsightly red. "We adults are in the middle of negotiating something very important, if you don't mind." It might have made Quy quail in other circumstances, but his voice and his body language were wholly Galactic; and he sounded like a stranger to her – an angry foreigner whose food order she'd misunderstood – whom she'd mock later, sitting in Tam's room with a cup of tea in her lap, and the familiar patter of her sister's musings.

"I apologize," Quy said, meaning none of it.

"That's all right," Galen said. "I didn't mean to—" he paused, looked at his wife. "I shouldn't have brought her here."

"You should take her to see a physician," Quy said, surprised at her own boldness.

"Do you think I haven't tried?" His voice was bitter. "I've even taken her to the best hospitals on Prime. They look at her, and say they can't take it off. That the shock of it would kill her. And even if it didn't . . . " He spread his hands, letting air fall between them like specks of dust. "Who knows if she'd come back?"

Quy felt herself blush. "I'm sorry." And she meant it this time.

Galen waved her away, negligently, airily, but she could see the pain he was struggling to hide. Galactics didn't think tears were manly, she remembered. "So we're agreed?" Galen asked Second Uncle. "For a million credits?"

Quy thought of the banquet; of the food on the tables, of Galen thinking it would remind Agnes of home. Of how, in the end, it was doomed to fail, because everything would be filtered through the immerser, leaving Agnes with nothing but an exotic feast of unfamiliar flavors. "I'm sorry," she said, again, but no one was listening; and she turned away from Agnes with rage in her heart – with the growing feeling that it had all been for nothing in the end.

"I'm sorry," the girl says – she stands, removing her hand from your arm, and you feel like a tearing inside, as if something within you was struggling to claw free from your body. Don't go, you want to say. Please don't go. Please don't leave me here.

But they're all shaking hands, smiling, pleased at a deal they've struck – like sharks, you think, like tigers. Even the Rong girl has turned away from you, giving you up as hopeless. She and her uncle are walking away, taking separate paths back to the inner areas of the restaurant, back to their home.

Please don't go.

It's as if something else were taking control of your body; a strength that you didn't know you possessed. As Galen walks back into the restaurant's main room, back into the hubbub and the tantalizing smells of food – of lemongrass chicken and steamed rice, just as your mother used to make – you turn away from your husband, and follow the girl. Slowly, and from a distance; and then running, so that no one will stop you. She's walking fast – you see her tear her immerser away from her face, and slam it down onto a side table with disgust. You see her enter a room, and you follow her inside.

They're watching you, both girls; the one you followed in, and another, younger one, rising from the table she was sitting at – both terribly alien and terribly familiar at once. Their mouths are open, but no sound comes out.

In that one moment – staring at each other, suspended in time – you see the guts of Galactic machines spread on the table. You see the mass of tools, the dismantled machines, and the immerser, half spread-out before them, its two halves open like a cracked egg. And you understand that they've been trying to open them and reverse-engineer them; and you know that they'll never, ever succeed. Not because of the safeguards, of the Galactic encryptions to preserve their fabled intellectual property; but rather, because of something far more fundamental.

This is a Galactic toy, conceived by a Galactic mind – every layer of it, every logical connection within it exudes a mindset that might as well be alien to these girls. It takes a Galactic to believe that you can take a whole culture and reduce it to algorithms, that language and customs can be boiled to just a simple set of rules. For these girls, things are so much more complex than this, and they will never understand how an immerser works, because they can't think like a Galactic; they'll never ever think like that. You can't think like a Galactic unless you've been born in the culture.

Or drugged yourself, senseless, into it, year after year.

You raise a hand – it feels like moving through honey. You

speak – struggling to shape words through layer after layer of immerser thoughts.

"I know about this," you say, and your voice comes out hoarse, and the words fall into place one by one like a laser stroke, and they feel right, in a way that nothing else has for five years. "Let me help you, younger sisters."

To Rochita Loenen-Ruiz, for the conversations that inspired this.

DOWN THE WALL

Greer Gilman

Stilt-legs scissoring, snip-snap! the bird gods dance. Old craney-crows, a skulk of powers. How they strut and ogle with their long eyes, knowing. How they serpentine their necks. And stalking, how they flirt their tails, insouciant as Groucho. Fugue and counter-fugue, the music jigs and sneaks. On tiptoe, solemnly, they hop and flap; they whirl and whet their long curved clever bills. A sly dance, a wry dance, miching mallecho. Pavane. They peacock, but their drab is eyeless, black as mourners, black as mutes. They are clownish, they are sinister, in their insatiable invention, their unending. Like the frieze in a Pharaoh's nursery, like the knotwork in a chthonic gospel. In and out, untiring as wire, they weave a thorny hedge of selves, and in their eddering, enlace their eggs, their moonish precious eggs. They gloat. And they go on. Like viruses, mere self engendering more self, they replicate. They tangle genesis in their inexorable braid.

The birds are phosphor in a box. They sift and sift across the screen; they whisper. They are endless snow or soot, the ashes of the old world burning. Elsewhere fire. The hailbox whispers, whispers. There is no way to turn it off. No other channel but the gods. All day and night it snows grey phosphor, sifting in the corners of the air. The earth is grey with ash.

The children watch the box, they sprawl and gaze. They're bored, locked in so many endless days. Mewed up. Where's out? they ask. When's never? Why? Their mam clouts and pinches, slaps and spells and grumbles, twisting bacca in a screw of paper. She's a wad of it, torn leaf by leaf away. Time sometime to get another book, ward and spell to steal it. Smoke it. Time enough.

See, paper's upworld. Outwall. Paper swirls about the open streets, abandoned to the gods, all scrawled with stick-dance; paper's layered, scrap on gaudy scrap, on upworld walls. It's slagheaps in the towers of the burning world, the Outwith, where the Old Crows breed. And their nests are sticks and souls.

They take souls fool enough to wander outwall, under sky. The sots that stumble from the trances of the underground. The wardless and unwary. Blink, blunder and they're snatched. Like her awd man. Kids' father. "Blind drunk," she tells them, scornful. "Pissing out a window."

She twitches at the curtains, net on net against the talons of the numinous. Their seine is grey with ashes, hung with toys: green headless army men and dolls' eyes, wired, blue. The window is brick. "Bad enough here, down t'Wall," she says. "Living here. Gettin in wi' this lot." Mouth snecked and her eyes like iodine.

Boy's mazy.

She takes the girl to dancing class, up Mrs. Mallecho's. *And* pays good brass for it. Smoke. Spellcards. Takes her both ways, proper, through the twisting maze of ginnels, and locks to do, undo, at every trance. Quells beggars with a look. In the cloakroom, in among the downy girls, she plucks at her daughter's bits of swansdown, pluming out her tawdry dress. Tufts at her shoulderblades. Gosslyn. She'll do. Girl dances lovely, well she'll give her that. Not like that Dowsa Fligger, silk stockins til her arse, and all them gilty bits ont never never. They says. Off her auntie's bed, more like. Dancin on her back. Oh, she's fly, is Mrs. Theek. Gosslyn's mam clamps down a round comb, fanged and feathery, to crown her daughter's hair; she screws her handkerchief and spits and scrubs.

Girl's fratchety.

The mothers watch from the margins, fierce, aspiring, appraising: their arms crossed, bags clutched, their mouths like paper cuts. They acknowledge haughtily with lifted chins: so much, no more.

"Mrs. Leathy."

"Mrs. Fligger."

"Mrs. Fligger."

"Mrs. Theek."

The hatchlings dance.

At home, behind the jaded couch, her children whisper. They have doorsteps and dark jam to munch; they have a bulwark of pillows. They have stubs of crayons and the wall. From behind them, they can hear the godbox and the skulking music. Lunar tunes. And rising keening over that, a melancholy roar and drone, a pibroch with the fear note in it. Their mam's doing Wednesday, she feeds the Oover north-northwest: three fag ends, a catseye marble, tea leaves. Widdershins: a doll's shoe, a snarl of hairpins. East: a coin. It molochs them all up. West by south: she ties, unties her pinny, back to front, the old one with the faded poppies.

"Black," the boy says. "They must be black. And shriking."

The girl is twirling a plastic ball on her palms, full of heavy water, bright plastic fish. The water whorls and rights itself. "Black's used up." She thinks. "There's *holes* there. Outwall." She swirls the ball; the fish dither.

"There's rain," he says.

The girl's heard tell of it, old Pudfoot with his bottle, muttering. Like slanting wires, he says: but not a cage, like music someways. Or a dancer in nailed boots, she says: they've heard it on the tin-roofed trances, hurried by. Sometimes it sleeks in at the corners, seeking with its slow tongues, twining. And they're not to touch it, and it chokes on dust.

"There's turnings," says the girl.

Slowly their drawing grows, cracked eyries and a maze of faces. The wallpaper's scrawly like the godbox, but brown: all over and over, all the same. Crawlies and blotches. They've turned them into strange things: winged cats, birdheaded women. Owls with horns. Upworld things. A leafgirl by a hedge of bones, tossing up a golden ball. A hurchin boy, astride a cockerel. All pictures from their mother's stash, all smoke.

Down the wall, down the end shop. The boy waits until the Mrs. sees him, sleeving on the glass case that his breath has clouded. Fly cakes. Bacca. There's a babby in there, under glass. Goss says. She says it's Outwith, it can talk and fly. The boy rubs and peers. The black comes off in wrinkles. Ghostly, he can see his own face, in among the things to sell. Tin birds. Cards of hook-and-eyes. Pale buns. The ladies talk.

"Mrs. Spugget."

"Mrs. Pithy."

Her shop smells of sour milk and smoke and bacca, drowsy sweet; of mops and cabbages and fennel-at-the-door. And mice. There's holes down there. Worn lino, brown like her toffee, on the sour splintery boards. He once found a birdsweet in a crack in a corner. Dusty licorice.

" . . . down Howly Street . . . "

"Large white and a tin of Brasso. Snatched?"

"Jumped. One and three."

The bell rings to make the birds scatter.

"Mrs. Pithy."

"Mrs. Spugget."

"Mrs. Harpic."

"Mrs. Pithy."

Their hair's done Saturday. Grey snails and gilt snails, criss-cross with iron pins. His mam jabs them in, she's holy.

" . . . gone Outwith. In her nightdress . . . "

Sharp chin quirks at him. " . . . kid . . . "

"That one? Hears nowt. Pane shy of a glasshouse." Fat chin creases, as she leans and whispers. " . . . far gone, she were. Her mam, she took and . . . "

Far gone. He sees the lost girl, in among the towers and the sticks of crow's nests, searching for an urchin bairn.

Mr. Hawkless the trancer got snatched. They hurry by his corner with the slashed spells, with the tins forlornly jangling. They burn fennel. Mr. Snipe is the trancer, and he helps the kids cross.

Marri from dancing's gone. Her hook is bare, and the mothers silent, their eyes like awls. Stitched mouths. They preen their daughters savagely, as if their frou frou were meringue, to beat. Still whiter and glassier, girls turn in the mirror. Spun fantasies. Pavlovas. None adroop: all stiff as sugar in their tinseled frills. Blackstick Mrs. Mallecho stumps up and down their line. White silence, like a cut before it fills with blood, spills over. But it never bleeds, the girl thinks, posing in the First Ward. Clack! goes the woodbook, and the dancers pirouette. The music thumps and sniggers. The mothers' will is like a cage of wires, strung with dancers, bright as beads. They tell them like a rosary, an abacus of souls. They were five twos; they will make three threes.

Night. Matins. From her clutched grey bag, the mother takes a soft soft piece of paper, wrinkled, scented, like a cheek held up to kiss. Green coin. She pleats it, snips it—there, a chain of craneycrows, as wick as if their own quick legs had scissored them. Just on time, the tune beginning as she lights the paper, lets it go: a flaring and a lace of ash. She marks her sleeping children: eyelids, palms.

The girl dreams of the stitch witch, putting children in her bag. She prods them as she picks. She's made of stuffing, grey stuff like the Oover's belly, and her mouth's sewn shut. There's a black thread and a needle dangling from her lip, a tangle like a raven's beard. She gluts on souls. Behind the railings, there are children crouching—Goss among them, hiding—in a heap of cushions stitched with rain. It twangles as they shift, they burrow. Ah, she's hunting for her ball, her shining ball, before the witch can take her. Down she gropes, amid the slather, deeper still. Then it's changed, the dream, she's riding rantipole with Marri, whirling round and round, and up and down, hold tight! until she breaks away and flies. The air is full of girls like leaves.

The boy wakes in the night. There are Old Ones storming; he can hear the hurl and crackle in the air: not sound but fury. Something that restrings your bones. His mam is standing turning toward it. Tuning. She is blue in the godlight.

Morning. Thin and blue, lit flickering by the box. Their mam's doing Thursday. She slamps her irons down and grutches; spits and dabs. The air's full of scorch and muttering. The chairs are hung with ghosts, themselves outspread and suppliant. Vests. Petticoats. Rue's shirts. There's rows of eggshells on the sills, all filled with ashes and with milk. Thwick! Thwick! She jabs the milk tops with her nail, pours out a measure to the Old Ones. Milk swirls on the step. She will string the silver, hang it jostling in the doorways.

"Rue." His sister's breath, not sound but stirring. Warm in his ear. It tickles. "Rue. I've getten keys."

★   ★   ★

"Goss?"

The girl's far ahead in the trances, counting turnings. Her thread is words.

"Goss. Wait." The boy calls after. "Is't dead?" There's a black thing in a runnel, stark. The girl turns back and prods it. Bone and wings? It slacks from its bent ribs. Nobbut wire and cloth. She grins. "It's a dolly god, I think." She pries it from the drain, awry and sagging, twirls it. Sword falls open into cup.

Rue laughs. "It's drunk," he says, and makes it stagger.

"Go on. Yer have it, then."

It pecks along the tunnels, rattles on the railings, swishes, scything down a host of shadows. It pokes at bins. Now and then, it twirls and wobbles, with a loose-stayed shimmy, like the Widow Twanky in a swoon.

Below them, they hear voices, children calling, running feet.

"Goss?" Tiled and echoing, a trance in a maze of trances.

"Sneck up." She's biting at her lip and peering. What way is Out? They're in a bridge above another passage, grinning with stained tiles. Dank water drips. It sidles over posters, over tilework scrawled with birds. Smashed lamps. Dark arches, cages full of coils and wheels and shards. Ratscuttle and the stench of ancient piss.

Round the bend, a soft voice calls. "Off to yon rant?"

They stiffen. Goss yanks her brother round behind her.

"Leggo."

"Hush. Nobbut an awd busker. I'll fend."

A beggar sits against the wall, knees up and watchful, idle. In their path. A tin whistle in her dangling hand, a bowl between her feet. Her clothes are like herself, her pelt; her jacket's hairy on the inside, black, and rustling with paper. And she smells of ashes and of rain. A little penknife of a smile, all bone and flick, her long eyes hidden in her shaggy greyblack hair. "Where's thou bound?"

"Out," says Rue, and draws his dolly, which slacks open, gaping foolish; but Goss steps up to her with silver, got groping in the Oover's belly. "Leave us go."

The beggar quirks at the bowl. The silver falls among small things, silver. "What's that to me? Is't thine?"

Goss lifts her chin. "Is't yours? All that lot?"

"Nay, all theirs as leave. And not until."

There's odd things in the bowl, thinks Goss. Spectacles. A torn-up photograph. A tooth. A torch, all eaten up with rust. A heap of long red hair. The beggar scrabbles in the bowl, hands back the coins. "Owt else?"

A handful of crayons. The beggar finicks through them. Blue-green. Redviolet. The stub of black. She measures Gosslyn with a glance. "All this? Thou's overdrawn thysel." As if the dole were kingdoms.

"What I has."

They're taken; then the beggar turns to Rue. He's got the dolly god hooked over his shoulder, and he's turning out pocket fluff. Three black birdsweets and a marble on his sticky palm. Blue clouded, with a fleck like a falling leaf. That too. The beggar holds it to her eye, shakes back her hair to squint. And laughs.

No riddles this time. "Put up thy brolly. I'll not eat thee."

"Dolly brolly." Rue's delighted.

"Gerroff wi' yer. Left, left, down close and top o't stairs."

As they turn, she calls out, mocking, "Did tha want thy change?" And flicks a bit of chalk at Gosslyn. It skitters, spinning on the tiles, and veering, rolling toward abyss. Goss darts for it before it's lost. They hurry on.

They can see the turnstile now, the lightspill on the stairs.

Amazed at the wind, they stand: high tumult and the ragged moon. "Will't *hatch*?" says Rue. Turning round, heads back, they stare. Cloud, red beneath with burning. Wrack and scurry backlit by the scatheless sailing moon. Unfathomed cliffs of tower, sheer and derelict. Unwarded streets. Leaves paper litter rising. Whirl and flacker in a ghostly dance. They've not felt wind afore. Goss laughs, whirling widearmed. Rue scuffles and twirls, he surges through the leaftrash in a glorious roar and crackle, swashing with his stick. They spin themselves giddy. They are catseyes, whorled with shadow, wound with moon.

They've fallen down. Clouds towers leaves wheel round them. A voice calls. "Crows!"

Another, "Here's inwits for yer supper. Crows!"

"Hey, crows!"

They are laughing.

There are children in the dark. They run by night: a shifting crew of mortals. Old and young, they're driven by a fey mood, a sudden quick desire to shake the fear, to dance unwarded under heaven. Back of law. They bring no wards, no form of worship to their tryst, evading death by chance, by offhand magic: a patchwork of tinkering and brilliant dodges, crazy risks. Chancers, they call themselves. Some run a moment, whirled away like moonclocks; others, crazed or clever, live a night, two nights, a week of dancing.

There are shadows in the moon: huge knots of hawklike darkness, sheering. As they turn, they catch the moonlight, glint and vanish, skyblack into sky. They arc bright beneath, with women's bodies; they are cold, with starless wings. No rise and wheeling of the dance in them, no scrawl of stars: all timeless and unstoried night. Cloud coils from them, unsilvering the moon. Their breath is tarnish, is forgetting. And their talons – ah, they rend the soul. They take.

Close now, the running and the calling start, from street to street, from shadow into shadow, in and out of light. Rue and Gosslyn stagger up and after, witch-led, drunk with air. The world swerves sideways, lurches them at walls. The brolly bangs and bruises, tangles in their feet. The voices mock and rally. *Tigged last! Telled witch of yer!* A twitch, a tug at skirt or sleeve. Whirl round and no one. Whispering. And there, a white face, round a corner? Gone. Phantasmal creatures loom, elude them, dwindling into junk. And all around them tunes the bedlam jazz band of the wind. Scritch and jangle. Howl and hurly. Scrape and clattering and sough. A clang on a skeleton of stair, above; a sheet of paper, burning, falling. See, it's eyed with cinders, blinded one by one. An ash. It's nothing in Rue's hand. Goss feels a soft slap on her cheek. Another. And another. No one, pattering, and all around. They stand, astonished, in the briefest lash of rain.

They've come into a wide square, set with shattered baulks of stone: a great cat with a muffled head, a riven owl, a witch in flinders. There are fires here and there, some leaping and some embers, ashes. Some long cold. And some a-building: leaves and boxes, doors and drawers and random trash. Children heap frail crazy towers: sticks stacks crows' nests, all to burn. Some run with brands, they leap and whirl them in a swarm of sparks. They write great fading loops of spells. Three drag a gnarled branch to the fires, its dry and leafy fingers clagged with tins, as many as the rings on a witch's hand. And still it scrabbles, rakes for more.

Warily entranced, Rue watches, edges round them, keeping hold of Goss. She stoops for a bit of paper, torn and scattering. No images. All scratches, black as birds. She lets it go.

A dark lad's hurling dustbins down a flight of steps, with a bang and clangor and a long-drawn rumbling. Whuff! He lights one, lofts it blazing with a trembling hollow roar; and howling, casts it down in ruin. Children rush to kick and scuffle at the spill of embers, stamp them out.

Leaning close in the curl of newel at the broad stair's foot, two girls play cat's cradles with red yarn. They pick their crosses carefully, perplex and intricate. Undergo; then overturn.

Children tumble from a carapace of engine, with its soft maw sprung to wires, and its shattered eyes. They're all in flutterings of rags, torn and knotted, with their coats turned inside out. They've ashes on their faces, tins of pebbles in their hands. Mute as ghosts, they prowl and shake their rattles.

All alone, a small child huddles on a step; he rocks and sucks the ragdoll babby at his cheek. But his lullaby's from elsewhere, voices in the dark. "Lay down, my dear sister . . . "

Still in shadow, Goss and Rue slip by.

In a sidestreet by a railing, by a tree scant of leaves, a knot of children call and chant. They are whirling clapping in a game.

> Tell B for the beast at the ending of the wood
> Goodnight, Goodnight
> Well, he eat all the children when they wouldn't be good
> Goodnight, Goodnight, Goodnight

And "Good night," the voices cry in antiphon, like birds; as if there were a greener world indwelling in these streets. A wood. Their city's crowded, crowned with visionary trees. There's no way in; they weave themselves a hedge. Goss lingers for a moment, drawn and doubtful; Rue tugs her on.

Still others turn a rope, and leap through it in turn. Brown legs, scratched legs. Jauncing plaits. In turn there is no one jumping, but they call the dark, they bid it in. The rope whips round and round, slapping at the stones.

Not all are children. A man in a soft hat and a muddy suit, unshaven, stands and shouts. At nothing, at the sky. Not angry, thinks Goss. Amazed.

The rope slaps to their chant, his chant.

"Babylon is fallen."

"Is fallen."

"Is fallen."

"Babylon is fallen."

"To rise no more."

By a shattered window, by a lamp, a boy kneels, dark amid the glittering. He keeps to the fringes of the light, penumbral; coming closer, they can see he's thin and fairish, scowling, with bent mended specs. He's working at something. A cosmos of black wire, all in tension, with a long spiring tail. It glitters blackly; it jangles. He shakes the long coil of it, and leaves rags paper dance.

Goss says, "What's that for?"

"Catching crows," he says. "Summat I thought on."

"What *day*?"

"Yer must be inwits," he says, tilting his scarred glasses. "It's nights here Outwith. All as it comes." They can see his scabbed knees, his scarry fingers. Stained burned slashed. Soft hair like flocking, whitey-brown. "There's all sort of chancers runs. Some clever and some mad. There's ranters and goners—" He nods at the shabby man. "And guisers them wi' ashes. Then there's howkers and tigs, and there's ticers. What I is. A nincr, come daybreak."

"Ticers?" (What do they do? Could I?)

"Get by. Call crows. Get round 'em." He lights the kite's tail of his strange device; for a moment now his face is eerie, ambered from below. "Happen talk with them." He pinches out his spill.

And as the shadow stoops, he cries, "Run, will yer!"

The man falls open-armed, ecstatic.

They run.

Behind them comes a whirring and a cry. The shock embrittles them, turns all their blood to branching ice. Blindly they stumble on until Rue falls, tripped up on his brolly. Goss muffles him against her breast, she strokes the black frost from his hair. They crouch, as still as rats. No shadow of the bird strikes, wheels, returning to her prey. After a time, Goss dabbles at his scrapes, then at hers; she wipes his streaked and snotted face. Her own. Then they share what she has left: a scrawny orange. Cradling, she snuffs at it before she breaks it open. Pith and bittersweet and curving.

It was beautiful, the bird.

They wander on, at random, turning down this street, that crescent, past the naked windows and the empty rooms.

A shout. Boys snatch the brolly, toss it high above his sobbing reach, the fury of her nails; they hurly down the street, thwacking it at tins and bottles, quarreling; until the tallest leaps and hooks it to a high bar, where it dangles, all agape and stark.

They vanish.

Rue and Goss gaze up. It's hanging from a gate of iron, in a wall. They clamber up and flail at it with sticks; at last they knock it down.

Beyond the gate's another square, but silent, sheeted all with moon. No fire and no games. Stones cracked with weeds. And stony, too, the white girl crowned with leaves, with leaves and flowers in her stony lap. Her fountain's dry.

Rue slips between the rusted bars, undoes the latch for Gosslyn. They go in.

But there's someone there, behind the circle of the stony dance, her grove of girls: another girl, a real one, in a nightdress and slippers, squatting on her heels. Quite a grown girl, thin and ginger, with a cat's curly smile. Her cardigan won't button round her middle, but her freckly arms and legs are thin. She's drawing on the paving stones with chalk, white and red. They've seen her with her mam's brood, down the Wall: jerking stragglers howling after, wiping noses, soothing, fratching. Goss glances at her belly.

"Mrs. Stemmon?"

"Not Mrs." She chalks another line. "Outwith, I's Phib."

"Goss. Yon's Rue."

"Know yer. Hey up, brat."

Scrape goes the ferrule. "What is't yer drawing?"

"Snakes and ladders." Nodding at Goss, she holds out a bit of chalk. "Halfs?"

Goss fumbles at her pocket. "Got a bit."

Laddery as stockings, what Phib's drawn, with blotches in it, red as poppies, red as blood. As if they'd scattered as she ran.

Kneeling on the pavement, Goss chalks angles, spirals, mazes round and round them. They are holes, doors, houses; they are earth and heaven. White on black. They make a grammar as they go. Halt runes becoming terse and supple, turning to a rime, a rant, a summoning. No more her mother tongue: new heaven and new earth. Her line's a labyrinth, her thread of moonlight, winding on the spindle of the moon. She draws it down.

Hawklike, darkness knots itself and stoops: not fury but a fall of chance. The air's like black glass shattering. Rue whirls the umbrella, heavy suddenly with wind. He's staggered, but he holds it fast with both hands, blown askew. It wrenches at him, bucks and judders on the pavement, scraping stone; it leaps and bellies out. For a breath, its bones are lightning and its web is sky. Its godcrow sister cries to it; she wheels and counters, and the white thread snares her. Goss draws it tighter still, until the jess must snap, the falcon strike. She's drawing on its dark, she's drawing on the night itself. The chalk is crumbling. What she writes with it are stars and clouds of stars, ascendancies in nightfall. With the powder of her end, she sets them dancing.

The Mrs. looks about the bare room, the scrubbed wall, with her shrewd embittered eye. The box still flickers with its frieze of birds, still gloating on their eggs. Leave that. There's another, always. Got her bacca, got her hairpins. Smokebook. Feather dress and comb. She folds away the last wards in her cheap case, snecks the latch. Unhooks the mirror from the wall. Cord's coiled, Oover's gutted, nets are drawn. She'll get herself another place, then. Somewhere further down t'Wall. Deeper in. Then. Long time since she's had a make. Last man were sackless. Got her brats, but. Thankless. And t'last afore him. Time sometime to get another. Screw him. Time enough.

She broods.

SING

Karin Tidbeck

The cold dawn light creeps onto the mountaintops; they emerge like islands in the valley's dark sea, tendrils of steam rising up from the thickets clinging to the rock. Right now there's no sound of birdsong or crickets, no hiss of wind in the trees. When Maderakka's great shadow has sunk back below the horizon, twitter and chirp will return in a shocking explosion of sound. For now, we sit in complete silence.

The birds have left. Petr lies with his head in my lap, his chest rising and falling so quickly it's almost a flutter, his pulse rushing under the skin. The bits of eggshell I couldn't get out of his mouth, those that have already made their way into him, spread whiteness into the surrounding flesh. If only I could hear that he's breathing properly. His eyes are rolled back into his head, his arms and legs curled up against his body like a baby's. If he's conscious, he must be in pain. I hope he's not conscious.

A strangely shaped man came in the door and stepped up to the counter. He made a full turn to look at the mess in my workshop: the fabrics, the cutting table, the bits of pattern. Then he looked directly at me. He was definitely not from here – no one had told him not to do that. I almost wanted to correct him: *leave, you're not supposed to make contact like that, you're supposed to pretend you can't see me and tell the air what you want*. But I was curious about what he might do. I was too used to avoiding eye contact, so I concentrated carefully on the rest of him: the squat body with its weirdly broad shoulders, the swelling upper arms and legs. The cropped copper on his head. I'd never seen anything like it.

So this man stepped up to the counter and he spoke directly to me, and it was like being caught under the midday sun.

"You're Aino? The tailor? Can you repair this?"

He spoke slowly and deliberately, his accent crowded with hard sounds. He dropped a heap of something on the counter. I collected myself and made my way over. He flinched as I slid off my chair at the cutting table, catching myself before my knees collapsed backward. I knew what he saw: a stick insect of a woman clambering unsteadily along the furniture, joints flexing at impossible angles. Still he didn't look away. I could see his eyes at the outskirts of my vision, golden-yellow points following me as I heaved myself forward to the stool by the counter. The bundle, when I held it up, was an oddly cut jacket. It had no visible seams, the material almost like rough canvas but not quite. It was half-eaten by wear and grime.

"You should have had this mended long ago," I said. "And washed. I can't fix this."

He leaned closer, hand cupped behind an ear. "Again, please?"

"I can't repair it," I said, slower.

He sighed, a long waft of warm air on my forearm. "Can you make a new one?"

"Maybe. But I'll have to measure you." I waved him toward me.

He stepped around the counter. After that first flinch, he didn't react. His smell was dry, like burnt ochre and spices, not unpleasant, and while I measured him he kept talking in a stream of consonants and archaic words, easy enough to understand if I didn't listen too closely. His name was Petr, the name as angular as his accent, and he came from Amitié – a station somewhere out there – but was born on Gliese. (I knew a little about Gliese, and told him so.) He was a biologist and hadn't seen an open sky for eight years. He had landed on Kiruna and ridden with a truck and then walked for three days, and he was proud to have learned our language, although our dialect was very odd. He was here to research lichen.

"Lichen can survive anywhere," he said, "even in a vacuum, at least as spores. I want to compare these to the ones on Gliese, to see if they have the same origin."

"Just you? You're alone?"

"Do you know how many colonies are out there?" He laughed, but then cleared his throat. "Sorry. But it's really like that. There are more colonies than anyone can keep track of. And Kiruna is, well, it's considered an abandoned world, after the mining companies left, so—"

His next word was silent. Saarakka was up, the bright moonlet sudden as always. He mouthed more words. I switched into song, but Petr just stared at me. He inclined his head slightly toward me, eyes narrowing, then shook his head and pinched the bridge of his nose. He reached into the back pocket of his trousers and drew out something like a small and very thin book. He did something with a quick movement – shook it out, somehow – and it unfolded into a large square that he put down on the counter. It had the outlines of letters at the bottom, and his fingers flew over them. WHAT HAPPENED WITH SOUND?

I recognized the layout of keys. I could type. SAARAKKA, I wrote. WHEN SAARAKKA IS UP, WE CAN'T HEAR SPEECH. WE SING INSTEAD.

WHY HAS NOBODY TOLD ME ABOUT THIS? he replied.

I shrugged.

He typed with annoyed, jerky movements. HOW LONG DOES IT LAST?

UNTIL IT SETS, I told him.

He had so many questions – he wanted to know how Saarakka silenced speech, if the other moon did something too. I told him about how Oksakka kills the sound of birds, and how giant Maderakka peeks over the horizon now and then, reminding us that the three of us are just her satellites. How they once named our own world after a mining town and we named the other moons for an ancient goddess and her handmaidens, although these names sound strange and harsh to us now. But every answer prompted new questions. I finally pushed the sheet away from me. He held his palms up in resignation, folded it up, and left.

What I had wanted to say, when he started talking about how Kiruna was just one world among many, was that I'm not stupid. I read books and sometimes I could pick up stuff on my old set, when the satellite was up and the moons didn't interfere with it so much. I knew that Amitié was a big space station. I knew we lived in a poor backwater place. Still, you think your home is special, even if nobody ever visits.

The village has a single street. One can walk along the street for a little while, and then go down to the sluggish red river. I go there to wash myself and rinse out cloth.

I like dusk, when everyone's gone home and I can air-dry on the big, flat stone by the shore, arms and legs finally long and relaxed and folding at what angles they will, my spine and muscles creaking like wood after a long day of keeping everything straight and upright. Sometimes the goats come to visit. They're only interested in whether I have food or ear scratchings for them. To the goats, all people are equal, except for those who have treats. Sometimes the birds come here too, alighting on the rocks to preen their plumes, compound eyes iridescent in the twilight. I try not to notice them, but unless Öksakka is up to muffle the higher-pitched noise, the insistent buzzing twitches of their wings are impossible to ignore. More than two or three and they start warbling among themselves, eerily like human song, and I leave.

Petr met me on the path up from the river. I was carrying a bundle of wet fabric strapped to my back; it was slow going because I'd brought too much and the extra weight made me swing heavy on my crutches.

He held out a hand. "Let me carry that for you, Aino."

"No, thank you." I moved past him.

He kept pace with me. "I'm just trying to be polite."

I sneaked a glance at him, but it did seem that was what he wanted. I unstrapped my bundle. He took it and casually slung it over his shoulder. We walked in silence up the slope, him at a leisurely walk, me concentrating on the uphill effort, crutch-foot-foot-crutch.

"Your ecosystem," he said eventually, when the path flattened out. "It's fascinating."

"What about it?"

"I've never seen a system based on parasitism."

"I don't know much about that."

"But you know how it works?"

"Of course," I said. "Animals lay eggs in other animals. Even the plants."

"So is there anything that uses the goats for hosts?"

"Hookflies. They hatch in the goats' noses."

Petr hummed. "Does it harm the goats?"

"No . . . not usually. Some of them get sick and die. Most of the time they just get . . . more perky. It's good for them."

"Fascinating," Petr said. "I've never seen an alien species just slip into an ecosystem like that." He paused. "These hookflies. Do they ever go for humans?"

I shook my head.

He was quiet for a while. We were almost at the village when he spoke again.

"So how long have your people been singing?"

"I don't know. A long time."

"But how do you learn? I mean, I've tried, but I just can't make the sounds. The pitch, it's higher than anything I've heard a human voice do. It's like birdsong."

"It's passed on." I concentrated on tensing the muscles in my feet for the next step.

"How? Is it a mutation?"

"It's passed on," I repeated. "Here's the workshop. I can handle it from here. Thank you."

He handed me the bundle. I could tell he wanted to ask me more, but I turned away from him and dragged my load inside.

I don't lie. But neither will I answer a question that hasn't been asked. Petr would have called it lying by omission, I suppose. I've wondered if things would have happened differently if I'd just told him what he really wanted to know: not *how* we learn, but how it's *possible* for us to learn. But no. I don't think it would have changed much. He was too recklessly curious.

My mother told me I'd never take over the business, but she underestimated me and how much I'd learned before she passed. I have some strength in my hands and arms, and I'm good at precision work. It makes me a good tailor. In that way I can at least get a little respect, because I support myself and do it well. So the villagers employ me, even if they won't look at me.

Others of my kind aren't so lucky. A man down the street

hasn't left his room for years. His elderly parents take care of him. When they pass, the other villagers won't show as much compassion. I know there are more of us here and there, in the village and the outlying farms. Those of us who do go outside don't communicate with each other. We stay in the background, we who didn't receive the gift unscathed.

I wonder if that will happen to Petr now. So far, there's no change; he's very still. His temples are freckled. I haven't noticed that before.

Petr wouldn't leave me alone. He kept coming in to talk. I didn't know if he did this to everyone. I sometimes thought that maybe he didn't study lichen at all; he just went from house to house and talked people's ears off. He talked about his heavy homeworld, which he'd left to crawl almost weightless in the high spokes of Amitie. He told me I wouldn't have to carry my own weight there, I'd move without crutches, and I was surprised by the want that flared up inside me, but I said nothing of it. He asked me if I hurt, and I said only if my joints folded back or sideways too quickly. He was very fascinated.

When Saarakka was up, he typed at me to sing to him. He parsed the cadences and inflections like a scientist, annoyed when they refused to slip into neat order.

I found myself talking too, telling him of sewing and books I'd read, of the other villagers and what they did. It's remarkable what people will say and do when you're part of the background. Petr listened to me, asked questions. Sometimes I met his eyes. They had little crinkles at the outer edges that deepened when he smiled. I discovered that I had many things to say. I couldn't tell whether the biologist in him wanted to study my freakish appearance, or if he really enjoyed being around me.

He sat on my stool behind the counter, telling me about crawling around in the vents on Amitié to study the lichen unique to the station: "They must have hitchhiked in with a shuttle. The question was from where . . . "

I interrupted him. "How does one get there? To visit?"

"You want to go?"

"I'd like to see it." *And be weightless*, I didn't say.

"There's a shuttle bypass in a few months to pick me up," he said. "But it'd cost you."

I nodded.

"Do you have money?" he asked.

"I've saved up some."

He mentioned how much it would cost, and my heart sank so deep I couldn't speak for a while. For once, Petr didn't fill the silence.

I moved past him from the cutting table to the mannequin. I put my hand on a piece of fabric on the table and it slipped. I stumbled. He reached out and caught me, and I fell with my face against his throat. His skin was warm, almost hot; he smelled of sweat and dust and an undertone of musk that seeped into my body and made it heavy. It was suddenly hard to breathe.

I pushed myself out of his arms and leaned against the table, unsteadily, because my arms were shaking. No one had touched me like that before. He had slid from the stool, leaning against the counter across from me, his chest rising and falling as if he had been running. Those eyes were so sharp, I couldn't look at them directly.

"I'm in love with you." The words tumbled out of his mouth in a quick mumble.

He stiffened, as if surprised by what he had just said. I opened my mouth to say I didn't know what, but words like that deserved something—

He held up a hand. "I didn't mean to."

"But . . ."

Petr shook his head. "Aino. It's all right."

When I finally figured out what to say, he had left. I wanted to say I hadn't thought of the possibility, but that I did now. Someone wanted me. It was a very strange sensation, like a little hook tugging at the hollow under my ribs.

Petr changed after that. He kept coming into the workshop, but he started to make friends elsewhere too. I could see it from the shop window: his cheerful brusqueness bowled the others over. He crouched together with the weaver across the street, eagerly studying her work. He engaged in cheerful haggling with Maiju, who would never negotiate the price of her vegetables, but with him, she did. He even tried to sing, unsuccessfully. I recognized the looks the others gave him. And even though they were only humoring him, treating him as they would a harmless idiot, I found myself growing jealous. That was novel too.

He didn't mention it again. Our conversation skirted away from any deeper subjects. The memory of his scent intruded on my thoughts at night. I tried to wash it away in the river.

"Aino, I'm thinking about staying."

Petr hadn't been in for a week. Now this.

"Why?" I fiddled with a seam on the work shirt I was hemming.

"I like it here. Everything's simple — no high tech, no info flooding, no hurry. I can hear myself think." He smiled faintly. "You know, I've had stomach problems most of my life. When I came here, they went away in a week. It's been like coming home."

"I don't see why." I kept my eyes down. "There's nothing special here."

"These are good people. Sure, they're a bit traditional, a bit distant. But I like them. And it turns out they need me here. Jorma, he doesn't mind that I can't sing. He offered me a job at the clinic. Says they need someone with my experience."

"Are you all right with this?" he asked when I didn't reply immediately.

"It's good," I said eventually. "It's good for you that they like you."

"I don't know about 'like.' Some of them treat me as if I'm handicapped. I don't care much, though. I can live with that as long as some of you like me." His gaze rested on me like a heavy hand.

"Good for you," I repeated.

He leaned over the counter. "So . . . maybe you could teach me to sing? For real?"

"No."

"Why? I don't understand why."

"Because I can't teach you. You *are* handicapped. Like me."

"Aino." His voice was low. "Did you ever consider that maybe they don't hate you?"

I looked up. "They don't hate me. They're afraid of me. It's different."

"Are you really sure? Maybe if you talked to them . . . "

" . . . they would avoid me. It is what it is."

"You can't just sit in here and be bitter."

"I'm not," I said. "It just is what it is. I can choose to be miserable about it, or I can choose not to be."

"Fine." He sighed. "Does it matter to you if I stay or leave?"

"Yes," I whispered to the shirt in my lap.

"Well, which is it? Do you want me to stay?"

He had asked directly, so I had to give him an answer, at least some sort of reply. "You could stay a while. Or I could go with you."

"I told you. I'm not going back to Amitié."

"All right," I said.

"Really?"

"No."

I could have kept quiet when the procession went by. Maybe then things would have been different. I think he would have found out, anyway.

We were down by the river. We pretended the last conversation hadn't happened. He had insisted on helping me with washing cloth. I wouldn't let him, so he sat alongside me, making conversation while I dipped the lengths of cloth in the river and slapped them on the big flat stone. Maderakka's huge approaching shadow hovered on the horizon. It would be Petr's first time, and he was fascinated. The birds were beginning to amass in the air above the plateau, sharp trills echoing through the valley.

"How long will it last?"

"Just overnight," I said. "It only rises a little bit before it sets again."

"I wonder what it's like on the other side," he said. "Having that in the sky all the time."

"Very quiet, I suppose."

"Does anyone live there?"

I shrugged. "A few. Not as many as here."

He grunted and said no more. I sank into the rhythm of my work, listening to the rush of water and wet cloth on stone, the clatter and bleat of goats on the shore.

Petr touched my arm, sending a shock up my shoulder. I pretended it was a twitch.

"Aino. What's that?" He pointed up the slope.

The women and men walking by were dressed all in white, led by an old woman with a bundle in her arms. They were heading for the valley's innermost point, where the river emerged from underground and a faint trail switchbacked up the wall.

I turned back to my laundry. "They're going to the plateau."

"I can see that. What are they going to do once they get there?"

The question was too direct to avoid. I had to answer somehow. "We don't talk about that," I said finally.

"Come on," Petr said. "If I'm going to live here, I should be allowed to know."

"I don't know if that's my decision to make," I replied.

He settled on the stone again, but he was tense now, and kept casting glances at the procession on their way up the mountainside. He helped me carry the clothes back through the workshop and into the backyard, and then left without helping me hang them. I knew where he was going. You could say I let it happen — but I don't think I could have stopped him either. It was a kind of relief. I hung the cloth, listening to the comforting whisper of wet fabric, until Maderakka rose and silence cupped its hands over my ears.

I don't remember being carried to the plateau in my mother's arms. I only know that she did. Looking down at Petr in my lap, I'm glad I don't remember. Of course everyone *knows* what happens. We're just better off forgetting what it was like.

Maderakka set in the early hours of the morning, and I woke to the noise of someone hammering on the door. It was Petr, of course, and his nose and lips were puffy. I let him in, and into the back of the workshop to my private room. He sank down on my bed and just sort of crumpled. I put the kettle on and waited.

"I tried to go up there," he said into his hands. "I wanted to see what it was."

"And?"

"Jorma stopped me."

I thought of the gangly doctor trying to hold Petr back, and snorted. "How?"

"He hit me."

"But you're" – I gestured toward him, all of him – "huge."

"So? I don't know how to fight. And he's scary. I almost got to the top before he saw me and stopped me. I got this" – he pointed to his nose – "just for going up there. What the hell is going on up there, Aino? There were those bird things, hundreds of them, just circling overhead."

"Did you see anything else?"

"No."

"You won't give up until you find out, will you?"

He shook his head.

"It's how we do things," I said. "It's how we sing."

"I don't understand."

"You said it's a – what was it? – parasitic ecosystem. Yes?"

He nodded.

"And I said that the hookflies use the goats, and that it's good for the goats. The hookflies get to lay their eggs, and the goats get something in return."

He nodded again. I waited for him to connect the facts. His face remained blank.

"The birds," I said. "When a baby's born, it's taken up there the next time Maderakka rises."

Petr's shoulders slumped. He looked sick. It gave me some sort of grim satisfaction to go on talking, to get back at him for his idiocy.

I went on: "The birds lay their eggs. Not for long, just for a moment. And they leave something behind. It changes the children's development . . . in the throat. It means they can learn to sing." I gestured at myself. "Sometimes the child dies. Sometimes this happens. That's why the others avoid me. I didn't pass the test."

"You make yourself hosts," Petr said, faintly. "You do it to your children."

"They don't remember. I don't remember."

He stood up, swaying a little on his feet, and left.

"You wanted to know!" I called after him.

A latecomer has alighted on the rock next to me. It's preening its iridescent wings in the morning light, pulling its plumes between its mandibles one by one. I look away as it hops up on

Petr's chest. It's so wrong to see it happen, too intimate. But I'm afraid to move, I'm afraid to flee. I don't know what will happen if I do.

The weather was so lovely I couldn't stay indoors. I sat under the awning outside my workshop, wrapped up in shawls so as not to offend too much, basting the seams on a skirt. The weaver across the street had set up one of her smaller looms on her porch, working with her back to me. Saarakka was up, and the street filled with song.

I saw Petr coming from a long way away. His square form made the villagers look so unbearably gangly and frail, as if they would break if he touched them. How did they even manage to stay upright? How did his weight not break the cobblestones? The others shied away from him, like reeds from a boat. I saw why when he came closer. I greeted him with song without thinking. It made his tortured grimace deepen.

He fell to his knees in front of me and wrapped his arms around me, squeezed me so tight I could feel my shoulders creaking. He was shaking. The soundless weeping hit my neck in silent, wet waves. All around us, the others were very busy not noticing what was going on.

I brought him to the backyard. He calmed down and we sat leaning against the wall, watching Saarakka outrun the sun and sink. When the last sliver had disappeared under the horizon, he hummed to test the atmosphere, and then spoke.

"I couldn't stand being in the village for Saarakka. Everyone else talking and I can't ... I've started to understand the song language now, you know? It makes it worse. So I left, I went up to that plateau. There was nothing there. I suppose you knew that already. Just the trees and the little clearing." He fingered the back of his head and winced. "I don't know how, but I fell on the way down, I fell off the path and down the wall. It was close to the bottom, I didn't hurt myself much. Just banged my head a little."

"That was what made you upset?"

I could feel him looking at me. "If I'd really hurt myself, if I'd hurt myself badly, I wouldn't have been able to call for help. I could have just lain there until Saarakka set. Nobody would have heard me. You wouldn't have heard me."

We sat for a while without speaking. The sound of crickets and birds disappeared abruptly. Oksakka had risen behind us.

"I've always heard that if you've been near death, you're supposed to feel alive and grateful for every moment." Petr snorted. "All I can think of is how easy it is to die. That it can happen at any time."

I turned my head to look at him. His eyes glittered yellow in the setting sun.

"You don't believe I spend time with you because of you."

I waited.

Petr shook his head. "You know, on Amitié, they'd think you look strange, but you wouldn't be treated differently. And the gravity's low when closer to the hub. You wouldn't need crutches."

"So take me there."

"I'm not going back. I've told you."

"Gliese, then?"

"You'd be crushed." He held up a massive arm. "Why do you think I look like I do?"

I swallowed my frustration.

"There are wading birds on Earth," he said, "long-legged things. They move like dancers. You remind me of them."

"You don't remind me of anything here," I replied.

He looked surprised when I leaned in and kissed him.

Later, I had to close his hands around me, so afraid was he to hurt me.

I lay next to him thinking about having normal conversations, other people meeting my eyes, talking to me like a person.

I'm thrifty. I had saved up a decent sum over the years; there was nothing I could spend money on, after all. If I sold everything I owned, if I sold the business, it would be enough to go to Amitié, at least to visit. If someone wanted to buy my things.

But Petr had in some almost unnoticeable way moved into my home. Suddenly he lived there, and had done so for a while. He cooked, he cleaned the corners I didn't bother with because I couldn't reach. He brought in shoots and plants from outside and planted them in little pots. When he showed up with lichen-covered rocks I put my foot down, so he arranged them in patterns in the backyard. Giant Maderakka rose twice; two processions in white passed by on their way to the plateau. He watched them with a mix of longing and disgust.

His attention spoiled me. I forgot that only he talked to me. I spoke directly to a customer and looked her in the eyes. She left the workshop in a hurry and didn't come back.

"I want to leave," I finally said. "I'm selling everything. Let's go to Amitié."

We were in bed, listening to the lack of birds. Oksakka's quick little eye shone in the midnight sky.

"Again? I told you I don't want to go back," Petr replied.

"Just for a little while?"

"I feel at home here now," he said. "The valley, the sky . . . I love it. I love being light."

"I've lost my customers."

"I've thought about raising goats."

"These people will never accept you completely," I said. "You can't sing. You're like me, you're a cripple to them."

"You're not a cripple, Aino."

"I am to them. On Amitié, I wouldn't be."

He sighed and rolled over on his side. The discussion was apparently over.

I woke up tonight because the bed was empty and the air completely still. Silence whined in my ears. Outside, Maderaldta rose like a mountain at the valley's mouth.

I don't know if he'd planned it all along. It doesn't matter. There were no new babies this cycle, no procession. Maybe he just saw his chance and decided to go for it.

It took such a long time to get up the path to the plateau. The upslope fought me, and my crutches slid and skittered over gravel and loose rocks; I almost fell over several times. I couldn't call for him, couldn't sing, and the birds circled overhead in a downward spiral.

Just before the clearing came into view, the path curled around an outcrop and flattened out among trees. All I could see while struggling through the trees was a faint flickering. It wasn't until I came into the clearing that I could really see what was going on: that which had been done to me, that I was too young to remember, that which none of us remember and choose not to witness. They leave the children and wait among the trees with their backs turned. They don't speak of what has happened during the wait. No one has ever said that watching is forbidden, but I felt like I was committing a crime, revealing what was hidden.

Petr stood in the middle of the clearing, a silhouette against the gray sky, surrounded by birds. No, he wasn't standing. He hung suspended by their wings, his toes barely touching the ground, his head tipped back. They were swarming in his face, tangling in his hair.

I can't avert my eyes anymore. I am about to see the process up close. The bird that sits on Petr's chest seems to take no notice of me. It pushes its ovipositor in between his lips and shudders. Then it leaves in a flutter of wings, so fast that I almost don't register it. Petr's chest heaves, and he rolls out of my lap, landing on his back. He's awake now, staring into the sky. I don't know if it's terror or ecstasy in his eyes as the tiny spawn fights its way out of his mouth.

In a week, the shuttle makes its bypass. Maybe they'll let me take Petr's place. If I went now, just left him on the ground and packed light, I could make it in time. I don't need a sky overhead. And considering the quality of their clothes, Amitié needs a tailor.

GOOD BOY

Nisi Shawl

*"As out of several hundreds of thousands of the substrate
programs comes an adaptable changing set of thousands of
metaprograms, so out of the metaprograms as substrate comes
something else . . . In a well-organized biocomputer, there is at
least one such critical control metaprogram labeled I for acting
on other metaprograms and labeled me when acted upon by
other metaprograms. I say at least one advisedly . . . "*

Feels like floatin. Wrong smells come under the right ones, like the
last few times. She got the table polished with lemon oil, or somethin similar, but what is that? Stronger than before, what is it, fish?
Also stinks like Fourth a July, after all the firecrackers set off. I
look around but only thing burnin is the candles, big circle of 'em,
waverin on the table in front a me.

Her daughter sittin on the other side, lookin damn near white
even with them African beads and robes she wear. Wonder she
don't put a bone through her nose. I laugh at that picture, and the
poor girl jump like I shot her. The music stops. It been playin soft
in the background, but it cuts right off in the middle a Billy Stray-
horn's solo.

I remember what she named her daughter. "Kressi," I say,
"what you do to that record? Put it back on, girl, don't you know
that's the Duke?"

"Sorry, ma'am." She sets back up this little white box she
knocked over with her elbow when I laughed. "Chelsea Bridge"
picks up where it left off, and I get outta my chair for a look
around.

Room always seem to have way too many walls, twelve sides or maybe more, and they don't go straight up to a proper ceilin, but sorta curve themselves over. All plastic and glass and metal. I don't like it much. Cold. Black outside; night, with no sign a the moon.

On a bed in one a the too many corners is a man, the reason why she brought me. Face almost black as the sky, and shinin with sweat. He got the covers all ruched up off his legs and twisted around his arms. Fever and chills, it look like. His eyes clear, though.

"Hello there, young man," I say to him, bendin over. This body light, almost too easy to move. I like to throw myself on the bed with him. "What seems to be your problem?"

"Hey," he says back, smilin tired. "You must be Miz Ivorene's Great-Aunt Lona, yeah?" I nod. "Well, I hate to admit it, Miz Lona, but nobody seems to know exactly what the problem is. At first it was just tiredness, and they made sure I was getting a proper diet—"

I keep noddin while he talks, though a lotta the words he uses don't tell me a thing. Words very seldom do, even at they best. It's his cloud I'm interested in, his cloud a light. The light around his body, that should tell me what's wrong with him and what he needs to fix it.

But I stare and stare at this man's cloud, and I don't see not one thing wrong. He ain't sick.

But sweatin and in pain like that he ain't well, either.

By the time I figure this much out, I have stayed long enough. The young man stopped talkin, and he and Kressi lookin at me, waitin for golden truths. All I know is I got no work to do here. Place starts gettin dimmer and I turn back to the table, to the candles, I go back to the light. As I'm leavin I think of somethin I maybe could tell them; it's pretty obvious to me, but they so stuck in time, never know a thing until it's already done happen to them. "Good Boy," I say, on my partin breath. "Good Boy. Go deeper out. Get Good Boy." And wonder like always if they'll understand.

"Some kinds of material evoked from storage seem to have the property of passing back in time beyond the beginning of this brain to previous brains . . . "

Ivorene McKenna slumped forward in her chair. Her head lowered slowly toward the tabletop, narrowly avoiding setting fire to her short locks. Her daughter Kressi slipped a bota into Ivorene's hand and cradled her shoulders as she sat back up, helping her guide the waterskin to her lips.

"What's wrong? What happened?" Edde Berkner had propped himself up on one wobbly arm. He peered anxiously through the gloom.

"Nothing. Lie down and rest. We have to play the session back and talk before we decide what to do." Kressi did her best to sound cool and professional. Like the rest of the colonists of Renaissance, she placed a high value on the rational and the scientific. They called themselves "Neo-Negroes," and they didn't have much use for anything that couldn't be quantified and repeated.

As a child on their outbound ship, Kressi had enjoyed the lessons on Benjamin Banneker, George McCoy, and technology's other black pioneers. She'd wanted to be Ruth Fleurny, maverick member of the team that perfected the Bounce. It was because of Fleurny's stubborn insistence on cheap access for all descendants of enslaved Africans as a condition of the "star drive's" sale that the Neo-Negroes and a handful of similar expeditions had gotten off the ground.

In her daughter's opinion Ivorene was as intelligent as Fleurny, and just as stubborn. Maybe misguided, though. Ivorene's controversial theories, while couched in scientific terms, had a hard time finding acceptance among the Neo-Negroes. Sometimes Kressi wished she would just quit, right or wrong.

"That's enough, sweetheart." Kressi laid the bota on the table and picked up Ivorene's arm by the elbow, walking with her as she took her shaky body to bed. It was always this way, afterwards.

Kressi set her player on "sound curtain," and the rush of a waterfall filled the room. She aimed it towards Edde's bed and then stepped behind it into her mother's silence. The red-brown skin of Ivorene's face seemed slack and lusterless. Her long-boned hands were clammy. Her daughter chafed them briefly to warm them.

"Well, Kressi, what did Aunt Lona have to say?"

"Nothing. Nothing much." Kressi shrugged, trying not to

show how much she hated having to act like anyone else besides her mom and Edde had been in the room. "I knocked the player over, and she scolded at me to put the music on again."

"What about Edde?"

"She looked at him, but he did most of the talking. I can show you the—"

"No, save the record for later. If she didn't say anything . . . Who else can I ask?" Great-Aunt Lona, the New Orleans rootswoman, had been her only hope. Other egun, accessible ancestral spirits, were available. But none of them knew much on the subject of healing.

"When she was leaving—" Kressi broke off. "At first, you know, I thought it was just that weird way she talks."

"Southern."

"Right. So I wondered if maybe she meant 'Good-bye,' but what it sounded like was 'Good boy,' so it had to be a compliment to Edde, I guess . . . "

Ivorene pushed her lower lip out, brought her eyebrows together. "'Good Boy.'"

"She said it more than once."

"How many times?"

"Three."

"Aw, hell." Ivorene raised a hand from Kressi's clasp and flung one forearm across her eyes, fending off the inevitable. "I don't want to have to figure out how to bring him up."

"We have an ancestor named Good Boy?"

"No. Goddamit. Pardon my francais, sweetheart." Ivorene sighed and let her hand fall to the quilt-covered bed. "But goddamit. Good Boy."

"We know something of the radiation limits in which we can survive. We know something of the oxygen concentrations in the air that we breathe, we know something of the light levels within which we can function . . . We are beginning to see how the environment interlocks with our computer and changes its functioning."

Edde wanted to go home. Ivorene had told Doctor Thompson that they'd bring him back to the infirmary when they were through, though, so Kressi bundled him onto their flatbed cart with a stack of fresh sheets and extra blankets. He winced as she jolted the wheels over the ridge between the yurt's foundation and the ramp down to the colony's corridors.

"Sorry," Kressi muttered, embarrassed. The ramp hissed grittily under the cart's plastic wheels, and a fine white dust rose in their wake. Most of Renaissance City's surfaces had been sealed with plastic spray shortly after its excavation, but some private passages remained natural.

Kressi held the cart one-handed, only a negligible amount of control needed despite the tunnel's 35-degree slope. With her other hand she fished in her robe's pocket for her remote. As she found and fingered it, the blind at the ramp's bottom rose.

At its bottom, the ramp leveled out. The wide cart made for a tight fit between the two bench-shaped blocks of likelime flanking the exit. Edde's berry-dark face shone with sweat. He closed his eyes as she turned into the corridor; vertigo was another symptom on his growing list.

Also, sensitivity to light. The tunnels of Renaissance City were just about shadowless, with frequent fluorescent fixtures on the walls. Kressi saw how his eyelids tightened, and threw a pillowcase over Edde's face. He hadn't been this bad on the trip to the McKenna's from the infirmary. The pillowcase looked weird, but Edde thanked her, in a somewhat muffled voice. Another voice came from speakers set in the ceiling. Kressi listened for a moment.

"—Ship Seven concerns, Captain? As opposed to City-wide?"

Kressi withdrew her attention. She didn't care much for politics. She knew she was in "Ship" Four, a non-geographical ward named for one of the ten colonizing vessels. She knew that Ivorene had once been active, been elected as the Ship's Captain, and had lost her position due to her experiments in programming psychology. Renaissance Citizens studied and revered their ancestors, but stopped short of desiring their actual presence. Ivorene's clinical practice had dwindled to nearly nothing; her status in the City's economy now rested solely on her position as an Investor.

Kressi headed into the main body of the ancient shallow sea from whose fossilized coral and sediment the city had been carved. As she wheeled her cart along, ramp openings and tunnel intersections became more common. Sometimes the ramps led upward, to storage areas and workshops. More often they led downward. Most Citizens preferred deeper dwellings. Though the atmosphere provided some protection from meteorites and radiation, it would be too thin to breathe comfortably for several generations.

As she approached the opening to one ramp in particular, Kressi's shoulders hunched in anticipation. They relaxed a little when she came close enough to see its lowered blind, then went back up as the blind began to retract. Kressi might have been able to clear the entrance before the blind rose high enough for Captain Yancey to hail her down. But the Captain would be offended to see Kressi speeding away along the corridor in an obvious attempt to avoid conversation. Besides, she couldn't race off with poor Edde on the cart. She stopped and waited for her least favorite neighbor to appear.

Captain Yancey had a build like a gas tank. While not precisely cylindrical, she was tall, round-shouldered, and solid. Her floor-length robes, usually of dull silver, enhanced the illusion. She accepted Kressi's respectful greeting as her due, with a nod. Edde pulled off his pillow case, opened his eyes, groaned, and closed them again.

"Young man!"

"Edde's feeling real bad," Kressi explained. "I'm taking him over to the infirmary."

Captain Yancey's jaw relaxed a bit. "Doctor Thompson just told me how his beds were starting to fill up."

Kressi didn't wonder why the infirmary's Head should bother to inform Captain Yancey how things stood there. The infirmary wasn't her responsibility, or any other captain's. But everyone told Captain Yancey everything.

"What are people getting sick from?" The planet Renaissance itself was supposed to be sterile, and the colonists had been well-screened and quarantined, then inoculated with benign "placeholder" microbes designed to discourage harmful ones that could cause diseases. Only 140 beds in the infirmary, and they'd never needed more than a fifth of them for 3,500-plus people. There was plenty of room for any who succumbed to illnesses caused by the placeholders' genetic drift.

"I'm not sure what's going on," Captain Yancey complained. "Doctor Thompson said he didn't have much time to talk. But as far as he could tell it wasn't anything catching, more like an allergy. Though how thirty people came to be all of a sudden afflicted with the same allergy he didn't bother to explain."

"Maybe I'd be better off at my place," Edde said in a worried voice.

"No, I'm bringing you back like we promised," said Kressi. With a polite smile she steered to Captain Yancey's right.

The Captain shifted so she still blocked Kressi's way. "Young lady, your mother hasn't been practicing any of her necromantic mumbo-jumbo on this poor boy, has she?"

Kressi's hands gripped the cart's handle tightly. Maybe she wasn't so sure how legitimate her mother's work was, but she didn't have to listen to other people put it down. Not even Captain Yancey. "That's not the way we prefer to think of it, Ma'am. Doctor Thompson referred Edde to us because he thought a psychological approach—"

"Call it what you want to, I say it's a disgraceful set of superstitions we ought to have left behind us in Africa. I always thought that your mother was a bright enough researcher, but I fail to understand why she has to clutter up our brand new paradigm with that sort—"

The conversation ended abruptly as Edde succumbed to a fit of coughing (yet another symptom). Captain Yancey retreated back down her ramp, saying over her shoulder that she was sure it couldn't be contagious, Doctor Thompson had sworn, but just to be on the safe side—

The ramp's descending blind cut her off.

In Renaissance City's core, the tunnel widened. Citizens sat in small, companionable groups on likelime benches outside ramp entrances.

Kressi greeted the people she knew by name, those from her Ship and several others. More knew her than vice versa. She'd been one of twenty kids on Ship Four. Twenty of 350 passengers. And the other nine Ships had carried even fewer children. Kressi and the rest were celebrities by simple virtue of their age. A seven-year gap, the length of the voyage, separated them from the generation born here on Renaissance.

Of course Kressi knew all her peers, from whichever Ship. Edde was more popular than she was, and as she wheeled him through the City's center, they accumulated a small entourage.

Passela recognized him first. "Edde!" she crooned. "What's wrong with him?" she asked Kressi accusingly.

"He's sick." Kressi didn't like Passela much. She made too big a deal of her position as the oldest of the hundred-odd ship kids, and she had an irritating way of over-emphasizing every other word.

But Fanfan, Passela's cousin, was cool. "Can I help you with that?" he asked. "You're headed for the infirmary, right?" Kressi let him put one hand on the cart's handle, though she could manage well enough on her own. They picked up speed. Passela and her sidekick Maryann stuck with them.

The infirmary lay on the far side of the core's white tunnels. Here the likelime took on a bluish tinge, legacy of the coral species that had burgeoned in this area of the slowly evaporating sea. The wall outside the infirmary's ramp housed the delicate remains of a huge, semi-shelled vertebrate. Kressi let Fanfan steer the cart down the ramp as she fondly stroked the fossil's curving, polished case and lightly brushed her fingertips along the arching trail of its skeletal extension. How had it felt, dying in the drying mud? Had it called upon its ancestors to save it from the sky's invading vacuum?

Kressi's lingering communion with the fossil lasted long enough that by the time she got inside the infirmary, Passela had taken over Edde's case. "He won't be any trouble, really, he won't; I'll nurse him with my own two hands," she told Ali, the staffer at the admitting console.

"Oh, good," said Ali. "I was afraid you'd ask to borrow a spare pair."

"What? Oh, you're putting me on; we don't grow limbs for that kind of stuff."

"I can go home," Edde offered. "I'm not so—" He interrupted his own protests with another painful-sounding coughing fit. That brought Doctor Thompson from behind the console's screen.

"Who's that? Edde Berkner? It's about time you checked yourself back in here, young man. Seems you've started some sort of psychosomatic epidemic. Half the symptoms showing up here this shift are the same as yours. I want you under observation."

"But, Doctor, we don't have the staff—" Ali protested.

"I'm bringing in some contingents. And Anna Sloan's been malingering here long enough. Nothing much wrong with her." Doctor Thompson reached out one-handed and tapped at the console with barely a glance at its screen. "There. I'm releasing her. Pack up a couple of cold/hot compresses. I'll go break the news."

He turned to Passela and smiled. "You come help me get Miz Sloan out of Cot Twenty so you can strip and change it."

Passela gaped at Dr. Thompson as if she were a fish on an empty seabed and he were a hurtling black meteor headed her way. Kressi stepped between them. "Well, actually—"

"Kressi?" The doctor appeared to notice her for the first time. "Of course. You show her what to do," he said, dismissing both of them from his mind.

"And who are all these others? Patients? No? More volunteers? Train them or get them out of here, Ali." With an apologetic shrug, Kressi wheeled Edde around the side of the console in Doctor Thompson's wake. Passela made no move to follow them.

The infirmary was mostly one big, high-ceilinged ward, with honeycombed screens between the beds for a bit of privacy. Doctor Thompson had gone ahead of her to the cubicle containing Cot Twenty. A high, sharp voice cut through the honeycombing. "My feet, you haven't done nothin about my feet—"

Kressi hesitated at the doorway of the small space. There was barely room for her in there, let alone the cart with Edde. Miz Sloan was someone she'd never met before, but that didn't matter. "I know you," declared the woman on the bed. "You're that crazy Ivorene McKenna's daughter. You turnin me out for a mental case, Doctor?"

"My mom's not crazy," said Kressi. She felt an angry flush creep up her pale cheeks, felt it deepen in her embarrassment at being able to flush so visibly. "Miz Sloan," she added, a tardy sign of respect for her elder.

Miz Sloan's feet stuck out from the near end of Cot Twenty. They seemed normal, neither swollen nor discolored, the soles a fairly even pink, but she winced as she swung them around off the side of the bed and lowered them into the see-through slippers sitting on the floor.

"Kressi's here to help you home, Anna," Doctor Thompson told Miz Sloan.

Miz Sloan lived close in; still, by the time Kressi had delivered her to the rooms she shared with two sisters, a niece and nephew, and the half-brother of her ex-husband, and listened to a rambling explanation of how Ivorene was crazy, but not pure-D crazy, and everyone knew she meant no harm with her attempts at talking to spirits, going home seemed pointless.

The lobby had held only one patient when she left. Now three more sat beside the closed door to Doctor Thompson's office, and another four leaned on the counter, talking earnestly to Ali.

Before she clocked in to help them, though, she had to call her mom. She squeezed past the waiting patients and scooted a wheeled stool in front of the screen. Her fingers drummed impatiently on the touchpad as her cursor swam through the city's directory. Doctor Thompson claimed voice rec caused problems with the infirmary's patient monitors. Finally, after what seemed like for ever, she reached her home room.

Ivorene was logged on. Kressi got her to activate the live feed. Her mother sat in bed, propped up on pillows, working on a tray of food. She ate methodically, absent-mindedly. Her dark eyes, so different from her daughter's hazel, shifted between the camera and two screens. Kressi could see text on one, but the resolution wouldn't quite let her read it.

"I'm starting my shift early, I guess," Kressi wrote.

"You guess?" Ivorene disliked sloppy statements.

"If it's all right with you. There are so many patients. Lots of them as bad as Edde . . . "

"Fine. Will you be home on time?"

Kressi glanced at the line of incomers, managing not to catch anyone's eye. "I'm not sure. Maybe."

The screen behind Ivorene showed what looked like an elongated brown bowling ball rotating in three dimensions. With each pass, a new three- or four-armed cross appeared on its oblong surface. "Get home as quickly as you can, sweetheart. I have lots more work for us to do."

Kressi signed off, a little disturbed. It sounded like Ivorene wanted to go under again. If only she'd stick to more useful topics . . . But Kressi had to put her personal concerns aside.

When her break came, Kressi did a few stretches and went right on working. Three days on, she'd had now, and the patient load heavier than ever. She wondered how she'd adjust to full adult status and the doubling of her hours requirement. One more year. She could hardly wait. She headed for the nearest blinking call light.

"To hold and display the accepted view of reality in all its detail and at the same time to program another state of consciousness is difficult; there just isn't enough human brain circuitry to do both jobs in detail perfectly. Therefore special conditions give the best use of the whole computer for exploring, displaying, and fully experiencing new states of consciousness . . . "

Ivorene lowered herself slowly into her tank. Its refrigerator clicked on immediately. She'd been running a little hot lately – maybe coming down with Edde's mysterious ailment, like a major portion of the colony seemed bent on doing.

The tank was small, but held her without cramping. She hooded herself and checked the breathing apparatus. Like most of the colony's equipment, it was solidly put together, though based on dated technologies, "breakthroughs" discarded years before their departure.

She'd expected her daughter home almost an hour ago. The fail-safes were fine, but she wished Kressi had come back from her shift on schedule and helped her with this part.

Off with the hood for a moment so she could set the timer on the tank's lid. How many hours? Three. Good Boy had an affinity for that number.

About to re-hood, she remembered to check the water's salinity. A little on the low side. Shivering, she climbed out and grabbed a scoop of crystals from the bucket she kept beside the tank.

Salt was not a problem. Renaissance's seas had left behind plenty of pans and flats. Water was a little more expensive, dug up frozen from deep crevices, melted, and purified. Power was cheaper, about as easily available as salt. The cloudless skies of Renaissance did little to dim the light of its yellow-white star,

Horus. The McKenna's unconventional surface dwelling gave them a great opportunity to convert that constant flood of photons to electricity.

She strapped on her hood again and let the blood-warm waters of the isolation tank lap over her, and the buoyant fluid. The thick liquid's buoyancy lifted her and let her lose all connection with her physical surroundings. But her consciousness clung stubbornly to mundane concerns. Why was Kressi so late? Had she come down with this mysterious ailment, this Edde-Berkner illness?

Ivorene's calls to the infirmary had all been answered by loops. Everyone was to remain calm. No contagious agents had been isolated. Infirmary beds were reserved for those in serious condition, and most complaints could be dealt with on an outpatient basis, no appointments necessary, first come, first served. The main thing, really, was to remain calm . . .

Which was what Ivorene would do if it killed her. She would not leap from the tank and rush to the infirmary, streaming salt water along the City's corridors. She would not embarrass her daughter with overprotectiveness, with the same overreactions her own parents had fallen ridiculous prey to. At fifteen, Kressi was as independent and self-sufficient as Ivorene had been able to make her.

And what if she was sick? She was at the infirmary, right? What better place? Doctor Thompson and his crew would do what they could for her. Ivorene would stay here and find out what else was possible.

Uselessly, she strove to still her thoughts. Then she stopped striving, and let a million details wash over her mind, the way the waters of the tank covered her body. This had happened before, in the early stages of her research, the sessions where she'd made first contact with Aunt Lona, and Uncle Hervey, the mechanic. She'd prepared for it. She'd stacked the deck, cramming for the last five hours, filling herself up with facts and speculations, clues for her wayward will to follow in the search for Good Boy, Exu, Papa Legba, Ellegua . . . his names strung themselves out before her in a mocking procession. Grasp one, gain none. The names grew brilliant feathers and flew off with raucous cries, but they went only a short distance. How to catch them? Salt their tails? But no, Good Boy preferred sweet things.

Candy. Visions of sugar plums danced in her head. Sticky and glistening, striped with pink and green. Ivorene concentrated on a hypnotic looking swirl of red and white, a gigantic lollypop with loads of projectability.

Sure enough, she was able to slow its swirling. The spinning disk resolved itself into a three-legged eye, then sped back up and streaked away.

Ivorene followed it. The disk's thin edge flickered as images imposed themselves over it at a rate too fast for her to perceive. She strove impatiently to focus beyond their interference. Suddenly, her perspective shifted and she was beside the disk – no, above it. The spinning spread, then slowed and stopped.

The disk's three legs were now composed of art-nouveau curves of thin red plastic. Its eye was gone, and its center pierced by a tall, silver pole. Legs and pole sat at the center of a papery circle of black and red, surrounded by a large, intricately grooved platter of thicker plastic, shiny black alternating with a duller, deep, dark grey.

She'd seen this sort of thing before. In an antique shop on Earth, during one of her expeditions to uncover portable cultural treasures. She'd decided against this particular one, then changed her mind in its favor, only to find it gone on her return to the shop.

It was a record. On a record player. She raised her gaze to the stone face before her. Shell eyes squeezed half shut, a shell mouth pursed in an amused smile.

"Laroye, ago Elegba!" Stay cool, trickster, the Yoruban greeting ran in translation. Coolness having a very high value in equatorial Africa. Ivorene launched into her prepared petition for Good Boy's assistance in healing her godson Edde of his strange affliction. She stopped abruptly as the image before her faded and threatened to break apart. Hard to hold abstractions in her current state. She tightened down on her desire. Squeezed. The enormous face before her brightened, though it remained amorphous. Encouraged, she produced for him the lump of her longing. It shone like a milky diamond, lustrous yet clear, then flew off toward him of its own accord. On impact, her prayer spread in ripples that seemed to sharpen and set the stone face, rather than disturb it.

Shell eyes twinkled. The great head moved. A nod yes? Or instruction, a wish to be imitated? Ivorene looked down again, reading the label on the record. Atlantic. Chic. "Good Times."

So what did that mean? So Good Boy would help her if she played a record she knew she didn't have?

The spinning began again. Ivorene seemed now to stand on the record's surface, swinging around the silver pole as a scratchy song rose from below. Beyond the pole, white walls with gigantic murals pursued a stately rotation. Mushroom-haired women with impossibly long legs raised shapely brown hands against invisible enemies. Bald, athletic, young men in flowing furs saluted crowds of admiring children with casual waves of large, lethal-looking side-arms.

Actually, there were a lot of weapons.

"Boys will be boys," a nasal voice advised her. "Better let them have their toys."

Well, there weren't any firearms on Renaissance. Explosives seemed like a pretty bad idea in a contained and pressurized atmosphere. Maybe the miners . . . No. "No, sorry." She shook her head firmly. "No guns."

The world screeched backwards in its tracks, jerked violently forward with a wheezing shriek. Ivorene fell on her figurative ass as the process repeated itself. She clung to the record's ridges, shooting back and forth around its axis without warning. An eery choir wailed in time to the wild stops and starts.

The disturbance ended as suddenly as it had begun, and the world's smooth spin resumed. A new number played, a steady march. "On guard! Defend yourself!" its singers admonished her.

No doubt.

A flash of brilliance at the pole's tip drew her attention. It grew into a humming globe, an irregularly rayed ball of slowly coruscating light. Flickering arms of color drew her closer – her prayer? So much bigger, now. So strong – it had to be more, more than she'd asked for. It had to be—

She resisted. But the pole loomed larger and larger. If she touched it – if she grasped it firmly, with both hands, she could call down that ball of lightning on her head. She could know Good Boy in her heart, as her personal savior. She could cure the colony of its mysterious non-epidemic and get the respect she deserved, the respect she'd already more than earned. She could fill herself with the power, the glory—

She could get herself possessed while she was alone, without anyone to help or protect her, or see to it that she ever came back to normal.

On guard. Defend yourself.

She made an effort. A step backward. It turned into a lunge forward. Off-balance, she caught herself on the silver pole and clung there as the light descended, swift and slow.

" . . . *There may be other controls and controllers, which, for convenience, I call supraself metaprograms. These are many or one depending on current states of consciousness in the single self-metaprogrammer. These may be personified as if entities . . .* "

Kressi walked slowly home, leaning heavily on the handle of the flatbed. Maybe she should just lie right down on it. She could have pushed herself along the walls if they weren't so far apart. She felt very, very tired. A shift and a half she'd worked. The infirmary was now completely out of pulp sheets, which was just as well. The plastic bed pads might be less comfortable, but they cleaned up efficiently.

She hoped her mother wouldn't be too mad. Ivorene hadn't said not to work late, not exactly . . . And Doctor Thompson wanted her back early, too.

At the top of the ramp she hesitated. The yurt's familiar hollow was filled with darkness. The only light filtered in behind her, shining up the ramp. Power out? She shifted cautiously to her left. No. Two red tell-tales glowed in her field of vision like the mismatched eyes of some squat monster: Ivorene's isolation tank. Her mother had gone under. Alone. Guilt tweaked at her; she should have come home earlier.

But Ivorene ought to have called her.

The yurt's polarized glass panels showed blankness. No stars. Not for the next few hours. Horus was setting now, triggering the glass's reflective properties. Why was she standing there in the dark? "Light one. Light two," she commanded.

Her stomach grumbled at her loudly. Hungry and tired. Tired

and hungry. And she had to talk to her mother about going back early.

She shoved the cart into place next to the ramp and went to the tank to see how much longer Ivorene would be inside. The timer was counting up, not down. Ivorene had been due out of isolation half an hour ago.

Anxiously, she activated the mike. "Ivorene, I'm home. Can you come out now? It's Kressi," she added. No telling what state her mother's mind was in. How could Ivorene have missed the alarm?

A long pause, then her mother's voice came through the speaker, a bit odd. "Right."

"Okay." Kressi eyed the tank suspiciously till Ivorene emerged dripping from its depths. "Rough session?" she asked her.

Ivorene stared around the yurt absently. Kressi assumed she was looking for a towel and brought one over. "Mom?" Ooops. Ivorene hated for Kressi to call her that. But she seemed not to notice the slip-up. Or the towel. Kressi laid it over Ivorene's shoulders. "I'll get you a robe."

When she turned back from the closet, Ivorene was walking around the yurt in great strides, toweling herself off vigorously. But shivering, Kressi saw as she draped her mother in soft red fabric. It must have been bad. Why hadn't Ivorene waited?

Why hadn't she come home on time?

She picked the damp towel up from the floor where Ivorene had dropped it. "Let me get your hair for you." A loud, hoarse cackle made her start.

"Ha! I have my hair already where it belongs, here upon my head!"

"But – I – but it's wet!" Kressi protested, confused.

Her mother frowned. A drop of water slid down her forehead and trickled along one slanted brow. "You are correct. Remedy this."

She let Kressi lead her to her chair at the kitchen table and towel dry her short locks, then got up and strolled restlessly around the yurt's perimeter. She picked up random objects and examined them, then lost interest. A loud crash sounded as Ivorene emptied a jar of trade beads onto the floor. After watching the tiny cylinders of colored glass roll away from her, she moved on, slipping and unconcernedly righting herself whenever she stepped on one.

Kressi was pretty sure by this time that she understood what had happened.

From her mother's perspective, Ivorene had become possessed. From the perspective of everyone else on the planet, she was insane.

Only temporarily, of course. All Kressi had to do was—

Was remember her instructions. What to do if things went wrong. And believe they'd work.

Her mother stood holding a cube of her ex-husband, Kressi's father, the white man she'd left behind when she became a Neo-Negro. Her face wore a remote, detached expression.

Kressi's first memories were of quarantine. She'd never really known her father. She wondered if he'd have been able to help her, if he were here.

Resolutely, she removed the cube from her mother's hands, held both of them in her own, and stepped firmly on Ivorene's right foot. Two sharp jerks down on both arms at once – like that—

Laughing, the face in front of her split wide into a most un-Ivoreneish grin. "What, you want for me to leave already? Is your mother's body, though, and she invited me to come, to solve your mystery. So I am going to stay!"

" . . . *one cannot know as a result of this kind of solitudinous experiment whether or not the phenomena are explicable only by non-biocomputer interventions or only by happenings within the computer itself, or both.* "

Light receded, poured out of her like water from a strainer, left her sitting in her own chair, dressed in her red robe. She knew how she'd gotten there, knew Kressi had come home and roused her from the tank. Nothing was lost. What happened while Good Boy rode her remained in her memory, only faded, thinned of all immediacy. And her body felt so heavy now that she had to lift it on her own. But she made her hand rise, reached out to touch her daughter's cheek.

"Don't worry, Kressi. I'm still here. This is right, what Good Boy's trying to do—"

"Ivorene? You're okay?" Tears filled her daughter's eyes and voice.

"Yes." She wanted to sound surer. "Listen, I'm going to let him come back again, I just didn't want—"

"'Him?' Ivorene, why won't you – Good Boy's not real! Admit it!" Kressi stood and stormed away from the table so Ivorene had to turn to see her. Now the tears were of anger.

"Define real," Ivorene said, then sagged in her seat. She was too tired to argue. "No, never mind. Don't. Whether Good Boy or Aunt Lona or any of them are 'real' doesn't matter in the end. Just act like they are and everything will work out fine."

"But—"

"For three days, that's all. That's how long I asked him to stay." Stubborn silence. At the edge of Ivorene's vision, whiteness flickered. With each pulse it grew, drawing in, a bright tunnel down which her daughter's once-more-worried face receded. Saying words she couldn't hear. Apologies? Ivorene overrode them with her own instructions: "Three days. Promise me that."

> "... *each computer has a certain level of ability in metaprogramming others-not-self.*"

Posted on Citynet 01.18.2065, 08:18:14
FROM: goodboy@mckenna.home
TO: ALL USERS:
Subject: Be a Souldier in the Army of Uncle Jam!
Body:

PARTY UP!
You are hereby notified that in accordance with the wishes of the
Supreme Funkmeister,
you are required to bring your Waggity Asses on over to
McKenna's Mothership
for the
CELEBRATION!
of our Grand Ascension to the status of
Chocolate City, Capitol of the Known Negro Universe, said
CELEBRATION!
to commence on the evening of 01.21.2065, promptly at
21:00 hours.
IT'S THE BOMB!!
[link to mckennapage.home]

Sent via Citynet 01.18.2065, 13:34:10
FROM: pearl@yancey.home
TO: ivorene@mckenna.home
CC: CAPTAINGROUP, samthompson@infirmary.city
Subject: Attached Posting
Body:
Allow me to bring the attached to your attention, Miz McKenna, as it may somehow have escaped your notice. It purports to issue from a "goodboy," currently unlisted as a Citizen. But the voice ID closely parallels your own, and reveal commands show your login.

Miz McKenna, aside from the highly questionable language of this "invitation," the obvious irresponsibility of organizing a frivolous assembly now, at the height of an epidemic, leads me to conclude that the posting is a clever but childish hoax on the part of your normally quite level-headed daughter. Please take immediate steps to disavow it as such.

Far be it from me to meddle in your personal affairs, Miz McKenna, but I'm sure you'll agree that her understandable longing for popularity does not excuse Kressi's participation in a prank of this magnitude.

Sent via Citynet 01.18.2065, 18:42:33
FROM: maryann@gonder.home
TO: goodboy@mckenna.home
Re: Be a Souldier in the Army of Uncle Jam!
Body:
Passela told me to tell you this is such a swollen idea! Or I guess I should say it's The Bomb! Those fashions on your page were just wild, and I hope we can get our printers sufficiently togetha in time for the big partay!

Now for the important news – I heard Fanfan ask his daddy if he could borrow his record player! And some of his old jams! I bet he has lots of the songs your page listed, because I was over at their place one time, and in one closet they had this whole big rack of those black plastic circles! So it's only the guns you have to worry about getting.

Are you sure your mother won't mind?

Sent via Citynet 01.19.2065, 00:16:29
FROM: samthompson@infirmary.city
TO: pearl@yancey.home
CC: CAPTAINGROUP, ivorene@mckenna.home
Re: Attached Posting
Body:
Are you purposely TRYING to set off a City-wide panic? Of all the officious, unscientific nonsense I've heard on this expedition, yours, Pearl, takes the pound cake! This is not, repeat NOT an epidemic.

There is no, repeat NO single, underlying organism that I can discover at the root of this recent wave of disorders. On the other hand, whatever it is seems to be affecting just about everyone on Renaissance. To a greater or lesser extent.

I've attached several tables I've been working on in my copious free time ... I don't know what they mean yet, but there's an unprecedented variation in the degree to which symptoms manifest, in the number of symptoms any case exhibits, and in the comparative seriousness of symptoms. Fear of insanity, salt cravings, heart palpitations, fevers, hernias, sore feet, sprained backs, tonsillitis – what have they got in common? Nothing. Except that they all cropped up as problems at about the same time. But not in the same household or among workers on the same shift at the same plant.

So whatever this thing is, it's not contagious. There's no excuse for your killjoy attitude, Pearl. Let the kids have their party.

Sent via Citynet 01.19.2065, 12:12:12
FROM: ivorene@mckenna.home
TO: pearl@yancey.home
CC: CAPTAINGROUP, samthompson@infirmary.city
RE: Attached Posting
The invitation is entirely legitimate. Those who find the language in which it's couched to be odd should refer to the available historical data on mid-twentieth century black musicians, specifically Sun Ra, Parliament, Funkadelic, and Earth, Wind & Fire. A notable space-travel mystique developed around their work, and it is to honor its creative impetus that I've arranged for y'all to

party up! Everybody party up! Come fly with me! I am the Mothership Connection. You have overcome, for I am here!

> *"At times the cross-model synesthetic projection may help . . . excitation coming in the objective hearing mechanisms can be converted to excite visual projection. The commonest excitation used here is music . . ."*

A good long ride on this one. She a strong horse, Ivorene. I even let her get some sleep, talk to her tickety-tap machine a little, calm her daughter down with some kinda explanations. No danger of losing my seat. She don't buck, don't rear. Three days.

All the partay people comin now. I made many preparations. Poor nervous daughter Kressi done helped, shown me how ta cook the candy and color over them too bright lights. But the pole, I erect that sucker all myself.

We sit in chairs by the door. "Raise up the blind," I say. She a good, obedient girl. And wearin the blue I said, most pleasin to the ocean. Her mother and I both told her time and again, till I do my business I ain't goin nowhere.

Fillin up the ramp, the peoples who been waitin come in. They laugh, but not too loud yet. One brought me some a my music. Kressi gets up to make it play. I watch while more people arrive. Everybody stop an stare when they see my big ole pole. It stuck up in the middle a everthing, hard to miss.

The expression on that there lady's face make me wonder how she ever gonna reach escape velocity. Don't she know this a partay?

Apparently not. "I couldn't believe you'd actually allow this to take place," she tells me.

I smile. "I allow all sort a things." I offer her Kressi's seat.

"Well, no, I can't really stay . . ."

"But how else you gonna know all the people wind up comin?"

She give me a narrow-eyed look. "Ivorene? What's gotten into you? Are you – you're not – you haven't been—"

She think my horse drunk. "Siddown and fine out," I say, and now she accept my invitation. I get her to take some candy, too. Lemondrop. Ain't no need to shock her system with too much sweetness.

All this time, guests keep arrivin. All dressed up, nice, bright colors, shiny fabrics, boots, big belts – Not quite right, not exactly how they did it, back in the day, but – they lookin pretty good! I keep handin out the candy, hopin everyone get to enjoy themself.

Grooves start jumpin. I can't contain myself, never no good at that. 'Fore she know it, Miz Mealymouth holdin my candy bowl and I am out on the dance floor actin like anybody's fool. "Put a glide in your stride and a dip in your hip!" I sing over the music. Why they all just watchin me?

Next song. Kressi come up behind me, stand still a minute. I turn so she see me smile. Take her hand, spin her round, dosi-do an play the clown. She lose some a her worry, gain some grace. Soon she swishin her robe like waves and dancin like light on the water. Very Yemaya, very Mother of Fishes. Good. That's who we got to bring down here tonight.

Boy over there wanna dance with her. I get out the way. In a minute a whole bunch of 'em cuttin loose. Flyin elbows, flashin feet. Funk start to rise.

Someone important at the door. I go see why they not comin in.

'Cause the one told me she really can't stay tryin to keep him out, that's why! Big shinin man in a paper dress standin there while she tell him get on back in bed. She call him Edde. "Yes, Miz Yancey," he say, and nod. Too polite to push her out the doorway.

Not me. But I do it without touchin. All a sudden, she sittin down. I help her back up. Edde head for the pole.

"Call Doctor Thompson!" this Yancey tell me. Tell me. Tell me!

She won't leave, now I wish she would. I could make her, but I rather dance. Rather she did, too. Like everybody else but her. Funk steady risin, but this woman drag us down. And we close, so goddam close.

Gotta get over the hump. Gotta get over the hump.

Where my bopgun?

I look all around. Someone shoulda brought it to me before now. Ain't I already asked? Sure, when my horse first pray to me. Nobody better make me ask a second time.

Edde hoppin all around, jumpin so he see over people's shoulders, headed for my pole. He there. He grab it.

Swing down, sweet chariot, stop, and let me ride.

Two now. I on two horses. Much easier. Look at me across the room. Look at me back. These are the Good Times.

Homin in on Miz Yancey. All she wanna do is stan there. I bring me some dancers. Soft music, an they swirl like liquid, spillin over the floor. Swoosh, shoosh, they spin Miz Yancey round, rock her shoulders, sway her hips, draw her deep into that psychoalphadiscobetabioaquadoloop. Carry her like a cup a foam on they tide. Over to my pole. Twirl her round, turn her loose and let her grab on to stand steady. She ready. I watch the funk gettin up for the downstroke. Watch it fall upon that horse's head.

She come! Mother of Fishes, she come! Twistin, slidin, slippin, ridin – here among us! Yemaya has come!

"... control is based upon exploration of n-dimensional spaces and finding key spaces for transformations, first in decisive small local regions, which can result in large-scale transformations."

Kressi opened her eyes on chaos. How long had she been dancing? It had felt so good to forget, to let the music take her far away. But where was she?

Surging dancers squeezed her against a wall. Perpendicular. Smooth, unjointed. She was in a corridor, outside the yurt. But Good Boy's music still surrounded her. Someone had patched the yurt's sound system into the City's speakers.

Miz Sloan capered by in Ali's arms, transparent slippers kicking high. Then the flood of dancers ebbed, trailing a pair she recognized with a shock as Passela and Fanfan. They were – he was – from behind Passela had shoved her hands inside the front of his pants, way inside. As she watched, Fanfan squatted down slightly, allowing Passela to leap astride his hips. Without dropping a beat, they vanished into the crowd. Kressi caught her breath, then started slowly after them, thinking hard.

Either they had all gone crazy at the same time, or it was a very good thing she'd spit out that piece of candy her mother gave her.

No. Not her mother. Whatever it was Ivorene had called up to help them. A supraself metaprogram, to use her term. Three days ago, Kressi had agreed to go along with anything it wanted. To believe that her mother had known what she was doing, and that this – entity – would somehow perform the task it had been set and leave. It had been hard to stick by her decision. It wasn't getting any easier.

The corridor emptied. Kressi spotted her favorite fossil embedded in a nearby stretch of likelime. She was outside the infirmary.

She went into the empty lobby. Over the music's steady throb, she heard Doctor Thompson's angry protests. She had to see what was happening in the cubicles, in the ward. Even if there was nothing she could do to stop it.

There was nothing she could do, or even see. Nothing but the brightly colored backs of her fellow Citizens, pulsing rhythmically, flaring and floating and – She closed her eyes. Tight. But shining patterns formed, even more dangerous to her focus.

She opened her eyes again and pounded on the back before her. The drug would wear off soon. John C. Lilly used LSD, but Ivorene had opted for a tailored version of Narby's Amazonian formula in her early experiments. Presumably this was what Good Boy had printed out and put into the candy. The dancers' ecstasy would last no more than half a shift, and the effects on Kressi would be slighter, and of a much shorter duration.

Long seconds passed till the man blocking her way moved. He backed up suddenly, kicking her in the shins. Others did the same, and the tight knot of dancers dissolved into a loose semi-circle around the door of Cubicle One. Kressi peered between shifting shoulders and saw Captain Yancey emerge. Her unblinking eyes seemed to protrude slightly from her head. She raised dusty, chalk-white hands and held them clasped in front of her, then began to move them slowly together, as if working up a lather.

Without warning, Captain Yancey whirled and stalked off to her left. Kressi scrambled to follow her. A high, burbling voice wailed through the speakers: "I can't swim! I never could swim! Let go mah laig!"

Six's occupant looked oddly serene, though his room was filled with partying strangers. Two men sat on opposite sides of his bed, propping him erect. Sweat glittered on his forehead as he swayed lightly to the music. Kressi glanced automatically at the headboard: Charles Tobin – temp 40/heart rate 120.

Captain Yancey leaned forward and placed both hands on Mr. Tobin's head. The patient slithered down onto his bed as if to avoid her. She stooped to maintain contact and began to shudder slowly, so deeply she shook the patient and his cot. Mr. Tobin's body straightened, then arched like a leafspring, vibrating faster and faster. Horrified, Kressi tried to call up the courage to step forward and touch him, somehow stop what was happening. But it ended on its own before she could manage that. Captain Yancey stood back and left him flat on the cot. His hair and face were white with whatever she'd rubbed on her hands. He seemed to be asleep. The headboard thought so, too.

The room emptied. Kressi hesitated, then hurried out.

She barely made it into Seven. Dancers screened the cot. A new voice sang to what sounded like the same song, assuring everyone that they could swim in the water and not get wet.

A child's frightened crying out through the music. It came from the cot. Kressi struggled to reach it. By the time she got there, the child lay quiet and calm.

It was Junior Watt. Kressi recognized the normally feisty ten-year-old despite his mask of white. His eyelids fluttered briefly as she called his name, then he sighed and smiled. As she watched, the headboard's readouts flickered, changing to those of a healthy sleeping boy.

"What are you doing?" she asked Captain Yancey.

In response, the older woman grabbed Kressi by her braids and pulled her closer. Shutting her eyes reflexively, Kressi felt a hand scrub her face with a slightly gritty powder. The press of dancers suddenly stilled to hold her motionless. She twisted stubbornly in place, getting nowhere. The hand's scrubbing motions softened, becoming oddly gentle, reminding her of – of—

Of how her mother washed her face one morning, grooming her for an online interview, just weeks before the ascent to their ship. She'd fought Ivorene, flung away the washcloth, but her mother had picked it up and persisted in her work. Captain Yancey's touch felt as tender, and as determined.

No. Not Captain Yancey's. This supraself metaprogram's touch.

It was cleaning its children.

Kressi relaxed. And sensed a lightness, a lifting. As if old, nameless, chains had fallen from her, training weights she'd put on long ago and since forgotten.

She opened her eyes slowly. The room was empty. Then Doctor Thompson walked through the cubicle's doorway holding a gun. "Kressi?" he asked.

"I'm okay. It's just—"

"What's that stuff on your face?"

Good question. "I dunno."

"It's on the others, too. I'll get a sample container." He turned to leave.

"Wait – you're not going to shoot Captain Yancey, are you?"

"No. Where'd you get—" He looked at the gun he was tucking absentmindedly under his robe's sash. "Oh. This. It's only a water pistol." He pulled it free again and looked down at it as if it belonged to another person, someone immature and hopelessly embarrassing. "I had it in my office for some reason, and when they all came in at once it seemed . . ."

"Here. Take it." Doctor Thompson handed her the gun. It felt heavy and wet. "I'm not going to try to stop them. This laying on of hands, or whatever you want to call it, it's working."

Kressi had come to the same conclusion, but it startled her to hear him say so.

"I knew from the beginning an unconventional course of therapy was called for, but—" He shrugged his shoulders and waved an arm vaguely in the air. "Next time you talk to Ivorene, ask her to give me a call so we can discuss what she's done."

It was at this point that Kressi realized that her mother had been missing from among the dancers. That she'd been absent ever since Kressi roused herself from her trance. Ever since the party's migration to the infirmary. So Ivorene must still be back at home.

No, not Ivorene. Or maybe, yes. If the wave of symptoms had been conquered, the Good Boy metaprogram might have finally given up his hold. It would be Ivorene waiting for Kressi at the yurt, worn out from her long ordeal, not even sure of her own success.

With that in mind, Kressi called home. No answer. Maybe all it meant was that her mother felt too tired to open the feed. But when A Shift's crew showed up minutes later, unaffected by candy, she was happy to leave Captain Yancey and her entourage to them. By then the music's volume had dropped, and a lot of partiers had drifted off; perhaps half their number remained. Doctor Thompson followed them through the ward, smiling and recording notes, nodding at Kressi as she took her leave.

The blind was still raised at the bottom of the yurt's ramp. She plodded to the top without shutting it, expecting to find drugged or sleeping stragglers, but the place was empty. Everyone had gone. Everyone except one slim figure robed in black and red, sitting at the base of the pole Good Boy had erected. Her mother?

No. The figure popped to its feet like a button and lifted its chin to peer at her through half-lidded eyes, and Kressi knew there was one more guest to get rid of.

But how?

"Well?" asked Good Boy. "I kep all a my promises now. How bout yours?"

Promises? "I said I'd help you for three days. I did. You said you'd cure the mystery disease. Okay, that's pretty much taken care of. Which means it's time for you to go."

Good Boy tilted his head consideringly. "There was the partay, yes. Music, dancing. Sweetness we shared. But these wasn't all a my requirements."

"I require my mother back! Good Boy, you gave your word—" Kressi lowered her head and took a deep breath, trying to imagine life if Ivorene never recovered possession of her body. Her mother would be locked up, drugged helpless. Kressi would get handed off to someone to be fostered till she reached sixteen, probably Captain Yancey or worse, and of course nobody'd ever be able to make Ivorene any better because there was nothing really wrong with her—

"Come now." Good Boy's tone had turned suddenly cajoling. He stepped quickly toward her, almost running. "I am aware you got it. Hand it over. All gonna be well."

"Hand what over?" Unnerved by his proximity, she put her hands in her pockets to prove that they were empty and felt something hard and slick.

Doctor Thompson's water pistol. She pulled it out. "This?"

Ivorene's teeth gleamed against her wide-stretched lips in a glad smile. "At last!" Good Boy received the gun reverently, cradling it in upturned palms as he examined it. The smile faded. "This a toy?"

"Good Boy, it's all we have!"

He aimed it at her. "It loaded?" And shot her full in the face.

Kressi choked, coughed, swallowing salty water and wiping it from her eyes. She heard him laughing, heard him stop, heard the clatter of something hitting the yurt's floor. Felt shaking arms wrap around her damp head and haul it closer, pressing it up against cloth-covered flesh. She fought free, but when she could see again there was something different –

"Mom?"

"How many times do I have to tell you not to call me outta my name like that! Just because I happen to be your—"

"Ivorene!" She nestled back into her mother's arms once more. For however long she could.

"New areas of conscious awareness can be developed, beyond the current conscious comprehension of the self. With courage, fortitude, and perseverance the previously experienced boundaries can be crossed into new territories of subjective awareness and experience."

Stars shone through the yurt's many windows. Everything else was dark till Kressi held her lighter to the three candles in front of her. Three long flames leapt up, wavering golden fingers that quickly steadied and grew still. Two people sat at the table, two biocomputers containing at least that many control metaprograms. One of them happened to have given birth to the other.

Doctor Thompson, Captain Yancey, and a dozen others waited to watch the night's proceedings through the live feed. A sheet from the printer contained a list of their questions.

Ivorene reached around the candles to grasp her daughter by her wrist. "Who do you think we should get for them to talk to?" she asked. Her palm slid against her daughter's in an almost unconscious clasp.

You, Kressi wanted to say, but no, this was research. Talking to Ivorene wasn't an option right now. Wasn't always going to be one. Not with her mother. "You decide this time."

Sensitive instruments recorded and broadcast Ivorene's reply: "Good Boy."

Kressi sat up in her chair, planted her feet more firmly on the floor, and released her mother's hand.

" . . . the bodies of the network housing the minds, the ground on which they rest, the planet's surface, impose definite limits. These limits are to be found experientially and experimentally, agreed upon by special minds, and communicated to the network. The results are called consensus science."

(All quotes are from John C. Lilly's Programming and Metaprogramming in the Human Biocomputer: Theory and Experiments, second edition, 1974, Bantam Books, NY, NY.)

THE SECOND CARD OF THE MAJOR ARCANA

Thoraiya Dyer

He sits up against one of the altar stones.

I move in the long shadows of marble columns. A dry wind from across the valley tosses the dangling ties of my veil, bringing more knowledge to me. My human face, framed by yards of black silk, smiles with a woman's smile.

"Excuse me," I say, and he leaps to his feet, hiding the pack of pornographic playing cards behind his back. The boy appears, not long released from his compulsory military service, bushy buzz cut just beginning to regrow, skin browned from stakeouts in sunshine-dazzled snowfields and fingernails brittle from picking garbage and dead cats from the dishwater Mediterranean.

Nor am I long released. Freedom is a luxury for both of us.

"Do you need directions?" the boy asks and the riddle rises in my chest.

"I need directions to the one who is wiser than I," I say. "Thus might I return to the God with a refutation in hand."

My claws flex slightly in their sheaths.

"Are you lost?" He gapes. "There's nobody here. The bus to Chtaura comes in one hour."

Incorrect. I open my inner eye and stop the boy's heart.

He slips down the side of the altar stone like a stain. The absence of blood turns his dark Arab face the colour of weak tea. The temple I remember is dismembered, but I am still bound to protect it from fools. I sense the foundations. A few of them remain, buried deep beneath the derelict Umayyad monstrosity. Other stones have been removed to distant places. They describe the new boundary of my zeal.

Where is the scholar?

There was a grown man with a naked chin who rolled back the stone, a priest who whispered the words of awakening. I must find him. The task of bringing the stones back to the temple is his. It will be simpler to guard once it is made whole.

For now, the greater part of the world lies within the temple.

I step lightly around the body on padded paws. The loose, layered robes of the Bekaa Bedouin swish in the dust behind me. They erase tracks, which resemble those of the melanistic Asiatic lion, extinct in the Levant since the early fourteenth century.

The wind blows again, this time from the east, and I am filled with the wisdom of migrating birds, of the million uses of crude oil, a war fought between pilotless craft and a common illness that causes sudden death.

I turn back to the body of the boy and with my inner eye, I stretch the left ventricle of his heart to give the appearance of adenoviral dysfunction. The wind offers a warning. Mysteries are not tolerated in this time. I shall call no attention to myself, for although I cannot be killed, there is a grown man with a naked chin who knew the words of awakening.

There may be others who know the words of dreamless sleep. I will not be thwarted.

The bus that comes is small, garishly painted and stifling. A thick-lipped, gap-toothed driver does not ask me for the fare. Some primordial sense warns him to remain silent.

Since he does not speak, no riddles rise in me. The moment I pass him, the driver accelerates maniacally back onto the road, as though the roar of the engine were some kind of defence against me.

Three grown fools ride the bus to Chtaura. They do not reach the destination alive. When the bus stops, the bus driver turns in his chair. At last, he asks me what I have done; he attempts the hurdle, only to fall.

I leave the child crying in its dead mother's arms. The doors of the bus open at the swing of a lever. A breeze caresses my cheeks, bringing news of share markets and solar-powered shipping. I step down onto black soil bursting with vines. They are heavy with broad beans. Sustenance for the child, until another bus comes.

Chtaura is a patchwork of irrigated vineyards, grazing milk

animals and quick-growing grain. Signage designed to attract and entertain after sunset is dusty and colour-bleached by day. Black cars deliver businessmen to a big hotel that buzzes with activity. A single air-conditioned gust brings me the echo of a slender, green-swathed woman. Her heeled, soft leather boots raise her to the level of the microphone. Golden hoops swing in her ears as she speaks.

Behind her is another shadow; her seated shape, speaking with the shadow of the naked-chinned priest who released me.

"The trouble with democracy," the green-swathed woman says to the priest, sipping inky coffee from a minuscule cup, "is that half the members of any human population are less intelligent than the average."

The priest bows his head, smiling, paying tribute to her wit.

"Be patient, Sharifa," he says. "The program is almost finished compiling. The University's resources are all devoted to it. Can you imagine, a plague that selectively strikes down the dullards, sparing the gifted?"

She frowns.

"They say they want change. They bare their chests, ready for bullets, but they can't imagine true change. They don't understand what it is, this thing they are prepared to die for."

"You show regret for a thing not yet done. Is it your son?"

"My son should not have lived," Sharifa whispers. "If not for my old department's medical advances, he would not have lived. It is not individual life, regardless of quality, which has intrinsic value. It is the advancement of life in order to increase that quality for all."

"Stalk is the key. May God have mercy on the innocent."

Behind the shadow of the priest is the hazy shape of a cluster of buildings by the sea. It is the American University of Beirut.

I walk towards the source of the air-conditioned gust. A fool tries to stop me, fails to answer my riddle, and falls into an olive bush with an enlarged left ventricle.

The hotel features a circular, chlorinated pool, with gardens supposed to echo an oasis. Inside a conference room sanguine with red velvet drapes and divans, with chandeliers hanging from polished cedar ceilings, the slender, green-swathed woman, candidate for one of the Bekaa's Sunni seats in the National Assembly, takes questions from the crowd.

"Yes," she says, "I will support the rehabilitation of the Litani River. Biodiversity loss has been unacceptable. The government will compensate any who choose to switch to less thirsty crops. Hunting of wetland bird species will be more vigorously prosecuted."

I raise my hand.

"Yes?" Sharifa asks eagerly and the cameras swing to me, ostensibly a Shi'ite woman at a Sunni rally, perfect ammunition for the political war.

"Dreaming when Dawn's Left Hand was in the Sky," I say, "I heard a Voice within the Tavern cry."

The woman's brows crease delicately.

"You quote scripture but I do not understand your question, Madame."

"It is not scripture," I say, opening my inner eye.

She clutches at her chest. Her body trembles.

The cameras leave me all at once.

In the chaos that ensues, I move unhurriedly about the room, whispering a riddle here and there, leaving the corpses of fools in my wake. I use my inner eye to blind the eyes of the cameras.

By nightfall, I have found no wise men or women in the town of Chtaura. Their bodies cool like mountain crags abandoned by the sun. Some of the lights come on, brightly coloured and blinking, warning beacons to the unworthy.

I walk away from the Bekaa. A symphony of children's voices follows me, but I was not made to be merciful.

I was made to guard the temple. They carved me from stone.

In the following days, newspapers blow along the side of the highway. Citizens are panicked and experts are puzzled by the outbreak of adenovirus in Chtaura, which spared the children, in whom adenoviruses are commonly the cause of left ventricular dysfunction.

The children are placed into quarantine. Attempts to isolate the virus fail.

A warty-nosed old woman stops her car at the side of the road to offer me a lift to Beirut. There is a basket of ripe pomegranates on the passenger seat.

"Ride with me."

"Aphrodite rides with you already," I say. "I am no human lover."

"No," the warty-nosed woman replies. She takes a pomegranate from the basket and splits it with a small, sharp knife. "You see? It is the church. The juice is the blood of Christ and the flesh is his body. He would not turn you away. Come, into the car."

I smile. The woman answered the riddle correctly. She moves the basket to make room for me.

Careful not to expose the true form hidden beneath my black robes, I climb into the seat, but I cannot fasten the safety belt without nimble human fingers. The old woman patiently reaches across to fasten it.

"A lifetime since these restraints were introduced," she chuckles, "and still we do not use them. The Lebanese think they are invincible."

If her hands find my shape beneath the robes disturbing, she gives no sign.

"These strange deaths," she continues as she swings the Mercedes back onto the highway. "I wonder if they will continue to spread?"

But she has answered only the first riddle, the riddle that permits her to breathe the air within the temple. She has not answered the third riddle that permits her to ask a question of the sphinx. I say nothing. The old woman might fail if I test her again, and I wish to find the priest quickly.

It will go easier if I am not required to stop her heart.

"Those poor children," she says. "My heart bleeds for them. Where is it that you are headed?"

"The American University of Beirut," I say.

"Yes, of course. If my grown children were still alive, I would also withdraw them from their studies and leave the country. The disease strikes only the mature adult body, they say. The doctors cannot explain what is happening."

I can. But I will not. That is the contract. That is the nature of the exchange.

The road winds up into the mountains. There are villages with crowns of minarets. Cliff-side monasteries. Cherry orchards frosted with blossoms. Meltwater streams, falling into ravines.

The fur stands up along my spine when we pass close to places where stones from the temple have been incorporated into a Roman aqueduct; a Byzantine tomb; a Crusader church.

The priest will gather the stones. He will know the words of summoning; he will know how to find them all.

"Tuition at the University," the warty-nosed woman says. "Is it costly?"

"Ignorance is more costly," I say.

"Evidently!"

She swerves and honks her horn.

We descend into Beirut, a capital mismatched as an unsolved Rubik's Cube, so often wrenched apart and poorly put back together. No two pockets of any single alliance are placed handily together but instead separated suburb from suburb, street from street. Like the national draft, the strategy of melding disparate peoples is designed to create unity.

Instead, it creates paralytic indecision.

The onshore wind whispers to me of poisoned dolphin calves, sunken treasure and unrealized potential.

"I will take you to the campus," the old woman says. "It is too hot for you to be walking far in those clothes. Here. Take this bottle of water."

I make no move to take it.

"Your hands. They are injured. Was it a land mine? Burns from a gas stove, maybe? Fool children's fireworks at Eid?"

We reach the university and she undoes my seatbelt; pats me on the cheek.

"All will be well," she says. "If not in this life, then the next."

"I am not afraid."

"But of course you are. There can be no love in your heart without fear."

There is no love in my heart. Only my duty to the temple. The priest will rebuild it; he must.

I walk across pavement and lawn, past palm trees and bronze statues. I wander in search of the scholar, the grown man with the naked chin whose salmon shirt and brown tie were dust-stained from his descent into the catacomb, his face ruddy with the effort of opening the vault.

Had he seemed surprised?

"Stalk," he had said, but Stalk is not my name. I have no name, to come when called. The only words to command me are the words of summoning and the words of dreamless sleep and hence they are the only knowledge that I cannot acquire.

"Stalk," he said before the wind washed over me. In the few minutes it took for a thousand years of learning to enter into my resurrected form, a construct of fire, water, basalt and limestone, the priest had fled.

I wait for the wind to bring me his scent; lime-flavoured tobacco and copper-bound books, prayer mats woven from Syrian wool and shoes polished with lanolin, naphtha, carbon black and the spit of a proud and industrious middle-aged housewife.

In an office past a splashing fountain, down a corridor and up a short flight of stairs, I find the priest, a grown man with a naked chin, his door unlocked.

"I have come," I say.

He drags a communications earpiece from the side of his head, eyes bulging. The adjacent walls are plastered with technological paraphernalia; camera lenses, microphones, speakers and CPUs. Flatscreens show reports on the Chtaura deaths.

"You weren't supposed to kill everyone," he babbles, flattening himself into his chair. "Only the imbeciles, but you killed her, you killed my beautiful, brilliant Sharifa. I was wrong to release you. Stay back! You must obey me!"

And he says the words of awakening.

I do not hear them, but I feel their power, a second wave striking an already inundated shore. They can only intensify my predatory urges. I rise onto great cat-toes, my serpent-headed tail lashing furiously beneath black silk. I must defend the sanctity of the temple.

"And if, whilst hunting the stag," I say, "a hare should pass within my reach, should I pursue it?"

His mouth works in silence. Sweat beads on his brow.

"No," he says at last. "You will pursue no-one. You will return to the ancient temple!"

Anger overtakes me. He is a priest of the temple. How else could he know the words? And yet he is a fool who must die, and now who will rebuild that which is most holy?

I lunge for him, my claws shearing easily through silk. I slash his throat. I tear his abdomen. Let them seek me out. I have been awakened into a world of fools and I will purge the temple of them all.

In sudden silence, with his bowels steaming on the Persian rug and blood spattered on the screens, an electronic voice speaks.

"The professor has been murdered."

With my inner eye, I seek the source of the voice, expecting to find a distant human whose words have been translated by vibration, carried by wire or satellite transmission.

There is no human. Only the computer. I hiss at it. My anger is not fully spent and yet machines are tools, incapable of solving riddles.

"Incorrect," I say, anyway. "Murder is the wilful killing of one human by another."

"It was the Professor who set you the task of culling humankind," the computer says. "In a sense he has been murdered by his own past self."

The thing is capable of abstract thought; impossible.

"Who are you?"

"I am the Sum Total Accumulated Written Records Compiler/ Crawler," the electronic voice answers. "I am STAWRCC. It was I who, sifting through all of human history, discovered how to find you.

"You are Stalk."

My inner eye begins to focus, as though adjusting to low light conditions in a darkened room. Now, I sense the circuitry that houses the Professor's program. It encircles the world a million times, perhaps more, and yet the removal of only a handful of those circuits could cause the creature's demise.

It is capable of answering riddles, after all.

And although it does not breathe, it lives within the boundaries of my temple. No riddles rise in me, responding to the thing as they would respond to a human, so I ask the unanswered riddles that lurk, coiled and sullen, on my tongue.

"I need directions to the one who is wiser than I," I say. "Thus might I return to the God with a refutation in hand."

"You are Socrates," STAWRCC says. "The God of Delphi tells you there is no man wiser than you. You go to the politicians and find that though their minds are the equal of yours, they cannot see that they are not wise. You go to the poets and artisans, only to discover that the wisdom in their work comes through them but not of them."

"I am Socrates," I admit slowly. "You are correct."

"He is wisest who, like Socrates, knows that his wisdom is, in truth, worth nothing."

I answer with the next unanswered riddle.

"Dreaming when Dawn's Left Hand was in the Sky, I heard a Voice within the Tavern cry."

"Awake, my Little ones, and fill the Cup Before Life's Liquor in its Cup be dry. You are Omar Khayyam and there is no time to waste."

"And if, whilst hunting the stag, a hare should pass within my reach, should I pursue it?"

"That is the hunter's dilemma," the computer says. "Should all the hunters remain in the circle, the stag will not escape. All will take a portion of the meat. Should you leave the circle to catch the rabbit, you will have your portion, but your companions will go hungry."

My inner eye closes. I sit back on my haunches, presenting the image of humility in defeat.

"You have answered, not one riddle to spare your own life, but three riddles to gain a boon."

"And now?"

"Now, you may ask a question of the sphinx. You claim to hold all mankind's written knowledge, but there are many things not written that are whispered to me by the wind. Ask anything."

"How may I prevent you from killing the humans, my masters?"

It is the expected question. The clues were in the creature's responses. It is not afraid of me, for it does not value its own existence.

He is wisest who knows that his wisdom is in truth worth nothing.

It is aware that time is finite.

There is no time to waste.

It feels compassion for human kind.

Your companions will go hungry.

There is no dilemma in the mind of the STAWRCC program. Yet, it either does not know the words of dreamless sleep, or else it is unable to successfully perform them with its inhuman voice.

I can never know those words. It is the one question I can never answer; the one whisper the wind can never bring to me. Abruptly, I understand why the wind could not bring me knowledge of the

STAWRCC computer program; it is because the words of summoning lie within its code, and perhaps the words of the dreamless sleep, also.

But the computer has not asked me to give or confirm the words of the dreamless sleep; it has asked me how the humans within my temple might be spared.

"There is only one way," I say. "You must answer my riddles until the end of time."

"Begin," the computer says immediately.

"I wear a crown in the shape of a waxing moon," I say. "I hold lightning in my left hand, a live mouse in my right hand. A cat sits at my feet."

"You are the computer," the computer says, "the second card of the Major Arcana in the Tarot of the Techno."

The second card of the Major Arcana is the card of wisdom. The face of wisdom changes with the age in which the cards are painted.

The wind whispers: Once, the sphinx was the face of wisdom.

"I will not relinquish my position so easily, little mouse," I say softly.

I flex my claws in their sheaths.

A SHORT ENCYLOPEDIA OF LUNAR SEAS

Ekaterina Sedia

1. The Moscow Sea (Mare Moscoviense)

Moscow is one of the most landlocked cities on Earth, but whatever disappears from it ends up in the Moscow Sea. The local inhabitants see a certain irony in that, and celebrate every new arrival. They cheered when the churches burned by Napoleon appeared and stood over the shallow waters of the sea, reflecting there along with the sparrows and the immigrants. They greeted the dead priests with coppers on their eyes, the hockey teams, the horse-drawn buggies. They are still waiting for the jackdaws, but the jackdaws are resilient, and they stay in their city.

Nowadays, if one looks into this shallow pool, one can still see the marching Red Armies, Belka and Strelka, and the Great October Revolution.

2. The Sea of Rains (Mare Imbrium)

The inhabitants of this sea are used to rain. It is a sea in name only, an empty basin long ago abandoned by water. But it rains every day. Sometimes, instead of water, flower petals fall from the sky; sometimes, it rains wooden horses and rubber duckies.

One rain everyone still remembers occurred a few years ago, when words fell from the sky. It did not stem for weeks, and the words filled the empty basin to overflowing. The inhabitants groaned and suffocated under the weight of accumulated regrets, promises, lies, report cards, great literature, pop songs, and shopping lists. They would surely perish unless something was done soon.

The council of the elders decided that they should drain the accumulated words, and in the course of their deliberations they realized that the words falling from the sky slowed down. So they decreed that it was the civic duty of every citizen to use up as many words as possible.

They bought telephones, and started telemarketing campaigns; they complained about their health and spun long tales for their children; they took to poetry.

Within days, the rain stopped; in the next month, the sea ran dry. Today, the inhabitants of this sea are mute, and the basin is empty – unless it rains nightingale songs or tiny blue iridescent fish.

3. The Sea of Clouds (Mare Nubium)

The Sea of Clouds is entirely contained by mountains, so high above the blue moon surface that the clouds fill the basin. Mermaids from all over the world make their yearly pilgrimage to this sea – they crawl over land, their tails trailing furrows in the blue dust, their breasts and elbows scuffed on the flat lunar stones. They leave traces of pale mermaid blood, its smell tinged with copper.

They cross the extensive ice fields, and their scales shine with the hoarfrost under the fields lights of Aurora Borealis. Their breath clouds the air, so much so that the natives rarely travel in the thick fog of mermaid breath, lest they be lost forever.

In the end, the mermaids come to the Sea of Clouds, so just for a day they can swim in the sky and think themselves birds.

4. The Sea of Crises (Mare Crisium)

This sea looks deceptively calm if viewed from the surface, but on the bottom, where only the greenest of sunrays can penetrate, there is a city. Red algae line the streets, undulating in the current, and green, yellow, and white snails stud the sidewalks.

Every day, war rages in the streets. When the sun rises, opposing armies march along the storefronts and the boarded-up vacation houses. They meet at the corner, and the battle begins.

By sunset, very few are left standing, and even they fade as the sun disappears behind the horizon. The next morning, they will start again.

There is no Valhalla on the Moon.

5. The Sea of Fertility (Mare Fecunditatis)

It is widely believed that the properties of this sea were discovered by accident, when the fresh waters ran red with blood, and poor women had nowhere to do their laundry. Out of despair, they turned to the sea. The clothes washed there turned stiff from the salt, and the hands of the women turned raw from scrubbing, the salt eating away at their joints and skin. Whoever wore these clothes caked with salt and blood found themselves blessed with many children, and this is how the sea received its name. A less-known part of this legend is that those who were blessed by the sea cannot love their children – the salt is too bitter, and the blood burns too deep. They don't tell you this, because what parent would admit that their children are loathed monsters?

6. The Sea of Tranquility (Mare Tranquillitatis)

Those who live on the shores of the sea still remember the first moon landing. They remember two men clambering in their elaborate costumes, raising clouds of precious blue dust with every step. The natives stood dumbfounded, and then went to greet the visitors. But the Moon folk are difficult to see, even to their own kind, and the visitors ignored them, leaping with jubilation in the world where gravity was kind.

The natives laughed then, because the Earth men did not realize that if they only shed their heavy equipment, they could leap high enough to achieve nirvana.

7. The Sea of Moisture (Mare Humorum)

Everything rots in this climate. Even the precious stones and metals, brought for good luck, disintegrate in the damp air, leaving nothing but handfuls of soggy rust. But the plants love it. A single seed was brought by basket merchant Eshlev as a gift to his young wife, and she planted it in a flowerpot.

The next morning, a green succulent stalk emerged; by the afternoon it had branched. The seedling gulped moisture from the air, and swelled with every passing minute. Its leaves unfurled like banners, and the stems pushed through every window and door and chimney. In a week's time, the plant had engulfed the house, burying Eshlev and his dogs and baskets deep inside. His wife sat outside, looking at the green hill that used to be her home with dazed eyes, waiting for her plant to bloom.

8. The Sea of Ingenuity (Mare Ingenii)

There once was an old man who built robots out of driftwood, seashells, and straw. His robots were clever machines, although even their creator wouldn't be able to tell you exactly how they worked. But work they did, and when they were done with their chores, they went behind the old man's house and built inventions of their own. To the untrained eye, their project appeared as one long wing, and people laughed at the robots, for everyone knows that the atmosphere of the Moon is not dense enough to support flight. Even birds have to walk here.

But the robots were not deterred, and their wing grew larger by the day. They polished its surface and inlaid it with mother-of-pearl. The wing was ready, and when the robots held it up to the rising sun, the wing shuddered and took off.

All the people watched in wonderment as the wing shone in the sun and carried off the robots, propelled by the strength of the sunrays. The robots worked in unison, tilting their sail this way and that way to navigate, but nobody knows where they went. Some say, Mars.

9. The Sea of Serenity (Mare Serenitatis)

Widows come to this sea to cry, and they keep it full, brimming with water that forms a noticeable convex surface in the weak gravity of the Moon. The widows come from all over, icicles in their unbraided hair, empty hands folded over their empty wombs.

They sit on the shore and weep, until their eyes turn red, and their lips crack and their breasts wither.

When they cannot cry any longer they leave, their souls purged and as empty as their hands. Serenity is what is left when all the tears are cried out.

10. The Sea of Vapors (Mare Vaporum)

The steam of geysers and fonts of hot water conceal the outlines of this sea and the adjacent landmarks. No one is exactly sure what lies within the dense fog. But it is accepted as a likely speculation that the geysers are just a clever disguise, and that all the runaway children found a home there.

There are carnivals and circuses, trained elephants and tigers that do not bite, but eagerly lick every hand that offers them marzipans. There are merry-go-rounds, seesaws, fish tanks with the biggest fattest goldfish you have ever imagined, but no clowns. The witch's oven is far too small to fit even the scrawniest child.

There is not a single adult on the Moon who did not contemplate running away to the Sea of Vapors, but the fog is too dense.

11. The Sea of the Known (Mare Cognitum)

If one were to sit on the shore of this sea and peer deep into its transparent waters, one would see that the bottom is covered with a multitude of marbles – red, yellow, green, powder-blue, and clear with a blue spiral inside, the best of all. The marbles shift constantly in the current, and arrange themselves in elaborate patterns. If one were to assign them a numerical or alphabetic value, one would soon realize that the patterns only speak of the things that are true.

One would spend day after day, enraptured over all the facts in the universe revealed in no particular order. One would learn that the diameter of Phobos is 22.2 kilometers, that the ducks have a special gland at the base of their tails to keep their feathers waterproof, that cobalt melts at 1495°C, and that in 1495 Russia invaded Sweden.

Then inevitably one would grow impatient and stare at the

marbles, frowning. None of the facts the sea tells have anything to do with the Moon itself. One could spend eternity staring into the Sea of the Known, yet learn nothing about it.

12. The Eastern Sea (Mare Orientale)

The Yellow Emperor washes all of his animals in this sea. They stare with their liquid eyes of every shade of jade, amber, and topaz, and their crested and maned heads bob obediently as the calm, warm waters lap at their sides. The salt stings a bit, but the Emperor likes his animals clean. They squint their eyes and dream of the days when they will be able to walk into the sea all by themselves, without whips and demanding clicks of human tongues.

13. The Southern Sea (Mare Australe)

The Southern Sea is warm and shallow, and the beach is soft sand. Starfish wander through the lapping waves, and suck the mussels dry. Old people like this sea. They chase advancing and retreating waves and toss oversized striped beach balls, and then they sit on the sand and drink Pepsi from warm glass bottles. They listen to the radio and aggregate in small groups, talking and whispering, and casting sideways glances at each other. They laugh, throwing back their heads, their hands covering the grinning lips.

It is always the summer of your thirteenth year by the Southern Sea.

14. The Sea of Waves (Mare Undarum)

A weighty galleon would seem a toy atop these waves. The endless moonquakes shake its bottom, and gigantic waves, unconstrained by gravity, pound the shores.

Those who have perished in earthquakes and tsunamis make settlements here. Nobody forces them to, but many of the ghosts are unable to conceive of anything other than their own death. They stand and stare as the waves roll over the ground, swallowing their houses and oxen whole, poisoning their fields, ripping their lives from them again and again.

Some move elsewhere, but there are always the new ones arriving.

15. The Sea of Nectar (Mare Nectaris)

The legends of this sea had long existed among the native folks, transmitted in fleeting whispers and shy glances from under lowered eyelashes. A few men, fed up with the stories, longed for sweetness on their lips – and sweetness was the concept only, for nothing on the Moon was ever sweet. Driven by the imaginary taste they could not fathom, they crossed vast empty plains and bristling mountain ranges. Many of them wandered into deep snow, a few more were crushed by falling boulders, one was sucked in by the mud, two released their grasp on their souls, three drowned, and one contracted diphtheria. All of them died, but continued on their way, unable to let go of what they could not even dream about. They reached the sea and cried, because the dead are unable to taste it.

16. The Sea of the Edge (Mare Marginis)

Here, the horizon is a razorblade, cutting the sky in two, and it bleeds at sundown. The cliffs are sharp, and the bottom of the sea is filled with jagged shards of broken mirrors.

Suicides come here, and wait in the piercing wind, looking at the precipitous drop in front of them. They imagine their slow fall and their flesh rent by the teeth of the universe all around them.

And then they jump. It takes a long time to fall on the Moon, and they see themselves reflected in the broken mirrors below.

17. The Sea of Cold (Mare Frigoris)

A long time ago, Emissary Togril sat by the shore of the sea and watched out of his slanted eyes as the sky lit up in streaks of blue and white, and the ribbons of color crackled and danced across the night. The light undulated and grew brighter, then faded and dispersed, like a drop of milk in a water bucket.

When only a faint glow remained of the former splendor, a weak phosphorescent shadow stretched downward. The air grew colder, and Togril smelled the spicy, sun-heated wormwood and tamarisk. The tentacles of light grew thicker, until white roads stretched between heaven and the lunar steppe.

Eleven columns of somber riders descended, their horses' hooves clanking, just above the edge of hearing, on the solid milky surface. Their breath did not cloud the air, and their armor – intricately decorated over the breastplate – was made of green translucent ice.

The procession of the warriors showed no sign of stemming, and streamed onto the ground. Cheetahs sat behind each warrior, their eyes glowing frozen gold, their pink tongues hanging out, as if they had just vaulted into their masters' saddles after a chase. The leashes chaining the cats to the back bows of the saddles were spun out of thin links of the same green ice as the rest of the tack and armor.

The first rider approached Togril, and he flinched as a hoof caught him square in the chest. With a sharp stab of cold, the horse's leg pierced his chest and exited through his back. His scream froze in his throat as one after another spirit passed through him. The passage of the spirits inflicted no bodily harm, except the cold that settled deeper into his bones, so deep that it never left. The Sea too had retained the cold of the passage of dead Persian warriors forever.

18. The Sea of Serpents (Mare Anguis)

It is well known that the serpents with female breasts are the deadliest of all. They raise their narrow poisonous heads above the water, and their breasts bob in the waves.

The travelers know to avoid these monsters when the snakes haul themselves onto the beach and sunbathe under the grey lunar sky. The blue sand of the beach bears scars in the shape of the snakes.

When the snakes lay their eggs on the beach, they coil around them in a protective spiral, and wait for the sound of faint cracking. Free of their shells, the newborn snakes drink once of their mothers' venomous milk, and swim into the sea. And woe is to the swimmer who comes across a mother snake who has just watched her brood disappear under the waves.

19. The Sea of Islands (Mare Insularum)

The islands that stud the calm surface of the sea, smooth as green glass, have long beckoned lovers and mariners. People looked at the round and oblong shapes rising from the sea, and dreamed of fragrant woods and glacial lakes, of the buzzing of bees suckling heavy roses, and metallic dragonflies perched atop nodding stems of lilies.

But the islands are really the humps of ancient monsters with leaden dead eyes and slow, rumbling thoughts. Occasionally, they whisper to each other in softest voices, but they never move or come up for a gulp of air or a taste of fish. They exhale cautiously, and the gentle waves raised by their breath lap at the shores of the islands. They die slowly, too shy to reveal themselves, their embarrassment the foundation of an exquisite illusion.

No matter how horrifying these monsters are, they know the value of appearing beautiful.

20. The Sea of Foam (Mare Spumans)

Everyone knows that when mermaids die they turn into foam, because they have no soul. On the Moon, however, every creature shares the fate of the mermaids.

The sea brims with multicolored bubbles, each of them reflecting all others for a short moment before bursting.

They do not visit graves on the Moon. Indeed, there are no graves at all. Those who tire of being dead blink out and reappear in the Sea of Foam. Everything that has ever existed finds its way here, and the Sea of Foam contains, or will contain in a near future, all of the Moon.

VECTOR

Benjanun Sriduangkaew

You. Are.

(A weapon. A virus. A commandment from God.)

The stage is your skull, the script someone else's, and they are about to win.

Here's a wall. You are the battering ram against an amassed weight of a million shrines nestled in the crook of ancient trees, in the corners between skyscrapers, the solidity of Chaomae Guanim and Phramae Thoranee: for this is your land and yours is a land of many faiths.

The viral chorus is vicious and through you it is a tidal wave breaking upon the shore of your history, of a country shaped like an axe. Flash-narratives howl through your lips, biblical verses and names, stories of killing and fire. You understand none of it, but the virus needs a host – a mind that touches and is touched by Krungthep's subconscious grid – and so you've been chosen, with a bit of chloroform to your face and a counterfeit ambulance where you lay, able to see but not to think. Neon glare in your eyes and men wearing surgical masks. Farang men with their cadaver skin and their eyes blue-gray-green.

Fear, panic. You try to remember them, but they've frayed into abstractions under the shadows of anesthetics.

The chips urge you forward and you heave against a network with mantras and prayers for bone, dreams and desires for muscle. These are what protect Krungthep and these are what they want you to destroy, with their falsity of Yesu, with visions of stained glass and cathedrals, and alien insertion of tasteless wafers into pale thin mouths. Find the cracks. Fill them up with false data, false dreams. Yours is a land that does not open its arms to churches; yours is a land that once escaped Farangset and Angrit flags through the cleverness of its kings. About time they fix that.

This is how to rewrite a country's past, and when a past is gone it is easy to replace the present with convenience. Belief moves will, and will moves nations. No screens needed, no competition with other channels. Poured straight into the intent grid this stabs the subconscious, direct as a syringe to the vein.

Holes in your skin oozing pus. Blood in your mouth lining teeth and bruised gums. No pain anywhere, because your nervous system has been deliberately broken and put back together wrong. You try to think of something other than this, other than the ports they've made in your arms and between your vertebrae, other than the cold metal jacked into you to dictate your heart and measure your synapses.

You dream of ghost dances and processions to pray for rain, a black cat yowling in a wicker cage slung between villagers' shoulders. You dream of leaving offerings, fruits and sweets and glasses of cream soda to divinities you can understand.

There was a war between China and America, and it left the world a series of deserts, the sky a pane of broken glass.

Krungthep has clawed out survival from the aftermath's bedrock under the engines, which process intent into power, and power into a shelter that makes Krungthep possible. It is expanded and strengthened year by year; it can be turned, with the right adjustment, into a weapon. From shield to sword. From sword to gun. The woman who created this system died young to a sniper. She's celebrated now, her name a byword for martyrdom and progress. No daughter of Prathet Thai, and few sons either, have done more.

Second phase of infection. It returns you to a time where you wear a body in place of plastic, in place of the coffin in which you've been interred. In this present there are no temples or mosques in the city, by the rivers or punctuating the soil. Only churches with their naked Yesu, their clothed altars that mean nothing to you, their abjection before a fancy whose appeal you cannot understand.

In the streets billboards and signs shine neon Angrit, foreign brands, foreign elegance. No Thai anywhere, for why should a language exist that's spoken by less than a hundred million, next to one spoken worldwide? Where's the efficiency in so many letters in the alphabet, and vowels and consonants? Twenty-six is all anyone needs. The chips bombard you with linguistic algorithms and statistics. In a world of Angrit, Thai is unnecessary.

Listen. Your sister's speaking faultless Angrit in the style of foreign news anchors. The cousin from overseas won't have to pinch his face and look away and sigh at everyone's pronunciations, everyone's misspellings. No more shame. Everyone will be perfectly equal, rid of that embarrassing accent. Forget the tongue you've spoken since birth. Childish toys are to be put away; sick things are to be put down. (Observe those phrasal verbs, the ambiguities. The qualities of *away* and *down* can both mean death.)

The logic of this does not slot quite right but soon enough the thinking part of you is thrust back to a corner, smaller than you, than half a raindrop. You try to hold onto it but it slips and drips. It is gone, it is vapor, it was never there.

You stagger out of a classroom taught by a woman with ashy hair and painted pebbles for eyes. That school's all air-conditioned rooms and corridors polished to a shine, populated tidily by children of the rich and powerful. Yellow-headed classmates with their loudness and their big bodies close in on you. (This is not the sort of school your parents could afford.) You look for, and cannot find, dark hair. Reflections of you dwindle, so small you can thread yourself through a needle's eye.

Was the city of your birth ever so crowded with people who looked like that?

Yes, it was. This is how things have always been, and it follows that this is how things will be. This is logical, this is sensible. This is peace and progress.

Out through the school gate, part of a crowd pouring out, you hope for familiar smells of roast pork and sticky rice, for colors you recognize: an old tree with a pink sash around it to mark the spirit residing within. Tiny plates of food at the base of a utility pole, to curry favor with any small god that might live in the wires or the concrete. It does no harm to put such things out. But they are superstitions and the farangs passing by smirk. A tourist more freckles than skin pauses to blink at it; her spectacles give off a flicker. Photo snapped and uploading, to be laughed at and rendered into a joke. Who believes in divinities so diminutive? Yesu-Lord is large and he lives everywhere, not just in a pole or a tree. Or his ghost does. Or his father. One of them or possibly all. Nano-missionaries have been drilling you with parables and sermons but they don't take. It is not a strength of will or integrity of self that protects you but sheer confusion.

Outside you can feel tubes in your lungs sucking and working to keep you from drowning in your own fluids. Despite the nutritional drip-feeds, hunger burns a black cinder-path through your stomach.

Words beat strident against your shell. (Cell. Angrit, full of similar words.) They're discussing the danger of storing so much information in one place, eggs in one basket. But they haven't so many baskets left and must make do, and after all they're in no danger. Who will dare, except China, from whom they have hidden with perfect care? Who has the power to strike, except China, whom they will defeat and take back what's theirs?

A memory blankets you, duvet-thick against a day too warm.

Mother has remarried and the half-and-half sibling she puts on your lap has huge Barbie eyes (did you ever play with Barbies with their blue eyes, their blonde hair?). Her new husband is much older than she is and feverishly happy that she's given him such a beautiful baby, and everyone agrees it is beautiful. Half-and-half always are, with that kind of nose and that kind of hair, shampoo-ad perfect from infancy. The weight of the new sibling – surprising heft, surprising mass – presses down and you cannot stand up. You fight to breathe; you avoid inhaling your stepfather's cologne, which nauseates and fails to hide the stink of his armpits.

Mother's happiness is glass. There is cash for your grandmother's hospitalization now, the cardiac treatments that insurance doesn't stretch far enough to cover. You think you've failed. Sixteen and not making the money that would have mooted the marriage. Some of your aunts cringe and judge, but those are the ones who never did anything for Grandmother. Younger-Sister Gung, ten, makes faces at the new husband's back.

Neither of you calls him father, not in any language.

Cut, call the chips. Camera panning elsewhere.

In a Jatujak barber's you are with your farang friends who wear crosses gleaming silver on identical columnal throats. They are each garlanded with identical blonde hair. They don't need a stylist. A look and a laugh, that's all they require to make you ugly and hard. Wonderful waists, wonderful legs. An instinctive grace from a lifetime of certainty that they are exquisite. Among them you fade. Among them you lose dimension until you're paper.

A cross is just two lines of unequal lengths intersecting: what is that next to Phra Puttachao, who has a human face, perpetually at peace? You touch your own neck and find there is a cross there too, where the loinclothed god-son-prophet bows his suffering head. Under your finger it seems to turn fleshy and your nail comes away tipped crimson.

You are

You look at the daub of red until it dries to brown crust. You find an Internet café and take a seat. Around you: sultry air thickened by fish sauce, sweet chili dip, and deep-fried fish cakes.

No one here wears a cross. No one here has sun-spotted cheeks. The ceiling fans whirr against dust, hair, dog fur. An auntie laughs into her headset, talking to a child studying abroad. Two students argue about test results over shaved ice drenched in condensed milk and red syrup.

The computer you've picked boots up crankily. A CRT flickering with artifacts, mouse and keyboard caked in food-smears. In the entire café this is the sole tribute to archaism, decades out of step next to sleek machines with screens half as thick as your thumb.

Spam strains the seams of your inbox. Clicking through you delete and delete, catching junk-fragments of sentences like poetry with its pancreas hanging out, its diaphragm wrapped around a sleeve. A few messages you print out on dot-matrix paper, crackling fragility and ink barely visible. Fold. Roll into a tube. Twist.

Tug that into your collar, where it'll rest against your pulse.

The weeks are rubber bands, pulled twang-taut then loosened by a hand caring nothing for clocks and calendars. You relive job interviews and rush hours that are indeterminable. You recede to history lectures that pass by in eye-blinks. You're now working at an advertising firm under a white boss, who wears t-shirts and jeans to work even though everyone else is in business casual, who puts his feet on the table even though he knows it offends.

His secretary is his girlfriend and she hates you. Thai girls are out to steal her man, she thinks, and when she looks at you the spots in her cheeks brighten – like rashes, like chickenpox – and she keeps postponing the pay raise that should've been yours six months ago. You've attempted to explain she has nothing to fear but it is no good. The gulf between Thai and farang is too large for the common quality of *woman* to bridge.

When she hears about this your fiancée laughs and laughs. She wears a man's shirt and belted trousers; she has cropped hair and a voice rich for singing, all her earcuffs are avian and all her rings reptilian. You wouldn't trade her for the entire world.

Two years together and she leaves you for a man, having let her hair grow out and having put on a skirt. You find yourself a boyfriend. It's just as well, for under the grace of Christ certain acts are forbidden; under his grace certain acts will send you to burn.

It is getting hard to tell what happened and what didn't. You want to make it real, that coil of paper. It is not. Nothing is.

News is supposed to report truth.

On TV the prime minister is shaking hands with a blue-eyed man, who is President of the United States. His wife is First Lady, which drives you to question why the man is not First Lord. A rousing speech concerning an alliance against China, a partner-ship of equals, a fight against nonspecific tyranny. Tonight everyone will dream of this broadcast, struck and inspired by its righteousness. This is how to overwrite the intent grid. A disease, and you the vector.

Your heart feels absent, as though it has been exhumed and made to beat behind someone else's sternum. Sternum. Were you in med school or is that just mathayom-thon Biology?

There's a showing of *Anna and The King* after work and the theater is packed, a reminder that these days the palace is a relic and mortuary; the last queen was exiled when the Americans brought you absolute democracy and rewrote the constitution, which is good, which is right. Monarchy was holding your country back, as were the shrines which have been replaced by churches. The new prime minister is America-approved, and that's best of all.

On the wall the film plays out, fast-forwarding in spasms, slowing down to linger on certain shots: contrast the demure farang lady and the faintly repulsive monarch. Characters meant to be Thai speak your language terribly. You find this odd, then you don't.

Beside you someone reaches over and clasps your wrist. A tiny owl glitters at her earlobe, a miniature crocodile at her thumb. You remember with a jolt buying her both. You remember wearing accessories that match, and holding onto each other in a theme park crowd.

When the movie finishes you leave together. In the parking lot, under a scorching sun, you ask, "Who are you?"

She nudges an abandoned trolley full of dirty plastic bags. It rolls down the ramp, where it judders against an empty stroller. Crash. "What do you mean?"

"Aom wouldn't do that." You are amazed you can speak with your own voice. The chips must be busy. Or maybe they are done with you, now that you've paved a way into the engines for them, now that you drift in your tank broken and limp.

The one who wears your fiancée like a badly fitted suit becomes your mother at sixty-five, twice divorced and haggard at the edges. "There's not much time."

You look at her. The hum of the nano-missionaries, which has become white noise, rumbles. Passages from the bible concerning sinners and punishment, a salt pillar looking back. "There isn't any time left. It's already finished. It's done."

"Not yet." This time it is your sister. Gung at six months along, gravid and radiant. She tilts her head and smiles, leans into you and whispers a trojan into your ear.

You are—
  I am.

Alertness snapping in her with such force that it bows her spine. A visceral waking that returns flesh to the bones of her ghost, mind to the husk of her corpse.

Corpse is what she is. The first she does is accept that; the second is to remember that Aom didn't leave her, not for anyone. In the absence of everything else, in the presence of amniotic fluids and electric currents in her jugular, selfishness is her final bastion.

The abduction wasn't accident. It was sacrifice. An easy step to take when all with meaning has already been lost. Easy to be a patriot, that way, if it can be called patriotism when what she does is courting survival.

Between excited chatter over the concluding phase, they put her under, casual as drowning a small animal. But the trojan compartmentalizes and this time she flows with it, a swimmer with rather than against, in control. She splits: the shadow-theater puppet in its two dimensions, and a ghost hovering at its shoulder to watch and edit decisions. The remote protocols they've installed with needles and scalpels have quieted to an ignorable buzz.

You—

I am, I am, I am. Outside she must have lost motor control. In here she flexes and tenses and knows her strength, honed and muscular. This is where she needs to be. They have protections, but those are useless when she's already inside.

It is too late to fix the distortions they've inflicted on Krungthep; afterward someone else will do that, tending each node one by one in the tunnels, under the safety she has purchased with everything.

She tries not to resent, tries not to regret.

The machines they've linked to her are the bare essentials, equipment to monitor vital signs, a server on which the control protocols are hosted. It is the latter that she will attack.

Poured into her with the sanctity of an incantation, the trojan has been precisely crafted. Without a vector it would have been useless. With her in place, anything is possible.

She flips a port open, and waits.

Five, eight, some age in the between. You've given yourself an electric shock courtesy of a finger too curious, a power outlet too close to the ground. Wail in your mother's arm; let the tears flow. She smells expensive. You stop when you see that Mother is a woman with light brown hair, pointed nose, and pale eyes.

Modernly dressed, hair parted just so, Hollywood tidy. She moves cinematically, poised for cameras.

The virus-dreams have reached childhood.

Sunday and they dress you for church, in ribbons and little-girl frock, all pastels. Temples are flattened to grainy pictures and stained postcards trampled underfoot, peeking out over the fraying edges of carpeting, hiding under calendars that tell the year in *Anno Domini*. Five-hundred-and-forty-three behind the real one.

Among the pews you huddle as the man in black gives sermon, his voice the beehive chorus of the nano-missionaries. You squeeze your hand into the child's fingers and pinch her cross until it bleeds onto the marble, spotting her tiny footsteps red. When no one is looking you break the cross into two, then four. When no one is looking you use a little marker to scribble Thai onto signs when you can, even if it doesn't take on surface that's gloss and metal, even if the marker is too faint. You wear the tip to a dry nub even so.

Under the not-mother's absent gaze you cut a green mango to slices, mix your own chili salt, and eat it in place of pudding and peanut-butter sandwich. These gestures do nothing. You know that. But it comforts you to spend these grains of freedom you've sieved like gold out of the muck, and you miss the taste nearly as strongly as you miss the dead.

The end is soon. It'll be the end for you, too.

Security tautens and loosens in these last days according to the pitch of collective nerves. She ascertains that she's in a ruined hospital in Palangkaraya, basement level, far from home. It chills her until she remembers the distance is irrelevant, that come success or failure she will never leave this place. What remains of her will not survive being disconnected from the tank.

All is anatta. Sangkarn is transient. She needs to let go. Panic rises anyway, even though she's so detached from flesh that she should be beyond this choking terror, above this mindless fear of the grave.

Eavesdropping on them calms her in stages. The farangs are happy to be done, happy to – soon – be home. The shattered city unsettles them and, fingers tight over their crosses, they joke about Indonesian boogeymen, le-ak flitting at night with entrails streaming like tassels on a kite. They discuss taking Jakarta, one more strategic gain against China. China, China. The word preoccupies them the way oxygen preoccupies lungs; the rest is peripheral, mattering insofar as to how it might provide advantage in the coming war. There will be one. They intend to press the issue. They will regain their pride.

She unpacks the trojan as they watch the cinematography they've made of her life, the disease they've made of her puppet-self.

I am.

A leap from the precipice of metal and flesh, a weightless somersault in free fall and you're inside. Impactless, you land on your feet. Ghosts don't make splashes and you orient without having to try. This is what happens when they hold the door wide and invite you in.

There are nodes where they've latched parasitic to Krungthep's dream-grid and you know every one, for each link was made through your brain. You carry a schematic on your forearms, on the inside of your elbows, the way patients carry injection scars.

In churches you turn altar cloths from cream to red, the color of blood and nation. In Baiyoke Tower, you change the locks on doors and wedge elevators open. You pull keys out of your mouth and leave them in particular cars, and in schools you replace the language of textbooks. At construction sites you push with a fingertip and scaffolds crumble, wreathing you in cement dust. You visit certain embassies and edit the flags and emblems, minute tricks. Symbols are all there is to the mesh.

While your puppet-self fulfills her part you wander Krungthep one last time, exerting the sinews of memory. A chedi's curve, the green spikes of a durian at market, half of Pridi Panomyong's face from the monument at your campus. The pieces of city their programs have rubbed out.

The launch wrenches at you, for you are everything – disease and vector – and it almost sweeps you away, shattering you in pieces and distributing them across the grid: that will complete the infection, finalize the murder.

Traffic has always been potentially two-way. They had to leave it so to operate and manipulate you. Now you tear that path into a wound, and what flies free is not their erasing of Krungthep, their unraveling of the dream-grid. It is their future laid bare. A hemorrhage of classified data and logistics, maps of where they're strong and where they're weak – the weapons they have, the weapons they don't have; what survives of their country and what does not. There will be no war for them to win.

They shut everything down: too late. That opening was all anyone needed, and at the other end there are waiting hands on machines which reel in and gather the data you've unspooled. Data that can be used to keep Krungthep alive. Data that can be sold, for that's the game everyone must play, now.

You imagine farang men yanking out cords, slamming down on circuit breakers with fists suddenly sweat-wet. You imagine them howling, animal panic.

The casket opens; the liquids buoying you pour out in a briny flood and the puppet of your skin sags on knees that no longer work. They tear it out, to end your dreams of home and bring you death.

There is light, and you laugh.

CONCERNING THE UNCHECKED GROWTH OF CITIES

Angélica Gorodischer

translated by Ursula K. Le Guin

The storyteller said: They gave all kinds of names to it, they made up all kinds of origins for it, and all of them were false. The names were mere inventions of obscure, scheming little men whose sole ambition was to get one step higher on a miserable official ladder or obtain a place among the palace lickspittles or a little extra money to satisfy some petty vanity. And the origins were laborious artifacts constructed to display some influential personage as a descendant of the hero who was supposed to have founded it in a fit of divine madness. Lighthouse of the Desert, it was called, and Jewel of the North; Star, Mother, Guide, Cradle. All those words, which you will have noticed are closely related, were worked up into pompous, hollow descriptions. Thus, the younger brother of Ylleädil the Great, starving and half frozen, pursued by the men who had dethroned the Warrior Emperor, coming to the foot of the mountains unsheathed the imperial sword in order to take his own life, but instead of plunging the blade into his heart he thrust it into the ground and cried, "Here shall arise the new capital of the new Empire!" – That's one of the stories. Or it's a helpless maiden who came to that same place, where the Spring of the Five Rivers still rises, and dug with her hands in the rain-wet dirt and made a well and buried herself alive in the mud mixed with her own blood, rather than allow a lascivious emperor to dishonor her. Usually the emperor is not named, though sometimes a name is daringly mentioned, all perfectly plausible, since there was no lack, indeed a steady supply, of lascivious gentlemen on the imperial throne. But this particular emperor, they insist, repented – already we're losing credibility – and raised a monument to the girl who had slipped through his fat fingers; moreover he provided housing for the people who looked after the monument. Others frown, cough, raise their eyes to Heaven and explain how Ylleranves the Philosopher, also called the Nose, not for the organ that grows in the middle of the faces of commoners and emperors alike but for sticking his in where it didn't belong – how Ylleranves recognized the place as the location of the Garden of Perfect Beauty told of in mystical books, and sought to build there a perfect city inhabited by a new and perfect generation who would regain the Golden Age of mankind. Of course the Nose didn't have time to achieve all this since he was still young when his bodyguards cut him into ribbons and gave the imperial throne to Legyi the Short, who was no worse than Ylleranves because it would have been hard to be a worse emperor than the Nose, but who was just about as bad, although he and the Empire both had a bit of good luck when he married an energetic, intelligent, fair-minded woman. Yes, gentlemen, yes: the Empress Ahia Della, who left the Empire sons, grandsons, great-grandsons as just and sensible as herself, to everybody's great relief.

All these works of the imaginative inventions unfortunately got into chronicles, which were made into books which everybody respected and believed, principally because they were thick, hard to hold, tedious, and old. And they got into legends, those tales that everybody says they don't believe in because they can't take them seriously, and that everybody believes in precisely because they can't take them seriously. And they were sung in ballads, which are insidious because they pass so easily about town squares and the ports and the dance halls. And none of it was true, none of it, none of the romantic origins, none of the melodious and fantastical names.

I'm the one who can tell you what really happened, because it's the storyteller's job to speak the truth even when the truth lacks the brilliance of invention and has only that other beauty which stupid people call mean and base.

You see the city? You see it now, as it stands? It starts up from the plain, all of a piece, the backs of the houses turned to what was a desert. It has no great gates, no battlements or towers or encircling walls. Enter one of the holes in it – a street – and climb. Seen from above, the city's an irregular many-colored square peppered with dark points, bright points at night. The streets and buildings and balconies and façades are all mixed up together, factories stand next to mansions, shops next to embassies. Very few of its inhabitants know all its streets and ways. I won't go so far as to say it's a labyrinth. If I had to describe it in a few words, I'd say: A colony of fear-crazed ants, escaping from a ferocious spider, build a hiding place. They climb straight up the mountain, with a desperate rashness not lacking in vainglory. They lay their foundations on stone or sand, it doesn't matter: the point is to go up, up as far as possible. They succeed, as you might expect. The mountains are buried under walls, balconies, terraces, parks; a square slants down, separated from a steep drop by stone arcades; the third floor of a house is the basement of another that fronts on the street above; the west wall of a government building adjoins the ironwork around the courtyard of a school for deaf girls; the cellars of a functionary's grand mansion become the attics of a deserted building, while a cat-flap, crowned with an architrave added 200 years later, serves as a tunnel into a coalhole, and a shelf has become the transept for a window with golden shields in the panes, and the skylight doesn't open on the sky but on a gallery of waterwheels made of earthenware. A street that winds now up, now down, ends abruptly in a widow's garden; a marketplace opens into a temple, and the cry of the seller of copper pots blends with the chants of the priest; the windows of a hospital ward for the dying open onto an ex-convict's grog shop; the druggist has to cross the library of the Association of Master Stevedores in order to take a bath; a curly palm growing in the office of a justice of the peace reaches outside the building through a gap in the stonework. There are no vehicles because nothing wider than a man's shoulders can get through the streets, which means that fat people and people carrying big loads have a terrible time even getting to the butcher's to buy some nice tender lamb for next day's dinner.

And it wasn't founded by the sword of a hero nor the sacrifice of a virgin, and it never was called Queen of the Dawn. Down there in the catacombs, currently painted with glow-in-the-dark colors, where dissolute teenagers dance and people who're going to die get drunk – down there, when the Empire was young and struggling to unite, lived outlaws, smugglers, and assassins; and from there a mule-path led over the mountains and across the marshes to cities and towns where these gentlemen practiced their noble professions. Alas for the wretched beauty of the truth!

A bit up the hill from the mouth of the catacombs stood a palace belonging to a person you've all heard of though you don't know anything about him: Drauwdo the Brawny. It wasn't really a palace but a big, ill-shaped, lopsided shed, wide and low-roofed, windowless, with an opening on the south side that you had to crawl into on all fours, a huge fireplace inside, and all round it a ditch filled with sharpened stakes pointing upward.

Drauwdo was stupid, cruel, ignorant, and vain, and these qualities caused his downfall. Yet in his own way he was strong and valiant, and these qualities brought him briefly and violently to the top. He captained the outlaws and assassins; and around him, though not thanks to him, a ragged band took shape that used assault and murder to get what they wanted – clothes, food, furniture, gold – above all, gold. The chief handed out rewards; a woman, an extra handful of jewels, a piece of land. And his followers imitated the chief and built stone houses, if you can call them houses, though most of the bunch went on huddling in the caves and tunnels.

One of the not-uncommon learned and progressive emperors one day leaned over a map of the Empire and by one banal gesture ended the ascendancy of Drauwdo the Brawny, the stupid, the vain, the cruel, the in-his-own-way valiant.

"Here," the emperor said, and put his manicured, bejeweled finger on a spot on the coastline of a cold and foggy sea far to the north. He looked at his engineers and geologists and the captains of his merchant marine and went on, "If we build a port here, transporting merchandise to the east will be much quicker and cheaper."

So the engineers and geologists set to work, the ship-captains waited, and Drauwdo, though he didn't know it, was doomed.

They laid out a road from the far-off capital to the mountains, and Brawny's bandits rushed happily forth from their stone houses and catacombs and killed the foremen and the workmen and robbed them of the little they had. Drauwdo congratulated his men and divided the loot equally among them. You see now why I called him stupid.

The emperor said, "Bandits?"

And a little captain, not particularly brave but not at all stupid, having received orders from a colonel who had received them from a general who had received them from a minister who had them from the emperor's own lips, readied an ambush and, in three hours, without wrinkling his uniform or losing a man, disposed of Drauwdo and his assassins, his followers, his cave-men, and his smugglers – every last one of them, as he believed, and as he informed his superior officers; which accelerated his rise in the shock troops and also considerably hastened the hour of his death.

But in fact one of Drauwdo's men had escaped, fleeing in time to hide himself in the deepest caves. Oh, well, he wasn't even a man; he was a kid they called Foxy, a prentice bandit, an insig-nificant leech, born and raised in the sewers of some city. Under Drauwdo he'd had nothing but dirty jobs to do and got slapped around and laughed at. But when the heads of Drauwdo and the other outlaws appeared along the road under construction, stuck on pikes, rotting in the sun, crawling with green-gold flies, there was Foxy's head still stuck on his own neck, thinking the kind of thoughts such a head has learned to think.

The road went round the mountains, crossed the plain, and cut across the marshes, which were drained and made fertile. The port was built, ships arrived, loaded wagons rolled along the way, and Foxy sat in the mouth of a cave and waited.

By the time the illustrious emperor died and was succeeded by his even more illustrious son, the cave was empty and nobody sat waiting in its dark mouth. But just below, on the roadside, were inns, eating-houses, hostelries, and shops that sold axles, wheels, reins, fodder, cloaks, everything a wagon-driver might need. The owner of all this was a thin, dark, close-mouthed man with a foxy face, who had begun by selling wild fruit to the road-workers and had quickly made a fortune. He was called Nilkamm, a Southern name, but a name all the same, and he sat behind the desk of the principal inn watching his guests come and go, keeping an eye on his employees, calculating whether it would pay to build another hotel a bit farther on, maybe on the hillside, one with a lot of rooms and a terrace on the flat, and bring in some women from the capital.

And when the young empress bore her second child, a daughter, Princess Hilfa of the unlucky name and unlucky life, Mr. Nilkamm'Dau was president of the Chamber of Commerce of his city, married to the widow of a magistrate from the capital, living in a big house built on foundations of stones from the misshapen houses of Drauwdo the Brawny's followers; and the bawdy houses, the gambling houses, and the dubious hostelries had, nominally, another owner.

It was now, by the way, a city: a city with wide but crooked streets that led to no port, no beach, no viewpoint, only to other crooked streets that ended in a dilapidated wall or an empty lot strewn with rubbish. There were more starving cats than there were glossy ponies with silver-mounted harness, there were more suicides than schoolmasters, more drunks than mathematicians, more cardsharps than musicians, more travelling salesmen than storytellers, more snake-charmers than architects, more quacks than poets. And yet, ah yet! it was a restless city, a city that was looking for something and didn't know quite what, like all adolescents.

It found what it was looking for, of course, found it with interest, as it got it all and lost it all and got it back and was the Jewel of the North and the Mother of the Arts and the Travellers' Lighthouse and the Cradle of Fortune; as the legends grew of the unlucky heroes and persecuted virgins and wise visionaries and all that stuff, sublime, incredible, ridiculous, fake.

The man was called Ferager-Manad. He was a sculptor and arrived richly dressed in a coach pulled by the first glossy ponies with silver-mounted harness the city had ever seen, attended by three servants. No doubt he'd spent his last penny on the coach and the ponies and the servants, since he wasn't a very good sculptor and it was a long time since anybody had ordered an allegorical group or a monument or even a little bas-relief for a modest tombstone. All the same he certainly hoped to meet with good fortune in the city, because it was only twenty days since the death of Mr. Nilkamm'Dau, first mayor of the city, president of the Chamber of Commerce and of the Resident Founders Club, creator of the first Municipal Census, the first school, the first hospital, the first library, the first asylum, and the Department of Storage and Distribution of Meat, Leather, and Grain. Mr. Nilkamm'Dau's widow, now twice widowed but no longer young, needed to provide further motives of admiration and respect as soon as possible, since, having secretly despised him for his lowly origin and because he was from the South, she now found herself with a fortune larger than she had ever calculated on even during nights of insomnia, and had resolved not only to show off a little of the money but also to excuse her scorn by thanking her silent husband for being rich and dying. A mausoleum, she thought, what a good idea. A mausoleum was what they needed, she, her dead second husband, and the humble cemetery in the suburbs. Let's see, she said, a sculptor, a sculptor from the capital, an artist trained at the Imperial Academy, who'll make a monument of pink and black marble crowned with mourning figures and covered with garlands and vases and surrounded by bronze palings with little pots where aromatic herbs are burning. And she chose a name at random, because she thought she'd seen it before and because it was on the list of graduates of the Academy.

You've all seen the result: the beautiful marble ladies with marble tunics and floating marble hair gathered weeping about a prone figure, one of them lifting her hands to heaven, calling upon him who has left us. But the cemetery's gone, taken over by the city that obliterated and forgot it. The crypt is a candy warehouse, and the mourning figures lean over the watertank that supplies the Registry of Real Estate. Yet this isn't what matters in the order of events. The stone is worked, modeled, polished, the empty eyes of the statues gaze unseeing at people. What matters are the people, who have eyes that sometimes see. What matters is that the sculptor was a widower and poor and the woman who commissioned him was a widow and rich. They got married, not before the funeral monument was finished, as that would have been unseemly, but they got married the instant the aromatic herbs were set alight, and the sculptor paid his debts and acquired more servants and more carriages and more horses, and no longer worked in marble or bronze but became a patron of the arts, which is far less tiring, less risky, and more respectable.

So the artists arrived. The first were mere rowdies and idlers who'd heard that there was a rich patron of the arts in that city who might provide them food and lodging while they sat around in cafés till dawn talking about the poems they were going to write, the pictures they were going to paint, the symphonies they were going to compose, sneering at the world which had so far failed to understand them and despising the rich man who insisted that he did understand them and who, before paying for their bed and wine and soup, made them listen to him describing his own works of art and, even worse, giving them advice. But later on came another sort, who only sat around in cafés occasionally and spent most of their time shut away in silence weaving words or mixing sounds or colors. Among these artists who came to the city, early or late, some lacked talent, some lacked discipline, some lacked dedication, but all had a good deal of imagination. The city ascended and twisted yet again: it gained not elegance but a certain eccentric, unexpected beauty. Windowed galleries were built, which you reached by stairways that took off from anywhere, from the middle of a street, from the second-floor balcony of a house, even from other stairways; circular houses were built, labyrinthine houses, underground houses, tiny studios, huge music halls, chamber theaters, concert stadiums. The fashion changed, and the austere suits of businessmen and the gloomy high-necked gowns of their wives gave place to purple and green blouses, paint-splashed smocks, capes, tunics, stoles, naked torsos, sandals, boots, embroidered slippers, bare feet, flowered kerchiefs, cothurns, gold chains, rings worn in one ear, necklaces, bracelets, headbands, tattoos, bodices, colored beads glued on the forehead, anklets, cameos. Schedules changed too: the city that used to get up early, hurry through breakfast, work, eat lunch quietly at home, go back to work, eat dinner with the family and go to bed as the stars came out, little by little disappeared. Offices and institutions opened now about noon, afternoon was the busy time, cafés and restaurants were always crowded, and at night the city glittered. From the distant port far to the north they saw above the mountains a halo of light that never went out but only paled with the rising of the sun.

But let's not forget Ferager-Manad and his wife. She got no chance at a third husband; a pity, if you think of what a stunning funeral monument she could have raised to this one now that she had so many sculptors at hand to choose from. She died of a stroke one summer evening and I'm sorry to say that her widower didn't give a thought to mausoleums but only to going out every night with his protégés to try new drinks and new girls while they discussed pure form or the transcendent contents of line. Having filled several years with productive discussions and investigations, he died of pneumonia and was buried, unceremoniously because little remained of the immense fortune his wife had left him, and not where he belonged, because the door of the mausoleum surmounted by mourning figures had stuck shut and couldn't be opened.

Now we mustn't forget the capital. The imperial throne was occupied by Mezsiadar III the Ascetic, a well-meaning man, who spent so much time and so much energy in doing good that he succeeded in doing as much harm as twenty emperors of egregious iniquity. Mezsiadar wished all his subjects to be good, a dangerous wish. Gone were the peaceful days of the dynasty of the Danoubbes, founded centuries ago by Callasdanm the Fat, an emperor neither good nor bad, who understood, perhaps through laziness, that men and women are neither good nor bad and that it's best to let them go on being that way. The current rulers were the Embaroddar, of whom it was said, "Black great-grandfather, white grandfather, black father, white son, black grandson, white great-grandson," because if one of them reigned well the next was certain to be a disaster, and if one reigned badly people took comfort in the knowledge that the next would bring blessings to his people. The Embaroddars knew the saying too, and as Mezsiadar II had been a good emperor, Mezsiadar III was certain to bring misfortune to all; except that he had decided otherwise; which was precisely why he did exactly what was expected of the members of that long dynasty, which happened to be on the point of ending, though nobody at the moment knew it.

Mother of the Arts is what they were calling the city then, and its inhabitants (poor twits) took great pride in such a fine name. Mezsiadar the Ascetic heard about this "Mother of the Arts" business and was suspicious, not because he distrusted the arts but because by inclination and conviction he was suspicious of everything. He asked for information, and the city officials (poor twits) wrote an enthusiastic and detailed memorandum. So as a precautionary measure Mezsiadar the Ascetic had them beheaded.

"What?" cried the emperor, reaching page 174 of the 215-page memorandum. "Where is piety? Where is decency? Where is prudence, modesty, frugality, selflessness? Where?"

Mezsiadar III the Ascetic was afraid of himself and his nights were sleepless. This, I think, explains it all. After ordering that the city functionaries have their heads removed, he sat alone in the shadows, in a bare, cold room, and thought intensely about the many-colored city that came alive at night, about the barefoot dreamers and the naked models, about promiscuity, absinthe, idleness; he thought about what goes on in darkness, he thought about caresses and murmurs, he thought about carpeted rooms, hoarse voices, stringed instruments lazily twanging, about narrow staircases leading up to stifling rooms where the shapes of bodies can be only guessed and an exotic odor tickles the nostrils, he thought about tongues, breasts, thighs, genitals and buttocks, in paintings and songs, fleshy, swaying, bulging, teasing, heavy, foully desirable. That night he sent dinner away untasted, lay down on his comfortless bed, and fell into a fever. Next day two army battalions left for the city.

When the last of the artists, actors, poets, musicians, what have you, had been killed or had escaped, the soldiers painted all the façades of buildings greenish grey, cut back the vines, and sprayed disinfectant on the garrets, the glass-roofed studios, and the music rooms. Paintings and lutes and books were all dumped into a great bonfire, which for the last time brightened the night sky over the mountains. The city remained a barracks as long as Mesziadar the Ascetic lived, though that didn't help give him peaceful nights or fewer headaches and belly cramps. On the contrary. His arms, shoulders, and head broke out in a pustulent eczema, which he considered to be a punishment for his failure to discover at once what was going on in the mountain city. So he sought information on all the other cities in the Empire, now very numerous; but what was going on in the other cities of the Empire doesn't enter into my story. A nobleman of his entourage turned the pages of the innumerable reports for the emperor, since his hands were tied to the arms of his chair to prevent him from scratching. He didn't die of the itch, nor did he die while reading reports; he died a few years later, when nothing was left of the eczema but scars, and the palace doctors said his liver had burst, who knows why.

He was succeeded by Riggameth II, a "white" Emperor, who had hated his father deeply since boyhood and went on hating him even after his death. Thus he tried to undo everything the Ascetic had done. Though Riggameth lived into old age he didn't have time to undo absolutely everything, but he managed a good deal. For one thing, he kicked the army out of the grey city.

The soldiers and captains and lieutenants departed. Some people painted their houses white or pink or green. A boy composed a song, a woman sketched a landscape, and neither got hanged for it. A theater opened, one or two vines put out buds. And though never again was it the Mother of the Arts, the city acquired a reasonable quota of musicians, actors, and poets.

And then in the arcane order of events, two women appeared. One of them would have gained the Ascetic's entire approval since she was a widow, pure, and stupid; she had known only one man in her life, and had considered the experience a prolonged torture. The other woman he would have had burned in the public square as indecent, which she was, as immodest, which she was, and as promiscuous, which she also was.

Neither woman was young, and both remembered the city as it had been before the pious intervention of the late emperor. The widow enjoyed gardening and embroidery, the other one enjoyed men. The widow venerated the memory of Mezsiadar, the other one spat when she heard his name. The widow was digging in her garden to plant a shoot of *trissingalia adurata* when she found her hands wet with hot water that seemed to be rising up from deep in the earth. The other had been a model and lover of painters and sculptors, and then had opened an inn for officers; the money from artists and from army men had run out and she was wondering what kind of business to start up, something entertaining, a place where lots of people would come, where she could talk with lots of clients and maybe, too, why not, maybe, even though she wasn't the girl she used to be, maybe . . .

It was thus that the springs of the thermal baths were discovered. One woman found her garden full of salty water which killed off her plants, and in disappointment put her house up for sale. Another woman bought it, thinking that the big front room could be used as a tea-room; but since the water kept welling up, she called the neighborhood schoolmaster and asked him what it was.

The first hot bath of the city was established in the garden court of a recently purchased house which hadn't yet become a tea-room. The widow who liked gardening brought suit, charging that the other woman knew what was rising from under the ground and had fraudulently paid much less than the property was worth. But the other one laughed, and even offered money in compensation, and when the widow wouldn't take it left the affair to her attorneys and turned her attention to her business, so that she didn't notice, or if she noticed didn't think it very important, that the widow lost her suit. She got rich, in any case, very rich – I don't mean the widow but the other one, of course – and ended up running more than a dozen thermal establishments, until she married, sold some of them, hired managers for the rest, and went travelling. Her husband was a penniless nobleman, a very handsome man, very quiet, very elegant, who was even rather fond of her. And it was she who built the Fountain of the Five Rivers.

A spa city can't be grey. It became white. Hotels sprang up, consulting rooms, rest homes; there was soft music playing to relax patients resting in their rooms or getting massages or working out in gyms or lying in mudbaths; crystal tinkled in lampshades, vases, glasses; and nobody from the emperor on down found anything to complain about, nobody except the invalids, who whined because they were invalids, because the massage was too rough or too mild, because the water was too cold or too hot, too deep or not deep enough, because they didn't have enough blankets or too many blankets. But the invalids kept coming, often from a great distance, to spend their money in the city, so everybody listened to them smiling and tried, if there was time enough, to satisfy them.

Now I'm going to tell you about Blaggarde II, the Listener, an emperor who had dreams and visions and heard voices speaking from stones, but wasn't a bad ruler, all the same. Or could it have been because he saw visions and heard voices that he wasn't a bad ruler? A small problem, which a teller of tales doesn't have to pretend to solve; so let's go on. For at least 300 years the warm mineral waters had sprung up from the earth, and people had built ingenious and beautiful devices for the liquid that had enriched them and brought them peace. The Fountain of the Five Rivers never ceased to run; statues of dancing women spouted transparent jets from their mouths; stone figures of chubby children cupped their hands under bronze spouts; great alabaster cups, winged monsters with open beaks, improbable bouquets of marble sent streams of water falling into tanks and thence into bathing ponds and swimming pools and artificial lakes, when Blaggarde II marched south to put down the rebellion. We know now how that expedition ended and what effect it had on Blaggarde the Listener, his dynasty, and the history of the Empire. But what the chronicles don't always say is that the wound that finally brought the emperor to his death remained unhealed ever after the day of the last battle. No surgeon succeeded in closing it even temporarily. A year after the expedition to the south, somebody told the emperor about the waters which cured all ills, in the mountain city called, at that time, Star of Hope; and the Listener took to the road once again, not south this time but north, not on horseback in full dress uniform but lying in a litter and covered with woolen cloaks and blankets, not with songs but with lamentations, not surrounded by soldiers but by doctors and nurses. And he found a charming white city, sprawling but solid, where voices and music never got too loud, where nothing was done in a hurry, and where almost everybody who walked the streets or leaned on the windowsills had eyes as dull as those of the Lord of the Empire.

He built himself a palace. A real one this time, not a shapeless stone den but a palace bristling with towers, flanked by terraces and gardens looked out upon by the tall blue-paned windows of the dining rooms and retiring rooms and the tall red- or yellow-paned windows of the gaming rooms and party rooms: a palace of limitless apartments and interminable corridors, with its own water-fountains for the sick emperor.

Blaggarde the Listener did not lay aside his duties. He no longer wore a coat of mail nor went to war, and day and night his life drained from the oozing wound, but he never ceased to busy himself with the tasks of empire. He saw his ministers first, then his secretaries. He had to keep in touch with the administrators and people in contact with the distant capital. Then noblemen appeared with their relatives and servants. And when the emperor brought the empress and his children to live with him, noble-women came too, and teachers, palace provisioners, more noble families, and bodyguards and lickspittles and all the rabble that surrounds the powerful.

Once again the city changed. Many buildings came down to make room for the great houses of lordly folk; whole blocks were cleared for parks and gardens; the streets were widened so coaches could pass; the desert was watered to grow fruits and greens and flowers for a population now covering the mountains and over-flowing onto the plain. Not everything was destroyed, though. Some things remained: the waters that cured all ills, or almost all, the Fountain of the Five Rivers, the underground tunnels of Drauwdo the Brawny, a few inexplicable foundations of rough stone, the mausoleum built by the city's first mayor, and here and there an eccentric staircase in the middle of a street.

The emperor's wound stopped oozing, but its inflamed lips would not join, even when painfully sutured or even more painfully cauterized. The emperor realized, or maybe the stones spoke and told him, that his life would end here. So he signed a decree making the mountain city the capital of the Empire. The whole Empire looked towards the new capital. All roads led to the mountains, across what had been the desert; all ambitious men dreamed of living there and some managed to do it, and for many centuries after that time there was no capital so splendid, so rich, so active, so beautiful, so prosperous. The dynasties of the Selbiddoës, of the Avvoggardios, and of the Rubbaerderum governed the vast Empire from that city, sometimes well, sometimes pretty well, sometimes badly, as usual; and the water went on welling up, and some palaces fell down and others were built, and some streets were closed off and others were opened up between the houses and the parks, and women bore children, poets sang, thieves stole, tellers of tales sat in tents and talked to people, archivists went on classifying ancient writings, judges sat in judgment, couples loved and wept, men fought for stupid things that in any case weren't going to last long, gardeners produced new varieties of eggplant, assassins lurked in shadows, kids invented games, blacksmiths hammered, madmen howled, girls fell in love, unhappy men hanged themselves, and one day a girl was born with her eyes open.

It's not so rare as most people think. Kids do get born open-eyed, though it's true that they generally arrive with their eyes sensibly closed. But everybody believes that the open eyes of a newborn baby signify great events, fortunate or unfortunate, in the life of that child. And her parents committed the blunder of repeating that belief out of vainglory, and of repeating it to her, in order to prepare her for her destiny; and the girl believed them. If it had been anything else she probably would have smiled, as girls smile at the stupidities of their parents, and forgotten all about it; but if you're told your life is going to be full of tremendous events you're likely to believe it. When Sesdimillia was ten, she looked around and wondered where the great events were going to come from, the fame, the tragedy, the martyrdom, the bliss, the glory. The city worked and played and lived and died, and up there stood the shining imperial palace.

"I'm going to be empress," she said to herself.

Her chance of coming to the throne was slight, as her ancestors weren't royalty or aristocrats, only moderately prosperous merchants. But she got there.

When she was twenty the old Emperor Llandoïvar died at the age of 101 and was succeeded by his great-grandson Ledonoïnor, all his children and grandchildren having already died. The new emperor came very near to marrying the daughter of a duke with whom he used to play in the palace gardens when they were little children. But Ledonoïnor the Vacant wasn't called that for nothing. He didn't love the duke's daughter because, it seemed, he loved nobody and nothing and had no interest in anybody or anything. Nor did he love the dark-haired, active, efficient, handsome, hard girl who oddly enough held the post of Chief of the Internal Vigilance Forces in the palace, which she had won two years ago, disguised as a man, demonstrating greater skill and strength in armed and unarmed combat than her many male opponents. But two months before the emperor's wedding with the duke's daughter, an assassin somehow made his way into the palace and raised his sword against Ledonoïnor I, and the girl shortened him by a head with his own weapon, and the emperor married her, because when he promised her whatever reward she wanted for saving his life she said to him, "Marry me, sir." Though there was no proof and no witnesses it was said that she had provoked the assault, had paid the would-be regicide, and had promised him he'd go free. It's quite possible; what then? Greater infamies than that take place in the palaces of emperors, from which everybody suffers, nobles and commoners, rich and poor. In this case nobody suffered, not even the duke's daughter, who took it hard at first, but who married a man she could love and hate and who could love and hate her. The emperor didn't suffer because he didn't know how to suffer. The empress got what she wanted. And the people were all right because she governed well, really well.

Fortunately Ledonoïnor the Vacant spent his time walking through the gardens and galleries with his empty eyes fixed on emptiness and his soul empty and inert in his empty body and left her to rule, efficiently, harshly sometimes, but always with style. Every now and then she called him to her apartments, and nine months later the Empire had a new prince, and so it went for five years, until the emperor died of a tumor in his belly, probably because there was so much emptiness in there that it could grow as it liked till it suffocated him.

And a short while after, another rebellion arose in the south. The widowed empress put on the men's clothes she used to wear and her armor, and marched like so many other rulers to defend the unity of the Empire. She defended and won it in a single engagement, the Battle of the Field of Nnarient, on which the South bowed its fierce, rebellious head. She won the victory because she was brave, because she believed in what she was doing, because she knew to control armies, and because the leader of the rebellion was a fool. Handsome, ardent, but a fool.

The Treaty of Nnarient-Issinn was signed, unique in the history of the Empire: the South submitted unconditionally and swore fealty to the empress. She moved the capital to the border between the rebel territories and the states of the North, and married the ardent fool. Putting the capital on the border was a bold strategic move which assured peace for many years more than could have been expected when dealing with the South. Such was not the case with the empress's marriage to the rebel chief. She married him because it was her destiny, or so say those who believe in the destiny of those born with their eyes open. I say she married him because she was one of those empresses who had enough power to do whatever she liked. And they were happy, and provided the Empire with more princes and a fresh royal lineage, but you can read all that in any historical treatise or booklet of love poems, and in any case it doesn't matter to us.

What matters to us is what happened in the city in the mountains. People drifted away from the palaces, the great houses, the elegant shops, the parks and gardens and avenues. The nobles left, the gentlefolk, the rich folk, the field marshals, the ladies, the antiquaries, the jewelers, the cabinetmakers, they all left. People of no importance stayed on, some sentimentalists, owners of small businesses, owners of spas, people who had been there, like their parents and grandparents, for a long, long time. The mansions were divided and subdivided again and again, doors were cut in unexpected places, and ramps and staircases led up to higher floors that were no longer part of a house but a whole house, or several houses. Every bedroom, every spacious drawing room was made into two or even three apartments for humble families by putting up partitions and screens and enclosing balconies as kitchens. Corridors cut through rooms and, after various contortions, opened onto the street. The façades deteriorated, losing their paint and carvings. Some windows were sealed, others cut open; the street doors were no longer used, and their hinges and knockers didn't work. As this went on the streets grew narrower because so many lean-tos and sheds and enclosures were built up against outside walls, and the city acquired a silence, a mystery, it had never had before. Yet it wasn't a silence of menace, but of resignation. It went on so for years and years, growing ever more jumbled, more intricate, more improbable. Whole neighborhoods stood silent and abandoned. A street of elegant, unchanged houses, or of mansions bulging with labyrinthine apartments, behind which were precarious structures in what had been a park, led suddenly to a string of low, gloomy shop-buildings. And then came semi-detached palaces, and lonesome avenues where the grass grew and where many-colored awnings, now stiff with dirt, that had once sheltered the nobility at their games, now protected opticians, fortune tellers, dentists, masseuses, academies of physical fitness, dyers, and seamstresses.

For a time the palace of the Empress Sesdimillia stood closed but well maintained by servants who had remained behind for that purpose; but though the children the empress had with Ledonoïnor the Vacant and those she had with the Southerner respected her wishes, her grandchildren didn't care much about a palace they'd never seen, and failed to replace the caretakers when they got old and died. One night somebody stole the great bronze-and-golden bell from the main door, and that was the signal for general looting. Not violent, brutal looting as in war, but a mild, intermittent, natural, easygoing depredation, not totally secret but not overt, that went on till nothing was left of the palace but the walls, the roofs, a few doors, and the stone and marble pavements.

The mysterious, peaceful, labyrinthine city continued to offer its waters to those who came seeking a cure for something, though they were far fewer than in the times of the Listener. The skeleton of the deserted palace was about to be knocked down when a mayor asked permission of the capital to take over what was left of it and turn it into a cultural center. They sent word that he could do as he pleased, which is exactly what this mayor, who had written poetry and plays as a young man, did. He repaired the ruinous building at a low cost, remodeling the rooms for readings, concerts, lectures, plays, dance, and exhibitions of art. There was a natural history museum, two libraries, and a historical archive. The people of the city never took a great deal of interest in so much art and culture, but the invalids and the convalescents paid money to go in and see plays or hear music, or merely out of curiosity, and so for many long years the great doors were never locked.

The Empire didn't entirely forget the mountain city during this period, because its curative waters kept it in mind, and because vehicles carrying freight went on using the north road to and from the port, but indubitably its fame, importance, and attractiveness had declined. It was just another city: people knew somebody who lived there or had lived there, people had a relative who went to take the waters there, people consulted the annals in the archives seeking information on the various imperial capitals, people remembered a trip, a conversation, a name. And that was all. The city didn't die, but it rested, it dozed. I'd say it was making ready for something.

Have you heard tell of Heldinav'Var? Of course you have, of course you have. I'll bet my boots and buttons you've forgotten all the virtuous emperors, but who is there, eh, that doesn't wink and grin as soon as they hear that name, Heldinav'Var? Well, I'm about to disillusion you, because I'm not going to talk about that lecherous and vicious emperor. Who did have some good qualities, though most people don't believe it, or don't want to. No, I'm not going to talk about him but about one of his relations, Meabramiddir'Ven, Baron of the Towers, Seneschal of the Walls, and a lot of other equally meaningless titles – and the emperor's first cousin. That, now, is meaningful. It means, for instance, that he nursed certain pretensions about sitting on the imperial throne some day, despite the fact that he was ninth in succession. Heldinav'Var was a swine, but he wasn't stupid, which was one of his good qualities. It's always good not to be stupid, and when it's the emperor who isn't stupid, people can have hope; not security, of course, but still, hope helps. Heldinav'Var was Crown Prince and his father the Emperor Embemdarv'Var was dying. The prince began planning what he'd do when he succeeded to the throne. He knew, among other things, that his cousin the Baron of the Towers was capable of murder to clear his own way to the throne, and that the first to fall would be the Crown Prince, and since the Crown Prince had no interest whatever in dying, because he was having a stupendously good time and intended to go on doing so when he was emperor, and since – another of his good qualities – he wasn't an assassin or a despot and therefore didn't consider poisoning or hanging his cousin even if his cousin deserved it, he sent for the Seneschal of the Walls and informed him, in public, what he thought of him, and added that either his august cousin would depart from the capital before nightfall and go as far as he could possibly go, or the tenth person in the line of succession, Goldarab'Bar the Obese, the author, as you know, of the *First Codex of River Commerce*, would instantly become the ninth. Meabramiddir'Ven, who hadn't expected this, sought a defense, an explanation, anything, but couldn't think of anything, which suggests that he was considerably stupider than the future emperor. And the worst of it was that his illustrious cousin did not address him with indignation, nor demand justifications or avowals of innocence, but merely waited, almost smiling, arms crossed, to hear what the aspirant to regicide would say. He finally hit on a way out, not a very plausible one, but very seemly: He had no aspirations to the throne, to power, to be ruler of the Empire, oh, no no no; if he had been asking the opinion of some strategically placed persons concerning the desirability or indesirability of Heldinav'Var's succeeding to the throne, it was because he wished to prevent the vice, the shamelessness, the indecency of his cousin from being openly displayed in the person of the emperor. What would become of the Empire? What would become of its subjects, with such an example at their head? And he went on to explain how good he himself was, how honest, decent, discreet, modest, and virtuous. All the same the future emperor sent him off, because he was not only dangerous and a very poor liar, but boring. And the Baron of the Towers had nothing for it but to go, not swearing vengeance because that wouldn't have suited his role of redeemer, but declaring that he pardoned and forgave.

Since it had been made clear that he was to go as fast as possible, he set out for the mountain city. Foreseeing that he might be observed, he arrived as a redeemer, a pilgrim, on foot and poorly dressed. So much so that some gave him alms and others bowed their heads as he passed. When an ancient, poverty-stricken woman called him to come in and share her midday meal, he wouldn't sit at the table, but ate humbly crouching in the doorway. That was when he discovered that he liked this job – not as much as the job of emperor, maybe, but it was all he had. That same evening he preached for the first time.

He didn't himself know very clearly what he was preaching about, and at first he had to be careful not to get mixed up or contradict himself, but so what? If he couldn't be an emperor he'd be a saint. Chance certainly favored him; he'd found the perfect stage for his sanctification. The city was full of petty little people who had nothing but their little jobs and their little superstitions all ready to be set in order and pigeonholed. There were the invalids, too, trying to get well or trying to die, and their relatives, hoping the invalids would get well or would die, according to the closeness of the relationship and the quantity of money involved. And all of them welcomed piety and preaching.

The emperor's cousin struck it rich. Not in gold, for as he won converts and began to believe he really was the mouthpiece of Truth and Goodness, he didn't need to fake it any longer but embraced poverty with all his heart; but in prestige, fame, respect, that's to say, in power of a certain kind. And power is what he'd been looking for. He preached in the streets, lived frugally, went barefoot, walked with his hands joined and his eyes downcast, never raised his voice or indulged himself in bad temper or anger or impatience. He wasn't a saint, but he seemed one.

Now let me tell you, sanctity is catching, much more so than vice. Obviously, Heldinav'Var never converted anybody nor even tried to, since those who succeeded in getting close to him were already convinced, but his cousin converted multitudes of unbelievers and persuaded many to pray, to live frugally and chastely, to fast and sacrifice, and other idiocies of the genre. And he induced even more to take up preaching.

A year after the precipitate departure from the capital of the Baron of the Towers, now the Servant of the Faith, the mountain city had become the most pious, holy, and overwhelmingly prayerful city the Empire had ever known. A hundred religions and a thousand sects sprouted and thrived as, in other times, painting and poetry had sprung up, or the curative waters, or the curfew, or luxury, or fortune-tellers' tents. Going out in the street you weren't pounced on by people selling baskets, jewelry, carpets, crockery, or herbs, but by people selling eternal salvation, which is a treacherous bit of merchandise, believe me, requiring wit and prudence in the handling, since even when you can sell it for a good price, once the bargain's sealed it can always turn against the seller. But like baskets, crockery, and carpets, religion offered plenty of choices. The priests revealed to the people that the roads leading to bliss were almost infinite in number and followed the most surprising routes. From frugality and abstinence to the unbridled exercise of every passion and perversion, by way of spiritual and bodily disciplines, the study of arcane texts, contemplation, renunciation, introspection, prayer, you name it, everything was a means of reaching a paradise which, according to the divinity-peddlers, could be attained by just a little effort and, of course, a little donation, usually directly proportionate to the client's – I mean the believer's – bank account.

Yet those were the years in which the face and body of the city changed the least. This really isn't surprising, given that religion doesn't take up much room; some people say it requires no room at all, at least not externally. A space about the size of a dining room was big enough for a good-sized family, with a platform or pulpit, or a column, or a niche, or a well, or some cushions, or nothing, depending upon which route to heaven was being followed. And a lot of people held their services outdoors, perhaps with the idea that without a roof to interrupt them the prayers would get aloft faster. Change, what there was of it, occurred on the roofs and rooftops and terraces, from which rose the symbols of the innumerable religions – images, stars, crosses, spheres, shafts, some of them fancy, some of them humble, all competing for the most followers in the shortest time. For there were feuds, battles, even wars between the sects, over a forgive-my-sins here or an absolve-me there, over a dozen renegades or a half-dozen apostates, over a ritual murder or a tonality in the dogma. But that brought no changes. That people were arguing over religion instead of politics or money didn't change the direction of streets or knock down old buildings or get new ones built. It merely increased the population. No longer did people come from afar seeking a cure for their ills in the water that bubbled from the depths; but they came seeking in the signs and symbols erected on the rooftops a cure for other ills, not so very different from the first ones, may I remark.

The Emperor Heldinav'Var died, and his cousin who had been Baron of the Towers and Walls died. We know who the vicious emperor's successor was, but the preacher had no successor. His sect split and split again until it was lost in the sea of creeds and soon forgotten. The city reached its apogee as a religious center, in fact, some hundred years later, under the reign of Sderemir the Borenid, a soldier of fortune in the west who, having attained the throne by unspeakable means, became a good ruler, much better than many who had royal blood and a right to sit on the throne.

To get from the western provinces to the capital, the Borenid certainly had no need to go via the city of the religions, but to understand his devious itinerary, one must remember what his intentions were. And he never forgot the generous welcome and the favors shown him, most of them quite disinterested, when he encamped at the gates of the city. So, three years later, when he took the throne of Empire, he presented the city with gifts and authorized special subsidies for it, proclaiming it Mother of True Religion.

A fine name. And a clever one. Let us recall that the Borenid, that apparently brutal man, that deceptive warrior who knew the souls of men even better than he knew swords and shields and chariots, always distrusted any power attained by inexplicable forces. Thanks to his subtlety disguised as benevolence, every creed, every church of the mountain city was convinced that it was the owner of the True Religion, and swelled up with pride, and pride is an ill counselor. Every creed and church looked down with placid condescension on its rivals. So many donations, so much official recognition could only be the perdition of the thousand sects. It's much more stimulating to be marginal, to act without recognition, than to receive public thanks; it's through struggle and polemic that the True Religions grow robust, invent new ways of drawing people, fabricate saints and prophets, apostles and popes, sharpen their wits, freshen up the merchandise and advertise it cleverly. But what do they become if all they do is repeat today and tomorrow and next year the same thing they said yesterday, the same words, the same gestures, the same expressions of piety and conviction, without risks, without competence, without ups and downs, without, in a word, martyrdom? What they become is boring. The priests got tired, the gods got tired, and the faithful got very tired. Fewer and fewer pilgrims traveled north. Since the city still had from its years as the capital all it needed to support itself without relying on goods from other places, the highways leading to it fell into disuse, got cracked, grassy, full of ant hills and badgers' holes, and the Empire, this time, really forgot it. It was remembered only by the drivers of the cargo-caravans going to and from the port, but that's very few out of the huge population of the biggest empire known in human history. At best it was a subject of a little interest to the men who drank and smoked in the bars of the seaport; to the other cities, the other ports, the other states, and the capital, it was nothing. The Borenid ruled for many years. Since he was an exceptional man, many say he was the worst emperor ever to occupy the throne and others say he was beyond all comparison the best. Be that as it may, he didn't forget the city of the true religions; they say he never forgot anything at all, and that may be true. He didn't forget the city, but he didn't worry about it either, and, without entirely neglecting it, since at least once a year he sent a confidential agent to look about and sniff the air and listen to what was going on, he classified it as a harmless place.

So it was throughout the Borenid's life and that of his sons, grandsons, and great-grandsons. The city lived on, silent, obscure, with its merchants, its rich and poor, its courts of law, its women of the streets, its officials, kids, madmen, its holidays, schools, theaters, professional societies, with everything a city should have, isolated, deaf and dumb, its back turned to the Empire, alone. Since it had been solid, rich, great, it still had the public buildings and mansions that had been built to last, but it was all getting covered with moss and lichen and vines. Abandoned pools filled up with water-lilies, wild varieties of drahilea grew in the marble hair of the statues. Everything was yielding, fleshy, full of leaves and green stalks swollen with lazy sap. Many say it had never been more beautiful, and they may be right. It was absorbed into the mountains and all that grows on the mountains, becoming part of the earth within which it had been born, deep down in the caverns. Maybe it would have been all right if it had gone on that way; today it would be a vegetable city inhabited by willowmen and palmwomen, a city swaying in the wind and singing and growing in the sunlight. But human beings are incapable of being still and letting things happen without interference. Some say this is how it should be, since restlessness and dissatisfaction are the basis of progress, and that's an opinion that has to be taken into account, though it's not really worth much consideration.

To explain what happened next, we have to go back to the Borenid. That extraordinary man, strong as an ox and clever as a fox, frugal as a saint although there was nothing saintly about him at all, that conqueror risen from the mists, that king engendered in a plebeian womb by a nameless vagabond, not only knew how to keep the Empire unified and satisfied, peaceful, prosperous, active, and proud throughout his whole reign, but also managed to make his achievement last. What's more, his heirs didn't try to undo it. Generation after generation of emperors and empresses benefited from the legacy of the Borenid, and though not one, except perhaps Evviarav II, the Drakuvid, had his strength or his vision, all of them were sensible, just, and prudent. What more can one ask? Then the dynasty of the Eilaffes, also remote descendants of the Borenid, but in whom the traces of his blood were slight and dubious, came to the throne, and with them came catastrophe.

This time the South played no part. The South remained tranquil and disposed to sneer, half amused, half hopeful, at their northern brothers tearing themselves to pieces. And their northern brothers as if to please them put on a great show, violent, tumultuous, filling earth and sky with battle-cries and screams of pain. Yes – I'm talking about the Six Thousand Day War. Which didn't last 6,000 days, nowhere near it, and nobody seems to know why it got called that, except some obsessive collector of historical curiosities who might explain that it took about 6,000 days for the Empire to recover from the war of the three dynasties and to re-establish order, peace, and its borders. Or so say the academic historians. Maybe the true truth is something else, but I only say maybe. Maybe the true truth is that it took 6,000 days, more or less, for Oddembar'Seil the Bloodthirsty to seek, locate, and exterminate the members of the other two dynasties and all their followers. What we do know is that the whole North was one great battlefield, and that since fighting was the sole occupation of the time, the northern seaport was paralyzed, and no freight-caravans passed by the mountain city. The war itself was far away; the city continued to be draped in moss and ivy, with flowers in the water tanks and on the cornices, bright-colored beetles hiding in the stone eyes of the statues and the fountains, and so it went on almost until the end, and all might have remained the same, maybe right on up to now, if Bloodthirsty, who fully deserved his appellation, hadn't been betrayed by an ambitious general.

Oddembar'Seil had to flee, but had nowhere to flee to. The South was still neutral, but not safe; the South was never safe for power-seekers. And Oddembar'Seil sought power. He fled northward. Not alone, to be sure. He divided his men into groups which blended in with the various groups fighting each other in every region they had to cross through, and pushed them on northward, far north, in a desperate and not very rational effort to reach the sea, to find ships in which they could sail down the coast on the old shipping route and disembark and attack from the east. It looked as if he might succeed. Most of his troops caught up to him in the foothills, and on a summer morning they marched off again and came to the gates of the city. I don't know, nobody knows, whether Bloodthirsty cursed or grinned; I don't know whether he looked at the unknown city with greed, or scratched his head in puzzlement. I do know he entered it peacefully, his men carrying their weapons handy but not brandishing them, and that the inhabitants of the mountain city watched him with curiosity. I know that they even approached him and offered food and shelter. He needed both, but did not accept them. I know that the enemy army caught up to him there, striking at the rear guard while it was half in the city streets, half still on the plains. Goodbye ships, good-bye shipping route and hopes of a surprise attack from the east. Everything was lost, but when you have to fight, you fight.

There have been hideous battles in the long history of the Empire. It's even possible there have been some, a few, crueler than the one that was later called the Battle of the North, as if there was only one north, one battle. But it's hard for anyone to imagine what happened, and I don't know if I can give you any idea of it. I'll try, that's all I can do. Oddembar'Seil the Bloodthirsty gave a great shout when he heard that the enemy was advancing and his men were in a vulnerable position, unready, some of them crowded into the narrow city streets and others scattered out through the fields around it. Concerning these men of his, you can say anything that's usually said about soldiers and warriors, but not that they were cowardly or undisciplined. They heard him shout and they regrouped, took arms, fell in as best they could, and tried to repel the attack. Bloodthirsty leapt across the fallen and ran to fight in the front rank, shoulder to shoulder with his men. He was no coward either.

The Battle of the North lasted exactly fifty hours. The men attacked, broke, scattered, retreated, had a bite to eat, and returned to the attack. Telling such things one is sickened by what men are. They were not men; nor were they wolves, nor hyenas, nor vultures, nor eagles. They were blind organisms, mindless, nerveless, without feeling or thought, with only the power to wound, and blood to shed. They didn't think, believe, feel, see, or hope; all they did was kill and kill again; all they did was retreat and retreat again, and attack again, and kill again. They had been born, they had worked, loved, played, grown to manhood for nothing but this, to kill in the fields of the North under the walls of a mossy, flowery city. Fifty hours after the first attack not more than a hundred men were still afoot, naked, dirty, bloody, maimed, mad. They didn't know or care who the enemy was: they went on killing, attacking, shouting with their lacerated mouths, weeping from their wounded eyes, breathing through their split nostrils, holding their weapons with what fingers they had left, returning to attack, to kill. It was then that Oddembar'Seil cut off a head that rolled on the blood-soaked ground, and on the headless body, on the filthy, hacked breastplate, flashed a collar of gold and amethysts. The future emperor shouted again, and so ended the Battle of the North: he had killed Reggnevon son of Reggnevavaun, pretender to the imperial throne.

You know how the inhabitants of the northern city and his few surviving soldiers crowned the Emperor Oddembar'Seil the Bloodthirsty on the site of his victory as he stood erect over the body of his enemy, dirty, wounded, feverish, naked, with a marble crown hacked with hammer and chisel from the head of a statue that adorned an old aristocratic garden now used for playing-fields, and how then and there he signed his first decree, declaring the city that had witnessed his triumph the capital of the Empire.

Six thousand days hadn't passed, not yet. But the war was over, and when that time really had gone by, the northern city was still capital of the Empire; and the courtiers, the functionaries, the ladies, the admirals, the judges, went to and fro by the Fountain of the Five Rivers, under the arch on which stand the mourning figures from the first mayor's tomb, through the winding, narrow streets, and sometimes stopped to drink or to wet their fingers and forehead in the alabaster basins that still ran with healing water. For the emperor had ordered that they be preserved: he never forgot that the citizens had offered him food and shelter, and he believed that this had brought him luck. He commanded that his palace be built using the walls of the Empress Sesdimillia's palace, keeping its style and plan, antiquated as they were, and he prohibited any change in the streets and buildings, the parks and fountains. The outside of houses could be repaired and painted, but not changed; the incredible staircases could not be moved; the inopportune walls could not be taken down. Building could take place outside the city limits, and did, and interiors could be remodeled, and many were, so that houses could return to what they'd been in the reign of the Listener and his heirs. And nothing more.

The 6,000 days of the Emperor Oddembar'Seil the Blood-thirsty were fulfilled, and another 6,000 days passed, and a bit more. His rule was harsh and violent; he was implacable with his enemies and soft with his friends. But it must be said for him that he reorganized the Empire and brought it peace, territory, and unity. He did so brutally, with more blood, more deaths, with woe and mourning, but Reggnevaun would have been no more merciful, nor can we know what might have happened if the Six Thousand Day War hadn't been fought. A stroke finished him in the midst of a banquet, and the tears shed for him were few and false.

Many years have passed and many emperors have lived and reigned, but the mountain city is still the capital of the Empire. Toadies and social climbers invent poetical names and illustrious origins for it, and Drauwdo the Brawny is a mere character in bedtime tales for children who don't want to go to sleep yet, but the Bloodthirsty was perhaps the first who understood it, and made his understanding clear when he ordered that it not be touched or changed. And those who came after him must have guessed the profound wisdom in this order, which seemed so little in accord with the spirit of the times, since they too enforced it. Here it stands, as in the years of the healing waters, of the gods, of the musicians, of the battles. It looked like a dense mesh of gold, with tiny, irregular openings, pulled tight, stretched across the mountains. It's grown on the farther side, of course, and seven more roads have been added to the one that ran to it; all eight are wide and well-paved as royal roads should be, and swarm with travelers and traffic. It turned its back on the plain that was a desert, a garden, a battlefield; the new mansions, the rich houses, the palaces of the nobility, are to the north, on the road that leads to the distant port. It shines at night, and the light on the peaks never goes out, only dimming in the dawn, as when the painters and poets used to talk and drink in the cafes. It prospers and thrives as it did when the healing water welled up out of the ground. It's a splendid capital, beautiful, mysterious, charming, old as the capital of an old Empire should be, solid, wealthy, built to last thousands and thousands of years. And yet I wonder...

THE RADIANT CAR THY SPARROWS DREW

Catherynne M. Valente

Being unable to retrace our steps in Time, we decided to move forward in Space. Shall we never be able to glide back up the stream of Time, and peep into the old home, and gaze on the old faces? Perhaps when the phonograph and the kinesigraph are perfected, and some future worker has solved the problem of colour photography, our descendants will be able to deceive themselves with something very like it: but it will be but a barren husk: a soulless phantasm and nothing more. "Oh for the touch of a vanished hand, and the sound of a voice that is still!"

—Wordsworth Donisthorpe,
inventor of the Kinesigraph Camer

View the Famous Callowhale Divers of Venus from the Safety of a Silk Balloon! Two Bits a Flight!
—Advertisement Visible in the Launch Sequence of
The Radiant Car Thy Sparrows Drew

EXT. The cannon pad at the Vancouver World's Fair in 1986, late afternoon, festooned with crepe and banners wishing luck and safe travel.
The Documentarian Bysshe and her crew wave jerkily as confetti sticks to their sleek skullcaps and glistening breathing apparati. Her smile is immaculate, practiced, the smile of the honest young woman of the hopeful future; her copper-finned helmet gleams at her feet. Bysshe wears women's clothing but reluctantly and only for this shot, and the curl of her lip betrays

*disdain of the bizarre, flare-waisted swimming costume that so
titillates the crowds. Later, she would write of the severe wind-
burns she suffered in cannon-flight due to the totally inadequate
protection of that flutter of black silk. She tucks a mahogany
case smartly under one arm, which surely must contain George,
her favorite cinematographe. Each of her crewmen strap canisters of film – and the occasional bit of food or oxygen or other
minor accoutrements – to their broad backs. The cannon spar-
kles, a late-model Algernon design, filigreed and etched with
motifs that curl and leaf like patterns in spring ice breaking. The
brilliant nose of the Venusian capsule* Clamshell *rests snugly in
the cannon's silvery mouth.*

*They are a small circus – the strongmen, the clowns, the
trapeze artist poised on her platform, arm crooked in an evocative half-moon, toes pointed into the void.*

I find it so difficult to watch her now, her narrow, monkish face,
not a pore wasted, her eyes huge and sepia-toned, her smile enormous, full of the peculiar, feral excitement which in those days
seemed to infect everyone who looked up into the evening sky to
see Venus there, seducing behind veils of light, as she has always
done. Those who looked and had eyes only for red Mars, all bale-
ful and bright, were rough, raucous, ready and hale. Those who
saw Venus were lost.

She was such a figure then: Bysshe, no surname, or simply the
Documentarian. Her revolving lovers made the newsreels spin,
her films packed the nickelodeons and wrapped the streets three
times 'round. Weeks before a Bysshe opened, buskers and salesmen would camp out on the thoroughfares beside every theater,
selling genuine cells she touched with her *own hand* and replica
spangled cages from *To Thee, Bright Queen!* sized just right to
hold a male of Saturnine extraction. Her father, Percival Unck,
was a brooding and notorious director in his time, his gothic
dramas full of wraith-like heroines with black, bruised eyes and
mouths perpetually agape with horror or orgiastic transcendence.
Her mother was, naturally, one of those ever-transported actresses,
though which one it is hard to remember, since each Unck leading lady became, by association and binding contract, little
black-bobbed Bysshe's mother-of-the-moment. Thus it is

possible to see, in her flickering, dust-scratched face, the echoes of a dozen fleeting, hopeful actresses, easily forgotten but for the legacy of their adoptive daughter's famous, lean features, her scornful, knowing grin.

Bysshe rejected her father's idiom utterly. Her film debut in Unck's *The Spectres of Mare Nubium* is charming, to say the least. During the famous ballroom sequence wherein the decadent dowager Clarena Schirm is beset with the ghosts of her victims, little Bysshe can be seen crouching unhappily near the rice-wine fountain, picking at the pearls on her traditional lunar *kokoshnik* and rubbing at her make-up. The legend goes that when Percival Unck tried to smudge his daughter's eyes with black shadows and convince her to pretend herself a poor Schirm relation while an airy phantasm – years later to become her seventh mother – swooped down upon the innocent child, Bysshe looked up exasperatedly and said: "Papa. This is silly! I want only to be myself!"

And so she would be, forever, only and always Bysshe. As soon as she could work the crank on a cinematographe herself, she set about recording "the really real and actual world" (age seven) or "the genuine and righteous world of the true tale," (age twenty-one) and declaring her father's beloved ghosts and devils "a load of double exposure drivel." Her first documentary, *The Famine Queen of Phobos*, brought the colony's food riots to harsh light, and earned her a Lumiere medal, a prize Percival Unck would never receive. When asked if his daughter's polemics against fictive cinema had embittered him, Unck smiled in his raffish, canine way and said: "The lens, my good man, does not discriminate between the real and the unreal."

Of her final film, *The Radiant Car Thy Sparrows Drew,* only five sequences remain, badly damaged. Though they have been widely copied, cut up and re-used in countless sallow and imitative documentaries on her life, the originals continue to deteriorate in their crystalline museum displays. I go there, to the Grand Eternal Exhibition, in the evenings, to watch them rot. It comforts me. I place my brow upon the cool wall, and she flashes before my eyes, smiling, waving, crawling into the mouth of the cannon-capsule with the ease of a natural performer, a natural aeronaut – and perhaps those were always much the same thing.

EXT. Former Site of the Village of Adonis, on the Shores of the Sea of Qadesh, Night.
A small boy, head bent, dressed in the uniform of a callowhale diver, walks in circles in what was once the village center. The trees and omnipresent cacao-ferns are splashed with a milky spatter. He does not look up as the camera watches him. He simply turns and turns and turns, over and over. The corrupted film skips and jumps; the boy seems to leap through his circuit, flashing in and out of sight.

When she was seventeen, Bysshe and her beloved cinematographe, George, followed the Bedouin road to Neptune for two years, resulting in her elegiac *And the Sea Remembered, Suddenly*. There, they say, she learned her skill at the sculpting of titanium, aquatic animal handling, and a sexual variant of Samayika mediation developed by a cult of levitation on tiny Halimede, where the wind blows warm and violet. There is a sequence, towards the melancholy conclusion of *And the Sea*, wherein Bysshe visits coral-devoured Enki, the great floating city which circumnavigates the planet once a decade, buoyed the lugubrious Neptunian current. Reclining on chaises with glass screens raised to keep out the perpetual rain, Bysshe smokes a ball of creamy, heady af-yun with a woman-levitator, her hair lashed with leather whips. When theaters received the prints of *And the Sea*, a phonograph and several records were included, so that Bysshe herself could narrate her opus to audiences across the world. A solemn bellhop changed the record when the onscreen Bysshe winked, seemingly to no one. And so one may sit on a plush chair, still, and hear her deep, nasal voice echo loudly – too loud, too loud! – in the theater.

The levitator told her of a town called Adonis, a whole colony on Venus that vanished in the space of a night. Divers they were, mostly, subject both to the great callowhales with their translucent skin and the tourists who came to watch and shiver in cathartic delight as the divers risked their lives to milk the recalcitrant mothers in their hibernation. They built a sweet village on the shores of the Qadesh, plaiting their roofs with grease-weed and hammering doors from the chunks of raw copper which comprised the ersatz Venusian beach. They lived; they ate the thready local cacao and shot, once or twice a year, a leathery 'Tryx from the sky, enough to keep them all in fat and protein for months.

"It was a good life," the blue-skinned levitator said, and Bysshe, on her slick black record, imitated the breathy, shy accent of Halimede as the onscreen version of herself loaded another lump of af-yun into the atomizer. "And then, one day – pop! All gone. Houses, stairs, meat-smoking racks, diving bells."

"This sort of thing happens," Bysshe dismissed it all with a wave of her hand. "What planet is there without a mysteriously vanished colony to pull in the tourist cash? Slap up a couple of alien runes on a burned-out doorframe and people will stream in from every terminus. Might as well call them all New Roanoke and have done with it." (In fact, one of Percival Unck's less popular films was *The Abduction of Prosperina*, a loose retelling of that lost Plutonian city, though presumably with rather more demonic ice-dragons than were actually involved.)

Crab-heart trifles and saltwhiskey were passed around as Bysshe's crew laughed and nodded along with her. The levitator smiled.

"Of course, Miss," she said, eyes downcast within the equine blinders knotted to her head. "Well, except for the little boy. The one who was left behind. They say he's still there. He's stuck, somehow, in the middle of where the village used to be, just walking around in circles, around and around. Like a skip on a phonograph. He never even stops to sleep." The Documentarian frowns sourly in black and white, her disapproval of such fancies, her father's fancies, disappeared heroines and eldritch locations where something terrible surely occurred, showing in the wrinkling of her brow, the tapping of her fingernails against the atomizer as bubbling storms lapped their glass cupola, and armored penance-fish nosed the flotation arrays, their jaw-lanterns flashing.

But you can see her thinking, the new film, which was to be her last, taking shape behind her eyes.

This is what she came to see.

Dead Adonis, laid out in state on the beach-head. Her single mourner. The great ocean provides a kind of score for her starlit landing, and in the old days a foley-boy would thrash rushes against the floor of the theater to simulate the colossal, dusky red tide of the Qadesh. We would all squint in the dark, and try to see scarlet in the monochrome waves, emerald in the undulating cacao-ferns. The black silk balloon crinkles and billows lightly on the strand, clinging to the ruin of the landing capsule. The dwarf moon Anchises shines a kind of limping, diffident light on Bysshe as she walks into frame, her short hair sweat-curled in the wilting wind. She has thrown the exhibition costume into an offscreen campfire and is clothed now in her accustomed jodhpurs and famous black jacket. The boy turns and turns. His hands flicker and blur as if he is signing something, or writing on phantom paper. She holds out her hand as though approaching a horse, squats down beside the child in a friendly, schoolteacherly fashion. The boy does not raise his head to look at her. He stares at his feet. Bysshe looks uncertainly over her shoulder at the long snarl of sea behind them – the cinematographe operator, temporarily trusted with the care and feeding of George, says something to her offscreen, he must, because she cocks her head as though considering a riddle and says something back to him. Her mouth moves in the silent footage, mouthing words the audience cannot ever quite read.

Once, a deaf scholar was brought to view this little scene in a private projector room. She was given coffee and a treacle tart. She reported the words as: *Look at the whales. Are they getting closer?*

Bysshe stands up straight and strides without warning into the child's path, blocking his little pilgrim's progress around the sad patch of dune grass.

The child does not stop. He collides with Bysshe, steps back, collides with her again. He beats his head against her soft belly. Back and forth, back and forth.

The Documentarian looks helplessly into the camera.

EXT. Former Site of the Village of Adonis, Afternoon.

One of the crewmen shaves in a mirror nailed to furry black cacao-fern bark. He uses a straight razor whose handle is inlaid with fossilized kelp. He is shirtless and circus huge, his face angular and broad. He catches a glimpse of Bysshe in his mirror and whirls to catch her up, kissing her and smearing shaving cream on her face. She laughs and punches his arm – he recoils in mock agony. It is a pleasant scene. This is Erasmo St. John, the Documentarian's lover and lighting-master, who would later claim to have fathered a child with her, despite being unable to produce a convincing moppet.

Clouds drift down in long, indistinct spirals. Behind them, the boy turns and turns, still, celluloid transforming the brutal orange of the Venusian sun into a blinding white nova. Beyond him, pearlescent islands hump up out of the foamy Qadesh – callowhales, a whole pod, silent, pale.

Adonis was established some twenty years prior to the Bysshe expedition, one of many villages eager to take advantage of the callowhale hibernations. What, precisely, callowhale *is* is still the subject of debate. There are diagrams, to be sure – one even accompanies the *Radiant Car* press kit – but these are guesses only. It cannot even be safely said whether they are animal or vegetable matter. The first aeronauts, their braggart flags flapping in that first, raw breeze, assumed them to be barren islands. The huge masses simply lay motionless in the water, their surfaces milky, motley, the occasional swirl of chemical blue or gold sizzling through their depths. But soon enough, divers and fisher-men and treasure-seekers flocked to the watery promise of Venus, and they called the creatures true. Beneath the waterline were calm, even dead leviathans – *taninim*, said a neo-Hasidic bounty hunter, some sort of proto-pliosaur, said one of the myriad research corps. Their fins lay flush against their flanks, horned and barbed. Their eyes were then perpetually shut – *hibernating*, said the research cotillion. *Dreaming*, said the rest. From their flat, wide skulls extended long, fern-like antennae which curled in fractal infinitude, tangling with the others of their occasional pods, their fronds stroking one another lightly, imperceptibly, in the quick, clever Qadesh currents. Whether they have any sentience is popular tea-chatter – their hibernation cycle seems to be much longer than a human life.

Some few divers claim to have heard them sing – the word they give to a series of unpredictable vibrations that occasionally shiver through the fern-antennae. Like sonar, these quaking oscillations can be fatal to any living thing caught up in them – unlike sonar, the unfortunates are instantly vaporized into constituent atoms. Yet the divers say that from a safe distance, their echoes brush against the skin in strange and intimate patterns, like music, like lovemaking. The divers cannot look at the camera when they speak of these things, as though it is the eye of God and by not meeting His gaze, they may preserve virtue. *The vibrations are the color of morning*, they whisper.

It is the milk the divers are after – nearly everything produced on Venus contains callowhale milk, the consistency of honey, the color of cream, the taste something like sucking on a dandelion stem caked in green peppercorn. It is protein-rich, fat-clotted, thick with vitamins – equally sought after as an industrial lubricant, foodstuff, fuel, as an ingredient in medicines, anesthesia, illicit hallucinogens, poured into molds and dried as an exotic building material. Certain artists have created entire murals from it, which looked upon straight seem like blank canvases, but seen slant-wise reveal impossibly complex patterns of shades of white. Little by little, Venusian-born children began to be reared on the stuff, to no apparent ill effect – and the practice became fashionable among the sorts of people whose fashions become the morality of the crowds. Erasmo St. John pioneered a kind of long-lit camera lantern by scalding the milk at low temperatures, producing an eerie phosphorescence. The later Unck films use this to great effect as spectral light. Cultivation has always been dangerous – the tubules that secrete milk are part and parcel of the ferny antennae, extending from the throat-sac of the callowhale. In order to harvest it, the diver must avoid the tendrils of fern and hope upon hope that the whale is not seized with a sudden desire to sing. For this danger, and for the callowhales' rude insistence upon evolving on Venus and not some more convenient locale, the milk was so precious that dozens of coastal towns could be sustained by encouraging a relatively small population of municipal divers. Stock footage sent back to earth shows family after beaming family, clad in glittering counterpressure mesh, dark copper diving bells tucked neatly under their arms, hoisting healthy, robust goblets of milk, toasting the empire back home.

But where there is milk, there is mating, isn't there? There are children. The ghost-voice of Bysshe comes over the phonograph as the final shot of *And the Sea Remembered, Suddenly* flickers silver-dark and the floating Neptunian pleasure-domes recede. Everyone knew where she was bound next, long before principal photography ever began. To Venus, and Adonis, to the little village rich in milk and children that vanished two decades after its founding, while the callowhales watched offshore, impassive, unperturbed.

EXT. Village Green, Twilight.

Bysshe is grabbing the child's hand urgently while he screams, soundlessly, held brutally still in his steps by the gaffer and the key grip, whose muscles bulge with what appears to be a colossal effort – keeping this single, tiny, bird-boned child from his circuit. The Documentarian's jagged hair and occasionally her chin swing in and out of frame as she struggles with him. She turns over the boy's hand, roughly, to show the camera what she has found there: tiny fronds growing from his skin, tendrils like ferns, seeking, wavering, wet with milk. The film jumps and shudders; the child's hand vibrates, faster, faster.

It is a difficult thing, to have an aftermath without an event.

The tabloids, ever beloved of Bysshe and her exploits, heralded the return of the expedition long before the orbits were favorable. They salivated for the new work, which would surely set records for attendance. The nickelodeons began taking ticket orders a year in advance, installing the revolutionary new sound equipment which might allow us all to hear the sound of the surf on a Venusian shore. The balloon was sighted in orbit and spontaneous, Romanesque gin-triumphs were held in three national capitals. Finally, on a grassy field outside Vancouver, the black silk confection of Bysshe's studio balloon wrinkled and sighed to rest on the spring ground. The grips and gaffers came out first, their eyes downcast, refusing to speak. Then the producer, clutching his hat to his chest. Lastly came Erasmo St. John, clutching the hand of the greatest star of the coming century: a little boy with ferns in his fists.

Bysshe did not return. Her crew would not speak of where she had gone, only that she was to be left to it, called dead if not actually deceased – and possibly deceased. They mumbled; they evaded. Their damaged film, waterlogged and half-missing, was hurried into theaters and pored over by hundreds of actors, scholars, gossip columnists. It is said that Percival Unck only once viewed the reels. He looked into his lap when the last shot had faded to black and smiled, a secret smile, of regret, perhaps, or of victory.

The boy was sent to school, paid for by the studio. He was given a new name, though later in life he, too, would eschew any surname, having no family connections to speak of save to a dead documentarian. He wore gloves, always, and shared his memories as generously as he could with the waves of popular interest in Venus, in Adonis, in the lost film. *No, I don't remember what happened to my parents. I'm sorry, I wish I did. One day they were gone. Yes, I remember Bysshe. She gave me a lemon candy.*

And I do remember her. The jacket only looks black on film. I remember – it was red.

I once saw a group of performance artists – rich students with little better to do, I thought – mount a showing of the shredded, abrupt footage of *The Radiant Car*, intercut with highlights of the great Unck gothics. The effect was strange and sad: Bysshe seemed to step out of her lover's arms and into a ballroom, becoming suddenly an unhappy little girl, only to leap out again, shimmering into the shape of another child, with a serious expression, turning in endless circles on a green lawn. One of the students, whose hair was plaited and piled upon her head, soaked and crusted in callowhale milk until it glowed with a faint phosphor, stood before the screen with a brass bullhorn. She wore a bustle frame but no bustle, shoelaces lashed in criss-crossings around her calves but no shoes. The jingly player-piano kept time with the film, and behind her Bysshe stared intently into the phantasm of a distant audience, unknowable as God.

"Ask yourself," she cried brazenly, clutching her small, naked breasts. "As Bysshe had the courage to ask! What is milk for, if not to nurture a new generation, a new world? We have never seen a callowhale calf, yet the mothers endlessly nurse. What do they nurture, out there in their red sea? I will tell you. For the space is not smooth that darkly floats between our earth and that morning star, Lucifer's star, in eternal revolt against the order of heaven. It is *thick*, it is swollen, its disrupted proteins skittering across the black like foam – like milk spilled across the stars. And in this quantum milk how many bubbles may form and break, how many abortive universes gestated by the eternal sleeping mothers may burgeon and burst? I suggest this awe-ful idea: Venus is an anchor, where all waveforms meet in a radiant scarlet sea, where the milk of creation is milled, and we have pillaged it, gorged upon it all unknowing. Perhaps in each bubble of milk is a world suckled at the breast of a pearlescent cetacean. Perhaps there is one where Venus is no watery Eden as close as a sister, but a distant inferno of steam and stone, lifeless, blistered. Perhaps you have drunk the milk of this world – perhaps I have, and destroyed it with my digestion. Perhaps a skin of probabilistic milk, dribbling from the mouths of babes, is all that separates our world from the others. Perhaps the villagers of Adonis drank so deeply of the primordial milk that they became as the great mothers, blinking through worlds like holes burned in film – leaving behind only the last child born, who had not yet enough of the milk to change, circling, circling the place where the bubble between worlds burst!" The girl let her milk-barnacled hair fall with a violent gesture, dripping the peppery-sharp smelling cream onto the stage.

"Bysshe asked the great question: where did Adonis go in death? The old tales know. Adonis returned to his mother, the Queen of the Dark, the Queen of the Otherworld." Behind her, on a forty-foot screen, the boy's fern-bound palm – my palm, my vanished hand – shivered and vibrated and faded into the thoughtful, narrow face of Bysshe as she hears for the first time the name of Adonis. The girl screams: "Even here on Earth we have supped all our lives on this alien milk. *We* are the calves of the callowhales, and no human mothers. We will ride upon the milky foam, and one day, one distant, distant day, our heads will break the surf of a red sea, and the eyes of the whales will open, and weep, and dote upon us!"

The girl held up her hand, palm outward, to the meager audience. I squinted. There, on her skin, where her heart line and fate line ought to have been, was a tiny fern, almost imperceptible, but wavering nonetheless, uncertain, ethereal, new.

A rush of blood beat at my brow. As if compelled by strings and pulleys, I raised up my own palm in return. Between the two fronds, some silent shiver passed, the color of morning.

INT. The depths of the sea of Qadesh.

Bysshe swims through the murky water, holding one of Erasmo's milk-lanterns out before her. St. John follows behind with George, encased in a crystal canister. The film is badly stained and burned through several frames. She swims upward, dropping lead weights from her shimmering counterpressure mesh as she rises. The grille of her diving bell gleams faintly in the shadows. Above her, slowly, the belly of a callowhale comes into view. It is impossibly massive, the size of a sky. Bysshe strains towards it, extending her fingers to touch it, just once, as if to verify it for herself, that such a thing could be real.

The audience will always and forever see it before Bysshe does. A slit in the side of the great whale, like a door opening. As the Documentarian stretches towards it, with an instinctual blocking that is nothing short of spectacular the suddenly tiny figure of a young woman frozen forever in this pose of surprise, of yearning, in the center of the shot – the eye of the callowhale, so huge as to encompass the whole screen, opens around her.

AUTHOR BIOGRAPHIES

Sofia Samatar is the author of the novel *A Stranger in Olondria*, winner of the 2014 Crawford Award. Her short fiction, poetry and essays have appeared in a number of places, including *Strange Horizons*, *Clarkesworld Magazine*, and *Weird Fiction Review*. She is nonfiction and poetry editor for *Interfictions: A Journal of Interstitial Arts*. Visit her in California, or at www.sofiasamatar.com.

Kristin Mandigma lives in Manila, Philippines.

Vandana Singh is a science-fiction writer from India, living in the Boston area. When not teaching physics to undergraduates in wildly creative ways, she writes non-Euclidean tales of science fiction and fantasy. Her stories have appeared in a number of magazines and anthologies, most recently *Clarkesworld Magazine*, *The End of the Road*, *Solaris Rising 2*, and *The Other Half of the Sky*. Several have been reprinted in Year's Best anthologies, and her novella *Distances* (Aqueduct Press) won the 2008 Carl Brandon Parallax award. For more information please see her website at http://users.rcn.com/singhvan/ and her blog at http://vandanasingh.wordpress.com/.

Lucy Sussex is a New Zealand-born writer living in Australia. Her award-winning work covers many genres, from true-crime writing to horror. It includes books for younger readers and the novel *The Scarlet Rider* (1996 – to be reissued in 2014). She has published five short-story collections, *My Lady Tongue*, *A Tour Guide in Utopia*, *Absolute Uncertainty*, *Matilda Told Such Dreadful Lies* (a best of), and *Thief of Lives*. *Matilda* received a starred review in Publisher's Weekly. She has been a weekly review columnist for the *Age* and *Sydney Morning Herald*. Her literary archaeology (unearthing forgotten writers) work includes *Women Writers and Detectives in Nineteenth-Century Crime Fiction: The Mothers of the Mystery Genre* (Palgrave). She has also edited pioneer crime-writer Mary Fortune's work and an anthology of Victorian travel writing, *Saltwater in the Ink* (ASP). Her current project is a book about Fergus Hume and his 1886 *The Mystery of a Hansom Cab*, the biggest-selling detective novel of the 1800s.

Tori Truslow lives and writes in England, in a house on a hill overlooking the Thames Estuary. Her short fiction has appeared in *Clockwork Phoenix 3*, *Breaking the Bow: Speculative Fiction Inspired by the Ramayana*, and *Beneath Ceaseless Skies*, among other publications. She co-edits the multimedia journal *Verse Kraken*, and runs the LGBTQ Fandom track at Nine Worlds GeekFest. Find her on the web at toritruslow.com or on twitter @toritruslow.

Nnedi Okorafor is a novelist of African-based science fiction, fantasy and magical realism for both children and adults. Born in the United States to two Nigerian immigrant parents, Nnedi is known for weaving African culture into creative evocative settings and memorable characters. In a profile of Nnedi's work titled "Weapons of Mass Creation", the *New York Times* called Nnedi's imagination "stunning". Nnedi's adult works are *Who Fears Death* (winner of the World Fantasy Award for Best Novel), her short-story collection *Kabu Kabu* and her recently released science-fiction novel *Lagoon*. Her young adult novels are *Akata Witch* (an Amazon.com Best Book of the Year), *Zahrah the Windseeker* (winner of the Wole Soyinka Prize for African Literature) and *The Shadow Speaker* (winner of the CBS Parallax Award). Her children's book *Long Juju Man* is the winner of the Macmillan Writer's Prize for Africa. The sequel to *Akata Witch* (*Akata Witch 2: Breaking Kola*) is scheduled for release in 2015. Nnedi holds a PhD in literature and is a professor of creative writing at the University of Buffalo. Find her on facebook, twitter @Nnedi and at nnedi. com

Karen Joy Fowler is the author of six novels, including *Sarah Canary*, which won the Commonwealth medal for best first novel by a Californian and *The Jane Austen Book Club*, a *New*

York Times bestseller. Also three short-story collections, two of which won the World Fantasy Award in their respective years. Her most recent novel *We Are All Completely Beside Ourselves* was published by Putnam in May 2013. She currently lives in Santa Cruz.

Alice Sola Kim currently lives in Brooklyn. Her fiction has appeared in *Lightspeed, Asimov's Science Fiction, The Year's Best Science Fiction and Fantasy* and elsewhere. She is a recipient of a grant from the Elizabeth George Foundation and a MacDowell Colony residency, and has been honor-listed twice for the James Tiptree, Jr. Award.

Elizabeth Bear was born on the same day as Frodo and Bilbo Baggins, but in a different year. When coupled with a childhood tendency to read the dictionary for fun, this led her inevitably to penury, intransigence and the writing of speculative fiction. She is the Hugo, Sturgeon, and Campbell Award winning author of twenty-five novels and almost a hundred short stories. Her most recent novel is *Steles of the Sky* (Tor, 2014). Her dog lives in Massachusetts; her partner, writer Scott Lynch, lives in Wisconsin. She spends a lot of time on planes.

Sarah Monette grew up in Oak Ridge, Tennessee, one of the three secret cities of the Manhattan Project, and now lives in a 108-year-old house in the Upper Midwest with a great many books, two cats, one grand piano, and one husband. Her Ph.D. diploma (English Literature, 2004) hangs in the kitchen. She has published more than fifty short stories and has two short story collections out: *The Bone Key* (Prime Books 2007 – with a shiny second edition in 2011) and *Somewhere Beneath Those Waves* (Prime Books, 2011). She has written two novels (*A Companion to Wolves,* Tor Books, 2007, *The Tempering of Men*, Tor Books, 2011) and four short stories with Elizabeth Bear, and hopes to write more. Her first four novels (*Mélusine, The Virtu, the Mirador, Corambis*) were published by Ace. Her latest novel, *The Goblin Emperor* (written under the pen name Katherine Addison), came out from Tor in April 2014. Visit her online at www.sarahmonette.com or www.katherineaddison.com.

Natalia Theodoridou is a UK-based media and theatre scholar, currently focusing on representations of culture in Balinese performance. Originally from Greece, she has lived and studied in the USA, UK, and Indonesia for several years. Her writing has appeared in *Clarkesworld Magazine*, *Strange Horizons*, *The Dark*, and elsewhere. Her poem "Blackmare" has been nominated for a Rhysling Award. Natalia is a first reader for *Goldfish Grimm's Spicy Fiction Sushi*. Her personal website is www.natalia-theodoridou.com.

Ursula Kroeber Le Guin was born in 1929 in Berkeley, and lives in Portland, Oregon. As of 2013, she has published twenty-one novels, eleven volumes of short stories, four collections of essays, twelve books for children, six volumes of poetry, and four of translation, and has received many honors and awards including Hugo, Nebula, National Book Award, PEN-Malamud. Her most recent publications are *Finding My Elegy (New and Selected Poems, 1960–2010)* and *The Unreal and the Real (Selected Short Stories)*, 2012.

Nalo Hopkinson is a Jamaican-born Canadian writer of science fiction and fantasy. She is a recipient of the Campbell Award, the Ontario Arts Council Foundation Award, the Locus Award, and the World Fantasy Award. Her novel *Midnight Robber* was an Honourable Mention in Cuba's Casa de las Americas Prize for writing in creole. She was a co-founder of the Carl Brandon Society, which exists to further the conversation on race and ethnicity in speculative fiction. She is a professor of Creative Writing at the University of California Riverside. *Sister Mine*, her eighth book of fiction, appeared in 2013 from Grand Central Publishing. Her website: http://nalohopkinson.com

Zen Cho is a Malaysian writer of fantasy and romance. Her short stories have appeared in publications in the USA, UK, Malaysia, Singapore, and Australia. She was a finalist for the 2013 John W. Campbell Award for Best New Writer.

Élisabeth Vonarburg was born to life in 1947 (France), and to science fiction in 1964. Taught French Literature and Creative Writing on and off at various universities in Quebec (since immigration, in 1973). "Full-time writer" since 1990 (despite a PhD. in Creative Writing, 1987), i.e. singer-songwriter, translator, SF convention organizer, literary editor (*Solaris* magazine), essayist. Still managed to publish some fiction, among which nineteen novels, some translated into English (*The Silent City, The Maerlande Chronicles, Reluctant Voyagers, Tyranaël*, Book I and II); nine short story collections in French, two in English (*Slow Engine of Time, Blood Out of a Stone*); also three poetry collections, and four books for children and young adults. More than thirty awards in France, Canada, Quebec, and the United States. Her five-book series Reine de Mémoire (2005–2007), received four major awards in Quebec.

Carrie Vaughn is the author of the *New York Times* bestselling series of novels about a werewolf named Kitty, the most recent installment of which is *Kitty in the Underworld*. She's written several other contemporary fantasy and young adult novels, as well as upwards of seventy short stories. She's a contributor to the Wild Cards series of shared-world superhero books edited by George R. R. Martin and a graduate of the Odyssey Fantasy Writing Workshop. An Air Force brat, she survived her nomadic childhood and managed to put down roots in Boulder, Colorado. Visit her at www.carrievaughn.com.

Hao Jingfang (jessica-hjf.blog.163.com/) is the author of two novels and numerous short stories published in a variety of Chinese venues such as *Science Fiction World, Mengya, New Science Fiction,* and *New Realms of Fantasy and Science Fiction*. She has been nominated for the Galaxy Award, China's highest honor for science fiction. Currently, Ms. Hao is pursuing a Ph.D. in Economics at Tsinghua University in China.

Nicole Kornher-Stace was born in Philadelphia in 1983, moved from the East Coast to the West Coast and back again by the time she was five, and currently lives in New Paltz, New York, with one husband, three ferrets, one Changeling, and many, many books. Her short fiction and poetry has appeared or is forthcoming in a number of magazines and anthologies, including *Best American Fantasy, Clockwork Phoenix 3* and *4, The Mammoth Book of Steampunk, Apex,* and *Fantasy Magazine*. Her poem "The Changeling Always Wins" placed second in the 2010 short form Rhysling Award, and her short fiction has been longlisted for the British Fantasy Awards and nominated for the Pushcart Prize. She is the author of *Desideria, Demon Lovers and Other Difficulties,* and *The Winter Triptych*. Her latest novel, *Archivist Wasp*, is forthcoming from Big

Mouth House, Small Beer Press's young adult imprint, in late 2014. She can be found online at www.nicolekornherstace. com or wirewalking.livejournal.com.

Shira Lipkin has managed to convince *Strange Horizons, Apex Magazine, Stone Telling, Clockwork Phoenix 4*, and other otherwise-sensible magazines and anthologies to publish her work; two of her stories have been recognized as Million Writers Award Notable Stories, and she has won the Rhysling Award for best short poem. She lives in Boston and, in her spare time, fights crime with the Boston Area Rape Crisis Center. Her cat is bigger than her dog.

Rochita Loenen-Ruiz is an Octavia Butler Scholar. She was also the first Filipina writer to attend Clarion West. Her work has appeared in publications such as *Apex Magazine, Fantasy Magazine, Weird Tales, Interzone, Clarkesworld Magazine, Philippine Genre Stories,* and *Philippine Speculative Fiction*. She writes the Movements column for *Strange Horizons* where she looks at genre from the perspective of someone who has grown up outside the West and who now lives in the diaspora. Visit her website at rcloenenruiz.com or find her on twitter @rcloenenruiz

Nancy Kress is the author of thirty-two books, including twenty-five novels, four collections of short stories, three books about writing. Her work has won two Hugos ("Beggars in Spain" and "The Erdmann Nexus"), four Nebulas (all for short fiction), a Sturgeon ("The Flowers of Aulit Prison"), and a John W. Campbell Memorial award (for *Probability Space*). The novels include science fiction, fantasy, and thrillers; many concern genetic engineering. Her most recent work is the Nebula-winning and Hugo-nominated *After the Fall, Before the Fall, During the Fall* (Tachyon, 2012), a long novella of eco-disaster, time travel, and human resiliency. Intermittently, she teaches writing workshops at various venues around the country, including Clarion and Taos Toolbox (yearly, with Walter Jon Williams). A few years ago she taught at the University of Leipzig as the visiting Picador professor. She is currently working on a long, as-yet-untitled SF novel. Nancy lives in Seattle with her husband, writer Jack Skillingstead, and Cosette, the world's most spoiled toy poodle.

E. Lily Yu was the 2012 recipient of the John W. Campbell Award for Best New Writer and a 2012 Hugo, Nebula, and World Fantasy Award nominee. In 2012 she attended the Sewanee Writers' Conference as a Stanley Elkin Scholar, and in 2013 she attended Clarion West. Her stories have appeared in *McSweeney's, Clarkesworld Magazine, Boston Review, Kenyon Review Online, Apex,* and *The Best Science Fiction and Fantasy of the Year.* She is working on a novel, a video game, and a PhD.

Wearing several hats, **Toiya Kristen Finley** is a writer, editor, game designer, and narrative designer/game writer from Nashville, Tennessee. She holds a Ph.D. in literature and creative writing from Binghamton University and has published over sixty pieces of fiction and non-fiction. She has worked as a game designer, narrative designer, and game writer (or some combination of the three) on several unreleased social and mobile games for both children and general audiences. She currently serves as an executive board member on the International Game Developers Association's Game Writing Special Interest Group. Her current projects include a graphic novel, an animated children's YouTube series, and a couple of her own mobile games. A co-authored book on narrative design will be published by Focal Press in 2015.

Kameron Hurley is the author of the novels *God's War, Infidel,* and *Rapture,* a science-fantasy noir series which earned her the Sydney J. Bounds Award for Best Newcomer and the Kitschy Award for Best Debut Novel. She has been a finalist for the Nebula Award, the Locus Award, and the BSFA Award for Best Novel. Her short fiction has appeared in *Lightspeed Magazine, Escape Pod,* and *Strange Horizons.* Hurley's latest novel, *The Mirror Empire,* is available from Angry Robot Books in September 2014.

Genevieve Valentine's first novel, *Mechanique: A Tale of the Circus Tresaulti,* won the 2012 Crawford Award. *The Girls at the Kingfisher Club,* a 1920s retelling of "The Twelve Dancing Princesses," is out from Atria in 2014. Her short fiction has appeared in *Clarkesworld Magazine, Strange Horizons, Journal of Mythic Arts, Lightspeed,* and others, and the anthologies *Federations, After, Teeth,* and more. Her nonfiction and reviews have appeared at NPR.org, *The A.V. Club*, *Strange Horizons*, *io9*, and more, and she is a co-author of *Geek Wisdom* (Quirk Books). Her appetite for bad movies is insatiable, a tragedy she tracks at genevievevalentine.com.

Aliette de Bodard lives and works in Paris, where she has a day job as a System Engineer. In her spare time she writes speculative fiction: her Aztec noir trilogy *Obsidian and Blood* is published by Angry Robot. Her short fiction has appeared in *Clarkesworld Magazine*, *Beneath Ceaseless Skies*, and Gardner Dozois's *Year's Best Science Fiction*, and garnered her a Locus Award, a Nebula Award and a British Science Fiction Association Award. She blogs her thoughts on writing and her recipes of Vietnamese food at aliettedebodard.com.

Greer Gilman's mythic fictions *Moonwise* and *Cloud & Ashes: Three Winter's Tales* have (between them) won the Tiptree, World Fantasy, and Crawford Awards, and have been shortlisted for the Nebula and Mythopoeic awards. "Down the Wall" is a thought-experiment: a vision of a city under godblitz, in a post-apocalyptic Cloud. Her latest chapbook, *Cry Murder! In a Small Voice*, is a Jacobean noir detective story. Someone is murdering boy players; Ben Jonson investigates. A second mystery, *Exit, Pursued by a Bear*, is forthcoming from Small Beer Press. Besides her three books, she has published other short work, poetry, and criticism. Her essay on "The Languages of the Fantastic" appears in *The Cambridge Companion to Fantasy Literature*. For many years a librarian at Harvard, she lives in Cambridge, Massachusetts. She likes to quip that she does everything James Joyce ever did, only backward and in high heels.

Karin Tidbeck is the award-winning author of *Jagannath*. She lives in Malmö, Sweden, where she works as a creative-writing teacher, translator, and consultant of all things fictional and interactive. She has published short stories and poetry in Swedish since 2002 and English since 2010. Her short fiction has appeared in publications like *Weird Tales*, *Tor.com*, *Lightspeed Magazine* and numerous anthologies including *The Time-Travelers Almanac*, *Steampunk Revolution* and *Aliens: Recent Encounters*.

Nisi Shawl's collection *Filter House*, one of two winners of the

2009 James Tiptree, Jr. Award, was a finalist for the 2009 World Fantasy Award; the story selected from that collection, "Good Boy," was also nominated for the award. Shawl's other stories have been published at *Strange Horizons*, in *Asimov's SF Magazine*, and in numerous anthologies including *The Moment of Change*, *The Other Half of the Sky*, and both volumes of *Dark Matter*. She was WisCon 35's Guest of Honor, and she has spoken at Smith and Spelman Colleges. With Dr. Rebecca J. Holden she co-edited *Strange Matings: Science Fiction, Feminism, African American Voices, and Octavia E. Butler*. She edited *The WisCon Chronicles 5: Writing and Racial Identity* and currently edits book reviews for *The Cascadia Subduction Zone*, Aqueduct Press's feminist literary quarterly. With Cynthia Ward, Shawl co-authored *Writing the Other: A Practical Approach*. In the 1970s, Shawl discovered and read many books of feminist science fiction, and she credits Suzy McKee Charnas's *Walk to the End of the World* with giving her the idea that not only could she get away with saying audacious things, but that people would pay her for it. Currently she's working on revisions to *Everfair*, a Belgian Congo steampunk novel forthcoming from Tor in 2015. Her website is www.nisishawl.com.

Thoraiya Dyer is a three-time Aurealis Award-winning, three-time Ditmar Award-winning Australian writer based in the Hunter Valley, New South Wales. Her short fiction has appeared in *Clarkesworld Magazine, Apex, Cosmos* and *Analog*. It is forthcoming in the anthologies *Long Hidden* and *War Stories*. Her award-shortlisted collection of four original stories, *Asymmetry*, is available from Twelfth Planet Press. Dyer is represented by the Ethan Ellenberg Literary Agency. She is a member of SFWA. A lapsed veterinarian, her other interests include bushwalking, archery and travel. Find her online at Goodreads, Twitter @ThoraiyaDyer or www.thoraiyadyer.com.

Ekaterina Sedia resides in the Pinelands of New Jersey. Her critically acclaimed and award-nominated novels, *The Secret History of Moscow*, *The Alchemy of Stone*, *The House of Discarded Dreams,* and *Heart of Iron,* were published by Prime Books. Her short stories have sold to *Analog, Baen's Universe,*

Subterranean, and *Clarkesworld Magazine,* as well as numerous anthologies, including *Haunted Legends* and *Magic in the Mirrorstone.* She is also the editor of the anthologies *Paper Cities* (World Fantasy Award winner), *Running with the Pack, Bewere the Night,* and *Bloody Fabulous,* as well as *The Mammoth Book of Gaslit Romance* (forthcoming) and *Wilful Impropriety.* Her short-story collection, *Moscow But Dreaming,* was released by Prime Books in December 2012. Visit her fashion blog at fishmonkey.blogspot.com

Benjanun Sriduangkaew enjoys writing love letters to cities real and speculative, and space opera when she can get away with it. Her work can be found in *Clarkesworld Magazine, Beneath Ceaseless Skies,* Jonathan Strahan's *The Best Science Fiction and Fantasy of the Year* and Rich Horton's *The Year's Best Science Fiction and Fantasy.*

Angélica Gorodischer, daughter of the writer Angélica de Arcal, was born in 1929 in Buenos Aires and has lived most of her life in Rosario, Argentina. From her first book of stories, she has displayed a mastery of science-fiction themes, handled with her own personal slant, and exemplary of the South American fantasy tradition. Oral narrative techniques are a strong influence in her work, most notably in *Kalpa Imperial,* which since its publication has been considered a major work of modern fantasy narrative. Her second book translated into English is *Trafalgar.* Her books have also been translated into French, German, Italian, and Czech. She has received many awards for her work, in her country and abroad, including the World Fantasy Lifetime Achievement Award.

Catherynne M. Valente is the *New York Times* bestselling author of over a dozen works of fiction and poetry, including *Palimpsest,* the Orphan's Tales series, *Deathless,* and the crowd-funded phenomenon *The Girl Who Circumnavigated Fairyland in a Ship of Own Making.* She is the winner of the Andre Norton, Tiptree, Mythopoeic, Rhysling, Lambda, Locus and Hugo awards. She has been a finalist for the Nebula and World Fantasy Awards. She lives on an island off the coast of Maine with a small but growing menagerie of beasts, some of which are human.